THE THINGS YOU FIND IN ROCKPOOLS: BOOKS 1-3

BOOKS 1 - 3 OF THE ROCKPOOLS SERIES

GREGG DUNNETT

CONTENTS

THE THINGS YOU FIND IN ROCKPOOLS 1
Book One

THE LORNEA ISLAND DETECTIVE CLUB 269
Book Two

THE APPEARANCE OF MYSTERY 523
Book Three

THE THINGS YOU FIND IN ROCKPOOLS

BOOK ONE

ONE

I SEE the body from my bedroom window. It's lying halfway up the beach, stranded there by the overnight tide. There's nothing else breaking the sweep of pale, silvery sand, and there's no mistaking *what* it is, even from this distance. It's funny, I've always known I would find something like this one day, living here. You see it all the time on the TV news, bodies wash up just like this. And now I've found one.

I grab my binoculars. They're big ones, they magnify ten times and it's hard to hold them steady. So, even though I press them up hard against the windowpane, all I really see is jerky snatches of skin, a ghostly white patch of belly, and a bright red color where a wound cuts into her back. Definitely a 'her'. I can see that. A female, young, lying dead in a puddle of blood and seawater in the middle of the beach. My beach.

I'm suddenly conscious of my breaths, visible as little clouds in the coldness of my bedroom. Could I be imagining this? Maybe I'm asleep and this is a dream? But the rest of the room looks real. My closet's open, I see my school uniform hanging inside. The posters on my wall look right, the periodic table, my 'Fishes of the Sea' chart with all the Latin names. I look closely at this, they wouldn't be right if I was dreaming because they're hard to remember. I look at the Striped Bass - *Moronesaxatilis*. I can't be dreaming.

I take another ten-times-magnified look. This time I notice the gulls. Some are wheeling above the body, others are standing on it, like it's a new rock that's appeared overnight. Then I see they're not just standing, they're bending over, pecking. Tearing at bits of flesh. I see one wiggling its beak right down in the eye. I drop the binoculars and think.

I should tell Dad. I know I should. But something makes me hesitate. Dad's been weird recently. He gets mad about nothing at all. And with something like this, there's going to be police and journalists, and Dad hates those people. If I tell him he might insist we have nothing to do with it. He might even say we're not going out this morning, and then I wouldn't get a chance to examine it. And how often do I get a chance like this? For someone like me this is an amazing opportunity. I mean it's sad too of course, but there's no point being too sentimental about these things. Mostly it's an amazing opportunity.

So I feel a bit bad about it, but right away I know I'm not gonna tell Dad.

I'm Billy, by the way. I'm eleven-years-old, but I'm a bit more interesting than most eleven-year-olds. Or at least, I am judging by the others that go to my school. I'm pretty sure you'd agree if you met them.

Luckily though, it's Saturday today, so there isn't any school. We have a pretty set routine for the weekends. First thing, Dad always goes surfing. He goes early in the morning because it gets busier later and he doesn't like going with other people. I always go with him, but I never actually surf. That would mean going in the water, and I don't go in the water. I don't just sit in the truck waiting for him, though. That would be boring. I've always got lots of projects going on. Like my treehouse project, for instance. I built it last year, from stuff Dad had left over from work. It's in the woods behind the dunes, although you'll never find it because I painted the walls in a camouflage pattern. It took ages too. I found out you can't actually buy camouflage paint, which makes sense when you think about it - all the separate colors would get mixed up in the can. But anyway that was last year's project. I've got other projects now. Better ones.

But obviously today I'm not thinking about my projects at all. Today there's a body on the beach. I decide to get Dad up and out of the house as fast as I can. That way I can be the first to the body. I can be the one who discovers it.

Dad usually gets up after me. He comes downstairs and makes himself a coffee. If it's not raining or too windy he always drinks it outside. He stands in our little yard on the clifftop and looks out over the beach to decide where he's going to surf that day. If there's a big swell, we go to our end of the beach, near the cliff, because the waves there are smaller and less powerful. But if there isn't much swell, we go to Silverlea, the town in the middle of the bay. It's more open to the ocean there. Obviously, if there are no waves at all, or if the wind is too strong, then we don't go surfing at all. But that's generally bad news because it means he'll be moody the whole day.

It's just me and Dad who live in our house. I don't have any brothers or sisters. Or a mom, not anymore. And Dad won't let me have pets, not after what happened with the seagull chicks. So it's just us. And we've lived here, perched up in our clifftop cottage, for just about as long as I can remember.

But this morning I make the coffee. And I make it in a really noisy way to wake Dad up, banging the cupboards shut, rattling through the cutlery to get a spoon. I need him to hurry if I'm going to be the one to discover the body, you see.

We have one of those silver stove-top coffee makers that screw together with the coffee in the middle. I'm not sure how much to put in, but I know Dad likes it strong, so I fill it right up. It doesn't take long before it's hissing and frothing away, and the room smells thick with coffee. I get a cup for Dad and bang the cupboard door shut again. Then I hear Dad going to the bathroom upstairs, the long trickle he always does. When it finally dies out I shout upstairs.

"Coffee Dad."

Then I go outside for another look. It's still lying there, no one else has discovered it. But I realize there's another problem. It's the waves. This morning they're small. That means Dad will want to drive to Silverlea where the waves are bigger. Normally this wouldn't bother me, because my projects are kind of spread out so it doesn't matter where Dad wants to go. But the body is here, at *our* end of the beach. If we go to Silverlea I'll have to walk all the way back, and there's a danger someone else will discover it while that's happening. I don't want that. I want to be the one that discovers it.

So when Dad comes outside to join me, coffee in one hand, I'm already thinking of a way to solve the problem. I look at him cautiously. He got in late last night and I think he was drinking too because he looks a bit rough.

"What's with all the noise this morning Billy?" Dad rubs his eyes. "I thought you were being murdered or something." He laughs and takes a sip.

"Jesus Christ. This is rocket fuel," Dad says, and I frown because I'm not sure if that's good or bad.

Dad puts the cup on the front wall. Then he yawns and stretches his arms over his head. He's only wearing a T-shirt and jeans, which pull apart so I can see all the muscles of his stomach. He's still brown from the summer, even this late in the year. He isn't wearing any shoes either, though the grass is wet from dew. Dad doesn't really notice the cold.

We stand in silence for a moment. Looking out at the view. Just in front of our wall is the old cliff path. It was closed a while ago because it got too dangerous, but I still know a way down. Beyond the path, there's just a big drop to the beach, all seven miles of it, stretching past the town of Silverlea, right up to Northend. To the right you can see the woods. To the left it's just ocean all the way. It's a pretty amazing view from our yard, really.

"Looks OK, huh?" Dad says, picking up his coffee again.

He means the waves look OK. You can see everything from up here, but Dad only notices the waves. That's why I think my plan will work. I wait a few moments before speaking; I let him watch what's happening below us. Watch the waves roll in.

The waves you see when you go to the beach aren't always the exact same size. They come in groups, or sets. So one minute, it might look like the waves are really big, but then, a few minutes later, they might be much smaller. Right now, while I'm letting Dad watch, it's pretty big. Actually I'm lucky, it's probably the biggest set of waves I've seen the whole morning. Perfect for my plan.

"It looks pretty big," I say as casually as I can. "It looks small at the moment, but it looked real big just before you came out. I reckon Littlelea."

If Dad had watched for as long as I had, it would be obvious I'm lying. It's obvious it's going to be better for surfing further along the beach at Silverlea, where it's less sheltered. But Littlelea is where the body is, so I need him to decide to surf there this morning. And to do that, I just have to convince him the waves are bigger than they really are.

Dad doesn't reply right away. We stand there together, looking out over the ocean. The body is visible enough if only he were looking for it, but he's not looking at the beach. His eyes are scanning the horizon, watching where the approaching swells begin to steepen into real waves. He waits, sipping at his coffee. And he's patient. As the minutes pass, the waves that had been unloading pass through, and it goes nearly flat. I do my best to look surprised.

"Looks a little small to me," Dad says finally, a funny note to his voice. "You feeling alright this morning Billy?" He turns to me, and for a moment, I'm worried he's going to get into one of his weird moods. But he's kinda smiling.

"Come on, we'll go into town. We can get breakfast after."

Town is what we call Silverlea. So we're going to drive two miles north, past the body, and then I'll have to run all the way back here to Littlelea to get to it. Obviously I'm disappointed. But getting breakfast afterwards is a consolation, because of where we get it. And I'll never change his mind now, so I might as well make the best of it.

Dad drains his coffee, winces and gives me a look.

"Leaving in five," he says then walks inside to get dressed properly. I follow, and in the kitchen I hurriedly shut down my computer. I grab my binoculars, a new notepad and my camera, and stuff it into my backpack. Dad walks past me as I'm putting my walking shoes on and he tells me to hurry up. As I step outside Dad swings his wetsuit into the open back of his pickup truck. It lands with a wet *thwack* on the ribbed metal base. His board's already in there; it pretty much stays there the whole time. I hesitate. When he's in a good mood he lets me ride in the back, even though it's technically illegal. But when he's mad I have to ride up front. I take a risk and climb in the back with the board, not making eye contact. He doesn't say anything at first, just pulls open the door to the cab, then before he gets in he says: "You see any police you keep your head down, OK?"

Then he gets in, and moments later, the engine roars to life and the truck judders. The smell of un-burnt gas fills the air. We bump down our lane to the main road, then Dad starts off down the hill, driving fast, using the whole road to smooth out the corners.

You can't see much of the beach from the road, just glimpses through the trees. Then once you cross the river you're quite low and the dunes block it out. But it's only a ten-minute drive and we don't see any other cars. I take that as a good sign.

We come into town the back way, crunching to a halt at the front of the parking lot by the beach. The Sunrise Café is right here, that's where we'll have breakfast, but it isn't open yet.

Even so, we're not the first car here. There are four other vehicles; I recognize two of them as Dad's surfer friends. I guess the others are probably people walking their dogs. I hope they've walked north, up toward Northend and not south down to Littelea, toward where the body is. You probably can't see the body from here, so I'm hopeful, but I won't know until I get down on the beach.

"Be back here at ten," Dad says. Years ago, he used to try and make me come surfing with him. But not anymore. He understands that I don't go in the water now.

"Sure," I say. "I'll see you later." I leave him as he sits on the flatbed of the truck to pull on his wetsuit. He doesn't bother to cover himself with a towel when no one's around.

I walk fast down the little path to the beach. It's easy at first because there's a wooden boardwalk, but then it runs out, and my feet sink into the soft sand. Then finally, I get to the stones. There's a strip of them, big flat stones the size of dinner plates. When I get there, I stop and pull my binoculars out of my bag. Even before I've gotten them focused, I can see something's wrong.

There are people on the beach. Right by where the body is. This far away, I can't see who, or what they're doing, but it's obvious they're standing right by it.

I feel a flood of disappointment. It's the dog walkers. Why couldn't they walk the other way? *I* saw the body first, over an hour ago now, and I wanted to be the first to get there. Now I don't even know if I'll get to see it at all. I expect the Coast Guard will be there soon. Or the police. They're all over the town these days.

I stand there for a while, feeling the disappointment wash over me, but it doesn't last long. After all, whoever turns up, they can't exactly move the body, it's a bit big for that. I suppose they might try and cordon it off, but there's no sign of that either. At least not yet. If I get a move on, I might still be able to examine it. I just need to get there fast.

So I set off again, walking just below the high tide mark. That's the best place to walk because the sand there is always hard and flat. Plus, sometimes, you find things washed up from the tide, which is a bonus. But today I'm not looking down. I keep my eyes focused ahead, trying to make out details as I get closer. Then, when I'm about halfway there, I see a police car driving slowly down the beach toward where the body lies. I puff my cheeks and sigh.

I know what you're thinking, it's not really normal for an eleven-year-old to want to examine a dead body washed up on the beach. But like I said, I'm not like most eleven-year-olds. I mean, probably, some of the kids at school would want to take a selfie with it or something stupid. But I don't want to do anything like that. I'm interested because I want to study it. Like a proper scientist.

If you know about Silverlea, if you've been on vacation here or something, you might wonder too at a police car turning up so fast, and so early in the morning. But that's just the way things are at the moment. This fall they're everywhere. It's all because of that girl. The one in the news. And if you consider it's not just on the local island news but the *real* news, next to stories about the President and earthquakes and stuff, you can imagine what it must be like here. The whole island is obsessed with it. How could a teenage girl just disappear like that *here*? It doesn't seem possible.

I met her, the girl who went missing: Olivia Curran. I might as well tell you now, since even walking fast it's going to take me a while to get there. She was staying in one of the cottages that Dad manages. She was here on vacation with her family, her mom and dad and her brother. They were staying in the Seafield Cottages. They're the expensive, beachfront ones, with views of the ocean from the bedrooms. Actually, they're just along from the lot where we parked this morning.

I wasn't supposed to meet her. I was just in the cottage next door when they arrived. I was fixing the wi-fi after the guests the week before had complained about it dropping out a lot. That's another thing I do, I configure the wi-fi for all the vacation cottages that Dad manages. Mr. Matthews, Dad's boss, he knows I'm really good with computers, so he lets me do it.

Anyway, I'd just finished fixing the problem as they were arriving. They had a Jeep or SUV or something and it was loaded up with bikes on the back and a roof box. I didn't talk to them, of course. All the Seafield cottages are self-catering, and when guests arrive, they get the door key from a metal box with a combination lock bolted to the wall. So I just ignored them like normal. But then I decided to get a snack from the cottage storeroom. There's a little stone shed in the yard of the cottages where we keep the spare linen and towels for the changeovers, and there's little packets of cookies, too, for the welcome packs we put in. So there I was, carrying my laptop in front of me, going out to the storeroom to get some cookies. That's when she must have seen me. Because when I came out, still with my laptop open, this girl came walking up to me from the cottage.

"Excuse me," she said, looking a little unsure. "Are you staying next door or something? We've just arrived and we can't get the wi-fi to work."

I didn't say anything. I couldn't, I had a cookie in my mouth.

"It's just I saw your computer. I wondered if you'd maybe figured it out." She had blond hair that was tied behind her head in a ponytail, but a few strands had escaped, and she had to brush them away from her eyes.

"Hey don't worry about it, forget I asked." She said and she started to turn away. I pulled the cookie from my mouth.

"I live here. I don't need to stay here. But I do configure the wi-fi for all the cottages that Mr. Matthews owns."

She turned back, she looked me up and down a bit dubiously. "Oh. OK. Well that's kinda handy I guess. Since, er, it doesn't *seem* to work." She trailed off and smiled. She had quite a pretty smile.

"It does work. I've just fixed it," I told her.

"Oh. . . Well, erm, I just tried and actually it kinda doesn't."

"Have you put the password in?" I asked her. Tourists are quite stupid so we put instructions about everything in Welcome Folders - even things like how to work the electric stove. "It's in the Welcome Folder which is on the. . . "

"Yeah. I found that. It connects OK, but then it keeps dropping out."

I was annoyed at this because I'd had the same problem earlier, but I thought I'd fixed it.

"Have you changed any of the settings?" I asked, a bit hopeful.

"*No.* 'Course not." She gave me a funny look. "We've only just got here."

I frowned. If only I hadn't gone to get a cookie, she wouldn't have caught me. I thought about going into cottage two and trying to connect from there, but the girl would probably try to come with me. And it would be quicker if I could connect direct to their router.

"I'll have to come in. I need to plug into the router. Is that alright?" Part of me hoped she'd say no, but she didn't. The girl - I didn't know her name was Olivia then - swung her arm out and around like she was doing theatre or something.

"Be my guest."

She did have a very pretty smile actually.

The router in cottage number one is on the sideboard next to the kitchen table. I could see right away the LED was flashing orange, when it should have been glowing steady green. It's all open plan, in the Seafield cottages, and the girl's dad was there too. He was putting groceries away in the fridge.

"Hello there!" he said to me as I walked in, but I didn't have to say anything because the girl answered for me. "It's alright, he's just here to fix the wi-fi."

I put my laptop down on the table and poked in my bag for the network cable.

The dad put more stuff away, but I could tell he wanted to say something. Eventually, he did.

"You're very young to be fixing computers," he said. He had the kind of voice adults use when they're being patronizing to kids. I turned slightly away and didn't answer.

"You know, it doesn't matter if you can't get it working," he went on. "We'll be on the beach most of the time anyway, won't we, Livvie?"

"Duh. Yes, it does matter," the girl cut in. "It might not for you, but this place was advertised as having wi-fi. What if you got here and there wasn't a bathroom, but it was advertised as having a bathroom? You wouldn't like that, would you?"

"It's alright," I said. I didn't want to hear them arguing. "It does this sometimes, but if I reboot from the admin panel, it solves the problem." I sounded more confident than I was, though, because I wasn't sure why it kept breaking like that.

"Well, I'll be very impressed if you're right. And Olivia will be very grateful." He paused, and I hoped he might go away, but he kept on filling the fridge.

"So you're the *Silverlea computer expert*?" He said it like he was pretending it was a real job title or something. "You hear that Will?" He spoke louder, trying to attract the attention of a boy, about fourteen, who was at the other end of the living room, fiddling with the TV. The dad turned back to me. "We can hardly get William out of bed in the mornings, let alone working a responsible job!" The dad laughed and I took the opportunity to ignore him.

I got the admin panel up on my screen, and I could see I was right, one of the settings had got corrupted. It was an easy fix but I still didn't know why it kept happening. I fixed it and made a mental note to google the problem later. Then I rebooted the router. I wanted to leave right away, but I knew I should wait until it came back on, just to make sure it was working now.

"So, what is there for young people to do around here?" the dad asked me, still with his 'friendly' voice.

I don't like it when tourists ask me questions like this. Like I said, I'm a little different, so it's hard for me to know what they like doing. This one time, a tourist asked me, and I started telling them about my project counting the eggs of greater black-backed gulls on the cliffs. They looked at me like I was crazy. I tried to tell them they're the biggest gulls in the world, with a wingspan the size of an eagle's, but I could see from their face they just thought I was weird. So I wasn't ever going to tell Mr. Curran about my crab project. But I had a moment of inspiration. I thought about some of the posters I'd seen around town.

"There's the Surf Lifesaving Club Disco next Saturday," I said. "It's the end-of-summer one."

"Ah. The Surf Lifesaving *Club Disco*," he said, like that was just the sort of event he was expecting to happen in a small town. "You see, Livvie, I told you there would be things to do."

She rolled her eyes, but she turned to me too.

"Do you need to get tickets?" she asked, sounding surprisingly interested.

"I don't know." I knew *I* didn't have to, I'm a local. But I had no idea about tourists. I was saved from answering, though, because just then the router's green light came on.

"You can check it now," I said to the girl. She already had her phone in her hand. She'd had it there the whole time, like she couldn't wait to get it connected. And now, she poked at the screen for a few moments.

"Hey, it works," she said, not looking up. For a minute, she continued, typing something into the screen with her thumbs. Then she looked up suddenly.

"Here you go. Silverlea Surf Lifesaving Club End-of-Summer Disco. Tickets available in advance or at the door."

Then she looked at me with a proper big smile on her face. "That's pretty cool, thanks." She really *was* pretty when she smiled.

I told all this to the police, apart from her being pretty of course, I kept that to myself. Even so I was worried it might have got me in trouble. After all, if she hadn't gone to the disco that night, then she couldn't have disappeared *from* the disco. But the detective who took my statement didn't seem to think it was important. She said Olivia would probably have heard about it anyway, from all the posters up in town and everything. But then, she wasn't a very good detective. She can't have been, since she didn't notice when I lied to her.

But I guess that explains why I've felt kind of involved in the whole Olivia Curran thing somehow. Right from the very beginning.

* * *

I'm pretty close now to the group on the beach. It's grown just in the time it's taken me to walk here. There's now a police car *and* a Coast Guard truck parked up either side of the body. And this close, the wounds look pretty shocking: they go right through the skin, and you can see the layer of fat. I walk closer, to get a better look at the wounds. I want to see how she might have died.

"Hey Billy," a voice calls out, and someone steps in front of me, trying to cut me off.

TWO

"Hi Dan," I say, not enthusiastically because I don't much like Daniel Hodges. He works as a lifeguard. He knows Dad quite well because they go surfing together, but I don't think even he likes him much. The reason I don't like him is because he acts like he owns the beach, like now, where he's trying to stop me getting to the body.

"I'm not sure you should see this, Billy. It's pretty grim."

"Is it dead?" I ask, and I'm immediately annoyed at myself. It's totally obvious it's dead, but sometimes, things come out of my mouth that I didn't mean to say.

"Yeah, it's definitely dead, Billy." He says, smirking.

I try to peer around him, and I'm close enough now to hear the other conversations going on. A man I don't know is talking to the police officer.

"Do you know what species it is?" he asks. He sounds like a tourist. There aren't many here in the winter, but you still get some.

"We're not sure. We've got an expert from the mainland coming," the policeman replies. He's wearing his uniform. Police uniforms always look so strange in real life. Really impractical. "They might be able to tell us."

I interrupt at once, glad for a chance to step around Dan.

"It's a minke," I say.

The policeman starts saying something about waiting for the expert, but the tourist turns to me.

"How do you know?"

"You can tell by the distance between the dorsal fin and the blowhole, and how upright the dorsal fin is. It's a female. A young one too."

"Yeah, well," the policeman says. "Like I say, we'll see."

"Minke whales usually only occur in the northern hemisphere, but you do get dwarf minke whales in the Southern Ocean and around Antarctica. But this isn't a dwarf one because they have different markings, so this is a just normal one," I go on. I was fairly sure about my identification when I first saw it, and up close, there's no doubt at all.

Dan moves back now to let me look at the body more clearly. Just behind its head is a large open wound cutting into the flesh. It's dark red near the skin, but deeper in the color is brighter. It's sitting in a depression in the sand, filled up with a mixture of seawater and blood. It's pretty small for a whale, not much longer than the Coast Guard truck.

"What do you think happened to it?" the tourist asks. "Do you think it was a shark?" He sounds thrilled by this, in his mainland accent. That's how I know he's a tourist, his accent. Plus tourists are always going on about sharks.

I look closely at the wound. "No. We don't usually get sharks around here big enough to take on a whale, even a baby one. And it doesn't look like a bite mark, more like a propeller injury. Probably it got separated from its mother when it surfaced near a ship."

"You seem to know a lot about whales," the man tells me.

"I know a lot about all the animals on Lornea Island," I tell him. "I'm going to be a marine biologist when I'm older. I'm already doing experiments." I'm suddenly feeling confident, so I ask the policeman, "What time is the whale expert coming?"

I'm hoping I might be able to stay long enough to meet him or her. They might be interested in my hermit crab study. Unless they're just whale experts. Sometimes, you get scientists specializing in just one species, or one genus. Others are more general. So they might be interested, or they might not be. It just depends.

"The guy's coming on the ferry now. He should be here around lunchtime," the policeman tells me, and I check my watch. I have to be back at Dad's truck at ten. I can wait for a little while, but not that long.

THREE

I STAY for as long as I can, and the policeman lets me take photographs of the whale, but then I have to go. I jog back, my bag thumping against my back. I'm looking to see if Dad is still in the water. He'll be annoyed if I'm late. But I should be OK. The waves are still good, so it's more likely that he'll be in longer than he said.

As it turns out, I get back to the truck just after him. He's got the door open and music playing into the parking lot, and he's drying his hair with a towel, his wetsuit peeled down off his chest. He's smiling and whistling, so I guess the surf worked for his mood.

"There's a dead whale on the beach," I say to him. "Down by Littlelea. It's a minke whale."

"Alright, Billy, how are you?" Dad says; he's being sarcastic, telling me I didn't say hello. "Have you had a nice time?"

"Hello, Dad," I reply, starting again. "Yes I have, thank you. There's a dead whale on the beach."

"So you say." His smile's gone already. "I wondered what was going on. I saw the police cars on the beach." He doesn't say anything else, but a look comes over his face. He doesn't like the police much. He never has.

"It's a female. A really young one too," I go on.

"You want to get some breakfast?" Dad asks, ignoring what I say. Dad's not that interested in wildlife. He goes to work, and he likes surfing, and that's pretty much it. But I don't mind too much. If he hadn't said anything, I was going to remind him about going to the café. I'm almost always hungry, and even if I'm not, I always want to go to the Sunrise Café.

The café is open now. It's actually the upstairs part of the Surf Lifesaving Club, and from up there, you get a really good view of the ocean. When Dad's changed, we climb up the wooden steps and sit by the window where we always sit. There are photos on the walls of people surfing on days when the waves are really big. Dad's in a couple of them, although you can hardly see who it is because his body's so small against the wave. The photos are all for sale, so that sometimes, tourists buy a photo of Dad and put it on their walls at home, like he's a famous person. You'd think he wouldn't like that, but he doesn't seem to mind. I don't notice them today, though. I get my camera out of my bag, ready to show off my whale photos.

"Hey guys, what can I get you?" I stop what I'm doing when I hear Emily's voice. She comes over to us with her little notepad and pencil. She smiles at me, and I can smell her perfume. Like warm flowers. Emily works at the Sunrise Café, but she's not just a waitress. She's only there to earn money while she does her doctorate. She's studying marine biology. She's a real scientist. I like Emily. I like her a lot.

"You can get me a full breakfast," Dad says, rubbing his stomach. "And coffee."

"Good surf this morning, Mr. Wheatley?" She smiles at him, but not for long; she's only being polite. Then she turns to me.

"And Billy. You having your usual?" That's a white roll with two sausages in it and lots of ketchup.

"Yes, please, Emily."

"And *coffee*?" she asks. She doesn't wink, but she gives me a secret look. I once asked for a coffee, I kind of wanted to impress her, and then I didn't like it. She realized and went and got me a hot chocolate instead. So now she always says it like this.

"Yes please. Have you seen the whale? It's a minke, a baby one."

"I've heard about it," she says. "Haven't had a chance to see it yet, though."

"I've got some photos. They're sending a whale expert from the mainland. He's going to be here this afternoon. Maybe Dad could drive us all down later on? Once Emily finishes her shift?" I look at Dad hopefully. It's a long shot, but you might as well try when he's in a good mood.

"Sorry, Billy. I've got to work. Window frames to paint."

Sometimes, I don't get adults. What's the rush? It's almost winter. There aren't any bookings for that cottage until next year. Surely he could paint when there isn't a whale expert in town?

Emily senses my disappointment and tries to make it easier. "I've got a few things to do here too, I'm afraid." She glances at Dad, like she's trying to communicate something.

"Dan'll be there, though, Mr. Wheatley. If you wanted someone to keep an eye on Billy, I mean?" Her face is bright and open. Optimistic.

You remember Dan Hodges, the lifeguard? Well, there was something I didn't tell you about him. He's sort of dating Emily. I guess that might be a little bit why I don't like him much. It's not serious, though. She's only with him because there's no one better around here. I'm sure when she's finished studying, she'll marry a famous scientist, not some stupid lifeguard. Maybe she'll even marry me when I'm a famous scientist. We can do research together.

Dad thinks for a moment. "OK. You can go down there if you like, Billy. See this whale guy, and then run on home from there?"

I'm disappointed that Emily can't go with me, but not that surprised. And I'm not too unhappy since it's a lot better than helping Dad to paint. He makes me do the sanding bit, which isn't as fun as painting.

"Just don't get cut off by the tide will you? You know when high water is?"

"I can look it up if you want," Emily says, pulling out her cellphone. She's got an app that tells her the tide times. I don't need an app. I've lived by the beach so long I've got a sense for the tides.

I turn back to Emily, who's smiling because she likes helping me out.

"It's alright." I say. "I've got some photographs of the whale. Do you want to see them?"

"Sure. But hold on. I'll get your order first."

Me and Dad both watch her walk back to the kitchen. She's wearing black pants and you can see the outline of her butt. When I turn to Dad, he's still watching.

"There was a tourist there who thought it might have been killed by a shark," I say when she comes back with the drinks. "But I told him we don't get that type of shark here. I reckon it was hit by a ship or something."

Emily laughs at the idea of it being a shark. Clear, fresh notes that ring around the room, and make people turn towards us. That's what I really like about Emily. She knows the sharks we get here are too small to attack a whale. She knows almost everything about the wildlife of Lornea Island, even though she's not a proper local. Emily's like me and Dad – she lives here now, but she wasn't born here. She used to come for vacations and stay with her grandma, until she died, and now Emily lives here all the time. Maybe that's another reason I like her. We're both not proper locals, but we know more than they do about the important things.

"It could be the sonar from the submarines that confused it. I read about that," I say. "How it makes them muddled up. Then it could have surfaced too close to a ship and got hit by the propeller."

She thinks about this for a moment.

"Yeah, it could be," she says. "Maybe they don't need that whale expert after all. You've got it pretty figured out."

I'm a little bit proud at this. Then the kitchen guy calls her name because our food is ready.

Dad's not watching this time as she walks away. Instead, he reaches for a newspaper that someone's left on the table. It's the *Island Times*. I once saw they printed a photograph of a dead dolphin that washed up at Northend. The woman who found it was in the shot too. That's why I wanted to be the one to find the whale, because I could have gotten in the paper. Although, thinking about it, the *Island Times* has gone a little crazy recently over the whole Olivia Curran thing, so maybe they won't bother putting in a picture this time. The headline in this week's paper is about Olivia again. It reads:

FOUR

I DON'T THINK that's a very good headline, since it sort of tells you they don't have anything new to say. They might as well say, "No news today!" But that's the kind of thing they've been printing every week. *Olivia - could she still be on the island? Olivia Case: Police believe she drowned. Olivia mystery: Police search continues.* Dad opens the paper and quickly skims the first three pages, which is all Olivia stuff. I flick through my photos on the back of my camera. Zooming in and out. Then Emily comes back, this time with our food.

"Here you go." She puts Dad's down and then mine. There's tons of ketchup in there, and the butter is spread thick and melting where the sausages are touching it. She sees Dad has the paper open.

"Anything new?" she asks.

He looks up at her, surprised, then shakes his head. "No. I don't know why the police don't just accept she drowned." Dad always says this. He thinks Olivia Curran decided to go swimming that night and got into trouble.

"I guess her parents are still hoping she'll turn up alive," Emily says. "It must be awful for them, not knowing. I just wish someone would find out what happened to her."

You get a lot of this kind of conversation around here these days. It's like people have gotten kind of obsessed with the Olivia Curran case. I don't really know why. It's not the first time a tourist has drowned. Everyone knows the water's dangerous, that's why there's a surf lifesaving club here. But when people drown normally, you get the body washed up a day or so later, and that didn't happen with Olivia, so no one knows for sure.

People don't normally talk about Olivia Curran to *me*, though. It's like a conversation that only adults are allowed to have. When they turn to me, they pretend it hasn't happened. Whatever it was that did happen. I know why: it's because everyone *really* thinks she got abducted and murdered. Or maybe she's not even dead yet, and she's being kept in a cellar somewhere, and raped every night. But Emily's different. She treats me like an adult. So I'm not that surprised when she turns to me and says, "Maybe you should turn your investigative powers to the Olivia Curran case, Billy? After all, you've solved the mystery of the dead whale in about five minutes." She smiles, to make clear she's kind of joking.

Dad reaches for the ketchup and gives her a look. Like he doesn't think this a very good idea.

"Don't get him started. He's got enough on counting his eagle eggs." He tries to roll his eyes at her, but she looks away and smiles at me. She knows about the great black-backed gulls; I told her all about them. I told Dad, too, but he still gets it wrong.

She leaves us with our food because she has to serve other people. I take a big bite of sausage and bun, so that the grease drips onto my plate. I know it's only a throwaway remark that she's made, but already I'm starting to think about it. Maybe I *should* turn my investigative powers onto the Olivia Curran case. The thought of it has kind of floored me. After all, look at the paper. The police don't seem to be getting anywhere, and I know from personal experience how incompetent they are. Maybe I can be the one to solve the mystery? I think about what the *Island Times* headline would say: *Local boy solves Olivia mystery!*

That would be even better than getting my picture in the paper with a dead whale.

And after all. No one knows this beach like I do.

FIVE

After breakfast, Dad goes off to do his painting, and I run back down the beach to the whale. By now, the tide is much higher, almost up to where the little group is standing, still surrounding the carcass. As I get close, I can see a second police car is there now. I hope it's brought the whale expert.

But when I get there, I'm disappointed. It's not the expert. It's Mr. Matthews. He's Dad's boss; he owns all the cottages that Dad runs, plus the big hotel on the other side of town. I don't like him much, but Dad always defends him. I reckon he makes a fortune even though Dad does all the work. He drives a really big car; you usually see it parked at the golf club. It's not here today. I guess he didn't want to drive it on the beach and get it sandy.

Mr. Matthews is talking with another policeman. He's older than the first one, and suddenly I realize I recognize him. Whenever there's a statement about Olivia Curran on TV he's always there. I think he's pretty important. I know it's him because he's got a funny mustache that only covers the lower part of his top lip, like there's a caterpillar resting there. And because he's black, and there's hardly any black people on the whole island. He's stroking his mustache now, as he talks to Mr. Matthews.

Another policeman joins them. It's the one I talked to earlier. He starts telling them that he thinks it's a minke whale, and how it was probably killed by a ship's propeller. Then Mr. Matthews pulls the senior police officer over to one side, which is where I'm standing. Mr. Matthews gives me a sort of smile of recognition because he knows I do the wi-fi stuff, but he doesn't say anything to me.

"Larry," he says to the police chief. "We're already getting a lot of negative coverage with all that's happening over this girl. I don't want to add to that with a. . . " He glances over at the whale. "With a *corpse* rotting on the beach." He says this last bit really quietly, but I've got good hearing. The important policeman is still stroking his mustache, like he's considering what Mr. Matthews is saying.

"I understand, Jim. Really, I do. We've got someone from the university coming on the ferry now. As soon as they're done, we'll see to getting it moved."

Mr. Matthews sighs and looks around the beach. There are about ten tourists hanging around the whale now, watching what's going on. Some of them are taking photos. And there's another five or six people walking down the beach from the town.

"I'm not sure you do Larry. Look, the tide'll be covering it in a half hour, anyway. How about I arrange for a boat? We can tow it out, get rid of it quickly and cleanly. Before the press get here. The town doesn't need pictures full of blood."

Again, I can hear all this, but I can't believe it. I want to interrupt and tell them the expert will want to do tests, to perform an autopsy. But I know I can't interrupt Mr. Matthews and the important police man. Dad could lose his job. I could get arrested.

"Come on, Larry. The goddamn tide's gonna wash it down in front of the town if we don't. It's going to look even worse. You can say it's a public health hazard. No one's gonna argue with you."

The policeman stands there for a moment. He's still stroking his mustache.

"You can get a boat here in time?"

"Sure."

The policeman makes a decision.

"OK. If you can get it moved, then do it. It'll be easier to tow out from here. Swell's bigger in town. We'll use that as the justification if anyone complains."

"Good man, Larry," Mr. Matthews says. "Good man." He pats him on the back, and he pulls out his cellphone and starts dialing right away.

I'm horrified, but there's nothing I can do, except hope the whale expert can get here before they tow the whale away. I don't know for sure, but maybe they can overrule the police chief. Like the shark expert does in that movie *Jaws*. But then, *Jaws* isn't a very realistic movie, especially the part where the shark tries to eat the whole boat. That would never happen; they might bite on a boat to see what it is, but when they found out it wasn't food, they'd go and eat a seal or something. I think this as Mr. Matthews wanders a little way away and talks on his cellphone for a while. Then he comes back and talks quietly to the inspector.

"All set. Kevin'll be here in forty minutes." Then he shakes his head and says something else, but this time, I think he's just talking to himself.

"Christ alive. First that girl and now this. We'll be lucky if anyone comes here next season."

After that, the other two policemen go to the trunk of the police car and come back with two shovels. They start digging a hole on each side of the whale's tail. Lots of people think whale's tails are called flukes, but they're actually made up of two flukes, one on each side. The right word for the whole tail is just *tail*, like I said. I go and stand as close as I dare, and try to push the sand back into the hole with my feet, but they get annoyed and tell me I have to stand back, so there's nothing else I can do after that. After all, they *are* the police. Instead, I just check my watch and frown a lot. It takes about forty minutes to get here from Goldhaven, where the ferry gets in, but I don't know which ferry the whale expert is on. I just hope he or she hurries up.

I'm thinking so hard about this, I don't notice that the policemen have already got a rope under both flukes. They wrap it around twice and knot it. Annoyingly, they do it well. By the time they've finished, the water is really close, and a fishing boat is waiting just outside where the waves are breaking. Like I told you, the waves aren't very big down this end of the beach today. As I watch, the men on the boat trail a buoy attached to a line from the stern, and it doesn't take long before it gets washed ashore and the policemen can collect it. Then they tie it to the line they've already got secured around the whale's tail. And then we all wait.

About fifteen minutes later, the tide has come in enough that there's water all around the whale, and it's sticking up out of the waves like a rock. The boat tries to pull it a couple of times, but before it's actually afloat, and they've got no chance. But they keep trying, with lots of shouting, and then, ten minutes later, the whale suddenly moves. For a half second, I make the mistake of thinking that it was never dead at all, but then I realize, it's just floating now, and the boat slowly begins to pull it out backward into deeper water. A wave breaks over it, and it disappears for a moment. When it emerges again, it looks shiny and clean, and then it rolls over so we see the white underside. And slowly it gets pulled out to sea.

A half hour later, you can hardly see it: the boat is pulling it out around the headland. I don't know where they'll dump it; away from the island, I guess. I watch until the boat goes out of sight behind the rocks and then turn away, still feeling angry about what's happened. As I do, I see a man standing on the dunes by the parking lot. I don't know him, but from the way he's dressed, the backpack he's carrying and the funny round glasses he's wearing, I reckon he's probably the whale expert.

SIX

DAD ISN'T HOME when I get in, so I light the log-burner and start to make dinner. Usually, I'd put the TV on while I'm cooking, but today, I don't. I'm too busy thinking.

I'm really angry about what happened with the whale. Not just because I didn't get to meet the whale expert, or tell him about my hermit crab study, but because I know the police did the wrong thing. If they'd waited until the expert got there, he could have measured the wounds, and taken samples and all sorts of things that would have been useful to science. But now, they can't. They threw away the biggest piece of evidence they had.

I can't help but link this with how the police have failed to find out what happened to Olivia Curran. That detective who interviewed me practically ignored my information about how Olivia heard about the Surf Lifesaving Club Disco. If they make those kinds of mistakes, what else have they overlooked? Then I think of Emily and the way her face gets all worried when she talks about the girl. I know why. It's because she's worried that whatever happened to Olivia Curran might happen to her too. So maybe I *should* investigate the case? Maybe I could solve it where the police haven't? After all, Dad's always saying the police are useless and corrupt.

In a funny way, I think me being a child might help too. Look at the way Mr. Matthews and the policeman were talking on the beach today - they moved away from all the other adults because they didn't want to be heard, but they hardly noticed *I* was there. And lots of people around the town treat me like that, like I'm sort of invisible. So perhaps it's not such a crazy idea for me to try and find out what happened? After all, I do all my projects, and I'm really good at those.

On the other hand, I am really busy already, what with my project and also school and things.

I don't know. I change my mind lots while I'm cooking. I make spaghetti bolognese because me and Dad both like that.

But then, when Dad comes home, he says he's tired, and he's in another one of his strange moods. I guess he must have done too much painting. The first thing he does when he gets in is open a beer. Then he takes his dinner without a word and sits down in front of the TV. Sometimes I'll watch TV with him, but tonight I'm still kind of annoyed with everything, and I'm thinking a lot, so I eat in the kitchen. Then I go to my room. I've got homework to do, but I don't get my books out. Instead, I open a new Word document on my computer and start typing everything I can remember about the Olivia Curran case. This is what I write:

Date of Mystery: August 26

Location: Silverlea Surf Lifesaving Club (End-of-Summer Disco)

Summary:

Olivia Curran was a sixteen-year-old girl staying for two weeks in number one Seafield cottages in Silverlea along with her brother (14), and parents (ages not known, but fairly old). Halfway through her stay, she attended the Silverlea Surf Lifesaving Club Disco, which is approx. fifty yards along the beach from the cottage. Her parents claim she did not return to the cottage that night or the next morning.

On Sunday, August 27, a police search was begun using officers from the island and then later from the mainland too. There were lots of police cars (I counted seven all parked together at one point). Some of the police had dogs, and there was a helicopter that landed on the beach. Lots of local people from the town helped to search too, but not Dad (and not me either). No one was able to find any trace of Olivia.

On Monday, August 28 (which was still vacation, so no one had to go to school), the search kept going but got even bigger. There were lots of police now, and Coast Guard launches in the bay with their little boats and divers. And a second helicopter that hovered around the town the whole day. The story was in all the newspapers too. It was the front page story in some of them. Some of the national ones, I mean, not just *The Island Times*.

On Tuesday, August 29, the search kept going. In the morning, the woman police officer came to our house to speak to Dad because the family was staying in our cottage, but Dad said he'd not even met them. This is when I volunteered my information about how Olivia found out about the disco. In the afternoon, Dad and I watched from the yard as all the police searched through the dunes for clues. They were still going after it got dark; you could see the flashlights waving around in the darkness.

I start to write the entry for Wednesday, but realize I don't have much more to say, except that the search carried on and no one found anything. And I could say that for every day since it happened.

I decide the most important part is probably the night she went missing. So I go on the Internet and go to the *Eastern Daily News* website. A couple of weeks after Olivia disappeared, they printed a timeline detailing her last known movements. I copy and paste it into my document too:

Timeline

Saturday 20:30 - Olivia arrives at the Silverlea Surf Lifesaving Club End-of-Summer Disco with her mother, father, and brother. She immediately joins another group of female teenagers whom she met and befriended in the previous week.

Saturday 21:00 - Olivia and friends eat from the BBQ, and the group are observed drinking and laughing.

Saturday 22:00 - Olivia and friends are among the first to begin dancing and continue doing so for around an hour, staying toward the front of the hall. Olivia seems relaxed and appears to be enjoying the party.

Saturday 22:37 - Olivia's family leave the party to return to their rental cottage, less than one hundred yards from the hall. Olivia's mother speaks to her daughter and tells her that she must be back with the family by midnight, which she promises to do. This is the last sighting of Olivia by a family member.

Saturday 23:00 - Olivia and her group of friends go outside the hall, but stay within the confines of the party, chatting and drinking further.

Between the hours of 23:00 and 01:00, there are various unconfirmed sightings of Olivia, both on the beach and within the hall.

Sunday 01:15 - The party winds down. Many of the guests have left by this point. Those remaining are young people and teenagers, and many are heavily intoxicated.

Sunday 01:30 - The disco officially ends, the hall is closed and the doors are locked. A group of young people remain outside for some time. Many then proceed to a party held at 45 Princes Street, in an apartment rented by members of the Silverlea Surf Lifesaving Club. There are conflicting reports as to whether Olivia attended this after-party.

Sunday 04:00 - The impromptu event at 45 Princes Street winds down, with most partygoers either returning to their homes or vacation accommodation, or sleeping over in the Princes Street apartment.

Sunday 08:00 - Susan Curran discovers her daughter Olivia did not return to the cottage but at this point assumes she has slept elsewhere. The family does not call the police until nearly midday.

Sunday 11:45 - Joseph Curran contacts Silverlea police station to report that his daughter Olivia Curran is missing.

It's late now. I read back everything I've written, and I'm not sure. I decide that Emily's idea for me to investigate the Olivia Curran case is a little crazy after all. Plus, I'm pretty tired. I click the 'x' to close the file, and the computer asks if I want to save it. I almost say no, but at the last moment change my mind. I think for a moment, then I make a new folder called "Limpet shells" and save it in there. I've noticed that not many people are interested in limpet shells, so if my computer is ever hacked, they're less likely to look in a folder with a name like that. Then I password-protect the file like I do for all my stuff, because you can never be too careful.

Then I get into my pajamas and go to sleep.

SEVEN

DAD WAKES up later than normal on Sunday. We go to Silverlea again because the waves are still small. When he's gone into the water, I think about going to find out if the whale has washed up somewhere. But I couldn't see it anywhere from the clifftop earlier, so I don't think there's much point. Maybe it's sunk. Instead, I decide to do some work on my hermit crab project. So I walk up the beach to Northend.

Northend is a strange place. Years and years ago, they used to mine silver from the headland up there. It's how the town got its name: Silverlea. It was proper silver too, real nuggets that they dug out there. There were tunnels running through the cliffs, right down to the beach in some places. But then, one day, there was a really big storm, and the waves brought down the cliff. Almost all of the mine collapsed. It was a big deal and loads of the miners died. But it was a long time ago, so it doesn't really matter anymore. The point is, all the silver nuggets they'd been mining and all the nuggets they had stored up, ready to ship out to the mainland, they all fell onto the beach too. And they got hidden there, in the sand and between crevices in the rocks up there.

And now you're still supposed to be able to find silver nuggets, in the rock-pools and buried in the sand up at Northend.

When I was little, me and Dad would spend hours and hours up at Northend, me with my little bucket and net and him with his sleeves rolled up and his shirt open, and we'd search in those rockpools, hoping to find our nugget of silver. I'd shout out to Dad every time I found something, and he'd come over to see. And it wouldn't be silver; it would be the tab from a soda can, or the foil-inside of a potato-chip bag, but he'd still smile and tell me I had to keep on looking and one day we'd find some. I loved searching for silver so much I'd refuse to leave, and later Dad would have to carry me back while I slept on his shoulders because I was so tired.

We never did find any silver, not a single bit. And these days, we don't look anymore. I guess I got too old. These days, Dad's got more into his surfing, and obviously, I can't do that because of the going-in-the-water thing. I still see the tourists, though, in the summer. With their special "Silverlea Silver Nugget" buckets and their "nugget nets," which are really just the normal kid's fishing nets on cane sticks that you get everywhere but a bit more expensive. The tourists never find anything either. I'm pretty sure all the silver has gone.

But that doesn't mean there isn't anything interesting up at Northend. It's perfect for my project.

It's about a half-hour walk along the sand to Northend, and the exercise means I’m warm by the time I get close. I can see the tide is still dropping, which is good, but I'm frowning again, this time because I'm not sure if it's low enough. I need the tide to drop right down so I can get around the headland. There's another little beach round there, which is where I'm going. Dad used to call it the 'secret beach' although it isn't really secret; it's just hard to get to, and some people say it's dangerous. There's a sign warning people. I go past it now. It says:

DANGER
Do not pass this point
On Rising Tide!

When I was a kid, I didn't used to like going past this sign. I was always scared we would get cut off and drown. Dad would tell me it was OK as long as you kept an eye out on the water, but even so, we almost got caught out a few times. He liked going past the sign, partly because he thought we had a better chance of finding silver in the pools around the headland because not many tourists would go round there. And partly because that's just what Dad's like.

These days I'm much more confident though. I know you get about an hour or so at low tide before the water cuts you off, so it's not really that dangerous, as long as you keep track of time. I'm pretty sure today's low tide is at eleven, but I'm not totally sure because I was still thinking about the whale when I looked. I'll just have to be careful, that's all.

When I get to the headland, there's just enough beach to walk round without having to scramble on the rocks. And when I'm round, the whole of the main Silverlea beach is out of sight, blocked by the rocks I've just passed. It's a funny little beach, this one. There's no other way to get here, no path down the cliff. You can't even see it from the clifftop above. That's why it's dangerous if you get cut off here. At high tide, there is no beach, and the cliff is too steep and unstable to scramble up.

Today I can't see anyone else on the secret beach, so I know I'm completely alone. And since there was no one walking the beach behind me, I know mine will be the only footprints on the sand here in this tide.

But I don't have long. I walk a little faster, over the hard, wet sand toward the end of the second beach. Toward the entrance of the hidden pools.

I found the hidden pools with Dad, years ago. We thought they were just caves at first, but later, Emily told me they were actually part of the mines. They're the old tunnels and chambers that had been dug at beach level all those years ago. Only now, they fill up and empty out with the sea every time the tide goes up and down. Hardly anyone knows about them though; there's just a tiny little entrance where you have to duck under a ledge of rock, and then you're inside. You have to take your shoes off, though, because it's wet inside. It's dark too.

I have a long look at the sea before I go in. I think the tides are neaps, when it doesn't go out that far. It's a bit risky, really. Especially since when I get into my projects, I sometimes lose track of time. I think about it, biting my fingernails as I do so. I decide I'll just have a quick look.

I dig around in my backpack for my special flashlight. Flick it on, then duck under the rock into the darkness. I won't stay long. I'll just see how many I can find.

EIGHT

I STEP THROUGH THE COLD, still water, my jeans rolled up to just under my knees. I keep my head down so I don't bang it where the rock ceiling is low. After that there's a high section where a rock has fallen out of the ceiling, and then another low part. I can't see much, there's no beam of visible light from my flashlight, but that doesn't mean it's broken. And when I get into the cave proper I shine it around. A few blobs of color glow back at me from the darkness. Then something reddish scuttles across the floor. The only sound is the slow drip, drip, drip of falling water droplets.

I should probably explain about my hermit crab project, and why I have to come up here to do it.

It all started with Emily. For her university course, she's studying jellyfish, a special venomous type that lives off the coast of South America (well, warmer waters anyway, they kind of live wherever they float to, since they're jellyfish). Anyway. She went for six whole weeks on a research ship last year to study them. Most little fish get killed when the jellyfish catch them in their tentacles. They get dissolved and eaten, but some special fish can swim around in the tentacles all they like without getting hurt. Emily says they have a special antidote in their blood. That's what she's studying. She's going again, soon, on the same ship, the *Marianne Dupont*. It's French. Or Canadian. Or something, I'm not sure. Anyway, I was a little jealous, and a little sad that she was going for so long. But obviously, I couldn't go because I've got school, and besides, it would be really expensive. But then Emily told me about some other research that her friend was doing at her university. And the cool thing was, the scientist doing it wanted volunteers.

It's all to do with hermit crabs. Their territorial range and population density. You see, no one really knows much about that because no one's done any research into it. At least, not until Dr. Ribald decided to study it. That's her name - the scientist, Emily's friend. Dr. Susan Ribald. She wanted people who live near rocky coastlines anywhere in the world to monitor their beach and record the numbers and distribution of hermit crabs. Obviously, it can't just be any people, though; it has to be professional, scientific people. And Emily suggested that *I* could do it because I'm very scientifically-minded. So that's what I'm doing. I'm doing Dr. Ribald's experiment.

There's lots of us around the world doing it, or at least there were. I think a lot of them have stopped now. The idea originally was we put a spot of paint on the shells of all the hermit crabs we could find in one particular rockpool on one low tide, and then count how many we can find in the same pool on the next low tide, and try and see how far the other ones have gotten. Well, I tried that, but it was really hard because I couldn't find any of the crabs again the next time I went to count them.

That's when I had my idea. The hidden pools up at Northend are inside a cave where it's *dark*. I already knew there were hermit crabs inside because I'd seen them before when I went in with dad. They'd freaked me out as a kid, the way they scuttled around in the dark.

So my idea was to get some ultraviolet paint; the stuff that glows in the dark, and one of those scanner machines they use in stores to test if the bills people are paying with are fake or not. So then, I just had to paint the crabs' shells with the glow-in-the-dark paint, and I'd be able to find them easily when I needed to see where they'd gone.

I told Emily about it, and she helped me write to Dr. Ribald, and *she* wrote back that it was a "really interesting idea" and asked me to report back on how it went, so I went on the Internet to buy all the stuff. I was too young to buy the scanner thing, but I found you can buy ultraviolet flashlights which look just like normal flashlights until you turn them on and think nothing's happened. And there's lots of different colors of the special paint.

That was earlier this year. Now, things have moved on. Inside the rockpool caves at Northend, I've now got over two hundred different hermit crabs. Some of them glow blue in the dark, some yellow, some green, and some red. And because they can't get out, I can find tons of them every time I go in there.

I shine my flashlight around today. A few crabs glow back at me, but not as many as usual. Dr. Ribald will be interested in that. I start to count them, and when I've done that, I'll put them all back in the correct pools. All the orange crabs in the rockpool with the orange rock, all the blue ones in the pool with the blue rock, and so on.

So that's what my hermit crab project is all about. I did tell you it was serious scientific research. And actually, because it's so important, I've decided I'm not going to investigate the Olivia Curran mystery after all. It would get in the way of my scientific work, and I'm sure Dr. Ribald would be disappointed by that. She says I've got an "unusually persistent approach".

An hour later, I've counted thirty-two crabs. Twelve are red ones, there's ten orange, eight are yellow, and the other two are blue (the blue ones are always the hardest to find because the blue paint doesn't glow very brightly). That's *a lot* down from the last time I came to look. I'm tempted to go a little deeper into the caves to look there, but I don't like going too deep. It's like you can feel the weight of the whole cliff above pushing down on you when you go too far into the cliffs.

And then, with a rush of panic, I remember the tide.

While I was counting, I had to stop and roll my jeans higher, well above my knees, because the water in the caves was rising, but I was so busy wondering where all my crabs were that I didn't stop to think about why. Now I know, it means the tide is pushing in. Outside, the water will already be at the entrance of the cave, and there won't be much beach left. I quickly grab my bag from the ledge where I left it and go toward the exit. When I get there, the water is up above my knees, the surge of the waves pushing in. I can't see the ocean - I can't see anything much, just the dim glow of the light through the water. I've never left it this late before, and for a moment I hesitate, wishing there was another way out, or that I could stay in here and wait until the tide drops again. But I know I can't do that. The caves get filled right to the roof; I know that because there are barnacles growing on the actual ceiling.

So I don't have a choice. My backpack is waterproof, but only when I fold the top over on itself lots of times. I take off my jeans and put them in the bag, so I've only got my underwear on. There's no one around, but I'd feel silly taking them off too. I can feel my hands shaking as I do it. I know I've got to move quickly. Then I look at the exit, a narrow kink in the rock with water sluicing through it. If I time it wrong, I'll try and wade through just as a big wave pushes in, but I can't see the ocean; I've got no way of timing it. I just wait until it looks like the water is draining back out, and I go for it.

If you were claustrophobic, you wouldn't like the cave entrance. It's really narrow. I stumble at one point on a rock hidden under the water, but the walls are too close for me to fall. Instead, I just bang my arm on the rock. But I'm OK. Moments later, I'm out -back into the world with its high, gray sky and the cliffs around me. I'm shocked how little beach there is left. I'm going to have to run to get back around the headland, or I'll be stranded on the beach here. I'm lucky the waves aren't too big today.

I have to wade around the headland, but I'm just in time. Less than ten minutes later, I'm safely back past the sign saying:

DANGER
Do not pass this point
On Rising Tide!

I get dressed again, but I leave my shoes off and walk the rest of the way back on the wet sand, letting the ends of the waves tickle my toes.

NINE

SOMETHING HAPPENED today to change my mind. I wouldn't want you to think I'm indecisive, but I *am* going to investigate what happened to Olivia Curran.

It's Monday today, so I had school. When I was younger, I went to Silverlea Elementary School, but last year, I started at Lornea Island High School. That's in Newlea, the capital of the island. It's twenty minutes away by car, or half an hour on the school bus. I catch it a way down our lane, and there's another girl who waits for it in the same place. Her name is Jody. Even though she's a year older than me we're kind of friends. Sometimes we talk while we're waiting for the bus, and while it drives down to Silverlea. She always stops talking then, though, because other kids get on the bus in Silverlea, and she doesn't want to be seen talking with me. It's OK though. I understand. It's not exactly cool to be seen talking with me.

But I'm getting a little ahead of myself. It's because I'm excited. Because I've got a *lead*.

This morning, waiting for the bus, Jody wasn't talking to me; she was busy on her cellphone. When the bus came, I sat at the front, and she walked to the back. I got out my book like normal; I'm reading a new textbook called *Marine Biology: Function, Ecology, Biodiversity* by Jeffery S. Levinton. They didn't have it in the school library, but I kept asking, and Mrs. Smith, the librarian, eventually ordered it for me, I think because she recognizes that it's important to nurture young talent. It's pretty hard to read, actually, but it's got lots of pictures too. Anyway. The point is I wasn't thinking about Olivia Curran while I was reading, or at least I didn't *think* I was thinking about her, but somehow I wasn't really reading the book either. Instead, my mind was kind of pondering things. Like, if Olivia Curran was kidnapped, or murdered, then who was most likely to have done it? And I was kind of running through all the possible suspects, and then from the back of the bus, some of the bigger boys suddenly started shouting, *"Pedo! Peeeeedo!"* and then laughing at each other about how funny they were.

I didn't really pay much attention at the time, but later on, when I got to school, that's when I realized the significance.

Mostly, I don't like school. I'm not interested in sport, or music, or any of the things that the other kids talk about. I don't know about the football players and singers they're always discussing. I don't mind the actual lessons, especially science, and some of the teachers are OK, but often, there aren't any teachers around, like in breaks and lunchtime. And when that happens, some of the kids sometimes give me a hard time.

That's what happened today, at lunchtime. I was going to the school library to read, but some older boys blocked my way in the corridor. They started by flicking my bag off my shoulder and asking what was in it. There actually wasn't much except *Marine Biology: Function, Ecology, Biodiversity*, but I didn't want to show that to them because, frankly, that's just the kind of thing that gets you into trouble with boys like that. And then one of them started calling me names. Again, that's not that unusual, they call me a loser and a loner quite a bit which I don't even mind too much since I don't want to hang out with them anyway. But today, the one who was on the bus this morning, he called me something else.

"Billy, you're such a fucking pedo, you know that?" It was Jared Carter. He lives in Silverlea. He's two years above me in school, and he's really stupid. I saw his English workbook once: a teacher was marking it while taking my class, and I finished my work early. I tried to read his work, and honestly, he's basically illiterate. It's shocking, really.

"He's a what?" One of Jared's friends started laughing at him, a tall boy with dark hair. I didn't know his name.

"A pedo." Jared said, sounding a bit unsure of himself now. He meant 'pedophile' by the way.

"How can *he* be a pedo? He's a kid. He's maybe a pedo's. . . I dunno, *bitch* or something. But *he* can't be a pedo, can he?"

"Why not?"

The tall boy suddenly slapped Jared around the head. He did it pretty hard. I took the opportunity to move a little way down the corridor.

"Hey! What you do that for?" Jared shouted. He sounded hurt.

"Because you're a fucking idiot, that's why. You don't even know what a 'pedo' is, do you?"

"Yeah I do."

"What then?"

And that's when it hit me. Just when Jared clammed up. You see, when he said it on the bus this morning it wasn't because he knew what it meant – he's too stupid for that. It was just because he saw the guy with the limp. And all the Silverlea boys shout that when they see him. It's like a Pavlovian response with them. Now I usually try to ignore the boys from Silverlea whenever possible, so I’d never paid much attention before. But then I hadn't been thinking about possible murderers or kidnappers before.

The way the guy limps does make him look a bit creepy too. I guess I'd always assumed that's the reason the Silverlea boys pick on him. But now, I needed to be sure.

"Hey, Jared," I said, hoping this wouldn't get me into trouble. "Why do you always say that guy with the limp is a pedo anyway?"

All the boys stopped and stared at me, like they didn't know I could actually speak.

"You know, the guy with the bad leg. You were shouting it at him on the bus this morning."

"The fuck you say? Pedo-boy?" the tall one said, turning on me again.

I'd started talking without really thinking about it. I wasn't sure now it was such a good idea.

"I just wondered why you all call him that," I said, my voice cracking a little.

"'Cause he fuckin' is. That's why," Jared answered, happy to be back on firm ground. He began advancing toward me.

"Yeah, but. . . Why, though?" I said, backing up a little more.

For a moment, I thought Jared was going to hit me, but the tall boy interrupted.

"He got done. My old man said. On the mainland, he got caught doing it with a schoolgirl." I filed this piece of information away for future reference, and since everyone was looking at the tall boy now, I took the opportunity to ask for more.

"Did he kill her?" I asked hopefully.

"No. You know, he just, fucked her. Or something. I dunno. Raped her, I think."

I was disappointed by this, but then, I guess if he'd killed her, he wouldn't have been allowed onto the island in the first place. He'd be in prison already.

"Do you know his name?" I asked. If I got that, I reasoned, I could google him and find out everything else I'd need to know. I could wrap the whole thing up tonight. But he didn't seem to know.

"No I fucking don’t. Weird-boy," the tall boy said now, and he took a step closer too. So now there was him *and* Jared, looking like they were going to hit me. In my experience bullies don't usually like to *actually* hit you, because then they might get into trouble. But if there's others watching them, then sometimes, they will, because they don't know any other way to finish a conversation.

"Are you going to fuck off, or am I going to have to fucking slap you?" Jared asked.

I decided I'd probably got as much information as I was going to get from Jared and his friends, so I shouldered my backpack and chose the first option.

Unlike Jared and his friends, I'm not a total imbecile. They think this guy is a pedophile because they’ve combined two pieces of information: he walks with a weird limp, and they’ve heard a rumor about his raping history. But I’ve now got three pieces of information. Because I know something else about him. Something that's directly relevant to Olivia Curran. I know *he was there the night she went missing*. I know this because I was there too, and I saw him, hiding in the darkness.

* * *

So that's what made me finally decide I was going to investigate. All those thoughts I was sort-of-having about who might be a likely suspect, and suddenly I had one. A real suspect. A suspect who really might have kidnapped Olivia Curran. But I could be the one who helped to get her rescued. So I didn't really have a choice. And it was easy to get started. Because of Jody.

I'm on the bus right now. On the way home from school. I'm waiting until all the Silverlea kids get dropped off, and it's just me and Jody left. I'm going to talk to her because I know she knows who the pedo guy is. Well, her dad does, anyway. I've seen them coming out of church together. Me and Dad often end up coming back from the beach at about the same time their service finished. And I see Jody and her mom, all dressed up, and sometimes I see Jody's dad too, talking to the pedo guy, with his weird limp.

Eventually, the bus gets into Silverlea, and the last kids get off so that it's just me and Jody left. We're the last stop, so I make my way to the back of the bus where Jody's sitting.

"Hey Jody," I say, real casually.

She looks up from her cellphone for a moment.

"Oh... Hey Billy."

But then she looks right back down at the screen again. While I was waiting for this moment, it seemed like it would be easy. Now that I'm actually about to ask her, it's a little harder. But I don't have long before our stop. She glances up again.

"Can I help you?"

Even though she doesn't really mean that I decide to go for it.

"I was just wondering something," I begin. "You know that guy, the one with the funny leg who lives down in Silverlea?"

She frowns at me.

"You know the one. He's always fishing late at night. Your dad knows him. I've seen them at church together."

"Mr. Foster?" She screws up her face.

"Is that his name?"

"I guess. Why?"

"Do you know his first name?"

"No. Why?"

"No reason," I say. Then I go on. "Do you know much about him?"

"Like what? What's with all the questions?"

I've already decided not to tell Jody that I'm investigating the disappearance of Olivia Curran, because we're not *that* close as friends. So now I don't know how to answer her.

"I just wondered."

“Why?”

“No reason.”

She scowls at me now for a long time. Finally she shakes her head.

"You are one weird kid, Billy Wheatley."

I think hard for a moment, wondering if I could try a different approach. But then I decide against it. Like I said, Jody sometimes forgets that we're friends. I don't care. I've got what I need. I've got his name. *Mr. Foster.*

TEN

I NEED to back up a little. I need to tell you how come I saw Mr. Foster on the beach that night. Like I said, I was there too.

I'm not really into parties or discos or things like that, but Dad likes them, so sometimes, I have to go along too. And as they go, the Surf Lifesaving Club disco is quite good because there's always a barbecue and I like barbecued food. I like that it marks the end of the summer too. Afterwards the town starts to empty out, and I get my beach back. Almost the whole town goes along, locals and tourists, and somehow the two groups mix like they don't in the middle of summer, when everyone's worrying about making money.

The afternoon of the disco, Dad had to drop off some speakers. We drove down to the club with them in the back of the truck. It was a hot day, so the beach was busy and there was nowhere to park. Dad had to leave the truck in the space you're meant to leave so that ambulances can get onto the beach in case there's an emergency. Dad normally doesn't worry much where he parks, but he's got a thing about ambulance spaces. So I got left in the truck with the keys in case we had to move, while he carried the speakers in, one after the other.

But it was late in the summer by then, and people were already leaving the beach, so it wasn't long before a proper space became available. So I decided to park the truck myself.

I'm not really allowed to drive, but I know how to do it. Dad taught me last winter in the parking lot down at Littlelea, when there was hardly anyone around. I was good at it too, except for when I scraped the paintwork. It was just a little bit and it wasn't my fault, because the post was too low, but Dad got real mad anyway.

This time, I was careful. I backed the truck slowly out from where Dad had left it. And then, when I was about to move forward into the space, this van swept past me and went into the space instead.

Maybe the other driver didn't realize I was going into that space; after all, it did take me a couple of minutes to back up, and I might not have been that straight on it. But still, it was annoying and it made me notice the driver. It was the weird guy, the one with the limp. I remember feeling angry at him, and then feeling kind of guilty about that because Dad says I shouldn't judge other people on how they look. But thanks to this guy I had to wait in the middle of the parking lot, until another space came available. So I just watched him, while he opened the back of the van and started taking his fishing gear out.

That's how I knew it had to be him later on. Lurking in the darkness.

"Hey, shift up," Dad said. He'd unloaded the speakers by now. "I'll put the truck on the beach. Locals' parking only, hey?" He gave me a grin. He likes to feel that the laws are only for the tourists.

I shifted over to the passenger seat, and Dad drove us down the little path over the soft sand and the stones until we were on the hard part of the beach. It's really good for driving on, but you're not supposed to do it. Only if there's an emergency, like if a whale body gets washed up, then the police and Coast Guard can drive down to it. Or if you're Dad and there's nowhere else to park. Anyway. Dad drove along the beach a bit, so no one could see his truck easily from the parking lot, and the ticket guy wouldn't give him a fine.

Then we walked back to the hall. I remember how busy it was inside. There were people putting up banners and decorations, packing cans of beer inside ice buckets and moving tables out of the way. I was given a job right away. I had to take the surfboards and the wet-suit rack out around the back, which took me quite a while because the wetsuits are heavy and they smell bad when people pee in them. When I finished doing that, and washing my hands, Dad was fanning the big barbecue with two paper plates, one in each hand, and Emily was laughing at him because he was going red in the face. Dad had a beer open on the table in front of him, so I knew then we'd be there for a long time.

It quickly went from busy to crowded, and by sunset, the band started playing. I got another job. The price for the disco included a burger or a hotdog and one drink – a can of beer or one plastic cup of wine for adults, Pepsi or Fanta for anyone who was under twenty-one. My job was to give out either a burger bun or a hotdog roll. Mrs. Roberts, who normally works in the store, stood next to me, giving out the drinks because I'm too young to deal with alcohol. Beyond her, Dad was cooking the meat, and Emily was helping him and giving people sauces. The barbecue couldn't keep up with all the people, though, so there was a line forming. That was the second time I actually spoke to Olivia Curran.

She was there with her family, but she wasn't *with* her family, if you know what I mean. Although they were right next to each other, they were in separate groups - the mom and dad and the brother were all together, and then Olivia had made friends by then with some other girls, and they were hanging out together a little way behind, like she didn't want to be seen with her parents.

When the dad came past, he remembered me, and he said something about how I seemed to have all the important jobs in town, I don't exactly remember what. But it reminded me I hadn't looked up that wi-fi problem on the Internet.

Olivia looked quite different, all dressed up for the party. She was wearing makeup, and her hair was pinned up. I almost didn't recognize her until she smiled. And then I remembered that.

At first she was busy talking with the other girls. They were all giggling and glancing over at the lifeguards. They were drinking beer and pretending not to look back, but really they were. Olivia didn't say anything to me when she handed over her ticket, but then she recognized me, and she did a little double take.

"Oh, hello," she said. That's when she smiled. "They make you do everything around here, don't they?"

I nodded. "Sometimes. Do you want a burger or a hotdog?"

"What's best?"

"The burger's bigger if you're hungry."

"Hotdog, please." She held out her plate, and I tonged a roll onto it.

"Thanks," she said.

And then her attention was back with her friends and the lifeguards. I told all this to the police officer too - the detective woman I told you about - but she didn't think that was 'significant' either. I already told you though. She wasn't a very good detective.

A while later, the line for food calmed down, so I got to eat. I had two burgers covered with ketchup and then a hotdog, too, which made me feel a little sick. It was dark by then, and the music was really loud. Inside the hall, people were starting to dance, and lots of the adults were getting drunk. Emily tried to get me to dance at one point, but I don't really like dancing, and eventually, I was yawning so much that I went to find Dad and tell him I wanted to go home.

But Dad was outside. He was chatting to his surfer buddies, and he didn't want to go yet because he was enjoying himself. Eventually, he agreed to take me, but then we couldn't go because he'd lent his jacket to someone who was cold, and now he didn't know where they were, and he still had the truck keys in it. I told him I could go and sleep in the back of the truck; I didn't mind. I often sleep in there when Dad wants a night out, but Dad said it would be too cold that night. But just then Jody and her mom walked by. They were going home too, and Jody's mom said to Dad that she could drop me off too. Dad thought this was great, because he'd be able to stay and drink more beer. But he said he'd be back in half an hour or so.

So I left with Jody and her mom. I think back now to when we went outside. I remember how quiet it was out there. I mean, you could still hear the party, but now the music sounded really far away, rather than pounding in your ears. And it felt empty too. Somehow you got the sense that everyone was at that party, the whole town was there. But then, just as I was getting into Jody's mom's car, I noticed this light on the beach – the only one. And I saw who it was – it was the weird guy with the limp. It looked like he was fixing bait to a hook, and when he'd finished he turned the light off and he disappeared into the darkness. But that's not the weird part. What's weird is this: Mr. Foster was just about the only person in the whole town who didn't go to the party. Even *I* went to the party. But this weird guy with his weird limp, the guy with the history of raping girls, he *didn't* go. But he was still *there.* He was there on his own, fishing from the darkness of the beach, or maybe just *pretending* to fish but actually just watching as people came and went. And choosing who he was going to take. And I'm the only one who knows about him.

ELEVEN

It's Tuesday evening now, and my head hurts a little. That's because I've been thinking a lot. I've been trying to remember more about that night, and I've been wondering what to do about it. And in the end I came to this important decision:

Even though I know Mr. Foster was on the beach that night, and even though I know about his raping background, I don't think it's enough to go to the police. Not yet. I need more evidence. And even though I don't really know how the police get evidence, I've got quite a good idea from what I've seen in movies. And what I've seen is, it's not too different from how scientists go about getting their evidence. And like I've already told you, I'm a pretty good scientist. So all I have to do is gather some evidence that proves Mr. Foster did it.

There's also a bit of me that doesn't want to tell the police just yet. Because if I do tell them about Mr. Foster being a pedophile, *and* being there on the beach, they'll probably just take over. They'll say I can't be involved because I'm only eleven. And then I'd miss out, and I've barely even gotten started yet. Or - and you have to remember what happened with the whale - they might miss something else, and then Olivia might never be found. So, between all that, I've got plenty of good reasons for my decision.

My homework sits ignored in my bag while I think over my options. I haven't even updated my crabs project with the data I got over the weekend, and Dr. Ribald won't be impressed if there's data missing – Emily told me once she's got a real temper on her. But instead of either of those, I open my secret Limpet file, and then a separate window on the Wikipedia page of the Olivia Curran case. After a little reading, I add the following information to my file:

Theories on what happened to Olivia Curran

1. Accident

Some people believe it is most likely that Olivia left the party at some point in the evening to go swimming. The water is at its warmest in late August, and it's common for people to swim in the evenings, especially if they have been drinking alcohol. Apparently, some people saw Olivia drinking alcohol that evening. The theory is that she might have swum out too far and been caught in a current, or even eaten by a shark (this would explain why her body was never found). Or she might just have not been a very good swimmer, and maybe forgot this with the alcohol.

However, there are problems with this theory. The first is that no one went swimming with Olivia, or can even remember her telling them she was going swimming (again, maybe they forgot because of the alcohol?). Secondly, the police didn't find a little pile of clothes like people usually leave on the beach when they go swimming. So maybe she went swimming with her clothes on (the alcohol again?) Third, her body hasn't been found, and the currents here tend to wash things onto the beach at Silverlea, not take them away from it. Like the whale body.

Overall, I don't think this is the most likely scenario, but I'm not able to totally discount it yet, so I think it's important to add it to my file. Then I add notes about the second theory.

2. Suicide

One of the newspapers covering the story said Olivia had a boyfriend who split up with her earlier in the summer (at her home, not here in Silverlea). It said Olivia might have been depressed and decided to kill herself. She could have done so by swimming out into the bay. And this might explain the lack of clothes on the beach (if you were swimming out to drown yourself, maybe you wouldn't worry about keeping your clothes dry?).

However. Olivia's parents then released a statement saying they were very angry with the newspaper, and that Olivia hadn't broken up with her boyfriend and had been looking forward to returning home and seeing him again. Also, just like the first theory - what happened to her body if this is what happened?

I'm not very impressed by this theory either. She didn't look very depressed when I saw her, not once I got the wi-fi working anyway, or at the disco. I carry on.

3. Murder / Abduction

The final theory is that someone abducted her.

Most of the evidence suggests this is what happened, and teenage girls quite often do get abducted. It explains why she disappeared without any warning and why no body was found. But the problem with this theory, at least according to Wikipedia, is that there are no obvious suspects. And the very public location of where Olivia went missing, and the poor illumination on the beach and in the parking lot, mean a very wide range of potential suspects.

Wikipedia goes on to say that the investigation is the biggest ever carried out on Lornea Island, but that so far, it hasn't found Olivia Curran, or even produced any credible leads. I stop reading and think back to that night. I try to remember what Mr. Foster looked like, the expression on his face when I saw him, lit up by his fishing lantern. He wasn't that far down the beach, now that I think about it.

Not as far as he should have been if he really was fishing. And I remember how, when he'd finished baiting his hook, or whatever he was doing - *or maybe when he saw me looking* - he turned off his light, and you couldn't see him at all. He was just hiding there in the darkness. But he would still have been able to see me. He'd have been able to see everyone. If Olivia had slipped out of the hall, he would have seen her in the outside lights. He'd have been able to sneak right up close to her. And with his fishing knife he'd have been able to grab her and… I stop visualizing it. I feel sort of cold thinking about it.

A little bit half-heartedly I decide to google the name “Mr. Foster”. I don’t have much expectation of success though, it’s quite a common name. It comes back saying:

"About 3,240,000 results (0.67 seconds)."

I try again, adding "Silverlea" to the search, but it doesn’t help much. Then I try "Lornea Island" and I get a bit excited because there's a *James* Foster who runs a care home in Newlea, but then when I follow some links I find a picture and see he’s not the right Mr. Foster.

I search for an hour, but I know I'm getting nowhere. If Mr. Foster has kidnapped Olivia Curran, then she'll be hidden in his basement, or chopped up in his freezer. Not up on the Internet ready for me to find.

No. If I'm going to find the proof I need to go to the police, then I need to be a little more inventive in finding out about Mr. Foster.

TWELVE

SILVERLEA ISN'T VERY BIG, and even with the extra police around, it's not very busy at this time of year. Even so, I don't know where Mr. Foster lives, and I can't exactly go down every street until I find his van. I *could* ask Jody's dad, since he knows Mr. Foster, but that's difficult because I've never actually spoken to Jody's dad before, and he's bound to ask why I want to know. If I tell him I suspect Mr. Foster of kidnapping and maybe murdering Olivia Curran, he'll want to go the police, and then I'll have exactly the same problem as before. I need to have more evidence before I tell anyone.

But I've got a plan. I know Mr. Foster likes night fishing. Not just from the night Olivia went missing either. I know because I often see him doing it. Or more accurately, on the weekends when Dad goes surfing, Mr. Foster is often there, too, limping around his van, packing up. He finishes his night fishing trips just as we get to the beach.

So, if I know I'm likely to see him at the beach, then I can follow him. I can use my bike. It's a mountain bike. Dad bought it for me, and one for himself, too, although his has got twenty-one gears and mine only has fifteen. When he bought them, the idea was we would go on rides together, but after the first ride we did Dad decided he didn't like it because he thought people drive too fast on the narrow lanes around here. We haven't used them much since then. But we've got a little outhouse and they're still in there. I just need to oil the chain and mine'll be ready.

It's a simple plan, I know, but that just means there's less to go wrong. I've already checked my bike over, and it's loaded into Dad's truck, ready for the morning. When Dad goes surfing tomorrow, I'm going to follow Mr. Foster home and find out where he lives.

THIRTEEN

SATURDAY DIDN'T WORK out so well. Dad didn't even want to go to the beach because it was windy and blowing onshore, which messes the waves up, and because he was out late the night before. But in the end, I convinced him, and we went down to Littlelea where it was a little more sheltered.

Then Mr. Foster's van wasn't in the parking lot. Dad decided to go surf anyway now that he was there, so while he got changed, I wheeled my bike down onto the beach and then pedaled along the hard sand by the water's edge, all the way until I got to Silverlea. It was hard work, and I was worried that even if Mr. Foster had been fishing from Silverlea, he might have already gone by the time I got there. And when I did get there, all hot and sweaty, the Silverlea parking lot was empty too. I cycled around the town a little because you never know, but I didn't find him. Then I had to cycle back along the beach to meet Dad. He was mad because he'd been waiting for me, and I was exhausted from the whole thing.

But that was Saturday. Today is Sunday, and the day is going better. There wasn't much wind this morning, so Dad was happy to go surfing. We drove straight to Silverlea, so I didn't have to cycle anywhere, and guess whose van I saw as we pulled into the parking lot?

That's right. Mr. Foster's.

But now I've got to move fast. I can see Mr. Foster too. He's limping back up the beach, a fishing box slung over one arm, his bundle of rods in the other.

Dad parks the truck at the front of the parking lot, close to Mr. Foster's van. Dad's decided the surf is "going off" this morning, so he's already out there in his head, thinking about the waves he's going to catch. So he doesn't notice how I'm focused on watching Mr. Foster. I watch as he puts down his fishing rods to get his keys. As he pulls open the battered van's back door.

"Look at that, Billy boy," Dad says. He's standing, looking at the sea. I glance over at it; a set of waves are lining up, and there's hardly any wind, so the surface of the water is all glassy and silvery.

"I'll be a couple of hours," Dad tells me, but I hardly hear. "It's perfect out there." He laughs as the waves start to break, peeling smoothly across the beach.

"You know you should stick around and watch for a while this morning. Instead of running off like you normally do."

"OK," I say. Obviously, I don't have time for Dad right now. I just need him to get going so I can follow Mr. Foster when he drives away. I've already got my bike ready, and I'm taking deep breaths, trying to fill my lungs with air. It's occurred to me that Mr. Foster might not live in the actual town of Silverlea itself. If that's the case, I'll have to pedal really hard to keep up with him.

"It'll be a good show. You can go up to the café. Watch from there. Get yourself a drink. Tell Emily I'll come in later and settle up, OK?"

Of course, I *could* use Dad's truck. He hides the keys in the suspension spring of the driver's wheel. But obviously, I don't have a license. You *are* allowed to drive in emergencies, though. I wonder if this counts as an emergency? Thinking about it, I'd probably be quicker on my bike anyway.

"Billy?" Dad interrupts me, shaking his head. "Did you hear me? I said go up to the café if you get bored." A troubled look passes over his face. "Jesus, kid, what's got into you these days? You're so caught up in your crazy projects. What is it today, anyway?"

It's so rare that Dad asks what I'm doing that I'm totally unprepared for this. Now is hardly the time for a detailed explanation of my crab project. Mr. Foster has already loaded his fishing gear, and he's shuffling his way around to the driver's door. He gets in; I can hear the door slam shut.

"Nothing much."

Dad doesn't say anything for a moment, but I can feel him looking at me.

"You know, it's about time you got in the water, Billy. We could surf together. Wouldn't you like that?" Dad says.

Not now, Dad, I think to myself. I can't believe he's trying this on me now. Just to get rid of him, I say:

"OK. But you should go now. The waves are real good, you said so yourself. You don't want to miss it." I don't mean it; there's no way I'm going in the water. But Mr. Foster is about to drive away. I'll say anything to shut Dad up.

But still Dad doesn't move. He's watching me. "OK," he says slowly. "Well, maybe I can give you a lesson? Would you like that?"

The exhaust pipe on Mr. Foster's van shakes as the engine fires up. The tires start to move with a crunch.

"OK, Dad, but I'll see you later."

To my relief, Dad seems content with that for now. He reaches down and picks up his board.

"Go to the café, yeah? If you get cold." He looks down the beach at the surf. Another wave is feathering, rising up from the surface of the ocean like a smooth hill of glass, about to pitch forward. Dad whistles.

"Check that out. We'll have you riding those in no time."

I can see he's gone, in his head, I mean. He can't help himself; he loves it when the waves are smooth like this, so I don't even have to reply to him. He turns and is soon jogging light-footed down the beach, towards the ocean. And it's just in time, too, because Mr. Foster's van starts backing out of its space, and then the gearbox crunches as he changes into first.

My feet press on the pedals and I reach the parking lot exit just as the van crunches past me on the gravel. I put my head down and push the gears as hard as I can.

FOURTEEN

THE VAN TURNS north out of the parking lot, along the seafront road. But immediately, I start falling behind. Then it turns inland again, up Claymore Street, which is where most of the stores are in Silverlea. It makes the turn almost before I'm even on the seafront road. It's so much faster than me. I didn't expect this problem.

What's worse, Claymore Street is slightly uphill. I haven't gone more than a minute before the van is almost out of sight. I'm pedalling as fast as I can, standing up out of the seat, breathing hard already; I can't get enough oxygen in to keep this up for long. I start to panic I'm going to lose him right away.

Then I get some luck. There's a set of lights on Claymore Street where it crosses Alberton Avenue, and Mr. Foster's van gets caught there. He sits there for a minute while I pedal up the hill behind him as fast as I can, standing on the pedals still and swinging the bike side to side underneath me. Out of the corner of my eye, I watch the light. It stays red, and I get close to him. But not for long. The light turns orange and then green, and then he's off again, straight on, still up Claymore Street. I get a blast of smoke in my face as he pulls away.

But then I have a big stroke of luck. While the lights were against him, another car pulled in front of him, and it's someone really old because they're driving real slow. It's only a few moments before Mr. Foster catches them up, but he doesn't overtake, I guess because he doesn't want to draw attention to himself. It's still faster than I can cycle, but at least they're not disappearing into the distance in front of me. For about three minutes, we go on like this, me still pedalling as fast as I can, and Mr. Foster's van and the old person pulling away, but not too much. Even so I know I can't do this much longer. If the old person turns off. Or if Mr. Foster keeps going out of town, where the road is long and straight and easy to overtake on, I've got no hope of catching him.

I put my head down and really go for it. But even so I feel my legs slowing, and I've got nothing left to give. There's a bend up ahead, and after that, we'll be out of town. I'm going to lose him. I'm probably going to die from cycling too hard, and even so I'm going to lose him. But then the blinker on Mr. Foster's van comes on. He's turning off the main road.

I don't know the name of the road he turns onto, and I don't get there until a full minute later. And when I do, I have to stop. I drop my bike and hold onto a lamppost with both hands. Then I collapse to my knees, on the verge. I feel like I'm going to throw up. It's like when you have to do running races at school; the four hundred meters is the worst. Sometimes, kids actually do throw up doing that one.

Finally, I recover enough to look up again. I'm on a small road that I don't know. There's no stores, it's just houses and I can't see the van anywhere. I think I've probably lost him.

When I recover a little more, I get back on my bike and keep going. I don't know where exactly, but I figure I might as well look around. Silverlea isn't big and behind the houses here it opens right out into fields, so maybe I can still find him. The houses at the back of town here are kind of small, not the type that get rented easily to tourists, and I think quite a few of them aren't lived in at all. It certainly looks that way.

The road Mr. Foster turned into branches out into several different minor streets. I take one at random and cycle all the way to the end, hoping to see the van parked somewhere, but I don't see it, so I return to the main road. Then I take a second one, with the same result. I think this is hopeless; I might as well go back. I could go to the café and get a hot chocolate. I could update Emily on my project. But there's one more street, so I might as well keep looking. I cycle down it slowly, checking out the driveways. Most are empty, and where there are cars they're pretty old. There's a bend up ahead, and I almost decide to turn around before reaching it, but figure I should check there too. And there it is: Mr. Foster's van.

I almost can't believe it. My heart's still going hard from the exercise, and now something else as well. Nerves I guess. I stop by a tree and wait, watching. The van is parked on the driveway of a single-story house, right at the end of the street. It looks run-down, and it's kind of tucked away. Behind it, there's a stack of big trees, like a little forest.

There's a fishing boat on a trailer in the front yard, an old, open-style one. The lights in the house are all off. Overall, it looks really suspicious. Exactly the kind of place you'd expect a pedophile murderer would live.

Standing there, I get a creepy feeling, like spiders crawling on my skin. It's worse because I know Mr. Foster is inside right now. He might be watching me, like he did with Olivia that night at the beach. He might be sneaking out of the back door right now, with his fishing knife ready. I mean, if he *did* take her, then surely he would be careful now? He'd be looking out for anything strange. Anything that suggested someone was onto him? It occurs to me now that this is a *really* quiet street. I haven't seen anyone since I turned off Claymore Street. There's no neighbors out in their yards, hardly any cars on the driveways. He could be sneaking toward me right now, in the cover of those trees. I start to feel really scared. I want to jump on my bike and just get out of here. I nearly do, but I stop myself. I need to get evidence to take to the police. It is scary, but I'll just have to be careful. That's all.

I take a deep breath. I lay my bike down on the grass verge and move closer, keeping myself behind the trunk of another tree just on the edge of his property. I can see into the trees now, and I'm sure he's not there. I'm close to his van now. Close enough to hear the engine ticking as it cools down.

I risk another look at the house, scanning for signs of life. This close up, I can see it better. There are two windows in the front. The bigger one has got the drapes drawn, which means I can't see in. The smaller window is the kitchen, and there's no drapes. I can see a section of countertop, an electric kettle, and one of those wooden trees of mugs. One of the mugs has got fish painted on it. It's too dark to see further into the room. The lights are still off.

I look for any signs there might be a cellar. Pretty much all murderers use cellars, and if Olivia is still alive, this is where she'll be. But I don't know how you tell if a house has a cellar or not. I mean, it's not like there's any windows, because they'd be underground. I decide there probably is one – I just can't see it.

I slide back behind my tree and think for a moment. I've made good progress: I know where Mr. Foster lives, and therefore I probably know Olivia's location, whether she's alive or dead. This is good. But I know I need more. If I go to the police now, they still won't believe me. I'm just a kid, they won't realize I'm really a scientist. Even if I could get them to listen to me, they might believe me just a little bit and send one officer to ask him some questions, and then *they'd* probably get kidnapped and be kept in the cellar or killed too. So it's definitely too early for the police. I need to do what I came here for. I need to do a stakeout of Mr. Foster's house.

You see stakeouts in movies all the time. The people doing them always get to eat takeout, or donuts. Usually, they argue a little, or have a heart-to-heart so you learn their back story. But it always works. They always see something important. So I know a stakeout is the right thing to do. But obviously, I can't just sit on the street eating donuts and watching Mr. Foster's house. But don't worry, like I told you earlier. I did a lot of thinking the other night.

I have another look at the front yard. I notice the boat again. It's an open boat, quite small, like the ones that people use to fish in estuaries, not the open sea. The stern is facing the house, and since the front yard isn't that big, the bow is almost buried in the hedge. It's got a faded blue cover tied over the top, with gaps between the ties where the wind has worked it loose. From the look of the rusted trailer, and the weeds growing up all around, it doesn't look like it's been used in a while. And winter is coming on and people only use that kind of boat in the summer. So Mr. Foster isn't likely to take it out any time soon. That makes it perfect for what I need. I lock my bike to a post so I don't have to worry about that, then I sneak back towards Mr. Foster's house. When I'm right in front, kind of hidden from view by the boat, I run across to it and lift the cover.

My heart is pumping when I get there. I have to stand on the trailer because it's higher than I thought. And the cover isn't as loose as I'd hoped. For a second, I think I can't get in, but I'm already committed, sticking my head and shoulders inside the boat, my feet in the hedge. The smell hits me at once, mold and decay. I suddenly start panicking. The idea hits me that I'm going to land right on top of Olivia's decomposing body. I frantically wriggle backward to get out, and drop down back onto the grass, breathing hard and in full view of the windows. I kind of half-hide under the boat, and I try to control my breathing. I tell myself to calm down.

It's just a boat smell. It's just fish guts and stagnant seawater. All boats smell like that when they get old or aren't looked after. I glance around at Mr. Foster's windows and around at the neighbor's houses too. I'm lucky. Still no one seems to have noticed anything, but I'm totally exposed, sitting under Mr. Foster's boat. If I don't move, someone is going to see me any second. So I take a deep breath and go again. I climb back onto the trailer and slide under the cover a second time. This time, I'm calmer, and I pull myself inside using the seat. I slither into the boat; my backpack gets stuck for a moment, but then it frees, and my body slides into the bottom of the boat with a bump.

It rocks at first, but then settles. It really does stink in here. It's so bad it's hard to breathe. It takes a few moments for my eyes to adjust to the darkness, but when they do, I'm relieved to see there's no body, just slimy wooden floorboards, and that I'm lying in half an inch of dirty water. I try and lift myself out of it, but I can feel the water soaking through my knees. I ignore this, slip my arms out of my backpack and retrieve my camera. Then I work my way to the back of the boat where I can best observe the house. There's a kind of cutout for the engine where most of the light in the boat is coming from. Through the hole, I can see the front of the house perfectly. With my heart still pumping, I settle down to see what's going to happen next. And it's not long before I spot something interesting.

FIFTEEN

It really does look suspicious, his house. There are pieces of render missing from the walls, and the paint is peeling off the window frames. And looking now, I can see that one of the windowpanes is actually cracked. And they're really dirty. The drapes behind are dirty, too, and faded, with a big yellow stain on the ones covering the big window. And now that I think about it, why does he have the drapes closed when it's daytime? It's very obvious now that Mr. Foster has things to hide. I decide I should just get set up, then get out of here. I don't really know how dangerous this is. And I'm pretty uncomfortable in here.

But then the kitchen light comes on. I freeze. I can see further into the room now, and a man walks through the doorway, comes into the room. It's Mr. Foster. I know it's him because of the limp.

I try to get lower, so he can't see me. But that makes the whole boat move again, rocking on its trailer. If he looks out of the window now he'll definitely notice. But I'm lucky – when I dare to look again, I can see him, still in the kitchen. He doesn't seem to have noticed anything. Then he walks out of the kitchen. Before I've even managed to take a photograph. I'm annoyed at myself. What if I don't see him again?

But a moment later, a strip of light appears between the drapes in the other window, and they start to open. Now I can see it's a living room. It's quite big, but strangely empty – the only things in it are an armchair, pulled close to a gas fire, and a big TV. And it's dirty. Strewn across the floor are pizza boxes and beer cans; an ashtray is overflowing with cigarette ends. And there, limping around the room with a black garbage bag, is Mr. Foster. I can't figure out what he's doing at first, but then I realize. He's tidying up. He's collecting the beer cans and crushing them before adding them to the bag. I feel a rush of excitement. I'm right, I know I am.

This is *exactly* how you'd expect a murderer to live. Alone, in a dirty, creepy house. And what's he doing now?

He's trying to destroy evidence.

I make double sure the flash is switched off on my camera, and then, very carefully, I take several photographs, trying to catch Mr. Foster's face. I get a couple of good ones. When he leaves the room, I review them on the camera, waiting to see which room he'll appear in next.

But then there's a disaster. The front door suddenly bursts open and before I have a chance to duck down I see Mr. Foster standing right there, just a few feet away. I almost cry out in panic as he comes straight towards me. All I can do is drop down into the belly of the boat, feeling the water soaking up my leg. He must have seen me through the window, or maybe he saw the boat move. I think about screaming for help. But I don't know if his neighbors will hear me. It's not the kind of area where you can rely on neighbors anyway. I hold my camera like a rock in my hand. It's my only hope. When he peels back the cover, I'll hit him with it and then jump out and run as fast as I can. I have a flash-thought of what it might be like in his dungeon-cellar, chained up next to Olivia. Even though I don't have much time, I still feel scared.

Then I hear him *right beside the boat*. There's a noise - I can't place it at first, but then I realize, it's whistling. Mr. Foster is whistling a tune as he comes to get me. I try to make myself breathe quietly, and I adjust my grip on the camera, getting ready to lash out with it. I wait. Each second lasts forever. But instead of the cover being peeled suddenly back, instead of his hairy hands reaching down to grab me, the whistling stops, and there's a new noise, a kind of metallic banging and then a crashing sound. And then quiet. For sometime, all I can hear is my breathing, short, fast breaths that sound incredibly loud. Is he still there? I don't know. Then I hear the front door shutting again.

I know it's probably a trap. I don't make a single move. I wait in the bottom of the boat, but the seconds tick by, then the minutes, and I wonder why Mr. Foster doesn't do something to catch me. Any second, I expect to see his face in the gap between the boat's side and its cover. But then something else happens instead. I hear the van's engine roar to life. I change position to look outside again, and I'm just in time to see Mr. Foster behind the wheel, backing out of the drive. He's not looking at me. I watch him turn in the street and drive off down the road.

What the hell is going on? I stick my head out from under the boat's cover, and immediately, I'm relieved to breathe air that doesn't smell of dead fish. I look around the yard, to where the noises came from, and I find one answer at least. I didn't notice when I climbed in the boat, but there's a metal trash can in the corner of the yard. I put two and two together with the black bag I saw Mr. Foster with before. He was putting the trash out.

Putting the evidence in the trash.

I climb completely out of the boat now and go to look. I cautiously lift the trash can lid. The black bag is there; it smells of stale cigarettes. I gently push the bag open. All I can see are beer cans and cardboard pizza boxes. I don't know what they mean, but I grab my camera and take photographs anyway.

Next though I'm uncomfortable. I know I've suddenly got an opportunity to actually rescue Olivia. Mr. Foster has gone, I don't know for how long he's gone, since he's left the lights on, but I know he's driven away. So if I can break into the house I might be able to find her and help her escape. But the thought of it is really scary. What if he comes back while I'm inside? Perhaps he *did* see me, and this is all part of his trap? I'm paralyzed with indecision for a moment. But I pull myself together for a second time. I'll hear the van coming down the street if he comes back. I've *got* to try and rescue Olivia. I have to be brave. Slowly, I approach the front door.

Up close to it, I can feel eyes on my back. I can almost sense someone right behind me. It's like when you're little and you're sure a monster is under your bed, but you're all alone, and you're too afraid to look. I spin around, ready to confront whoever's there. But there's no one. I'm alone in the street. The windows of Mr. Foster's neighbors are blank and empty. I watch for a long while, but nothing moves, apart from the wind swaying the branches of the trees.

I turn back to the door and gently push against it. It doesn't move. I turn the handle and push a bit harder, but still it resists. I put more weight behind it, but it's obvious now it's locked. I feel a puff of relief and wonder if I've tried hard enough. But I go to the kitchen window next, running my fingers around the frame to try and pull it open. It's too cold this time of year for people to have the windows open, but maybe he hasn't locked it shut. But it looks like he has, or more likely, he just never opens it. I think for a minute about breaking the glass and forcing my way in, but I decide against it. I know he's a pedophile and probably a murderer, but it's still wrong to go around breaking people's windows.

I move instead to try the living room window. But it's no good there either; it's locked shut too. I inspect the cracked pane. It looks like it cracked when someone tried to pull it shut, and the frame is still sticking out. I could get my penknife and prize it open. Maybe I could get in. But then I think of something. I'll only hear Mr. Foster's van if he comes back in it. What if he's parked around the corner, and even now he's sneaking silently back to catch me? I go really cold, thinking of this. And that's when I notice it.

SIXTEEN

It's on the floor behind the door. Maybe a little bit hidden, but definitely looking totally out of place in Mr. Foster's weird, run-down house. It's a pink backpack. I recognize the brand, some of the girls at school have the same one, it has a big red heart logo on the front. Now what would Mr. Foster be doing with a girl's pink backpack like that?

For a while I'm just frozen to the spot, staring at it. I don't know what it means – the bag being there – but I get a bad feeling from it, like a foreboding. It's like my mind is reaching out into darkness to understand the implications. But I can't grasp them. Only that it's bad. Real bad.

And there's another thing. Up to now this all felt just a little bit like a game. Or one of my scientific experiments. Important, obviously, but maybe not something totally real. But that's changed now. Looking at that pink bag, so out of place, I know this is real. And I know that Mr. Foster really could be back at any moment. He really could be sneaking back to catch me. A fully grown man, twice my size, and with no neighbors to see when he drags me inside. I just want to get away from here. Right now. As fast as I can.

So I don't try to get inside anymore. Instead, I get on with what I came here to do. You see, I never planned on staking the house out myself. I always knew I'd only have a couple of hours at best, and the chances of seeing something in that time isn't very high. I need to watch for much longer. But that's not a problem. I've got technology for that.

I was hoping there'd be a tree or bush, but the inside of the boat is much better. It's hidden from view, but close enough to the house so the lens will capture anything that goes on. It's even sheltered from the rain, which is good. I mean, obviously, the camera is waterproof, but sometimes, rain gets on the lens and makes it hard to see anything.

I use a couple of clamps to fix it to the back of the boat, so that it's facing the house. I'm using my latest and best camera. It's a Denver WCT-3004 Wildlife Camera. It's motion-activated, and when I bought it, it had 258 reviews on the Internet of four or five stars. There were a few one-star reviews, too, but they were mostly from people who couldn't figure out how to set it up correctly. They didn't worry me at all because I'm good at setting these cameras up now. I've had lots of experience. It was expensive, though. I spent most of the money I earned from setting up the wi-fi networks. But it was worth it for one thing. The Denver WCT-3004 has *infrared night vision*. That means that even if Mr. Foster sneaks out in the middle of the night, I'll still see him.

When I'm happy that it's all set up to record and the clamps holding it are tight, I back slowly away, making sure I've left nothing that will give away what I've done. Then I walk back to where I've left my bike. I look around carefully while I do, in case Mr. Foster is hiding somewhere, but I don't see him. I feel a lot better when I've cycled away. I feel good, actually. At least someone is doing something constructive to find poor Olivia Curran. And I get that familiar feeling that always comes when I set up a camera. I can never wait to see what I'll catch.

SEVENTEEN

FEELING good doesn't last long.

"Billy, where the *hell* have you been?"

Dad's mad. I'm barely halfway across the parking lot before he's shouting at me.

"I've been waiting a half hour for you. I looked in the café and everywhere."

I squeeze my brakes and see right away what's happened. It's the wind: it's changed direction. It was blowing offshore this morning, which was good for the waves, but it's swung around. Now it's onshore, which surfers don't like because it ruins the waves. Behind Dad, standing with his hands on his hips, I can see the smooth, pretty lines of swells from earlier have been replaced with messy white-capped chop.

"I told you not to go far. I *told you* that. Now, get your goddamn bike in the back, and let's get going."

I open my mouth to tell him all about Mr. Foster and his creepy house, and how I'm going to catch him for abducting her, or murdering her, or whatever he's done. But the words don't come out. Instead, I let Dad grab my bike and watch while he throws it into the back of the truck so it scrapes the paintwork. He'd be so mad if I did that. Then he climbs into the cab and revs the engine too loud until I get in beside him. I don't try to get in the back. I'm not allowed to ride there when he's in a bad mood.

"Jesus, boy." He carries on as soon as I shut the door. "What did I do so wrong with you?" He shakes his head,"You know Craig's son James?" He asks, and I don't get a chance to say I do, "he goes surfing with Craig every weekend? Even when it's big, he gives it a try. He *tries*. But you? I can't get you anywhere near the water." Dad shakes his head again. "Where did I go so wrong?"

It's not really a fair comparison. James is *two years* older than me, and he's really sporty. He's even on the school football team. And anyway, Dad's got lots of friends to go surfing with, so why is it so important *I* have to do it with him? I buckle my seatbelt in silence and wait for the storm to pass.

"Where do you go anyway?" Dad says a few minutes later, as we're driving out through town. "We come to the beach every weekend, and you're always busy. Where do you go? What do you do?" We come to a rest at the traffic light that caught Mr. Foster earlier.

"Come on, Billy, tell me."

This time, he really does seem to want an answer. I calculate quickly. He's still in too bad a mood to risk telling him the truth.

"I told you before," I say. "I'm doing a study on the territorial habits of hermit crabs," I begin, but he cuts me off.

"Oh Christ. You're still doing that? Jesus. You're not a kid anymore, Billy. You can't just. . . " He lifts both hands from the steering wheel, but then stops. He puffs his cheeks out and holds his face in his hands.

"Shit. *Shit. Shit. Shit*." He surprises me by punching the steering wheel. The light turns green, but we don't move. Then there's a horn behind us. Dad winds down the window really angrily, then leans out.

"You wanna fuck off buddy?" he shouts at the car behind. But then he starts going anyway. I'm too scared to look behind in case the other driver is going to get out to have a fight, but then I do look, just as the other car makes a turn. Then Dad and me both sit in silence for a while, him driving slowly, me pretending to look out of the window.

A few minutes later, when we're out of Silverlea, Dad pulls over onto the verge. The road around us here is deserted. For a long while, Dad doesn't say anything. He just sits there, staring out of the windshield.

"Billy, I'm sorry," Dad says eventually. His tone is changed now. He's much calmer. He sounds weary.

"I didn't mean to lose it like that." He sighs and stops talking again. There's just the sound of the engine rumbling away in front of us.

"I just worry sometimes. You know, Billy?" Suddenly, he's talking again. "I worry that it's just the two of us and that. . . That maybe I'm not such a great dad. I worry about you hanging out on your own all the time." He looks across at me and waits until I look back at him. "I don't even know if it's safe. Since that girl went missing."

I don't answer. I don't even move. I'm too surprised at him suddenly bringing that up.

"You know what I mean? I know it's hard, being here, just the two of us. But we have to stick together. We have to make it work."

I don't answer.

"I'm gonna make it up to you. OK, Billy?"

He looks at me, and I still don't say anything. I'm not even looking at him.

"Billy!"

I turn to look at him. But still I don't say anything.

As I watch, Dad opens and closes his mouth a few times, like he's trying to figure out what to say next. Eventually, some words come out.

"Listen buddy, I saw Pete out in the water today. You know Big Pete? Runs the surf store over in Newlea? We got chatting when the wind came in. How about we head over there this afternoon? We could pick you out a board. Your own surfboard? Get you set up. You'd like that, wouldn't you?"

The best thing to do when Dad's like this is to go along with whatever he comes up with. But I wasn't expecting that.

EIGHTEEN

I GUESS I should tell you about Mom. Now that we're getting to know each other a little better. I mean, I should tell you what I *know* about Mom, which isn't that much because I was very young when it all happened, and Dad doesn't like talking about it. I mean *really* doesn't like talking about it.

I don't much like talking about it either, to be honest, but maybe you've been wondering why she's not here with Dad and me in the house.

Mom worked as a nurse in a hospital. Not here, not on Lornea Island; we lived on the mainland then, a long way away, I don't even know where since Dad gets all weird when I ask him. But the way Dad tells it is like this: One evening, she was driving home from work. She was on her own in the car, and it was raining real hard. It was so late, there was hardly anyone else on the freeway. And probably, she was tired, too, because she'd been working, saving people's lives. Up ahead of her, a tractor-trailer truck jackknifed. The truck was carrying one of those steel-sided shipping containers, and somehow it ended up sideways across the road. The driver didn't have time to do anything. All his lights had gone out, and it was on an unlit part of the road. It was just there. This steel box blocking the whole freeway. Just bad luck. Mom's was the first car to get there. Dad told me once it would have been over quick for her. But I sometimes wonder about that. Sometimes, when Dad's driving me to Newlea, I spot a tree or a building on the side of the road, and I count how many seconds we take to reach it, and I imagine what it must have been like for Mom. When she hit the brakes and nothing happened, except the car skidding forwards on the wet road. I wonder if she knew. And how that felt.

So I don't know what happened. Sometimes, I think Dad isn't telling me everything. I don't really know if she tried to brake, or if she tried to steer around it. I don't know what was in the container, or if she died the moment she hit it, or if they took her to hospital and she died slowly.

I don't remember the funeral. Maybe I didn't go? Mostly I just remember things from here, from Lornea Island. I've figured out we moved here soon after it happened, but I don't know *why* Dad chose here. I don't think we'd been here before. We don't have relatives here. As far as I know we don't have relatives at all. I guess maybe Dad wanted to make a fresh start. Maybe he thought it was better if we lived in a place that doesn't have freeways? I don't know. Like I said, Dad doesn't talk about it, and I stopped asking him a long time ago.

We don't go back. To where we lived with Mom, I mean. Dad doesn't like to be reminded of anything from that time, and it's too far away anyway. So we don't go back, and we don't talk about it, and if I ever do ask, or if something comes up on TV that maybe reminds me of before, and what happened, Dad just tells me we've got to move on with our lives.

So now you know. And you can stop wondering.

NINETEEN

"HEY, *Sammmmm*, how's it going, man?"

"Hey. . . buddy. How ya doing? You cool?"

We've just walked through the door of *The Green Room* surf shop, and that's the assistant and Dad talking and high-fiving the way surfers do. I don't say anything as I've gotten myself a little bit upset telling you about Mom. I'll be OK in a minute, though.

The assistant has got blond hair down to his shoulders, and he's wearing shorts even though it's cold. The yellow hairs on his legs are sticking up like fur. He's really excited to see Dad though. This often happens. It's because Dad's kind of a celebrity for the local surfers. Sometimes, there are surfing competitions, and when people persuade Dad to enter, he usually wins, especially when the waves get big. So they all like to hang out with him.

There's a strong smell of rubber in the store, from all the wetsuits, and there's a TV on the wall, playing a surf video. I don't get surf videos. They all show the exact same thing, just people riding waves over and over again. Actually, maybe that's why the assistant looks excited: he's just so bored from watching the video.

"Did you catch it this morning?" the assistant asks. "Pretty *awesome*, huh?"

"Yeah, it was OK. Until that wind came in anyway."

"Oh yeah. That was a bummer, man. So, you buying? Or just hanging?" He looks equally hopeful about either option.

"Actually. . . " Dad looks kind of awkward for a moment. He scratches at his ear. "Pete said he'd do me a deal. . . He let you know?"

"Yeah, sure. He said you might drop in."

"Cool. Well, actually, I'm looking for a board for my son here."

The assistant notices me for the first time. Or maybe he saw me when I came in but assumed I'd wandered in by accident. I look a bit out of place in surf shops.

"Yeah. . . Awesome." I can feel the assistant's eyes on me, and there's a flicker of recognition between us.

"Hey, dude," he says to me, the first words he's *ever* said to me. "I never knew you were *Sam Wheatley's* kid." He tilts his head to one side, like he can't quite get past this. I don't say anything.

"So, you gonna be a local legend like your old man, huh?" I can hear the forced enthusiasm in his voice, and still I say nothing.

"You gonna win the Island Championship when you're older? Maybe even go on tour, yeah?"

A couple of times, after there's been a big surfing competition, I've heard people say that Dad could have done the surfing tour. If he hadn't had to look after a kid, that is.

"No," I say finally, just to shut him up. I look at Dad. He's the one who brought me in here.

"Yeah, we're looking for a board, aren't we, Billy? Say hi to. . . um." It's suddenly clear Dad doesn't know the assistant's name. The guy jumps in quickly to put this right, like he's more embarrassed about it than Dad is.

"It's Shane. You remember, right? Shane."

"Yeah, yeah, sorry buddy." Dad hits the side of his head, like it just slipped his mind. "Yeah, say hi to Shane, Billy."

"Hi Shane" I say, raising a hand to wave. Then Shane launches into his sales pitch. Although he's looking at me, it's Dad he's trying to impress.

"So, you're after a new board? Well, you've come to the right place. We got these new Micro Machine boards for grommets. You thinking thruster? Quad fin set up - "

Fortunately, Dad interrupts him.

"Billy's not. . . He's not quite at that level yet," Dad says. "We're looking at something more at the beginner end of things. But nice, though. Something decent." Dad looks at me and smiles.

Just then though Big Pete himself comes in. He sees Dad and they start talking about the waves this morning, so for a few minutes, Shane and me are just standing there, until Pete suggests that Shane should show me the boards.

"Yeah, sure. Cool." Shane nods enthusiastically. "Billy, you wanna come with me?"

I don't have much choice, so I follow him into the board room where the walls are lined with racks, each housing a surfboard resting on its tail. He goes to one wall and starts pulling boards out, looking at them. I don't know what he's looking at; they all look pretty much the same. I can hear Dad still chatting with Big Pete next door.

"So, what's the story with you then, Billy? How come you're only learning now, I mean?" Shane asks me. "I mean, it's cool and all. No big deal, I'm just wondering, with your old man being. . . You know."

I shrug and don't answer. I'm certainly not going to tell someone like Shane about my thing about going in the water. It's not because I'm embarrassed about it; it's not a big deal. It's just that Shane's an idiot. I'll tell *you* if you like.

The thing is, I'm just a bit scared of the sea, that's all. I know it's kind of odd for someone who lives on an island and all that. Especially someone who lives in a house overlooking the beach and who's going to be a marine biologist when they're older. But then, this kind of thing isn't that uncommon. Did you know, for example, that Neil Armstrong was afraid of heights? So are most airline pilots.

It's not that I'm scared of the water exactly, anyway. It's just I don't like going out of my depth. Or any deeper than my waist, really. Everything else is fine. I don't mind the rockpools. And I can swim OK if I need to. Dad saw to that. He made me go to swimming lessons for years. I'm OK in a pool, where there's lifeguards, and I don't actually go out of my depth. It's just the open sea I don't like. There's something about how big it is, and how deep it is, and the currents that can pull you out. It gives me the shudders. I just don't like it.

I feel my heart rate going up now, thinking about it. And I start to feel hot too. The room and all these surfboards begin to wobble in my vision. I can see Shane's face, too. Suddenly, he's looking really worried about something. He's not exactly spinning around, not yet anyway, but I can feel it going that way. White dots of bright light appear in front of my eyes, and I can hear my breathing sounds funny: it's gone fast and heavy. Suddenly, I feel a hand on my shoulder.

"Hey, Billy, you OK? Seen anything you like?" My dad's back. His voice sounds distant, though. I hear him talking to Shane. "Bill's a little nervous about the water. It's not a big deal. He can swim just fine, and we're gonna work up to it real slow. Aren't we, Billy?" He's crouching down beside me now. Then he slaps me on the back. "We're going to figure it out. Catch you some waves."

Slowly, my vision returns to normal, and my breathing slows. Dad's hand is still on my shoulder, and he's gripping me tight. Holding me up, pushing me on.

"How about that one?" Dad says, pointing to one of the boards. Shane pulls it out for us to inspect. It's blue, and it's got three dolphins painted on the top. When I was younger, I had a thing for dolphins. I wonder if he remembers.

"Yeah, that looks cool," he says. "What you reckon, Billy?"

One hour later, I'm all set with my new surfboard and wetsuit. We're driving back home, and Dad's telling me over and over how nice the rails are and how great the graphics look. I'm wondering how the hell I'm going to get out of actually using this stuff.

Oh. And I think dolphins are one of the most overrated animals in the sea. Just so you know.

TWENTY

IT'S late on Friday evening now. I've been at school all week. I was hoping I'd get the chance to go back to Mr. Foster's to pick up the memory card from the camera, but what with school and the evenings getting darker, I didn't manage it. And the weather's been bad too; it's hardly stopped raining all week. And now the weather's gone really crazy. I've got a weather station on the roof of the house. It tells me the average wind speed and the maximum gust. Tonight, it's averaging forty-four knots, and the biggest gust was fifty-five knots. That's an actual storm, as classified by the Beaufort Scale.

Storms are pretty scary up here on the cliff, but they're exciting too. With the big gusts, the whole house shakes, and the wind howls like we're surrounded by wolves. Sometimes, I like to go outside and lean into the wind, not too close to the cliff edge, though. The clouds scud through the sky like they're on fast-forward; and even at night the sea is more white than black.

The wind is supposed to peak about now, and then drop off quickly. I hope so, because I won't get any sleep until it does. Not with the wolves howling like that. And I need to sleep because Dad will definitely be up early tomorrow for the surfing. And that means I can get to Mr. Foster's house at last. There'll be a full week of recordings to pick up. Maybe Dad will even surf all day. Then I'll be able to go through the recordings tomorrow afternoon and pick out the best parts to give to the police. Then they can arrest Mr. Foster, rescue Olivia, and everything can go back to normal.

I'm sort of wondering, too, whether I should become a detective *and* a marine biologist when I'm older. I think I'd like to, but I don't know if you're allowed to do two jobs. I don't know anyone who does. Except Emily obviously. She's a waitress and a scientist, although what she does in the café isn't a real job for someone as clever as her. And thinking about it, I'd rather be a marine biologist than a police officer. Most of the time, the police just sit in their cars, eating donuts.

I'm tired now. I didn't have a very easy time of it in school this week. If I'm honest, I'm a little bit worried, too, because this is the first weekend since Dad bought me the surfboard. At some point, I'm going to have to explain to him that I'm not going to use it. I shudder a little at the thought of that. And under the sound of the wolves, I can hear the roar of the ocean, like it's trying to remind me all the time. Then my window rattles like someone's trying to break in. I know there isn't, really; it's just the storm. I check the reading from my weather station. That last gust was fifty-eight knots. I won't sleep until this storm dies down.

TWENTY-ONE

THE STORM BLEW itself out about three, but Dad's up at first light. The wind has gone, but the swell is *huge*. Obviously, I'm not going anywhere near it, but even so, the bay looks kind of awe-inspiring from up here on the cliffs. Out to sea, the swells are like great folds stretching right across the whole seven miles of the bay. Closer to the beach, where the waves break, they're forming into enormous round caverns that rear up and hang in the air for longer than looks possible. And then when they finally do crash down, each one does so with a bellowing *crack* that makes the windows rattle. Then, in the aftermath, all this crazy white water tumbles in toward the beach like a tsunami. Even the beach looks wild. It's covered in long streaks of foam, wobbling like jelly.

You'd think only mad people would want to go in the water today, but you should see Dad. He's singing to himself, and his eyes are open wide. I guess he looks like a mad person, come to think of it. But he loves days like this. Days like this are his thing.

It's colder after the storm. I'm shivering in my sweater, and I put my shoes and socks on before I come downstairs. But Dad's there just in bare feet and his jeans.

"Hey, buddy! You seen the swell?" He's eating a big bowl of muesli as I come into the kitchen. I glance nervously at the corner of the room, where my new surfboard has been leaning up against the wall since we got back from The Green Room. Dad follows my eyes.

"Whoa there. Sorry, big guy. I know I promised to take you out this weekend, but I don't think it's a day for you. It's kinda big out there today."

There's a *crack* from the bay below us as another wave explodes down. Both our gazes go to the window, which shakes in its frame. Beyond it, we can actually see the lines of waves; they're breaking that far out. Dad whistles.

"Maybe in a few years, huh? We'll get you out there on a big 'un. I tell you there's no feeling like it. Not even. . . " He doesn't finish the sentence but shovels the last few spoonfuls into his mouth.

"We might be able to do tomorrow. Later on?" He says when he's finished chewing. "This swell's not forecast to stick around too long. Maybe we'll get you in the water tomorrow huh?"

I don't say anything to this. There isn't much point because Dad isn't really listening to me. It's like he's not even here in the kitchen with me. He's only thinking about one thing.

"Anyway, we better get going. Get down there before the wind kicks in. You ready?"

I haven't had breakfast, but I nod anyway. If I hold him up, he'll only get frustrated.

I have time to grab my backpack and a chunk of bread before I hear the engine on the truck. Then I go outside. There's no question where we're going. No one could paddle out through the giant waves pummeling Silverlea, not even Dad. But at Littlelea, the rivermouth shapes the waves better, and the cliff gives some protection, so they're smaller - it's just where people go when the waves get big like this. So I chuck my bike in because I know I'm going to have to get along the beach to get to Mr. Foster's house and retrieve my memory card.

I climb in the back of the truck, and take a bite of bread. I go to sit back against the cab, like I normally do, but my bike's in the way. Instead, I have to squeeze in down one side. And Dad's board bag is kind of pushing against me, so I shove it out of the way to get more room. And that's when I see something.

I don't know what it is at first, but it's flashing in the light, almost like a tiny mirror. It's something small, whatever it is, caught between the side of the truck and the floor. I try to get closer to get a good look at it, but at that moment, the truck bounces over a pothole, and I bang my head against the side of the truck. Dad's driving too fast. I rub my head and blink. I almost give up on the thing, but then it flashes at me again. Something shining and sparkling in the light.

I try again, more carefully this time. It's probably just a nail or a screw - there's always stuff like that from Dad's work - but then, it looks a little too shiny for that. I try to get my fingers in there, but they're too fat to get down the gap. I can't even touch it, let alone pull it out to examine it. But now I'm a little closer, I realize why it looks familiar. Why it looks so out of place. It's a girl's hairclip. The part flashing in the light is the diamond on one end.

Obviously, we don't have many hairclips in the house, between Dad and me. But the girls at school wear them, so I know what they are. And I know they don't have real diamonds in them too. That's not why this one interests me. It's not that I think I've found some treasure. I look around for something like a piece of wire or a stick to fish it out, but I can't see anything. By then though, we're already pulling into the parking lot at Littlelea. There's already four or five other cars there, all surfer friends of Dad. They all come out on days like this, although a lot of them stay on the beach watching when it's really big.

We skid to a halt on the loose gravel, and Dad's door is open before the engine has even died away.

"Hiya, boys," he shouts to the group, who are all watching the waves roll in. It's big enough that you don't even need to climb the dunes to see it today.

"Day of the year, huh? Day of the year!" Dad gives a kind of whoop and turns to me. "Jump out, Billy, I gotta grab the board."

So I don't get a chance to prize out the hairclip, if that's actually what it is. I'm a little bit frustrated by this, but not for very long. I've got important things to do today. I've got to get my memory card from the camera outside Mr. Foster's house and get my evidence. So I put the clip out of my mind and get my bike ready. I hang around for a little while, until Dad's suited up. It just seems polite since they're all so excited. Then I begin pushing my bike through the dunes.

TWENTY-TWO

THE BEACH IS QUITE BUSY. People come down to watch when the sea is rough like this. The tide's almost up, too, so everyone is pushed up together near the dunes.

I like storms. You always get strange things washed up when the waves get big. All the flotsam that's floating around in the ocean gets pushed in. And the jetsam too. (The difference is that one is accidentally put in the ocean, and the other is dumped from ships. I don't know why they need separate words for that.) One time after a storm, the beach was covered in dozens of plastic butter-containers, and the butter was OK to eat too. I collected tons of it, and we ate it for weeks. They must have come off a container ship. That's flotsam, I guess, although it makes more sense to just call it butter. Or plastic. Another time, I found an old fishing buoy that was covered in these really strange creatures. I'd never seen anything like them before: they looked like snakes. Or maybe aliens. Or alien snakes. They were stuck onto the buoy, but their heads were writhing around, like they were trying to get back into the water. I looked them up; they're called goose barnacles. Over in Europe they eat them as a delicacy and they're really expensive. I always look out for them now, not to eat, they look disgusting. But so I can sell them. But I've not seen anymore.

All I find today are a couple of coconuts, which I don't bother to collect because I've got lots of those already. Oh, and a big dead crab, which reminds me of my hermit crab study. It'll be good to clear up this Olivia business and get back to work.

So when I get to Silverlea, I hurry up a little and cycle through the town until I get to Mr. Foster's house. I can still hear the sea booming, even from up there, but other than that, it's eerily quiet, and it occurs to me that actually lots of Mr. Foster's neighbors' houses are just empty. In fact, when I look, all of the neighbors' houses look exactly the same as when I was here last week: the drapes drawn in exactly the same way, the driveways still empty. It gives me a chill to think of that.

Mr. Foster's van *is* in the driveway, though. I was hoping it wouldn't be, because it would be easier to switch over the memory cards that way. But no one said being an investigator would be easy. I lock my bike up like before and watch the house for a long time from behind the tree. The drapes are open, but this time, the lights are off, and I don't see any movement inside. Eventually, I go for it, running over to the front of the boat again, where I'm a little bit protected from view if anyone in the house does look out, and I sneak back inside the cover and inside the boat. Straight away, I see my camera setup is still there, and I crawl forward to where it's clamped on.

I wave my hand in front to see if I can hear the little noise it makes when it switches on, but there's nothing. The battery's dead. I'm not unhappy about this. The battery life depends on how much recording it's done. If there's nothing to record, it will last almost two weeks. It hasn't managed a week this time. That means it's done a lot of recording.

I unclip the camera, slide out the old battery and card and replace them with fresh ones, then refit the camera. The house is still dark. Perhaps Mr. Foster isn't there after all? Maybe he's gone for a walk. I hang around for a little while, but nothing happens, and what I really want to do is download my videos. So after a while, I roll back out the boat and sneak away.

TWENTY-THREE

I CYCLE ALL the way back through Silverlea and along the beach to Littlelea. The tide's fully high now, which means there's no hard patch of sand to ride along. I'm worn out when I get back to the truck.

"Yo, Billy. We've been waitin' on you," Dad says when I get there. He's in a good mood, sitting in the passenger seat of Pete's truck, which is the same as Dad's, but it's got ads for *The Green Room* all down the side.

"Tide's got too high. We're gonna grab some breakfast, then head out again when it's lower," Dad says. Or he says something like that. The important thing is the word 'breakfast'.

I put my bike back in Dad's truck, and we drive all the way back to Silverlea again, the place I've just exhausted myself cycling back from. Honestly, sometimes, I can't wait until I'm an adult and can decide things for myself. I'd rather go home to download my card, but it wouldn't do any good to argue.

The Sunrise Café isn't busy, so we all sit together near the window. Dad and his friends are all going on and on about the 'drops' they took and how clean the wave faces were and how hard they had to paddle, and obviously, I'm not listening because I never listen to that kind of talk. I'm wondering if I can get away with opening up my computer here and looking through the footage from outside Mr. Foster's, and deciding I probably can't. Then, all of a sudden, I realize they've stopped talking about surfing, and now they're talking about Olivia Curran. But before I understand exactly what they're saying, Emily comes over to take our order.

"Hi, guys," she says, giving me a wink. Then she looks surprised. "Why the long faces? I thought you'd all be loving these waves?"

"Yeah, we are," Big Pete says. "But Karl here was just saying how it'll probably be a day like this that finally washes that girl's body in." Karl works for the Coast

Guard, here on the island. But I don't know him very well because he's a bit strange.

"They're gonna step up the search for the body. Next week," Pete goes on, but then he stops. There's a moment of silence as everyone thinks about this, then Pete waves his hands like he's dismissing the subject.

"Hey. Forget I mentioned it. It's too nice a day. Say you got pancakes this morning Honey?"

Emily's smiles at him, like she's happy to move on.

"Sure do." She writes all the orders down on a notepad and walks back to the kitchen. I'm pretty sure she knows that all of Dad's friends are watching her walk away because she walks a bit funny. When she's out of earshot Karl opens his mouth again.

"Is she still seeing that lifeguard?"

"Think so," Pete replies, still watching her. "Why? You fancy your chances do you?" And he laughs. I kind of snigger a bit too because Emily would never date someone like Karl.

"Not me. I heard she's high maintenance," Karl says. Like I said, Karl is a bit strange.

* * *

A half hour later, and only a few moments after I finish eating my sausage sandwich, Dad pats me on the shoulder.

"Right, Billy boy," he says. It's the first thing he's said in a while and his voice sounds tense now, like his earlier good mood has completely gone. "We gotta get going. I gotta go to work."

"I thought you were going surfing again?" I say. I thought we'd be going back to Littlelea, and I would be able to walk up the cliff to the house to download the card.

"Don't have time. I gotta paint the chalets up at the hotel." I start to interrupt him to tell him he said he was going surfing again, but he talks right over me with what sounds like false cheeriness: "And *you* gotta help this time."

Big Pete gives him a look like he's surprised too. But he doesn't say anything. I think fast. I've got to download that card as soon as I can, but you've got to be careful arguing with Dad. Especially in public.

"Is it alright if I do my homework instead? I've got a ton of math to do."

"Do it tonight," Dad says.

"I was gonna do geography tonight."

Dad doesn't say anything at this, but looks at his friends and sighs. Most of them are married and sometimes he complains that they don't know what it's like having his responsibilities.

"*Shit*. Whatever, Billy. Whatever you want." He shakes his head like I'm being unreasonable; then he lays down a couple of notes on the table.

"Pete, give this to Emily when she comes out, will you?" Then he gets up and we leave, Dad and me, even though the rest of them are soon heading right back to the beach.

We ride together up to the hotel. On the way, Dad starts asking me about what I'm actually doing in math, like he's sorry about getting mad but doesn't want to say so. But I tell him it's algebra, and then he doesn't know what to say because he doesn't know anything about algebra. Dad didn't even finish high school. It's probably not his fault, but that's why he's just a handyman. It's not really the point though, I don't actually have any math homework anyway.

We arrive at the hotel and park right in front of the chalets. There's two rows with five in each. He's still in his mood when he goes into one of the chalets with his paintbrushes and stuff. I go into another and set myself up at the little table.

I plug the card into the computer and set it to download the video. The window pops up: it tells me there's five hours of footage in 118 separate clips. That sounds like a lot, but actually it's less than normal. When you set up the camera traps, a lot of the time, they start recording just because the wind moves some leaves. It's a pain to watch it all. You can view it on double fast-forward speed to make it easier, but – actually - I've got a whole lot of footage I've never even watched yet.

I start watching them now, one after the other, thinking maybe I'll grab a Mountain Dew from the fridge. I noticed there's a packet of cookies on the shelf too. It's one of the perks of having access to apartments all over town. I can almost always get cookies wherever I am. But I don't get my soda. Because then I see a clip that makes me forget all about it.

TWENTY-FOUR

I WAS RIGHT ABOUT MOST of the clips not being much use. There was a weed growing up the back of the boat - I told you it was overgrown there - and the top of it must have been moving in the wind. That did two things. First, it kept setting the camera off, so a lot of the clips only show this stupid plant waving its leaves around in front of the screen, and nothing else happening. But worse than that, there were times when the whole plant got stuck right in front of the camera, so you can't see the house at all, just a close-up of out-of-focus green.

For a little while, I worry that all the later clips are going to be just green, but then the plant moves again. I guess the wind direction changed.

The first clip where anything actually happened was this: Mr. Foster opens the front door, then shuts and locks it behind him, and limps to his van. Then you see the front of the van back slowly out of the picture. Thirty seconds later, the recording stops, which means nothing else happened. I save this clip to my investigation folder, although I don't know the significance of it yet. Then there's quite a bit more green where the plant gets in the way, and by the time the camera is working again, the van is back, and the lights are on in the house. The camera only seems to have picked up any movement from inside the house when Mr. Foster comes really close to the windows. There's a couple of other clips where you can just make out someone's moving inside the house, but I don't bother saving them because I get impatient and scan another clip a little later on. And that's the one that almost makes me stop breathing.

It was filmed at four thirty-seven on Sunday afternoon, still the same day I set up the camera. On the screen it's just getting dark. The lights are on in the house, both the kitchen and the living room, so you can see inside really clearly. The thing that sets the camera off is the drapes are moving in the living room window. Someone's shutting them. But it's not Mr. Foster. It's a girl.

It's only a short clip. For most of it, you can't see her face clearly, but you can see she's a teenager, and she's got long blond hair. Then, just before she closes the drapes completely, she pauses and looks straight out of the window. And in that moment, you can see exactly who it is.

I've found Olivia Curran. I've really found her.

TWENTY-FIVE

"I DISAGREE, sir. I don't think she drowned."

Detective Jessica West, a mainlander, was only in the meeting as a courtesy, she wasn't supposed to say anything, much less interrupt her commanding officer as he summarized the progress made in the month since Olivia Curran had gone missing. Lieutenant Langley kept talking, assuming she'd realize this and shut up. But Chief Collins held up a hand to stop him, turned to her.

"Why not?" he asked.

Now the small room went quiet and all eyes turned to her.

As far as most of the island officers felt, West shouldn't have even been there at all. The Lornea Island Police Department was small, but it was capable, and they understood better than most the nature of crime on the island. But when this case had come along the Chief had been quick to send out a plea for spare resources from neighboring forces. It turned out to be a good call. With almost the entire town of Silverlea present when the girl went missing it had been a stretch to take statements and organize the search, even with outside help. But that's why the Chief was the Chief, he tended to call the big decisions right.

"I just don't see why she would suddenly decide to go swimming." West began, wishing she had something stronger to say. "Without saying anything to anyone."

Langley looked as though he might just continue with his summary. He shook his head.

"Thank you for your input Detective, it's noted." He looked through his notes until he found something. Then he began reading again.

"We've had nine accidental drownings on the island in the last five years. Nearly half of those were folk who took a swim at night. In one case without telling anyone where they were going." He turned to West, as if hoping to pacify her. "People underestimate the currents. They get drunk. They think the ocean looks beautiful. They don't know how dangerous it can be."

"And in those other cases, how often did the body not get washed up?" This was Detective Rogers. He too was a mainlander, brought in to help the case, and he'd been assigned to work with West. But since he was an experienced detective, it had been easier for him to fit in. And perhaps because he was a man. Langley hesitated in answering him.

"Usually they're in the water about a week. Obviously in this case it's been longer. But that's not unheard of. The whole east coast of the island is a nightmare of cliffs and sea-caves. It could be anywhere along there." He turned to the chief now. "That's where we need to focus, keeping the search going. Not on some fantasy investigation."

The chief sat behind his desk, his chin resting on one hand, listening. He drummed the fingers of his other hand a few times and observed his officers.

"OK. Tell me again about Joseph Curran. You're happy there's nothing there?"

"No previous convictions, not even a speeding ticket. We've spoken to his friends and colleagues. Nothing unusual about his relationship with his daughter. Just your typical family guy." Langley shook his head. "We've turned him inside out, the mother too. There's nothing there. If the Curran's did it they're goddamn criminal geniuses, without a motive."

The Chief nodded. "The boyfriend?"

"Luke Grimwald. They'd been seeing each other for a few months. Friends said it wasn't anything serious. He was on the mainland. No way he could have gotten here."

"What about the brother? Have you looked into him?"

"William Curran? He's only fourteen sir."

"It happens."

Langley hesitated a beat. "The Currans left the party to take him back to their rental apartment. She was seen multiple times after they left. The mother reported she checked in on him before she went to bed."

"OK," the chief seemed satisfied with that. "And there's no one else here on the island she knew?"

"No."

"And there's nothing else you're following up right now? Nothing come up?"

"No."

The chief mused over this for a moment.

"All of which leaves two possibilities. Either something happened to her - she was taken by someone with no connection to her, who no-one saw even though the whole town was there. Or for some reason she went into the water." He drummed his fingers again.

"She went into the water," Lieutenant Langley said. "This is Lornea Island. We don't get people *taken* here."

There was a short silence in the room. West was the one to break it.

"What about her clothes? Where are they if she went swimming?"

Langley turned to face her. "It was a low tide. She would have left them near to where she went in. It's too far to walk from the top of the beach. So when she didn't come out, the tide washed them away too.

"And they disappeared just like the body?"

"Either that or she didn't even bother taking them off in the first place."

"There's nothing to suggest she was suicidal."

Langley shrugged. "It's the sort of thing parents hide."

Detective West and Langley glared at each other.

"But why didn't she *tell anyone* she was going swimming?" West said again.

"You've got to understand the nature of the island, detective." Langley was beginning to sound frustrated. "This isn't the mainland. We're not chasing serial killers here, no matter how much fun that might sound to you."

West opened her mouth to reply, but Detective Rogers shot her a warning glance. She closed her mouth again.

"I think that's enough Lieutenant, Detective." The chief interrupted them all. "We're going round in circles now,". There was silence for a few moments, apart from the rasp as the chief stroked the ends of his mustache.

"As you all know. The reason for this meeting is to make a decision whether to continue working this case at the current level of resources, or whether to scale it back to something a little more sustainable. Obviously in an ideal world we'd investigate every crime, and potential crime, to its natural conclusion. But I'll let you all know when we're operating in an ideal world." The joke did little to lighten the mood. The chief didn't seem to notice.

"The Currans have sought - and received - a lot of media interest in this case. I responded by focusing the entire investigative capacity onto the case. And bringing in outside help," he nodded to Rogers and West. "It's frustrating when that level of effort doesn't pay dividends." The chief drummed his fingers on the desk again. "However, this is the bottom line. Without anything concrete to go on I've no choice but to scale things back to a more sustainable level. I'm also inclined to agree with Lieutenant Langley that the most likely scenario is the girl went into the water and didn't come out." He stopped and turned to West.

"Notwithstanding your concerns Detective."

Langley was nodding his head.

"It's therefore a decision that makes itself." The chief turned to the two mainland detectives. I'll be certain to highlight to both of your commanding officers that you've been a big help over here. But I'll also be informing them I'll be releasing you at the end of the week. I want to thank you both for volunteering to come over and help. I know everyone here shares the sentiment." He stopped and straightened the papers on his desk. The meeting was over.

TWENTY-SIX

Detective West and Detective Rogers sat at the near-empty bar as the late-evening news came on. The TV was a small, flat-screen model that looked too cheap among the mirrors, gleaming glasses and dark woods of the Silverlea Lodge Hotel bar. Neither West nor Rogers had been in the mood to talk anyway, so they both turned to listen. The volume was low, but the place was so quiet, they had no problem hearing.

The presenter had that overly made-up look you only really get on local TV news. She sat on a lime-green sofa beside a pile of newspapers. She held one up to the camera.

"A development came today in the case of missing teenager Olivia Curran." The presenter had the characteristic accent of Lornea Island locals: the thickening of the vowels that West still wasn't used to.

"It seems the girl's parents have taken out full-page ads in major newspapers across the whole country. They're appealing to the public for any information about what might have happened to their daughter. Jim, what more can you tell us about that?" She turned, and the image cut to a man standing by a newspaper stall on a city street.

"That's right, Jenny," he said, pressing one hand to his ear and ignoring the irritated looks of pedestrians passing behind him who had to step off the sidewalk to get past. "This case is already one of the higher-profile investigations that Lornea Island has ever seen, and with full-page ads in most of the major national newspapers, that looks set to continue. As you know, there have been *no* arrests so far, and police still don't seem to know what happened to Olivia, or even if she's still alive."

The man stood there, listening while the first presenter asked another question.

"Tell me, we've heard previously from the Lornea Island Police Department's

Chief Collins that the police are scaling back the investigation, as no leads have come up. Is this in some way pushback from the parents on that issue?"

"Well, Jenny. Olivia's parents have not explicitly said that. Their only comment was they simply want to do everything they possibly can to find their daughter. But the timing of these ads does seem a remarkable coincidence."

The report cut back to the studio and its lime-green sofa. The female presenter turned to face the camera. "And of course, if you have *any* information regarding Olivia Curran and what might have happened to her, you can reach the Lornea Island Police Department at the number below." She smiled sadly at the camera for a few seconds. Then her face brightened as she began a new story about a girl's football team.

West turned away. She'd seen the ad that morning. Everyone in the department had. It was simple enough, showing a large photograph of Olivia Curran's face and the words:

Have you seen Olivia?

Then there was a brief summary of what happened the night she went missing, and a number to call.

"You know, it's clever what they're doing," said Rogers. He was in his forties, a big man, but from what she'd seen working with him, straightforward. One of the good guys. "I don't know how much ads like that cost, but the fact that they've spent it makes it *news*. Gets it on TV. That'll spread it far and wide. You watch if it doesn't."

West thought for a moment.

"Well, they do run a PR company," she replied eventually. "What do you expect?"

Rogers seemed not to hear her.

"Even little things, like just using her first name in the ad. You notice that? You ever notice how the most famous people just go by one name? Elvis? Cher. I dunno. . . OJ. They're trying to do the same for the Curran girl." He shook his head. "They're not giving up. They're damn persistent."

"Persistent?" West said. "They've lost their daughter. They're desperate, and everyone knows we've gotten nowhere. Wouldn't you do everything you could to keep the investigation going?"

"We haven't gotten nowhere. We've followed up all the leads, and they go nowhere. Which points to the likelihood that she almost certainly went swimming and drowned. At some point, you've got to give up."

"Except that there's no evidence she went swimming. No clothes on the beach, no telling anyone what she was doing, and of course, no body."

Rogers looked at her. West went on.

"I'm only saying it to you since no one else will listen to me."

"You have to work the odds. The odds here - she probably went swimming."

West didn't answer but pressed her lips together.

"I told you, when we first got here. The secret to being a detective is solve the ones you can solve, and let the rest go. It's tough, but there it is." Rogers took a swig of his beer and turned back to the TV.

West kept watching him, feeling conflicted. She liked Rogers. She'd liked him from the moment they'd arrived together, on the same ferry, and been made temporary partners in the Curran case. It wasn't that everyone else here had treated her badly. On the contrary, even though she was young. Even though they all knew she had only just qualified as a detective, they'd still sent her out speaking to witnesses, taking statements. But as the leads dried up she had found herself assigned more and more to the monotonous tasks that no one else wanted to do. Her and Rogers too. The two mainlanders.

She sipped her wine.

"It could all be a bluff," she said, with little conviction in her voice. "Go all out in public about how desperately you miss your daughter, and that way no one'll ever believe you're the one who took her."

Rogers shook his head. "It's not him."

"What about the statistics? Four out of five cases where children are abducted, the Dad did it."

"Still leaves one out of five where he didn't. And she probably wasn't even abducted."

West laughed suddenly. Rogers looked at her surprised, then finished the remainder of his beer. Then he set the glass back on the bar top.

"You want another one?"

She hesitated - she was on her third glass of the night, and she rarely drank more than one.

"Come on, it's our last goddamn night on Lornea Island. And we've earned it."

"Have we? I don't think we have much to celebrate."

"Don't talk like that, Detective. First thing you've gotta learn in this job, you're never gonna win 'em all. You don't remember that, you're gonna go crazy."

West smiled. In the month she'd worked with Rogers there must have been at least ten "first things" she had to learn. Not that she minded. He had over ten years' experience of major investigations, while this was her first real case.

"Go on then. One more," she said, sliding her empty glass toward him.

Rogers raised a hand, the bartender came over. He was in his twenties, dressed in a crisp white shirt, and more used to serving tourists than the two detectives who had been staying in the hotel for the last month. It had been the bartender's hope to get the detectives to talk about the case since they'd arrived, but they'd barely made it into the bar, until this evening. Tonight, he knew, was his last chance.

"Same again, Detective Rogers?"

"Sure."

The bartender unstopped the bottle he'd opened for West earlier in the evening and emptied it into her glass, the golden liquid swirling round. When it didn't quite reach the full measure, he pulled the cork from a second bottle and topped it off comfortably over the measure line. Then, as he stood pouring Rogers' beer, he asked as casually as he could,

"So, I hear you guys are on the boat tomorrow?"

West waited for Rogers to tell him they couldn't talk about the case, but he didn't say that.

"That's right."

"What's that all about, then?" The bartender went on.

Rogers shrugged. "Like the TV said. You can't throw unlimited resources at one case. No matter how influential her parents are, or what stunts they pull."

The bartender used a flat wooden stick to wipe the creamy foam so that it sat flat and level on the top of the beer.

"So that's it? You guys are just giving up?"

"No one's giving up. There's still detectives on the case. Just not us."

The bartender set the beer down carefully in front of Rogers, then frowned. "I still don't get it," he said.

A look of irritation appeared on Rogers' face, and West smiled to herself; she felt she'd gotten to know that look over the last few weeks.

"Get what?"

"The whole thing. How come you guys are here. . . How come you're going even though the case isn't solved. . . "

Rogers sighed. "Look. It's like this. Lornea Island is a small place, right? So when a big, difficult case like this comes along, the police department has to ask for help from neighboring forces. That's where we came in." He pointed at himself and West. "We came over to help out at the start of the investigation. But crime doesn't stop elsewhere. We've done what we can, now we gotta go back. It's that simple."

The barman's head tilted to one side as he considered this.

"So you guys are like the special agents, the supercops?" he said. West looked at him more closely than she had before. She noticed a tattoo partially hidden under the sleeve of his shirt. She guessed the guy read a lot of comic books.

"I wouldn't say supercops exactly," Rogers was saying. "But yeah, it's something like that."

"Actually, we're more like the lowest of the low," West said abruptly. "We're the detectives our own departments could spare." She smiled at the bartender, aware that Rogers was screwing up his face, scowling at this description.

"It's more about who's available. You need guys who can up-sticks in a moment's notice. They can't be in the middle of a case. They gotta have an understanding family," he coughed. "Or not mind leaving their family for a while." The bartender began nodding.

"I get it. So now you gotta go back? Solve some more crimes?"

"That's right." Rogers looked happy for a moment.

"Before you know what happened to Olivia Curran?"

Both detectives went quiet.

"Yeah," Rogers said eventually.

West pulled her glass toward her and sat stroking the stem. The bartender retired to the other end of the bar and resumed his slow washing of glasses.

"I know you're right, but it still doesn't feel great to have failed at my first real case," West said. "Leaving when we don't know what happened to her."

Rogers shrugged. "That's the job, Detective. You work a case. Maybe you crack it, maybe you don't."

"So it doesn't bother you, even a little?" she asked.

"Nope. And it shouldn't bother you, either."

"I know." West looked into her glass; the hotel bar was reflected on the surface of the wine. "It does, though. I guess I'd just like to know what happened to her."

Rogers watched her for a moment, then laughed. "Well, I guess you will now. The amount of media coverage her parents just bought, this case is gonna be in the papers if she does ever turn up."

She looked up at him, surprised at the sound. He had a nice laugh.

"Anyway. We're supposed to be talking about something else," Rogers said, forcing a more upbeat note to his voice. "Aren't you looking forward to getting back to the mainland? To *civilization*?"

Jessica West thought about what she was returning to the next day. An image formed in her mind, her one-bedroom apartment, in a cheap part of town, the lease signed in a hurry after it all went wrong with Matthew. Work was better though, she supposed. After five years in the Hartford Police Department she'd been successful in her Detective Exams at her first try. The city was a curious mix, the home of many major insurance firms but fast-climbing the poverty rankings. Domestic abuse cases were common. So were random shootings. Was that really more civilized than here, where outside, she could smell wild heather and hear nothing but the sound of the ocean?

"I never cleaned out my fridge," she said thoughtfully. "Before I came here, I mean. I'm dreading what civilizations I'll find in there."

Rogers made a face. Then, watching her closely he went on.

"What about your boyfriend?" He looked away, as if he wasn't that interested. "What did you say his name was? Matthew? Doesn't he look after things like that?"

West had noticed him using the same voice when he'd be taking statements, when he'd thought the witness might be about to say something interesting. She bit her lip for a moment, then decided to come clean.

"He's not really a *boyfriend* as such. Not anymore." She watched him as she spoke, knowing it was the wine making her open up, but not minding so much. Rogers frowned again, his big, bearlike face revealing the effort of trying to fit what she was saying now, with how she'd described it when he first asked about her circumstances.

"We split up a while back. When I came here, I made out we were still together. I just thought it was simpler that way. I didn't want any complications. You know?" She looked at him, searching his face to see if he got it.

There had seemed good reason for the lie. Even back in Hartford, male officers outnumbered women by four to one, but the Lornea Island Police Department was fifteen years behind. It consisted entirely of male officers, most of whom had done little to hide the fact they were checking her out when she turned up. It was a small department, too, the kind of place where everyone knew each other's business, or expected to.

"I get it," said Rogers, nodding but still frowning because he didn't really understand. He waited a beat, then went on. "So what happened? With this Matthew, I mean?"

Normally, West would have steered the conversation onto other matters, but this was her last night on the island. It was almost certainly the last time she'd ever see Detective Rogers. And, she guessed, she was ready to talk.

"I had quite a different kind of life, before I joined the force. He's kind of a hangover from that. We tried to make it work but. . . " She stopped, changing her mind about getting into this. "We grew apart. Actually, it's one of the reasons I volunteered to come over for the case. He was having a hard time accepting it was over."

"What kind of a hard time? He get violent?" Rogers narrowed his eyes.

She smiled, but shook her head. "No, nothing like that. It's just my life changed a lot when I signed up. It was tough for him."

Rogers grunted but seemed to accept the explanation. He didn't ask what it was she had done before signing up. West guessed it didn't much matter. Once a police officer, always a police officer.

"How about you?" West asked, "Why'd you volunteer to come here. To be a *supercop*?"

Rogers glanced up at the word, then smiled.

"I used to come here as a kid." Rogers looked around. "We even stayed right here in Silverlea." He shrugged. "I guess that got my interest. Plus my ex-wife has recently decided to do everything she can to make my life a misery."

"I'm sorry."

"Don't be. But don't end up like me. I'm a walking stereotype. My ex-wife won't talk to me, and I see my kid maybe once a month." He grinned at her, and she found herself considering the man sitting opposite her again. He wasn't bad-looking; she'd thought that the moment she was assigned to work with him. Blond hair, receding a little. Maybe twenty pounds overweight, but he carried it well. Looking at him, she was once again reminded of a bear. A friendly bear with huge hands.

A silence stretched out between them, but a comfortable silence. They watched each other. The mention of Rogers' wife had triggered something in West's mind. She hadn't considered him as anything other than partner and colleague until that moment. Now another aspect of him came into focus. As a man. An apparently available man.

She turned away. What the hell was she thinking? Throughout her short career as a police officer, and her even shorter career as a detective, she'd been warned by senior female colleagues not to get involved with anyone she worked with. The office gossips would ensure she'd never live it down. To date she had followed that advice. But she'd been with Matthew then. And there was an easy way to dismiss the warning voices. Come tomorrow she would never see Detective Rogers again. She would never see the guys at the Lornea Island Police Station. Tomorrow morning, she would pack up her gear and drive to the port. She would climb on the ferry and return to her old life, never to come back to Lornea Island. And the way she was feeling about that, a little human company might be welcome.

She sighed. She looked across at him wondering if he was thinking anything remotely the same as her. She finished her drink.

"Fancy a nightcap?" She asked.

TWENTY-SEVEN

IT TOOK a while for West to recognize the dryness of her throat and the bitter taste in her mouth, but then it had been a while since she'd drunk that much. And even then, she couldn't figure out why her hotel room seemed different. It looked more or less the same, but somehow reversed, like it had been turned into a mirror image of itself in the night. Then she remembered. It wasn't *her* hotel room at all. It was the one across the hall from where she had been staying the last month. She looked across the other side of her bed and sighed.

"Oh Shit," she said, but quietly enough that she didn't wake him up.

She covered her face with her hands as last night began to come back to her. He'd agreed to her suggestion for another drink. That turned into another, and they'd ended up taking the bottle of Jack Daniels from the bar. She dimly remembered sitting on the bed, staring at Rogers' suitcases, packed and ready to go. What happened after that, she didn't want to think about. She glanced over at the bottle now, nearly empty.

It doesn't matter, she told herself. *I'll never see him again. I'll never see any of them again.*

She sat up in bed and looked across into the mirror. She took in her tired-looking face, the crumpled clothes surrounding the bed.

A swim, she thought to herself. *I need to go for a swim.*

Ten minutes later, and still driven on by the alcohol in her bloodstream, she was striding down the beach. The October air raised goosebumps on the bare skin of her arms and legs and the sun, still low, stayed hidden behind a thick blanket of clouds. For a mile to the north, and five miles to the south, she couldn't see another figure on the sand. She breathed in the freshness, questioned her sanity, and listened to the low roar of the waves.

The hotel had a heated indoor pool she could have used. But it was tiny, barely long enough to fit in five strokes before she had to turn around. And they kept it too hot, unlike the pools she was used to. No - if West needed to make peace with Lornea Island, with her failure on her first major case, and with whatever mess she'd gotten herself into last night - the ocean was what she needed.

She reached the lower part of the beach, where the wet sand was washed by the long surges of water, the final gasps of waves that had broken much farther out. She set down her towel where she thought the water wouldn't reach, and hoped the tide was going out. She took two deep breaths, then strode forward, still clumsy from the drink. Moments later, she was in the water, the coldness splashing up against her body. It made her gasp, but she forced herself to carry on. To focus only on keeping her legs moving.

When the water reached her stomach, she leaned forward and dived under. The cold knocked the breath from her body, and she came up at once. But after a few panted breaths she tried again. This time when she dived she forced herself to glide for several long seconds. She kept her eyes open, watching the green-yellow sand slide past underneath. Then she angled her body up and rose through the shades of green to the surface, where she fell automatically into a smooth, powerful stroke.

Under the water, her arms swung beneath her, pulling forward with an easy rhythm. Her breathing became light, just a subtle roll of her neck, alternating from one side to the other. Her movements were smooth, all trace of clumsiness gone. As if she belonged in the water.

She swam straight out to sea, powering through the small breaking waves as they rolled toward her. West swam until her body no longer felt the cold of the water. Then she stopped. Treading water, she looked back at the hotel. Already, last night felt washed away.

Then she widened her gaze. From out here, the beach was breathtaking. A vast sweep of sand, the little encampment of Silverlea midway along, the low cliffs of Northend feeling closer than they must actually be. She hadn't had the time to do the tourist thing of searching for silver, of course. Well, maybe she'd have to come back one day. She turned to the other end of the beach; the higher, more severe cliffs of Littlelea were half-lost in the mist.

She'd stood on those cliffs just a few days after she'd arrived. She visited a boy and his father who had been at the party. She'd taken their statements. A strange boy, what was his name? Billy. *Billy Wheatley.*

She grimaced at the thought, and began swimming again, this time along the beach. But as her head fell to the side she noticed a figure walking down the beach to where she had left her towel and clothes. The figure waved a hand. She stopped, brought back into the moment. On a whim she took a full breath of air and let herself sink down, feet first, into the water. Once her head was covered, she exhaled and looked up, watching the bubbles disappear above her to the surface, watching her hair swirl, until the water turned too dark to see. She felt a moment's fear, that her feet would never touch the bottom and she was letting herself sink forever, but then she felt sand under her feet. She bent her knees until her arms touched, too, in the darkness now, and she grabbed two handfuls of sand. For a second, she stayed there. Her eyes were open, but they saw nothing. She wondered what creatures might be observing her from the shadows. She wondered if Olivia Curran's dead eyes were somewhere staring back at her.

When she surfaced she swam fast back to the beach, enjoying the feeling when the swells picked her up and accelerated her towards the shore. When she felt the bottom she walked out. The cold made her skin feel like it was glowing.

"Thanks," she said, taking the towel that Rogers held out to her. She bent forward, rubbing the water from her hair.

"You swim pretty good, Detective West." Rogers took care to avert his eyes from the thin fabric of her swimsuit as she wrapped herself in the towel.

"I grew up swimming," she said.

"I grew up swimming too. I can't swim like that." He pulled his eyes back to her face and smiled at her.

"No, I mean I really grew up swimming. Since I was five years old, my dad decided I was going to be a swimmer. We went every morning before school. Then since I was seven, every day after school too."

"No shit? You were serious about it?"

"Dad was. He had this dream I'd win him an Olympic medal."

He watched her for a beat, to see if she was serious.

"So did you?"

West's childhood flashed before her eyes. The early years, when it was just Dad shouting at her from the poolside, stopwatch in hand. Driving to competitions in Dad's Volvo that smelt of chlorine from her constantly wet hair and towels. Then, later on, when it wasn't just her but Sarah too, and it wasn't just Dad but a team of coaches and nutritionists and physiotherapists. It might have ended with Olympic success - although she knew Sarah always had the greater chance. But it wasn't how it ended. It was too much to explain to Rogers. And did she even want to?

"No." She said, looking away.

"Why not? What happened?"

Without thinking West rolled her shoulders around, feeling for the burn she still remembered from after a race.

"I wasn't good enough." She turned away, not wanting him to see her face.

Rogers sounded dismissive. "Well you look pretty good to me. I had no idea I was working with an athlete."

West had heard the same sentiment before. It always annoyed her.

"I never achieved anything when I was a kid. Too busy getting drunk and chasing girls." Rogers went on, flashing her a grin.

"Can we not talk about it please?" West replied.

There was a silence, just the burr of the wind rolling down the sand.

They walked in silence for a while but West felt frustrated. Thinking about her past highlighted the sense of failing, again. By leaving Lornea Island and the case unsolved she was failing again. Just like she'd failed her Dad. Just like she'd failed Sarah. There had been nothing she could do that time, but now she was *supposed* to help. She was a police detective. She was supposed to put things right this time. Yet a girl was still missing. Another family left in limbo, not knowing whether their daughter was alive or dead. It didn't feel good.

With a jolt she realized Rogers was speaking again.

"Anyway, I'm guessing you didn't check your cellphone this morning? Given how it's on the floor of my hotel room."

West brought her mind back to the present.

"No. Why?"

"The chief wants to see us."

She stopped.

"Why?"

"I don't know."

"How do you mean?"

"He didn't say. Just that he wanted us to come in."

"When?"

Rogers checked his watch. "He said to be there at nine. That's in about ten minutes. That's why I came down to the beach to get you. You think I just fancied a stroll?"

"He didn't say anything about why?"

"No. Just that it was urgent. Maybe he wants to say goodbye and thank us for all our hard work."

"Didn't he do that yesterday?"

"Maybe he wants to do it again?"

West didn't reply. But her mind latched on to the meeting. It offered a chink of hope.

TWENTY-EIGHT

IT TOOK JUST ten minutes for West to shower and get dressed. They drove the twenty minutes to the police station together. A few of the uniforms were sitting around, on a break. One of them, a guy named Deaton, gave Rogers a friendly shove as he passed.

"You just can't keep away from the place, can you?"

Rogers grinned back, but shrugged when Deaton asked what they were doing. West said nothing, and no one spoke to her, but Lieutenant Langley did glance up at her as she passed. He nodded in greeting.

"Detective Rogers, Detective West. . . " The chief said from the window. He waved at two chairs in front of his desk and poured them coffees from the percolator he kept for his own use. They sat. West looked around his office, she hadn't expected to see it again.

He kept the small room neat. There was a well-stocked bookshelf, and the books looked used. Perhaps that was how he intended on spending the last few years before retirement? On his desk there was a newspaper.

"So, I understand you're both booked on the midday ferry?" Chief Collins said, taking his own seat and smiling at them.

"I'm sure you're both anxious to get back to family and friends." He raised his eyebrows. West felt Rogers glancing across at her. She nodded noncommittally.

"But I'm sure you'll also be aware of yesterday's little development." His eyes shifted to the newspaper, which lay open on the Currans' advertisement. His face remained neutral. He took a sip of coffee.

"I spoke with Joseph Curran by telephone yesterday afternoon," the chief went on. "He informed me he intends to purchase another round of ads next week, then another *every week* until his daughter is found, or he runs out of money. Whichever comes sooner." He stopped, and sent the detectives a wan smile.

"As you know, the Currans have rather a lot of money." He gave a small laugh this time. Then he made a steeple with his hands as if praying.

"As of eight o'clock this morning, when I got in, we've logged twenty-seven calls. Tip-offs, from people who think they've seen her, across the whole country." The chief watched the two detectives as he said this.

"Anything relevant, sir?" Rogers asked, his voice gruff and low against the Chief's clipped, precise tones.

"Nothing obviously so, no. Langley and Strickland are looking into them as we speak. And if Langley's right - and the girl went into the water - there won't be anything relevant. Just a lot of work, following up dead end leads. But if Langley's wrong. . . " The chief's eyebrows flicked up on his face. "Well, there's just a chance something might come out of it. Which brings me to why I've asked you back here." His fingers started drumming on the desk.

"I'll get right to the point. I spoke to both of your commanding officers last night. I've explained how our circumstances have changed, and how we could benefit from your assisting us here a little longer. Ultimately, they're both willing to release you - if you're willing to stay on, that is."

West realized she'd been holding her breath. She took a gulp of air.

"You're not scaling back the investigation after all?" she said.

"Officially, no. Unofficially, yes. Clearly, I cannot continue to dedicate my entire criminal investigation division to a single case. There may not be much happening on Lornea Island, but we do still have other crimes to investigate." He smiled.

"Lieutenant Langley will remain in nominal charge of the investigation, as before, but if you agree, you two will become the main active investigative unit. The search of the Silverlea sea cliffs will also continue with the help of the Coast Guard."

"So we'd be digging into the leads the Currans' ads generate?" Rogers said.

The chief took another sip of his coffee.

"That's about it. I'd suggest you also go back over the case. Review everything. It's possible something was missed."

"But unlikely?" Rogers questioned. The chief didn't answer him.

"We wouldn't be able to keep you in the hotel any more, but there's a number of apartments in Silverlea that become empty this time of year. You'll have a bit more space." He smiled again. "You'll still be neighbors."

"How long are we talking here?" Rogers asked.

Chief Collins shrugged. "Assuming we don't find anything and the Currans don't decide they're wasting their money, I'd look to review the situation after three months. Every case has limits. Even when the victim's parents run a successful PR agency."

There was a silence.

"I know you weren't expecting such a long stay on the island. And you're probably itching to get back to friends and family."

Two images flashed through West's mind. Her apartment back in Hartford, and an image of Matthew. They were gone almost as soon as they appeared. She felt the weight of disappointment lifting. This was a second chance. An opportunity to not fail. Then another thought occurred to her. Another image formed, this time it was Rogers' hairy back, turned away from her in the thick white sheets of the hotel bed. Was that going to be a problem?

She wondered if Rogers would stay. He'd been clear he thought the case was hopeless. If he left as planned that would be simpler, she reasoned. No worries about their night together becoming common knowledge.

But Rogers' voice interrupted her thoughts.

"I could stay here a little more sir. I don't have too much to get back to right now."

"Good man. Good man. Detective West?" The chief's attention swung over to her.

She tried to think fast. The idea of everyone in the department knowing she'd slept with Rogers didn't bear thinking about. But then she blinked it away. Who the hell really cared? There was never any doubt how she would reply.

"Me too, sir. I'd like to stay as long as it takes."

She glanced at Rogers, and their eyes met for a moment before both looked away.

TWENTY-NINE

MY HEART IS BEATING like a drum as I sit and stare at the image on the laptop. I've got the image paused on the screen so she's frozen there, staring out at me. The girl the whole of America is looking for. Olivia Curran.

I've found her. I've caught her on my wildlife cam. I actually pinch myself because it doesn't feel real. I pinch both arms until they hurt, but afterward, she's still there, frozen on my laptop screen, looking out the window, right at the camera. But then questions begin to bubble up in my mind. She looks so normal. Why isn't she locked up in the cellar?

I check the date of the recording. Six days ago. I nudge the video a few frames forward. It's not *that* clear, actually. The windows are dirty, and because the lights are on in the house, she's backlit, so her face is in shadow when she looks out. And these few frames forward, her expression has changed.

I zoom right in to try and figure out if she looks scared or not. It's hard to tell, but she's definitely not smiling.

What does it mean? If she's in the living room, maybe that means she's just escaped from the cellar, or wherever he's keeping her? But if you'd just escaped from a murderer, you wouldn't go and close the drapes, would you? Why doesn't she run away? Why doesn't she make a run to the front door and escape?

Then something else occurs to me. Something obvious that you've probably already worked out, but it makes me feel really happy. *Olivia Curran is alive*. Even though the TV news people always talk like she might be alive somewhere, it's been obvious for months that no one really believed that. Even the parents, when they stare right at the cameras and pretend to speak directly to Olivia, saying how much they love her and how they just want her to come home, you can tell they don't believe it. You can tell from how much they're crying that really, they think she's already dead.

But she's not dead. She's alive, and I'm the one who found her!

I re-run the video a few more times, trying to take it all in. Maybe the police will want me to help on other cases? Will I be able to fit it in with my schoolwork? Will I be famous? Like that French boy, Tintin? I used to like reading those stories when I was little. Only he's not real, of course. Not like I am.

Then suddenly, I notice something in the video. Mr. Foster's van is in the driveway. I can't see him, but this means he must be in the house too. That brings me back down to earth. Wondering again what she's doing there? It sends a little shiver down my back too.

My next thought is I have to tell the police right away. But there aren't many other clips left, so I decide I'll just quickly look those over before I do anything else. And I'm glad I do, because the very next clip changes everything. And not in a good way.

Clip number 00753 starts with the front door opening. That must be the movement that triggers the camera because the recording starts with it half-open already. But immediately, you can see something strange is happening. The inside of the house is glowing red, like the inside of a volcano, and all around it, it's black. It takes me a moment to realize what's going on, but then I get it. It's a *night-time* clip. The camera is recording in infrared. The red glow coming from the house is just because the air in there is warmer than the outside. Then a monster with bright-white face and hands appears, limping into the shot. But it isn't really a monster. It's Mr. Foster, with his features all distorted by the heat signature. He comes out and props the door open with something that looks black against the red background; I guess it's a rock from the path. Then he goes out of shot, to the van. I guess he opens the back doors of the van because I see a little bit of red come into the corner of the frame, which is probably from the interior light, which gives off some heat. Then Mr. Foster comes back to the house, pauses on the doorstep, and has a long look around. Then he disappears inside, and then - and this is where it gets really interesting - he reappears. But this time, he's carrying something.

Actually, that's not the right word. He's *dragging* something. Something big, like a slightly bent trunk of a tree. It's hard to figure out what it is, since the colors are so strange, but I've seen quite a few infrared videos since getting that camera so I work it out. It's a carpet. A badly rolled-up carpet. It's bigger than he is, and Mr. Foster is holding onto one end and struggling to get it out of the front door. Then he drags it right past the camera, and it slowly disappears out of the left side of the shot. A moment later, the van door shuts again.

I can't see what's inside the carpet, but from the lumpy way it's rolled up, there's definitely something in there.

The clip ends with Mr. Foster going back and closing the front door, then getting into the van and driving off. Then there's thirty seconds of nothing while the camera runs in case there's anything else to catch.

I'm stunned. I watch the clip three times, and on the third time, I start taking screengrabs when there's a particularly clear shot of him with the carpet. It's obvious there's a body in there. It *has* to be her. It *has* to be Olivia. Sometime between 16:37 on Sunday afternoon and this clip from 02:12 on Monday morning, he must have killed her. All my excitement from before just evaporates. It's replaced by a kind of unreal horror.

And then a horrible thought hits me. If I wasn't a kid, if I'd done a real stakeout in a car, with coffee and donuts, then I could have rescued her. I would have seen her at the window. I would have called the police then. But it didn't happen like that. I used my camera instead, and now she's dead. I had a chance to save her, and I failed.

It's my fault she's dead.

I can't describe how it makes me feel. I've never felt it before. Crushed, I guess. Hollow. And horrified. But also panicky. My next thought is that I *have* to hide the evidence. Before anyone finds out that I could have known and blames me for it. My hand hovers over the *delete* key.

NO! Think Billy. Think.

I'm too late to save Olivia Curran, but Mr. Foster has a *history* of this. He's done it before, so he'll do it again. Unless someone stops him.

I realize my mouth is dry so I go and get that soda. I eat the cookies too. I try to pull myself together. I've got to be professional. It's just like doing science. In science, you have to collect and present all the information you get so another scientist can see what you've done and come to the same conclusions. It must be the same with criminal investigations. I need to send the police all the information so they come to the same conclusion, and arrest Mr. Foster. I just won't tell them who I am. That way, they can't blame me. I mean, it's not as if I actually killed her; I did my best. I'm only a kid, and at least I *found* her. That's more than the police did.

And once I've made the decision, it's easier. My breathing slows down, and my fingers start working again. I open the Word document and start writing up my notes. I label all the important video clips and embed the screen grabs alongside the correct file names. I make a timeline of when each event happened, and figure out what time Mr. Foster must have killed her. Then I remember I haven't finished watching all the clips yet, so finally, I go back to viewing the last few, and sure enough, there's Mr. Foster returning to his house the next day. I note the time: 05:55. But I'm so engrossed in my work that I don't notice the door to the chalet opening behind me.

"Billy, can you. . . " a voice begins. Then, "*What's that? What the hell are you doing*?"

Dad's voice swings from calm to mad in the space of two sentences.

THIRTY

I'VE GOT the video player screen open in a corner and I'm pretty quick to minimize that, but all it does it give more space to the investigation file in Word open underneath. I fumble with the keypad, trying to close that. It's open long enough, I reckon, for Dad to read the title:

INVESTIGATION INTO THE OLIVIA CURRAN ~~MYSTERY~~/MURDER

"What the *hell* is that, Billy? You said you had math homework. You got out of helping because you had math. Did you lie to me?"

It's really hard to snap back into Dad's world after what I've been doing, and I can't understand why he's so *angry*. I could tell him that I finished, but then he'll be annoyed that I didn't come and help him. Anyway, I don't think of it in time.

"*Investigation into the Olivia Curran Mystery*? That's not math. What the *hell* are you doing?"

"It's nothing," I say, and I close the laptop screen. I feel my face flush hot. "It's just a project I have to do. For. . . for PD."

I don't know why I tell him that; it's just the first thing that comes into my head. It's not a good excuse, but I'm pretty sure it's better than telling him what I've really been doing. I can't imagine how mad he'd get if he knew she was dead and I could have saved her.

"PD? That Personal Development bullshit? You're studying that girl for *Personal Development*? That's sick." It turns out it was actually a good excuse because Dad always gets angry when he hears about PD. I think it's because they didn't have it when he was at school, so he can't figure out what it's for.

"Jesus. That's. . . That's not right."

Dad seems thrown off balance by this, so I keep going.

"Yeah, it's about keeping safe, you know, from pedos and stuff."

"Pedos?"

"Pedophiles. They're people who like to - "

"I know what a goddamn pedophile is, Billy." Dad cuts me off.

"I'm just not sure the school should be giving you projects on them." He stops for a moment, looking at the closed computer. Then he looks right back at me.

"You're not lying to me, are you, Billy?"

I hesitate for just a second. Maybe I should just tell him. After all, what I'm doing here is unquestionably adult stuff. Surely I can tell Dad? But I feel another flush of guilt that I was too late to save Olivia, and I push away any thought of telling him. I'm going to tell the police; then they can deal with it. Dad never needs to know. No one ever needs to know that I could have saved her. I shake my head.

"No."

For a little while, the only noise is the sound of Dad breathing, irregularly because he's still angry. I think I'm out of the woods, but he doesn't let up.

"Then let me see. Let me see what you were working on. Open it up. Right now."

He's called my bluff. I can't let him see the detail – it's all about Mr. Foster and how he killed her. And it's too late to be honest now. Not now I just lied to Dad. I can't let him see my computer, but he leans over me and lifts up the laptop lid. The screen comes to life.

Welcome Back user: Billy Wheatley

Enter Password:

"What's your password Billy? Put it in. Let me see what you're doing."

I hesitate. There's something about the way Dad's standing over me that's just plain scary.

"Put the goddamn password in, Billy. Put it in NOW."

His voice is so loud it makes my fingers jump onto the keyboard, but I stop myself just before they press out the word that's throbbing in my head. All my passwords are variations on one two-word root, with different endings and numbers to make them more secure. But Dad doesn't know the root. I start to type.

Incorrect Password

"Um," I say. And I try again. Typing the same word in a second time. The computer makes the same dud sound, and I'm still locked out.

"What the hell are you doing, Billy?"

"I can't get into it. I changed the password the other night, and I forgot what it is."

"Bullshit. . . " Dad slams the little table with his hand, and the empty soda can falls off and onto the floor. I freeze, not knowing what to do. Then Dad's anger turns to frustration. He can't figure out what to tell me to do.

"I've got it written down at home," I say. "I can open it again there. It's just I keep changing my password for security, and I forgot." I pretend to try again, still typing in the wrong word because, obviously, I haven't really forgotten my password. I'd never do that.

"Billy, are you lying to me? Are you really studying what happened to that girl for PD?"

There's not much else I can do but nod.

"I swear, Dad." He makes a big sighing noise.

"That's just. . . This whole damn town's gone crazy over that girl." He scratches his head, and I notice he's gotten white paint on his hands. Some of it rubs off on his hair. "The whole damn country. She just went swimming. She drowned. That's it. I don't know why people can't just *fucking* drop it."

"Do you want me to help you with the painting?" I say a few moments later. Clearly, I can't go back to working on the computer now, and if I help out, he's more likely to forget about asking to see my PD homework when we get back. Dad sighs again.

"Yeah, why not? I'm in chalet six. You can do some sanding."

THIRTY-ONE

It's late now, and Dad's asleep. He didn't even remember about checking on my homework when we got home. I did a lot of sanding for him, and that made him forget, and my arms ache. I still had to run upstairs when we got home and quickly make some pretend homework I could show him in case he did remember. Just a summary of how the police have got nowhere. I copied and pasted it from Wikipedia mostly. But then, when I went downstairs, Dad was on the sofa with the TV on, one beer open, and another lined up on the arm of the chair, so I didn't even bother telling him about it. Instead, I went back upstairs and got on with what I really had to do this evening: organizing my information to give it to the police.

I know where to send it. There's been these ads in the papers for weeks, asking for information about her, and there's a phone number and an email address. It says you're allowed to be anonymous, but if you send a normal email, you're not really anonymous, are you? They could just reply and ask who you are, or at least see your email address. But I know a way around that. You can get email addresses that can't be tracked, and then you can send the actual email through lots of different countries like Russia and Australia and funny countries like Bolivia and Poland too. I don't know exactly how to do it yet, but I've read about it, and I understand the basics.

This is what I write to the police:

URGENT

To the attention of Chief Larry Collins.

I am emailing to tell you Olivia Curran is dead. She was being held prisoner at 16 Speyside Drive by Mr. Foster, who is well-known around town as a pedophile. Most of the time, she was locked up in the cellar, but unfortunately, last Sunday she escaped, so he killed her. Here is a picture of her closing the drapes before he killed her.

Here is another picture of him hiding her body in some carpet and taking it out of his house in the middle of the night. It's not very clear because it is taken with the infrared mode of a Denver WCT-3004 Wildlife Camera (not the new version, unfortunately, which has the higher resolution).

I have also seen that Mr. Foster has a pink girl's backpack in his house, which probably belongs to Olivia. I'm sorry I don't have a photograph of this because I forgot to take one. But I expect you'll find it in the house when you raid it.

I do think you should arrest Mr. Foster immediately so he doesn't kill any other girls.

Signed

HK

I think about signing it "Anonymous," but it's a hard word to spell so instead I put those initials that I just typed randomly, and then I attach the two screen grabs and package up the email to send. After a little reading, I download a remailer program from the Internet. Then I set up a VPN (that's a virtual private network, in case you don't know) and install a new browser that doesn't track IP addresses. Finally, I use something called Guerrilla Mail to create a temporary email address, which I use to set up a *permanent* Gmail account in a false name (Harry King, so if they ever do track it, it'll match my initials). I didn't need to do that last step; I could have just sent my message with the Guerrilla account, but I didn't like the logo for the account much. It was a man with a bandana and a rifle. You'd have thought they'd just use a monkey.

It was a lot of work. It's now almost midnight, and I've finally hit "send" on my message. The police will get it in the morning. Well, they'll get it now; even though the message goes all the way around the world, it only takes a few seconds longer than a normal email, but I don't think there's anyone there at this time of night. What I'm trying to say is that tomorrow, the police will do a raid on Mr. Foster's house and arrest him.

It's a shame I was too late to rescue Olivia, but at least he'll go to prison, and then the town can get back to normal. The beach too. I've been worried about the Coast Guard search teams tramping all over my hermit crab study. I'd like to get back to doing that too. I like being an investigator, but I think I prefer being a marine biologist.

I get undressed and put my pajamas on. I can hear Dad snoring while I brush my teeth. When I get into bed, I find my mind is still buzzing, and I can't get to sleep. For some reason, I start thinking about my password again. I decide I'm going to tell you what it is. Not so that you can break into my files, of course, and not the *whole* password. I won't tell you the end part where I have some funny characters, but then, that part isn't very interesting anyway. I'll just tell you the first bit, because I feel like we're getting to know each other by now. And I don't really have anyone else to talk to. But you have to *promise* that you won't tell anyone.

You promise, right?

The first part of my password is: **BabyEva**

THIRTY-TWO

I CHECK the local TV news as soon as I get up, but I'm not really expecting anything yet. Probably, the police are still eating their breakfast. They won't have even read my email yet. It's hard, but I try to forget about it.

Dad goes surfing again, from Silverlea, and with the tide being low, I decide I can get into the caves and do a hermit crab count. I make sure I've got all my gear and run up the beach to Northend as soon as we arrive. I feel I've neglected my study a bit. I hope Dr. Ribald doesn't mind. I guess she'd understand if she knew.

It's a beautiful day, the first good weather we've had in a long time. The sun feels warm on my back, almost like summer, and I run along that hard part of the sand you get just before the water, and sometimes, I have to make sudden detours up the beach when big surges of waves rush up the beach. It's fun, and by the time I get to Northend, I've stopped wondering if the police have raided Mr. Foster's house yet.

Then I take my shoes and socks off, put them on my usual rock, and roll up my jeans carefully. Part of me doesn't want to go in the caves, where it's cold and dark. It's too nice a day out here. But I do it anyway. I step into the cold, clear water of the rockpools by the entrance. They sparkle in the sunlight, and I see a shimmer of silver where a shoal of tiny fish darts away from my foot. I almost decide to stop and try to catch them. It reminds me of being a kid, searching for nuggets of silver. But I'm not a kid anymore. I've got work to do.

I step carefully through the seaweed until I get to the cliff face, where a small black opening marks the entrance to the caves. The water's pretty deep in the entrance, and you have to duck down, so it's kind of intimidating, but I've done it so many times now I don't even hesitate. I duck down under the rocky ledge, move forward with my back bent, and stand up inside the cave. In front of me, it's pitch-black at first. You'd think no light could ever reach in here, but the truth is a little bit of sunlight does get in through the cave entrance. Gradually, my eyes adjust until I can make out the interior shape of the cave. It's almost circular, this first chamber, with smooth bumps on the walls and ceiling, like the rock has been growing in here. Size-wise, it's about half a tennis court, but that's only the first chamber. It goes back further than that, but the rockpools don't, so there's no need for me to go that far.

I switch on my ultraviolet flashlight and start to shine it around at the water I'm standing in. Like usual, I'm a little worried that it's not working because it doesn't send out a beam of light like a normal flashlight. It's only when you catch something that glows in ultraviolet that you know it's actually on.

I focus my eyes on the bottom of the pools as usual, but all I can see at first are my feet glowing blue when the flashlight shines on them. And then I see some anemones. They look purple with the light, but they glow much darker, so they take a while to spot. I keep sweeping the flashlight from side to side, trying to catch the brighter yellows, reds, and greens of the crabs.

I search for a long time, until my feet feel cold and shriveled from the water, but there's nothing. For a while, I think I'm not going to find *any* of my crabs. That would be a disaster. But then I shine the light under a ledge of rock, far back into the cave, and a strange blue light shines back from under the dark water. It's pretty deep, and I have to put my whole arm in the water, so my sleeve gets wet, but I pick up the crab and pull it out to inspect it. It looks like just a shell; the little pincers and legs have retracted almost completely inside. I don't need to read the small number 13 painted on the back of the shell to recognize it as one of my favorites. For some reason, I called this one Gary.

I record Gary's position on a notepad hanging from around my neck. Then I put him back where he was and continue my search, eventually finding two other crabs, one is number 27 and the other doesn't have a number because I haven't managed to paint them all on yet. Then I run out of time. It means a lot of crabs have gone missing. I stay a little longer to try and find them, but for some reason today, I don't much like being inside the caves. A long time before I really need to, I find myself ducking back out of the cave and back to the sunlight.

I sit down on the rock where I leave my shoes. My feet feel the warmth of the sun, and I decide to knot my shoes together and hang them around my neck. Then I just sit there for a while, thinking about things. Three crabs from the two hundred I originally painted isn't very many, and I wonder what might have gone wrong. The first time I tried to do this experiment in the rockpools at Littlelea, I had the same problem of losing all the crabs. I thought I'd solved it with my ultraviolet light idea, but now I'm not so sure. I ponder if it's a useful scientific result to say that hermit crabs actually move around a lot more than people think. I consider emailing Dr. Ribald and asking her, but she still hasn't answered my last email, and I was hoping to send her some actual results before bothering her again.

So I'm a little glum as I set off back down the beach to meet Dad. But with the sun still out, I go back to my game of getting as close to the surge of the water as I can without letting it catch me. Then, halfway back, I change the game and jump in the puddles of water left on the beach, which have now been warmed up by the sun. It's like jumping into little sandy baths. And slowly, my mood improves. The problem with my study, I decide, is that I haven't been able to give it the attention it deserves. It's pretty hard, doing a scientific study *and* going to school. And when you add on catching a killer on top of that, it's not surprising that things aren't going that well.

But now, I can get back to things. The police will definitely have caught Mr. Foster by now. And thinking about that, I remember that I have to recover my camera from Mr. Foster's boat. I'm excited about that because it will have captured the whole police raid. I think about whether I could put it on YouTube. If I used a false name.

But when we get home (it's Sunday, and Dad isn't working for once) and I check the local news, there's nothing about a raid. In fact, there's nothing at all about the Olivia Curran case. I look on my computer in my bedroom and search all the sites I can think of, but still, I can't find anything. I think about it for a while and decide that maybe the information is going up the chain of command. That's what happens to important information. And maybe specialist officers are coming from the mainland. Maybe the FBI. The ferry gets in at two on Sundays, so maybe they'll catch him after that?

THIRTY-THREE

It's Wednesday evening now. Four days since I sent my evidence to the police. Four days and *still* they haven't done anything. What worries me is that Mr. Foster could easily murder again.

If you looked at me and Dad right now, you'd think we were just sitting together watching TV, but actually, a new idea is forming in my mind. The program we're watching is one of those late night shows where grown-ups talk about news and politics. Normally, I'd be upstairs on the Internet, but I'm disappointed after not finding anything about the raid on Mr. Foster. Tonight, I wanted to see if there might be an update about it on the show. There isn't. But it gives me an idea all the same.

They're not talking about anything interesting. It's about a hospital where people keep dying, more than usual I mean. But what's interesting is *how* they came to be talking about it. Apparently, there was someone who worked in the hospital, called a "whistle-blower." This person spent a long time trying to tell everyone about the bad doctors, but no one listened. So eventually, they went and told the newspapers about it. Then the newspapers printed a story, and *then* the bad doctors got found out. That's how they came to be talking about it on this program too. And that gives me an idea. It's just the same as with me. If the police aren't going to arrest Mr. Foster on their own, I can force them to by being a whistle-blower. I can send the information to the *Island Times.* They'll make a story from it, and then the police will *have* to do something.

At first, I don't really think about it seriously. I just like the idea of it. I like the idea of doing something. But the more I think, the more convinced I become that it's the right thing to do. Look at it this way:

If I *don't* tell the *Island Times*, and the police *don't* do anything, then Mr. Foster could easily decide to kill another girl. He might be planning it right now. I did the wrong thing before, and Olivia Curran ended up dead. If I do the right thing now, I could save another girl's life.

There's also the question of timing. The *Island Times* comes out once a week, on Fridays, so I don't have much time to sit around thinking about it. If I don't send the photographs now, tonight, I'll miss this week's paper. That would give Mr. Foster a whole week to kill another girl.

The more I think about it, the more certain I become. I *have* to be a whistle-blower, *and I have to do it right now*, before I even go to bed. That way, the journalists will get it tomorrow morning, and they'll have all day tomorrow to put it in Friday's paper. Then the police will have to go and arrest Mr. Foster.

Upstairs, I open up my laptop and get to work. I couldn't figure out from the program whether it was illegal to be a whistle-blower or not, but I decide to use my new Harry King Gmail account again to stay anonymous. Then I decide it might be safer to set up another one, so it's different than the police one. By the time I've gotten all that set up, and routed the email through fifteen different countries, it's really late, so I don't have that long to write the actual email. But I know what I need to send them: the same photographs that I sent the police. Olivia Curran's face at the window, and then the picture of her dead body being dragged out of Mr. Foster's house, with his face looking all burning white like he's some kind of monster.

Just before I send it, I have a moment's worry that this isn't the right thing to do. What if I get into trouble? But I make myself stop thinking like that. Being a whistle-blower is scary; that's what the TV program said. But if I don't do it, someone else could die.

My finger hovers over the button. One click, and my message will fly twice around the world, then land in the inbox of the *Island Times*. I can't take it back. I screw up my eyes and press my finger down onto the keyboard. When I open my eyes again the email is gone.

THIRTY-FOUR

WEST WOKE to the sound of rain battering the windows of the cramped, damp apartment which had become home. She was alone, the duvet on her double bed supplemented by two blankets. As long as she slept in pajamas, she was warm enough, just. She got up, pulled back the flimsy drapes above her bed, and looked out at the low, leaden sky. Fat raindrops ran down the glass, smearing the backs of the houses that blocked her view of the ocean.

She stumbled to the shower cubicle, where her elbows knocked the sides and threatened to break the thin plastic walls. She opened the tap, and a thin trickle of water leaked out. She let it fall on her hand until it got as hot as it was going to. With a grimace, she stepped inside.

As quickly as she could, she began washing her hair. Working the shampoo in, she heard the sound of the shower next door. Then next door's cubicle door shutting, the sound of water hitting a plastic tray identical to the one she stood in. Then, irritatingly clear, the sound of cheery whistling.

It was new, this morning optimism coming from next door. She put her head to one side and considered for a moment what it might mean. She'd only been inside Rogers' apartment a few times, but that was enough to know it was as unsuited to the onset of winter as hers was. And they had made almost no progress with the case. The Currans had made good on their promise, publishing their seventh round of ads only two days previously, but all it produced was noise, nothing of value. That didn't explain Rogers' exuberance. She went back to squeezing the shampoo out of her hair.

He was alright Rogers. He'd not so much mentioned the night they spent together, not to her, or more importantly, to anyone else. And they'd slipped easily back to the working relationship they'd had before. Most of the time, when she looked at him, she was able to forget they'd spent a drunken night together. And when she didn't forget she felt a kind of warmth about it. It was something in the past, but she didn't exactly regret it. That didn't mean his good mood didn't irritate her though.

Once she'd dressed and gathered her things, she found Detective Rogers relaxing in the plastic sun lounger on her little porch, watching the rain drip down from the roof overhead, smoking his first cigarette of the day. He greeted her with a quick flick of the eyebrows, then stubbed his cigarette out.

"Morning," he said. "You ready to seize the day?" There was a breeziness to his voice that West studied, trying to see what was different about her partner. He climbed to his feet. The keys were on the table beside him.

"You wanna drive this morning?" he asked, noticing her looking. Rogers never asked if she wanted to drive.

West's first job of the morning was to pick up the mail bag from Sergeant Wiggins. He was a cheery soul who had taken to counting the letters for her each morning. Mondays were the worst, since she and Rogers didn't work weekends. Today was a Monday.

"Just twelve today. It's definitely drying up," Wiggins said. And it was true. Even with Joseph and Susan Curran's latest round of newspaper ads, and an appearance on a popular talk show, the public interest in their daughter's case was fading away. West thanked the Sergeant and carried the bag to her desk, clearing away two empty coffee cups before sitting down. Rogers was already sitting down opposite her, frowning at the screen of his terminal.

West pulled open the Velcro closure on the mail bag and pulled the letters out.

"How many you got?" Rogers asked.

"Twelve. You?"

He ran a finger down his screen, counting in his head.

"Twenty-seven," he said, when he'd finished. He didn't take his eyes off the screen, and she didn't expect him to say anything more, but his good mood that morning seemed to make him more sociable. He went on, leaning back in his chair.

"It's incredible, isn't it? Even now, two months after she disappeared, we've got twenty-seven crazy people emailing to say they've seen Olivia Curran. I mean, clearly, they haven't. They've just seen a teenage girl who looks a little like her." He glanced at her pile of letters, then looked at her. "You still think it was worth staying?"

She bit her lip before answering.

"There's still a chance."

They'd developed a basic screening system. Green meant the tip-off was of the lowest possible credibility. They would do just enough work to confirm its status as junk, then it would be filed and forgotten. Nearly all the leads that came in were green leads.

Occasionally, a lead was flagged as orange. Orange meant there was some limited reason to think the information *could* be credible. Orange leads got scheduled for further investigation, although they would join a queue and wait their turn. An orange lead might require a phone call or a number of calls to be validated, or more likely invalidated. If they were particularly lucky, an orange lead might necessitate a trip out of the office. Real detective work, as Rogers put it. More often than not, though, the orange leads could quickly be downgraded to green.

Then there were red leads. Or rather, there remained the hypothetical possibility that red leads existed. A red lead – if it ever came in – would be one that contained information that was obviously credible or immediately relevant to the investigation. But in nearly a month of searching, there'd been no red leads. No one in the station really believed that one would turn up now. Too much time had passed. Except West. Even after all this time she still felt some belief, when she opened a letter or email, or listened to a phone message, that it might lead them somewhere. Rogers had taken to mocking her about it, although he did so with a grudging respect for her dedication.

The first envelope West opened that morning contained nothing but a handwritten note on a sheet of stationery that had a watermark from *City Garden Grand Hotel*. It was hard to read the spidery black ink, but after a moment, West deciphered the words. An anonymous sender claimed to have seen Olivia Curran in an open-air swimming pool in Manila in the Philippines. There were no details, not even the date the sighting was supposed to have taken place. Her gut feeling was this information was worthless, but she turned to her PC and typed "Manila" into the search bar of the investigation database. Nothing came back. She tried "Philippines", then "City Garden Grand Hotel" with similar results. She tried different spellings, in various ways that people might have gotten wrong. Nothing. There had been no previous sightings of Olivia Curran anywhere in the Philippines.

On a whim, she typed "swimming pool," and five listings came back. Five other people believed they had seen the missing girl in swimming pools. Three in the United States, one in Argentina, and one in France. Satisfied, she clicked the button to create a new listing. She scanned the letter and attached the digital version to the entry, then filed the original copy in the day's file - should it ever need to be reviewed, it could be found linked via the date. She typed the details of the "sighting", added the keywords "Manila", "Philippines", and "swimming pool", then coded the entry as green. Then she reached over and picked up the next envelope.

Three hours passed.

"How you getting on? I'm getting hungry here." Rogers' voice interrupted her work.

She flicked through the remaining envelopes. "I got three to go. I want to get them done before lunch," she said, expecting him to let her get back to it. But he didn't.

"I got another two sightings in Paris."

"Paris?" she said. She searched her mind. Paris had come up before, was it…something?

"Yeah, but don't get excited. They're worthless. They both took photos. Wrong age, wrong height. One of them was fat. How's she going to get fat in two months? They reckon she's been hiding out eating donuts on top of the Eiffel Tower?"

"France, though," West said, remembering. "I had some sightings in France the other day." She looked thoughtful.

"And you're still wondering if it can really be a coincidence? Well, it's not. I'll tell you what it is." Rogers leaned forward.

"What you've got is three hundred twenty million Americans who know this girl's missing and think that's tragic because she's *pretty*. Then, when these people go on vacation, which sometimes they do, they stop staring at the floor and look around them for a change. And when they do that, suddenly, they start noticing people. Including teenage girls who are pretty and look a little like Olivia Curran. Believe me. That's why France keeps coming up. A lot of Americans go on vacation to Europe at this time of year."

West had heard this theory from Rogers before, but he was refining it as time went on. She had to admit it seemed to match the evidence they were building up.

"I thought you were supposed to go to Paris in the springtime?" she asked, but he ignored her. Her concentration broken, she asked another question.

"Anyway. How come you were whistling in the shower this morning. Isn't yours cold?"

He looked up, pretending to be surprised, but unable to restrain a grin.

"Cold?"

"Yeah."

"No."

"What do you mean '*no*'?"

"I mean it's not cold. Well, not anymore it isn't. I got Tommy's brother to take a look at it. He's a plumber. If anything, it's a little hot now." He mimed shrinking back from hot water.

"Tommy? Who's Tommy?"

"Tommy! You know, the skinny guy from Patrol. We were in the bar the other night, and I was moaning about the shower. He said his brother could take a look for me."

West thought for a moment, feeling a little snubbed that no one had invited her. But then she'd not made much of an effort with the guys.

"You didn't get him to look at mine as well?"

"I didn't know yours was cold." Rogers made a face like this was obvious. "Was I really whistling?"

She ignored that.

"Did you get the guy's number?"

"No." Rogers shrugged. "You *heard* me? You were listening to me in the shower?"

"No. I wasn't listening. I was in the shower at the same time, and I heard you in there, whistling."

"Did you have the toothbrush glass up against the wall to hear better?"

"Don't be an idiot."

Rogers just grinned at her.

West shook her head and looked away.

"Come on." Rogers said.

"Come on where?"

"It's lunch time. My stomach's rumbling."

THIRTY-FIVE

ROGERS DROVE THIS TIME, even though the diner was only a few minutes' walk. They sat in their regular booth and Rogers chewed slowly through his usual turkey sandwich. West watched him, not feeling hungry enough for her order of chicken soup.

"Can I ask you a question?" West said after a while.

"I dunno. Can you?" Rogers replied, not looking up. West was used to the sarcasm and barely heard it.

"If you're so sure we're wasting our time here, why did you stay? "

Rogers didn't answer at first. He picked up a paper napkin and wiped the grease from his mouth, then he folded it and placed under the edge of his plate. He looked at her.

"Who says we're wasting our time?"

"You do. All the time. You complain about how all the leads are junk."

"They are junk."

"So why are you here?"

Rogers shrugged.

"I told you."

"When?" West frowned.

"That night," he glanced at her for a moment then looked away. He went on quickly.

"I told you, I'm in no hurry to get back home and face my ex-wife." He looked thoughtful for a moment. "And maybe you've taught me something."

"What?"

"I dunno. Don't give up? There's always a chance? You seem to believe it anyway."

A frown appeared on West's face and Rogers laughed.

"Are you finally realizing that detective work isn't very glamorous? Not like they show in the movies. Feeding a database and hoping to come across the needle in a haystack. That *is* the job. And it's the same job here or back in New York. At least here I can take refreshing walks on the beach." He smiled. They both knew he'd yet to take a walk on the beach.

"Seriously. I'm not a complicated guy. I like it here. I like the people. It makes a nice change from the city. And it's a long way away from my ex-wife."

"So you don't think there's any chance of solving the case?"

He plucked a toothpick and scraped at a gap in his teeth. "It depends if there's a case to solve." West looked away.

"How 'bout you? You ever going to tell me why you stayed?"

The question surprised her.

"What do you mean?"

"Back on the beach that day, you started telling me something, then you clammed right up."

She felt her face redden slightly.

"No I didn't."

"Yes you did. You were saying how you were all set to be a swimmer. But then you stopped and joined the police. That's not exactly a natural jump. And you're just about the most determined person I ever came across. So there's gotta be something behind it."

West was about to tell him he was wrong. But then she'd started with the heart to heart. It seemed only fair to give her side.

"Go on," Rogers said, still picking at his teeth.

"OK," West said slowly. "If you really want to know. It happened when I was nineteen. I'd done quite well. I was swimming in the Nationals. They were being held in Florida that year. We were swimming there. . . " West paused and looked down at the table for a moment. Rogers narrowed his eyes but let her take her time.

"I was there with my best friend, Sarah. We grew up together. Like, we were never apart. Never. We went to the same school. We both swam. We pushed each other on. We were. . . Close. Very close."

Rogers waited.

"Sarah Donaldson. Do you know the name?"

"Should I?"

"Maybe. Maybe you would've. She would have medaled in Beijing, no doubt." West stopped talking suddenly. There was no reason to tell the story she had begun. It only caused her pain.

"Would have? What happened?" Rogers prompted.

For a long moment West said nothing. She considered brushing him off again. But she knew that now she'd begun he wouldn't let it go.

"We were sharing a room together. Sarah and I always shared. The night before the competition, she was restless, full of energy. She was always like that before she raced. Usually she'd use the gym or something, to bring her down a bit. But the hotel didn't have a gym. So she decided to run a few K's. She asked me to go with her, but I preferred to rest before races." West looked up at the ceiling of the diner, as if the story still hurt. Then she looked back at Rogers and continued talking.

"It wasn't late or anything. The hotel was in a good part of town. There was no reason to worry about it, no reason to think twice. But when she wasn't back an hour later, I started to get worried. I told my coach. We waited for her together. And when she wasn't back by midnight, we called the cops.

"I'll never forget that night. No one could sleep. We were just waiting. Just praying that she would walk back in the door. And everything would go back to normal." West paused for a long time. Rogers gave her time.

"But it didn't. They found her body the next morning. Dumped behind some bushes in a park. The guy - *the monster* - raped her and then strangled her." West's voice cracked a little over the final words.

"He get caught?" Rogers asked after a pause.

West nodded. "Not at the time. A few years later he did. A traffic cop caught him in the act. He did it four more times in the meantime."

"Jesus."

"It wasn't just that." West said, a moment later. "I'm not drawing a direct link between Sarah's murder and me joining the force. That would be… An oversimplification. But at the same time. . . You could say I never really had the same focus after that. I never lived up to my potential." She shrugged. "Not that that matters."

This time Rogers looked confused.

"Swimming. I didn't qualify. My times went way down. Eventually I got dropped from the team. It never seemed important after that."

"Shit." Rogers said.

"How 'bout you?" West said, trying to force her voice to sound brighter. "Why did you join up?"

"Dad was a cop. Granddad too. I never had much imagination as a kid."

"Good reason. Better than mine," West said.

"Jesus Jessica, I'm sorry. I shouldn't have teased. About you being determined. You've got good reason."

She flashed him a smile, breathing a little deeply.

"You wanna get back to it. You wanna keep searching for that needle?" Rogers asked, and West nodded.

Neither of them knew it yet, but the needle they had been hunting for so long was sitting waiting for them at their desks.

THIRTY-SIX

THEY FOUND it right after lunch. West finished up her remaining leads and looked up, intending to offer Rogers help with his. She had to wait though, since he'd gone to get more coffee. There was a vending machine in the corridor with which he had developed a love-hate relationship. He walked back. Placed a cardboard cup in front of West.

"How many damn shirts am I gonna wreck before figuring that machine out?"

West smiled her sympathy and took her drink. "I'm all done here," she said. "You want some help with yours?"

"Sure."

She pulled her chair around the pair of desks so she could see his screen. He was still fussing over his shirt so she clicked open the next email and began to read it out loud to him.

"OK. Here we go. Urgent, written in capital letters. *To the attention of Chief Larry Collins.* Yeah, right. Like he's going to read this personally. *I am emailing to tell you that Olivia Curran is dead. She was being held prisoner at 16 Speyside. . .* " Suddenly, her hands stopped, and she read on in silence. She felt him stiffen beside her.

"Shit. Ollie, what's this?"

The email filled the top half of the screen; an image took up most of the bottom. It was too dark to make out what it showed at first, but it looked creepy. They both looked closer. It showed a man dragging a carpet from a bungalow in what must be the middle of the night, the image captured by infrared camera.

"The hell is that?" Rogers said, leaning in close. They both read the rest of the email.

URGENT

To the attention of Chief Larry Collins.

I am emailing to tell you Olivia Curran is dead. She was being held prisoner at 16

Speyside Drive by Mr. Foster, who is well-known around town as a pedophile. Most of the time, she was locked up in the cellar, but unfortunately, last Sunday she escaped, so he killed her. Here is a picture of her closing the drapes before he killed her.

Here is another picture of him hiding her body in some carpet and taking it out of his house in the middle of the night. It's not very clear because it is taken with the infrared mode of a Denver WCT-3004 Wildlife Camera (not the new version, unfortunately, which has the higher resolution).

I have also seen that Mr. Foster has a pink girl's backpack in his house, which probably belongs to Olivia. I'm sorry I don't have a photograph of this because I forgot to take one. But I expect you'll find it in the house when you raid it.

I do think you should arrest Mr. Foster immediately so he doesn't kill any other girls.

Signed

HK

"Scroll down," West said, and when Rogers did so, a second image came up. A girl's face at a window, this time taken in the daytime, but the same bungalow.

"Jesus!" Rogers spilled more of his coffee. "Is that her? Is that Olivia Curran?"

THIRTY-SEVEN

"We should do this more often," the woman said, resting her head on the man's shoulder. She was late thirties, him early forties. Her hair showed gray at the roots; he was no longer lean and fit like when they met, but growing a gut. Their girls, now four and six, ran onto the beach, oblivious to the cold weather.

"It's good to get away," he said, letting her head stay there for a while. "We all need to reset every now and then."

The girls had done their best on the journey, but three hours in the car and then two more on the ferry were plenty. Now they were like wild animals released from months of captivity. Running this way, then that, bending down to inspect pebbles and dig holes in the sand with their hands.

"So what do you want to do?" the woman asked. The man watched his children for a while before answering. "I think we should just tire them out and make sure they get an early night," he said at last, and she lifted her head to look him in the face.

"Oh yes?" She cocked an eye curiously. "And why would that be?"

"Don't you get all coy on me. I'm talking about a quiet meal in the hotel restaurant with a good bottle of wine. I'm not proposing anything after that."

She smiled. After a moment, she spoke again.

"When did we last have a meal out together?"

"Oh, a decade ago. Maybe more. Come on." He got up and strode down the sand to join his daughters. "Let's do a competition. Who can find me three types of shells? The winner gets a piece of chocolate cake."

In less than ten seconds, the older girl had presented her father with three types of shells, two white and one blue, and the younger girl was almost in tears at the thought of missing out. But he diffused the situation by resetting the challenge.

"OK, now you have to tell me what *types* of shells they are."

"What types of shells?" the girls asked, confused.

"Yeah, I'll help you with the first." He picked the blue shell from the girl's hand and held it up so they could both see. "This is a mussel shell. When they're alive, there are two of them, like this." He found a second blue shell on the beach and held them together.

"The little animal would live in here, and when it gets hungry, it opens up like this and lets the seawater flow in, and it filters out little bits of food."

"Daddy?"

"Yes, Chloe?"

"What's this shell here?"

She held up a second shell. He peered at it, confused. Then he pulled an iPhone from his pocket and began tapping on the screen.

"I'll have a look. You find some more shells," he said while he worked, and the girls went away, used to such interruptions.

His wife watched him from where she sat, on a patch of pebbles so her trousers wouldn't get sandy. She was a little disappointed that he was on his phone so soon, but it was probably a work email. Best to answer it so he could focus more completely on the family. She enjoyed watching him with the girls, when he did find the time.

"Chloe?" he said.

"Yes?"

"It's a slipper limpet," He showed her the screen on his iPhone. "Do you see? Apparently, they live in big clumps like this. The bottom one is always the female - that's the girl - and the little ones on top are the boys. When she dies," he stopped, corrected himself, "or just goes away for some reason, then one of the boys becomes the new girl. What about that? Can you imagine? So all the girl slipper limpets started off as boys."

As weird as this fact was, Chloe was used to the world not making sense, and simply held her head to one side for a moment to consider it, and then moved on.

"Where do they live?"

The man consulted his phone again, but it didn't immediately help, so he guessed. "In the rockpools, I guess. Tell you what. We'll have a real competition. We'll take our shoes off, and whoever can find the most interesting thing in the rockpools, they'll win the piece of chocolate cake."

Excited screaming greeted this suggestion, and the girls pulled off their shoes and socks and picked their way carefully through the pebbles to where the bigger rocks began. Only the woman stayed where she was, stretching out her legs and letting the low November sun warm her face.

It was her idea, the mini break to Lornea Island. She'd come a couple of times as a child, and she liked the thought of taking her children, too, but it had never happened. Then a pretty hotel with an indoor pool popped up on her Facebook feed. It looked lovely, and when she clicked the ad, she saw it was on Lornea Island. It's funny how coincidences work, she'd been thinking, what with Lornea being in the news so much these days. So she booked it. Her only caveat was she didn't want to go to Silverlea - the town where that poor girl actually went missing. Instead, they were on the other side of the island, facing the mainland, the sea here calm and unthreatening. Not many people came to Lornea in the off-season, meaning the hotel was cheap. The family room was actually two rooms, one with bunk beds for the kids, and a door dividing them and the main room. She and Peter would be able to dine in the hotel restaurant while the girls slept. A rare chance for an evening together. What happened after that was on her mind just as much as it was apparently on his.

She watched the three of them now, picking their way across the rocks, stopping by the many pools and bending down to investigate. Her husband had his trousers rolled up to just below the knee; their younger daughter, Sarah, had taken her leggings off completely. She shook her head in exasperation, the girl would get cold, but her excited whoops filtered back up the beach to the woman, and she let it slide for now. She breathed in the smells of the beach. The salt and the muddy odor of the seaweed.

Suddenly, a scream broke the quiet calm. And when the noise should have stopped if, say, one of the girls had seen a large crab, or splashed herself, it carried on, getting louder and more piercing. More desperate.

The woman was on her feet and moving without knowing how. She ran down the sand, ready to throw herself upon whatever danger her daughters faced but not yet understanding what it was. Her attention focused on Chloe, standing in the middle of a deep pool of water, her hands on her face, shaking in terror. The man was running toward her, too, as well as he could over the uneven surface.

"What is it?" the woman called out, but no one answered. The only noise was the screaming. She got to the rocks and didn't pause to remove her shoes, but carried on, crashing right through the first pool. She looked up to see her husband sweep Chloe off her feet and carry her to a large flat rock, away from where she'd been standing. Moments later, the woman was there as well, terrified at the look on the faces of her family. Her husband was still holding Chloe, and she lifted Sarah too, asking over and over as she did so,

"What is it? What happened?"

His face was white with shock. He looked at the children for a moment before answering, as if he didn't want them to know. But they were the ones who'd found it.

"It looks like a hand. A human hand. Chloe found a hand in the rockpool over there."

THIRTY-EIGHT

IT'S FRIDAY NOW, and there's still nothing in the *Island Times.*

I checked online this morning. Nothing. Then, just after registration, I sneaked up to the library before class. I had to ask the lady if today's paper had come in yet, and she looked at me really funny because she was actually reading it, at her desk. I told her I needed it for a school project, and she sighed but let me look. I skimmed through the whole paper really quickly, and there wasn't anything about Olivia Curran. I don't understand it.

I'm sitting in math now, trying to make sense of it. There's two possible explanations. The first is I didn't send the email correctly. I realized I can check that tonight. It's a bit complicated though, not just a case of looking in the "sent" folder of my secret Gmail account. It has more to do with tracking to see that the email didn't get bounced from any of the foreign servers I routed it through. It's hard to explain, but trust me. The second possibility is that I sent the email fine but just too late for the *Island Times* to include in this week's paper. You'd think they would be able to manage it, but one thing I've noticed about adults is they always take *forever* to do anything. Even important things.

It's like with math. I like math, but the stuff we do at school is so basic. Today, we're doing fractions. I could do fractions when I was six. We're only halfway through the class, and I've finished both worksheets already. I'm about to put up my hand and ask for some more work when the door of the classroom opens.

I glance up automatically, not really to see who it is; it's just that the noise gets my attention. It's probably one of the boys, coming back from the restroom. They all pretend they need to go all the time; I think it's a kind of joke. But that's not what it is. It's the principal, Mr. Simms. And I can see him looking right at me.

He mouths something to my teacher. I think he says: "A quick word." Then the teacher, Mrs. Walker, goes over to the door, where they whisper to each other.

Then she looks over at *me*; I'm sure of it this time. Then I see there's more people behind them. A man and a woman. I don't know who they are.

"Billy," Mrs. Walker says then. Her voice sounds funny. "Could you come out here for a minute?"

I feel a pang of alarm. A few of the kids in class are looking at me now, wondering what I've done. But there's nothing I can do. I push my chair back, and it squeaks on the floor, drawing even more attention. I feel the eyes of the whole class on my back as I walk over to the door.

When I get there, Mr. Simms puts his hands on my shoulders and guides me out into the corridor. Then he closes the class door so it's just me and him and the two strangers in the corridor. Mr. Simms nods to them.

"Billy Wheatley?" one of them says, the man. He's really big, with blond hair on the backs of his hands. "My name is Detective Oliver Rogers, and this is my colleague, Detective Jessica West. I believe you two already met?" There's a hardness in his voice, like he's being sarcastic.

I fight to hold back the panic. Detectives? The police? My mind is buzzing, trying to figure out what's going on. Then the man's words register, and I look at the woman. I don't recognize her. I don't know what's going on.

"Hello, Billy. I took your statement when Olivia Curran first went missing. Do you remember?"

I stare at her face. Dimly, I think I might recognize her. She was the one who didn't think my evidence was significant. The not-very-good one. Is that what this is about? They've finally realized the mistake they made?

I nod, then look down at the floor, waiting to see what happens next.

"Billy," the man says. The man detective; I've already forgotten what his name is. "We'd like to ask you some questions about an email you sent to the Lornea Island Police Department and later to the newspaper, the *Island Times.* We'd like to ask those questions at the police station. Your principal has agreed to accompany you there until we can track down your father, and then he can sit in with you. Are you OK with that?"

There's this heavy silence in the corridor. I don't know what horrifies me most: the thought of going to the police station, or going with Mr. Simms. I've never even spoken to him before.

"Do I have to?" I ask, my voice coming out in a squeak. The two detectives look at each other.

"Come on Billy. We just need a little chat," the woman says. She puts her arm out, like she's inviting me to go with her, and reluctantly I start walking.

THIRTY-NINE

It's not a real police car, just a red Ford, but they put me in just like they do in the movies, pushing my head down so I don't hit it on the roof, even though I've gotten in lots of cars before without any problems. Then the woman detective gets in beside me. Mr. Simms goes in the passenger seat. He doesn't say anything. He just pretends to be interested in the view.

We drive to the Newlea police station. It's on the main road, and I've driven past the front with Dad lots of times, but we've never gone into it before. We drive through these big black gates, and I'm a little surprised to see there's just a small parking lot inside; I don't know why, but I was expecting something more. There are lots of real police cars here, though, with the black-and-white markings of the Lornea Island Police Department. The man drives to the end, but there's no spaces, so the woman detective says she'll take us in, and he goes off to park somewhere else. I never knew the police had to do that; I always just assumed they would be able to park anywhere they liked.

The woman detective leads us inside into a kind of front desk area, where a policeman in uniform is sitting behind a big desk. The woman stands next to me while he asks my name and address, and writes it down. Then he asks Mr. Simms' name and address. Mr. Simms isn't allowed to call himself Mr. Simms, and I find out his first name is Paul. The policeman writes all this down in a book, an actual book, not a computer. Then the woman detective starts talking to Mr. Simms.

"We're going to take some fingerprints from Billy now. They'll help us eliminate him in the event that he's contaminated any crime scenes."

Mr. Simms nods like he thinks this is a good idea, and we all go into another room. My brain is working really fast, but I don't understand. Why do they want my fingerprints? Do they think I might have been involved? Do they think I might be Mr. Foster's accomplice? I try to think of what I might have touched. There was the boat, of course, and the windows - when I checked to see if the windows were locked. Why didn't I wear gloves? I've got lots of pairs of gloves.

"Billy, could you follow me, please." The woman detective's voice cuts through the chaos in my head.

There's no computer in the fingerprint room either. The woman detective tells me to roll up my sleeves, and then she presses each finger into an ink pad, and then on a piece of paper with a little square box for each finger. We do both hands, and after that, she takes palm prints too.

"OK, Billy, you can wash your hands now." She points to a sink on the opposite wall, and I wash them really well. I don't like the feel of the ink on my hands. It makes me feel guilty of something.

Then the man detective comes back. He sticks his head in around the door, so I guess he managed to find a space for the car.

"The dad's on his way. We're gonna take him straight in."

I get led to a room with the words "Interview Room 4" stenciled on the door, with a lightbulb inside a little grille just above the entrance. It's switched off at the moment. There's not much inside, just a table and chairs, an old-fashioned tape recorder on the table. There aren't any windows.

Before we've even sat down the man detective starts talking to Mr. Simms.

"Thank you for coming sir, but Billy's father has now just arrived, so we won't be needing you after all. I'll arrange for you to get a ride back to the school."

Mr. Simms nods at this. I glance over at him and think he looks disappointed all of a sudden. But then another policeman leads Dad into the room, and I can't really pay any attention to Mr. Simms anymore, because Dad's in a crazy mood. I mean, I know this isn't a normal situation, but Dad's real mad.

"What the hell's all this about?" he says at once. He seems to take in the detective who's still standing by the door.

"You. What's this about? Why has my son been dragged to the police station?"

"He hasn't been dragged here sir. He's agreed voluntarily to answer some questions."

"He's not under arrest? Then you can't hold him, he's just a kid anyway. Whatever he did. Come on Billy. We're getting out of here *right now*." Dad walks right around the table to where I'm sitting and goes to take my hand, but the man detective manages to get in between us.

"We'd prefer you do this voluntarily," the woman says. "But if you refuse, we can arrest Billy for attempting to pervert the course of justice and obstructing a police investigation."

No one says anything for a few beats.

Then the man detective speaks.

"Sir, I'm going to need you to calm down and take a seat."

For a moment I think Dad's still going to push past him. I'm holding my breath.

"Right now sir."

I've never seen Dad look like this before. His eyes flick around the room like he's trying to figure out if he can escape through a window or something, and then he just stares at me, shaking his head. Slowly Dad takes a seat.

The detectives sit back down again too. Across the other side of the table from us. They're both still breathing hard though. Then the man detective presses some buttons on the tape recorder.

"For the tape," he says. "The Officers present are Detective Oliver Rogers and Detective Jessica West." I make a point of remembering this time. When he's finished giving our names too, he slides a piece of paper across the desk to me.

"Billy. This email was sent to Chief Larry Collins of the Lornea Island Police Department on Sunday, November nineteenth. Do you recognize it?"

I look down at the paper. It's a printout of my email. Underneath are the two photographs I sent. All signed by HK. I try to think really fast, to work out why they think I sent it. Whether there's any way they can trace it back to me? I'm pretty sure I routed the email the right way. I glance up at Detective Rogers' face. He looks angry still. The woman looks a little bit friendlier. I do remember her better now. She gives me a little smile, just for a second, like she's encouraging me. But I shake my head.

"No? You don't recognize it? You sure about that?" While Detective Rogers talks he reaches for a clear plastic bag from the floor. I hadn't seen it there until now. But as he fiddles with the ziplock I get a dread feeling in my stomach.

"You did a good job with the email Billy, I'll give you that. We tracked it through…" He glances at his papers. "Here we go. Azerbaijan, Russia, Bulgaria. . . Then we lost it in Colombia. So instead, we visited Philip Foster to see if he'd noticed anyone unusual watching the house." He fiddles with the bag a bit more.

"And this is what we found." He pulls my camera out of the bag and turns it over and over in his hands. Eventually he stops playing with it, and when he does he's got the label at the top. He holds it up and shows it to Dad. I put it on for when I was recording animals. In case someone found the camera and thought it was lost. It says:

Property of Billy Wheatley
Clifftop Cottage, Littlelea
IMPORTANT SCIENTIFIC WORK
DO NOT TOUCH!!!

"Bit of a schoolboy mistake wouldn't you say?" He smiles at me, but I just look down at the table.

"And then there was the second email. You didn't do such a good job with that one, the *Island Times* was able to trace it all the way to Venezuela before they lost it. Fortunately, the editor has a good relationship with the chief here and passed it over at that point. If they'd printed this," he shook his head and glances at Dad. "If they'd printed this, we'd all be having a very different conversation here today." He pauses.

"Billy… Look at me." Reluctantly I pull my head up, and eventually I nod.

"Billy this is a very serious situation. We could be looking at juvenile court,

Youth detention facilities. But this gets a whole lot easier if you cooperate. Now did you send this email?"

This time I nod.

"For the benefit of the tape, Billy Wheatley is nodding his head."

"And this second email," Detective Rogers holds up another sheet of paper. "To the editor of the *Island Times*. Did you send this one as well?" Rogers slides it towards me so I can see better but I don't need to. I nod right away this time, and I'm surprised when a tear plops down onto the table in front of me.

"I was only trying to help," I say. "I wanted to find Olivia Curran because no one else could find her. Only when I did, it was too late, but that wasn't my fault. I didn't do it, I didn't help him kill her. You believe me, don't you?"

"Again, for the benefit of the tape, Billy Wheatley is nodding."

"I only sent that one because you weren't doing anything. I know she was already dead by then, but he could still be out catching another girl. Have you arrested him yet? He could be killing someone right now - "

"Is that the missing girl?" Dad asks suddenly. He's looking down at the email in amazement. "What the hell is going on here Billy?"

The two detectives look at each other. Detective Rogers is the one who breaks the silence.

"If you'll let me sir I'll explain. Your son here has formed the opinion that Philip Foster is connected with the disappearance of Olivia Curran. With these emails, he's wasted a large amount of police time. Had the *Island Times* printed those photographs, he could have caused irreparable damage to any trial resulting from this investigation. That's why he's here today."

"But that's her isn't it? That's Olivia Curran?" Dad interrupts him. "If he's found her, what does it matter how he did it?"

There's another silence and I take the opportunity to fill it.

"She was in his house. I saw her at the window. That's why I sent the emails. I push the emails back across the table to the detectives, so the picture of Olivia is right in front of him.

Detective Rogers doesn't even look at it. "Billy. Philip Foster has a sixteen-year-old daughter who comes to visit him on weekends. We've confirmed that your photograph of the girl in the window is of Mr. Foster's daughter. You also mentioned a pink bag you saw. That also belongs to Mr. Foster's daughter."

I stare at Detective Rogers. I can feel my mouth hanging open. Out of the corner of my eye, I see Dad rubbing his face.

"What about the cellar? Didn't you find anything in the cellar?"

"There's no cellar in that house, Billy."

"Well. . . " I screw up my face in confusion. "The carpet, then. What was he doing taking a carpet out in the middle of the night if he wasn't disposing of a body?"

Detective Rogers gives a really big sigh and pours himself a glass of water.

"The mystery carpet." He shakes his head. "Would you like a drink, Billy? Mr.

Wheatley?" He looks at Dad, who nods; then he pours us each a glass. When he speaks again, it's more Dad he's speaking to.

"Philip Foster is in the process of renovating his Silverlea property as a vacation let. It seems he wanted to avoid paying any charges to dispose of the carpet at the dump site." He pauses for a sip of water.

"Mr. Foster took the carpet to the dump in the middle of the night and left it in front of the gate. We've confirmed with the site that a carpet was found there in the morning after your son took this photograph. It was carried inside by the site staff when they arrived at work. They're sure it didn't contain a body. Furthermore, we've had a team of officers searching through the garbage to find that carpet." He pauses. "A lot of garbage. We finally located it yesterday. There are no traces of blood, or anything suspicious." Rogers turns to Dad again. "It seems Mr. Foster used it to wrap up some damp plasterboard. That's why it looks heavy in the image your son sent."

"So in a way, Billy, you have drawn our attention to a crime. But it's a crime of illegal waste dumping. Not murder. Meanwhile, the investigation has had to divert resources from legitimate lines of inquiry, to this wild-goose chase."

There's a long pause while they all seem to take this in. Then Detective Rogers turns back to me.

"You've caused a lot of people a lot of hassle. And you've accused an innocent man." Detective Rogers sits back and makes a steeple with his fingers. Then he looks annoyed when Detective West asks me a question.

"What was it that made you think he was involved, Billy? Philip Foster, I mean?"

It's the first question I've actually been asked to answer, and it takes me by surprise. There's so many reasons, I don't have them ordered in my mind.

"At school," I say before I've really thought about it. "At school, they call him a pedophile. And I saw him at the beach that night. He was fishing. And he walks with a limp. It's weird." I didn't mean to say the last part. I look down at the table.

West sighs. She glances across at Rogers, who shakes his head.

"Look, Billy," she says. "We understand you've tried to help. You've gone about it precisely the wrong way, but we understand your intentions were good."

She glances at Detective Rogers, and he nods at her before she goes on.

"Philip Foster used to be a schoolteacher. On the mainland, and in a pretty tough school by all accounts. There was a child - a fourteen-year-old girl – who made an accusation against him." She pauses to take a breath.

"We've checked it out. There was nothing in it. No evidence, no witnesses, no history, nothing. And the girl involved had a reputation for inventing stuff." She looks up at Dad. "Maybe the girl just took against him for some reason? We don't know. But there was no action taken against him. The complaint wasn't upheld."

She takes another breath, like the next bit is difficult.

"But it seems the girl's father wasn't satisfied. He followed Philip Foster home from school one day with a baseball bat. He managed to break his leg pretty bad before someone pulled him off. Mr. Foster and his wife came to the island to try to start afresh."

Then Detective Rogers butts in. "Until you came along Billy."

He gives me a hard look. He's about to say something else when I think of something.

"But I *saw* him," I hear myself interrupt. "Even if he didn't do the thing on the mainland, I *saw* Mr. Foster's van the night Olivia went missing. And his fishing light on the beach. He was on his own, at the beach where she went missing. In the dark. So how can you be sure he didn't do this?"

Detective Rogers stares at me for a long time. Then he shuffles around in the pile of papers in front of him until he finds the one he wants.

"Philip Foster *was* on Silverlea beach that night. He was fishing until 22:30, at which time he gave up, having caught nothing. Between 22:30 and 23:15, he was drinking with several people at the beach party, including one Brian Richards." Rogers looks up at Dad. "He's a neighbor of yours, I believe, Mr. Wheatley?" Dad says nothing.

"Mr. Foster's daughter was also at the party, and they left together, at about 23:15, driving directly to Newlea and arriving at his home just before midnight. His wife confirmed that he stayed there the rest of the night.

"Philip Foster is not involved in the disappearance of Olivia Curran."

At that moment there's a knock on the door. I barely register it, but Detective West gets up . Detective Rogers' eyes stay fixed on me.

We sit there in silence for what feels like forever. And then, just when Detective Rogers opens his mouth to speak again, Detective West calls out to him from the door.

"Rogers. You better come out here. There's been a development."

FORTY

DETECTIVES WEST and Rogers barely had time to grab more coffee before they joined what looked like the entire Lornea Island Police Department in the small briefing room. At one end a pull-down screen had been deployed, and projected onto it was the faded image of a hand, roughly cut off halfway down the forearm. Even though it was packed full, the room was quiet. Lieutenant Langley and Chief Collins stood at the front, waiting for everyone to file in.

"Can we get those blinds down, please," Langley ordered, while the chief watched the room. "And hurry up."

The room darkened. The image on the screen changed from a half shadow to a clear, full-color image, the skin's yellows, purples, and greens deepening. The colors were all wrong. The image sickening.

"Well, I guess I have everyone's attention," Langley said. He didn't wait for anyone to reply.

"As some of you know, the hand and partial forearm from a young white female was recovered from the rocks to the west side of Goldhaven beach earlier this morning. We won't have the full pathology report for some time, but from a birthmark on the wrist here," he tapped the screen, causing it to wobble and the image to distort, "there's little doubt it belongs to Olivia Curran.

"Moreover, we don't need to wait for pathology to tell us the hand was cut off deliberately. Which means this inquiry will now become a murder investigation."

A few hushed murmurs started up, but Langley talked over them.

"It's also clear from the advanced state of decomposition that Olivia died at or about the time she went missing, on August twenty-eighth this year. But the arm was removed later, probably within the last week. We'll get more precise timelines as they come in."

Langley paused and looked around the room. "I want to be clear. This is not in any way connected to the information received by Detective Rogers and Detective West relating to the Silverlea resident Philip Foster. I know a lot of you have worked hard on that, but we need to move on from there." He gave Rogers a sympathetic look, which seemed to have hardened by the time it moved across to where West was standing.

"So. Any thoughts on what we have?"

There was a momentary pause. Then they all came at once.

"How was the arm removed?" One of the other detectives asked.

Langley turned to him. "We'll have a better idea later for sure, but I'd say a saw or some kind of serrated knife."

"It couldn't be an animal? Bitten off by a shark?"

"No."

"A boat or something? It get chewed off by the prop?"

"No. You can see the marks from here." Langley pointed at the screen, and it *was* obvious. "Whoever did it wasn't an expert either. Unless they were working blindfolded."

"Where exactly was it found?" This was one of the patrolmen.

"It was partially buried in the rockpools. Some kids found it. They were pretty freaked out."

"Where was it exactly?" West interrupted.

"Goldhaven beach." Langley replied.

"That's the ferry port right?" Rogers asked.

"Yeah." Langley sounded impatient. Like everyone there should know this.

Then the patrolman came back. "The coastline up past Goldhaven is full of ravines and crags. It's a great place to hide a body."

"And a hell of a place to search for one," another said.

"It's going to be even worse if we're looking for lots of different body parts." Langley said.

The patrolmen looked at each other. They knew they'd be the ones doing the searching.

"What are the currents like around there?" The first asked. "I mean, could it have washed up there from this side of the island?"

The other patrolman answered by shaking his head. He was one of the oldest on the squad and an avid fisherman. He knew the currents. "I wouldn't say so. Anything that goes in the water here is either going to go north or south, not around the back of the island."

"I want that checked out. Get onto the Coast Guard about that," Chief Collins interrupted, directing his order to Lieutenant Langley, who nodded.

"I don't want any other civilians coming across body parts." Collins said, and there was another pause. Longer this time.

"What if it's *just* an arm?" West said into the silence. "What if there's no other parts to find."

Langley looked at her.

"What?"

"I mean, why would someone just cut an arm off? And the arm with the birthmark too?" West asked. She was aware that all the heads were turned to look at her.

"What are you saying?" Rogers cut in. "I don't get it."

"I don't know. But why cut off an arm weeks after you've killed someone?" West said. "What would be the point?"

"The killer went back to try and tidy up?" Rogers replied, but he didn't sound convinced.

There was another pause. This time, Langley interrupted it.

"Clearly, we need more information. The chief and I have discussed our next move. One," he jutted a finger in the air. "Let's get her found, either the rest of her body, or any other parts that may be washing around. Speak to the Coast Guard. Speak to local fishermen, oceanologists at the university if you need to. Draw me up a plausible area where that arm could have come from, and then a plan to search it. I want her found before anyone else does.

"Two. Goldhaven is now an area of interest. We've had no reason to focus our attention there until now. Well that changes. Let's go door-to-door. Let's find out if anyone saw anything suspicious. Either in the last two weeks when we think the arm was removed, or back when she first went missing. Rogers. West. I want you on that.

"Three. This case is now this department's number one priority. Everything else is on hold. Everything. We already have the attention of the entire nation on us, thanks to Mr. and Mrs. Curran. We can expect that attention to explode when this news gets out. Well I want the next headlines to be about how we've captured her killer. Is that clear?"

No one moved when he finished speaking, but he let the silence draw out for a few seconds.

"Well, go on, then. We're not going to catch anyone sitting here. Get organized and get going." He snapped off the power to the projector, and the image faded to white.

FORTY-ONE

Rogers drove them both to Goldhaven, they sat in near silence, lost in their thoughts. They arrived to find the beach closed, with patrolmen from the mainland stationed every fifty yards along the short promenade. They were turning away the few tourists who still remained.

The tide had come in by now. The rockpools where the arm was found were hidden underwater. Still, a police team worked in a rough line, performing a fingertip search of the high tide line where dried curls of seaweed lay mixed with sticks and random pieces of plastic. It wasn't a pretty beach: a few patches of sand, then rocks that extended to the heavy stone wall, forming the entrance to the harbor. It was the first time West had been back to Goldhaven since arriving on the island. It made her realize how beautiful Silverlea was, with its white sands stretching unbroken for miles in either direction.

"Come on. We better get on with it," Rogers said.

They separated, each with a list of streets to work, and West began the task of knocking on doors. About half of the houses were empty. Where people were home they knew nothing. Then one woman invited her in. She told West in a low whisper how she'd noticed a green van parked in front of her house for about a week, around the time Olivia went missing.

"Why did you think this was strange? West asked.

"Because I hadn't seen it there before," the woman whispered back.

"Do you know who it belonged to?"

"No."

"Is there any other reason why you think it might be relevant?"

The woman screwed up her face in thought for a long moment. "No," she said.

"Okay. . . I don't suppose you got the license plate?" West asked.

The woman shook her head sadly as if this failure could cost the police dearly.

It was probably nothing, it was *clearly* nothing, but it all had to be noted down, along with everything else. Vehicle make, color. It would all have to go in a new database, similar to the one West and Rogers had worked on so diligently for the previous three months, and which was now worthless.

And so it went on. Door after door, resident after resident. Hour after hour.

"Anything?" Rogers asked when they met up again, once it was too late now to knock on any more doors.

"Uh huh." West said.

"You alright?" Rogers asked.

"Sure." West said.

Neither of them spoke much on the drive back to Silverlea. After a while Rogers switched the radio on. A voice was explaining with a note of excitement how he was standing on Lornea Island, where the police were now focusing on the port town of Goldhaven.

"Earlier today, we saw Chief of Police Larry Collins confirming the dramatic news that Olivia Curran, the missing teenager, is now known to have died at or around the time she disappeared - the worst possible news for her parents. And it was on this very beach where the grisly discovery of Olivia's hand was found sometime yesterday.

"Chief Collins wasn't able to say whether this discovery means the police are any closer to solving the mystery that has gripped the island for the last few months. But there's no question that this find will only increase pressure on a police department already heavily criticized for having made little or no progress in this case."

Rogers switched the radio off and sighed.

"I need a beer. You wanna stop off for one?"

West rolled her neck around as far as the car's headrest would allow.

"You go. Drop me off at the station if you like."

"Come on. Come for a beer."

West didn't answer.

"You sure you're alright? You seem kinda quiet. I thought you'd be happy. We got a lead. This is a real case at last."

"Happy?" West replied sharply. "The girl's dead. We're too late."

Rogers drummed his fingers on the steering wheel.

"Come on Jess. We knew that three months ago. But there's a real case to investigate now. And a real lead. There's a chance of catching this guy."

"Is there? Maybe that's the problem," West said, suddenly much more vocal. "What are we doing here going door-to-door? And why isn't Langley doing it? We're the ones who've worked this case. And he just steps back in and takes over. . . " She stopped.

"Langley was always in charge of the case. What'd you expect? This thing explodes into the highest profile case the island's ever seen and he's just gonna hand it over to a couple of mainlanders? Come on. Come for a beer. You look like you need it."

West didn't answer.

"Look I'm not saying I disagree with you. But at least things are moving. Come on. Come for a beer and we'll be grumpy together."

"I can't." West replied. "I need to get to the station to finish up on the paperwork from that kid."

Rogers frowned at this. "What you gotta do?"

"Type up a report," West sighed. "And get the kid's fingerprints in the system. I don't suppose it matters now, but the chief asked me to put them in there, in case the kid's been sticking his nose into a crime scene."

"Christ, Jess, you don't need to do that. First thing you learn in this job: when the shit hits the fan, you *delegate*. Stick a note to Diane. Get her to do it. Come on. One beer." He sensed he was winning and gave her a weary smile.

"One measly beer."

"Oh what the hell," West said. "One beer."

Rogers laughed.

"What?" West asked.

"Nothing. I was just thinking: we sure scared the crap out of that poor kid."

FORTY-TWO

WHEN THEY COME BACK into the room, Detective Rogers doesn't even sit down before he starts talking again.

"Billy. Let me be crystal clear with you. I do not want to see you again. I do not want to hear from you again. You don't go *anywhere near* Philip Foster, or anywhere near this investigation. At all. Ever. Do you understand me?"

I don't say anything. They don't tell us what they were talking about outside the room, but suddenly they seem in a hurry.

"And you, Mr. Wheatley. You better keep your kid on a much tighter rein from now on, or you're gonna lose him. Do we understand each other?" I look at Dad and after a while he nods.

"Good. Detective West will sign you out." He leaves the room. The next thing, the other Detective is leading Dad and me out of the station. Dad has to sign some papers and then we walk outside. Suddenly it's just Dad and me. I can't believe how quick that just happened.

I feel a bit better outside, but also I feel scared because Dad's obviously still mad, and there's no one around now to calm him down. Dad doesn't have his truck, the police brought him in without it, so we have to get a cab. Dad asks the driver how much it'll be, and the man says thirty dollars. I can see this makes Dad madder than ever, and he doesn't talk to me the whole way home. So I just sit there, looking at my feet all the way and trying not to snuffle. When we get home, I try to walk upstairs, but Dad doesn't let me.

"Sit the *fuck down*, boy. Now it's my turn to set you straight on a few things."

I do what he says, taking the furthest seat I can at the kitchen table. Dad doesn't sit, though. He paces up and down. He's shaking. I've never seen him like this.

"Do you know what you did today? You almost fucked us. That's what."

He sits down, but it's like he can't contain himself if he's still. He gets up and starts pacing again. Now he's slapping the wall when he gets to each end.

"The police. The *goddamned* police. I don't know why the hell they let us go like that. I thought we were fucked. Jesus fucking Christ. I thought they were gonna. . . " He stops, he comes really close to me.

"You *cannot* go around drawing attention to us like that, Billy. You just fucking can't. Not with. . . " Suddenly, he turns and slams his fist into the wall cabinet where we keep the mugs. It jumps so it's not level any more on the wall, and there's a huge crashing sound inside. It stops his rage for a moment, though. He stands there staring at it, then looks at his fist. There's blood on his knuckles. Then there's more smashing as the more glasses make their way to the bottom of the cabinet. Neither of us says anything about it.

"You just can't do it, Billy. You just can't draw attention to us like that. Haven't I taught you that? Haven't I told you hundreds of times how we need to keep our heads down? You *don't know* who might be looking for us."

I don't know what he means by that. I don't feel like saying anything, but I don't like the silence either.

"Who's looking for us?"

Dad doesn't answer me at first. Instead, he sits down again and puts his head in his hands so I can't see his face. He's still doing that when he does speak.

"No one. No one's looking for you, Billy. No one's looking for us."

I don't understand what's going on, so I don't say anything. Then, after what seems like forever, Dad takes his hands away and looks at me again.

"How come I didn't know what you were up to? Haven't I been looking after you right?"

I don't know if Dad wants me to answer this, so I don't know what to say. It doesn't really make sense. Dad doesn't look after me; I look after myself. I screw up my face in confusion.

"I've tried to do right by you, Billy. It's just you're. . . You're not like how I expected you would be. You know? If you knew how much I gave up for you" Dad shakes his head, he gives a little laugh. There's a little smear of blood on the tabletop from his knuckles.

"We're going to do better. You and me. We're going to do so much better. We're going to *do* stuff together. Like we used to. You remember how we used to search for silver up at Northend? We'll do stuff like that." His eyes travel to the surfboard he bought me, still propped in the corner of the room, unused, and I sort of hoped, forgotten. "We'll go surfing. That's what we'll do. I'm gonna teach you to surf. I'm not good at much in this world, boy, but surfing's one thing I can do." And with that, Dad starts to cry. Big, fat tears appear in his eyes and roll down his cheeks. He doesn't seem to care at first; then he wipes them away and sniffs loudly.

"Come on, fuck off upstairs, kid. I got to clear up this fucking mess." He walks over to the cupboard and opens it. A shower of broken pieces rains out onto the countertop and the floor. He swears again, then laughs.

"We'll talk again later, huh?"

Thoroughly bewildered, I go upstairs before he changes his mind.

FORTY-THREE

I'VE JUST SEEN the news. I might have been wrong about Mr. Foster, but I was right about Olivia Curran being dead. They've just found part of her body in Goldhaven. It must be why the police stopped interviewing me so suddenly. They must have just found out.

I cry for most of the night. I just can't stop myself. I think about all that happened in the police station and all that Dad said, and although I don't understand why I'm crying, the tears still come. I don't sleep at all.

I don't even go downstairs the next morning. I'm missing school, but to my surprise, Dad doesn't even come up to tell me to get dressed. When I do finally go down to the kitchen, Dad's already gone out. He's tried to tidy up. The cabinet has been taken off the wall and placed on the floor; I guess he'll fix it later. The trash is full of pieces of broken mugs, and there's an opened can of soup on the countertop, with a note from Dad propped up behind it. I sit back down at the table and read it.

Hey Billy,

Sorry I lost my temper yesterday. It was just the shock, that's all. I gotta go out today, but we'll spend time together, just you and me. We'll get your new board wet, OK?

Love,

Dad

I eat the soup, tears still flowing from my eyes every now and then. I try to think. I try to make sense of everything that's happened.

I think first of all about Olivia Curran. She *is* dead, but not like how I thought it happened. Mr. Foster didn't do it. I got that all wrong. And just thinking about it now makes my face burn red. How much I messed that up. But then it wasn't my fault, there was so much evidence. And if Mr. Foster didn't do it, then who did?

Then my thoughts turn to Dad. Why was he so angry? I mean, I understand why he'd be a little mad, but I've never seen him like that before. He hardly ever swears in front of me and he's *never* used the F-word like that, so many times. And that thing with the cupboard. It was like he wanted to hit *me. Why?* I don't understand. And where's he gone now?

I don't leave the house the whole day. I just sit and think. And after a while I don't feel comfortable downstairs so I go back to my room. I don't have a lock, but I shift my desk so it blocks the door. I just think the whole day. I sit and think. And some things start to come clearer in my mind.

FORTY-FOUR

DAD MADE me go to school again today. It was OK, though. No one knows about what happened at the police station, and to be honest, no one there really cares about Olivia Curran. It's harder at home. Dad keeps trying to talk to me; like he's pretending that suddenly he's really interested in everything I'm doing. It's weird. It's kinda creepy.

It's Saturday morning now. Or at least it will be when I get up. Dad will want to go surfing, but I'm not going with him. I'm going to sneak out before he gets up. I'm just going to try and stay out of his way until I can work out what's going on. I just think it's the best thing to do. So I get up an hour early and as quietly as I can I go downstairs. I can't stay the whole day without food though, so I pour some cereal into a bowl, and I've just added the milk when I realize he's there in the doorway, watching me.

"Hey, Billy," Dad says. "You're up early."

His voice sounds wrong. Like he's suspicious of me. I freeze with my spoon in the air, milk and Cheerios dripping back into the bowl.

"I was trying to tell you yesterday," he goes on. "We're gonna get you in the water today. Try out your new board." His tone changes. There's a false cheeriness now, like he's pretending that everything's OK, when really, the last few days have been horrible.

"We won't get too many days this late in the year when it's OK for you. So we're going to do it. OK? You and me."

I regret having my breakfast now, just the sight of it makes me feel sick. I slowly put the spoon back down.

"I was going to check up on my hermit crab project," I manage to say. My voice sounds croaky. But Dad ignores me.

His voice stays calm but I can hear he's mad underneath it. Like he's planned out exactly what he's going to say if I try to object. "Listen, Billy. What you did the other day, with the police, that's serious. OK? It means things are going to change around here. No more running around on your own. No more crazy *projects*. You're going to come out with me today, and you're going to come surfing. And you know what? You're gonna enjoy it. You and me. Together. OK?"

I don't know what to say back to him. There's a hardness to his voice that I don't recognize. For some reason it worries me. It scares me. Normally if he said this I'd try telling him how I've got schoolwork that has to be done, or that Dr. Ribald really needs my results this afternoon. . . Or something. But today, I don't say anything. Maybe I'm just worn down by all that's happened.

"I understand about your thing with water. Believe me, I do. But you'll be fine. I'm gonna take care of it. I'm gonna take care of everything." Dad's still talking. I don't even hear the rest of what he says, until he finishes with:

"So no arguing, eh? No feeling 'sick'. No urgent schoolwork. We're going surfing this morning. That's all there is to it."

I don't eat any more. Instead I wait in the yard while he gets the gear ready and loads it in the truck. I look out over the bay and it occurs to me that I might not find a way out of this. It's not a big day for waves, not a huge day at least, and it's milder than it's been for a while. But the thought of having to go out there into the water makes my stomach feel like someone's kicked it. I hear the snap and rumble as the waves break and roll in towards the sand. I begin to imagine myself walking out there, the water creeping higher and higher up my body until I can't even touch the sand any more with my toes. I feel that dizziness around the edge of my vision. I hear that buzzing.

"Get in the truck Billy," Dad says.

FORTY-FIVE

SOMETHING MAKES me rebel just a little bit and I climb into the back, along with the surfboards. I guess I just don't want to travel in the front with him while he's in this mood.

He's already got the passenger door open for me, and he kind of sighs when I ignore it, but he doesn't say anything. He just shoves the door shut, a bit too hard, and gets in on his side.

I feel the truck vibrate as the engine starts and we roll out the drive and down the bumpy lane to the main road, taking the turn-off to Littlelea. I'm relieved by this, at least. The waves will be smaller there. Before I know it, we're pulling into the parking lot. We're here so early there's no one else around. Dad's door jerks open and he jumps out.

"Get your suit on, Billy." He snaps the words at me.

"Aren't we going to have a look at it first? To see if it's OK" I ask, because sometimes, Dad does this and decides the waves aren't good enough to go in.

"No need. It's perfect for you."

I don't move.

"Jesus Billy, you're almost twelve years old. Now get your goddamn suit on."

I try to think of anything I can say or do to get out of this, but I can't. So slowly I start picking at my shoelaces. Dad keeps talking. I don't really listen though.

"You know Donny? His kid's only eight, maybe nine years old, and he's *ripping*. Absolutely ripping." Dad pulls my board out from the back of the truck and puts it down on the grass, talking all the time. And that's when I see it again. That thing I saw before, stuck down in the gap between the side of the truck and the flatbed. I thought it was a hairclip before. Maybe the bumps we've driven over have jiggled it a little looser, because it's easier to see this time, and it *is* a hair clip; I can see that easily now.

"Billy. *Get your suit on*!" Dad says again. He throws the suit at me and then he goes to his seat to put his on. I do what he says, but as I pull the rubber suit over my legs, what I'm actually doing is scanning the floor around me for a piece of wire, or a nail, or anything I can use to dig that hairclip out. I don't even know why I suddenly think it's so important. Actually, that's not true. I've got a horrible feeling I do know.

These last few days, when I've been thinking about things, I spent a lot of time online, reading all the news about the Olivia Curran case. It's everywhere again, now they've found a bit of her body. In one story I saw a photograph of her, taken on the day she went missing. It was taken by one of the friends she made that week. It shows Olivia standing with another girl, their arms around each other's shoulders. I didn't know why but something made me study that photograph. Something made me look at her hair. It was pinned up. It was pinned up by a hair-clip with a flower decoration with little diamonds in it. And I remember it from when I gave her the hotdog roll that night. And it looks exactly like the one lodged in the back of Dad's truck.

"Right, Billy," Dad interrupts me. "Listen up,' cause this is important. We're going to walk out until you're about waist deep, and then we're both going to paddle right out the back. We'll use the rip from the river to get us out beyond where the waves are breaking. OK? You might have to duck under a couple of waves, but not many. OK?" He stares at me now, and his voice changes, goes quieter.

"Jesus, Billy, don't play the sick card on me now. I don't know what you're doing to look so white, but just pull yourself together. Huh?" Then he sits down next to where I'm pulling my boots on. He tries another approach.

"Listen, buddy, I know you get a little worried about the water. But it's OK. It really is. I'm gonna be with you the whole time. And as long as you listen to me and keep out of the breaking waves, you'll be absolutely fine. You'll love it."

I don't say anything. My brain's making connections faster than it ever has before. I'm still thinking about that hairclip. What it means, stuck there. I get this strange sense that I'm about to understand the whole thing. That it's all just about to fall into place. It's like suddenly, the world around me has become transparent, coherent, understandable. But then Dad's voice changes back to the harsh tone it's had all morning.

"Billy. You've caused a *shitload* of trouble recently, and I'm trying really hard with you. Really, I am. Now, you're going to get in the water today, and you're going to give it a good shot. You understand? No fu - " He stops, mid swear word, as another car drives into the parking lot. It stops a few yards away and a man gets out and whistles to a dog. It's not anyone we know, but he gives a friendly wave as he shuts the car door. Then Dad leans in close to me, and his voice is a low growl.

"Christ. Just don't fucking embarrass me. OK, Billy?"

I feel like I'm going to cry again. I can feel my bottom lip trembling, and that whole sense of understanding disappears in a puff. I tell myself I'm not going to cry. I sniff a little, but then I nod my head. Dad puts his hand on my head and ruffles my hair.

"Good boy. It's gonna be fun. I promise you. Good-sized, clean waves. No crowds to worry about. That's the beauty of getting here early. There's hardly anyone else around. Not like later on. Come on. I'll wax your board for you."

Dad jumps back down and crouches next to my board. His board is already waxed and ready to go, the truck keys hidden behind the wheel. While his back's turned, I take my chance. On the ground near the back of the truck is a small piece of wire, and I jump down and grab it, then climb back into the truck, and on my hands and knees I try to wiggle it into the gap behind where the hairclip is. It's not quite long enough, and all I can do at first is move it. I pull my wire out and try to straighten it to make it a tiny bit longer. It almost works. Twice I snag the clip and think it's going to come loose, but something is holding it in place. I try again, my hands beginning to shake with nerves because I know Dad will be finished any second. And then I get it: my wire catches firmly on the decorative flower with the diamonds in it.

"*Billy*! What the hell are you doing now? Get out of there!" Dad's voice sounds loud. He's right behind me. I don't have time to look at the hairclip, but I press it into my palm and turn around so he can't see what I've got, or what I've been doing. He's right there, his face near to anger.

"Billy. Come on. Get down. We're going *right now*."

I climb off the truck again, the hairclip pressed into my palm. Dad thrusts my board at me, and I have no choice but to take it, and try to tuck it under my arm. He picks up his too, and leads me away from the truck.

At first, Dad's behind me, and I don't dare open my hand to look at what I've got. I can hear Dad's breaths right behind me, and then his board bangs into mine.

"Fucking hell," Dad curses, stopping at once. "Jesus, will you not stop right in front of me?" He overtakes me, inspecting his board where they bumped, but there's no damage; it was just a knock.

"Come on, speed up."

With Dad in front of me, I finally have a chance to look at the hairclip. I unpeel my fingers and look at it. It's just a girl's silver hairclip, a flower pattern on the top with diamonds arranged where the petals would be. I think back again to the photograph I saw the other day. It's the same design; I'm sure of it. The same clip Olivia Curran was wearing. But what's worse, now that I've gotten it loose, I can see what was keeping it stuck in place in the truck. On the other end of the clip is a small but recognizable clump of hair and skin, colored black with dried blood.

FORTY-SIX

The Records Division of Lornea Island Police Department employed two people: Sharon Davenport, a young technician in her thirties, and her boss, Diane Pittman, an older woman who had worked there for longer than anyone could remember, and who had a reputation for ruthless efficiency. Had the task of processing the paperwork generated by Billy Wheatley's activities fallen to Mrs. Pittman, she would almost certainly have acted upon it more quickly. And that might have made all the difference.

Unfortunately, Diane Pittman didn't work Saturdays. So it was Sharon Davenport who found the paper card imprinted with Billy Wheatley's fingerprints in her in-box, with Detective West's handwritten instructions to enter them into the national fingerprint database. The detective hadn't stated that this was urgent, so Sharon delayed acting upon it until she had written a long email to her sister, answering a series of questions about the plans for her upcoming wedding.

With that done, Sharon turned to the fingerprint card. Sharon had grasped most of what went on with Billy Wheatley, and she didn't fully approve. In her view, he seemed a nice kid who had simply tried to help. To be rewarded by being marched around the station and given a talking-to by those detectives from the mainland was a bit much. The boy had been close to tears, and that father looked mad enough to near kill him. And now he would have his fingerprints locked away in the database until he was sixteen.

But she did understand *why* they had to be entered - there was a possibility his prints might have contaminated a crime scene, especially now the poor girl had turned out to be dead after all. So there was no question of Sharon not fulfilling her duty. And so, at about half past nine, she picked up Billy's fingerprint card and walked over to the terminal with the scanner.

The computer used to input fingerprints in the Lornea Island police station sat at the back of the technicians' office. It wasn't the most up-to-date piece of equipment. It looked like a standard scanner and computer, in fact it was – the only difference was the software loaded onto it. The scanner converted the inked prints into digital files, and the computer could then upload them to the central database. They would be indexed and filed, and then could be searched for by any authorized internet-connected computer. Should a fingerprint containing the same pattern of loops and swirls be found linked to any crime or investigation anywhere in the United States, and in a great number of other countries, too, it would come up in a matter of minutes. All Sharon had to do was create a new entry, with Billy Wheatley's details as written on the card. But when she tried to do so, an error message came up that Sharon hadn't seen before. Eventually, she reached for a telephone.

"Langley. What is it?"

"Oh, I'm sorry, Lieutenant Langley. It's Sharon here from the tech office. I've had something strange come up on the Billy Wheatley file."

"Wheatley? Who the hell is that?"

"Billy Wheatley. He's the boy that Detective West and Detective Rogers brought in the other day."

"Then you need to talk to Detective West or Detective Rogers." Langley was putting the phone back down when Sharon spoke again.

"I think it might be important."

There was a sigh. "As important as looking for whoever cut Olivia Curran's arm off? Because that's what you're interrupting here."

Sharon paused, not sure how to continue, but she realized that the lieutenant was still on the line.

"It's just, I was adding his fingerprints to the system. But something strange happened."

There was another sigh, then: "What?"

"Well, it's strange, really. He's already in there, but under a different name, and the entry under it doesn't make any sense."

"Like I said, I'm kinda busy here. Are you planning on getting to the point?"

"Well, it's just. . . It says he's listed as a missing person. And he's at risk because his father has tried to kill him on at least one previous occasion."

FORTY-SEVEN

It feels like the world should freeze, but it doesn't. My legs are still working; I'm still following Dad down to the water. Now we're at the bottom of the dunes stepping onto the hard, wet sand of the beach. Ahead of us, the ocean stretches out, a set of waves now coming in and breaking with the steady roar, like airplanes taking off from a distant airport.

I can hear my breathing, fast and panicky. The hairclip is burning in my hands. Part of me wants to drop it, to recoil in horror from the blood and just *get it out of my hands*. But I can't. If I do that, Dad will see it, and he'll *know*. He'll know I know.

But what *do* I know? Thoughts begin to flash through my brain like flickers of lightning. Too fast to properly understand them. What does this mean?

Dad killed Olivia Curran?

No. No. That's just crazy.

My legs work automatically. Following him down the beach toward the water. The open sea that I hate so much. That so terrifies me.

Dad killed Olivia Curran?

It kind of explains things. The moods. Why he got so angry in the police station.

No.

I shake my head and the thought is gone. I almost laugh. It's so crazy. But there's water pressing behind my eyes.

"So I'm gonna stick real close to you, OK?" Dad turns to me and waits a moment so we're walking in step. He suddenly looks different. So big and strong, so in his element, readying to enter the water. This is his world. He must see how my face looks, but if he does notice, he deliberately ignores it.

"You just paddle hard at first. We've gotta punch out through these little waves."

We reach the end of the beach. Dad places his board on the sand to fix his leash. I can't do the same, because I still have the hairclip in my hands. I look around, desperate for somewhere I can put it. Not to throw it away now, and not just because he'll see, but because I know how important it is now. But there's nowhere. It's mid tide at the moment, and all the beach around me will soon be covered by water. If I leave it anywhere here, I'll never find it again, and I can't think of any excuse to return up the beach to someplace where I could hide the clip. Wait, there's one thing.

"Dad. I need the bathroom," I say.

"Just go in your suit," he replies.

"Not that type," I say, almost openly crying now.

This stops him for a breath or two, but not long.

"No way. No way, Billy. You're getting in there right now. No excuses. We're gonna bust this stupid phobia of yours right now. You hold it in, or you take a shit in your suit. I don't much care which right now. Now put your leash on."

Dad stands there watching me, and I've got no choice. I bend down and put the board on the sand, and then try to wrap the Velcro around my ankle, but I can't with the hairclip in my hand. I do the only thing I can do. I reach up to where the suit is tight against my neck, pull it out as if I'm adjusting it because it's uncomfortable, and I drop the hairclip down inside my suit. As I do so I catch a glimpse of the end, the sliver of hair, skin and blood. I feel it lodged there, trapped between my chest and the suit.

"Let's go. Let's get some waves." Dad tries a final attempt at making this sound like something fun, and we push forward into the water.

I've got boots on but even so the water flows in and runs up my leg. I register it's cold, but distantly, like it's not affecting me. Like I'm watching someone else wading out. Then the first wave hits me. This close in, it's only a line of frothy white water, but it still goes right up over my thighs. It feels like it's reaching up to grab me and pull me deeper. My breaths come fast. Suddenly the cold hits me. It's icy. I feel the panic rising.

Think. I've got to think. What does it mean, the hairclip? The question is hammering in my brain. Does it mean Dad is involved? Does it mean Dad killed her? *Dad killed Olivia Curran?*

I know it makes sense. He was there on the night she went missing, he parked his truck out of sight on the beach. He said it was so he wouldn't get a ticket, but what if there was another reason?

And then, when I wanted to go home, he wouldn't take me. He said he wanted to stay. I went home with Jody's mom. But he made me tell the police we came home together. Dad made me lie to them.

The thoughts come rushing at me so fast I can't even think them all. I'm being crazy. Dad told me he got back a half hour after I did, about eleven. Olivia Curran was seen lots of times after that. So it couldn't have been Dad. Unless he was lying. I was asleep. I don't know when he got back.

My hand goes to my chest. I feel the outline of the hairclip with my fingers.

Olivia Curran's hairclip. That was stuck in the back of his truck, glued there with dried blood. I feel like I'm going to be sick.

Dad killed Olivia Curran.

Another wave hits me. It's deeper now, and it almost washes me off my feet, but I feel his hand in the small of my back, keeping me upright and pushing me forward. I try to recoil but I can't. Dad's behind me, pushing me out towards the waves. Horrible, freezing waves pulling at me and trying to hold me underwater.

A third wave hits, and it rips the board from my fingers. I feel Dad's hand move quickly to my head as my feet slip from the sand. Dad pushes me down under the water, and suddenly, vision turns to green and bubbles as my face goes under. I pull in a breath of salty water. I kick out, panicking wildly. My foot connects with the seabed, and I push off. My head is above the water again, and I see Dad right there, close to me. I suddenly understand. Suddenly, the full horror of it hits me. Of course Dad killed Olivia Curran. That's obvious. And he knows I know it. That's why we're here. Here too early in the morning for anyone else to see us. Here in his world. He's going to drown me. He's going to kill me so I don't tell anyone.

He says something, I don't hear what. My brain is racing all of a sudden, thoughts zapping around my head like the finale of a fireworks display. Maybe it's my life flashing before my eyes before I die. I suddenly see Mom's face. Clear as if she were really here. I see her eyes, cold and empty. I can't help myself. I scream. My mouth floods with salty water.

I cough and splutter, and I try to fight through the water to get away from him, but I'm too deep now: the river rip is pulling us out to sea fast. And now another wave is coming. Some of Dad's words break through into my brain.

"Duck under. It's easier if you duck under the wave." But I don't. I try to stand and jump at the approaching wall of water. This time, it totally knocks me off my feet, and I'm pushed backward and underwater. I feel my bottom hit the sand this time before the wave's energy passes and I fight my way to the surface. Only to see Dad striding purposefully through the water - barely waist deep for him - toward me. He takes my arm and leads me forward.

"There's a rip here. Get on your board and paddle."

I hesitate. I wonder if I could run to shore, escape him. But what then? And in my hesitation, my body responds to his command almost on its own. Maybe the result of my whole life with Dad. Listening to him, doing what he tells me.

My dad is taking me out to sea to drown me. And I'm doing exactly as he says.

FORTY-EIGHT

I LIE on my board and start to paddle. I almost slip off, but the wax grips my chest. I register the hairclip pressing against me, but my attention shifts to the arrival of the next wave. Lying down on my board, it suddenly looks much bigger. A wall of white water that towers above me.

"Dive. Duck now," Dad shouts, and my arms try to do what he says, to copy the way I've seen him and a thousand other surfers duck underneath the waves as they paddle out. I press down on the board's nose, but it hardly responds at all, and when the wave hits, it smashes into the gap between the board and where I'm performing an awkward push-up above it. It sweeps me off at once, and I get a second mouthful of water, and suddenly, I'm rolling around. I don't know which way is up. My head grazes the sand, and I can feel my board pulling against my leg. I surface again, and I hear my own voice crying out. But Dad's there again. I feel his strength shoving me back on top of my board. His voice telling me we're going to do this. He's not going to let me fail.

"Paddle. Come on, Billy. Just move your arms."

Gasping for breath, I do what he says, straight toward another wave. But this time, when it almost hits, I feel Dad giving me a mighty shove on the back, and the energy he gives me pushes me into and then through the wall of water. I'm not paddling or ducking this time. I'm gripping the sides of the board for all I'm worth.

"Now. Paddle again, Go left a little. That's where the rip is."

My fear of Dad is outdone by the terror of this moving, roaring water, so I do what he tells me. And it's slightly easier now. Around me, the water is bubbling and fizzing in a way I've never seen before, and the next wave hasn't broken yet: it's coming toward me like a low hill. Although I stiffen and ready myself for another tumble when it reaches me, this time it just lifts me up, and then I slide down the back as it rolls underneath. Dad's still beside me and a little bit behind. I feel my speed through the water surge every now and then as he gives a shove from behind. Two more unbroken waves come toward us and pass underneath. I can feel the power of the rip now, pulling us out, as if on a conveyor belt.

Dad's alongside me now, encouraging me to keep going. My throat is hurting from where I've swallowed the water. My arms hurt from the paddling; it's the rip pulling me out, not my paddling. But even so, I can see we're making progress.

Dad's pulled ahead, and he stops for a moment, sitting up on his board to look around.

"Come on, Billy, a little more. We're almost out." My pathetic strokes pull me closer to him, each one an effort now. I'm out of breath and stop when I draw level. I look at his face, and part of me wants to feel reassured I'm here with him, but part of me is terrified. Is he going to push me under again? What does it feel like to drown?

"Don't stop. Keep going in case another set comes in." He gives me another shove, further out into the ocean, further away from the safety of the beach. This time, I just put my head down and try and do what he says. I try to ignore the way my arms burn. I kick my legs like they taught me in the swimming pool, even though I can feel they're out of the water and doing nothing. Slowly, painfully, we creep further out to sea.

Finally, Dad stops us.

"That'll do. Take a rest."

I stop paddling but stay lying down on my board, my breath coming hard from the effort and the panic.

"Sit up, try to breathe slower."

I ignore him. If anything my breathing speeds up.

"*Sit up, Billy.* Like this. Sit on your board."

His voice brings me back, and I try to do what he says, sitting with my legs dangling down into the water. It's hard. After a few lurches to either side, I fall off, and my head goes under again. To right myself, I put my legs down, expecting to feel the sand underneath, but this time, it's not there. I sink right under and still don't feel it, and then, panicking again, I try to reach the surface, coming up spluttering and crying.

"That's it. Try again. You'll get it," I hear Dad say.

I grip my board like I'm some drowning sailor whose ship has sunk. Then, when my breath returns, I clamber back on, and try again to sit like Dad. This time, I manage it, although I don't feel secure, like I could fall off again at any moment. But I look around. I try to get my bearings.

We're about four hundred yards from the rocks, and maybe the same distance away from the beach – it looks miles away though. There's no other surfers out here with us. No one on the beach would even see me - I've tried to watch Dad from the beach a thousand times. With the waves, you can't see anything. Dad could push me under right now. No one would see. No one could stop him.

The only thing in my favor is the ocean has gone flat. It's off-set. While we were paddling out, it was like the waves would never stop coming, but now it's like a flat, calm day.

Dad's just sitting. Looking out to sea. He seems to be ignoring me. Maybe I could paddle away from him? But I know all the strength in my arms is gone.

Instead I just sit there, wondering. Why did he kill Olivia Curran? What does he get out of it? Maybe he's just one of those people who like it. Maybe he kills people all the time. Maybe our yard is full of dead people that he's buried there.

Maybe he killed Mom.

That thought hits me like electricity. A while back I tried to find out more about Mom online. He wouldn't tell me anything, so I went through all the newspaper archives. I thought of all the keywords that would have been used when the accident got reported. *Nurse, freeway, jackknifed truck, accident, killed, Laura Wheatley.* All I really wanted was to see what she looked like. Dad doesn't keep any photos of her, and I just wanted to see her face.

But I didn't find anything. Well, that's not quite true. I found plenty of nurses who had crashed on the freeways, over the years. But never one named Laura Wheatley. I couldn't figure it out at the time. But now I know. Mom didn't die on the freeway. Dad killed her. Now he wants to kill me.

I look at him now. He's still watching the horizon, and now lumps are beginning to define themselves - a new set coming in. And this time, my arms move without my thinking at all. Dad's distracted, and this is my only chance to escape him. I start to paddle as fast as I can. I don't even think which way. I'm not sure I think at all. I just paddle away from the man who wants me dead. But I haven't gone ten strokes before he sees.

"Hey. What you doing? Billy!" he shouts after me. Then I can sense him moving back into the paddling position on his board. Almost instantly, he halves the gap I've built up, just from a few strokes.

"Billy. Where are you going? There's a set coming. Stay with me."

But I don't. If anything, I paddle harder, and my panic must be flooding my body with adrenaline because now it doesn't hurt, and I feel my hands begin to grip the water better, begin to pull me forward better than before. I don't quite hear what Dad says next, only random words piercing my head.

"Wrong way. . . Get washed. . . Stop. . . "

I look up and see I'm heading in, towards the sand. Good enough. If I can make it to the beach, I can run to the rocks. I know the rocks. There are places I can hide, places where Dad might not be able to find me. It's my only chance.

For a strange half minute, it's just the two of us paddling, me a few yards in front. I can hear Dad behind me, his voice becoming angrier and angrier. If he catches me now, I know he'll do it now. He'll hold me under until I drown.

"Billy, there's a wave. Turn around."

But I don't turn around. It's a trap. And then I feel my legs rise up above my head. And then everything seems to happen in slow motion. The wave hits me from behind and from the side, and I get pulled up its face. But it's not a broken wall of white water or an unbroken glassy hill this time: it's actually breaking right here. It picks me up in an instant. It sucks me inside it, turns me upside down, and then it throws me forward and slams me down into the water. The violence of it is numbing. I didn't have any time to take a breath of air, and now it's too late. It's just a whirlwind of water and sound, and I'm tumbled this way and that way, and this time, I don't hit the bottom at all. I'm just stuck there underwater, rolling over and over, no breath in my lungs.

My eyes are open. I can see cascades of bubbles all around; I have no idea which way is up. I just keep spinning. Flailing around with the bubbles.

It goes on forever. It feels like it holds me for minutes, the water roaring around my head. And I can feel it happening. I can actually feel myself drowning. I realize I've got my eyes shut again, and I open them in a desperate attempt to see where the surface might be. But it's black this time, none of the green water I saw earlier. I suck in a half breath of water, desperate for anything, but my body stops me. I feel vomit flood into my mouth and throat. I'm running out of oxygen. I'm going to die. To drown. I can feel it. It's like I'm split: exactly half of me doesn't care, wants to suck in a lungful of ocean and let it happen, but the other half is still fighting, terrified of what comes next. Terrified of the darkness that I'm sinking toward.

And then something touches me. My board? Dad? I don't know. Whatever it is, I feel it push down on me, sending me deeper. But then it slips off, and I'm alone again. It's too late now. I open my mouth a little; it floods at once, and a reflex makes me close it again. And maybe I can start to feel the power of the cyclone of water reduce just a little, and around me I can see bubbles in the blackness. But instead of rising up around me, they're falling down. Down toward the bottom of the ocean.

I suddenly get it. *I'm upside down*. I'm upside down. I've been swimming toward the bottom to try and get to the surface. I fight to twist my body around in the water and change direction. It's my last fight. If this doesn't work, I know I'll give up. I'll give in to the screaming from my lungs, and I'll take a final breath of salty water, and then I'll die. I almost feel it already.

But I do fight, and I do feel it's easier, swimming upward, and the water isn't black anymore, it's green again, and that gives me a boost, and then it's almost white where it's just foam and bubbles, and suddenly my head breaks clear. I snatch a gasp of air before I sink under again, but it's enough to have me kicking my legs like crazy, and the next time my head bursts clear, it stays there, and I draw in a mix of water and air, coughing and sputtering. I stay like that for a minute, holding onto the side of my board, which is still there beside me, tied to my leg by the leash. Then I see Dad. The wave must have rolled me quite a long way in toward the beach because he's thirty yards away now, further out to sea, and another wave is about to hit him. I watch as he turns to meet it and ducks neatly under. Then he's lost from sight behind the rolling wall of water.

I know I have to take the opportunity. I climb on the board and start to paddle again, this time heading directly toward the beach. If I can get ashore, I can get to the rocks. I know places I can hide there. I don't know what I'll do after that, but I'm not thinking about that now. I just don't want to drown.

I feel the wave pick me up from behind, like before, but it's less violent this time. For a half second, I'm riding the foam, but then it tumbles me off again. The panic returns, but I keep my mouth shut this time, and the wave returns me straight to the surface. My board is right there again, waiting for me on the end of its leash, and I can climb on again, and I keep going to the beach. I hear Dad calling out to me, but a long way away. I can make it. I know I can. Then another wave hits. This time I'm ready for it. I grip the front of the board and I hold on. The wave catches the surfboard and picks it up, sending me sliding along in front of it, and suddenly, I'm racing toward the beach, covering the distance fast. I've seen how surfers do this when they want to come ashore. They just lie there, waiting, while the wave carries them in. I do it now, and I hold on for maybe twenty seconds before I'm pitched sideways and off again into the water. But this time, I immediately hit the bottom. I've ridden the final wave back to the shallows. I don't dare turn around to see where Dad is. Instead I struggle to my feet and try to run, but the water is like treacle, and it's flowing back out to sea, so I move like in slow motion. Then I hear Dad again, shouting. He must have ridden a wave in too. I glance behind. He's thirty yards away from me. I have to run. I have to reach the rocks. I have to get there before Dad catches me.

At last I'm free of the water, on the sand. I make a final effort. I drop my head and try to sprint. But I only get a few steps before something grabs at my leg and I fly forwards. My arms flail through the air, and I fall heavily, gritty sand grates against my face and goes in my mouth. What tripped me? Did he throw something? I try to move, but already I can hear Dad's footsteps closing in on me. I hurt all over. I try to crawl but something tugs at my leg again. I look down and follow the black line of the leash to where it anchors me to the surfboard. That's what tripped me up. I think to unstrap it, but there's no time. Dad's running towards me now. I crawl anyway, towards the rocks, dragging the board along behind me but he closes the distance in seconds. He steps on the leash and grabs my leg, pulling me back towards him. I scream. There's no one to hear me but I do it anyway.

I'm not going to go quietly.

FORTY-NINE

"Can you say that again please?" Lieutenant Langley said.

"It says he's listed as a missing person. And he's at risk because his father has tried to kill him on at least one. . . " Sharon Davenport began.

"Where are you?"

"I'm in the records office."

"Wait there. I'm coming down now."

Two minutes later Langley was leaning over the younger woman as she sat in front of her terminal. Langley peered at the screen.

"Do you see here, where I tried to create a new file for William Wheatley, yet his prints are already in the system? They're under the name of Benjamin Austin. . . " Davenport began again. She rotated her chair to give the lieutenant a better view.

"Yeah. Uh-huh. Who's the father? I don't see that."

Sharon Davenport typed quickly into the search box. An hourglass icon appeared, rotated, and a few moments later the screen refreshed.

"Jamie Stone," Sharon Davenport read. "Wanted by Oregon State police for murder, attempted murder, perverting the course of justice and - oh my - child abduction." She turned now and looked at the lieutenant.

"Print that off. Right now." Langley said, as he picked up the phone on the woman's desk.

* * *

The first two police cars arrived at the clifftop cottage just after eleven, ninety minutes after Lieutenant Langley finished his call. West was in the second car, her weekend canceled at short notice, not that she'd had any plans. It had picked her up from Silverlea and then driven, sirens-on, until they reached the bridge that led to the spread-out settlement of Littlelea. There they'd switched the noise off so as not to alert the residents of the clifftop cottage of what was about to happen.

The patrolman at the wheel swung into the long driveway too fast, scraping the side of the patrol car down an embankment lined with blackberry bushes, but no one inside the vehicle mentioned it or even seemed to notice. They already had their pulse rates maxed out. You could taste the thumping adrenaline in the air.

The first police car drove right up to the house, the driver of West's car stopped a little way down the drive, blocking it off as a potential exit in case Stone tried to escape. West pushed open the door and continued on foot, her firearm heavy in her hand. She reached the little front yard of the cottage just as the occupants of the first car were banging on the door. She scanned the scene, her heart pumping so hard the noise of it was a distraction. She waited, breathing hard, readying herself to give covering fire as she'd been trained to.

There was no response to Langley's shouts. He thumped on the wooden door one more time. Then, with a signal to an uniformed officer next to him, he retreated out of the way. The uniformed officer was standing ready with a heavy steel battering-ram, painted bright red. She remembered it from training, they called it the BFK, or Big Fucking Key. The door resisted the first blow, but on the second, there was a splintering of wood, and it swung inward. Langley entered first, his gun held in front of him. West's training came back to her again, entering half-finished properties where plywood villains and schoolchildren would swing out mechanically for her to either blast or ignore. Her mind raced. Would the boy be here? A flesh-and-blood version of the simulations.

She nodded to Rogers, who was standing beside her by then. Then she went through the door.

It led straight into the kitchen, smaller than she remembered. A few cups and bowls were left on the countertop. There was a faint smell of coffee. One of the wall cabinets was resting on the floor, a faded patch above it showing clearly where it had hung until recently. There were stairs leading directly from the kitchen, and from there, she heard the shouts of "clear" as the men before her searched the rest of the cottage. Now the stairs creaked as Langley came back down, his shoes thumping on the bare wood.

"Not here." He shook his head. Then he turned to the patrolman. "Get on the radio and report it." Langley went outside.

"Well, where the hell is he, then?" Rogers said to no one in particular. "*Shit.*"

They checked around the house, then Langley made them wait outside while he organized the scene. They stood by the low wall, looking out over the beach. There were dots in the water, swimmers perhaps, surfers more likely.

"What a fucking disaster," Rogers said, kicking at the wall. "I can't believe we had the son-of-a-bitch. Right there in front of us."

West frowned. "You reckon it's him? You reckon Stone is responsible for Curran too?"

"You reckon he isn't? You saw him. He was. . . " Rogers screwed up his hand, searching for the right word. "He was *tight* when we talked to him. Like he was holding something in. Didn't you see it?"

West didn't reply.

"I reckon he was just waiting for us to spring something on him. I bet he couldn't believe his fucking luck when we let him go."

West thought back to the interview with Sam and Billy Wheatley - as they'd known them at the time.

"He did seem kinda nervous," she said.

"He'll be halfway to fucking Mexico by now," Rogers replied, not really listening to her. He puffed out his cheeks, fat like a hamster.

"Maybe," West replied.

"Not maybe. For sure. Wouldn't you be?"

"I'm just saying I don't know." She looked around. "This doesn't look like a place where everyone's left for good."

"What does the place need to look like, then? You hoping for a goodbye note?" Rogers turned away and stared out into the void that dropped away in front of the cliff. A silence hung in the cold air.

"No," West said eventually. "I'm just trying to get my head around this. This guy kills Olivia Curran, and his son comes up with some elaborate, crazy tip off about someone else killing her. Does that make any sense?"

Rogers was spared from answering because Lieutenant Langley came up to them.

"Stone works for the guy who owns the big hotel in town. James Matthews. He may even be working today. I'm gonna tear this place apart. You get over there. See what you can find out."

They turned to go, but Langley had one more thing to say.

"Oh. And if you find the fucker. Try not to let him go this time, will you?"

FIFTY

THEY TOOK the squad car and drove down the hill toward Silverlea. Coming up to the bridge, they had to slow down. Ahead, another squad car was parked side-on, blocking the road. Two uniformed officers were standing in the road, stopping all cars and checking the occupants. Rogers flicked on the siren for a couple of seconds until the civilian cars in front cleared the way.

"Anything?" he asked, slowing beside the officer, who shook his head.

"No sign of either of them, sir," he replied.

"Well, keep looking." Rogers bit his lip and drove on.

They drove in silence down the pretty lane that led to the Silverlea Lodge Hotel.

"You reckon they'll remember us?" Rogers asked as they came to a stop outside. West didn't answer. Instead she pushed open the door and jogged up the steps.

The receptionist looked up from her desk, and her face broke into a smile.

"Good morning, Detective Rogers, how nice…" she began brightly, but Rogers cut her off.

"Hi, Wendy. Afraid this isn't a social call. We need to speak to the boss. You know where he is?"

"Mr. Matthews?" She looked flustered for a second but gathered herself.

"Well normally he'd be playing golf on a Saturday, but I did see him pop in earlier. Would you like me to check if he's still in his office?"

"Yeah. Do that." Rogers said, and waited right in front of her as she picked up the phone.

"Small place," Rogers said to West.

"What?"

"Small place. Lornea Island. Everything's connected to everything else."

Before West could reply, Wendy spoke again.

"You're in luck, Detective Rogers. Mr. Matthews is still in his office." She paused, covering the receiver with her hand. "Would you like to see him now?"

"Yeah, we would. It's this way, right?" Rogers didn't wait for her to reply, instead walking behind the desk and into the corridor behind it. West followed him, the flustered Wendy a few steps behind. A few yards away, they came to a door labeled 'Manager'. Rogers knocked three times and was about to knock again when a voice from inside said to enter. They did so without hesitation.

"James Matthews?" Rogers asked of the man seated behind the desk. Matthews was dressed in golf clothes and he still had the phone in his hand. He returned it to the receiver, a look of confusion on his face.

"Detective Rogers and - "

"Detective West, sir," West said. She pulled out her badge and flashed it. Rogers did the same. "Is there a problem?"

"You might say that," Rogers said. "Can you confirm that a Sam Wheatley works here at the hotel? He gave your name as his employer."

"*Sam*? What's this about?"

"If you could just answer the question," Rogers said.

"Well, I could, but I'll need you to tell me why first."

"We're investigating the murder of Olivia Curran. Could you tell me if Sam Wheatley works for you?"

Matthews looked like he was beginning to anger. "Look, Detective Rogers, I think I should advise you I'm a very close friend of your boss, *chief* Larry Collins."

"And I advise you I'm losing patience fast. Does Sam Wheatley work here at the hotel or not?"

James Matthews stared at Rogers, growing red in the face. West interrupted the two men.

"Mr. Matthews. It is urgent. And important."

For a long moment, Matthews continued to stare at Detective Rogers, but then he looked across at West and gave a tiny shake of his head.

"Of course, have a seat."

There was only one chair in front of the desk. Rogers grunted at it, and West sat down. Matthews took a deep breath, then exhaled slowly.

"Detective West." Matthews held up a finger as if he'd just placed her. "You're the two officers who stayed here at the beginning of the Curran inquiry." He tilted his head to one side.

"That's right."

"Well, I trust you had a comfortable stay? I made the rooms available to the police department. I wanted to do my part."

"We appreciate it, sir. Now, about Sam Wheatley. Can you confirm that he works for you, and do you know his present whereabouts?"

Matthews raised both hands as if in defeat.

"He does work for me, but not here. He looks after the maintenance of my vacation cottages. But I'm sure he's not involved in any way."

"And is he working today?"

"Look, I've spoken with Larry; I know all about the poor girl's hand being found in Goldhaven. And I'm sure Sam Wheatley has nothing whatsoever to do with that."

"If you could stick to just answering the questions," Rogers said, now pacing up and down at the back of the office. There was another chair here, and Rogers pulled it forward to the desk and sat down.

Matthews frowned again. He turned back to Detective West.

"I'm afraid I don't know. He does work a lot of weekends, but he essentially arranges his own schedule. I could call him if you'd like?"

"What number do you have for him?" Rogers cut in. There was a pause.

"I'll check," said Matthews. Another pause while he searched on his computer and then his cellphone. He found a number and showed it to Rogers, who wrote it down in a notebook he produced from his pocket. Rogers nodded at the phone.

"Try it."

Matthews dialed the number. The others waited while Matthews listened in silence for a few moments. Then he hung up.

"No signal."

"OK," West said a few moments later. "We're going to need a list of all the places he could be working. The cottages you mentioned. Can you get that for us right away? We can have those checked out."

Matthews sighed lightly, but he picked up the phone again, dialing a single digit on the phone's keypad, and gave clipped, clear instructions to whoever was on the other end.

"It'll be here in a few minutes." He smiled thinly at the two detectives.

"Thank you, sir."

Rogers dug his cellphone from his pocket and checked for messages. There were none, and he shook his head at West.

"What can you tell us about Sam Wheatley? How long have you known him? How did you come to employ him?" West asked.

The manager stayed silent for a while before he answered.

"I wouldn't say I do know him *well*. I think I met him. . . seven, eight years ago. Maybe more. As I remember, he came to the hotel, asking for work. Our old maintenance man was retiring at the time. I said I'd give him a chance."

"And did you perform any background checks? Check his references?"

Matthews paused. "It's a long time ago, but for a position like that, I wouldn't normally dig too deeply. May I inquire why you're asking?"

Both detectives ignored the question.

"And do you know him socially?" West asked. "Could you give us the names of any family here on the island? Or close friends?"

Matthews shook his head. "We've never really socialized." He thought for a moment. "I believe he's a surfer. You could try asking around that crowd."

West glanced at her partner.

"Does the name Jamie Stone mean anything to you?"

"No. Should it?"

Again, the detectives ignored the question.

"Is there anything else you can tell us about Sam Wheatley? Anything that might tell us where he is?"

Matthews shook his head again. "I only know he's extremely reliable, and he's never been any trouble. To be honest, I know his son a little better, he's something of a computer whiz kid. He fixes the Internet connections in many of our cottages."

West glanced across at Rogers, who had looked up from his phone at this.

"Billy Wheatley?"

"That's right."

There was a knock at the door, and it opened a crack. A girl hovered outside, holding up a sheet of paper. Matthews waved her in, and she approached the desk, glancing at the two detectives but not making eye contact.

"Thank you, Cheryl," Matthews said, then waited until she had left the room. He studied it for a while, then picked up a pen and began to scribble on it. When he'd finished, he held it out to Detective Rogers.

"This is a list of our properties. I've circled the ones that Sam's working on at the moment."

Rogers took it from him and glanced at it. Then he dialed a number on his cellphone and began issuing instructions for patrolmen to visit the properties Matthews had indicated. When he'd finished, his cellphone beeped loudly.

"Thank you, Mr. Matthews. You've been most helpful," West said, rising from her chair.

"Well, I hope so. I hope you're able to find him. Although I say again, I don't believe for a moment Sam Wheatley has anything to do with whoever killed poor Olivia."

"Well. Thank you anyway." She rose to leave, but Rogers stayed in the chair beside her. He was staring at the screen of his cellphone.

"We got it," Rogers said to her.

She didn't reply, but his eyes flicked to her face, and he spoke again.

"Langley's got his truck. Abandoned by the river."

FIFTY-ONE

It was late on Sunday evening when Chief Collins called the meeting. He had one of the patrolman fetch take out, and the four of them - Langley, Rogers, West and the chief - sat in his small, neat office, eating pizza in silence. It had been a long day with no opportunity to eat. When they'd finished the chief kicked things off, summarizing what they knew so far about Jamie Stone.

"I spoke today on the phone with one Randy Springer. He's chief of police out in Crab Creek, where this all happened. He was pissed about me calling on a Sunday, but he remembers Stone well enough."

"Springer is certain Stone is our man. He says he knew he'd resurface sooner or later. Stone's the type that's always gonna offend again." The chief paused and appeared to think for a moment.

"He says Stone is violent and extremely dangerous. He'll be armed, and if he's cornered he won't hesitate to shoot his way out." Collins paused again for a beat or two.

"Springer made a big point of that. He said to shoot first and ask questions later." The chief looked around at his team. "So I don't want anyone taking unnecessary risks. Especially with the boy involved. Assuming the boy is still alive."

There was quiet in the room as all the detectives considered this. Even though she hadn't eaten all day West hadn't touched the pizza. She'd listened to what Stone had done with a growing sense of horror. She thought of how it must have been for the boy to live with him. But more than that, she thought about how she had missed two opportunities to rescue him. It twisted her stomach. The chief went on.

"OK, let's get to some details. Langley. The pickup truck. What do we know so far about that?"

Langley pushed himself off the wall where he'd been leaning and read from his notebook. "It's a red Ford, '97 plates. Discovered unlocked in a rural parking lot down by the river. Fresh mud down the side like he'd been off-roading this morning. River water in the footwells."

"Anything in it? Any sign of the kid?"

"Surfboards and wetsuits in the back. They looked like they'd been used this morning too. Other than that, not much. We saw footprints, though, a large male boot and a kid's sneaker. Leading straight to the highway. I'm thinking they went surfing this morning, came back to the house and saw we were there, then fled through the backroads. Abandoned the pickup when they realized we had roadblocks set up."

"OK." Collins thought for a moment. "No cameras out that way, I suppose?"

Langley shook his head.

"Forensics?"

"There's no lab on the island big enough to take it, so it's being wrapped to go on the ferry tonight. We should have something by tomorrow afternoon."

"OK. Keep on that. I want to know the minute there's anything back. How about the vacation places he looks after? Anything there? Rogers?"

"He's not hiding out in them. We're keeping an eye."

"Keep on that too. It's cold out there tonight. If they're on the run they're going to need somewhere to hide out. Empty properties are going to be mighty tempting." Collins said. "Escape routes off the island?"

Langley took this point up. "We're watching the port and going through the CCTV. No one matching their description got on the boat today. Course, he could have a private boat we don't know about, but there's no sign of one. And nothing's reported stolen. We're working on the assumption he's still on the island somewhere"

"How about the house? Anything?"

Langley shook his head. "Nothing. We'll keep looking, though. We'll tear it apart."

"Alright. There'll be time for that."

Collins stayed quiet for a moment, not looking at any of them. He stroked his mustache.

"OK. Let's think back to his alibi. West, you took his statement didn't you. What did he say?"

Detective West had printed out copies; she handed them around now. She cleared her throat.

"He claims he didn't meet the Currans when they began their vacation. They picked up the key to the cottage from a strongbox. He claimed he didn't even know who the daughter was, not until it made the news. He *was* at the party though." She hesitated.

"He told us he left around eleven p.m. To take his son home. Olivia was seen after that time, so it wasn't followed up."

"The son confirm they left together?"

"At the time he did," West said. "But then I found this. Take a look." She handed out a second statement.

"This is from Linda Richards. She lives nearby to the Wheatleys. She says she was taking her daughter home from the party and offered to take Billy Wheatley back at the same time. Stone was talking with friends and wanted to stay longer. So the boy did come home when he said he did. But Stone didn't."

Langley leaned forward, skimming the document for himself. "How did this get missed?"

No one answered him.

"Who took Linda Richard's statement?" the chief asked.

"Strickland, sir." West replied.

The chief stroked his mustache and blew out his cheeks. There was a silence in the room.

"You didn't pick up anything weird about Stone? When you took his statement?" Langley asked.

"Like what?" West asked.

"Like it was *bullshit*." There was anger in Langley's voice.

"No. Not at the time." West replied. "There was no reason to."

"And how about when you had him sat in front of you. Here at the station? You didn't sense anything then?"

"We were focused on the boy. There was no reason to consider his father a suspect at that time."

"Jesus, what a fucking mess." Langley said.

West opened her mouth to say something but the chief stopped her.

"That's enough. We need to look into this. If Stone didn't leave at eleven, when did he leave? Who saw him after that? We gotta build a case against this guy as well as catch him."

West listened as the chief gave his orders, but she wasn't fully focused. She couldn't get Langley's anger out of her mind. Was it her fault they'd let Stone slip through the net? Should she have realized there was something not right about Billy and his father?

"OK, let's wrap up for now," the chief said, interrupting her thoughts. "Langley, Rogers, go home, get some rest. I want the search back on as soon as it gets light. West, you wait here for a moment. I'd like a word."

The other officers gathered their things and filed past her. Langley gave her a stare as he walked past. Rogers raised his eyebrows. When they'd gone, Collins quietly shut the door. Then he went back to his desk.

"Sir?" West asked a few moments later, concern written on her face.

The chief didn't answer at first. Finally, he looked up.

"Detective West. You need to know something. In addition to speaking with Chief Springer this afternoon, I've also been called by two journalists. It's only a matter of time before they discover we took a statement from Jamie Stone two months ago and did nothing, and then had him in the station this week. And let him go." He glanced up at West. His face was grim.

"Sir. . . "

"When that happens," Collins talked over her. "We're going to take a hammering. If they get your name – and I may not be able to prevent that - it's possible *you're* going to take a hammering." His eyes rested on West. She couldn't read his thoughts.

"If it does indeed turn out that you interviewed a killer on two occasions, there are going to be people, inside and outside the department, who hold that against you."

West felt her face flushing hot. There was nothing she could do to prevent it. She opened her mouth to speak again but he held up a hand.

"Don't misunderstand me, Detective West. I'm well aware that killers can make very good liars. I'm also aware that this department is under extreme pressure." He paused. Then swung on his chair, and looked out of the window.

"You know, I came here thinking I'd see out my years away from the limelight," he said; his voice suddenly a lot lighter. "I'd had enough of psychopathic child killers and the media circus they exploit. You realize, after a while, however many you catch, there'll always be more. It's a sickness within our society." He turned back to her.

"This is a small department, Detective. On a small and isolated island. The people here have conservative views. A woman detective. A black chief of police. These are difficult concepts for some people here. We both need to be aware of that."

West didn't answer. She didn't grasp what the chief was telling her, and he didn't give her the time to process it.

"Detective. I believe it would be advantageous if you were out of the way for a little while, just until we catch Stone. Should it take longer than I hope, there's a danger of attitudes toward you hardening."

West still didn't understand.

"Out of the way? What do you mean?"

The chief stroked his mustache again. "I've made some arrangements. I want you to look into Stone's background. Speak to the boy's mother, the rest of the family. Reassure them we're doing everything we can to find him. Last thing we need is them throwing their weight around. And they knew Stone. Maybe someone there will know something to help us find where he's hiding."

West frowned. It seemed like a longshot.

"But sir I want to find him. I want to be here."

Collins spoke sharply. "No. Langley has that covered. He'll search the whole damn island. If Stone is still here, Langley will find him. In the meantime I want someone on the mainland. I want to hear firsthand what this guy did."

"But. . . " West opened her mouth to voice another objection, but Collins stopped her.

"No buts Detective. I've told Chief Springer to expect you tomorrow lunchtime. You should speak to him first. He sounds like the kind of man who would demand that."

"*Tomorrow lunchtime*? How can I even do that?"

As if on cue there was a knock at the door. At Chief Collins' command it opened, and Diane Pittman put her head in around the door. She glanced at West to check who she was before speaking.

"The helicopter is on its way, sir. They say half an hour. They're asking where to head for?"

Collins' eyes flicked to West.

"You're still staying in Silverlea, aren't you?"

"Yes, sir."

"Can you be packed and ready to go in half an hour?"

She blinked at him twice before replying. "Yes sir," she said.

"Good." He turned to the older woman, still standing holding the door half-open. "They can land on the beach." The chief looked back at West. "They'll pick you up there."

For a moment, she didn't understand that he was dismissing her. Then she got it, and stood up slowly, her mind whirling. But he called her back.

"Oh, and Detective?"

"Yes?"

"If anything doesn't smell right over there, you let me know, won't you?"

FIFTY-TWO

OUTSIDE THE CHIEF'S OFFICE, the building was quiet, but not the normal Sunday evening quiet. Tonight, the place had the feel of being deserted, the entire department having been involved in the day's search. Coffee cups stood full and cold on desks. Computers, left on, looped *Lornea Island Police Department* screensavers.

Detective West entered the office in a state of shock. She almost didn't see Rogers waiting for her. Lounging in a chair that wasn't his own, and twirling a pencil around his fingers.

"What was that all about? He's not pissed we didn't see through Stone when we interviewed the boy?"

"No."

"It's not what Langley said is it? 'Cause the guy can be an asshole. And it wasn't just you. If there's an issue there, it's on both of us, and I don't mind telling him that." Rogers was getting up a head of steam. West interrupted him.

"He wants me to go out to Crab Creek - where Stone first killed. He wants me to look into all that. In case there's something there that could help."

Rogers frowned.

"How's that going to help? He's *here*. We need to catch him here."

West didn't answer.

"Well. When?"

"Now. Literally now. Tonight. The chopper's picking me up in a half hour."

Rogers screwed up his face in confusion.

"I guess you need a lift then."

They drove together to the apartments. West packed quickly, throwing two changes of clothes into an overnight bag. As she zipped it up her cellphone beeped as Pittman sent through messages about her flight details. Then Rogers drove her down to the Surf Lifesaving Club and right onto the beach. West waited in the front seat, her bag at her feet. They barely spoke.

Moments later, a bright light appeared in the sky, coming over the headland from the north. Only as it came close was it possible to make out the rotor blades and the shape of the helicopter. And then, when almost overhead, it slowed and descended, with a flood of noise and raising tiny tornadoes of seawater from the beach. It looked clumsy from inside the car, a little bit unreal. The left sled touched the sand first.

"Well, I'll keep you informed," Rogers said when it had settled. The rotors continued to thrash around and he had to raise his voice against the noise. Inside the chopper the pilot gestured at them.

She nodded, then glanced over at him. He had a distant look in his eyes, like he was itching to get back to the search for Stone.

"Yeah, me too," she replied at last. She put her hand out to open the door.

"We'll catch him for you," Rogers said hurriedly. "We'll nail the bastard."

West hesitated for a moment, remaining silent, then pushed open the door.

Outside, the noise was deafening. A wash of hot, exhaust-laden air was billowing toward her, heavy with sand that stung her face. West stooped down and covered her head to protect it from the blast. Around her feet, small puddles of seawater shivered like they were alive. She ran toward the helicopter, reached its glossy painted side, and slid the rear door back. She climbed in and hauled the door closed, having to use both arms to get it to move. When it thumped into place the noise was cut by half. It was warm inside too. The pilot turned to look at her and said something she didn't hear. Then he pointed to the earphones resting on the hook above her seat. She reached up to retrieve them.

"Welcome aboard, Detective," a voice said into her ears. "Could you strap yourself in, please? We'll take off right away." His mainland accent surprised her. She'd become accustomed to the islanders' way of speaking by now.

"Boston Logan, right?" the pilot said, and this time, she nodded at him.

"What time's your flight?"

"Ten forty-five."

"Gonna be tight, but we'll do our best. First time in a chopper?" he added, and she nodded.

"How do you know?"

"You can always tell by the look of terror." In the dim lighting of the aircraft's cabin, she thought she saw him smile, but then he turned back to his controls. She had barely finished fitting her belt before the engine note rose. Slowly at first, but gaining in speed, the helicopter lifted off. The ground, the beach, the sea, all dropped away below them. It felt like being drunk in an elevator. Then they spun around so the view from West's window changed. The town slid away. Instead, she could see the darkness of the dunes and then the ocean. She found herself gripping the armrest, then forced her hand to relax. They gathered speed, flying out over the water to skirt around the cliffs. It didn't feel like it, but by now they were moving fast, because they were already at Littlelea. She tried to see the boy's house, on the clifftop, but couldn't find it. Then she realized she was looking in the wrong place. It was disorienting.

Then she saw it. Billy Wheatley's clifftop cottage, the home he had shared for so long with a murderer, a child killer. From up there, it looked even more precariously perched, right on the edge of the cliff. It was fitting somehow. The boy had lived such a precarious life. Was that life over already?

Now level with the cottage, she could see the lights of the search team, still working, two – no – three squad cars in the narrow driveway. Then the pilot banked hard around to the right and out to sea, so that the black rocks of the cliffs were flashing past their left hand side. West flinched and pulled herself back from the window, as if that might help should the pilot lose his grip of the aircraft's controls and send them smashing into the dark rock face.

Then the cliff disappeared behind them, and they roared past the smooth tower of the lighthouse that squatted on the rocks. And then there was just water below them. A dark sea, flecked with flashes of white where the chopper's lights reflected off the waves. West turned to look behind. She could see the island, the lights of the towns, shrinking away. The pilot made another course adjustment and increased the power. The engine note changed. There was a whine of hydraulics. A clunk. The pilot's voice came through the earphones again, clear and familiar, without its island drawl, yet somehow missing something as well.

"I'm gonna explain your situation to Boston Flight Control. They should give us a good route in but I'm not promising." He adjusted one of the controls above his head. "Whoever booked your flight must really want you to get to wherever it is you're going," he went on. "Or maybe just get you away from here."

It was just a light hearted comment but West didn't feel like replying, and it was dark enough in the cabin that she got away with silence. Outside, the darkness blinked to the navigation lights and she watched the patterns in the rolling waves below. She wondered whether there was any real reason for taking this trip. Or if she had just been sidelined.

FIFTY-THREE

After the isolation of three months on Lornea Island, the mainland felt enormous. The two runways of Boston's airport reached out on giant arms into a harbor filled with ships, their superstructures lit up to make them look like a watery extension to the skyscrapers of downtown. The city itself stretched out behind the airport, yellow ribbons of freeways snaking around it. A billion tiny points of light, each one of them representing a human life, just like her's with its unique path around the spinning planet. She was back in civilization, and she didn't know if she wanted that.

The section of the airport reserved for helicopters was to the north, nearly a mile from the passenger terminal, but West found an airport security car was waiting for her. It raced across the tarmac, orange light flashing, dwarfed by the jet liners trundling into position to disgorge their passengers into the terminal or launch them shooting into the sky. The car dropped her off at a side door, the driver getting out to unlock it for her. When he closed it behind her she found herself in the main passenger check-in area, so bright it hurt her eyes. She shouldered her bag and ran for the desk.

Her sense of dislocation continued when she got there. In her line a family argued over the weight of their suitcases. Everywhere was a mass of people. People all living their own lives. People too busy to care about the strange, quiet Lornea Island that lay out in the Atlantic darkness. Out of sight just over the horizon.

She knew she should interrupt the family, explain to the check-in clerk how she was about to miss her flight, but she held back. The sudden vastness of the airport intimidated her. To her relief a second desk opened up, and the clerk called her forward.

West felt a little better when she boarded her flight. Maybe it had something to do with getting out of the airport, where so many people milled around. Maybe it was just relief for catching the plane. Whatever, they took off, and she found herself straining to see Lornea Island through the small window. She thought she'd caught a glimpse of it before they bumped their way through the cloudbase up into the night above.

It was a short flight to Washington Dulles and there was drizzle when she was back on the ground. West had to wait an hour in the concrete and marble for her connecting flight. The only reminder of where she had been now were the newspapers, a few of which carried small articles reporting the developments in the Olivia Curran case. When she took off again she tried to sleep but the cramped seat wouldn't let her body relax. So instead, she read the file, cover to cover. Then she flicked through the in-flight magazine, before finally feeling her eyes heavy enough to let her sleep. She rested her head against the window and outside the massive engines powered her across the mighty American continent.

Her jet landed at two thirty in the morning, Pacific Time. But that was five thirty in Lornea Island, off the East Coast, so it left West fresh enough to rent a car right away and begin the four-hour drive south to Crab Creek. She got there at seven and checked into a motel. By then, she didn't much care that the room smelled damp. She set her alarm for nine, then lay down on the lumpy mattress and went straight to sleep. Her breathing, still gunked up from the aircraft's stale air, was the only sound to accompany the low buzz of the refrigerator.

FIFTY-FOUR

"I DON'T KNOW what you expect to achieve by coming here, Detective. Like I told your boss, it's all there in the file."

Crab Creek's Chief of Police Randy Springer had rolls of fat barely held in check by his uniform shirt. His forehead glistened with beads of sweat. He shook his head now, or tried to; the thickness of his neck limited its available movement.

"Chief Collins wanted me to come and speak to you personally. It's such a high-profile case."

"Yeah. I know all about that," Springer said, looking annoyed. "I just reckon you'd be better off over there catching the bastard rather than sitting here." He fixed her with a stare but then didn't seem willing to hold her eye. He snorted, like something from his throat had gotten stuck in his mouth.

"Well, I'll tell you what I told your boss. Jamie Stone is a sick son-of-a-bitch. One of the worst I ever came across. A lot of folks around here will be happy if you shoot him dead the moment you lay eyes on him." He sniffed this time and looked around. West wondered if he was going to spit out whatever had entered his mouth.

"Could you tell me about it?" she heard herself asking.

"I told you. It's in the file. You *have* read it?"

"Yes. I read it on the flight, but it would still help to hear it from you. You actually worked the case, right?"

"If you've read the file, why are you asking me that? We do have crime to solve here, you know."

West waited, unsure of what to say next. She wondered if he was actually going to refuse to tell her.

"OK." He appeared to give up. "Where you want me to start?"

She thought fast. The file had been poorly written; it assumed the reader had background and sometimes inside knowledge.

"Maybe start with the family. They're well-known around here. Is that right?"

Chief Springer took a deep breath, but then, before he replied to her, he picked up a telephone on his desk.

"Laura, bring me some coffee, will you? I'm going to be here awhile." He made it sound like that wasn't his choice, and he didn't ask West if she wanted any. He put the phone down and looked at her.

Suddenly, he smiled. West didn't smile back.

"Yeah. You could say the family are known." He spoke as if only a fool wouldn't be aware of that. "The Austins own a lot of real estate around here. Hotels, couple of shopping malls. Then Bill Austin served as mayor. Stepped down last year. He'd be the boy's grandfather."

"So an influential family, then?"

"A reputable family. A good family. Tell me again why is this important to you?"

"I'm just. . . building a picture."

He sighed. "Building a picture," he repeated to himself, then blew out his cheeks.

"What about the mother?" West asked. "What do you know of her?"

"Christine?" He raised a pair of pink, oily hands in a shrug. "She was a good girl. Never in any trouble."

"Did you know her? Before it happened?"

"Knew of her. Least a little bit. Most folks did. Pretty girl like that. . . Hard to miss." Chief Springer's eyes strayed to West's face, and she felt him examining her with a casual gaze. He didn't seem to like what he saw.

"The file says she was committed to a psychiatric hospital after it happened. Is she still there, or has she been released now?"

"Why do you wanna know that?"

"Excuse me?"

"Why is that relevant?"

West frowned, "I'd like to speak to her. I'm trying to establish her whereabouts. The file doesn't actually give the name of the hospital..." She began paging through the file to show him, but he just shrugged. West stopped looking.

"So is she still there?"

"I wouldn't know."

"Well what's the name?"

He shrugged again. "Have to ask the family, I guess."

There was a pause. West took a deep breath, telling herself not to get frustrated.

"She was young, wasn't she? When it happened? Twenty-one, twenty-two, something like that?"

"If that's what the file says. . . "

"And he was too?"

In response, the chief pointed to the folder she was holding.

West looked down at her lap and smoothed the fabric of her skirt down her knees.

"Perhaps you could just tell me what happened? In your own words?"

"I could, Detective West. And I will, just as soon as I get my coffee." He smirked at her.

A few painful moments later, there was a knock on the door. The girl West had seen sitting outside the office walked in, carrying a cardboard holder with two take-away cups planted in it. Someone had written the word 'Chief' on one of the cups. Chief Springer pulled it out of the tray and flipped the lid off, while Laura handed West the other cup, smiling conspiratorially at her as she did so. Once she'd gone, the chief made a thing about pulling open his desk drawer and adding sweetener to his coffee. Only then, did the chief start speaking again.

"OK. Here we go. Yeah, he was young. And he wasn't exactly the kind of guy anyone would want coming home with their daughter. Least of all a society guy like Bill Austin. He was a nobody, a high-school dropout. Beach bum, you know? No job, imagined he was going to make a living for himself from surfing. But that was just fantasy. He was going nowhere, fast. And then he lucked out by getting Christine Austin pregnant, and then he even managed to screw that up."

He paused for a moment and sipped his coffee. West just waited for him to continue.

"No way she wanted his kid but she left it too long to do anything about it. And then when it came out there were two of them. Twins. Non-identical. Obviously, *he* couldn't provide for them - no job, no family money to fall back on. So it all turned sour. Christine and the kids moved back to the parents' house. A big old place out of town. Nice place. That's where the lake is. Where he did it. He was still living. . . I forget, somewhere in town." He waved his hands like this wasn't an important detail.

"He'd visit them, but it was always difficult, you know? Stone didn't get on with the family. You can't blame them. Guy like that ruining their daughter's life and still hanging around. Like a bad smell." The chief stopped again, as if he was thinking about this.

"I notice in the file," West said to prompt him, "there's nothing on what his motive might have been."

He scowled at her.

"Motive, opportunity? That's what you look for when you don't have solid witnesses who can tell you who did it."

"Yes. . . " she replied slowly. "But we're wondering if it might help us understand more about what happened in the Curran case."

The effort of speaking seemed to have left the chief out of breath. He was almost panting now, his forehead shiny with sweat.

"What about you let me finish up, now as you got me started?"

West was surprised at the unmasked distaste in his voice, but she nodded quickly.

"So like I was saying. It went on like this for a while, him hassling the family, her trying to move on. But it wasn't sustainable - you know what I mean?"

West nodded again.

"Christine has a brother. Smart guy. Paul Austin. Works for a law firm up in the city." Chief Springer sipped his coffee again. Then he sighed.

"And he came down to visit one weekend, and when he gets there, the front door is unlocked. He can't understand. It's never like this. He goes inside. He searches the house, but there's no one there. *That's strange,* he thinks. And then he hears screaming coming from the grounds. He runs out there, and that's when he sees it. He sees this guy who's been hassling his sister. This *Jamie Stone.* He's standing in the lake. He's holding Christine Austin down under the water, trying to drown her. One of the twins is on the bank, strapped into a stroller - that's Ben. His sister, Eva, she's floating face down in the lake. *Stone's already drowned her.*"

It was nothing that West hadn't read already, but hearing the words spoken gave them a power she'd not felt before. It was warm in the room, but she felt cold. Her brain furnished her with the file image of the dead baby photographed on the banks of the lake, the skin yellowed except where the purple bruises shone out. The girl hadn't gone without a struggle. West said nothing and waited.

"Paul runs straight into the lake. He tries to get Stone off his sister. But Stone sees him coming. He times a punch and lands Paul on the head with it. They fight, but Paul comes out on top. He drags Christine to the shore. She's conscious but in no state to do anything. Stone's picking himself up by now, but Paul can see the other kid, Eva, floating out into the lake. He knows Stone could get away, but what choice does he have? He goes for the baby, but once he gets there, he finds it's too late for her. And by the time he gets back to the shore, Stone's disappeared. And he's taken the other kid with him. Ben's gone.

"We searched the whole state for them. Looked everywhere he might have dumped a body, but we didn't find anything. He got away." Chief Springer looked away for a moment, a wistful look on his face.

"I was the first on the scene."

West said nothing. The chief looked back at her. "So like I said. There's a lot of folks around here who'll be very happy if you find Jamie Stone and put a bullet through his evil skull."

FIFTY-FIVE

For a few moments the only sound is our breathing, both of us out of breath. Slowly I open my eyes to look at Dad. His face is fixed in a crazed smile. Then he laughs, throwing his head back to the sky.

"That was one hell of a wipeout buddy! I thought you weren't gonna come back for a while out there!"

He laughs again. The noise of it fits the empty beach, just the two of us here, slick in our wetsuits.

"C'mere, kid. Come here." He grabs me now, he pulls me close to him, so that we're stuck together like two seals.

"Hey stop it. C'mon. Stop crying," he pulls back and looks at me, still holding onto my shoulders.

"I guess it was a little bigger out there than I thought." He laughs again, then slaps me around the shoulder. "But you did well. You went out there. You caught a wave. Shame you tried to run up the beach afterwards. But it's progress."

Slowly I lift my head. I look at my Dad. I don't really know what's going on. One minute he was trying to kill me. The anger written on his face. Now he's acting like nothing happened, nothing like that anyway.

I'm limp like a doll as he squeezes me again.

"But I get it. I get it now. I really do. You don't like the water. Some people don't. If that's you, that's you." He laughs again. "The way you panicked out there. . . I've never seen anyone react like that. You looked like I wanted to kill you." He laughs and squeezes me harder.

Dad kneels down beside me and undoes the leash that's still wrapped around my ankle. Then he picks up my board and his, and tucks them both under one arm, and wraps the other arm around my shoulder.

"Let's get you changed; then we'll get some breakfast. Not the cafe. We'll go someplace different. Someplace nice."

I walk with him, not sure what to think. It feels like suddenly my old dad is back. The dad I remember from when I was little. The dad who used to take me rockpooling, who had time for me. The dad who would sit in my room because I was scared the monsters under my bed would eat me while I slept. Then, with a sudden empty feeling in my stomach, I remember. I put my hand to my chest, feeling for the hairclip. The clip with the bloodied hair that I pulled from the back of his truck. The proof that tells me that version of Dad really has gone forever. I feel myself shrinking away from his grip again, and he looks at me, worried. He smiles, as if that's going to reassure me. I keep my hand on my chest, trying to feel for the bump under my suit that tells me the clip is still there, but all I feel is my chest rise and fall, in time with my too-fast breathing.

We get back to the truck, and Dad turns the radio on. It's playing Jay-Z and he turns it up louder. Dad still likes the kind of music that's meant to be for younger people. He throws me a towel, and then pulls open his door to get changed.

I pat my chest again, feeling for the bump of where the clip is. I can't feel it. So I reach behind my back to pull the zipper down on my suit. Carefully, I pull the rubber off my shoulders and then look down at the space where my chest has been. There's no hairclip. I study my chest. I look pale and skinny, even more so than normal, like the seawater has shriveled me up. There's a faint indentation that I think shows where the clip was, but the actual hairclip isn't there. Hurriedly, I pull the rest of my suit off, wrapping a towel around my waist even though there's no one else in the parking lot. Still no clip. I turn my suit inside out and inspect it, then look on the ground around me. But I know it's not there. It must have gotten flushed out of the suit when I was being rolled around underwater. It's out there somewhere, sunk to the bottom of the ocean, where it'll never be found again.

Suddenly, I feel pressure on my nose, and just in time, I lean my head forward. A run of water comes flowing out of my nose, not just a few drops, but enough to fill a cup. Dad sees and laughs.

"That's a good one, Billy. You've swallowed half the sea out there, buddy."

I don't answer. I look at my chest again, but now, where I thought I saw the indentation from the hairclip, there's nothing, except a faint reddish patch on the skin. It could be nothing, could just be where the wetsuit rubbed against my skin. As I get dressed, I look again in the truck, to see if there's anything more where I found it. The little gap where it was stuck is still there, and when I close my eyes I can see how the clip looked, when it was lodged in there. But when I open them again, it's gone. Gone forever.

"Tell you what, Billy. I've got to head into Newlea later anyway, so how about we grab an early lunch there? We'll drop the boards off at home, then go get some burgers. How's that sound?" Dad asks, and I nod slowly. I don't know what to think anymore. So once we're changed, Dad loads the boards up and flings the suits in the back in a big wet heap. Then we get in and drive back up the hill to drop the boards off. And that's when everything goes really crazy.

FIFTY-SIX

DAD'S WHISTLING as he drives. I don't understand why his mood has changed. From trying to kill me, to wanting to buy me lunch. And I'm just sitting here next to him, not saying a word. It's like I'm floating or in a dream or something. I'm sitting next to Dad, but at the same time, I'm sitting next to a murderer. Part of me wants to push the door open and escape; the other part wants to tell him everything and let him hug me and tell me it's crazy. In the end I do nothing. I just wrap my hands around myself against the cold. I can feel my body shaking.

We turn off the road and into our little driveway. The only place it goes is our house, but there's a bend halfway along which hides the house from the main road. We go around the bend now, and Dad's whistling stops. He hits the brakes.

Up ahead, there's two cars, both painted black and white, with the blue police lights on the roof going slowly around, even though there's no one inside.

"The fuck. . . ?" Dad says, and we just sit there for a moment. There's a gap in the hedge a little bit further on, and you can just see the house through it. Dad quietly rolls the truck on so we're level with it, and we both look through. There's more cars, some marked, some not, and there are people going in and out of the house.

"Shit," Dad says, and he puts the truck into reverse.

I'm thinking now, not fast enough, but I'm thinking. The police are here. This is real. It must be. And I have to act. The police are here. *They can save me.*

I look down at the door handle, and I wonder what would happen if I open it. Would I have time to run to the police? Or would Dad catch me before I could get there?

But I'm already too late. We're already moving backward.

"Fuck it," Dad says. He's instantly angry again. "The fucking cops." He spins

around in his seat so he can see behind better and speeds up. I'm worried we're going to veer off into the hedgerow.

He doesn't slow down where the lane meets the road. It's an awkward turn, even when you're going forward. But he goes for it anyway, backing out onto the road and spinning the truck around. We're lucky, though, it's clear. Then he rams the truck into first and accelerates so hard I get pushed back in my seat. He's checking in his rearview mirror all the time, and I turn around, too, expecting to see the flashing blue lights chasing us, but there's nothing there. The road is empty. He doesn't say anything. He doesn't say where we're going, or why. He doesn't say why there are police at the house. And I don't ask. Neither of us needs to say anything. The silence says it all.

When we get to the woods, he pulls off the road into the area where there's picnic tables and you can park to go for a walk. He drives behind some trees and stops. But he leaves the engine running. I look over at him and wonder what he's thinking. I realize he's checking the road again. We can't see it clearly because the branches of the trees are in the way, but we could see if any cars go past. Finally, I say something, mostly because it'll seem weird if I don't.

"Why are there police at our house, Dad?"

He looks at me suddenly, like he'd almost forgotten I was there. He's about to answer, but then we hear a siren. We both sit there for a moment, trying to hear where it's coming from, and then Dad pulls the truck forward so we're deeper behind the bushes. Then he kills the engine. I can see the flashing light now, bright though the gloom of the forest. The car flashes past, not coming from our house, driving toward it.

"What's going on, Dad?" I ask.

He stares at me again, like he can't believe I'm here. I guess he thought I'd be dead by now and he wouldn't have to worry about me.

"Billy. . . This is going to sound weird, but we've gotta go somewhere for a while."

"Why?" I say.

"We've got to get off the island."

"Why?" I say again. Even though I know the answer, I can feel the panic rising in me. I can hear it in my voice.

"I don't have time to explain now. Just trust me." Dad starts the engine again. "We're gonna go get the ferry."

We spin around again, and this time, Dad looks both ways before rejoining the main road. He keeps the speed down, and he checks in the mirrors almost as much as he looks out of the front.

"We'll get to Goldhaven, we should make the midday boat. That gets in by four. We can find a motel somewhere, figure out what to do," Dad seems to be talking to himself, but then suddenly he stops. We're out of the woods now; it's open land around us, and up ahead, the bridge over the river. And there, blocking the road in both directions, are two more police cars.

"Motherfuckers," Dad says. He slows to a halt and then puts the truck into reverse again, and backs up the main road into the woods. Then he stops again and just sits there with the engine running, thinking.

"Do you think they're looking for. . . ?" I don't know how to finish my question. *You? Us?*

Dad doesn't answer anyway. Then, suddenly, he beats the steering wheel with his fists and swears again. Then he smiles at me, a manic smile.

"Want to do a little off-roading, Billy?" he says.

He doesn't wait for an answer. He spins the truck around so we're facing back into the woods, and we drive on for a half mile, until we come to a track on the left. It's not a real road; you're not supposed to drive on it, but it's wide enough for the truck. We bump our way down it, and eventually break free of the trees. It's kind of marshy land here; no one comes here much, except maybe some bird-watchers.

Eventually, we come out by the river, about a mile upstream from the bridge where the police are waiting. It's not a big river. In the summer, it sometimes dries up, but this time of year, when it's been raining a lot, it's pretty full.

"What are you going to do?" I ask.

"I told you. We're gonna get the ferry."

"Won't they be waiting there too?" I ask, and Dad just looks at me. We drive along the riverbank for a while and then we come to a section where the banks are low. In the summer, you can easily get across here. I'm not sure about now. Dad edges the truck forward, down toward the water. He doesn't hesitate. He just drives right in.

The truck lurches from side-to-side as the wheels find hollows hidden under the water. I grip the door, worried we're going to roll at one point. The water's right up to the grille on the front of the truck, and out on my side, I can see water, almost up to the window. Dad's revving the engine hard, and we're pushing through the water, a big wave rolling out in front of us.

"C'mon, c'mon," Dad's muttering as we go through the water. I see water coming in through where his door shuts, but he ignores it. Then I feel the same is happening on my side. We hit something, and the truck stops dead, rocking back and forth. Dad swears again, then turns the wheel full lock, and somehow we edge past the obstruction. We're more than halfway across the water now, and heading back uphill, almost on the other bank. Dad's still muttering. Willing the engine to keep going. I can see we're going to make it now. We hit the bank, and the big truck struggles to grip, but with the engine roaring, we climb out of the water and over the neat grass where people come for picnics in the summer. There's another little parking lot here, and a track that leads back to the main road, past where the police are waiting.

There's woods this side of the river, too, although they're not as thick, but they protect us from the police on the bridge. We're going to make it. But suddenly, there's a roar above us and the sound of rotor blades hammers through the air. The helicopter seems to appear from nowhere. I guess it must have taken off from the beach, and now it's flying upriver, straight toward us. Dad guns the engine until we're in the trees again, and then he slows to a stop and stares up through the windshield, trying to spot it. We both see it together, coming overhead and banking into a turn. We don't see it clearly, just glimpses through the branches, but it looks like it must have spotted us, but then instead of staying overhead, it keeps on going, and we see it following the road out of town, the road we need to take across the island toward Goldhaven. There's no need for me to ask if Dad thinks the helicopter is there to catch us.

He doesn't move for a long moment. The chopper is hovering stationary now, not too far away. It seems to be keeping an eye on traffic on the main road. I guess they know what vehicle Dad's got, and they're looking out for it.

"Come on," Dad says suddenly. He pushes the door open and steps out. I don't move, so he says it again.

"Come on, Billy. We're gonna walk from here."

"To Goldhaven?" I ask, but he shakes his head. "No. They'll be watching the port anyway. We'll take the back way into town. I know somewhere we can hole up. Until I find a way out of this."

I still don't move, but he's already at my side of the truck. He pulls open the door.

"C'mon, kid. Let's get going." I unbuckle my seatbelt and step out of the truck. Then he leans in after me and opens the glovebox. Inside, there's his wallet and phone, and tucked under the folder where he keeps the car's documents, I catch a flash of black metal. My mouth falls open. It's a gun. I've never seen Dad with a gun before. He hates them. For a moment he tries to hide it, but then he sees there's no point. He kind of shrugs like what did I expect, then he tucks it into the waistband of his jeans.

It's cold, but Dad makes us walk fast, under the cover of the woods, and we get to the main road in no time. I've driven along this road lots of times in Dad's truck, but I've never been here on foot. I'm surprised how fast the cars are going as they zoom past. It's not busy, but there's always a car or two in sight. The helicopter is still visible, too, but it's a mile or two away. Dad takes my hand, like I'm still a kid, and he pulls me across the road.

"Where are we going?" I ask, stumbling behind him as we push through the undergrowth into the cover of the woods the other side.

But he doesn't answer.

FIFTY-SEVEN

DETECTIVE WEST DROVE BACK up the ocean highway she'd driven down only hours before. This time, in the day light, it was beautiful; the sunshine bounced and glittered on the waters of the Pacific. The climate was drier here than Lornea Island, the ocean seemed fresher, the air cleaner.

After an hour, the road snaked inland, cutting through huge fields. She was flanked on her journey by towering power lines that guided her toward the edges of the city. She had the road to herself at first, but as she neared Portland the traffic increased, and soon she had to concentrate, hands gripping the rental car's plastic steering wheel. She followed the GPS to the city center, where the traffic thinned a little, till it was mostly just cabs. Towering above her, tall buildings of glass and steel spoke of money and power. She pulled into a parking garage, left the car and continued on foot.

The offices of Austin, Laird & James occupied two floors high up in a smoked-glass tower. The atrium was so big there were full-size trees inside, presumably to make the experience of passing through metal detectors under the watchful eyes of security guards feel a little more natural. If so it didn't work. For West, as she rode the elevator up to the law offices, it felt like an environment designed to protect the wealthy and the powerful, and to send a message to everyone else. Don't challenge us. You don't belong here.

The receptionist was very pretty and looked very bored. She was filing her nails as West flicked open her badge and ID. Judging from how she kept on filing, nothing about West impressed her.

"I'm here to see Mr. Paul Austin," she said, trying to smile confidently. "I telephoned earlier."

The girl raised one finely-plucked eyebrow and took West's ID. She examined it carefully, then did something on her computer. There was the sound of a printer and she pulled out a visitor's card with West's details on it. The receptionist slipped the card into a plastic wallet and asked West to clip it to her lapel.

"Mr. Austin's in a meeting at the moment. I'm afraid I'm not able to disturb him." She smiled like this rather pleased her.

West checked her watch.

"We arranged to meet at three. He said he could fit me in."

There was an unmistakable challenge in the girl's answer.

"But you only made the appointment this morning. Normally, it wouldn't be possible to see Mr. Austin at all on such short notice." She smiled again. "If you'd like to wait, I can have some coffee brought over." West looked around, wondering who would do it if the receptionist wasn't going to move herself. She declined the offer anyway, and went to wait where she was told, on a suite of black leather sofas and smoked-glass coffee tables that matched the windows. There was nothing to read there except the company brochures, which explained the firm's specializations. Or rather didn't explain it, since West wasn't able to get past the language of *derivatives manipulation, disintermediation, discretionary trust protection* and *estate efficiency frontiers*. West flicked through the glossy document, then tossed it back down on the table and watched the receptionist, who moved onto her other hand. After twenty minutes, West returned to the front desk, only for the girl to repeat that Mr. Austin would see her as soon as he was able, but that she couldn't say when that might be. West refused another coffee.

Back on the sofa, her cell chirped, and she dug it out of her bag, happy for the diversion. It was a text from Rogers:

Call me if you get a minute.

Since she apparently had plenty of minutes, she hit the button to call him. He answered at once, his gruff voice taking her straight back to Lornea Island.

"I thought you'd want to know," he sounded tired. "It's Stone's pickup. The lab found traces of blood and hair in the back."

"Olivia Curran's?"

"Right blood type. And the hair's the right color. We should have the results of DNA tests in a couple days. But it looks like it. And that will positively link Stone to our case. If there was any doubt." There was a pause on the line. "Are you getting anything useful out there? Where are you now?"

West lowered her voice. "I'm just about to meet with a Paul Austin. He's the brother of Billy's mom, Christine. He's the one who disturbed Stone drowning the family in the lake. Or at least, I think I'm meeting with him. He's an hour late already."

"They not treating you right out there?"

"The chief out here thinks I'm wasting everyone's time. We should be putting everything into catching Stone."

"Well, if he'd caught him, Stone wouldn't have been able to murder Curran in the first place. You remind him of that if he gives you shit," Rogers said.

They were quiet for a second or two. West noticed the receptionist was on the phone; she hadn't heard it ring.

"Anyway, I'll keep you informed. I just thought you should know." Rogers sounded like he was preparing to hang up.

"I am confused about one thing, though," West spoke quickly, not wanting to end the call yet.

"Go on," Rogers said after a beat or two.

"I still don't get why Stone would drown one of his children, and then disappear with the other, and apparently try and bring him up as normal. Does that make sense to you?"

There was another pause while Rogers thought this over. At the same time, the receptionist put her phone down and stood up to walk across to where West was sitting.

Rogers sighed. "Some sort of psychopathic guilt? You're over-thinking this, Detective. If he's the kind of guy who can drown a baby, and murder a schoolgirl then go back and cut off her arm, we don't need to wonder too much about his motivations. The guy's a sick fuck. That's it."

The receptionist stopped just short of where West was sitting and waited. She was close enough to overhear her and West felt a buzz of irritation.

"I gotta go. Text me when you hear about the blood," West said, loud enough for the girl to hear. She killed the call and looked up with a smile.

The receptionist smiled back, but it was less self-satisfied than before. West felt a small victory that the 'blood' might have just unsettled her.

"Mr. Austin will see you now."

"Why thank you," West said.

Paul Austin's office was at least four times the size of Chief Springer's, but the view was a hundred times better. Floor-to-ceiling walls of glass revealed half the city and the river that wound its way through. Low hills dusted in mist graced the horizon. It was distractingly beautiful. Then she saw Paul Austin, and she was distracted further. He wasn't just handsome, but ridiculously so. Like a model from a Christmas perfume ad.

"I'm sorry to keep you waiting, Detective West." His voice purred, soft and sensual. "My two o'clock meeting ran over." He shrugged with a knowing look. As he did so his features softened slightly giving him an edge of vulnerability. West had to fight not to stare at him. He was her age, tall and tanned. His white teeth were perfect, set within unusually red lips. His eyes were so bright and so blue they almost looked fake, like a movie star touched up for a poster. He wore a dark blue suit that complimented his eyes, and underneath, a thick, cream cotton shirt, with slim silver cufflinks peeking from the sleeves.

"I'm afraid I'm normally booked up for weeks in advance," he explained. "But this is important so I've canceled my three thirty. I hope that's OK? Do have a seat, please." He held out a hand to an informal area of his office where more sofas were arranged. West felt herself sinking down, and any irritation she'd had in the waiting area slipped away. Paul Austin picked up a phone and ordered coffee in a quiet voice. Then he sat opposite and leaned in toward her.

"So. I understand Jamie Stone has resurfaced at last?" He was close enough that

West couldn't help but catch the fragrance of his aftershave. Fresh and musky. She had to resist breathing it in.

"We believe so," she said.

"And he's now implicated in the Olivia Curran homicide case?"

West fought to maintain her sense of sharpness. "That information hasn't been released yet. May I ask how you became aware of it?"

"Chief Springer. He telephoned me this morning. He thought I might not be able to clear space in my schedule unless I was told the importance of the meeting." There was a slight roll to his eyes, as if to acknowledge the police chief's deficiencies. "The family has maintained a very good relationship with the police." His blue eyes watched her face.

"I see."

"We've never stopped searching for Stone. To get justice for Christine. It's just terrible we weren't able to locate him before he could strike again. I understand he was hiding as a janitor?"

She answered before she realized he'd flipped things so that he was asking the questions.

"He was working for a hotel in the resort town of Silverlea, on Lornea Island. Do you know it?"

"I'm afraid not," Austin shook his head. He continued with his line of questions.

"And I understand you interviewed an eleven-year-old boy you believe to be Benjamin Austin? Christine's son?"

His voice was so soft she couldn't tell if his use of the word 'you' implied the Lornea Island Police Department, or her personally. "That's correct," she said carefully.

He didn't say anything. Instead, he brought his hand to his mouth and pressed his knuckles into his lips. Then he looked away. West thought she'd seen a tear appear in the corner of his eye, but when he looked back, it was gone.

"I'm sorry, Detective. I was only informed this morning. It's a lot to take in. Could you tell me what he was like? Did he appear abused? Was he healthy?"

"Physically, he seemed normal. Healthy. He. . . You may know, he contacted the police anonymously with information regarding the Curran murder. It turned out to be false, but given the subsequent development of his father now being implicated. . . " She stopped.

"I'm not an expert, but I would assume that hints at some. . . psychological issues."

"Of course," Paul Austin said. Then he continued in an even voice that West was unable to read.

"And you don't know where either of them are right now?"

She tried to answer in a positive way.

"We're looking everywhere we can. The search underway is the biggest in the history of the island's police department. We've brought in dozens of officers from the mainland," West said, uncomfortably aware of how inadequate that might sound in such opulent surroundings.

He nodded. "We'd like to do everything we can to help. I'll say that right away. If Ben can be brought back to us, that will be something positive to come out of a horrible situation. That's the priority for the family." Austin stopped. There was an undercurrent to his words that suggested that if Ben couldn't be brought back, he wasn't ruling out further action. Or perhaps West simply imagined it, intimidated by the display of wealth. Then Austin smiled. "Baby Ben," he said. Suddenly, he looked lost in thought.

"That's what we used to call him. And his sister. Baby Ben and Baby - " He stopped and screwed up his eyes, only to be interrupted by a knock on the door. The receptionist came in, carrying a silver tray loaded with coffee.

"Thank you, Janine," he said to the girl, his voice a little husky with emotion. West caught the way she looked at him, an expression that revealed such glances were why she turned up for work each morning. And probably why she spent so much time on her face. When she'd poured the coffee, her body seemed to pull itself into him as if attracted by a magnet. If he noticed he hid it well.

"Thank you Janine," he said, then waited till she left the room. "Anyway. How exactly can I be of help to you, Detective?"

It was a question West didn't welcome, given she didn't really know herself.

"I'm here to speak to everyone involved in the original case. To see if there's anything that might help us locate him now."

"Such as?"

She hesitated. What clues could possibly exist from a ten-year-old open and shut case?

"It's more about getting a better understanding of the crimes he's accused of here."

"*Accused of*? That's an interesting choice of words, Detective."

West hesitated. "I only say that because he hasn't been convicted of anything. Just a point of process."

"I witnessed him trying to murder my sister. There's no doubt as to what he is. He's a cold-blooded killer." West felt the blue eyes fixed on her, and she had to look down to avoid their stare. She pulled out a notebook and pen. It was more a prop than anything she needed, but it helped her change the direction of the interview.

"Did you know Jamie Stone well?" she asked. "Before he disappeared?" She clicked the pen so it was ready to write.

"No."

"But he dated your sister? They had the twins together?"

"Clearly."

"Well. You must have met him? Spoken to him, many times, I'd have thought?"

For a second or two, West thought he wasn't going to answer.

"Yes." He said at last. He seemed suddenly tense, then he made himself relax. He smiled at her.

"He came to the house once or twice when I was there. At garden parties and so on. We were very different."

"How so?"

"He was. . . rough. He wasn't the kind of man any of us expected Christine to become involved with. He was. . . more like a guy you'd meet in a sports bar. The type that would get into fights."

"He was violent?"

"Evidently so. Murderously violent."

"But you saw him being violent?"

"I saw him drowning my sister."

West glanced up from the notebook.

"I'm sorry."

Paul Austin was holding his head up high. She looked down again.

"Mr. Austin, where is your sister now?" She looked down at her notes. "I understand she's in a private institution, but I don't have the name?"

"Why would you need to know that?"

The sharpness of the reply surprised her. "As I said, I'm just trying to talk to everyone who knew Stone before he disappeared. He doesn't have any family so she knew him better than anyone else. I'd like to ask her if there's anything she might remember that might help us."

"I'm afraid that won't be possible."

West didn't respond at first, and when she did, she chose her words carefully.

"Mr. Austin, I'm investigating the murder of a teenage girl. It's possible your sister could assist in that - "

Austin cut her off.

"It's not possible."

"Excuse me?" West felt her voice rise in indignation. She told herself to cool it.

"It's not possible that she could help. She doesn't know anything about where Stone went after he disappeared. Believe me, I've asked her many times."

"Nonetheless, I'd like to ask her myself." West met his eyes once again. She felt she had to fight to maintain her focus against their piercing intensity.

Paul Austin was the one who looked away first.

"Detective," he began, then paused to allow himself a small sigh.

"I doubt anyone can truly understand the experience my sister went through. Stone *drowned* her daughter, in front of her eyes. He was in the process of drowning her, too, when I happened upon the scene. Christine was moments away from death. Perhaps some people might have come back from that, but not Christine. I'm afraid my sister hasn't yet recovered. She is not able to answer questions. It's unlikely she ever will be."

There was the buzzing sound of a cellphone, and West looked expectantly at the lawyer. But he raised his eyebrows.

"Yours, I believe," he said.

She realized he was right and scrambled for it, further flustered to see it was only a text and she needn't have rushed. She was slipping the phone back when the contents of the message flashed up on the screen.

Positive ID on the blood in Stone's truck. It's Curran.

She hesitated for a moment. Her mind absorbing the words. Then she pushed the phone back down into her bag. She noticed Austin watching her, as carefully as ever. She found her mind had gone blank, and it was Austin who spoke next.

"Detective, I appreciate this is going to be difficult to handle, but I have spoken to my father already this morning. He's agreed that for the sake of Christine, and for my mother's sake, too, we would like to remain as far away from this case as possible. Whatever this Stone creature has done this time has, mercifully, nothing to do with our family. Therefore, I'll be putting a team together to ensure that the Austin family is kept at arm's length from any trial and from media attention. I trust you'll understand why we feel like this." Paul Austin leaned forward and clasped his hands together. West breathed in another breath of his scented air.

"What about the boy? Billy - Ben?"

The lawyer didn't miss a beat. "Our thinking is further predicated upon the boy's case. He'll be returned here to the family. That's exactly why we insist our family is kept out of this as much as possible. It's vital that he is protected from any untoward media interest." Austin paused.

"That's assuming you're able to recover him before Stone goes on another killing spree, of course."

Paul Austin checked his watch. It was a slim, gold-bracketed model. West was reminded of the in-flight magazine she'd fallen asleep to the night before. It was full of ads for expensive brands, models pretending to be people just like Paul Austin. She realized how tired she was.

"I appreciate your coming to see me in person, Detective West. And I will further appreciate your keeping me personally informed, but alas, I do now have another meeting."

Before she could stop herself, West found she was getting to her feet. At least she stopped herself from walking to the door.

"Mr. Austin, if I could just get the name of the hospital where your sister is staying?"

"As I say, she's in no condition to answer questions on this matter."

Austin continued ushering her out, but something made West stop. She felt like, despite her best efforts, the entire meeting had been undertaken on his terms. She shook her head and refused to move.

"Sir, if and when Stone is captured alive, your sister will be a key witness in any trial that takes place. I *need* to see her."

The lawyer answered quickly, for the first time not picking his words as carefully.

"Detective, we both know you have no jurisdiction in this state and are in no position to insist upon anything."

They stared at each other, both breathing hard.

"The state police have agreed to cooperate fully. It feels to me like you're not," West heard herself say.

Austin looked away. He sighed again.

"Detective. You're trying to do your job. I'm trying to protect my sister." He looked down at the floor, as if considering what to say next. He seemed to come to a decision.

"I apologize. As I say, this has been an extremely challenging morning. My sister is staying at the Paterson Medical Facility. It's a private hospital. I can arrange for you to visit if you would like?"

"Thank you, sir." West felt flustered, unsettled. "I *am* just doing my job." She said. She didn't understand what had triggered the sudden change in his approach. She felt like she didn't understand much of the exchange that had just taken place. But Austin nodded as if the matter had been settled entirely amicably.

"I will telephone her doctor to arrange the visit. Janine will give you the directions."

"Thank you, sir."

West was about to leave when another question occurred to her, just one of the many she'd meant to ask.

"Does she know? Does your sister know about Billy, I mean? That he's still alive?"

A strange thing happened with Paul Austin's deep, blue, powerful eyes. They filled with water. He blinked and looked away. When he looked back, the eyes were back to normal, and she wasn't sure if she'd seen them wet at all.

"Detective West, if you're able to answer that question for us, my family will be most grateful."

FIFTY-EIGHT

DAD KEEPS us walking at a fast pace, so we don't talk much, and we stick to the woods. The noise of the helicopter fades away, leaving just the sounds of leaves and sticks cracking underfoot. We don't see anyone the whole way, even though it takes nearly two hours to get into Silverlea by the back way.

Dad looks more nervous when we get into the streets, there are a few people around but they don't pay us any attention, and we don't see any police. Even so I wonder about shouting to them, screaming for help, but I don't trust my voice, and I know Dad's still got the gun. It's tucked into his waistband, hidden by the hem of his jacket.

At one point, I see Mrs. Roberts, from the store. She's in her car. Dad sees her, too, and he turns me sharply so we're looking into the window of a real-estate agents. I watch the car go past in the reflection, and only when it's out of sight does Dad get me moving again. Then we turn off the main street, and we're in the quieter residential area again.

"Where are we going?" I ask. I'm getting tired, my face feels tight from where I was crying earlier, and I feel like I'm about to start again any minute.

"We're almost there," is all Dad says in reply.

And then, a couple of houses further on, Dad swings open a little gate, and we walk up a path to the front door of a little bungalow. I don't understand, though. I know who lives here.

"Why are we here?" I ask, but Dad just rings the bell; then he raps on the door with his fist, real urgently.

I hear a voice inside telling Dad to calm down, that she's coming.

FIFTY-NINE

"SAM? What the hell are you doing. . . " Emily starts asking when she answers the door. Then she notices me. *"Billy?"*

"Are you alone?" Dad asks, and she doesn't answer, just screws up her face in confusion, still holding the edge of the front door.

"Are you here alone?" Dad asks again, and this time, Emily nods.

Dad doesn't say anything. Instead, he grabs my hand again and pulls me inside, pushing past Emily, who gets pushed backward out of the way.

"Shut the door," he says.

"*What the hell*? What the hell is going on, Sam?" Emily asks.

Dad doesn't answer. He lets go of my hand and paces up and down in the hallway. Then he disappears into the other rooms, and I hear him closing all the drapes. I just stay with Emily, waiting for whatever is going to happen next.

"Hi, Emily," I say.

She's breathing really hard, and she stares at me for a minute.

"Hi, Billy. Do you know what's going on here?"

I shrug. "Dad killed Olivia Curran, and now he's trying to escape from the police. He tried to kill me too."

She stares at me like I've gone completely crazy. She opens her mouth to say something back, but doesn't get the chance because Dad comes back into the hallway.

"Em, I need your help. I wouldn't ask if I wasn't desperate, but there's police all over our house, a roadblock on the bridge. There's a helicopter looking for me. You've gotta help us get out of here. We've got to get off the island. Can you drive us to Goldhaven? Right now?"

Emily is breathing really hard, and she pulls her eyes off me like it's a struggle and focuses on Dad.

"*Goldhaven*? Why?"

"I'll explain on the way. There's no time now."

She opens her mouth again a couple of times and then closes it again. Finally, she manages to get a sentence out.

"I can't. I'm meeting Dan," she says and looks at her watch. "In about half an hour. It's my day off."

"Fuck Dan," Dad says in a low voice, like he hopes I don't hear. "This is important. This is serious."

They stare at each other.

"But won't they be watching the ferry port, if they've got all that looking for you?" Emily asks in the end.

That's what I said, I feel like saying, but I don't say it.

Dad doesn't speak either. He just looks around, like he suddenly feels trapped by the walls around him.

"What's going on?" Emily asks. "Billy said - "

"I'll tell you later. I'll explain everything. Just not right now." Dad's eyes flick across to me as he says this, and I know he means he won't say it in front of me. He doesn't want to admit he tried to kill me.

"You've got to help us, Em. There's no one else I can turn to."

We all stand there for a moment. Still in the hallway.

"I'll call Dan, say I'm not feeling well. You can stay here and work something out. No one's going to look for you here," Emily says. Her voice still sounds incredulous, like she can't believe we've just walked in.

Dad's suddenly nodding. "OK. And let us borrow the car. We'll leave it for you at Goldhaven. You can pick it up later - "

"Sam!" Emily almost shouts this, and Dad shuts up.

"They'll be waiting for you at the port. You can't just run like this. You've got to think, Sam. You gotta be smart."

I've never heard Emily talk like this before. She sounds scary, and it stops Dad dead.

"Sit down. I'll make coffee. I'll call Dan, tell him I've got a headache."

We all go into the kitchen, and Dad and me sit, watching Emily as she goes around putting the coffee together. About halfway through, she looks up at me and smiles.

"How about you, Billy? Do you want your usual? I think I've got some chocolate here somewhere."

I nod and smile back at her. She says it like we're in the café and everything's normal. She says it to make me feel safe. But my smile doesn't last long. I've got so many questions, and although I'm scared to ask most of them, the confusion is even worse.

"Dad," I start, cautiously. "Why are we here with Emily?"

Dad looks away from the wall where he's been staring, lost in his own world. He looks up at me and half laughs. Then he shakes his head. He says to Emily,

"Christ, I've got half the island's police force chasing me, and he wants to know that. Do you want to tell him, or should I?"

"I think you'd better."

I look at them both, mystified. "Tell me what?" I say.

A few moments later, Emily puts a mug of hot chocolate in front of me and a coffee in front of Dad. She sits down, takes a sip of her coffee and holds the mug in front of her, blowing the steam away. She doesn't say anything, but she looks at Dad.

"OK. Billy," Dad begins. But then he stops and looks down at the table. "I don't know how much they've taught you about this at school. I guess it's that Personal Development class, isn't it?" He rolls his eyes. I just wait.

"The thing is, Emily and me, we've been. . . kind of. . . " He scratches his head. "We've been kind of seeing each other. For a little while now." He glances at me to see how this is going.

"In the café?" I ask.

"No. Well obviously, yes. . . Look, I'm not talking about in the café. I mean, it's been here mostly, at Emily's house, when Dan's not around." He stops and looks at me.

"You know what I mean by *seeing* each other?"

I know what "seeing" means, but it doesn't make sense.

"Like Emily's your girlfriend?" I say, although that doesn't sound possible.

Dad sounds relieved. "Yeah. That's it. Sort of. You're OK with that, aren't you?"

"But Emily is *Dan's* girlfriend," I say.

Dad looks at Emily. She looks away.

"Yeah. That's right. But sometimes, people don't really want to be with the person they're with, and they see other people too. Just to see if that works better," he says. Then he sounds a little more certain.

"That's why I haven't been able to tell you. I didn't want to hide it from you, I swear to you, Billy."

"I'm sorry, too, Billy," Emily says.

I look over and see her blue eyes watching me, her mug half-hiding the rest of her face. I think of everything we've shared. All the times we've discussed my projects, and her research. She puts the mug down. She looks so pretty. I can't help but think of my daydreams. I've never told her. I've never told anyone, but sometimes, I can spend hours imagining what it would be like if I were a bit older, how Emily and I would go off around the world, doing science. How maybe we'd even get married. I feel my face going red. I feel - I don't know - angry? Angry and awkward and kind of embarrassed. But also just confused.

"You're Dad's *girlfriend*?"

She smiles at me now, then nods her head. "Not exactly, but I guess that's a way of looking at it." She smiles at me again, her eyes all big. "Oh, Billy, I'm sorry I couldn't tell you. Adults are such funny creatures." She reaches her hand across the table and takes mine. Her hand feels soft; she's got pretty, slim fingers. I let her squeeze my hand for a while.

"What about Dan?" I ask, a moment later. Emily gives my hand a final squeeze and pulls her's back.

"Dan doesn't know," she says. "No one knows. Apart from you, now, obviously. We had to keep it a secret at first to see if it was going to work." She looks at Dad now. "If it does, then maybe we'll tell people. You and. . . and Dan too."

Dad glances at her, looking troubled still. But mostly, he's watching me. I feel like I'm about to start crying, so I look down at my hot chocolate. I try to pick it up, but my hand shakes, and some goes on the table.

"Sorry," I mumble, and Emily makes a big thing of cleaning it up with a cloth. Then they're both sitting down and looking at me. I try again to drink the chocolate, but it's not good; it tastes old. I look at the carton, and I can see it's the old branding. They changed it years ago; it's got new colors now and everything. Actually, now I notice, the whole kitchen is really old-fashioned. I saw it in the hallway too. It looks like an old lady should live here, not Emily.

"Why is your kitchen so old?" I ask suddenly.

Emily looks confused for a moment, then laughs. It's amazing how much it lightens the heaviness of the atmosphere, that laugh. Her face is so pretty when she smiles.

"This is my grandmother's cottage, Billy. Or at least it was. She passed away earlier in the year. I haven't gotten around to sorting it out yet."

There's a silence, and the magic of her smile fades throughout the room. Then Dad takes over.

"Look, Billy. Em and I need a little space for a while. How about you go and find the science channel or something. Leave us to have a talk?"

Part of me wants to say no. Wants to ask what's going on, why we're here. Why he's suddenly pretending to be nice to me. But I can't quite get over what Emily just said to me. Normally, I'd be able to talk to her; I can tell her anything, or I could. Now, I'm confused. I need some time to think about everything. And I haven't forgotten the gun in Dad's jeans.

I look at Emily, hoping she might help, but she's nodding along with Dad. So I just do what he says. I pick up my drink with two hands and get up from the table.

"Good boy," Dad says, and he shuts the door behind me.

SIXTY

I GO into the living room like Dad says. I kind of hoped I would be able to hear what they're talking about, but they're talking quietly. The living room is decorated like the rest of the house. The walls have flowers on them, but they're stained yellow. The floor is brown carpet. There's a window, but when I go to look, it's locked, and I can't find the key anywhere. I guess Emily's grandma was one of those old people who worried all the time about burglars. A lot of old people are like that.

I wonder if I should try to escape anyway. I could just open the front door and run away. Maybe I could go to a neighbor and ask them to call the police. For a long time, I think about it. But it's scary. Maybe Dad would come after me. Maybe he'd shoot me this time. And now that we're with Emily, maybe I'm safe again. Maybe he's decided not to kill me after all. I don't know; it's all too much to think about. So I stop thinking. I sit down on the couch and wait for whatever is going to happen next.

I don't drink my hot chocolate, though. There's definitely something wrong with it, probably because it's so old. It's probably something her grandma had in the cupboard for years. I feel a bit sick about drinking it, but I don't want to offend Emily so I pour it away into a plant pot in the corner of the room. I mash the dirt around so you can't see where I did it, then wipe my hands on the carpet. It's brown anyway.

I think I'd better do what Dad says, so I look for the TV remote, but instead of finding it, I see Emily's laptop on the sofa, half-hidden under a cushion. I stare for a moment at its bright blue lid. Normally, I wouldn't think of looking at it, but I wonder if I could get online. Maybe I could find out what's happening. Glancing at the door to make sure Emily hasn't come in, I quickly open it up. Emily's icon is a starfish. I stare at that for a moment before I notice the cursor blinking, asking for the password. I have no idea what her password is, so I shut the laptop, feeling guilty for even trying. I slip it back under the cushion and sit back on the couch. I get the sudden feeling of everything hitting me at once.

Dad and Emily are like *boyfriend and girlfriend.* I remember things that have happened. Things that seemed a little strange at the time. Like when I wanted her to come and see the whale with me, and she said she had to work. Emily doesn't work Saturday afternoons. She never has. Did she say no to looking at the whale because she was with Dad? I think how often Dad's come home late from work recently. Crazy late, really. I feel my face going red as I think about it. He was with her. And the part that really gets me is I was at home, daydreaming about her and me going off together on a research trip or something. My face gets hotter still.

I tell myself to stop. I hardly ever had that daydream, really. And I never meant it. I see the remote at last and turn on the TV. I start to flick through the channels like Dad said, to find something with science in it, but instead, I find a cartoon. It's been years since I watched any kids' TV, but I find I can't make my finger press the button to move on. The sound is down low, but it's just a bunch of cartoon animals anyway, a dog and a rabbit running around. I put the remote down and leave it on. I'm surprised to suddenly feel my cheeks are wet. I grab the cushion and wipe my face. Then I pull the cushion close and wrap my arms around it. I let the tears flow.

It feels like hours later when Emily comes in. I'm curled up on the couch, still watching cartoons. I've been flicking between Cartoon Network and Disney Junior, and I've almost forgotten where I am and why I'm there. Emily's got her hair tied up behind her head, and she's gotten changed. She's wearing a baggy sweater and leggings. She still looks nice.

"Hey, Billy, how you doing?" her voice is soft.

She reaches out and puts a hand on my head, ruffling up my hair.

"This is all a bit much, isn't it? How are you feeling?"

Because I don't know what to say, I don't say anything, and she goes on talking.

"What you said earlier. About your dad. . . about Sam somehow being involved in that girl's death. That's not right. That's not what this is about."

I look at the cartoons for a moment before suddenly answering. I don't feel ready to talk about it.

"How do you know?" I say, because I can't exactly ignore her completely.

"Sam's told me everything. It's not about Olivia Curran. And I promise you it's not about you, Billy. He didn't try to kill you, Billy. That's just crazy. He would never do anything to hurt you."

I hear her words, but against the pull of the TV they sound weak. The cartoon world seems so much easier to face. The truth is I'm exhausted by it all. I want to turn away from Emily and pretend this isn't happening. But what happened this morning flashes through my head. I can't pretend.

"I've got evidence."

She does this funny thing where she tries to give me a comforting smile but also frowns a little.

"What evidence, Billy?"

My nose starts running, so I sniff. "I found Olivia's hair clip in the back of Dad's truck. It had blood on and everything."

Emily touches the hair on the back of her head. It's not like Olivia's. Emily's got brown hair. She touches her fingers on her own hair clip.

"Billy, you couldn't have." Her voice is reasonable and calm.

I shrug. "I did."

She smiles at me, but it looks fragile.

"Billy, sometimes, people imagine things that aren't really there, or make mistakes, think something is important when really, it isn't. When we're under a lot of pressure, I mean."

"I didn't imagine it." Suddenly, my voice sounds angry. It surprises me. "It was the clip she was wearing that night. It had blood on it."

Emily stays quiet for a moment.

"Can you show me, Billy? I'm sure there's an explanation. If you can show me, I can help explain."

I shake my head and look away. "I put it inside my wetsuit. It got washed away when Dad took me in the water."

"So it's gone?" she says slowly. Then she's quiet again for a moment, thinking. I think I know what she's going to say next, that this probably means I imagined it, but she doesn't say that.

"Did you look on the beach for it?"

I'm surprised by that.

"I didn't get the chance," I say. "But I lost it out in the water. No one will ever find it now."

She nods. Her eyes go big, and then she smiles. She slips down and sits next to me on the couch, putting her arm around me and pulling me close. She's never done this before, and I'm a bit uncomfortable because my face is close to her boobs. I feel like it's wrong but I try to remember how they feel. Soft and warm. I can smell her perfume really strong now. Flowers.

"Look, Billy." She squeezes me harder so my whole face is pressed against her side "You remember how things went with Mr. Foster? You were so certain he was responsible in some way. And then. . . Well then he wasn't. Well, this hairclip - if that's what it actually was - it's probably the same. I don't know what, exactly, but you must have the wrong idea."

I want to believe her. I want to believe I've got this all wrong somehow. To just press my face against her and make this alright, but that won't work. I'm here. In this strange room. Everything's changed. Different now. I push myself away from her.

"But I saw it, Emily. I *saw it*." For some reason, I'm pleading with her now. "I held it in my hand." I snatch up my sweater and show her my chest, where the imprint has now long since faded away. "I put it right here. It had blood on it, and *hair*, like a little tuft of blond hair. It was the same clip that Olivia Curran had. And then, right after that, Dad tried to drown me. He pushed me underwater. Just as a wave was coming. He chased me." The tears are flowing now, and I don't care. I don't even wipe them away.

"*Billy, no*. Stop it. Your dad wouldn't do that. He didn't do that."

"I saw it, Emily. I saw the proof."

"Then where is it now?" Her voice is sharper now. "Did anyone else see it? Did you take a photograph?"

I don't say anything to this. Just shake my head.

She bites her lip.

"Look. Your dad's explained a lot of things to me that do make sense. He's very nervous about telling you. God knows I can understand why. He's cooking some food. He's going to tell you everything once we've eaten, and then - "

"There's something else that will prove it," I interrupt her. "Tell me your password, and I can prove it."

"What?" Emily looks startled. I pull her laptop out from under the cushion.

"Tell me your password," I say, opening the lid.

She looks uncertainly at her computer. Then, without saying anything, she leans over and quickly types a word. I try to see what it is, but I'm too slow. The computer boots up; the desktop photo is an underwater shot of a coral reef that she took herself. She emailed the same photo to me from her last trip on the *Marianne Dupont*. She looks at me.

"Open the Internet," I say.

She does so, and we wait together.

"Now what?"

"Give it here."

I pull the laptop onto my knees and type in the address for my weather station, then I log in to the admin account. It's not just an online thing; it's something I've actually got fitted to the roof of the cottage. There's an anemometer which measures the wind direction and strength, a thermometer, and best of all, there's a webcam. I was the first person to set up a webcam on Silverlea beach. At the start, I would get tons of hits from people wanting to have a look at the surfing conditions, or just look at the beach, before they came here. But then the Surf Lifesaving Club copied my idea and put up their own weather station. And because they had a better camera, and you could see the waves better from where they are, they get all the hits now. But I still kept mine going because you can use the data for research.

The webcam takes a photograph every fifteen minutes. Every photograph gets uploaded to a database that you can access online. So you can go back and see exactly what the beach looked like at any time you want, for the last three years.

Unfortunately, though, when I bought it, I couldn't afford a very good webcam. Mine is just a static image with a wide-angle lens. That means you don't only get to see the ocean. You can also see the edge of the cottage roof on one side of the frame, and down to the yard on the other.

The back end of the site loads up. I click into the search box and set it to load the images from August 29, earlier this year.

"This is the view from our house on the night Olivia Curran went missing," I tell Emily. "You remember we were all at the Surf Lifesaving Club Disco?"

Emily nods, watching what I'm doing.

"About ten thirty, I got tired, and I asked Dad to take me home. But he wanted to stay and drink more beer. So Jody's mom said she'd take me home. Then later, when the police asked me about it, Dad made me lie. He said he'd get into trouble if they found out I was home alone."

"Go on, Billy," Emily says. I select the right time. The cam's view looks normal again, dark and empty.

"That's eleven o'clock. Just before Jody drops me off." I click forward. In the next image, there's a pool of light on the yard.

"Eleven fifteen. The light is from the kitchen window. I left it on for Dad because he said he wouldn't be long."

I flick through the next image, and the next, and the next.

"One a.m.," I say. "He's still not back. He told me he got back at about eleven thirty." I show her the next eight images. Finally, I get to the 5:00 a.m. image. This time, the pool of light has gone, but there's another difference. Even in the darkness, it's possible to see that Dad's truck has appeared in the driveway.

"Dad told me he got back at eleven thirty that night. I remember really well because that's the time he made me say to the policewoman. But *he* lied to me. He actually got back at five a.m. Because he was out there doing whatever he did to Olivia Curran. Then hiding her body."

There's this really long silence. Emily is staring at the laptop. When she finally says something, her voice is really quiet and soft.

"Oh, Billy," she says. "Oh, my poor boy." She takes the laptop, and it looks like she's going to shut the lid, but in the end, she just puts it back down on the coffee table and puts her hand on my hair again.

"Oh, Billy," she says again. "The reason your dad didn't come home until five that morning. He was with me. That was the night we got together."

SIXTY-ONE

THE RECEPTIONIST GAVE West the address for the Paterson Medical Facility and told her an appointment had been made for that afternoon. West made her way back to the rental car and drove for three hours. At first, she passed several small towns, but for the last hour, she seemed to be driving through entirely empty country. And then, when she arrived at what her GPS said was the right location, West found nothing but an empty stretch of single-lane road, fields on either side, with only a few stands of trees to break the monotony of the horizon.

She stopped, not bothering to pull off the road, since she hadn't seen another car in a half-hour. She left the engine running. She must have overshot by a few hundred yards since the GPS told her over and over to turn around where possible. So she switched it off. She held onto the steering wheel for a moment, thinking, but then she realized how tired she was, and how it was affecting her thinking. She killed the engine and got out of the car.

She felt a little better right away in the fresh air, but looking up and down the road, she still saw nothing that looked like a hospital. She pulled out her cell, hoping to google the place, maybe find a number to call, but she had no Internet connection. There was reception for a call, though, so she dialed Rogers. Maybe he could locate the place and tell her where it was. He could update her on the search for Stone at the same time.

The phone rang, and she held it to her ear, waiting to speak. But on the sixth ring, it clicked over to voice mail. Annoyed, she shut the call off. She leaned on the hood, wondering what to do next.

Then she noticed a small tarmac road that led off the main highway. It looked far too small to be of consequence, but just before it, there was a sign; whatever it said was obscured by a tree. For want of anything better to do, she walked back down the road toward it, then squinted up when she reached the front of the sign. In small letters, it spelled out the words:

Paterson Medical Facility

Private Road

Still a little confused, West walked back to her rental car and backed up. She used her turn signal out of habit and drove into the lane.

It took her through a stack of trees, and beyond these it dropped down into a hollow. At the bottom, she saw the facility: a plain, characterless building. As she pulled up, a man in a white doctor's coat walked out and stood waiting for her.

She pushed open the car door and he stepped forward and stretched out his arm. "Welcome. I'm Dr. Richards. We've been expecting you." The jacket was open and underneath it West saw an expensive blue shirt. He wore metal-framed glasses with thin lenses. He smiled.

"I'm Detective Jessica - " West held out her badge, but the doctor waved it away.

"Detective West. Yes, I know. Paul's explained everything. Please come inside."

They climbed the steps and walked inside. The room was smaller than West had anticipated, and a man sat watching a bank of security screens. He didn't move as the doctor pulled a form from a plastic tray and began to fill it out with the date and time of her arrival.

"What exactly is this place?"

"The Paterson is a private residential medical facility. We offer a safe and secure environment for clients with very specific needs."

"You're pretty hard to find."

He slid the form across the desk for her to sign.

"Yes. Our profile is deliberately low key," the doctor said. "It helps our residents."

West hesitated, then signed the form and passed it back.

"I'm sorry, how do you mean?"

The doctor scooped up the form, then slid it into a plastic holder and held it out to her again.

"Our location here is part of our appeal. We cater to residents who are unable to cope in an uncontrolled environment. They benefit from not coming across too many people they're not familiar with."

"Like a secure hospital?"

"No, quite the opposite. We're out here so that our clients are free to roam almost wherever they like without running into danger. You can walk ten miles in any direction without coming across a house or a farm." He smiled.

"Please, can I get you a coffee, or perhaps something to eat?"

"I picked something up on the way." The refusal was automatic, and West wasn't sure why she said it.

"*Really*? I don't know where." Dr. Richards looked perplexed for a moment. "Like I say, there's not a lot around here." He smiled again and shook his head, as if this wasn't relevant to anything.

"Anyway, perhaps we could have a quick chat inside my office before we go to see Christine. I understand Paul already told you this may be a wasted trip?" He opened another door and led her into a spacious office, with a large antique wood desk. She took a seat and waited.

The doctor offered her coffee again before settling his side of the desk. "I understand you want to ask Christine a number of questions about what happened to her, and the man who attacked her. Is that right?" The doctor raised an eyebrow.

"I'm hoping she might have some information that will help us locate him."

"I think that's unlikely."

"Why?"

"Christine doesn't like to speak about what happened. . . " Dr. Richards paused. "I don't know how much Paul explained to you, but Christine is suffering from post-traumatic stress disorder." He waited until she shook her head to show he hadn't said.

"Many people misunderstand the disorder; they believe it's a temporary reaction or that it can be cured. Both assumptions, unfortunately, are false. In Christine's case, her reaction was very strong: it resulted in a permanent change in her brain. The best we can do for her is manage it with medication, and shield her from triggers by avoiding unsolicited social encounters.

"Are you saying I can't see her?" West asked.

"Not necessarily. But I am saying you're unlikely to gain anything useful from doing so. And that your questions will upset her."

West thought for a moment.

"I'd still like to see her. To ask if she's able to help."

The doctor nodded.

"I can't prevent you. I'll need to stay with you while you speak to her."

"OK," she said, then paused. "Can I ask you something before we meet her?"

"Of course."

"Has anyone told her whether her son is still alive?"

"Yes," the doctor said. "Yes, we've tried to speak with her about that."

"And what did she say?"

The doctor sighed. "She said very little. Perhaps if the boy could be brought back, they could be reintroduced to one another over a period of time. But I understand he's now missing again. Is that correct?"

West hesitated, then nodded.

"Well, perhaps we should get on, and then you can get back to trying to locate him. Shall we?"

Dr. Richards rose and showed her out of the office. They went down a long corridor lined with black-and-white photographs of fields and farmland. Eventually, they came to a door. It had a small window with wired glass.

"Are you ready, Detective?"

SIXTY-TWO

"Billy, Billy?"

I look up. I don't know how much time has passed. It might be five minutes; it might be an hour.

"Did you hear? Your dad just said dinner's ready."

I don't move. I'm not hungry anyway.

"Come on, Billy, you've got to eat. And your dad wants to say something to you."

I want to stay where I am, but I find myself following her back to the kitchen, like a lost puppy. Dad's wearing an apron with an image of a kangaroo on it, with a little joey poking out of the pocket. He gives it a little shake and looks at me like I should be laughing. I just stare at him.

"I made spaghetti," Dad says. "Come on, you'll feel better once you've eaten." He opens a drawer and rummages around for a spoon. The food smells nice. I can see the waistband of Dad's jeans. I wonder where he's put the gun.

We all sit down, like we're all part of a happy family. Dad spoons the spaghetti onto the plates like this is how we always eat. He's got a beer open, and I notice Emily is drinking wine. There's a glass of water in front of my place.

"Cheers," Dad says, lifting up his can. "This was a little unexpected, but let's say thanks to Emily for helping us out." She picks up her glass and tings it against the can. I don't move. They exchange a funny look.

I poke around at my food, because that's better than looking at Dad. I still don't understand. I'm trying to make sense of all this. If he didn't kill Olivia Curran, then why are all the police after him? What's all this about?

"So Emily told me," Dad starts talking. He sounds all casual, like I'd just mentioned to her how I'd bought a new motion camera, instead of thinking he was a murderer. "About what you think this is all about."

He gives a little kind of half laugh, but then his voice gets more earnest.

"Billy, I understand how confusing all this must be. What happened today with the police." He stops. He hasn't even picked up his knife and fork yet.

"But I promise you, it's not what you think it is. It's got nothing at all to do with that." He shuts up and watches me for a moment.

"I don't know *anything about* Olivia Curran. I swear to you. I never even laid eyes on the girl. Never met her, never spoke to her. I've got nothing to do with it."

His voice sounds like honey, thick and smooth. I want to believe him. But I know what I know, so while he's speaking, I do my best to think about the hair clip. I try to remember exactly what it looked like. But it's hard. I can sort of see it, but it's not clear anymore. A fleeting thought occurs to me: Maybe Emily's right. Maybe I did imagine it all, or just made a mistake. . .

"And this thing about trying to push you underwater. . . " Dad's still talking. He's smiling at me, in a way he hasn't smiled for a long time.

"That was me being. . . just being an *idiot,* Billy." I see his eyes flick to Emily, then back to me.

"It's just that there was this big wave coming. That's how you get through the waves; you duck under. You know that, right? 'Course you do. You gotta hold your breath, and then you pop right out the other side." Dad starts tapping the table.

"But you panicked. That got you caught in the impact zone, so every other wave caught you too."

"But you were right. It was way too big a day to try and get you out there. I was just. . . I was frustrated. I feel like we should be doing more together. Father and son." He stops and shakes his head.

"Billy, you've got to believe me. I would *never* hurt you. You're the most important thing in my life. Bar nothing." He sighs. "Look at me, Billy. I'll never hurt you. You gotta believe me on that."

I want to believe him. He's Dad. I want to believe every word he says. But I'm not sure. I look down at my pasta; the cheese is melting over the top. I haven't eaten for hours. I don't feel hungry but my stomach is growling now I've seen the food. I nod, mostly just so he'll let me be.

"I'm gonna eat my dinner now," I say. He smiles.

We don't talk about any of it after that. Instead, Emily starts talking about her next trip on the *Marianne Dupont.* That's the name of the research ship she goes on; I told you about it. But with everything that's been happening I kind of forgot - she's going again later this week, back down to the Caribbean, to do more research into her jellyfish. If things were normal I'd be jealous. But now I just don't know.

After we've eaten, I help Emily clean up the kitchen, and Dad sits, drinking more beers. By that time it's late, so Emily shows me a room where I can go to sleep. It's old and musty, and it smells of old ladies, but I don't really care. I don't have a toothbrush, so I have to use my finger, and then obviously, I don't have any pajamas, so Emily lets me use one of her T-shirts, and that smells a lot better than the bed. I can smell her flowery perfume on it, and I use that as a kind of defense against the old-lady smell from the bed linens and the pillow. I'm so tired I'm asleep in seconds.

SIXTY-THREE

CHRISTINE AUSTIN WAS SITTING in a wingback armchair with a blanket over her knees. She was nodding her head to the TV show in front of her, which was on mute. A line of drool was hanging from her lips. The doctor noticed and wiped it smartly away. West was shocked by the age of the woman. She would be in her mid-thirties, but she looked much older. Her jowls hung from her face, and her skin was pallid and sickly. Her eyes were unfocused. She didn't appear to notice them come in, didn't react when the doctor used a paper tissue to wipe her mouth. He glanced at West, as if to say: *Don't say we didn't warn you.*

"Christine? Chrissy? There's someone to see you. Do you feel like talking today?" Dr. Richards spoke loudly but kindly. To West's surprise, the woman turned her head and looked in her direction.

"Chrissy, this is Detective West. She's from the police. Do you mind if we sit with you for a while?" Without waiting for a reply, the doctor sat down on a sofa next to Christine and indicated to West to do the same.

"Chrissy, Detective West is the policewoman who found Ben. The one I told you about. She'd like to ask you some questions." The woman's eyes moved across to West, but they were heavy and dulled.

The doctor stopped speaking and smiled at West as if encouraging her to go ahead. West opened her mouth to speak.

"Christine. . . " It felt strange, speaking with the doctor watching her. Almost like she was being judged. West pressed on anyway. "I'm part of a team investigating the murder of a teenage girl in Lornea Island. We believe your former partner, Jamie Stone, may be involved in some way. Can I ask if he ever mentioned Lornea Island to you? Did he have friends there, or relatives? Anywhere he might be able to go and hide out?"

It was impossible to say whether Christine heard what she was saying or not. She watched West speak, but gave no reply.

"We're searching for him now. And for your son. . . Ben. If there's anything you know about Stone it might help us find him. . . "

Still Christine said nothing. West glanced across at the doctor, who smiled sadly at her. She felt frustrated. This was clearly a waste of everyone's time. Just like Paul Austin had said. And the doctor. Just like she knew herself.

"Anything at all might be useful. Did he ever talk about going anywhere special? Did he own any property anywhere that he might go to?"

Still Christine said nothing, and then she turned back to the television. The doctor began shaking his head. He opened his mouth to speak, and West sensed he was going to tell her it was useless. Even though she knew he was right, it still irritated her.

"Christine, I saw your son, Ben. I saw him last week. I spoke to him. He's eleven years old." She reached out and took Christine's hand. "I just wanted you to know, we're going to do everything we can to find him. To bring him back for you." West squeezed the hand gently, and saw the woman turn back toward her. Deep within, behind the swirl of clouds in her eyes, she thought she saw a spark.

"Ben?" Christine said. When she spoke, her voice was weak. West nodded and held her breath. "That's why I'm asking for your help. We believe he's still with Stone."

The woman seemed to consider this. She moved her head in a slow nod, then it seemed like she forgot why she had started nodding but kept on doing it anyway, nodding over and over. Then she turned away from West so that she was watching television again.

"We're trying to find Ben," West continued, trying to regain her attention. "Is there anything you can tell us to help find Ben?" But this time, Christine appeared to ignore her. There was a pause. Then Dr. Richards interrupted quietly.

"I think we should probably leave it there." He didn't wait for an answer before going on.

"We'll leave you to enjoy your afternoon, Christine. The detective is going now." West felt her irritation harden, but she didn't argue. Instead, she pulled out her card, meaning to give it to Christine. But she hesitated, passing it from hand to hand.

"Dr. Richards, is she able to use the telephone?"

He saw the card and guessed what she had in mind. "It's better if I take it. If she talks to any of the staff, they'll come to me, and I can call you." He smiled.

West nodded, then turned back to Christine.

"Is that OK? If you think of anything that might help, you can talk to Dr. Richards, and he'll call me. We'll do everything we can to find your son. I promise." She reached down to touch Christine's hand again, but she seemed to be gone, sucked back into the silent world of her TV show. West was about to pull her hand away, but then something happened. With a speed that seemed impossible given the woman's condition, she suddenly twisted violently in her chair. She grabbed West by the arm, nearly pulling her off the chair she was sitting on, and before Dr. Richards could react, she thrust her mouth up against West's ear.

"Tell him I'm sorry," she said, in a low, rasping voice. "Tell him for me. Tell him I'm sorry."

West was startled. She had one knee on the floor where Christine had pulled her down. She saw Dr. Richards was moving toward them, clear alarm on his face.

There was just time for Christine to spit a few more words into West's ear before Dr. Richards reached her shoulder and pulled her sharply away.

"Chrissy," he hissed. Then when he'd separated the two women, and Christine had gone back into her passive state, he apologized to West.

"I'm so sorry, Detective. She doesn't normally do that. Are you OK?"

West was still kneeling on the floor. She looked at Christine, now back to watching the TV, nodding slightly to the tune in her head as if nothing had happened.

"I'm fine. It's fine," she said, getting to her feet. She stared at Chrissy, wanting to ask her what she had just whispered into her ear. But something stopped her. The doctor's presence stopped her.

"I do think we should leave Christine now. She's clearly tired," Dr. Richards said, and this time West didn't argue. The doctor lead them away. He continued to talk all the way back down the corridor, and it was only when she'd left the hospital that West realized she hadn't given her card to the doctor. When Christine had lunged at her, it must have fallen onto the floor.

SIXTY-FOUR

THERE WAS no helicopter flight back to Lornea Island for Detective West. Instead, she caught the ferry for the final leg of her journey. She texted Rogers from the boat, and he was there to pick her up.

He talked the whole way back to the police station, explaining the detailed searches of the empty self-catering apartments that Stone might have access to, the discovery of the boy's treehouse, in the woods set back from the Littlelea beach parking lot, with its camouflaged sides and its basic camping equipment. But ultimately, the failure to locate Stone.

"There's something we're missing," he said when he was finished. "Some connection we're not seeing yet. But we'll get him. We'll get the bastard."

West listened to him in silence, and now sat staring blankly out of the windshield.

"You OK?" Rogers asked.

She shook her head as if he'd woken her from a trance.

"Yeah. Yeah, I am. Just tired."

"Long flight, huh?"

"Long everything."

"So how about you? You find out anything useful out there? Anything that might help us find him?"

She answered slowly.

"I'm not sure. At first, I thought maybe the chief only sent me out there because he wanted me out of the way for a while."

"And? What do you think now?"

"I still think that. But one strange thing happened."

"What's that?" Rogers asked, as he swung the car into the police station's parking lot. He took the corner too fast and had to brake sharply to avoid a patrolman who was walking to a car. The patrolman was near retirement, a man in his sixties. He walked around to the open driver's window and called in with mock seriousness.

"Don't think I can't book you for dangerous driving just because of your shiny detective badge." He laughed at his own joke.

"I'm just testing your reflexes Bill. Get you ready for your next medical," Rogers shot back.

The patrolman noticed West and nodded at her stiffly. He backed away and Rogers edged the car forward into a space.

Rogers forgot to ask West what she found strange. She didn't bring it up again.

West reached the end of the office where her desk stood. She looked out of the window, at the familiar view of the parking lot and the back of the stores opposite. It was all as it had been before. Not surprising given that she'd only been gone a couple days. But it felt wrong somehow, as if the distance she'd traveled ought to be marked in some way.

On her desk was a note, telling her to report to Chief Collins when she got in. She found him talking with Lieutenant Langley, who stayed while she talked through who she had seen, but their focus was clearly on the local search for Stone. When she was done, Langley told her to help Rogers, who was checking through the boy's laptop computer. He did little to conceal his opinion that this was unlikely to produce anything of value, and went back to talking with the Chief. She left the office and found Rogers slouched back in his chair, his big hand toying with the mouse.

"What have we got, then?" she asked.

"Pull up a chair, Detective," Rogers said, sitting up straighter. "Pull up a chair."

She sat next to him, opened a fresh page in her notebook, and clicked her pen so it was ready to use. He raised his eyebrows at this.

"It's possible you're being a touch optimistic," he said. "It's a hell of a mess in here."

"How do you mean?"

"I mean, welcome to the inside of Billy Wheatley's head. Take a look around."

West leaned in toward the laptop screen; it was filled with folders. She took the mouse from Rogers and clicked a couple at random. They opened into new folders, each just as packed and chaotic as the last.

"Wow. He's got a lot of stuff in here," she said.

"Yeah. So here's the story. The kid's laptop was found in his bedroom. At first, no one could get into it because it's got a password set up. So we give it to the IT boys. No problem, they go in via a different route, or whatever they do, disable the password - I dunno. But what they can't do is restore any order. It's just a mess of files, random names, pretty random content too. Check this out." He clicked back a few times and opened a file named "Weather Sensor." A screen of thumbnail images popped up.

"What are they?" West squinted at the screen.

"They. . . " Rogers smiled and opened one. "Are hermit crabs painted with fluorescent paint." He watched her face, then laughed as she turned to him, her face screwed up in confusion.

"It's some experiment he was doing. Don't ask me. There's tons of this kind of stuff, though. He's like some schizophrenic version of Charles fucking Darwin."

"Is any of it relevant?"

"That's what I'm trying to figure out. I don't think so is as far as I've got. I did find this, though." This time, Rogers pointed to a printout on the desk. It was headed:

INVESTIGATION INTO THE OLIVIA CURRAN ~~MYSTERY~~/MURDER

Below these words was a summary of what happened to Olivia. Mostly, it looked lifted from the internet.

"What's this?"

"He was running an investigation, or trying to. He had this in a folder about limpets."

West looked at him questioningly.

"They're little triangle things that cling to rocks."

"I know what a limpet is. I just don't see the connection."

"Neither do I. The boy's nuts; I told you. And I'm not finished yet. Then there's these." He turned back to the laptop and clicked open a new folder.

"I think you'll enjoy this, Detective," he said.

The new folder opened to show six more folders, and when Rogers opened the first of those, it showed a long list of video clips. Rogers clicked one at random, a file called 00013_07_07_16 12:34. The little laptop ground its gears for a while. Then a video player box appeared.

"Here we go," Rogers said.

The image was of a small clearing in a wood. The horizon was unsteady, and there were drops of water on the lens, which made it confusing to see what was going on at first. But then a small red fox wandered into the frame, and sat on the ground in front of the camera. It began to scratch itself with its hind leg. When it was finished, it looked around casually, and eventually, it got up and walked on, this time out of the other side of the screen. The image didn't change at all for thirty seconds. Then the clip ended.

"What the hell?" West asked.

"Hey, that's a cool one," Rogers said. "I like that." He clicked another one. It opened to show the exact same forest clearing, but this time, a black rook was hopping through the frame.

"It's his wildlife camera files," Rogers said. "I kind of wondered after we'd interviewed him why he had that camera-trap thing. Well, this is why. This is what he did with them when he wasn't spying on people. He spies on animals."

"Have you watched them all?"

"Christ, no. There's far too many. Thousands. Tens of thousands, maybe. He's pretty into it."

He quickly clicked back through to the desktop. "I found the files from where he was spying on Philip Foster in a different folder. I guess he watched all of those. Fucking loony."

Rogers clicked away and opened another folder. He scrolled right down to the bottom and opened the last file. It showed the front of Philip Foster's house, with a patrolman in the foreground. He appeared to notice the camera and then leaned in close until his face filled the screen. Rogers laughed. "The moment we found the camera." He closed the file so there was just the folder visible. "Say, what were you saying outside? Something strange happened..?"

West found herself distracted and didn't answer. Something about the files had occurred to her, but she couldn't tell what.

"So what was it? The strange thing?" Rogers prompted.

She shook her head to clear the half-thought. She tried to focus properly.

"It's something the kid's mom said."

"The mom? You said she was a wacko too. PTSD? Never recovered from the attack?"

"I didn't say she was a wacko."

Rogers lifted his hands from the desk in mock apology. He waited for her to go on, but West didn't say anything.

"Well, what'd she say?"

West made a face.

"I'm not sure. It was a strange thing. She seemed to want to say it without her doctor hearing. She kind of whispered it, right in my ear."

"Whispered what?"

"I'm not sure; I didn't hear it clearly. But it might have been: *don't trust them*."

"Don't trust them?"

"Yeah."

"Don't trust who?"

"I don't know." West shrugged. "I've been wondering that all the way back. But then I'm not even sure that I heard right. It could have been something else." West let her eyes rest on the screen. There was something about that folder that bothered her. Something she still couldn't place.

"You said she was in a state, drugged up and whatever. It's probably nothing."

"I know."

"I mean, you're not seriously questioning the case out there, are you? We've all read it; it's watertight. Two eyewitnesses who knew him. Stone fleeing like he did. And now what he's done here too. . . "

West didn't answer.

"Come on Jess, don't find problems where they don't exist. That's the first rule of detective work."

"No, I'm not doubting it," West's voice was tight and she heard herself sounding uptight. She softened it before she went on. "It just affected me, I think. To see how much damage you can do to someone with a single crazy act. She's my age, Christine Austin. But she looks twice that. And they say she'll never recover. It just makes it seem more real, actually seeing her like that." West paused and looked at Rogers, as if searching for something in his face, a sign that he understood. But he looked away.

"Yeah, well. It makes it all the more important that we catch the son-of-a-bitch."

West was silent.

"Jess? You hearing me?"

"Shit. Ollie, give me the mouse," West said.

"What? What is it?"

"Just give it to me."

SIXTY-FIVE

SILENTLY, Rogers did what West asked. She leaned in closer to the little screen, clicking as she went.

"There."

"What?"

"Look at that column there." Her finger pointed at the two files they'd just played.

"What?"

"It gives the date it was last accessed. Today."

"So?"

"Well, look at all the others."

Rogers looked. After a while, he turned back to her.

"I don't get it."

"They're all the same. All the same dates. Same times too."

"OK. I can see that, but so what?"

"Well, either he looked at each and every one of these files on the exact same time and day he downloaded them off the camera - which is impossible - or more likely, just like you, Billy hasn't watched these files."

Rogers sat back in his chair and tapped his fingers on the edge of the desk, his eyes narrowed in thought.

"OK. But so what?"

West hesitated now.

"I'm just wondering if he had any of these camera traps set up on the night Olivia Curran went missing."

Rogers turned to look at her, then burst out laughing.

"Jesus, Jess, I've heard of long shots, but that's ridiculous."

"Why? These are *hidden* camera traps, set up around the town. Why wouldn't he catch something?"

"Because. . . Well, I don't know. But how do we check anyway?"

"Well, that's easy enough. They've all got the date and time on them."

It ended up being harder than West said. It took them two hours to understand that Billy had four cameras, two which worked in daytime only, and two which also recorded in infrared. Between them, he'd collected and saved tens of thousands of video clips. The vast majority were apparently unwatched. They also ascertained that two of his cameras were deployed and recording on the night the teenager went missing. They created a new folder and copied all the clips from that night. Then they arranged them in chronological order starting with those captured around the last time Olivia was seen alive.

"So. Detective," Rogers said when they were finally finished. "Are you ready for this?" He rubbed his hands together.

"Shut up Ollie," West replied. "We've been looking for a needle in a haystack for the last three months. We've got to find it sooner or later."

He raised his eyebrows and grinned at her.

"Just play the damn files."

The first dozen clips showed nothing of interest at all, perhaps the wind had moved vegetation to trigger the camera. The thirteenth clip showed a small mouse-like creature. Rogers spent some time debating whether it was a mouse or a vole. West ignored him. Then the next clip began.

The view the camera had recorded showed a scrubby open-heathland setting; the camera appeared to be fixed by a vague pathway - the sort of track made and used by animals as much as humans. West suddenly realized she could place it.

"This is somewhere around the Silverlea Lodge Hotel, isn't it?" she said. "I recognize the landscape." But Rogers didn't answer, because at that moment, a figure entered the frame.

It was a male, young - late teens or early twenties - and he was stumbling along the path. Then he stopped, put his hands to his mouth, shouted something, looked around for a moment, and then carried on. He looked drunk. The time of the clip was 12:47a.m.

The two detectives watched until the clip stopped. When it had finished Rogers immediately clicked to play it again.

"What's he saying?" West asked.

Since the only sound up to then had been wind noise, they'd had the sound turned down low. Rogers found the laptop's volume control and increased it. Then he replayed the clip for a third time. Again, the figure stumbled into frame, looked around, and put his hands to his mouth. This time, they heard what he said, a loud call:

"Where are you?"

"I know who that is," Rogers said.

West looked at him in surprise. "Who?"

"It's Daniel Hodges. He works at the Surf Lifesaving Club in Silverlea. Some people thought he'd shown an interest in Curran before she went missing."

"What's he doing?"

"I'd say he's looking for someone."

"Who?" West asked the question automatically, but she wasn't surprised that Rogers didn't answer. He turned to his own computer and typed the man's name in the investigation database. Quickly, he pulled up the statement that had been taken from Hodges in the days after Curran went missing. They read it together quickly on screen.

"He says he was at the disco all night, then went to the party on Princes Street."

"No mention of going wandering around the heath, looking for someone?"

"No."

"Then what's he hiding?" West asked. "We gotta go see him. Find out who he's looking for."

"We'd better get Langley first," Rogers said.

West made a face. "Really?"

Rogers shrugged. "It's his investigation."

* * *

Soon, there were four detectives crowding around Billy's laptop, viewing the clip over and over again.

"How about the other clips?" Langley asked after a while. "There anything else to see?"

"No. Just this one. You make anything of it?"

Langley thought for a long moment, then shook his head.

"I don't see that it changes anything. We've got Stone, a fugitive with at least one previous murder on his record, plus he's got Curran's blood in the back of his truck. So what if this guy was running around drunk?" He shook his head. "I don't think it's anything." He stood up from where he'd been leaning in to see the screen.

West felt a burst of irritation. She opened her mouth to argue, but then stopped herself.

"You mind if we go check it out anyway?" she asked, keeping her voice calm. "At least find out who he was looking for? It might tie in somehow."

Langley looked at her for a moment like he suspected some sort of trick. He shrugged.

"Be my guest."

West glanced at Rogers and grabbed her coat.

SIXTY-SIX

THEY FOUND him in the first place they looked, the Silverlea Surf Lifesaving Club. He was dressed in a one-piece blue overall, pulled down to his waist to reveal a sleeveless white vest and the arms of someone who worked out. It was cold inside, with the door open and a cold breeze blowing off the sea. He stood at a workbench, attaching a buoy to a shiny new shackle that was wedged in a vice.

"Daniel Hodges?" Rogers said.

He looked up, his brows knitted together. "Yeah?"

"I'm Detective Oliver Rogers, and this is Detective Jessica West. We're investigating the murder of Olivia Curran." They both flipped open their badges. Hodges didn't move, but his eyes widened.

"I already spoke to the police. When she went missing."

They both ignored him, but Rogers went on.

"The door was open; I hope you don't mind us just walking in?" From his voice it was clear he didn't care whether Hodges minded or not. West watched the young man's face carefully as her partner spoke. She noticed a look sweep over his features. It could have just been irritation at Rogers' manner, the normal reaction anyone would have to the words 'detective' and 'murder'. But it looked like something more.

Hodges shrugged unconvincingly. "Whatever. What do you want?"

"I wonder if we might ask you some questions."

Hodges put down the large wrench he was holding and wiped his hands on a rag.

"What about?"

"What are you doing?" Rogers asked suddenly, pointing at the buoy.

Dan Hodges looked at him warily, as if he couldn't understand why the police would want to know this.

"They mark the bathing zones. We take them in for the winter. I'm servicing them." He pointed over at the wall, where a row of similar buoys lay with their chains laid out.

Rogers stepped forward as if this was something of interest to him. West hung back, still watching Hodges' face.

"So what's this about?" Hodges asked again. "I gave a statement when that girl went missing. I said I didn't know anything about it. Anyway, I thought you'd found the guy you wanted? Sam Wheatley? It's all over the news."

"You're a friend of Sam Wheatley, aren't you? You wouldn't know where he was, by any chance?"

"No." Hodges seemed to recoil at the thought of this. "And we're not friends. I just see him around. I never liked the guy."

"Oh, really?" Rogers said quickly. "Why's that?"

Hodges seemed to sense he'd made some kind of mistake. He hesitated but then fudged an answer.

"I dunno. He's just. . . He's kinda weird. Too quiet. Like he's always judging you but never coming out and saying it."

The two detectives exchanged glances. For West it confirmed her partner was getting the same bad feeling she'd had since she walked in here. It seemed to rattle Hodges more. Rodgers didn't back off.

"What do you mean exactly?"

Hodges looked more uncomfortable. "He's kind of full of himself. Thinks he's God's gift just because he wins a few surf competitions."

"You ever fought with him?"

"*Fought?* No."

"You ever argued?"

"No. . . "

"Why not. Are you scared of him?" Rogers leaned in close to Hodges.

"No, I'm not scared of him. . . I just, I mean we just kinda keep away from each other."

"You sure about that? I mean you're clearly in good shape." Roger's nodded at Hodges' bare arms, "but then Wheatley looks like he can take care of himself too."

"No, look you've got the wrong idea. I hardly know the guy. It's just from what I've seen, he looks the type that's capable of doing something like this."

There was near silence, just the sound of Hodges breathing too fast, and the whistle from the wind outside. Rogers - who was nearest the workbench - reached out and ran his finger down the upper surface of the buoy, where it was faded by the sunlight. Then he continued past the clearly defined waterline to where it was coated with a film of dark green seaweed. He pulled his hand back and inspected the surface of his finger, turned slightly green from the algae. Hodges watched him in silence.

"You can't always tell from how people look on the surface, what's hidden underneath." Rogers said, apparently suddenly fascinated with the algae. Then he looked at West, and held up his finger to show her too. She took it as her cue and stepped forward.

Even though, she felt nervous as she pulled a notebook from her jacket pocket. She sensed the importance of this moment. She flicked her notebook open to gain a few seconds thinking time. She riffled through a few pages.

"Mr. Hodges," she began, her voice neutral but feeling the tension underneath. "In your statement, you said you spent the night of August twenty-ninth here, at the club disco, and then went on to Princes Street for the after-party. Is that right?"

He nodded.

"You made no mention of going anywhere else."

"No."

"But you did go somewhere else, didn't you?"

She looked up at him, as if she were simply checking a fact they were all aware of. Hodges' face was white. She didn't give him any time to reply, but carried straight on.

"Daniel, when you gave this statement, we were dealing with a missing person inquiry. It's now a murder investigation. You're aware of that, aren't you? You understand how much more serious that makes it if you lie to the police?"

"I didn't lie. I didn't go anywhere else. I don't know what you're talking about," Hodges said, his voice thick and deliberate. He had his feet planted squarely apart, and for some reason, he picked up the wrench he'd been using again. It was a heavy, oversized tool, painted red and well-worn. He seemed to realize at once how this must look, and he quickly set it back down again. But if he hoped West hadn't noticed, he was wrong. She hadn't planned to do what she did next, but something about his eyes, so clearly full of panic, made her take a risk.

"Mr. Hodges, you also stated you didn't know who Olivia Curran was. That you had never spoken to her. That wasn't true either, was it?"

Hodges' answer to this was hard to hear, a sort of grunted denial. West ignored it.

"You see, the problem is, Mr. Hodges, we have a videotape of you and Olivia Curran going off together, around midnight. Up toward Northend."

She sensed rather than saw Rogers swinging around to stare at her, but she didn't take her eyes off Hodges' face. She didn't know why the lie had come to her, but she knew right away it was right. His eyes widened, then flicked to the left, toward the door. For a crazy second she thought he was actually going to run for it. His mouth dropped open. He swallowed.

"How?" He said.

West fought hard to keep her face neutral. It felt like the floor was dropping out from underneath her. She heard her voice reply.

"A hidden, infrared wildlife-camera captured you both. It recorded the time and your exact coordinates. Very unlucky on your part." She offered him a sympathetic smile, more confident now with every passing moment.

"What happened, Dan? Did you have a fight? Did she do something to make you angry? Was it an accident?"

"No. *No*." Hodges put his hands to his hair and let them fall slowly down his face, scraping on the stubble he wore on his chin. For a long moment, he just stared at West.

"You don't understand. It wasn't me. It wasn't. I didn't do anything to her. You gotta believe me." He looked around the room. Piled up against the far wall were stacks of blue plastic chairs.

"I need to sit down," Hodges said, and West nodded. Silently, Rogers stepped across and got them all chairs, placing them in the center of the room. He managed to catch West's attention as he did so, his eyes full of questions.

Hodges sat down and leaned forward, his hands on his knees, arm muscles bulging. Forehead creased in concern.

"You *were* with her? With Olivia. That night?" West asked.

Daniel Hodges swallowed again. He looked past the two detectives at the open door and the sea beyond it. He ran a hand through his hair again.

"Look, I couldn't say anything. My girlfriend would have found out. She gets crazy jealous, even when it's nothing. Something like this she'd probably kill me." He laughed a little, like this was an attempt to lighten the mood. But then he seemed to regret it. "That was stupid, I know. But at first, no one really believed anything serious had happened to Olivia. People thought she'd just run off. Like teenagers do sometimes. And once everyone knew it was serious, it was too late. If I'd have said something then people would have suspected me. And I didn't do anything. I swear to God. I didn't do a thing."

"What were you doing with Olivia Curran that night?"

Hodges sat there breathing hard for a long time. Eventually, he spoke.

"Look, she and her friends had spent the whole week sunbathing down by the lifeguard tower. And she'd been giving me the eye." He glanced across at Rogers. "You know what I mean?" Rogers just stared at him. Hodges looked away.

"Well, that night, she was doing it again. Looking across at me. It was obvious what she wanted."

"What did she want, Daniel?" West asked.

He looked at her, still breathing hard.

"She said she wanted some air. So I took her out on the beach."

"Did she resist?"

"*No*. No. It was *her* idea. Look, I swear to you, it wasn't like that." He shook his head, frustrated. "When she said *air*, she was. . . up for it. She had *condoms* and everything." He said the word quietly, then stopped and stared up at the ceiling.

"There were quite a few people hanging around outside that night, so I said we should go up the beach towards Northend. You can go in the dunes up there. . . " He stopped, suddenly aware of how this might sound.

"Not that, I don't. . . I don't do this all the time, just. . . Sometimes."

"Then what happened?"

Hodges was breathing so hard now it was as if he'd been running.

"We were making out on the beach; we were lying down on the sand. Then she said she needed to go do something. At the time, I thought she meant she needed the bathroom. So she went up into the dunes - and that's it. She disappeared. I figured she'd changed her mind. Went back to the party, I don't know. It said on the TV she had a boyfriend back home. I figured in the end, she must have felt guilty."

"So what did you do? When she didn't come back?" Rogers asked.

"I waited a while. Then I went looking for her. But when it was obvious she'd gone, I went back."

Rogers and West exchanged questioning glances. Rogers turned back to him.

"And you didn't think it was important to tell any of this to the police?" Rogers said. "Even after her *severed arm* was found?" He stared at Hodges. West could hear the anger in his voice.

Hodges turned to face Rogers. "I'm sorry, man. Like I said, I was scared. I was scared half to death. But I don't know anything. You gotta believe me."

There was a long pause during which no one spoke. Hodges broke it.

"So what happens now? You guys gonna have to arrest me or what?" He looked around, as if he was worried about who was going to close up the club. West was recording what he'd said in her notebook.

"You say you didn't come forward at first because you were worried about your girlfriend finding out?"

"Yeah."

"What's her name?"

Hodges didn't answer at first. He stared at West.

"Does she really have to know about this?"

"I'd say your girlfriend knowing about this is a very, very long way down your list of problems."

Hodges continued to stare for a moment, but then he looked away.

"Emily. Emily Franklin." He buried his head in his hands.

* * *

"You took a hell of a risk there, Detective," Rogers said when Hodges was out of earshot. He'd asked to be allowed to get changed before they took him into the station. Rogers had checked the changing room carefully before agreeing, and now they stood outside - the only possible exit - waiting for him.

"I don't know," West said, her eyes still wide from the shock of what they'd heard. "You were pushing him pretty strong. His reaction just seemed wrong."

"Well, it worked," Rogers said. She didn't know if he meant his approach or hers.

"So you believe him?" she asked a moment later. She knew they didn't have long to talk together before he would be back, able to hear them again.

"I don't know. You?"

She shrugged. "The thing I don't get: If Hodges killed Curran, how does her blood and hair get in the back of Stone's pickup?"

Rogers frowned in thought, but shook his head.

"I don't know. There's something else that's strange too."

"What's that?"

"*Emily Franklin*. I recognized the name. The kid, Billy, there's a whole chain of emails between him and her on his computer. It's like they're friends."

"Why's that strange?"

"Apart from the age difference? Because she knew about his crazy-ass investigation into Philip Foster. He sent her updates. And she didn't exactly dissuade him from it either. I'd say she egged him on."

They both thought for a moment.

"You know what's gonna happen?" West said a few seconds later. She said it before she'd really thought about it.

"We're gonna take Hodges in, and Langley's gonna take over. He'll say thank you very much, take all the credit and we'll be back to tidying up the damn station." She could see in his eyes that he agreed with this, but he looked uncomfortable.

"So what're you saying?"

"Just that. . . that we've gotten this far. Let's dig a little bit more."

Rogers glanced at the changing room door. They could hear footsteps behind it; Hodges was changed and coming out.

"Franklin lives a street away from here. I looked her up earlier. You want me to wait here with Hodges while you go talk to her?" he said quickly. Then the door opened, and Hodges stepped out, this time dressed in jeans and a worn wool-sweater.

West thought for a moment. Then nodded. Rogers acknowledged her with a scowl.

"Right. Change of plan, Dan! You and I are going to wait here till a squad car picks us up." Rogers checked his notebook and found the address for Emily's house. He scribbled it on an empty page, then ripped it out and handed it to West.

"This is gonna piss Langley off," he said, raising his eyebrows.

SIXTY-SEVEN

When I wake the next day, I don't know where I am. I have this weird feeling that something's not right, and then I remember that everything's not right, and I wish I was still asleep.

There's a knock on the door. Emily opens it and asks if she can come in. She's got a cup of hot chocolate in her hand. She smiles at me and asks how I am, then sets it down on the bedside table and sits on my bed. It's the same hot chocolate as the other night, so I can't drink it.

We have breakfast, sitting around the table in the kitchen again. But this time, we all sit in silence. Dad's in a really bad mood, and although I've still got lots of questions, I'm too scared to ask them. Then Dad tells me to go back to my room. He says I'm not allowed to go into the living room in case someone looks in from the street - he thinks it would look strange to leave the drapes closed. I think it's because he doesn't want me to watch TV, though. I saw him watching something on the news, but he turned it off when I came in. So I sit in my room. Only it's not my room, it's Emily's dead grandma's room. There's a stack of old *National Geographic* magazines in there, the ones with the yellow covers. They're really old; they go right back to 2005. Eventually, since there's nothing else I can do, I sit and read through them.

I make three piles of the magazines. The first is ones I haven't looked through; the second is ones I've skimmed through, and there's an interesting article I want to read. The third is ones where I've read all the interesting articles. There's a couple of good ones, something about lobsters and how they go to deeper water when a storm approaches. They line up in little columns, each one searching for the lobster in front of it with its feelers. I don't know how the one in front knows where to go.

Even so, it feels like the day really drags. A couple of times, I leave the room, but both times, Dad tells me to go back. He's really worried about anyone seeing me from the road. Him and Emily spend the whole day in the kitchen, talking, sometimes really loudly, but not clear enough for me to hear. We have takeout later on. I eat it in my room.

The next day is pretty much the same, apart from Dad going out. I don't know where he goes. He borrows a baseball cap and sunglasses from Emily, and he goes in her car. Emily tells him to be careful, and he just looks at her, but I can't tell how he looks because of the sunglasses. When he goes, he locks the door from the outside. I ask Emily if I can watch TV. She says no at first, but then she lets me. We watch it for a bit, until the news comes on. And Dad's the first story. There's a picture of our pick-up being loaded onto the ferry, on the back of a big, flat-bed truck. You can't see it properly because it's under a tarp, and the newsreader says it's going to a laboratory on the mainland because Olivia Curran's DNA was found in the back. I want to watch more but Emily turns it off. Then she comes to sit with me in my room and read *National Geographic*. I try to ask her what's going on, and where Dad's gone, but she won't tell me. Instead, she just says how when she was a girl, she used to come and visit her gran, and she would look forward to the latest issue of *National Geographic,* and how it got her interested in marine biology. Normally, I'd be interested in stuff like that, but I don't really care at the moment.

Dad comes back about four. He and Emily disappear into the kitchen to talk where I can't hear, and they stay like that until it gets dark. Then they come out, and Emily shuts the drapes in the living room. We eat dinner in front of the TV, but Dad won't let us watch the news. We watch sitcoms instead.

We're all sitting there, just the noise of canned laughter and the clattering of our forks against the plates, when Dad suddenly starts talking. It's been so long since anyone really spoke to me that I'm surprised.

"We can't stay here. You know that, don't you, Billy?"

I jerk my head up, then look back down at my dinner. I'm not ready to talk. I go on eating like I didn't hear.

"I said we can't stay here, Billy." He picks up the remote control and turns the volume right down. I look at him, and he just watches me carefully.

"At Emily's?" I say.

"Here. On Lornea Island. We can't stay. We've got to get away."

I wonder about asking why, but I don't really want to think about all that again. It doesn't feel nice to think about it. I nod instead.

"I know."

"Emily and I have come up with a plan. I need to tell you about it," Dad says.

I can feel my heart start beating real fast. I don't want to talk about it. I want to go to bed.

"It's going to be a big change for us. But we can make it work. It's a good plan."

I don't say anything to this. I want to look back at the TV, but I feel this might make him mad. Eventually, he continues.

"I'm sure you know that Emily is going off on this research ship this week. She's going down to the coast of Central America. Did you know that, Billy?"

"Yeah," I say. "She's looking at the venom in jellyfish there, and why some fish survive and some don't."

"Yeah, I guess so. Well, Billy, how'd you like to go with her?"

I don't know if it really does, but it feels like my mouth drops right open.

"What?" My mind races. Like, as a scientist? How would that be possible? What about the police? What about *Dad*?

"The ship docks here on the island Thursday night. Emily reckons it'll be easy enough to get aboard. Then she's got her own cabin, so we'll stay in there. We'll keep hidden. She'll make sure we get plenty of food and water. It'll be fun. Like going on a cruise." Dad smiles at the thought.

"Then what?"

Dad stops smiling. He takes a deep breath in, then holds it for a long time.

"Well, Emily thinks there are plenty of smaller places where it'll be easy to get off again, maybe in Mexico, maybe Venezuela. We'll sneak off the ship. Then we'll find somewhere nice where we can be safe. We'll start over."

I blink at him. "But what about school?"

He holds up a hand. "We'll find you another one. I'll get some work. We'll find a nice little place somewhere." He gives me another smile. "Billy, I had a little stash. Some cash, some other bits and pieces, hidden out in the woods. That's where I went today, to dig it up. My emergency stash. That'll see us through for a few months. Long enough to find somewhere nice. Somewhere we can start again."

"But they speak *Spanish* in Venezuela! I don't speak Spanish."

I look over at Emily. "Are you coming?" I ask. I feel a little angry. I get the sense this is her idea. She hesitates.

"The idea is that I come back and try to help from here. You and your dad will be somewhere safe, where the police can't bring him back easily. But I'll be working with lawyers and things, helping them to understand how they've made a terrible mistake."

"How long will that take? How long will we have to stay there?" I turn back to Dad.

Dad takes a very long time to answer this.

"Not forever, kid," he says finally.

SIXTY-EIGHT

I LIE in bed thinking for a long time. I'm going to live in South America. That one fact just keeps pressing into my mind, crowding out everything else. I try to imagine what South America is actually like. Ironically, there were lots of articles in *National Geographic* from South America; it all looks like rain forest and people living in little huts. Little brown children in a classroom with an old-fashioned blackboard and no glass in the windows. Actually, that might have been Africa, but really, what's the difference?

I close my eyes and try to imagine what it might be like. Me and Dad living in a hut somewhere. Just outside the front door, we'd have the beach - fine, white sand - then a wide bay of turquoise water, so warm you can be in bare feet all year round, and protected by a coral reef offshore. I can almost see the hut: bamboo roof, a balcony with a hammock. Shaded by coconut palms that I climb every morning to get breakfast. There'll be a village nearby, but I won't go to school there. If Dad can get away with whatever he's done, there's no way he can make me go to school. Instead, I'll do my research. But this time, it'll be really important research. I'll do something on turtles. We'll be on the kind of beach where they bury their eggs. I'll tag them; maybe I'll paint their shells with the ultraviolet paint. I'll still have email and the Internet and everything. Maybe visiting scientists will come and stay with me. They'll sit on the balcony in the evenings and listen to how it all began with hermit crabs in the silver rockpools of Lornea Island.

But I can't hold the daydream in my mind. It's like a bike tire with a slow puncture. Reality keeps piercing it so it deflates, and I have to try and blow it up again. I can't make it stay feeling real. I try to build from what I know. Emily's research ship, the *Marianne Dupont*. I've seen tons of pictures aboard there. Both official ones from the websites and the ones Emily's taken on her trips. Whatever happens, I'm going to go on the *Marianne Dupont*. I know I'll have to stay in her room, and I won't be able to see all the science happening and everything, but that's something, isn't it? Through the whirlwind in my head, I'm able to make myself a little bit excited about that. I try to hold that in my mind as I fall asleep.

I guess I must doze off for a while because something wakes me up and brings me right back into the room. I don't know what the time is, but then there's a sharp click, and I see the door opening, light from the hallway leaking in. I see Dad peering in at me. Quickly, I pretend to be asleep. A moment later, he pulls the door softly closed again. But the latch doesn't work very well, and once he's gone, the door stays open.

The bungalow is all on one floor, so Emily's room is next door. And for a while, I lie there, listening to the soft sounds of them going to bed. My thoughts about South America are still fresh in my mind; it's nice to let the images play in my head. Just to lie there, not really thinking at all. Then the hallway light clicks off, and the bungalow goes dark. I turn over and try to go back to sleep. But now that I'm awake, I can't. The sound of Emily's grandmother's house is so different from our house. There's some light still, from streetlights outside, I guess. We don't have those. At home, if there's clouds and you can't see the stars or the moon, it's just pitch-black.

And I can hear murmured voices, too, coming from next door. Dad and Emily. I kind of expect them to go quiet in a minute, but they don't. I try to go to sleep anyway, but I've kind of got myself awake now. I wonder if going to get a glass of water might help. I do that sometimes at home.

I try to just forget about it, but once I've got the idea in my head, it becomes all I can think of. I'm not really thirsty, but on the other hand, I haven't really drunk much all day. I know I'll just sleep badly if I don't get up. For a long time, I try and resist it and go to sleep, but eventually, I give up. I push the covers off and pad to the door. I push it open and step out into the quiet of the hall.

Only it's not that quiet. For some reason, they've left the door open to Emily's room, pushed to, but not closed. And I can hear them still talking. There's still a glow of light coming from the door. I don't mean to listen. It's just I have to go past their door to get to the bathroom.

"You've gotta tell him sooner or later." It's Emily's voice, soft and concerned. "I don't understand why he isn't demanding to know more now. I guess he's just. . . overwhelmed by it all," she says. I freeze.

"He's scared, I guess." That's Dad's voice, lower, gruffer. "Scared of what he thinks he might find out."

"That's why you've got to tell him, Sam. He'll understand. That's why you've got to tell him the truth."

I can't hear Dad's reply, just the low murmur of his voice. Then Emily replying. I realize I've crept right up to their door now; I'm still out of sight behind it, just listening, struggling to hear what they're saying.

"Alright. Alright. He's your son. You know him best," Emily says. Then there are more noises, like the covers moving.

"God, you're tense." Emily gives a half laugh. "Come here."

I half-turn to go onto the bathroom, but I don't move away from the door. I realize I can see though the crack between the door and the frame. They've still got a light on, Dad's bedside light. I can see them both in bed. Dad's sitting up, staring at the ceiling. Emily's lying beside him, in a T-shirt like the one she lent me; she's rubbing his shoulders.

"Em, no. I don't think I can tonight," I hear Dad say, but she doesn't stop.

"Come on, Sam. When am I going to get another chance?"

Then, to my surprise, she stops what she's doing, reaches down, and pulls her T-shirt up and off over her head. For a stunning second or two, I can see *everything*. I have to slap my hand over my mouth to stop myself gasping out loud.

I've seen boobs before; on the beach in the summer, sometimes, girls take their bikini tops off when they're sunbathing in the dunes. But they're not supposed to do it, so they always go a long way away to do it. You're not supposed to look either, but sometimes, you can't really help it, can you? One time, I was birdwatching, and I had my binoculars, and this woman was sunbathing very close. I looked at her for a long time, but in the end, I felt dirty, so I stopped. And anyway, that woman was lying on her back, so it was kind of hard to make out where her boob started and the rest of her stopped.

Emily's boobs are really white, except for the middle bits that are pink and sticking out. They're swaying from side to side. I only see them for a few seconds then she leans in close to him, pushing herself against his back. She puts her arms around him, slides them down his belly.

"Em, not tonight, come on," Dad says.

I'm still shocked. I've just seen Emily's boobs. I've heard Dad's surfer friends saying she's got nice boobs. Though they call them tits, but I don't like that word. I realize I'm holding my breath. I try to remember what they looked like. Like white wobbly coconuts. I force myself to breathe.

"Em, no. Come on," Dad says again, a bit more forcefully this time. I'm staring through the crack now, my face pressed up against the doorjamb. Emily rolls on top of him now. I can see her long hair falling over both their faces. Then, with one hand, she reaches behind her and pulls the covers looser.

"Come on, Sam." Her voice has changed now; it's gone deeper. Breathy. Then she lets out a big sigh.

"I've missed you, Sam Wheatley," she says. Then she reaches out again, and this time, she turns the light off, and everything goes black. I still don't move, and all I hear is the sound of them moving on the bed, the mattress creaking a little bit.

I'm not an idiot. I know what's happening. I know what they're going to do. Everyone talks about it at school. We've even done lessons on it, although the teacher was so embarrassed he just handed out worksheets and pretended to mark homework while we filled them in. And obviously, animals do it all the time; otherwise, they wouldn't be there, would they? I know *what* they're doing, and I know I shouldn't watch. I should just get my drink and go back to bed. But now, my eyes are adjusting to the darkness. Emily's room looks out on the yard, so there's no streetlights, but the moon is really bright. As I watch, Emily rolls off Dad so she's lying on her back; then she arches herself up and pushes her underwear down and kicks them off her feet. Her limbs glow almost white in the gloom, but there's a darkness where they meet her stomach. There's hair. I catch my breath when I see it.

Then she does the same to Dad, laughing as his shorts get stuck. I have to look away when I see it. He's never tried to hide anything when he's getting changed, but it looks totally different now. Horrible. Huge. Then Emily does something disgusting: it looks like she's going to put it in her mouth. I can't look at that. I have to look away.

When I look back, he's lying on top of her, and I can hear him panting. Fast and short. I can see him going up and down; it almost looks funny. I can't see much of Emily, just her legs, stretched apart and wobbling in the darkness. I know I really can't watch any more now, but as I'm about to move away at last, Dad starts jerking like he's in pain. I see Emily's hands scratching at his back.

And then I see something I hadn't noticed before. There's a mirror next to the bed, and in the reflection, I can look around Dad and actually see Emily's face. And in the half-light, I get the scariest feeling she's looking in the mirror. Not at Dad, not at herself, but looking right at me. I feel her eyes locked on mine, and as I watch, the tip of her tongue comes out, and she runs it around her lips. I'm frozen to the spot. Then she closes her eyes and starts twisting and writhing, like a fish when you pull it out of the water. Suddenly, she screams so loud that Dad stops and tries to get her to be quiet. I use the moment to run away, back to my room and back into my bed. I lie there in silence, still thirsty and panting and shaking. All I can see are her eyes in the mirror, staring at me. That tongue running around her lips. And with every breath I take, I can taste the warm summer flowers of her perfume embedded in my T-shirt.

SIXTY-NINE

The next day is Wednesday. It turns out to be the longest day of my whole life. Everything changes on Wednesday.

It starts badly enough. I'm really embarrassed as we eat breakfast; I can't even look at Emily or Dad, so I just stay quiet. But Dad's not talking much either. Emily is trying to be sweet like normal, but I won't look at her. Then her cellphone goes off, and instead of answering it in the kitchen, she takes it into the other room. She's gone for a long time, and we can hear her voice rise more than once during the conversation. When she comes back, it's obvious there's something wrong. She looks at me, like she wants me to go away, and she says to Dad,

"Sam, we've got a problem."

"What?"

"That was Dan."

Dad sighs. He looks at me, too, but he doesn't get up from the table. Do you remember I told you once that people sort of forget I'm there? It's why I thought I'd be a good detective. Well, that's kind of what happens now. Or maybe because they've told me the plan now, they think it's OK that I hear. Anyway, they keep talking even though I'm right here, listening to it all.

"What does he want?"

"He's wondering what's going on. He wants to see me."

"Well, just say you don't want to see him."

"Sam, I can't do that. I'm going away for five weeks. We planned to spend some time together before I go. I can't have a headache forever."

Dad looks annoyed.

"Well, go see him, then."

Emily shakes her head. "He wants to come here, Sam. You know what his place is like. . . " She says the next bit more quietly, "there's no *privacy* there."

Dad gets up now. He paces up and down the kitchen.

"Well, he can't come here, can he?" he says in the end. Emily just looks frustrated. She made coffee before I got up this morning. She sees Dad's cup is empty and fills it up again.

"Sam. . . " She stops. She looks sad. "Sam, I really want to help you, but I didn't ask you here. I'm risking everything to help you out. I'm risking going to prison. All because I believe you didn't do what they're saying you did. But you've got to help *me*. He's already suspicious." She stops suddenly and covers her face with her hands. I wonder if she's crying. She sits down at the table. I wonder if Dad is going to hug her or something, but instead he just stares out of the kitchen window.

"I'm sorry," he says. "Look. When can we get on the ship?"

Emily sniffs a little, but when she takes her hands away, there's no tears I can see.

"Tomorrow. They're getting into Goldhaven tomorrow lunchtime; then we sail Friday at nine a.m. We can drive to the port and sneak you on tomorrow night. There's no security, just a key to get into my cabin. And I can pick that up before."

Dad nods. "OK. So what about Dan?"

"He wants to come around today. I think he wants to spend the night."

There's a silence after she says this. I think about what I saw last night. I can't help but imagine Dan in place of Dad.

"OK," Dad says. "OK. Well, maybe we could go to one of the cottages. They're mostly empty this time of year."

"Yeah," Emily says, but her brow is furrowed as she says it. "Only. . . "

"Only what?"

"Well, it's just - well, you've seen the news. Don't you think they'll be keeping an eye on them? They know you keep keys to them." Emily's eyes are round like stones. She bites her lower lip, and Dad stares at her. Then he rubs his head, like he's got the beginnings of a headache.

"So you don't think that's a good idea?" he says, and holds up his hands. "So tell me what *is* a good idea, will you? Just tell me what you want us to do." It sounds like Dad is getting angry, but he seems angry with himself, like maybe because he's not thinking straight. Emily looks a bit shocked and shakes her head.

"We can't go home!" Dad rubs his head again, wincing. He does sometimes get headaches. He looks pretty ill. I wonder for a moment if sex does that to you?

Emily watches him for a while. Then it's like she remembers I'm there.

"Billy, you know the old mines up at Northend?"

I look up, surprised.

"Yeah?"

"Did you ever go right inside? Past where the tide gets to? You can get to the old bunk room. In the old days, it took a long time to get up and down the shafts, so they put living quarters down there. It's a little dark and dusty, but it's all still there. You could hide out there tonight and during the day tomorrow. Then, when it gets dark, we'll go to the ship."

Her words seem to hang in the room. It feels like my brain can't quite make the leap from the photographs of South America, and the *Marianne Dupont*, to how the old mines look, pitch-black and the floor covered with pools of water. I can see Dad's struggling with it too.

"The old mines?" I say. My voice sounds squeaky all of a sudden.

"Not where you've been doing your experiment, Billy. You keep going up the old shaft and you get to a room. It's dry. It's. . . " She stops.

"Look, Nan had a thing for candles." She gets up and opens the cupboard under the sink. She pulls out three packets of thick white candles, not the decorative kind. "Nan was always prepared for power outages. There's enough here to keep lights going for a few days. She's got battery lanterns too. And I've got sleeping bags. Camping gear."

Dad doesn't say anything. He looks like he's thinking. He takes another swig of his coffee, then looks at the cup, a puzzled expression on his face.

"Sam, you've been here for *three days*. You need to move. It's only a matter of time before the police show up. You need to get away. Think of Billy. What's going to happen to him?"

There's a long pause.

"What's going to happen to me?" I say.

Emily pushes her chair back so fast it makes a loud squeak on the floor. "Nothing, Billy. Nothing's going to happen to you. We're going to get you on that ship, and then your dad's gonna figure everything out. I promise you." She gives me a hug, and suddenly, I've got her hair in my face, sweet and soft. I can feel her heart beating against me.

When Dad speaks next, his speech sounds slurred. Like he's just tired out by everything that's happening.

"You know this place? You've been there?"

I can't understand him at first, so it's Emily who answers. "Yeah, I know it. I used to go when I was a kid. A few of us used to hang out there. But hardly anyone else knows about it."

Dad stares at her for long minutes. I can't tell what he's thinking, but it doesn't really look like he *is* thinking. I'm a little worried about him.

"It's the safest place for you." Emily's eyes flit down to Dad's coffee, which is empty again. She glances at the coffeepot on the side, but doesn't offer a refill.

"How do we get there?" Dad asks, and I know he's really considering it. I don't like the thought of it. Emily lets go of me and steps away.

"We'll have to go this afternoon. The tide's low at four, and from the beach is the only way in. It'll be almost dark by then. We won't see anyone. Even if we do, they won't be able to see our faces."

Dad nods.

"OK," he says. "OK. I guess it's the only way." His voice still sounds odd and he presses his hand against his forehead. Like he's trying to squeeze a headache away.

I don't say anything. I'm wondering how Emily knows that low tide is at four o'clock, without needing to look it up.

SEVENTY

EMILY ALREADY HAS a big backpack filled with things she needs for her *Marianne Dupont* trip, but she empties it and puts all that in a holdall. Then we fill the backpack with supplies for our night in the caves: food, two sleeping bags - we're lucky that she has an old one and a new one at the house - extra blankets, lots of candles, and water. In a way, it's fun, but Dad's weird all day. He comes in and out like he wants to help, but then it's like his head hurts so much he can't do anything, and he goes and lies down instead. Emily gives him aspirin. She looks worried about him, but he tells her he'll be fine. He wants to rest now so he can stay up tonight and watch out for us.

The day goes by real quick. And at three, Emily makes a flask of hot coffee, and another one of hot chocolate. She gets me to pile all the gear in the hallway. She tells me how we've got to be gone by four to catch the tide.

The last hour ticks by real fast, because I don't want it to. At 15:45, I check my watch and hope Emily doesn't notice the time. But she looks at her cellphone.

"Come on, Billy, help me get the car loaded," Emily says. She opens the front door. But it's cold outside and I shiver. Emily sees and shuts the door again. She goes to the hall closet.

"Here. I'll lend you a coat, Billy. You'll need it for the caves." Emily smiles at me and holds a jacket out. It's the one Dad lent her on the night of the disco.

"I borrowed it from your Dad. I wanted to wash it before I gave it back. Never got around to it," she says.

I just stand there, staring at the jacket.

"Come on, Billy, put this on. We gotta load the car up." She pushes Dad's coat into my hands. Her voice cuts into my mind. Then it keeps on cutting. Her voice is a razor blade slicing through skin. I feel myself free-falling. I don't answer her. I just blink.

"Billy?" she says. "Are you OK?" She opens her arms to give me another hug, and it's all I can do to not shrink away from her in terror, because something horrible happens. It's like her skin and flesh have vanished from her face, and all I can see is a skull, her eyes still there but red like a demon's.

"Billy?" her voice says, but it's not her voice. It's a demon's voice, deep and pure evil.

"Put the coat on, Billy. It's time to go."

I shake my head, and the apparition is gone. In front of me, it's just Emily again, holding out Dad's summer coat.

We go out to Emily's car. It's the first time in three days I've been outside, and the air tastes fresh and cool. It's like when you've been thirsty all night, and you wake up and have a drink of water. It clears my head. I stand there for a minute in the driveway, just looking around.

"Come on, Billy, get in," Emily says, holding the back door open. I know I'm supposed to lie down there so no one can see me. She's going to cover me in a blanket.

"Hang on," I say. I run back inside. Into my room. I look around wildly, but there's no paper. Nothing. But the window's fogged. It's the best I can do.

"Billy!" Emily's at the bedroom door before I realize it. "We've got to go."

"Where's Dad?" I ask.

"He's already in the trunk. Come on. I don't want to leave him in there too long."

I go out to the car and climb in the backseat. Emily arranges the blanket over me. Even so, it's cold. I feel the car sink as Emily gets in the driver's side, then the chassis shuddering as she turns the key.

SEVENTY-ONE

EMILY FRANKLIN LIVED NEARBY and West drove slowly down her street, squinting in the rapidly approaching night to see the house numbers. It was a quiet road. No traffic at this time of day, this late in the season.

Forty-nine.

Franklin's address was further up and West accelerated. A car came toward her, its headlights on. West tried to get a look at the driver, but she couldn't see until the car drew level. A woman, youngish. No one else in the car. West hoped it wasn't Franklin. She followed the numbers down until she found Franklin's bungalow and pulled up just short. The lights were off, there was no car in the drive. West thought again of the woman she'd seen driving away.

She got out and walked up the short pathway to the front door. She knocked. When no one answered, she knocked again, louder this time.

"Damn," she said out loud. She looked around, hopeful that maybe a neighbor would be available to tell her where Emily might be, or when she might return. But the street was empty, the night drawing in. The windows in the neighboring buildings were blank, either dark or with the drapes drawn.

She walked to the bungalow's front windows and tried to peer in. The drapes were drawn here, too, but there was a space at the side where they didn't quite close properly. It was dark inside, but she could make out a couch and a gas fireplace. It looked like the kind of place you'd expect a grandmother to live in, West thought, not a twenty-two-year-old.

She carried on. There was a passageway that led around the back of the house. The gate was shut but not locked; even if it had been, the fence was low enough to jump over. She pushed it open and carried on, into the bungalow's backyard. She came to a door and tried the handle, but that was locked. There was another window, though, and she peered in. A double bed, slightly more modern furniture here, a dresser with various bottles and products on it. She squinted and saw a few she recognized. They shared the same brand of shampoo.

There was one more window, on the other side of the back door. She almost didn't bother with it, since the drapes were closed here as well, but when she did, the frown on her face deepened. She dug in her purse for a flashlight but couldn't find one; then she realized she could use the light on her cellphone. She spent a moment remembering how to turn it on; then she shined it at the window with the closed drapes. And what she saw made her pulse jump forty beats a minute. For a long moment she stood there, rooted to the spot, the adrenalin beating through her body.

SEVENTY-TWO

I'M LYING on the floor in the back of the car, breathing through a blanket that smells of mold and cats, and for some reason, I'm thinking about what happened in Mr. Foster's boat. That all seems like such a long time ago now. It all seemed fun then.

I can feel - I don't know how, maybe from how the car's tires are still running smooth - that Emily is still driving through the town. I think of the stores and houses we must be passing. I don't know why I have to lie down here; there won't be anyone around now anyway. It's almost dark, and Silverlea will be empty. Then the car accelerates, and I know we're on the road out to the hotel. Soon, we'll slow down and turn onto the track out to the heath. You're not supposed to drive down it, but us locals do sometimes. There's a little part at the end where you can leave a car and hike the last mile out to Northend.

Northend. The caves. Just thinking about them now gives my heart a jolt. I don't want to go into the caves. I don't really know why; I mean, maybe it's obvious, they're dark, and wet, and kind of claustrophobic. But what I mean is, I don't want to go into the caves with *Emily*.

Kerrump.

The floor drops away beneath me, then comes back hard, knocking the breath out of me. That's the drop-off from the tarmac onto the forest road; Emily's taken it too fast. I think of Dad in the trunk; is he going to be ok? What about the exhaust fumes? He already looks ill.

Emily slows a little, and the car rolls around as the wheels find the potholes. It's a long road. I walk it sometimes when I'm going to check my projects. I mean, I *walked* it sometimes. I guess that's all finished now.

I feel the car shudder and roll around as we go down the lane. It makes me feel sick. Suddenly, I think I'm going to be sick, and I don't care anymore what Emily says. I push the blanket up off my head and climb back up to the seat. I'm panting hard, and I roll the window down to get some air. Emily turns to look at me.

"You should stay hidden, Billy," she says. Outside the window is just heathland now. It's almost dark; the car's headlights pick up the potholes in front of us. I ignore Emily and put my face to the open window. The air streaming in feels cold, but it helps wash away my nausea.

"Well, I guess it doesn't matter here. There's no one around."

I sit back on the seat. We're near the end of the lane now. At the little area where you can park, and Emily slows, but she doesn't stop. Right at the end, the lane continues onto the beach, and that's where she goes. We slow for a minute, and the rear of the car slews around when we hit the sand, but she guns the engine, and moments later, we're on the hard sand below the high tide mark. You're not supposed to drive on the beach.

Emily accelerates hard now, and we're flying along the sand. We're heading directly for the first headland at Northend. It's weird, being here in the dark, and driving here. She slows when we get to the rocks and she picks her way carefully. And then when we're round onto the hidden beach she accelerates hard and then slows. We fetch up next to the rockface at the final headland. We're there. Right by the entrance to the cave. My cave.

Emily's door opens, and I see her walking past the back window. She pops the trunk and helps Dad out. He looks drunk.

"Come on, Billy. Get out, grab your bag," Emily says. I do what she says, getting out of the shelter of the car and stepping onto the wet sand. It's cold outside. I push my arms into the straps of the backpack. Emily swings my door shut, then locks the car with the key remote.

She switches on a flashlight. It's still not really dark enough, but it's comforting anyway, to see a little pool of light. I look at the cave entrance. It's dark in there, I know. It's just one night, I tell myself. It'll be alright. Then we'll be on the *Marianne Dupont*. We'll sail down all the way to South America. Where there are turtles. And I won't have to go to school. It'll be OK, I tell myself.

Emily was right about the tide. It's real low, at least twenty yards from the cave entrance. It's so low there's not much water in the rockpools at the entrance. We don't even need to take our shoes off. Emily digs out another flashlight and gives it to Dad. He tries to take it but drops it, and it clatters onto the rocks and goes out.

"Dad?" I say.

"It's alright, Billy. He's just tired. Once we're inside, he can lie down. He can rest. We all can. I'll stay a while before going back to see Dan." I ignore her. I don't want to hear it.

"Dad, *Dad*," I say to him. "I don't want to go in there."

I don't know if he hears me. He's fiddling with the flashlight, flicking the switch on and off, but there's no light coming out.

"Dad." I hear my own voice cutting through the gloom. The blackness of the cave entrance seems to be sucking me in. I know what it's like in there, but it's never felt this threatening before.

"Billy." Emily's voice is sharp, determined. "You've got to do this. You've got to help your dad. Sam, will you tell him?"

Dad's light suddenly flicks on, and he grunts in surprise, like he hasn't been following anything else. He points it around, at the cliff face, at the sand and rocks at our feet. He points it into the cave, but the light is swallowed up by the blackness. I can hear him panting.

"Em, I'm not sure," Dad says slowly, his speech slurring again. "I don't know what's wrong, but I don't feel too good. I'm not sure. . . " He stops, and there's a silence, apart from the wind blowing around the rocks.

"It's fine, Sam. You're fine," Emily says. She sounds frustrated. "We've just got to get you inside, get you laid down on a bunk. Come on. Sam, you go first, Billy in the middle. I'll go at the back. I'll show you where to go with the flashlight beam."

"Em, I'm not sure about this. Not sure at all." Dad doesn't move.

Then Emily snaps. She leans in close to Dad and starts talking to him hard and sharp. I don't catch all of what she says, but it's stuff about how we have to hide, and how there's nowhere else to go. How it's not too bad inside. That there's bunks to sleep on. When she stops, there's still enough light for me to see he's nodding. Then he turns to me and gives me a squeeze.

"OK. Come on, Billy. Let's get in there and get set up." He lets go, and he starts walking into the cave entrance.

"Be careful, it's low there," Emily says from behind me. I feel a light push in the small of my back, and she prompts me forward after Dad. I follow the yellow beam of his flashlight into the hole in the cliff face.

SEVENTY-THREE

THE MESSAGE WAS WRITTEN BACKWARD, stubbed into the condensation in the glass by a shaky finger. Childish letters. Even so, the first word was easy enough to understand:

HELP

Then the writer had obviously realized the need to conserve space. Next, it said:

Northend Caves
She wants to kill us

There were droplets of water beginning to run down from some of the letters, in some cases fresh enough that West guessed this couldn't have been written that long ago. An hour, maybe less? Maybe much less. She thought again of the car she had passed moments earlier. Then, with her phone in her hand anyway, she snapped photos of the message. As she did so the droplets continued. Her mind was racing.

Northend caves? She'd never heard of them, not specifically. She knew about the rockpools. You couldn't spend any time in Silverlea and not know about the famous rockpools, but she didn't know there were caves too. But it wasn't a big surprise; it was the right kind of coastline. She tried to think clearly. The rockpools were only exposed at low tide; you couldn't get to them otherwise. Presumably, that would be the same with caves? That was just a guess. But she did know it was low tide now. Very low, she'd noticed it when she was at the Surf Lifesaving Club, the surf had seemed further away than usual. It hadn't meant anything at the time, but now. . .

Now it would be coming in! How long would it take to get back to the station and organize a response? Too long, she knew at once. She had to move now. She ran back around the bungalow, dialing Rogers' number as she did so. When she got to her car, she looked around again at the street, wishing it weren't so quiet and empty.

Her cell connected. She held it up to her ear, willing it to give her Rogers' gruff voice. Instead there was just a busy signal.

"Shit," she swore. Then she tried to think. She got into the car and sat, scrolling through the contacts until she got to Langley's number. She dialed it and waited, wondering how she could explain everything to Langley so he'd actually act. When she got an identical busy signal, she slammed her fist down hard on the steering wheel.

"Fuck it." She killed the call again. She realized it would be each other they were speaking to, discussing what Dan Hodges had revealed. She could try someone else, but she didn't want to waste any more time. If Billy Wheatley was being taken into the caves at Northend, then every minute counted. She felt for her gun, holstered around her belly. Normally, she resented the hell out of wearing it there. But now she felt grateful for it. If Rogers was on the phone to Langley, they wouldn't be long. She texted Rogers to say where she was going. Then she started the car.

SEVENTY-FOUR

IT'S cold and black inside the caves. I can hear our feet scuffing on the rocks, and splashing through the rockpools. There's the occasional plop of water falling from the roof.

"Keep going back. It gets drier further in." Emily's voice comes from just behind me. My own path, deeper into the cave, is illuminated by her light. My giant shadow dances on the walls ahead, like an ogre luring us in.

"The cave gets tighter, and there are rocks to climb over. There's a way through," Emily says, and we push on. We go deeper inside than I've been before. She's right, though; the floor is mostly dry now, and the walls are bare. Dad stops. He shines his light around in front of him, but it's just solid rock. There's no way forward.

"Where now?" he asks, his voice still thick.

"Keep going," Emily replies.

"I can't. There's nowhere to go," Dad says.

She doesn't reply for a moment, but then her flashlight plays on the wall in front of us. The tunnel is blocked. We can't go any further. Emily fixes the light on Dad instead.

"Hey," he says, squinting into the light and putting his arm up.

She sounds different. "Then I guess we must be here."

Dad's voice sounds strained with the effort of talking.

"Em, what's going on. Where's the room?"

Emily ignores his question.

"You don't sound too good, Sam. How are you feeling?"

"I. . . I. . . " There's confusion in Dad's voice. "Em, what the hell are you doing? Where's the room you talked about? Get that goddamn flashlight out of my face."

"And how about you, Billy?" I still can't see her in the darkness. "How are *you* feeling? You seem to be coping a little better than Sam here. Aren't you feeling sleepy?"

I don't know what she's talking about. I'm not sleepy. I'm just cold and scared.

"Emily, where's the room? With the beds?" I say.

"Here." I feel Emily's hand touch me in the darkness. She pushes something toward me.

"Here. Light some of these. Let's all see what we're doing here, shall we?"

It's the candles. She's given me a bag of them; then a moment later, a lighter. Her flashlight shines at the plastic bag but then she brings it up to my face. It hurts. But I take a candle out and use the lighter to guide a flame onto the wick. I notice how my hands are shaking as I do it.

"Put that one on the floor somewhere and light a few more," Emily says. "You can melt the bases to make them stand up."

I do what she asks, and soon the cavern around us is illuminated with pockets of a wobbly yellow glow. The outlines of the walls and roof are visible around the candles; they look wet and lined with slime. I can't see anywhere where we can go deeper. I can't see any rooms. Then Emily flicks her light off, and slowly, the puddles of light seem to grow stronger as our eyes adjust. Now we're standing in a narrow cavern, blocked at the far end.

"Emily, where's the room?" I ask again. I can see her now, instead of just her flashlight, but she's still a vague shape in the gloom.

"Haven't you got it yet, Billy? I had an idea you'd worked it all out."

I don't answer. I've seen what she's holding, but Dad hasn't yet. "Em, what the hell's going on? We can't stay here. Where's this room you talked about?"

"Shut up Sam. Shut. The. *Fuck.* Up." Emily spits. Then Dad sees what she's holding too. Emily has backed away a few feet. In her hand is Dad's gun, pointed at him.

"Em, what's. . . ? What are you doing?" Dad says; it's a struggle for him to speak. "How'd you get that?"

"I said shut up, Sam. Take your pack off, sit down, and shut up."

"No. How'd you - "

"I said *shut up*." She lifts the gun out in front of her. "I want to do this in a way that doesn't cause you any pain, but it works just as well with the gun. So don't think I won't shoot you. *Sit down."* She screams the last words, and Dad struggles to do what she says.

"You too, Billy. Take your pack off. Sit on it. Next to your dad." The floor is flat rock, slightly sloping toward the cave's entrance - a long way away in the darkness.

"It wasn't hard to get the gun, Sam. I pulled it from your waistband as you got into the car. You're so drugged up you didn't even notice."

"Drugged?"

"Don't tell me you're not feeling it?"

"What?" Dad's breath comes short and fast. "How?"

She laughs. "How? You've been in my house, expecting me to cook and feed you the last three days. I've been increasing your doses all the time."

"With what?" he asks after a while.

"Sleeping pills mostly. Poor old Gran left all sorts in the bathroom when she died. I mixed in some rat poison this morning. It works slowly, should be kicking in now."

Dad doesn't answer. Even in the gloom, I can see his face is astonished.

"Why?" he asks.

I can hear Emily's breath now. It sounds like she's hyperventilating. Or maybe it's me. I can't take my eyes off the muzzle of the gun. A black hole in the blackness. She doesn't answer Dad.

"Billy, there's two flasks in your bag. Get them out."

"Why, Emily?" Dad's voice rasps out beside me. Then he bursts out coughing; it echoes through the darkness around us.

"Get the flasks, Billy."

"Why?" Dad begins to struggle to his feet.

"Sit back down," Emily says at once, but Dad doesn't stop.

"*Sit back down*, or I'll shoot your stupid-fucking son through his stupid-fucking head."

Dad stops. I turn to look at him, and his mouth is open as he stares at Emily.

"Get the flasks, Billy. There's coffee and chocolate. They'll send you to sleep. It's a painless way out."

I still don't move. I can't process what she's saying. A painless way out of what?

"Billy, I'm giving you five seconds."

"One."

"Two."

"Three."

"*Four*. Last fucking chance, Billy. I don't want to do it this way."

"Do what she says, Billy. Just do it."

On hearing Dad's voice, I finally move. I almost can't open the backpack, my hands are shaking so hard, but I manage it. I slide out one of the flasks, the bigger one. I set it on the ground and dig around for the other. I'm not sure, but it feels like I might have wet myself. I'm glad it's dark so neither of them can see me. My hands close around the other flask. I pull it out and look at Dad.

"Now each of you are going to have a nice hot drink and then this'll be over."

"Emily," Dad starts; he sounds a little more with it, I hear this and feel a tiny burst of hope. "What is this? What are you doing?"

"What am I doing?" She sort of laughs "I'm trying to get my life back."

For a moment there's just the sound of her breathing hard.

"Drink up. Drink up and I'll tell you." She shines her flashlight at Dad's flask.

"Come on. Do it now."

Slowly, Dad opens the lid and pours enough to fill half the cup. Wisps of steam disappear into the cold cave air.

"More. Right to the top, please."

Dad adds a little more.

"Now drink."

Dad doesn't move. "What's in it, Emily?"

"Drink it now, or I shoot Billy. It's your choice, Sam." She aims the gun at my head. "Alright," he says. He raises the cup to his lips. He winces, and lowers it again.

"Drink it.

"It's too fucking hot."

Emily laughs again, manically. "Jesus does it matter?" I can hear her breathing again.

"OK. Well let it cool down. It won't take long." She stops.

"You want to know what this is about? You want to know? Get up Billy. Get up."

I hesitate, but then I hear my own voice ask:

"What?"

"Take your dad's light and go over to that wall." She shines her own light a little way from where we're sitting. "See that pile of rocks? Move them out the way. See what's underneath."

I don't move. I look at Dad, still holding his cup with one hand. For a moment, we just stare at each other. Then he hands me the flashlight and nods at me.

Unsteadily, I get to my feet, and I make my way to where Emily said. Where the cave's wall meets the floor is a pile of loose, flat rocks; not big rocks, the size of a head at most. They sit in a small pool of water; the cave floor is low here. There's a smell too, and I can hear something, a kind of dull scratching. I shine my light on it. The gray rocks have flecks of quartz that reflect the light.

"Pull the rocks off, Billy. Your investigation is about to be successful. You're going to solve the mystery of what happened to Olivia Curran."

Slowly, I put my fingers on the first rock. It's not really on the main pile, but I pull it back, and it clatters to the floor beside me. Underneath is just the rock floor, an inch of water, and when my flashlight sweeps over the area, I see color.

At first, I don't get it. There's something red, something else that's bright green. Whatever they are, they're *moving*. Then I see. They're *shells*. Cockleshells, snail shells. Hermit crabs. *My* crabs. I see a number, black paint on a circle of white. Number 13. Most ignore my light. A few scuttle away back to the darkness.

"Keep going." Emily's instruction comes from behind me. "Just a few more stones."

I lift another, and there's a new color, purple, some kind of cloth. The smell is horrible. And then I lift one more rock. Underneath, there's a human arm. The hand is missing, and the white bone is poking out of the end. But it's the rest of it that's truly horrible. The skin is moving so much it looks alive. Only it's not skin: it's a carpet of crabs, all kinds, some painted, most not, latched on and feasting away.

I drop the stone and stagger backward. Then I trip and fall to the floor. I feel a sharp pain in my back. My light goes off, and I panic. I scream into the gloom, and I crawl back to Dad as fast as I can. I grab him, knocking the cup from his hand.

"What is it, Billy? What's there?" Dad asks.

"What do you think it is, Sam? It's the stupid little bitch that caused all this."

"What? Who are you talking about?"

"You still don't get it, do you? Who has everyone been looking for around here? Who are the police accusing you of killing, Sam?"

"Olivia Curran?"

"The very same."

"I don't understand. *You* killed her?"

Emily doesn't respond for a moment. Then she uses her light to pick out Dad's cup.

"Don't think I didn't notice that Sam. Fill it again, and this time, you can drink it hot. Then we'll talk."

Dad does it as slow as he can, but all the while, she's got her flashlight trained on his hands. The gun, too. Dad hesitates before raising it to his lips, but Emily seems impatient to talk.

"She was flirting with Dan. The whole week. Silly little bitch. He thought I didn't notice. But I could see them from the café. Don't you think Dan would know that? If he wasn't thinking with his dick. And then the night of the disco. She was like a bitch on heat. They tried to slip out together; I knew they would. Dan's done it before. Well, this time, I followed him. I didn't plan to hurt the stupid girl. I just wanted to confront them. They walked a long way, though. North, toward the dunes. That's where Dan likes to take them. Silly little tourist girls. To fuck them. How's the temperature, Sam? Still too hot for you? Remember, that's the easy way out here."

Dad doesn't move, but she doesn't seem to care now.

"They were on the beach. I was in the dunes, watching. She said she needed to go pee. She came right toward me. I couldn't move without her seeing me. She was going to discover me there, watching them. It would have looked like I was in the wrong, and I couldn't have that. There was a stone at my feet. I picked it up. I didn't decide to do it - it just happened. I swung it at her head. I didn't even mean to do it hard, but it was heavy, my arm swung faster than I intended."

Emily laughs, her voice eerie and weird with the shadows and flickering lights of the candles. Me and Dad are silent. My whole body is shaking now.

"I was at a total loss for what to do for a minute. I thought about trying to stop the blood, but when I touched her head, I could feel the skull was broken. I could press bits of it right into the brain. I knew then I had to sort it. I thought about just leaving her there, but we were halfway up to the caves anyway. It was low tide. I figured if I could get her in here, no one would find her. People would think she went for a swim and drowned."

"How did you get her here?" Dad asks. Emily's beam of light is slipping down from Dad's cup. I see what he's doing, trying to distract her.

"I was wearing your jacket. Do you remember you lent it to me? Your keys were in the pocket. I'd already passed your truck on the beach, so I knew where it was. I ran back. I drove it with the lights off; I almost couldn't find her again - God, that was a moment. Then I did find her, and I managed to get her in the back. I drove to the cave entrance, and it was easier there because I could drag her through the water.

"Then I got back to the party. You asked me where I'd been. I don't know, I must have looked pretty wild - I *felt* wild. I *needed* something to take me down. I told you to come home with me. You barely stopped to worry about poor Billy at home on his own. Do you remember that night, Sam? Do you remember what we did? The way we fucked? Death and sex, who knew they were such a combination?" She laughs again.

"And once I've dealt with you two, you know what I'm going to do? I'm gonna go fuck my boyfriend's brains out. What do you think about that?"

"You're not going to drink that, are you? Well, time and tide wait for no man, Sam."

Three things happen all at once. There's a spurt of light from where her voice is coming from, I feel Dad's body jerk, and there's a huge bang that echoes back and forth. It's the gun. She's fired it. I can smell it at once. A smoky, oily smell. For a second, I wonder if I'm hit. If I'm dead already, or dying, but I know I'm not. But Dad's grip on me has changed. It's almost gone.

"Well, well. I wasn't sure your gun would actually work," Emily says. She shines her flashlight over Dad's body again. I can see his hands have gone to his stomach. Even with the light, I can't see much. It's too dark, but I can hear him gasping, fighting for breath.

"Turns out it does," Emily says. "Now, where was I?"

No one else says anything. It's just Emily. Only it's not her, it's a monster in her place.

"I had to come back. To cut the bitch's hand off. Do you remember?" Emily says, but somehow Dad interrupts her. His voice sounds terrible, but he's speaking. Interrupted by shallow breaths, but loud enough to hear.

"Emily, you don't have to do this. You blame it all on me. Everything. Take Billy and go to the cops. Tell them it was me. Don't hurt Billy - "

She listens for a moment but then cuts him off.

"I *said*, I had to come back and cut the bitch's hand off. The police were searching this side of the island, they'd have found the body. My first idea was to move the whole thing, but that proved impossible. So I sawed her arm off. I dumped it in Goldhaven. I knew that would change where they were searching. And it did. Everything would have been OK." She stops.

I turn away to look at Dad. His back's slumped against the cave wall, but he's leaning on me now more than anything. I can see there's a black stain spreading out from his belly, but he's still breathing. I can hear it. Then he coughs, and I feel a spray of something wet on my face.

"Dad, are you OK?" I say. He doesn't answer.

"And it would have stayed OK if you hadn't turned up at my door. What was I supposed to do? The whole island is searching for you, thinking you killed the Curran bitch and you come to hide with *me*? Can you imagine what that was like? Can you imagine what I was thinking? And then we saw the news, didn't we Billy? We saw how the police found her blood in the back of your truck. I couldn't let you go then. They'd have caught you – they were always going to catch you – and you'd have told them that I had the keys that night. They would have worked it all out. I couldn't let that happen Sam. So that's *why* we're here. It's your fault. It's all your fault."

She almost yells this last part, but then makes an effort to calm herself down.

"But now. *Now,* when they finally find Olivia Curran's body they're going to find two more bodies. One of them Sam Wheatley, *already* a killer. The other his son, his final victim. They'll think you killed the girl Sam, because no-one else knew where she was. Do you see? They'll think something drove you to return to the scene of your latest crime. Perhaps the guilt of it finally got to you? Perhaps you always planned it this way? I don't suppose they'll care too much. The little flask of hot chocolate laced with drugs will tell the story well enough. That bullet in your stomach isn't perfect, but they'll just assume Billy did it. Do you hear that Billy? They'll call you a hero. The tide will wash any other evidence away. There'll be no trace of me." I can see her face in the gloom. She's smiling. She's triumphant.

"And talking of the tide. We need to hurry up. I've got to get out before the tide gets too high. Which means Billy, it's your turn. How do you want to go, Billy? A nice cup of hot chocolate, or shall we get this over with? It's time to choose."

SEVENTY-FIVE

THE SWEEP of the car headlights picked out the sign:

DANGER!
Do Not Pass This Point
On Rising Tide!

West barely noticed it; her eyes were fixed on the impression of tire marks in the wet sand. She'd picked them up as she drove along the beach, a diagonal track leading from the dunes down toward the headland at Northend. For some reason, they were easier to see from a distance: they stood out as something unnatural, not part of the regular patterns of the beach. Close up, they were harder to see. In places, they stopped completely, where the sand was covered with a shimmering layer of water in the dull moonlight. Only on the drier patches could she see them clearly, light impressions in the hard sand. But it was easy to see where they led, up to and around the headland at the north end of Silverlea's great sweep of beach.

She kept the gas pedal pressed to the floor until she reached the headland. Here there were barely twenty yards of beach left exposed at the foot of the cliff and the sand was pockmarked with rocks that stood in little pools of still water. The headlights picked them out and West steered between them, feeling the proximity of the ocean and the surf. She didn't know where she was going now, just that the tire marks led this way.

Around the headland, the beach widened into another beach. A kind of secret cove she hadn't known was here. It was too dark to see for sure, but it looked cut off on the land side by looming cliffs to her left. For a moment, she didn't know where to go - the tracks had vanished - but then her headlights picked out the shape of a car ahead of her, stopped by the cliff face at the far end of the cove.

It wasn't moving; its headlights were off. West switched hers off as well, plunging the beach around her into momentary darkness. Quickly, her eyes began to adjust to the moonlight. She saw the car was parked hard up against the cliff face. She couldn't see any people. No figures near the car or in it. But there were plenty of hiding places.

She drove on slowly, stopping twenty yards from the other car and feeling exposed and vulnerable. As she watched it, the final reach of a wave washed right up to its tires, then pulled back, like the ocean was reaching out to it, testing the strange object nearly in its grip. West guessed this meant the tide was coming in, probably it had got closer to the car since the driver left it there. But what the hell was a car doing parked here in the first place?

West swallowed, then pulled out her gun. She adjusted her grip around it; the weight giving her some comfort. On a whim she leaned across and searched inside the glove box. Among the papers, she found a flashlight. She pulled it out and mentally crossed her fingers that it had full batteries. She aimed the flashlight at the floor and clicked it on, relieved to see the car's foot-well flood with light. She clicked it off again. Then she took a deep breath and pushed the car door open. In a single movement, she stepped out and dropped down. She moved to the back of her car, using the body of the vehicle as protection in case of attack. But nothing moved. The only sound was the low roar from the ocean. West realized she'd been holding her breath and forced herself to exhale. Still from behind the car, she flicked the flashlight on. The beam shone powerful and yellow through the darkness. It picked out shadows in the cliff face; the other car's lights reflected back as if they'd been switched on.

Still nothing moved. There were no signs as to where the car's occupants had gone. Then she saw the entrance. In the cliff face beside the car, a black hole of a cave entrance, partially blocked by a low roof. *The Northend cave.* She hesitated for a moment. Then, with her gun supported over the flashlight, she closed the gap to the cliff face in a run.

She crept up to the side of the car, then shone her beam inside. It was empty. Casting the light around, she saw nothing of interest, just a blanket balled up on the back seat. She glanced up. In front of her, the cave entrance seemed to draw her in, a deeper shade of black even than the darkness of the cliff face. She approached and peered in, the flashlight sent a shaft of yellow inside. It picked out the wet rock wall in places, but in others only seemed to accentuate the darkness. She hesitated, unsure of what to do. Then there was a sound that made her jump.

At first, she didn't understand it. The noise seemed to 'pop' out of the cave entrance, followed by a lower sound. But then her brain placed it. It was a gunshot, muffled by the millions of tons of rock pressing down on the cave. She listened for more, her own weapon trembling slightly in her hand now. She considered for a moment, barely believing she could really be in this situation. A part of her mind was screaming at her not to go inside the cave. She felt the cold grip of fear. And yet. . . Another part of her felt something else. A rush of something – exhilaration? Duty? Somewhere inside the blackness of the cave something terrible was happening. And this time she wasn't a helpless teenager searching the midnight streets of Miami too late to help her best friend. She felt the fear, but she pressed it aside.

She turned around and swept the light across the beach one more time, hoping that maybe Rogers was on his way, or Langley and the guys. But there was no one. She was on her own. She took two deep breaths and stepped cautiously into the darkness.

She used her hand to shield the beam from her flashlight, giving her just enough light to move carefully into the cave. The floor was made up of irregular rock, some parts filled with pools of seawater. The water was so clear and still, it was nearly impossible to see which were filled with water, and she stepped into one that soaked her shoes, the water was cold, but she kept going. The walls were wet too, her light picked out the colors of minerals dissolved in the rock. The ceiling was low and it dripped water onto her. She shivered. Then she stopped and listened. There was a sound up ahead, hard to make out yet as it was coming from much deeper inside. The only other sound was her breathing, it felt frighteningly loud. She pressed on, deeper into the cave.

When she was maybe fifty yards into the cave, the sound became clearer: a woman's voice speaking, then laughing, then the voice again. West stopped again and listened.

"So how do you want to go, Billy? A nice cup of hot chocolate? Or shall we get this over with?"

West gently snapped off her light again. She tried to pick out which direction the words came from in the darkness. She'd seen how the cave seemed to narrow toward the back, and with her own light extinguished, she now saw the glow up ahead of her. The cave had narrowed into more of a tunnel, and she'd come to a bend. From beyond the bend, there seeped an eerie glow that changed in intensity, almost seemed to flicker. It was enough light that she could creep forward, one hand on the slimy wall to guide her passage. She could hear the voice more clearly now.

"Come on, Billy. Time's running out. I don't want to shoot *you, not after all we've been through. But I will. Then I'll put the gun in your dad's hand, and that's how they'll find you. They'll think he shot you. I'll put your prints on it, too. They'll think you got a shot into him before he got you. You'll be a hero, Billy. Shall we do it that way? So you can be a hero?"*

The cave was silent for a moment. There was no answer to the woman.

"Of course, you won't be Billy the hero, because you're not Billy. Do you even know that? Do you even know your real name? I can tell you if you like. We've got just enough time for that story. If you'd like, Billy?"

The woman paused again. Then there was the sound of her laughing. It echoed around the cave.

"It's Ben. Ben. *Your dad ever tell you that? He ever call you that by mistake? In the early days maybe. I guess you'd be too young to remember."* There was a pause.

"You don't even know why you're here, do you? You don't know what any of this is about. It's a shame. It's a shame that you need to die."

West crept forward, right up to the bend in the tunnel as the woman spoke, hoping all the while she wouldn't dislodge any stones to give her position away.

"Do you want to know? Before you go? I've got a few minutes Billy, but no more. I feel like you deserve to know. After all we've been through. When you were born, Billy. When you were Ben, you had a sister. A twin sister. Do you remember that? Do you remember her?" Another pause.

"No? Well your Daddy killed her. That's what this is all about. He went mad. He murdered *your sister. He drowned her. And he was right in the act of drowning you, too, when he got caught. It's all over the news, if only he'd let you watch it. That's why you came here. To Lornea Island. Your dad was trying to escape justice."*

West flattened herself against the rock wall. She held her breath and risked a glance around the rock. She caught sight of a bizarre scene. The end of the cave was illuminated by flickering candles, creating an eerie light. In the center, a woman stood with a gun, casting obscene shadows on the rock walls. She had the gun pointed at a shape on the floor. It took West a moment to see what this was, but then she picked out a pair of eyes. It was the boy, Billy Wheatley, and something else, an adult body, slumped against the wall.

"It wasn't Dad." The voice was so quiet West almost didn't hear it.

"What?" The woman replied.

"It wasn't Dad."

It seemed the woman didn't hear Billy because she went on.

"Your Dad's a killer, Billy, a killer no different to me. . . "

"It wasn't Dad that hurt Eva."

The woman stopped what she was saying.

"He tell you that did he? Because he gave me the same bullshit story. He said he was framed. That your mom did it. She had postpartum depression or some bullshit excuse. He tried to explain it all away. How your mom's family were embarrassed about it, wouldn't let her see any doctors. . . "

"I said Dad didn't do that. I remember. It was mom. I remember it all."

There was a silence in the cave, only broken by the dripping of water from the roof somewhere. West found she was holding her breath again.

"That's a lie." The woman's voice rang out, angry now. *"You were too young to remember. You're just saying that because that's what he told you to say…."*

"It not a lie. He didn't kill anyone." The boy's voice was clearer too. Defiant. *"It was Mom. She was singing while she did it. She'd been singing the whole day. That nursery rhyme, Row Your Boat. Only she wasn't singing it right. She was singing it like this." The boy's voice broke into fragile song:*

Row, row, row your boat,
gently down the stream,

Drown your babies in the lake,
life is just a dream.

"We were having a picnic by the lake and Mom wouldn't stop singing, even though it was making Eva cry. And then she picked her up and walked into the water. Eva was screaming and struggling but Mom just kept singing and smiling. And then she was pushing Eva under the water. I was strapped into my chair. I couldn't move. And then Dad turned up, with Uncle Paul. They stopped her but it was too late for Eva."

There was a moment of silence.

"Dad's not a killer. He's a good person. You're a killer. You're evil."

"Shut up."

Another silence, before the woman went on.

"Well, well, well. Maybe poor old Sam was telling the truth after all. He said to me your mum's family knew their reputation would never survive what happened so they blamed it all on him. He said they had friends inside the police. They had contacts. Power. They all closed ranks against him. He didn't stand a chance.

"But it doesn't change anything Billy. You know that don't you? The whole country believes Sam is a violent killer. When they find him in here, with you dead and Olivia Curran rotting away in the corner there. There's only one conclusion they can draw. I'd like to tell you otherwise. I'd like to say I'll clear your dad's name for you, but I can't. It doesn't fit with the plan you see. The only plan, once stupid Sam came knocking on my door. I'm sorry Billy. It's nothing personal, but we have to get back to business now. The tide's coming in Billy. It's coming in fast. It's time."

West felt her pulse climbing fast. She took a breath.

"No? Nothing? Nothing more to say? After all we've been through. I'm a little disappointed. Well goodbye Billy. Maybe I'll see you in the next life."

The woman straightened her arm, aiming the gun. But West was already moving. Her gun came up, too, and with her other hand, she switched on the flashlight, sending the powerful beam toward the woman.

"Armed police! Drop your weapon!" She screamed the words out in a voice that sounded terrifying even to her. But there was so much adrenaline surging through her, she barely felt in control of her limbs. She dropped automatically into a lower firing position, but as she did so, her front foot slipped out from underneath her on the slime-covered rocks. For a split-second, she fought to keep her balance as her foot skidded away, but in a sickening moment she knew her weight had gone too far. Her foot flew out in front and she slammed down onto the hard rock, her back hitting first. Her flashlight beam drunkenly slewed up to the roof then went out. She lost sight of the woman.

The next thing West saw was red-orange light splashing from somewhere in front of her, then the cave exploded with deafening noise. West heard the whistle of bullets, and fragments of rock flew past her ear. Then something hit her shoulder. It didn't hurt at all but it felt substantial, spinning her around like an angry shove, and knocking her back to the ground. It knocked her gun from her grip, too, and sent her flashlight flying so that the head of the light hit her in the face. There were more shots. More noise. A scream.

West knew at once she was hurt, already the pain was coming in waves, each more extreme than the last. She was still on her back on the wet floor. Gasping for air, shock coming on, but knowing the next few seconds would be her last if she didn't do something. She couldn't believe the element of surprise had been taken away so cruelly. She ordered herself to ignore the pain, and began feeling around the rock floor, desperate to find her gun. She splashed through pools of water blind; her eyes were still replaying explosions of red and yellow light. But somehow her senses had registered the direction the weapon had gone, and with an audible gasp of relief, her fingers reached it. She pulled it toward her, holding it in two hands now, pointing it wildly into the darkness. She swung around, her eyes now beginning to readjust to the gloom of the candlelight. She saw where the boy had been. He was gone. The woman too.

And then she saw something else. Or rather she sensed it. A shadow, a figure behind her in the darkness. She tried to turn. To get her gun up, but she knew she was moving too slow. There was a noise, weird at first, as the micro-seconds played out. West felt like she had time to wonder what the woman was swinging at her, a rock? Her own gun? And how would it feel when it connected with her head? But there was no time. No time to move, no time to get her own gun up, much less to fire it. And then West felt something connecting hard with the side of her head, snapping back her neck. For a blinding moment, she felt the shock of it smash into her brain, but then she felt her legs go underneath her, and there was nothing she could do to keep consciousness.

SEVENTY-SIX

When she came to, West saw a single pool of light. It took her a moment to work out what it was, then her brain forced it to make sense: a candle illuminating a crevice in the rock face. Surrounded by darkness. The effort of it made her head throb, and when she tried to move, lightning flashes of pain exploded from her shoulder. She cried out into darkness, her own shouts bouncing back at her from the walls. She let her head fall back on the rock floor and lay there panting loudly. She knew where she was, but something about it felt different. She couldn't understand what.

There was a noise. Then a blinding light burned into her face, she cried out again and screwed her eyes shut. She pulled her good arm in front of her face. There was nothing she could do now, no way to escape. Her mind presented her with how she must look. Lying broken on the floor. The woman standing above her, holding the gun, above it the flashlight blinding her against the darkness. Her finger squeezing against the trigger, her eyes empty. West barely had time to gasp before the bullet hit her. She could almost feel it cutting through the flimsy, hopeless protection her hand would offer, before it ripped through into her face.

"Are you alright?" a quiet voice asked her. It sounded quite wrong. Devoid of threat. West managed to quell her panic.

"Who's that?" she panted, a few seconds later, trying to push the light away.

"It's Billy," the voice replied. "I thought you were dead."

West fought to make sense of the wild inputs of information into her brain. The training she'd done kicked in. She remembered specific phrases, drills meant to help her focus on what was important, to allow unnecessary details to pass for now.

"Billy, the light. Don't shine it in my eyes," she said, and when he lowered the beam, she went on. "The woman with the gun. Where is she?"

"Emily? She went."

"Went? Where? Where did she go?"

"I don't know. She just went."

"When? How long ago? How long have I been unconscious?"

"I don't know. Not long. Half an hour maybe? A bit more." The boy's voice was quiet, calm but mournfully sad.

"Are you hurt?" West asked, struggling to sit up a little. The pain in her shoulder kicked in again, but it was manageable this time. "Did she hurt you?"

"No. I hid. When all that shooting started, I hid behind a rock. Down there somewhere." The boy pointed the flashlight out into the gloom, but the beam stopped where the chamber curved around. "She looked for me. She was real mad looking for me. But she couldn't stay long, because of the tide."

West's professional senses were still flooding her with information. With options. The need to assess and stabilize the situation she found herself in.

"The man on the floor. Your dad? Where is he? Is he. . . " She found herself stopping. Not wanting to say the word 'dead'.

"He's over there. She shot him." The boy's voice sounded tiny inside the blackness of the cave. She remembered, the noise that drew her inside the cave. The gunshot. Christ, that felt like a lifetime ago.

West fought to focus. Jamie Stone was dead. Not a priority. So what was important now? The whereabouts of the woman. She presented the danger. She was armed. An active killer.

"Where did she go?" She asked. "Where did Emily go?"

"To the ship. She had to get out before the tide came in. If you don't get out in time, you get trapped. Like we are."

Finally West understood. "The tide?" She remembered how, outside the cave's entrance, the waves had already reached the car's tires. "We need to move. We need to move now." She struggled further to pull herself up, wincing as her shoulder gave way underneath her.

"We're already cut off," the boy said, deadpan and with no urgency. "The sea's already coming in. I went to look."

That was it. That was what felt different. The noise - of the waves crashing into the rocks outside the cave - it was different now, to how it had been. Louder, and there was the sound of water moving inside the cave. And now that she looked, the floor was wetter. Not just from the pools of standing water, but there was flowing water on the floor. West struggled to her knees, sending more pain shooting back from her shoulder. She gasped and made an ugly, wounded noise.

"Are you going to die too?" the boy said now, his voice pure misery this time. "Are you going to leave me alone?"

West made a huge effort and got to her feet. As she pushed herself up she saw stars from the intensity of the pain, but she clenched her teeth until she was upright and the pain receded.

"No. I'm not going to die, and neither are you. We're going to find another way out." West took a few steps further into the cave, seeing through the gloom by the single remaining candle. The boy followed.

"There isn't another way. That's why she took us here. She told us it was to hide until she could get us onto the ship, but that was a lie. I started thinking it might be yesterday, but I didn't really know. It was all really confusing. I didn't know what to do. Then when we got here she started telling us all about it. Like she was proud. And then she shot Dad because he wouldn't drink the poison. It was in the coffee flask. But I wouldn't drink it because I don't like coffee and the hot chocolate was old. . . "

West fought to cut through the boy's words to what was important now.

"Wait. Then, we'll wait here. We'll stay here until the tide goes back down." Even as she said those words, West wondered if she would be able to do that. Her shoulder felt cold and useless. She still didn't know if the wound was a gunshot or a ricochet. And now she was standing, her head throbbed where it had been struck. She didn't know if she was losing blood.

"We can't do that," Billy said. "The barnacles go right to the roof of the cave. Look."

West didn't answer. But her eyes followed the beam of Billy's flashlight as he shined it up at the ceiling. He was right. There were different levels marked out on the walls, different zones populated by different types of life, but a few shells clung on, even at the highest parts of the roof. As Billy swung his beam around, West saw her own flashlight, and she reached down to pick it up. With the two beams, the cave felt slightly less threatening, the darkness less dense. But what it illuminated was more threatening than anything. From behind them, the ocean roared as it flowed in and out of the cave's entrance. The floor ran with seawater. West turned away from it for a moment, as if not looking could make their situation different. She saw the crumpled figure of Sam Wheatley, lying on one of the few remaining dry patches. She moved closer.

"That's Dad. She shot him." Billy said, keeping close to her. He seemed to take care not to let his light fall upon the figure lying on the floor, but West swung hers down. She barely recognized the man who she'd last seen in the interview room. She crouched down and put a trembling hand to his throat, feeling for a pulse. There was no sense of hope, just the demands of procedure. She closed her eyes to concentrate, expecting to feel nothing, just a cold, clammy softness. But she felt movement, the throb of life.

"He's alive, Billy. Your dad's alive," she said. Even in their situation, it felt a relief to say the words. She reached out and pulled the boy to her. He didn't resist and she felt his small, frail body shaking against her. Then she put her head down and tried to think. The desire to delay, to consider the options, to rest a little, was so strong. But she heard the sound of another set of waves pouring into the cave entrance.

"Billy, how deep was the water in the entrance, when you looked?"

"I dunno. There's a rock that you have to duck under. It's already beyond that, so we can't get out."

West remembered it: the rock she'd struck her head on. "Then we've got to move *right now*. We'll have to duck under it and swim out. You can swim, can't you, Billy? I bet you're a great swimmer aren't you, living here on an island?"

He didn't answer at first. When he did, his voice sounded more uncertain, sadder than ever.

"I can't swim in the sea."

West heard the words with a sense of growing disbelief. That was the last thing she needed to hear. She thought fast. He wasn't a big kid; in open water, she'd be able to carry him easily enough. How hard could it be to pull him through the cave entrance?

"I'll take you. Just trust me."

"But what about Dad? Please don't leave him here." She realized he was sobbing now.

There was a booming sound. West guessed what it must be: waves crashing into the entrance of the cave. If the waves were still hitting the entrance, it couldn't be that deep yet.

"We'll find a way, but we've got to move *now*. Hold the light on your dad." West set her own flashlight down and pulled off her top. She fed it underneath Stone's back and tied it as hard as her shoulder would allow against his stomach. Then she put the flashlight between her teeth and she slipped her arm beneath the man's shoulder. She began to pull. She almost stopped at once, the pain in her own arm was so intense, but she choked it back and tried again, managing at least to adjust his position. To her surprise, he moaned. He was conscious.

"Billy. Help me," she said.

The fact that the floor was both slippery and already awash with seawater helped and hindered them. It made it possible to move the weight of Jamie Stone's body, but only with repeated falls. Ignoring the pain in her shoulder, West kept trying, the boy helped, too, and together they succeeded in dragging him out from the back of the cave and into a wider area that was now knee deep with water. Here, it was easier. Although they kept stumbling, the man's body was fully afloat here, and she could pull him much quicker away from the end of the cave.

It was easy now to pull Stone through the water. But more of a challenge to keep his head above the surface. The water was getting deeper. Already, it was up to her waist. She could see Billy ahead of her, struggling as the surges came up to his chest. But where to go next, she didn't know, and her flashlight beam was zigging crazily around the walls and the roof.

"Show me the way out Billy. Show me where to go," she panted. She could hear him breathing hard behind the light. She reached down and gripped his father's shoulder again, lifting his head out of the water. There was almost no pain in her arm this time.

A rush of water flowed in against them. He shone the beam ahead of him, showing the way, but their way ahead became blocked. There was nowhere else to go. The water ahead was too deep and roof too low. Billy stopped. He held the flashlight above his head and let the angle from its beam drop until it played upon the moving water.

"It's through there. The only way out is through there."

West focused on the black water surging and retreating. She was up to her chest now, the boy almost up to his neck. The powerful current ebbed and flowed as waves pushed in and pulled back out.

West thought back to when she'd walked into the cave, an hour or less before. The roof had been low in one part, she'd had to duck. This must be where they were. But it hadn't been low for long. If they could just get under the restriction they'd be outside. Safe. They just had to get past this restriction – under the water.

"Billy, we're going to have to swim. You're going to have to hold your breath."

The boy didn't move.

You'll be OK, Billy. You can do this."

"No, I can't."

"Come on, Billy. It looks worse than it is. You just need to swim a short way. Please, Billy." West heard the desperation in her voice. She wondered if it was possible to swim out with the man, then come back for the boy. Or maybe she should do it the other way around. Whichever way would leave one or the other alone. Would she ever find them again?

"Billy, you've got to do this." For some reason, her mind conjured up a memory from her childhood. A young version of herself exhausted in the shallow end of the pool, her father shouting at her from the side. Just another length. Do it. You've got to do it. It was such a vivid memory she could even remember the way the warm water from the pool's pump would flow out against her body. With a jolt, she came back to the present.

She realized he was nodding. Then his voice rang out, louder and clearer than she'd heard it before.

"Dad didn't do it. He didn't do any of it."

West had almost forgotten what Jamie Stone was accused of. It seemed irrelevant to the circumstances that she'd found him in.

"I know," she said.

"Not just Olivia Curran. Everything else people are saying. I was there. No one knows I know, but I remember. I remember. . . "

"Billy, I know. *I know.* But tell me outside. We'll tell everyone when we get outside. But you've got to come *now*. You can do this. Just duck under the ledge. It's a short swim. I'll be right behind you."

He shook his head, the flashlight shaking as he did so.

"I can't do it," he said. His light slipped an inch under the water, the beam turned the water from black to a deep green. It almost looked beautiful.

"You've got to do it. Do it for your Dad," West said.

SEVENTY-SEVEN

The boy swayed in the darkness, the surges of water reached his mouth, causing him to splutter. Then he shook his head.

"No. I can't do it."

West fought the desire to scream at him. Every moment they delayed, the water got deeper, the distance they had to swim underwater grew longer, and the currents against them grew stronger.

"I can help you. I can help you do it Billy. But I can't do it for you."

"No."

"Billy, you either go now and live, or you die in here."

West's light played on Billy's face. She saw it crumple in misery. But this time he nodded at her. As she watched he gulped at the air. Then he nodded. He breathed again, and then he dived under.

For a second, West was so surprised he went she wasn't prepared to follow him. She saw his light sliding under the water toward the rock face. She almost panicked when she saw it dimming as it moved away from her. Then she snapped into action. She clamped her hand over Stone's face and took a deep breath of her own. Then she dived forward, keeping her eyes wide-open to follow the light.

Underwater, the noise was horrible, a constant roaring, and she could see almost nothing – just a gleam of Billy's flashlight ahead of her. She failed to sink deep enough, and she felt her back and her arm scraping up and across the roof. She felt the man's body catch on the roof too. But she kept going, fighting to make progress against the water that flowed against her. Then it went dark as another wave struck. She felt herself sticking as the power against her increased. She began to panic, not knowing which way to fight toward. But Billy's light was a constant, guiding her onwards. She strained toward it, feeling how the air in her lungs was running low. She tried to tell herself to stay calm. She could swim up and down an Olympic swimming pool underwater, Dad saw to that. But this was different, much harder than she'd imagined. She smacked her head against the side and nearly cried out, losing a gulp of air as she did so. And then suddenly Billy's light disappeared. The burning in her lungs was doubled by a panic she couldn't control, but then she felt the flow against her reduce. The power of the waves was weakening, Billy must have made it out, and she couldn't be far behind. She made a final, desperate effort and felt herself scrape forward once again, still dragging Stone behind her. And then she broke the surface. Just for a second. She gulped at the air before another wave plunged over her. But it was enough to give her another burst of life, and she swam now, more strongly. There was no cave roof above her now. She saw the moon, still low in the sky, oblivious to the drama it was illuminating.

"Billy," she called, swimming away from the cliff face and looking around. Her feet touched bottom, there was firm sand underneath her feet. She looked up at the black cliff face. After the darkness of the cave's interior, the night felt almost like daylight. Immediately, she could see lights, on the cliff top and out to sea. Boats, she realized. A thudding sound hammered overhead. A helicopter.

Most of the lights were on the tiny strip of beach that still remained, at the foot of the cliff. There were people there, visible from their flashlights. As she swam towards it, Stone's body began to spasm. She knew she had to get him out of the water. She released her grip from his mouth and nose. She fought her way through the water, willing the searchers on the shore to spot her. She called out to them, but every time water filled her mouth. Her shoulder throbbed from keeping him afloat.

"There!"

A spotlight from the beach shone onto her. A figure waded out into the water. Moments later she felt Rogers arms around her. She leaned into him. Whatever it was he was saying, she was too tired to hear. Too far gone to focus.

"Jess, are you OK? - I need some help here!"

Somehow she nodded.

"Christ," Rogers said. He began pulling her towards the shore as others came to help.

"We've got her," Rogers said. "Emily Franklin. We saw a car tearing back up the beach. She opened fire when we tried to stop her. But we've got her."

She nodded again.

"Is he alive?" Rogers took over pulling Stone's body. They were nearly at the beach now.

"I think so," West said, then the scene on the beach became more clear. Men with flashlights, shocked faces. "Where's the boy? Where's Billy?" Rogers hesitated. He shook his head. "He's not with us."

West stopped. "What? Didn't he come out? He was ahead of me."

Rogers hesitated again and West made a noise like a wounded animal. She turned around, looking around desperately at the dark boiling ocean. She realized she was still holding Jamie Stone's body. She pushed it over to Rogers.

"Here. Take him, get him ashore. I'm going back for the boy."

"No. It's too late," Rogers began, but she didn't hear him.

She dove back into the black water, towards the cave entrance.

SEVENTY-EIGHT

When West regained consciousness, she was in bed in a private hospital room, her shoulder heavily bandaged and arranged in a hoist suspended from the ceiling. An ECG machine on her bedside tracked her heart rate with a soft rhythmic beep. A TV on the wall in front of her played silently. Outside the window, she could glimpse a city, she didn't know which one. By the foot of her bed, Detective Rogers lay asleep in an armchair; he'd pulled up a small plastic chair to raise his legs, and he was covered by a light blue blanket.

"Hey," West said, but her voice was so weak he didn't wake up. For a moment, she considered trying to shout louder, but her throat hurt. And she realized she didn't know how long he'd stayed awake. She didn't know how long she'd been here. Nor how she came to be here. Let him sleep, she thought. In search of some answers she picked up the TV remote control, which was sitting on her bedside cabinet. She tried to raise the volume on the TV, but the batteries weren't good. So instead, she threw the control at Rogers. It hit him in the chest and then clattered onto the floor.

"Hey," she said again.

Rogers awoke with a start, and then began to rub his face and yawn loudly. He blinked as he looked around, confused.

"What time is it?" he asked.

"I have no idea. What day is it?"

Rogers pushed the smaller chair away with his foot and sat up straighter in his armchair. He was wearing jeans and a sweatshirt that she didn't recognize. They didn't fit well.

"How are you feeling?"

West considered the question for a moment. "Groggy. My shoulder hurts. Where's the boy?"

Rogers hesitated, a frown on his face. "You don't remember?"

"Remember what?" A sense of dread filled West's mind. "Is he dead?"

Rogers' face changed. The frown turned to a kind of amused disbelief.

"No. Far from it. He's running around the station telling Lieutenant Langley how to conclude this investigation. No one can shut him up from all accounts."

This time West frowned, struggling to remember. "What happened?"

"You really don't remember?"

Fragments of it were already coming back to West. The crazed way she had worked her arms underwater, freed this time from the drag of pulling Stone's body with her. Ignoring the massive pain in her shoulder. "When you first tried to get out, he only got half way. He stopped in an air pocket." Rogers began, but she knew. She'd swum too fast. She hadn't taken the time to fill her lungs with air. She got inside the cave and felt her muscles begin to seize. Her lungs screaming. She was unable to resist rising to the top, but instead of finding the surface and cool air, there was just the blackness of rock. She fought it till the last, clawing her way forwards - no longer in search of the boy - now just in a desperate last fight to prevent her body sucking in salty water as it shut down. And then the air pocket. The boy's light. His frightened face. And then nothing.

"He pulled you out. God knows how the kid did it. I mean I've been down there. Had a look. It's not *that* far, but Christ. To swim through when it's filled with freezing water. In the dark. Christ. The kid's a god damn hero."

Rogers looked at her seriously.

"And so are you Detective. So are you."

"How about Stone. Did he make it?" West said a few moments later.

"He came out of surgery last night. The bullet somehow managed to miss anything vital. He lost a lot of blood though." Rogers shrugged. "Doc's think he'll make it."

West breathed a few times, the act of it hurting her throat still. "How about her? Emily Franklin?"

"We got her. Langley's with her now."

"I saw her threatening to shoot the boy. She was trying to frame Stone for Curran's murder. Set it up like a murder-suicide."

"We know. The boy's told us everything. There's still a few bits left to piece together, but it looks like she set up the whole relationship with Stone just to cover up killing Curran. Dumb schmuck had no idea what was going on." He raised his eyebrows.

"And what happened before? Billy's twin. . . ?"

"That too. The guy doesn't have too much luck with women does he?"

West frowned.

"Christine Austin left a message on your answer phone. It was pretty confused but she was talking about when Eva Austin was murdered. She claimed responsibility. The Oregon State Police are with her now. They think she was suffering from postpartum depression when she did it. Seems her family covered up what really happened and blamed it on Stone. To protect their reputation. They believe your visit triggered something."

"It wasn't me. It was hearing about her son being alive."

"Well. Who knows? But you were the one that insisted on going to see her. Without that who knows how this would have ended?"

Rogers took his feet down from the chair. He rolled his neck around. Then he turned back to West and spoke a final time.

"It's not all good news. We recovered Olivia Curran's body from the cave." There was a moment of quiet in the room, when the only noises were the soft beep of the ECG, and the city sounds from outside.

SEVENTY-NINE

I'M SITTING in the office of someone really important from the hospital. I'm wearing the clothes the hospital lady gave me. They're a little big for me, and they probably came from a dead person, but they're better than wearing the blue gown I was given first of all, so I don't mind. Detective Rogers is here with me. He let me sit in the big leather chair that swings round. I didn't like Detective Rogers much before because he's like a big bear. But actually, he's OK, although he does ask a lot of questions. That's what we're doing. What we've been doing for hours. Or it feels like hours. I've been telling him everything that happened inside the cave, and earlier, at Emily's house. He writes it all down. I can tell he believes me this time. He's really impressed too. Especially about the part when I swam through the cave entrance. I got stuck halfway in the high part. Then just as I was trying again the other detective got stuck there too so I pulled her out. It was just like when Dad took me surfing and I got pushed underwater by all the waves. I thought Dad was trying to kill me then, because I thought he'd killed Olivia Curran. But he wasn't trying to kill me. He was just trying to save me.

* * *

Detective Rogers keeps bringing me candy and soda from the machines in the hallway. I've got it all stacked up on the desk in front of me. Detective Rogers tells me that Emily is going to go to prison.

"Why do you think she did it?" I ask him. He stops writing and thinks about this for a while.

"It's early days, kid, but a lot of folk have come forward saying Ms. Franklin has had issues for a while now. Your Dad too, he says she made his life hell when he was dating her in secret. He was trying to break it off with her, but she kept threatening to tell you." He hesitates. "You ever see it yourself? You spent time with her."

I think for a bit. I picture Emily, leaning over my shoulder. Helping me with my science homework, telling me the teachers at school are kind of stupid, and I shouldn't listen to them.

"No," I say.

* * *

"Can I go in the helicopter again?" I say, a moment later. "When we go back to the island? I didn't really get to enjoy it the last time."

Detective Rogers shakes his head in a funny way but doesn't answer me. Then there's a knock on the door. A doctor comes in and tells Detective Rogers that Dad's awake again. He had to have an operation. To remove the bullet. I asked if I could keep it. As a souvenir. But they said the police would need it for evidence.

The doctor talks with Detective Rogers for a while, talking about how Dad's operation went. They both look happy enough.

"Can I see him now?" I say suddenly. The doctor hesitates. He looks at Detective Rogers.

"I don't have an issue with that. But you'll have to keep it short." He looks at Detective Rogers, who shrugs.

"OK by me."

Detective Rogers gets up and holds the door open for me. "Come on kid," he says.

* * *

Dad's lying in a bed. He's connected to lots of tubes and machines which beep every few seconds. He looks really white but he's got lots of stubble. I can see the top of his chest. Below that it's just bandages. Everything smells of antiseptic. When I come in, he turns his head to look at me.

"Hello, Billy," he says.

"Hi, Dad," I reply. Suddenly I feel really worried. I don't know where to look.

Dad looks away too. He glances over at Detective Rogers, and a look passes between them. Then his eyes come back to mine.

"They told me what you did. What Detective West did."

"They said I might get a medal. I might get my picture in the paper. Do you think I might get my picture in the paper? Do you think that might happen?"

"It might." Dad says.

"Is that going to be OK?" I ask. I remember how Dad doesn't like that sort of thing. He looks at Detective Rogers again, who clears his throat, and looks a bit embarrassed.

"All the charges against you have been dropped." Detective Rogers says it in his gruff voice. "Both here and over in Oregon. There's a hell of a mess to sort out still but. . . " He doesn't finish his sentence, just fades out.

"I guess it's OK then," says Dad.

I don't move.

"Billy. Come here, will you? Give me a hug."

I walk over to him slowly and put my arms around his shoulders. Only gently, but I can feel him flinch anyway.

"Are you OK Dad?" I suddenly feel a bit worried. I didn't really hear what the doctors were saying, I was a bit too excited. "Are you going to die?"

Slowly Dad begins to smile. "I don't think so kiddo."

But I'm worried now. I feel my eyes begin to prickle like when you're about to cry.

"Is everything going to be OK?" I say. I can't help myself now. I'm properly crying.

"Yeah." Dad says. He pulls me closer and holds me tight. It feels good. I cling onto him.

"I think so. I think we're going to be OK."

THE LORNEA ISLAND DETECTIVE CLUB

BOOK TWO

ONE

I KNOW I'm in trouble. I'm just not sure what for.

I'm sitting outside the school principal's office. Lined up against the wall on a hard plastic chair. Just opposite is the school secretary, sitting at her desk and glowering over her glasses which hang from a chain round her neck. It's like she's wondering if I'm the type that might make a run for it.

The thought has crossed my mind. Principal Sharpe has a super scary reputation. But there's nowhere to run. Besides, I'm curious to know why I'm here, and if I run away I won't find out. And anyway, I'm not the running away kind.

I'm serious about Principal Sharpe's reputation though, everyone's afraid of her, not just the students. Once I was doing biology with Miss Jones, and we had to label the parts of a praying mantis in our work books. And because I was sitting right at the front of the class, I heard Miss Jones muttering when she saw the picture how it reminded her of Principal Sharpe. I don't think she meant the principal looked like one, she was talking about the way the females trap and eat the males after they've mated with them.

"Excuse me Mrs. Weston," I ask the secretary. "Will I have to wait here much longer?"

Mrs. Weston stops typing and frowns at me.

"The Principal will call you when she's ready."

"It's just I was in my math class you see, and math is very important..."

"*When she's ready.*"

She gives me a death stare so I give up. Then when she looks back at her computer I glance around at the little alcove where she's sitting. She doesn't get a proper room, but she's tried to make it nice anyway. There's a big yucca plant on the floor next to her, and as I'm looking at that I notice a gecko sitting half way up the trunk. I assume it's a gecko, it's definitely not any of the local species of lizards we have here on the island, and it has really big toes. I lean in closer, only stopping when I hear Mrs. Weston stop typing and peer at me. I wonder where it came from. Maybe someone kept it as a pet and it escaped? Maybe it lived in the plant and no one's ever noticed. Or maybe Mrs. Weston keeps it as a pet?

I'm suddenly interrupted by a loud commotion from the other end of the corridor. I look up to see Mr. Richmond marching another student towards me. He's pushing a girl, and he's got one of her arms behind her back like he's the police and she's been arrested. He looks *super* mad. But actually, if anything, the girl looks madder.

"*Sit down here and don't move.*" Mr. Richmond hisses at the girl when they get level with me. For a moment I think she's going to disobey him, but then she drops down into a chair, leaving her legs splayed at awkward angles. Unfortunately for me it's the chair right next to mine.

It's my fault too. There's only three chairs here, and if I'd been smarter I'd have sat in one of the end ones. Then, if someone had come along, they could take the other end chair and there'd still be another chair empty in the middle. But I'm not used to coming to see Principal Sharpe, so I didn't think of that.

I do my best not to look at the girl. I watch Mr. Richmond instead, as he talks to Mrs. Weston. I suppose he's telling her what the girl's done, but I don't hear what it is because he's talking in a very quiet voice. Then he turns to go. As he does so he notices me, and he gives a little surprised start. That's probably because I'm a really good student and he wasn't expecting to see me here. I get ready to explain to him that there's been some sort of mistake, but Mr. Richmond doesn't actually ask me anything, he just gives me a disappointed look and then he goes away. Then Mrs. Weston goes into Principal Sharpe's office, presumably to tell her she's got another student to deal with as well as me. I take advantage by moving to the other end chair so that I don't have to sit right next to the girl. It's better too, as I'm closer to the yucca. Maybe I can identify what type of gecko it is.

"Do I smell or something?"

That's the girl speaking.

"What?"

"I asked if I smell."

"What? Oh. No. Well I don't know..." The truth is I didn't notice. But I'm not going to lean over and sniff her, that would be weird.

"I don't think so."

She stares at me for a long time, then flicks her head like I'm not worth her time. I feel quite relieved by this and go back to watching the gecko. I'm not sure what they eat. I suppose flies and stuff, but maybe they actually eat yucca plants. I'll have to look it up later on...

"Well this is *bullshit. Isn't it?*" The girl interrupts again.

I don't answer. I try to keep my mind on the gecko. I think I read somewhere that you can find them anywhere in the country now, because of Global Warming and also the way bananas are transported...

"So what you here for?" It's the girl again. I drag my mind back.

"I don't know."

"What do you mean *you don't know*? How can you not know?"

"I don't know."

"You don't know how you don't know?"

I think about this for a second.

"No."

She glowers at this, then flicks her head again.

"Actually I don't know either. Except it's all *fucking bullshit*."

I turn to look at her. I get that she's mad about being dragged here, but I don't think that swearing in front of the Principal's office will help her case, whatever it is. I consider her for a second, while she's glaring at the opposite wall. She's a bit older than me, and dressed mostly in black. She's wearing massive Dr. Martens boots, and I guess her dark hair must have been dyed blue, because it doesn't look a very natural color to me. I don't get the chance to see anymore because then she turns back to look at me. I look away, but for a long time I can feel her staring at me.

"You're that kid aren't you?"

I don't answer at first, but there's no point denying it.

"Yeah."

The girl doesn't say any more, but I sense her continuing to stare at me. I'm almost relieved when Mrs. Weston comes back out.

"Billy Wheatley? Principal Sharpe will see you now."

TWO

PRINCIPAL SHARPE IS SAT behind her desk, writing on some papers. She doesn't look up.

"Close the door." She's still not looking at me, but I do what she says, then stand there, waiting.

"Sit."

There's one hard chair in front of her desk, and then a couple of comfy chairs by the window. I take a guess and sit on the hard one. Still she doesn't look at me, she just keeps writing. Finally she stops, then puts the pen down. Then she does look at me. Right at me. It's hard but I do my best to look right back.

"I'm sure you know why you're here?" She asks, and one of her eyebrows goes up in a sharp arch. I feel a strong urge to nod, but the problem is, I really don't know. All I know is the teacher in my Math class had a message I had to see Principal Sharpe right away. It didn't say why.

"I have to say I am incredibly disappointed in you Billy. What were you thinking?"

I'm hoping these are all rhetorical questions, because I don't how to answer them. She's still looking at me so I lower my gaze to the floor. But then there's silence, and I end up glancing up again. I think Miss Jones is wrong, she's not really like a praying mantis at all. She's more like a bird of prey, settling on its favorite post.

I guess they were rhetorical questions, because then she goes on.

"Billy. I'm aware you are one of the more *unusual* personality types in this school. I understand that." She stares right at me. "But that does not give you the right to take liberties."

I blink back at her now, trying to work out what she's talking about. In the end I have to say something.

"Yes."

"And as I'm sure you're perfectly aware, there are robust and clear procedures to deal with any..." she hesitates, and for the first time she looks away, just for a moment.

"With any *issues* you feel you may have at the school." She's back to staring.

There's a very long silence.

"OK." I say.

I'm beginning to wonder if I might get through the entire conversation without knowing what it's about. She shakes her head and continues.

"And ironically, in the circumstances, some might consider that what *you* have done constitutes bullying." She tips her head on one side and falls silent again.

But this time I have a sense of what this might be about. It was that word 'bullying', and the way she said it, stressing the 'ing' part. I open my mouth to reply, but then change my mind. I bite my lip instead.

This time both her eyebrows go up.

I bite my lip again.

"Oh," I say in the end.

"Oh indeed," Principal Sharpe says, then she shakes her head.

"I'm actually confused Billy. Did you somehow think this wouldn't come to my attention? Did you think I wouldn't find out? I'm genuinely curious. Because surely you can't have thought it was a *good idea*. I give you more credit than that."

Before going any further I want to be sure I've got it right – the reason she's angry I mean – so I interrupt her, just a little bit.

"Is this about the Kickstarter idea?"

Principal Sharpe sighs sharply. "Yes Billy. This is about your *Kickstarter* idea."

There's another silence.

"In which you publicly accuse several students of this school of bullying behavior, *and* identify this school as having a significant bullying problem."

I try to remember. It was quite a few weeks ago and I've forgotten exactly what I wrote. I haven't forgotten the idea, because it was a good idea. And I wanted to act on it quickly, because sometimes when I have a good idea, a few days later I forget about it, and I didn't want that to happen this time. No, I've just forgotten the exact words I used.

"I'm probably not actually going to make it now. The invention I mean."

She opens her mouth to reply, but then closes it again. She looks a bit frustrated.

"That isn't the issue Billy. The issue is how you've named students on a public forum when they have no right to reply. And how you've attacked the reputation of this school." She lets out a slow sigh.

"I'm just grateful it was brought to my attention before one of the boys involved happened upon it. Or their parents."

I'd better explain. Especially since Principal Sharpe just called Kickstarter a forum, which it isn't. But then she's a grown-up, and lots of grown-ups don't really understand the internet very well. You see, Kickstarter is a website for making good ideas actually happen. You post your idea – like for a new invention, or a book or a film – and then if enough other people agree it's a good idea, they give you the money for the idea to get made. It's nothing like a *forum*. They're places where people talk online, though I don't think anyone uses them these days.

"I'm very disappointed in you Billy. You've a good reputation in this school. You're not a troublemaker, but to undermine the school's good name like this... To accuse your fellow pupils. It's quite outrageous."

Principal Sharpe has a computer on her desk and she angles the monitor so I can see it. To my surprise she's got my Kickstarter web page on the screen. I see the logo I made at the top, with the words 'BullyTracker' in red, next to a little picture of a radar tower with little circular radio waves coming out of it. I thought it explained the technology behind BullyTracker really well actually, you see the idea is to get all the bullies to wear this special tracker device – probably it would be an ankle bracelet that they can't take off – like the ones criminals wear, and then everyone who wants to keep out of the bullies' way can use their cell phones to see exactly where the bullies are *in real time*. You could even set up a little alert so people get a message when the bullies are getting too close. It's clever isn't it?

"While I appreciate the sentiment behind this idea, to name these boys is quite wrong. I just hope we can get it down before I get a call from their parents."

"I think they're probably bullies too."

"*What?*"

"Their parents. At least, they certainly look like bullies. Just grown up..."

"*Billy!* I've not called you in for a discussion on this matter!"

I hesitate for a second.

"Well why have you brought me in?"

Principal Sharpe looks away, like a small bird just flew past the window and she thought about catching it. Then she turns back to me.

"The issue is that none of these boys has any opportunity to refute your '*claims*'. And the way you're misrepresenting the school is extremely damaging."

"But it's not *mis*representing the school if it's accura..."

"*The reason I called you in Billy is because you're going to delete it. Right now.*"

She shouts loud enough that Mrs. Weston can probably hear her outside. And that girl too. It shuts me up though.

She slides the keyboard towards me now, but it's not a wireless one, and it gets stuck when the cable isn't long enough. She has to fight for a few moments, to free up more cable. Finally she gets it in front of me.

"I assume you can log in from here?"

I can feel my forehead crunching up in a frown. I told you how lots of adults don't understand the internet. I've got a copy of the whole thing at home anyway, so even if I delete it here it won't mean anything. I glance up at her, wondering if she really doesn't know that. But she stares right back at me, her face white with veins sticking out of her neck. So I don't say anything. Instead I type in my log-in details. Then she *keeps* watching me, so I have to curl my arm up over the keyboard to stop her seeing my password from the keys I press. From the other side of the desk I hear her sigh.

"I'm not actually sure how to delete it," I tell her, while the page loads. "I haven't ever deleted a Kickstarter before."

"You're a smart boy Billy, I'm sure you'll find a way."

I don't answer, but turn my attention to the screen. Actually it's really easy. Moments later the screen says:

Are you sure? This Kickstarter has been backed!

I didn't know that. I look up to tell her.

"It's actually been 4.2% funded."

I expect her to be at least a little bit impressed by this, but she doesn't say anything.

"I set it for 50,000 dollars, which means it's actually raised 2100 dollars..."

"I'm well aware of how Kickstarter operates." Principal Sharpe replies. Even though she isn't, since she just called it a forum. Her voice is ice-cold, but I persevere. After all this is important.

"So it only needs another 47,900 dollars and it will get made. You know I really think this system could help lots of people..."

She sighs again. "Billy, have you done *any* work on it? On actually creating the device? Or the software that would operate it?"

"No. But that's why I put in the bit about the school. I thought maybe if someone at Google saw it they might want to build it. And they'd want a place to test it, once it was made. So they could do it here. At Newlea High School."

"And you didn't think to check that with me first?" she snaps. "The school principal?"

I don't answer at once. Maybe I should have checked.

"I didn't think you'd mind," I say. "You're always saying how you won't tolerate bullying and everything?"

Now Principal Sharpe sighs really loudly.

"Billy. It's my job to ensure that Newlea High School is a safe and welcoming environment for all students..."

"But it *isn't*. There are bullies everywhere. And no-one ever does anything about it."

She gasps at this, like this is somehow shocking.

"Billy... Billy that's... That's simply *not the case*. There are *procedures* in place.... Rigorous procedures..." She composes herself before going on.

"Billy, if you feel you are being targeted by bullying you only need to speak to your class tutor, or to *any* teacher. Or you can come direct to me."

I don't answer. If *that* worked I wouldn't have needed to invent BullyTracker, would I?

"*Are* you experiencing problems with bullying? Billy?"

I take a long time to reply. I can't help but think about what Dad's always telling me. How we just have to ignore it. To keep our heads down and not make a big deal. How things will get better. Eventually. Even though they never do.

"No."

She looks exasperated and rubs her forehead. "Well. . . Well then I suggest we simply delete this and we'll put this episode behind us."

I look at the screen again. The funding amount is displayed in big green letters. $2100. I don't have a copy of *that* at home. It seems such a shame to lose it. But I don't have much choice.

I press delete.

THREE

SHE GIVES me one after-school detention. Just one. Actually I get the sense it's a token punishment, like she has to do something, but knows that I didn't really do anything wrong. Or maybe she realizes that detentions won't have much effect on someone like me who actually *likes* doing school work. It must be hard for teachers when they have extraordinary students.

I don't get my usual bus home. Instead I sneak onto the Holport bus that goes down the west side of the island. I've been doing that for a while now, since Dad got his new job down there.

When we get into Holport I run down to the harbor. Dad works near the big square basin where all the fishing boats unload their catches. There's these little cranes where they hoist up the plastic pallets of fish and load them on trolleys, before a fork-lift pulls them into the warehouse. But all the boats are finished for the day, so there's no one about right now. As I look around my feet crunch through piles of dried fish scales that look like snow. Everything smells of fuel oil and fish gone bad in the sun.

Dad doesn't work on one of the boats, though he wants to, because that's where the real money is. Dad works onshore, in the warehouse. That's the big, flat-roofed building next to me, where they take all the fish that comes in, and auction it off. Dad doesn't get involved in that either. He just washes the auction house down when all the fish have been sold. He has this big pressure hose, and he has to blast all the fish guts and scales back into the water.

When I get there, the big, double doors are open, and I stick my head inside. I'm used to the smell now, a mix of fish and the chemicals Dad uses – but it's still not very nice. I see him at once, dressed in his overalls and boots, limping along in the far corner of the warehouse.

"Hi Dad! Did you make a bag for Steven?"

In response he shuts off the hose and points to a plastic sack just behind the door.

“Thanks," I say, then add. "How long you gonna be?"

He looks around the warehouse. "Gimme an hour." He says. Then he turns the hose back on and goes back to spraying it at the floor.

"OK." I shout over the noise. "I'll see you at the truck."

I grab the sack – it's quite heavy, but that's mostly the ice. I make sure it's properly closed, then heave it over my shoulder. Then I go back outside and dump it in Dad's truck, along with my school bag.

Dad used to have a much better job. He looked after the vacation properties for Mr. Matthews, who owns the Silverlea Hotel, but he lost that a couple of years back after the whole murdered tourist thing. It's kind of a long story, but basically this teenager went missing, and the police thought that Dad killed her. Obviously he didn't, but it was the second time Dad got blamed for murder, so – well – some people thought there was no smoke without fire. I guess Mr. Matthews was one of them, because he told Dad he didn't need anyone to look after the vacation properties any more. But then, a few weeks later, we found there was someone else doing it. So we knew that wasn't the actual truth.

Then for a really long time, Dad couldn't get any other jobs at all because it seemed no one trusted him. He says he only got *this* job because it's the kind of thing no one else wants to do. And it is a bit disgusting. But it is handy for Steven.

Since I've got an hour to kill, I walk out of the commercial harbor towards the marina. I like it here too. I like looking at all the boats. There's all sizes and shapes, from stubby little yachts to massive motor cruisers. You're not allowed actually onto the floating pontoons, unless you have a boat of course, but that's OK because I know the code to open the gate. I look around to make sure no one's looking, then I quickly unlock it and step through.

I really like the way the deck moves when you walk on it. It's like you're already on a boat, even before you get to the boats. I walk out now. I do this quite a lot, looking at all the different boats and deciding which type I'm going to have when I'm older. Probably it'll be one of the little ones, with just a small cabin, because I'm going to be a scientist when I'm older, and they don't earn very much money. I was going to be a detective for a little while, after everything that happened with Dad, because I thought the police could do with some help, but then I changed my mind because I realized my science was more important. And anyway, I don't think detectives earn that much either. And they certainly don't have much time to go out on boats.

I keep walking, out to where the bigger sport-fishing boats are tied up. Some of these are really flash, with huge flying bridges and blacked out windows. I don't like these much, but they're interesting, in a funny way. You see, tourists like to rent these boats out, the ones who have lots of money. The skippers take them out and help them catch fish and give them lots of food and beer. It's something I've been thinking about a lot lately.

The boat I do like is right at the end. It's 39 foot long, or 11.8 meters, and though it's still a charter fishing boat, it's a bit older and looks nicer for it. More friendly somehow. It's called *The Blue Lady*. There's a little offshoot to the pontoon that lets you walk right out alongside it, so I do that now. And then, because there's no one looking, I reach out and touch the boat as well, running my hand along the cool steel railing. They used to be shiny, but now they've gone a bit dull from the weather and the salt water. This boat isn't being used for charters at the moment, because the man who owns it got too old. So it's just been sitting here, with no one using it, or even looking after it. Not once since Dad started work in the fish warehouse.

I look around the harbor. Some of the restaurants are putting out their tables for dinner, but no one's watching me. So very carefully I put both hands on the railings, and then I step across the little gap of clear blue water between the boat and the pontoon. Right away I feel it dip under my weight, but only very slightly, because it's quite a big boat. Then I climb down so I'm standing in the cockpit at the back. The wooden floorboards are scrubbed clean. There's a ladder leading up to the bridge, where the skipper sits with a view out over the top of the boat. And there's glass doors that let me see into the cabin. It's light and clean inside, there's a little kitchen area, and a little table for charts, and then stairs too. I've seen from the internet that there's two bedrooms and a bathroom too, but I've never actually seen it for myself. I know the door is locked, but I try it anyway, and when it doesn't open I press my face up against the window, trying to imagine how it would be, inside the cabin out at sea. Being in charge.

I stay like that for a while, then I climb up the ladder to the bridge. This is my favorite part of the whole boat. Up here you can see all around. There's a fabric roof that keeps the sun off, and a plastic screen for the wind, so it's sheltered and feels protected. I sit on the captain's seat and put my hands on the wheel. Then I look at the other controls. There's a GPS, a depth gauge, and the one I'm most excited about, the fish finder. The way it works, it sends out sound waves into the ocean below, and if there's something down there, like a shoal of fish, then the sound bounces back and you can see where it is on a little screen. But it doesn't just bounce off fish, which is why my idea is such a good one. You could use it to find anything. You could use it to find...

"Hey kid!" A sharp voice suddenly cuts in, from close nearby. I give a little jump in surprise.

"The hell you doing up there?"

A man is standing on the pontoon right beside the boat, in the blue uniform of the private security firm that patrols is harbor.

"You here with someone?"

I consider telling him about Dad working in the warehouse nearby, but I change my mind.

"No."

"Then get the hell down from there."

For a second my daydream wants to come back, to ignore this interruption. This is *my* boat and I'm far out in the ocean doing important scientific...

"Are you deaf or just plain stupid? I said get down from there. *Right now*."

Reluctantly I let the image fade away and do what he says. I climb down the ladder, then step off *The Blue Lady* and back onto the pontoon. I don't look at the security guard, but I feel him glaring at me the whole time. Then he blocks me off from leaving by holding out his hand.

"I seen you before haven't I? Hanging around here?"

I don't answer. I try to get past again, but he's still blocking my way.

"This is private property. No public access. You can't read the signs?"

"This one isn't private. It's for sale. They want people to look at it, so they can sell it." This stops the man for a moment, but only a moment.

"And what? I'm supposed to believe a punk like you's gonna buy it? You clear off, you hear me? I ever see you climb on the boats again, I call the cops. You got that?"

At last he drops his arm, so I can walk past, but he stays standing in the middle of the walkway so I have to go close to the water to do so. And I get a weird feeling he's going to shove me in as I step by, but he doesn't. Then, I sense him, following close behind as I walk back up the pontoon to the gate. And all the way I feel my face burning red.

Back at the fish warehouse I wait while Dad gets changed out of his overalls, and when he comes out we walk together to the truck. On the way we go past a yacht broker, it has all the ads for boats for sale in the window. I try to steer Dad a bit closer as we go past. And when we're level with it I point at one of the ads.

"Look Dad, *Blue Lady* is still for sale."

But Dad just ignores me.

FOUR

Dad goes for a shower as soon as we get home. He takes ages because it's so hard to get the smell off. So I go up to my room and check on Steven. Before I even get to my door I can hear he's excited, and jumping up and down in his cardboard box. And the moment I open the door there's this big explosion of flapping and squawking and load of loose feathers fly around.

Steven almost bowls me over, but I manage to sit down at my desk. Then there's a noise like a helicopter and he's up there too, striding back and forth because he's so excited.

I open the plastic sack now and see what Dad's got. I pick out a little flatfish, a plaice. I hold it out and Steven steps towards me, squawks loudly, and then delicately takes it from me. When he was little I had to train him not to peck at me, because even then his beak was very sharp. Now he could easily bite my finger off if he wanted to. He swallows the plaice whole, tipping his head back and flapping it around until it curls up and goes down his throat. Then straight away he wants another one.

It was Dad who called him Steven. He thought it was funny because of someone called Steven Seagal, who is a famous actor from the old days and whose name sounds like 'seagull', although not *that* much. I'd never heard of him but Dad said I wasn't allowed to keep the chick unless I went along with the name. It's all a bit silly because there's actually no such thing as a seagull, not technically. There's just different types of gull, like Black Backed Gulls, Common Gulls, or Ring-Billed Gulls.

Steven is a Herring Gull. I've had him since he was a baby. I found him on the beach, near the cliffs. He must have fallen out of his nest, and when that happens to the chicks, the parents can't do anything, they just have to leave them to die. So that's why I had to keep him and bring him up myself. And he's not a baby anymore. Now he's about the size of a chicken – a big brown-and-white chicken, with a black beak and pink legs. And he *really* likes fish. Which is why it's helpful that Dad can get the scraps from the fish warehouse to feed him.

I give him about half the fish scraps, until he tells me he's full by shaking his head. Then he stretches out his wings, they're so big they almost touch both sides of my room at once. He flaps them a bit, then bounces around the room, and then he just goes and stands in his box and preens himself. Steven can actually fly already, but Gerry – she's from the Lomax Wild Bird Rescue centre and she's helping me to look after him – she said I should keep him inside for a bit longer so that his wings get the chance to grow stronger before he starts using them. But pretty soon he'll have to move outside, because he's quite messy now.

Once I've fed Steven I make dinner for me and Dad, then I do my homework, and after that I do some work on my new project. But I'm still feeling a bit down because of what happened with the security guard. So in the end I pick up my laptop and go down and sit with Dad in the lounge. It's a bit weird, because he isn't actually watching TV at all. He's got the sound off and it's a sitcom, and Dad doesn't usually watch stuff like that.

"You alright Dad?" I ask eventually. He doesn't look at me. He just stares at the screen.

"Dad?"

He turns round. He gives a weak smile. "Sure. Aches a bit. That's all."

Dad got shot a couple of years ago, back when the whole tourist-girl-murder thing was going on. They sort of fixed it, but his hip still aches sometimes.

He smiles again, a bit stronger this time.

"School good?" He asks. I hesitate, wondering whether to mention everything that happened with Principal Sharpe and my BullyTracker idea. In the end I just shrug.

"It's OK," I say.

Dad's smile fades away, and he turns back to the TV. So I tell him about something else, since he's in a talkative mood.

"Dad," I say. "I was kind of looking at bank loans. The other day, on the internet." I don't look at him, I know he won't like this.

"That way you wouldn't need to pay the whole fifty thousand in one go. You just need some of the money, then you pay the rest in installments. As you get the customers I mean?"

I risk a glance at him. But his expression is familiar. It's really frustrating. It's like he's totally resistant to my idea, even though it's actually a really good one.

"I'm just saying you wouldn't need to clean the fish warehouse. And it would be better for your hip."

Dad takes a deep breath, but he doesn't say anything.

"I've sort of been working on a website," I tell him. "To show you."

I'm good at making websites. It's kind of a hobby of mine. I think it's really important that children know how to do things like that. Making websites. Coding. Using the internet.

"I put all the species on it, that people could see. And then if you click the species name it takes you to a new page with more information about them. I reckon they'll like that. I really think they will."

I open my laptop to show him, and I've already got the site loaded up. There's lots of pictures of the *Blue Lady*, one taken from the yacht broker's website, and then others that I took. And then around the edge I've put all the different types of whales, and dolphins and porpoises you'd be able to see if you hired Dad to take you out.

"I thought you could call it *Blue Lady Boat Charter*."

Dad looks at the screen, and for a moment I see him smiling, but then it fades away.

"Billy. Believe me, I would love nothing more than to buy that fishing boat you're obsessing over, and run charters or track poisonous jellyfish – or whatever it is you think is gonna make us rich..."

"It's whale watching," I interrupt. "It's taking tourists out to see the whales. It's really popular in some places, but no one is doing it on Lornea Island. Even though we get lots of..."

"But it ain't gonna happen Billy. Not now. Not for a few years at least."

I don't reply. We've had this conversation before so I know what he's going to say.

"I told you. I gotta show the guys at the fish dock I can work hard, even with this goddamn hip." Dad sighs, then turns to me.

"And I tell you Bill, I'm close to getting a space on a boat. Then all I gotta do is haul nets for a few years. I can put a little aside every month. Then maybe, in a year or two..." He glances at the screen again.

"But if you get some sort of a loan?"

"Billy they ain't gonna give a guy like me a loan. OK? I told you this before. It ain't gonna happen, and even if it did..."

He lapses into silence. I guess he's tired, because sometimes he gets angry when I try to talk to him about this. And because I know it's pointless I shut my laptop and start to walk away, heading for my room. But just as I do he calls out.

"Hey Bill, I ain't saying I don't like your dream. It's a nice dream. It really is. You just gotta work out what's a dream and what's reality. You know?"

He looks so sad I don't want to make him any sadder, so I just nod.

"Sure Dad."

FIVE

I'VE NEVER HAD an actual detention before, so I'm quite looking forward to seeing how they work. But it turns out to be very boring. We just have to sit in the computer lab after school and do the exact same homework that we'd do at home anyway. It's not much of a deterrent is it? I guess that's why the bad kids get them over and over again.

Mr. Coyne is the only teacher here. He's sat at the front marking books, and he's not even very strict, so some of the students behind me are chatting to each other.

I just ignore everyone. Or at least I mean to, but then I do something silly. I glance around to see who's talking and I notice the girl who was outside Principal Sharpe's office the other day. She's sitting on her own, and she looks up at the exact same time as I do. I almost don't recognize her, because her hair isn't blue anymore, it's purple. Then when I see it is her, I can't stop myself raising my hand to wave hello. She stares back, then rolls her eyes and looks away, so I feel a bit embarrassed about that.

But then, about half way into the detention, she sneaks forward and comes to sit at the computer next to me. I look up at Mr. Coyne, a bit worried, but to my surprise he's put headphones on and doesn't notice.

"So? You figure it out?" The girl whispers to me.

"Figure what out?"

"You figure out why you're here?"

"Oh. Sort of."

I turn back to my history homework, but it's awkward, because now she's sitting right next to me.

"Well?"

"Well what?"

"You gonna tell me?"

Obviously not. But I have to tell her something.

"I was late."

"You don't get sent to see Sharpe for lateness."

"Don't you?" I ask. I didn't know that. "I was late a lot."

I feel uncomfortable with how close to me she is now. And the way she sits there staring. In silence.

"I have to do my homework now..." I start to say, but she cuts across me.

"You know there's loads of rumors about you." Then when I don't reply, she goes on.

"About when you were a baby... About how your mom went crazy and drowned your sister, and then tried to drown you..."

I don't answer. It's not really something I talk about with strangers.

"And then how the cops blamed your dad, so he kidnapped you and brought you up here in secret. Is it true?"

"It's not really something I talk about with..."

"So it isn't? I didn't think it was."

"I didn't say it wasn't true."

"So it is true?"

I don't answer that.

"Alright. You don't *have* to tell me." She looks away now, like she's suddenly bored. It annoys me a bit.

"It is true. I just don't like to talk about it with strangers."

"I'm not surprised. That's mental."

She doesn't say anything for a moment so I turn back to my homework.

"So where's your mom now?"

I put my pen down and sigh. I might as well tell her. Maybe then she'll go away.

"She's in a secure medical facility. Out in Oregon."

"Like a prison?"

"No. It's a secure medical facility. It's more like a hospital, just she's not allowed to leave. I'm allowed to visit too, if I want to, but the judge said I don't have to."

"And have you? Visited?"

"No."

"I don't blame you. *Fuck her*."

I look up at Mr. Coyne, but he didn't hear. He's still nodding his head to his music.

"I mean. I thought *my* Mom was bad but...."

She rests her fingers on the desk in front of her, and taps out a little beat with her fingers.

"So what? You just live with your dad now?"

"I really need to do my homework actually..."

"And your dad was accused of killing that tourist girl? What was her name?"

"It's due in tomorrow."

"Olivia something? Curran – Olivia Curran. But it wasn't your dad was it? It was that waitress from Silverlea. Fucking psycho waitress killed her and hid the body in some caves."

"She wasn't exactly a psycho. It was more of an accident."

"But she did hide the body in a cave? And then she tried to kill you in the cave too."

"Yeah. Sort of."

The girl laughs. But quietly.

"My dad died," she says suddenly. And then we're both silent for quite a long time, before she speaks again.

"I've been googling you. There's tons of stuff about Olivia Curran, but not much about you..."

"That's because the newspapers weren't allowed to print my name. I was under thirteen at the time it happened."

"Uh huh." She says.

"But I knew *your* name."

I look up at her. I don't understand this.

"So I did find something interesting."

There's something in her tone of voice that sounds like she's teasing me a bit.

"What?"

In response she logs onto the computer in front of her. It takes a while because the computers here are really slow. But when she finally gets online I watch as she types in the letters of a web address. And as she does so I get this horrible sinking feeling.

SIX

THE WEBSITE COMES UP. It's dominated by a large logo. A man holding a magnifying glass. There's a headline too:

The Lornea Island Detective Agency

The girl scrolls down and starts reading.

"*The Lornea Island Detective Agency is the best private investigators in Lornea Island for solving your crimes and catching murderers...*" She looks at me, one eyebrow raised up.

"Specializing in cases too difficult or secret for the police," she goes on. *"Whatever your mystery, we can help."*

I don't say anything.

"Does that sound familiar Billy?"

"No. Why would it?"

"Oh I don't know. *Catching murderers...* Didn't you do that? Didn't you help to catch the psycho waitress who killed the tourist girl?"

"She wasn't exactly a psycho... And I didn't *help* catch her. I did catch her."

"*Specializing in cases too difficult for the police.* You're pretty cocky aren't you? For a geek."

"I'm not a geek. And I've no idea what you're talking about. This has nothing to do with me."

"Oh really?" She scrolls down again. Right to the bottom of the site. Then she looks at me and smiles.

"That's odd, because it's got your name on it."

I don't have to look – I already know – but after a moment I glance at the screen, and sure enough at the bottom of the website it says this:

Website Design by Billy Wheatley

"That's probably why it came up when I searched for your name." The girl laughs again. "I thought that maybe you just did the website design, which is terrible by the way..."

I look at her, surprised by this.

"No really, it's seriously awful. My *sister* could do better and she's three years old."

I feel my forehead furrowing into a frown. The girl clicks to the '*Contact Us*' page.

"But then I saw this. The email address you've left is BWhealtley1995@gmail.-com. And that just has to be you."

She looks at me, triumph on her face.

"It is, isn't it? You're actually running a detective agency?"

"I'm not running..." I begin, but I stop. It's hard to explain.

"Billy Wheatley – Private Eye!"

"I'm not actually running it... I mean I don't have any..." I try to work out what to say, it's complicated.

"It's just that, after everything that happened with Dad and the murders, I had this idea that maybe I could maybe help the police again. But it never happened. I didn't even get around to finishing the website...."

She doesn't seem to be listening. She's clicked onto the 'Our Services' page, which lists surveillance, vehicle tracking, phone tapping, debugging equipment and polygraph testing.

"So how do you do all this?"

"What?"

"Phone tapping. Polygraph testing."

"Oh. I don't."

"So why does it say..."

"I just copied the text from a site in Los Angeles."

"A real detective agency? You copied the text?"

"Sort of copied it. I improved it too."

She laughs at that.

Suddenly she holds out her hand.

"Amber."

"Pardon?"

"Amber. My *name*. It's Amber."

"Oh."

She rolls her eyes. "This is where you're supposed to say *How nice to meet you Amber*."

Obviously I don't.

"It's very nice to meet you too *Billy*." She picks up my hand and shakes it for me. She's got very soft hands.

"So have you got any clients?"

"What? No. I told you, I didn't even finish the site. I'm surprised you even found it. I should take it down, I just forgot. I just like to make websites sometimes, it's like a hobby..."

"Or you could not."

"What?"

Amber looks at me. There's a strange expression on her face.

"You could not take it down."

I frown again, unsure what she means.

"No, you see, I thought for a while I wanted to be a detective, in the police, but I'm too young for that, and I didn't want to wait. That's why I made the detective agency site. But then I decided I wanted to concentrate on my science work instead."

"Science work?"

"I'm a marine biologist. Or at least I'm going to be. So I started doing a population count of grey seals on Littlelea Point, and then I must have forgotten to take the detective agency site down."

I stop. It's nearly true what I'm telling her. All except for one thing. The real reason I didn't take the site down was because it's one of the best I've ever made. I was rather proud of it.

"It really does look shit." Amber says.

"Pardon?"

"The design. Well it isn't *designed* at all. It's just thrown together. You need to think about it. Make it look professional."

It's the first time in nearly a year I've looked at the site. And now I have to admit, it's not *quite* as good as I remembered it.

"I was gonna add something else to the logo." I say, "I don't know, maybe add an eye into the magnifying glass. You know, so that it looks really big, like you're looking at it through the glass."

Right away Amber shakes her head. "No. See that's the mistake everyone makes. With designing stuff. You don't want to add things. You have to take away. You've already got way too much going on. You should strip it back. Simplify it."

Without asking me she grabs my pen and starts drawing on the cover of my folder. I'm about to tell her to stop, but the lines she sketches out stops me.

"Just choose one element. Like the eye. That's a good idea, but..." Her tongue pokes just a little bit out of the corner of her mouth as she draws. I focus on that for a moment, then look at what she's actually drawing.

"Mmmm. Maybe something like that could work."

I look up at her, and I sort of realize my mouth is hanging open.

"It's only rough. It would take a bit of time to do something decent," she says.

"That's amazing. I've never seen anyone draw that well."

She looks at me, with an expression I've not seen yet. I realize she's kind of embarrassed. And a bit pleased too.

"It's kinda my thing. I like art."

Art is my least favorite of all the subjects. I don't see the point of it.

"I don't see the point of art."

She looks at me and tips her head onto one side. "Well it takes all sorts doesn't it? That's why I'm here actually," she looks around at the detention room. "Painting on the wall of the gym. Sharpe called it 'vandalism', but it's art."

I don't answer this either. I just stare at the logo she's drawn. It really is amazingly good.

"Can I keep that?" It is on my folder after all.

She pushes it back in front of me. "I can do you a proper one if you like. Help you design the site right too. That way you might actually get a client."

I'm about to explain how that would be silly, since I'm not going to be a private detective anymore, when Mr. Coyne suddenly gets up and tells us to pack up our books. Apparently the detention's over. The room fills with noise and movement as the other students get ready to leave. All except Amber and me. We don't move at all.

"Only of course you won't. Get a client I mean. Because the only interesting thing that ever happened in Lornea Island was all that shit that happened to you. And now that's done nothing interesting is ever going to happen again." She shrugs.

"But still. It might be fun to try."

I think about this for a moment. Most of the other students have already filed out of the room.

"Come on Billy," Mr. Coyne says now. "Amber. Time to go."

"Actually the average homicide rate in the U.S. is 4.9 deaths per 100,000 head of population. And since the population of Lornea Island is 140,000, it means there's approximately six people murdered here. Every year. Statistically."

She stops and looks at me for a long time before answering.

"You *actually* know that? Off the top of your head. Without having to look it up?"

I shrug. "I looked it up, when I made the site."

She smiles at me. "You're fucking mental Billy Wheatley."

"Amber Atherton! Watch that language if you don't want to be here tomorrow night too."

She glances up and gives Mr. Coyne a sweet smile.

"Sorry sir." Then she walks back to her original seat and starts packing up her books. I do the same.

But as I'm leaving she comes close to me again.

"I'll email you something cool. Maybe we actually will get a client."

SEVEN

IT TAKES me ages to get home, since I'm too late for the school bus, and then I have to walk the last mile because the normal bus doesn't go right to our house. Then I have to feed Steven, and then cook for Dad, and all that makes me forget about Amber. But just when I'm going to bed there's an email from Amber. She's attached the logo she drew on my folder, only it's even better this time.

So obviously I have to put it on the actual website to see how it looks. And while I'm doing that Amber starts messaging me, and we end up working together on the rest of the site. She sends through suggestions for how to make the words better, and then we find pictures of people doing detective things – like stakeouts in cars and following people – to make it look more realistic. By the time we've finished it's nearly three in the morning. But the website does look better. It almost looks like a real detective agency site.

But then, the next evening after school, Amber starts messaging me again, with a whole new list of things she thinks I need to do to make the website better, so I do that. But then the next night she does the same again, and then the night after that as well. It's annoying and in the end I get a bit fed up, and just send her the log-on details so she can do it herself.

Anyway. That was all a couple of weeks ago, and it's not very important now, because something else has happened. Something really... Well, something really weird actually.

* * *

It all started last night. I was working in the kitchen, since Steven kept climbing on the keyboard if I used my room, when there was a knock at the front door.

I guess for some people that might be normal, but for us it's not. I don't get any visitors, because I'm not really keen on people, and if Dad sees friends they usually go out to a bar. So I shouted to Dad to come answer it, but he didn't answer. So I had to get up to answer the door myself.

Then it was dark outside, so the man standing there was silhouetted and I had to squint to see if I knew him. But I didn't.

"Hello?"

The man doesn't answer, but I can see he's kinda nervous.

"Can I help you?"

The guy steps forward into the light. He tries to smile, but it keeps slipping from his face.

"You don't remember me, do you?"

I stare back for a moment and try and make sense of him. The guy's about Dad's age, with greasy yellow hair, and yellow stubble too, like he hasn't shaved in a while. I'm pretty sure I'd remember him.

"No."

The man tries to smile, but he still looks nervous.

"Is your dad in?"

"Yes."

There's a long silence as we both stand there, waiting.

"Well, you wanna go get him?"

I don't answer this right away. Instead I look at him more closely. He's carrying two bags. One is a small sports holdall, the other is a plastic bag from the store in Newlea. I can see from the way they're stuck to the outside of the bag that it's got cold cans of beer in it.

"Why?"

At this the man gives a kind of nervous laugh, like I've made a joke. But I obviously didn't. I'm thinking about that when I head Dad's voice behind me.

"Billy, get away from the door." His voice is tight, anxious. The next thing he's pulling me back from the doorway. It surprises me so much I try to push him off.

"Billy, I said *get away from the door*."

It's not that I'm scared, it's just a surprise. Then there's another silence. Then the man starts laughing, but it's not a normal laugh.

"Jamie! *Fuck me*. It's really fucking you." The man drops his bags and holds out his arms, like he thinks Dad might want to hug him. But Dad doesn't move.

I just stare at them both. Then I realize something. He just called my Dad *Jamie*.

"So you gonna invite me in, or what?"

My dad's name is *Sam*. Or at least. He's been called Sam almost my whole life. But he did use to be called Jamie, back before we came to live on Lornea Island. He had to change it when the police were looking for him. With the whole murder thing.

"What the hell are you doing here?" Dad's voice breaks into my thoughts. His voice is cold.

The man at the door laughs though. Properly this time.

"That's all you got? I ain't seen you in – what? Ten years? And that's the best you got?" He shakes his head. "Fuck Jamie..."

"I don't use that name no more," Dad breaks in.

The man stops, then holds up his hands. "I saw that. It's Sam now, ain't it? Sam Wheatley?"

Dad doesn't reply. He doesn't even move.

"Come on man. You gonna let me in or leave me on the goddamn doorstep? I come a long way..."

I look at Dad. He's still like a statue. I can't tell if it's anger or fear. But then he steps aside. The man on the doorstep smiles and picks up his bags. He comes into the kitchen. He looks around.

"So. This is where you been? All these years?" He smiles. He's got really yellow teeth. "It's nice." Then he sees me again.

"So what do I call *you*?"

I don't answer.

"It used to be Ben... I remember how you were this little..."

"It's Billy," Dad says.

"*Billy*." There's a flash of teeth again, they match his stubble. And they're sharp too, like an animal's.

"You don't remember me? Not at all?"

I look at him again. At his greasy hair. His sharp yellow teeth. He's holding out a hand now, for me to shake, and I see it's got a tattoo on it. A snake that twists round his wrist and out of sight under his sleeve. I'd remember that if I saw it before.

"Tucker and me were friends," Dad says suddenly. "Back in Crab Creek. Before you came along."

I already told you, back when that girl was asking, about how I came to live here on Lornea Island because my Dad had to get away from the police back in a place called Crab Creek. They thought he'd murdered my sister, but it was actually my mom because she had something called postpartum depression. But because Mom's family were rich and Dad wasn't, they were going to blame him for everything. So he came to live here where no-one knew anything about him.

The man – I suppose his name must be Tucker – lowers his hand. Then he laughs, a bitter laugh.

"We were more than just friends Billy. We grew up together. Did everything together. We were like brothers."

I look to Dad to see if this is true, but he won't meet my eye.

"Then when it all kicked off, and your dad had to get the hell out of there, he came to me. I hid you in my truck, the both of you. We had to go cross country to avoid the roadblocks on the state line, then we just drove. Day and night. All the way across the country. That was a trip and a half, eh Jamie?"

I look at Dad again. There's a vein sticking out on his neck that only happens when he's super stressed.

"It's Sam." He says, quietly.

Tucker appears to consider this for a few seconds.

"Sure. *Sam*" He nods. Then he turns back to me again.

"We had you in a cardboard box on the back seat... Took turns driving. Fed you cookies... We made it all the way to New York, then... Well..." Tucker looks at Dad, and smiles again, but a different smile this time.

"That was the last I saw of you." He shrugs and shakes his head. "What happened, *Sam*? When we got to New York. Where'd ya go? What the hell happened?"

Dad folds his arms across his chest before he answers.

"You know what happened. We had to disappear. Completely. I couldn't have anyone know where we were."

The man – Tucker – is suddenly mad. "But I wasn't *anyone*! I was your best goddamn buddy. I drove you five days across the goddamn country... And you just leave me? You don't even tell me you're going?"

There's an awkward moment when neither of them speak. I look from one to the other.

"I couldn't take the risk," Dad replies, in the end. "I had to make a fresh start. Somewhere…"

"You were worried I was going turn you in? Is that it? You thought I might be tempted by that reward?"

"No, 'course not." Dad stops. Then he goes on. "But if you *knew* where I was, I'd always have that worry... Christine's family getting to you... Putting pressure somehow..."

Christine is my Mom's name. I've almost never heard Dad even say it.

"I never liked those stuck-up..." Tucker stops, glancing at me. "Christine's folks. You must've known I'd never betray you to them."

"Yeah," Dad replies at last. "But I never knew if..." He stops again.

"What?"

"If you knew where I was, I'd always have to worry about..."

"About what?"

"I don't know. About you getting loaded and shooting your mouth off in some bar."

Right away Dad looks like he wishes he hadn't said that. Tucker just stares for a long time, then he pulls out a chair and sits down.

"Oh Come on *man*," Dad goes on. "I grew up with you. I *knew* what you were like. I couldn't take that risk? I couldn't take *any* risk, not with Billy to look after."

All the anger in Tucker seems to have evaporated. He just shakes his head, and kind of mutters instead.

"I had your back man! I would've looked after you. Your best fuckin' interests." Then, when he looks up, he's smiling again.

"Well anyway. I'm here now. So you got a beer for your old buddy?"

Dad hesitates again, but not for long. Then he goes to the refrigerator and pulls out two cans of Budweiser. He hands one to Tucker, then holds on to the second himself.

Tucker opens his at once and takes a deep swig. I can see his Adam's apple bobble as the beer goes down his throat.

"You know I would never have betrayed you. *Never*."

Dad shakes his head again.

"I'm not saying you would have. I just thought... I dunno, it was hard to think straight at the time. I figured if I could disappear completely, that was my best chance." Dad still hasn't opened his beer, and he taps the top now with his fingernail.

"I didn't want it to end the way it did. I swear." He doesn't take his eyes from Tucker as he says this.

Tucker drinks more from his can. His hands are so strong he dents the sides of the beer can, I think he does it without even realizing.

"It hurt man. Fucking hell. It hurt. I looked for you. I went round every goddamn motel and cheap hotel in the whole of New York state. But..." Again he shrugs. "It's a big place."

Tucker glances at me and sends me a big yellow smile.

"Long fucking drive back too."

No one says anything for a moment. Then Dad does.

So how'd you find us?"

Tucker looks surprised by the question at first. But then he laughs.

"You made the news man! I mean, you were already famous, after your earlier disappearing act, and getting accused of killing the kid…" He smiles at me, then shrugs.

"All I know is, one night, I'm sittin' watching the TV, mindin' my business. And suddenly there's something on the news about *Jamie Stone.*" He turns back to me.

"That's your Dad's name, or least it used to be. Until he gets accused of drowning your sister. Trying to drown you. That's why it was news - when he turned up again - ten years later. They were saying he'd got mixed up in some business about a murdered tourist, in some place called *Lornea Island.* I'd never even fucking heard of it." He stops, laughs bitterly and turns back to Dad. "I guess that was the point, huh? Sam?"

He grins at Dad, waits for him to answer, but Dad doesn't say a word.

"I knew it was bullshit. Just like the first time. There's no way Jami... No way *Sam* would ever do something like that. But all the same. It told me where you were."

Tucker stops to drink more beer, and Dad just taps on the ring pull on his.

"So for a while, you make the news every night. About how the police on Lornea Island had you down as this psycho murderer, and then they finally catch you and work out it wasn't you after all. And then – like magic – all the Crab Creek shit gets cleared up too. They talk to Christine and she admits to everything..." He stops and looks at me.

"That's your mom. You know about her?"

I don't mean to, but I give a little nod. He watches me, like he doesn't know what to make of it. Then he goes on.

"Post-partum depression they called it. Real bad case, I guess. Anyhow. There's my old buddy, suddenly innocent of everything, and I'm thinking, surely this means Jamie's finally gonna put in a call to his best friend in the whole goddamn world? Now there's nothing to stop him."

Tucker drinks again and sniffs loudly. Dad doesn't move.

"And I wait, because I ain't changed my number or nothing. But I don't get no call. So in the end I think to myself, well – Jamie always was the quiet type, not wanting to make a fuss. So I figure, if I want to see you, I'm gonna have to come here myself, and look you up." He tips his beer can vertical and drains the rest of it, then crushes the can in his fist and bangs it down hard on the table.

"So here I am!"

EIGHT

RIGHT AFTER THAT, Dad tells me I have to go upstairs, because of school tomorrow. But it was only 11.00, so I knew it was actually because he wanted to talk to Tucker in private. So then I try to listen to what they were saying from upstairs, but they were talking too quietly. Even when I put the toothbrush glass from the bathroom onto the floor to amplify the sound, I could only hear that they were talking lots, not what they saying. So eventually I had to go to bed.

When I came downstairs this morning, I was wondering if the whole thing might have been some weird dream, but right away I saw there were loads of beer cans left in the kitchen – much more than Dad would normally leave. From the state of it, it looked like they'd been drinking the whole night. And that made me wonder what time Tucker actually left. And *then* I saw the lounge was darker than usual, and there was this shape on the couch, with a pair of feet sticking out. So I knew it wasn't a dream. And that he hadn't left at all. He was still here.

So after that I gathered all the beers cans and put them in the recycling, because otherwise they make the kitchen smell. Then I fixed my breakfast. And then I had the idea to google Tucker, to see if I could find out anything about who he was, and why he might be sleeping in our lounge. But that was no good because he never said what his second name was. So I just searched for Crab Creek, where I was born. I've never been back there, and to be honest I haven't thought about it much, since it's such a long way away, and Dad doesn't like to talk about it and I don't know anybody from there anymore. So I was looking on Google Maps, at how it's 3159 miles or 49.8 hours (without traffic) to get there from Lornea Island (plus the ferry crossing which is four hours). When suddenly Tucker walks into the room.

He's dressed only in his underwear, and he stops and stretches right in front of me, reaching up and nearly touching the ceiling. He's got muscles all over him.

They're in places where I didn't even know you could *get* muscles. And the tattoos aren't just on his hand, they're all over his body. He's got this big green dragon thing that wraps around from his stomach all the way to his back. It looks like the sort of thing that Mafia hit men have on them.

"Morning Billy," he says to me. He finishes his stretch then rolls his neck around. His joints crack like microwave popcorn. He starts poking around the kitchen.

"You got any coffee?"

I don't answer at first, but when he turns and looks at me I don't feel I have any choice.

"Yeah."

"That's nice. You wanna make some for your dad's old buddy?" He grins at me.

I hesitate for a moment, but eventually I drop my spoon and push the chair back. He smiles again, then goes over to the window.

"Whoa... That's a hell of a view you got here," he says.

I don't answer, pretending all my attention is on the coffee.

"I didn't see it last night. I heard it. I heard the sea, but it was dark...

I feel him turning to me. "You're right on the clifftop. You can see for miles."

I don't know why he's telling me this. It's not like I wouldn't have noticed.

"You surf?" he asks. "Like your old man?"

I stiffen a bit at this. I had a bad experience surfing with Dad.

"No."

He goes on like I haven't said anything. "We used to go all the time. Your dad and me. When we were kids. We used to skip school if the surf was pumping, hell even if it wasn't pumping…"

"Dad isn't good at surfing anymore," I interrupt him. "When he got shot it took away his flexibility."

Tucker stops. "Yeah. He told me 'bout that. Tough break." He turns away from the window.

"So what about you?" He asks me. "What do you do?"

I don't know what he means by this, so I don't answer. Instead I just hand him his coffee, and he winks at me.

"You got school?" he asks. This should be fairly obvious since I'm thirteen years old and it's a Thursday. What else am I going to do?

"Yeah."

"I never much liked school," Tucker says. Sipping his coffee. Then he raises it up, like he's saying it's good. "And school never much liked me neither." He nearly laughs at this but then doesn't. Instead he asks me a question, which takes me a bit by surprise.

"You mind if I borrow that computer of yours?" He points at my laptop, which I've closed so he doesn't see I've been trying to google him.

"I just have to check something onli.... Whooa! *What the fuck is that*?"

He says that because right at that moment something happens. Steven wakes up. He's sleepy in the mornings and I usually take his box down to breakfast with me. Now he squawks and raises up his wings, then flaps them really hard.

"*Jesus fucking wept!*"

"It's only Steven."

"Steven? It's got a name? Fucking hell kid. You've got a *seagull* for a pet?"

"He's not a seagull, he's a Herring Gull. And he's not a pet either. It's illegal to keep wild birds as pets in the United States. As soon as he can fly I'll let him go."

Steven settles down now, and folds his wings back up. Then Tucker leans in close to his box. With a nasty grin he reaches out as if he's going to poke him. Steven watches him with one eye, then just before Tucker actually touches him he flaps his wings really hard and takes off. He's so big now it makes quite a commotion in our small kitchen, and Tucker jumping backwards doesn't help. Steven lands on the cabinet where we keep the cups.

"Fuck me!" Tucker says again, when he recovers a bit. "Looks like he can fly already."

I don't answer him.

"Anyway," Tucker grins at me, then looks at my computer again. "You mind? I just gotta check something online."

I'd forgotten about his question, but now I have to think about it. And as I do, I'm not exactly comfortable about the idea. It's not just that I've just been googling him, there's also a lot on my computer that I wouldn't want anyone to see.

He slurps at his coffee, the steam hiding his face for a second. I try to think fast.

"Don't you have a phone you can use?" I say in the end. "We get good reception, even out here."

"Don't have one." Tucker suddenly grins broadly. "Don't trust those things. You know what I mean?"

"What?"

Then I realize it must have been a kind of joke because he puts his hands up, like he's giving up.

"Hey, sorry I even asked. Don't worry about it. I'll ask your dad when he gets up."

I'm still trying to work out what he's talking about, when he puts the coffee down with a bang.

"Say. I gotta take a piss." He sniffs loudly, then walks towards the downstairs bathroom. As he goes I hear him talking to himself.

"Steven the Seagull. I get it. Like the guy in *Under Siege*. Man I loved that movie..."

For a few moments I don't move, I'm still a bit stunned by how strange this all is, that he's still here, wandering round in his underpants and sleeping in our lounge, and I don't know anything about him. I look into the lounge now. I see his clothes draped over the chair, all messy. I'm about to look away, when I get an idea. Whenever I need to get something from Dad's wallet - like cash for groceries, or his credit card - I have to fish it out of his jeans pocket. So If Tucker's jeans are there, then maybe I can get his surname from his credit card? If I do that, then I can google him after all.

It's just an idea, and I know I probably shouldn't do it, but at the same time, where's the harm? It's not like I'm going to *take* it. And surely I've got a right to know who's in my house?

There's a sudden, quite unpleasant noise of urine hitting the toilet bowl which means I've only got seconds before he's back. But seconds are all I need, so I get up and run into the lounge. The drapes are drawn and there's a musty smell that isn't normally there. And I'm worried suddenly, because I can't actually hear the bathroom from here, so I don't know whether he's still weeing or if he's already finished. But I'm committed now, so I reach down to pick up his jeans. I can feel from the weight that there's something in the pockets. But it's awkward, because the material is twisted. And then I don't want to touch the bit around the fly, where his groin goes, because that would really be disgusting.

So very carefully I untwist the jeans, and straight away I can feel something hard and square in the back pocket. I reach in to pull it out, but then stop in surprise. Because it's not a wallet in my hand. It's a cell phone.

I stare in surprise. It's a proper one, with a touch screen and everything – not one of those ones that old people like, that can't connect to the internet. But didn't he just tell me he didn't have a phone at all? I try to rewind in my mind. Yeah. He said he didn't trust them, or something like that? If that's the case, why has he got one in his pocket?

I press the button to wake the phone. I don't know why - he'll probably have it locked with a code, but I do it anyway. But nothing at all happens. It doesn't even light up. After a moment I realize why. The phone's actually switched off. Or maybe the battery is dead. Maybe that's why he wanted to use my computer. But why wouldn't he just tell me the battery was dead on his phone? Or ask if I've got a charger, I've actually got loads. I decide I should try to switch it on to check, but then I realize I don't have time for that, since cell phones take ages to boot up. So instead I turn back to his jeans, still confused, but thinking I can still get his surname from his wallet.

But then, right above me, I hear the stairs squeak. I know the sound, I know exactly what it means. It's Dad, coming down. Normally he'd sleep later than this on a weekday. But I guess because Tucker's here, he's got up early.

Really I should give up, I've only got seconds before Dad will see me, but I don't stop. I really want to know now, and I only need one glance at Tucker's credit cards to see what his surname is. So I scrabble with the jeans again, this time pulling out his wallet. I open it up and fumble a plastic card out, all while listening for Dad's voice. The card I pull out is a driver's license. It's hard to see it in the half light of the room, but it's got a picture on it. Tucker, but in a suit and looking much smarter than he does in real life. I'm already slipping the card back into the wallet as I read the name, getting ready to shove it back into the jeans pocket. But then I stop. Because it doesn't make sense. It doesn't make sense at all.

Tucker's name is Peter Smith.

I do a double take. I check the picture again, then re-read the name. Peter Smith.

I shove everything back and drop the jeans back on the floor. I try to walk as calmly back to the kitchen as I can. But Dad's already there. He gives me a funny look, like he's wondering what I'm doing in there.

"I left my school bag," I say. Then I sit back down at the kitchen table, hoping he won't say anything.

I feel his eyes studying me.

"You know Tucker stayed over last night? You might want to give him a bit of space."

Then the toilet flushes and Tucker walks back into the room, whistling. Or at least, the man my dad is pretending is called Tucker walks back into the room.

I told you it was weird.

NINE

Before I go to school I take my computer upstairs. I use it to google whether Tucker is a nickname for people called Peter. But before I even finish typing the question, the auto-complete tells me that sometimes Tucker *is* a nickname, but for people called William or Thomas. But more usually it's just a name. It comes from old English, where it meant someone who made cloth. Or something like that. So when I go downstairs again, and Tucker's in the lounge getting dressed, I ask dad about it.

"Is Tucker's real name Peter?" I watch him carefully as I speak, but I don't let him see that I'm that interested.

"Peter?" Dad frowns at me. "No. Why do you ask that?"

"Oh, no reason. I just thought it was a nickname."

Dad keeps looking at me for a few moments but he says nothing. If he's lying he's doing it well.

"OK. Well anyway, I gotta go to school. I'll be late for the bus."

Dad's still staring at me as I walk out of the door.

I'm still trying to make sense of this at school. I hardly listen to my morning classes which would matter if I wasn't a good student and already way ahead of the class. And I'm still thinking about it at lunchtime. But then I check my phone, and there's an email that does totally distract me. In fact it changes everything. This is what it says:

Dear Sirs,

I found your agency on the internet and have decided to engage your services. I would like you to investigate the disappearance of my dear husband, Henry Jacobs. I have lived half my life praying that the mystery of what happened to him would be solved. And as I am now nearing my own end, I would like to know I have done everything I can to find out.

I trust you are more used to getting this type of letter than I am in writing it, and that you will know how to proceed from here. Certainly you seem to be a very trustworthy and professional looking company which gives me great confidence that you will succeed, even in this most difficult of cases. I shall look forward to you letting me know what happens next.

Sincerely

(Mrs.) Barbara Jacobs

At first I'm baffled as I read it. Then I remember about the detective agency website and how it must be to do with that. And then the text messages start pinging in.

WTF? Billy is that you jerking me around?

Then:

This is for real! No fucking way!

And finally:

Meet me in the library you retard.

These all come from Amber. I remember now that Amber added her email address to the 'contact us' page of the detective agency website. I didn't think much of it at the time, but then I never thought anyone would contact us anyway. I don't know what to think now. But I do what she says.

"Billy! Over here," she whistles at me from over by the computers. Which I don't like because you're not supposed to even talk loudly in the library, let alone whistle.

"I've tried googling 'Henry Jacobs' but there's like, six million people with that name, so that's not going to work."

I look on the screen, open on google's search results.

"Have you got any ideas?"

There's a notebook open on the desk and she's written 'Henry Jacobs' in capital letters at the top. Then she's underlined it twice. The rest of the page is empty.

"I can't believe we've actually got an actual client!" Amber says before I can answer. "This is so fucking cool!"

I sit down next to her.

"What else do detectives do?" Amber asks. "Apart from googling people I mean?"

"I don't know."

"You don't know?"

"No, why would I know?"

"You're the detective."

"No I'm not."

"You made the website."

"Well… OK but. Look have you actually replied to her?"

"Not yet. I thought we should work out what to say first."

"Oh. Good." I hesitate. "You mean about whether we should take the case or not.?"

"No," Amber looks at me. "I mean about how we're actually going to find him. We're definitely going to take the case."

I hesitate again.

"I'm not sure," I say in the end.

"I hoped we could get something from google that we could follow up on. Like a lead..."

She stops, then turns to look at me. "What did you say?"

"I said I'm not sure we should *actually* get involved. I mean, we're not *really* private detectives and if this is important to this lady, and it kind of sounds like it is, then shouldn't she go to a real detective agency?"

She frowns.

"Why?"

I'm a bit confused by Amber's attitude. I mean, isn't it obvious? I guess I'm maybe just a bit distracted with this strange business about Tucker/Peter at home. Why would Dad be calling him Tucker, or pretending his name is Tucker, if his real name is Peter? I have a few theories already – that's he's some sort of secret agent, or living a double life, or in the Witness Protection Scheme...

"*Fuck* Billy. If this is your attitude, why did you waste my time getting me to make you a private detective agency website?"

"You didn't make it, I did!"

"I made it better!"

I'm taken aback by this.

"It was alright before..."

"It was crap. And anyway, I'm the one who advertised it."

"You *advertised* it?"

"Of course I did. Otherwise no one would ever find it. We'd never get any clients."

"I didn't want to get any clients!"

"What? Why would anyone start a detective agency if they didn't want clients? You'd have to be a moron."

I open my mouth to tell her I only made it because I liked making websites. But suddenly that doesn't seem a very good reason. I close my mouth again.

Amber stares at me for a long while, then turns away.

"Fuck Billy. You really are weird you know that?"

But then she turns back.

"And anyway. It's too late now, because we've got a client now."

We don't talk to each other for a few moments. I watch her click on some of the google links in front of her. One *Henry Jacobs* is the director of a golf club in Arizona, another a doctor in Vancouver. She glances at both and then clicks away, dismissing them.

"The thing is," I say. "She's not *actually* going to want to hire us, is she? Not once she knows we're just kids. She's going to want adults."

"I already thought about that," Amber replies at once. "We'll do everything by email. We'll tell her we have to do it that way so that no one can find out our true identity. For security."

I stare at her.

"Would you hire a private detective who wouldn't even meet you?"

"Of course I would." Amber says. "It's how they all do it. It's standard practice."

I feel my face tighten into a frown. "Is it?"

"I don't know. But that's the point! You didn't know if it is or isn't. So neither will she. Besides she's already said she wants to hire us. She's already decided."

I puff out my cheeks. I suppose that might work. I feel like all my objections are being dismantled rather unfairly.

"Well how would we actually go about finding him though? It doesn't look like Google is much help."

Amber turns to me. Suddenly she looks excited again. Eager.

"That's why you're here. You're the one that found that tourist girl. You *solved* that case. How did you do that?"

I think for a moment. It is true. They even gave me a medal.

"I just kind of worked it out."

"Then just do that again." Amber's face breaks into a broad smile.

"*Come on Billy.* This is so cool. This is awesome. We've got an actual case to investigate. Just like on TV. Like in the movies. It's going to be so much fun."

I hesitate at this. One thing I know from everything that happened before is that doing detective work is nothing like they show it on TV. I suppose this doubt shows on my face.

"Look even if we can't find him, we still get paid. Two hundred dollars a day. Even if we don't find him."

"Really?"

"Yeah. That's what the terms and conditions say. Think what you could do with that money!"

I don't say anything. But I do think about it.

"Come on Billy. Don't be a dork about this!"

In the end I don't exactly say yes, but I don't exactly say no either. So then we have a go at writing an email we can send to Mrs. Jacobs. But it's really hard to know what to say. There's a ton of questions we need to ask about her husband if there's any chance of us finding him, but it's almost impossible to ask by email because the questions we need to ask all depend upon what her answers to the questions before were. And even worse than that, it's really hard to work with Amber because she keeps suggesting really stupid questions in the first place. So by the time the bell for afternoon class starts, we've hardly got anywhere. In the end I tell Amber that I'll work on our reply to Mrs. Jacobs tonight.

But even as I walk out of the library, I'm not sure if that's true. I think it might be better to reply to Mrs. Jacobs and tell her to go to a proper detective agency, because it sounds like this is something really important to her, and not just a game that we should be playing.

And that's what I've just done, this evening. I told her I was sorry about her husband, and I lied a little bit and said I had worked with the other agency and they were really good, and I was sure if anyone could find her husband they would. I know you're not supposed to lie, but I think in the circumstances that's OK.

I copied Amber into the email, so she knows too. I expect she'll be mad tomorrow, when I see her at school. But that's just too bad. I can't just do everything that people want me to do.

Oh. I almost forgot to mention. Tucker/Peter (whatever his name is) is still here. He was in the lounge with Dad when I got home from school. They were drinking beer and watching a ball game. Dad told me to come in and watch it with them, but I said I had homework to do. Then later on Dad called me down for dinner, but I said I wasn't hungry. That was a lie too, because actually I'm starving. But I didn't want to sit with him. He's made the lounge smell funny and I just don't trust him.

TEN

I ASSUMED THAT TUCKER/PETER would be gone by the time I got home from school on Friday, but he was still here. Then, when I woke on Saturday morning, he was still here. There was a huge pile of beer cans and the kitchen was a mess which I had to clear up. When he finally got up him and Dad went surfing. Dad hasn't been surfing for ages. He used to go all the time but then he got shot and like I said, it messed up his flexibility. But somehow Tucker/Peter persuaded him, and they dug a couple of Dad's old boards from the shed in the yard. Tucker/Peter even asked if I wanted to go, but I told him I was busy. It's true as well. I had to teach Steven how to fly.

Then Tucker/Peter and Dad went out drinking on Saturday night, and he stayed all Sunday as well. And then this morning, when I got up for school, he was *still* here.

And what with everything I've found out about him – how he lied about not having a phone, and how he's lying about his name, I'm obviously not delighted about leaving him in the house. I don't have a lock on my bedroom door, so I've come to school with my laptop computer, which makes my school bag really heavy. That's the most important thing, but I've still had to leave my binoculars, my camera traps and all my other equipment unsecured at home. I tried to hide it, but what with Steven following me around and uncovering everything I tried to hide, it wasn't very easy. I did have one good idea though. I remembered something I once saw in an old James Bond movie, about how you can stick a hair over the gap between the door frame and the door. It doesn't stop people going in, but at least you find out *if* they have broken in. If the hair's not there when you come back it means the door has been opened.

And anyway I'm still thinking about all this when I bump into Amber in the corridor. She's got her head down looking at the screen of her phone. And when she looks up I see a strange look on her face. Like she is pleased to see me, but then she isn't pleased to see me. That doesn't make any sense because I thought she'd be mad with me for saying no to Mrs. Jacobs.

"Hi Amber," I say. She kind of slides the phone away so that I can't see what she was looking at.

"Hey Billy," she says. Then she looks past me, like she doesn't want to stop and talk.

I'm a bit confused because of her not being mad and everything.

"Are you still mad about that email I sent?"

Again she looks past me, but then she seems to change her mind. There's an open classroom door next to us, and she pokes her head in, checking that it's empty. We're not allowed to go into classrooms when we don't actually have classes in them.

"Come in here," she says. "We need to talk."

"We're not allowed to go into..." I begin to tell her, but she just grabs me by the straps of my backpack and pulls me inside.

She shuts the door behind her, and I can tell she's excited about something, but she doesn't know how to say it.

"I got another email," she says at last. "I was just reading it."

I frown at her, not understanding.

"From Mrs. Jacobs. The old woman."

I still don't understand.

"I emailed her back, last week. Asking for more information about what happened to her husband."

"No," I correct her, after some thought. "*I* emailed her back, telling her that we couldn't help her. I told her she should go to that agency on the mainland."

"Yeah, you copied me in," Amber looks annoyed for a moment. "But she doesn't want an agency on the mainland. She wants *us* to investigate."

"How do you know that?"

The look on Amber's face changes from annoyed to awkward.

"Because she told me. I sent her an email right after you did, explaining how you thought we were too busy, but that we could move things around and still fit her in. And she said how important it was for her to have someone on the island to investigate her case."

"Oh," I say.

"And it's a *proper* mystery. She told me all about it. How her husband went to the store forty years ago and just disappeared. She has no idea what happened to him. He just vanished. Wouldn't it be cool to solve that?"

I think for a second. "I guess... But how? We tried to find out more by email before, and it's just impossible…"

"That's why I arranged to see her. Today, after school. Why don't you come with me?"

My mouth drops open. Amber is two years above me in school, you'd think she'd be smarter than this.

"But... You *can't* meet her. She's gonna see straight away how old you are?"

"I know," Amber concedes. "It *is* a bit awkward. I thought that I could put on different make up. You know, make myself look older. Then if that doesn't work, we could tell her how we've got a boss who's older, but who has to keep his identity a secret. You know, so that he can work incognito."

I just stare at her. So that eventually she looks a bit embarrassed.

"Yeah OK, forget that. But you know, the weird thing is," Amber goes on. "I actually get the sense it doesn't actually matter."

"What doesn't?"

"How old we are. I just get the idea she's a bit crazy. Like, mad enough that she won't even notice how old we are."

That's ridiculous, so I don't say anything.

"And it might mean *the case* isn't that hard either. You know, her whole problem could be that she just doesn't have a grip on modern life. The internet and everything. So we might be able to solve the case just because we understand all that. You know, because we're young."

This all sounds highly unlikely to me.

"And anyway, why *shouldn't* we investigate it? The truth is you did find out what happened to that tourist girl that got murdered. You found her. You solved it. When the police couldn't."

That *is* true, but even so. I shake my head and go to turn away, but Amber stops me.

"So what do you think?"

"What do I think about what?"

"Do you think it's a good idea?"

"No. I think you're completely mental."

Amber's face breaks into a wide smile at this.

"I know. But will you come?"

"Come where?"

"To meet her. I was just thinking, if we go together it'll look..." Amber begins.

"I'm not going." I interrupt her. "I think you're mad. And besides. I've got other things to do. Important things."

"What things?" She says at once.

That question takes me by surprise, and I think of the true answer. I've still got work to do on the *Blue Lady* project, then I've got to do more flying lessons with Steven. I've got homework to catch up on... But then I think about home. How Tucker/Peter is probably still there, and how I'll have to hide in my room so that he won't try to talk to me. I don't want to mention any of this to Amber. Given how she's completely crazy.

"Nothing."

"Well come on then. Come with me. See what you think. You know we could actually *help* this lady. She's really worried about it. If we can find her husband it would really help her. And I know you wanna do that."

I don't reply.

"And it'd be so *cool* Billy, to have a real mystery to investigate."

Amber fixes me with big, round, sparkling eyes. She puts her hands together, like she's begging me. In the end I have to look away.

"She's just going to tell us to get lost when she sees how old we are."

Amber shakes her head. "No she's not. But even if she does, we don't lose anything." She tips her head to one side. Like the way Steven does when he wants something.

"And anyway she's *expecting* us now. We don't want to let her down."

I give up. And maybe I'm a little bit interested to see what happens too.

"OK," I say. "I'll come. But only so we can tell her we can't take the case. Like I said.

"Sure," Amber replies.

"OK, good."

Honestly, just the idea of it is crazy.

ELEVEN

AMBER DOESN'T HAVE A CAR, but she tells me she can borrow her mom's. So after school we walk to her house to get it. She makes me wait in the kitchen while she gets changed. Luckily there's no one home, so I look around a little bit. There's plastic children's toys everywhere, and it smells nasty too, like baby food and diapers.

When Amber comes back down she's wearing lots of makeup and she's in this suit thing. She definitely looks a lot older. She looks quite... well, I suppose, professional too.

"Stop staring. *Weirdo*."

"I'm not staring, you just look..."

"What?" Amber smoothes down the skirt onto her thighs and turns sideways. "Power dressing turns you on does it?"

I don't really know what she means, and I don't like the funny voice she's doing, so I'm glad when she stops.

"I borrowed it from Mom, OK? She used to work in an advertising agency. She had to dress smart for clients. Though that was all before *that thing* came along." She points at a photograph on the wall. It's a little blond baby. Actually there's loads of photos of it, everywhere in the house as far as I can see.

"My half-sister, Grace. Mom remarried after Dad died and then she came along. Mom gave up work and decided to turn herself into Parent of the fucking Year." Amber kicks a large plastic xylophone out of her way.

"Ow! Never felt the need to give up work when I was a kid. I hardly ever saw her."

I don't say anything.

"Anyway," Amber goes on after a moment. "We have to get out of here before she comes home. If we want the car that is."

That makes my head jerk up. “I thought you said you could borrow it?”

"I didn't say we could *borrow* it, I said we can *use* it."

So after that we hurry outside and she unlocks an old Toyota Corolla that's parked on the driveway. I keep looking around anxiously, expecting to see her mom turn up and start shouting at us, but there’s no one around. Amber fires the motor clumsily, and backs off the drive.

"I put the address in my phone." Amber steers with one hand as she opens the maps app on her cell phone. She stares at the screen as she pulls off down the street. A van is coming towards us, I can see the driver frowning as we slowly drift into its path.

"Erm, Amber..." I begin, but I'm interrupted by the van honking its horn.

"Fucking hell!” Amber looks up just in time to swerve out the way. Then she tosses the phone to me. “Hey can you find it for me?"

* * *

I quickly realize that Amber’s not a very good driver, which kind of helps me not to think about where we’re going, and what we’re doing. I read out the directions and we take the road that goes towards the west side of the island. I don't know it well, only that there are no beaches here – it's all tall, craggy cliffs and a long drop down to the sea, which makes Amber's driving even more scary, especially when the road goes near to the edge. But even so I can’t shake a feeling we shouldn't be doing this. A couple of school kids pretending to be private detectives. As if we really have any idea how to find this poor woman's husband. But I don't say anything. It wouldn't be safe to distract her.

Eventually we make it down to the southern tip of Lornea Island. There's no town here, just a few houses dotted around. One of them is bigger than the others.

"Wow!" Amber whistles as she stops at the address marked on the phone. "Check that out!"

I see what she means. Mrs. Jacobs' house is enormous. It's set back from the top of the cliff, and there's a gravel driveway leading up to it. It looks like the kind of place you'd expect to be met by a butler.

Amber pulls forward again, and as she does so, Amber starts humming to herself. I realize she's nervous. I don't know if that makes me feel better or worse.

"You know, I really don't think this is such a good idea," I say.

"Mmmm. Me either," Amber replies. But when she's stopped the car and pulled on the parking brake she looks across at me. Her eyes are shining with excitement.

"But we're here now aren't we?"

She gets out, and after a moment I do too. I figure that Mrs. Jacobs is probably going to take one look at us and tell us to go away. And at least that'll be the end of it.

By the time I get to the front door. Amber's already pressed the bell.

TWELVE

I HEAR the buzzing noise from deep inside the house. Then, moments later a voice too. A distant 'I'm coming', and then a long silence. Eventually we hear the shuffling of feet as someone comes to the door. Then it opens, just as far as the chain allows.

"Yes?" The voice is sharp. Angry.

"Hello, Mrs. Jacobs? It's Amber. From the detective agency?"

I can see an old woman through the slot in the door, screwing up her face, like she's trying to hear better.

"The what did you say?"

"The detective agency." Amber repeats it louder. "We're here about your husband."

"My husband?" The voice changes now, incredulous. "I don't have a husband. Not had one of those for years."

Amber turns to look at me, a goofy look on her face. But then she tries again.

"I know. You contacted us about finding him. You emailed us." She pauses. "Do you remember?"

The old lady snaps back at once. "Of course I remember, I'm not senile, if that's what you're implying?"

The door suddenly slams shut, and we hear the fumbling of the chain. A moment later it opens again, properly this time.

"*Is* that what you're implying, young lady?"

Amber takes a step back. "No, I just…"

"Good, because if you were we wouldn't be getting off on the right foot. Not at all." Mrs. Jacobs glares at Amber, who looks like she wants to run away. I take the chance to examine Mrs. Jacobs. She's tall and thin, but kind of elegant. Except she seems to be wearing two blouses, and she's got the buttons mixed up so they're all in the wrong holes.

"Who's this, your little companion here?"

She turns on me so quickly it makes me jump, and I'm not able to reply before Amber talks over me.

"This is Billy. Billy Wheatley. He works for the agency too. He's one of our junior investigators." She glances over and mouths that I should go along with this, so I do. But then, when I look back at Mrs. Jacobs something weird has happened. It's like there's suddenly a different figure standing there. Or maybe I just notice more about her now. She suddenly seems much more stooped over and frail now. Her face changes too. It looks more lined, more sad. She doesn't say anything for a while. But when she does it's like we're starting all over again.

"I'm sorry, who did you say you were?"

So Amber tells her a second time. But now she nods.

"Amber. Mr Billy. From the detective agency. Yes of course. Please, won't you come in? I've been expecting you."

It's weird. It's like we've just met two completely different people in the same body.

* * *

We go inside a huge hallway. It's decorated like a museum, with portraits on the walls of men in suits. One is on horseback. The floor is made of marble and above us is a huge chandelier. I look around, and notice Amber is doing the same.

"I was in the garden enjoying this lovely sunshine. Perhaps we could talk out there?"

We follow Mrs. Jacobs' curved back through several other dark rooms, all with the drapes closed. It seems to take forever, and at one point I think I see a stuffed fox's head hanging up, but I can't be sure. Finally we come to a patio door and step back out into a large garden enclosed by a high wall. It's nice enough, with flowerbeds everywhere and a big lawn, but I can't help notice we can't get out easily if we need to.

"Would you like some iced tea?"

She has a tray of it ready, on a wrought-iron table. We sit down.

"Thank you," Amber says, and Mrs. Jacobs pours us each a glass. Her hands shake as she lifts the jug.

"It's so lovely of you to come and see me," she says, her voice frail again. "It's been such a long time."

I'm not sure what to say to this, so I just smile and look at Amber, who raises her eyebrows just a tiny bit. She turns back to the old lady.

"We're here from the detective agency Mrs. Jacobs. You contacted us about your husband?"

For a second Mrs. Jacobs' face fills with a strange look. She continues to pour the tea into her own glass, but doesn't stop even when it's full, so that it pours all over the table and then flows over the edge and onto the ground below. It takes her ages to notice and stop pouring, but eventually she does. Then she sets the jug down.

"Yes, of course. Excuse me. I forgot for a moment."

She smiles. It's a sad smile, she looks lost.

"Yes. That is quite the mystery."

"Could you tell us exactly what happened?" Amber asks. She pulls out a notebook and balances it on her knees.

But Mrs Jacobs doesn't seem to hear. She looks at me instead. "I should have baked some cookies or something. I had no idea you'd both be so young"

"We're actually older than we look…" Amber begins, and I stiffen. This is the moment I've feared and I hope Amber's not going to try her idea of saying we've got an older boss who doesn't want to reveal his identity. That's such a stupid idea.

"Oh don't worry about it dear. I expect it's like policeman."

"Excuse me?"

"Private detectives are like policemen. They get younger all the time."

Mrs. Jacobs gives me a smile, and I realize Amber was somehow right. Our age isn't an issue, because Mrs. Jacobs is completely crazy.

"I'm sorry, this is all rather difficult for me. I've been a long time thinking about this."

"That's OK Mrs. Jacobs," Amber says. "If you could just tell us what happened, in your own words."

It sounds to me as if Amber spent all of last night practicing lines like that, but it seems to work because Mrs. Jacobs nods. She takes a moment to compose herself, then she begins.

"It was December 8th. 1979. I remember we'd just put the tree up and all the decorations and the children were so excited, they were still young enough to believe in Santa and all the magic of presents." She smiles at me for a moment, almost like she's not sure if she needs to pretend Santa's real – for my sake. Then her face turns serious again.

"It was evening time, the children were in bed and Henry said he was going to the store, up in Newlea. I usually bought the groceries, but what with Christmas coming up we'd run out of a few things. So he got into his car and he drove away. And that was the last anybody ever heard of him."

She looks at me again, and shrugs as if that's all there is to it. Amber's busy writing down what she said, so I ask the next question.

"Maybe he had an accident? Did you check the hospitals?"

"Well no." Suddenly she gives me a really big smile. "That's a very astute question Mr. Billy. I can see why you're a detective. No. We checked all the hospitals and he wasn't in any of them."

I'm quite pleased to be told I'm astute, so I try again.

“Did you ever find the car?"

"Another excellent question. Yes. The car came back. But Henry didn't."

Amber seems to have decided she's going to be the one who writes things down, so I keep asking questions.

"How do you mean?"

"Like I say. The car came back from the store. Or at least – I went to bed, thinking that perhaps Henry had stopped off for a drink somewhere and wouldn't be back until late - he did that sometimes. But when I woke in the morning, the car was back, but no groceries, and no Henry."

"Well perhaps he came back, and then went away again, but not in his car?"

"I suppose that's possible. But the fact remains, that no one's ever seen or heard of him since."

She watches me closely, a bit too closely, it makes me feel awkward while I try to think of another question.

“Did you go to the police? What did they say?"

I look over to Amber to make sure she's writing all this down, but then when I look back at Mrs. Jacobs, she seems changed again. Her posture is more slumped. She looks frail. It's like a cloud has slid over the sun.

"Mrs. Jacobs? What did the police say?"

She doesn't reply.

I look over at Amber and frown again. I don't understand what's happening here at all.

"Mrs. Jacobs, did you go to the police about your husband?"

"When did we last see each other?" Mrs. Jacobs asked suddenly. "I think it's slipped my mind."

Amber and I look at each other, totally confused.

"We didn’t. We haven't actually met before," I tell her in the end.

"Really?" She peers at both of us, like she's struggling to recognize who were are.

"And who are you again?"

Amber steps in again, but this time her voice is different now, less confident. "We're from the detective agency," she says again. "You asked us to find out what happened to your husband."

Then Mrs. Jacobs screws up her face, like she's desperately trying to make sense of this, before she finally says.

"Yes, of course." She puts a hand to her head and leaves it there, pressing against her temple. I slide my eyes again to Amber.

"I'm so sorry. I must seem rather… muddled. You see I get so forgetful these days. I do want to know what happened, but I just... forget."

"That's OK Mrs. Jacobs," Amber says. "You were telling us whether you went to the police? What did they say?"

Mrs. Jacobs looks like she’s thinking for a long time. But when she finally speaks she shakes her head.

"I'm sorry. I don't... I just can't bring it back. It's like, it's all in here, but I just can't get at it. It's so frustrating. It's why I thought you might be able to help. A professional agency like yourselves."

I look at Amber. Trying to send her the message we really shouldn't be here, since we're not really a detective agency at all.

"Coconuts!" Mrs. Jacobs says suddenly.

"What?" Amber asks.

"Coconuts. I remember something about coconuts."

"What about them?"

"I don't know. They were important. In some way."

"In what way?"

There's a pause. "I don't know. Palm trees maybe... It's difficult to remember..." Mrs. Jacobs stops. She looks frustrated.

Amber tries again. "Did you say you can't remember if you went to the police, or you can't remember what they said?"

"There was snow on the ground. Not much, not enough to go tobogganing. Do you like to toboggan Mr. Billy?"

I have no idea what to say to this so I stay quiet.

"More iced tea?" Now she pours more drink into my glass. It's already full so that it overflows like before, and runs all over the table a second time.

I've seen enough at this point. Mrs. Jacobs is completely mad, and there's no way I'm getting involved investigating a mad lady's case. I don't have time for things like that.

"Mrs. Jacobs," I begin. "The actual reason we came today was to tell you we're not able to take on the case." I feel Amber's eyes shooting towards me, but I don't care.

"We can recommend the agency on the mainland, but we're too..."

"Oh no." Mrs. Jacobs interrupts me, and there's something about her voice that makes me stop.

"Oh no, it has to be you."

There's silence.

"Why?"

"Because I have a *feeling*." She taps her nose, like this makes perfect sense, which of course it doesn't. "I had it when I found your lovely website. I had it when your colleague here arranged this meeting, and I have it now. A *feeling*, that you're the only one who can help me."

I've no idea what to say to this, so I don't say anything.

"And I won't take no for an answer."

I swallow. "Yeah well that's really nice and everything, but..."

"And if it's about the money Mr. Billy. As you can see I'm quite comfortably off."

"It's not..."

"Mr. Billy, I've read the terms and conditions on your website very carefully. I understand there's no guarantee of success, but I'm prepared to take that risk. Here..." She reaches down beside her chair and there's a purse I hadn't noticed before. She pulls it onto her lap and brings out a checkbook in a leather case. She tears off the top check and holds it out to me.

"Five thousand dollars. That should be enough to get you started. Obviously there'll be more when you find out what happened." She smiles, and wafts the check in front of me, close enough that I can read her spidery handwriting. I swallow again.

“Here. Take it.”

I don’t mean to, but I do what she says. It’s five thousand dollars after all. More money than I’ve ever seen before.

"Now, I do tire easily, so I'd like to take a rest now, if you don't mind?"

I open my mouth to tell her again that we can't take the case. But no words comes out. I can’t stop thinking, obviously I shouldn't take the money - the old lady is very clearly insane. But *five thousand dollars?* And all we have to do is find this lady's husband. But then how on earth are we going to do that? Anything could have happened, and it was forty years ago.

“You know I do sometimes wonder if whatever happened to Henry has just slipped my mind.” Mrs Jacobs interrupts my thoughts.

I stare at her, and then move my eyes across to Amber, who’s grinning in delight.

“Now if you don’t mind, I must take my afternoon nap.”

THIRTEEN

As we step out the front door and crunch back across the gravel, I feel Mrs. Jacobs eyes on me. When she's in the car Amber starts laughing, but I wish she wouldn't.

"*Do you like to toboggan Mr. Billy!*" Amber says as she starts the engine.

"She's fucking insane. That was hilarious." She turns the car around, and I ignore her. I lock eyes with Mrs. Jacobs again, standing on the doorstep, and for my last view I feel really sorry for her. She looks really sad and lonely so I don't feel like laughing.

"So? What do you make of her?" Amber asks, when we're back on the road. Thankfully she's driving much slower this time.

"I think she's a bit mad," I say.

"A *bit* mad? She's fucking batshit crazy."

"Yeah," I say after a while. Since that probably isn't an unfair description.

"What do you think about her husband though?"

I just shrug.

"It's weird though isn't it?"

"What is?"

"That he just walked out and disappeared? I mean how can that happen?"

I think about this for a while before answering. "We don't exactly know that he *did* walk out and disappear. He could have just died normally. Or he could still be living with her, and she just hasn't noticed."

Amber thinks for a moment. She laughs again, then stops.

"Well either way, we have to find out," she goes on.

I look across at her.

"But she's mad. We can't take money from a mad person." But even as I say it, I think again what I could do with that money. How it could change Dad's life.

"Why the hell not? What's five thousand dollars to someone with a house like that?" Amber turns to me, so that she's not looking at the road anymore.

"It's not how much she's got," I say, more firmly than I actually feel. "It's whether it's right to take it when she's mad. Whether it's ethical, I mean."

Amber says nothing for a while. Then she repeats the word 'ethical' in a funny voice.

"What exactly is *ethical*?"

I don't answer her.

"Look Billy," Amber tries again. "I'm not suggesting we *don't look* for him. We'll do the work we're being paid for. And like I said, it might be easy. If she's just forgotten what happened to him, or if nothing ever did, and she's just a bit mad, then it might be easy to solve. We'll tell her what happened and she can – I dunno – write it on a post-it note and stick it next to her bed. That way she can read the truth every morning when she wakes up."

It takes me a few moments to work out why I don't like her logic here.

"Yeah but she's not just *a bit mad* though is she? She's batshit fucking crazy."

Amber laughs really hard at this.

"Come on Billy. We've got to give it a go at least? I tell you what. Don't cash the check. If we can't help her we'll just give it back. That way there's no ethical problem."

Again I think about what I could do with the money. How I could use it to put Dad back on the right path. Then I notice that Amber is still staring at me, ignoring the road that she's driving along.

"Come on Billy." She makes a thing of fluttering her eyelids at me, though I know she's doing it ironically.

"Could you keep your eyes on the road please?"

She doesn't. "Pretty please Billy," she laughs, pursing her lips. I think it's only luck we're on a straight bit of road, and Amber hasn't driven off the cliff edge already, but there is a bend coming up.

"Amber!" I say.

"Billy..." Now her eyes are almost closed and she's making a kissing face.

"OK. OK, just look at the road will you!"

And with that Amber laughs, and looks forward again.

So like that we sort of take on the case.

FOURTEEN

DAD'S not in when I get home, so I grab some food and take it up to my room.

I'm about to open my bedroom door when I remember the hair. The one I stuck across the entrance, like in the James Bond film. I almost don't bother checking, since my mind is so on the Mrs. Jacobs case now, but something makes me stop. I put down my plate and carefully I examine the door frame. For a moment I don't understand it, because I can't even find the hair that I left. And then I realize the implication of this. That's the whole point of it. It means someone's been into my room while I was out. It can't have been Dad. He knows not to, and anyway he's been at work all day. So that only leaves one possibility. Tucker. Or Peter. Or whatever his name is.

I stand, on the upstairs landing for a moment, thinking about this. Then things get worse. From inside my room I start to hear a strange noise. I don't know what it is, but it's coming from inside my room. It sounds like – I don't know – it sounds almost like a weird breathing noise. I start to get a bit worried, since I'm alone in the house. I wonder if he could *still* be in there. I think about getting some sort of weapon, I could probably find a baseball bat in the shed somewhere. Then I realize this is all ridiculous – I can't be scared to go into my own bedroom. So I tell myself not to be stupid and take hold of the door handle.

"Hello?" I call out, trying to make myself sound totally confident. The noise stops, but no one answers. Then the noise begins again.

I can feel my face frowning tightly. I grip the door handle and very quickly I turn it, and push the door open. Then I get a real shock.

For a second I don't see anything out of place, then there's a loud screeching noise and then a large fluffy football of brown feathers throws itself at me and starts pecking at my face. Two long wings beat around my ears.

"Urgh! Steven! Get off!"

I try to push him away, but he's so eager to see me he almost knocks me back into the hallway. He must have been hungry, here on his own. I get him sat on my arm and go into the room. Then I see what the noise is, he's been trying to eat the corner of my desk, scratching at it with his beak. It really is time I released him. He's going a bit crazy locked up in here all day.

I share my dinner with Steven, which kind of means he eats most of it. And while that happens I start researching Henry Jacobs. But there's so many people with that name that I don't find anything, even when I add other keywords like *Lornea Island*, or *disappeared*, or *murder.* It's a bit disappointing actually, and I'm pleased when I hear Dad coming home. I get up to see him, but then I hear Tucker's voice as well. Or whatever his name is. And I don't want to see Tucker, so I stay upstairs. Dad shouts up the stairs to see where I am, but I shout back that I've got to do homework. And then, after a bit more work, I go to bed.

* * *

I have school the next day. Actually I've been having a few issues at school. I didn't tell you, because it's not really a big deal, but since you're here, you might as well know. It's just some of the boys in my class. They're idiots, the problem is, they're quite *big* idiots. I expect you probably had kids like them when you were at school. Or if you're still in school, you probably know kids like them right now. They're the type who sit at the back of the class, messing about and complaining that school is boring. It's so ironic though, because the only reason the classes are boring is because we have to do such basic stuff so that they'll understand it.

Today one of them brought in a bag of candies – jellies shaped like little Coke bottles – and they spent the lesson sucking them to make them sticky, and then flicking bits of them at the teacher, Miss Smith, when she tried to write on the whiteboard. She didn't notice at first, just wondered why they were laughing so much, but then she did notice, and she did the worst thing possible, which was to try and pretend it wasn't happening. I don't know why they don't train teachers not to do that. It never works, it just makes the whole class laugh along with the idiots. That's what happened this morning, until more and more people were throwing the sticky bits of candy at her every time her back was turned.

Anyway, what happened next was this. I was trying to get on with my work, when I felt something hit *me* in the back of my head. And when I touched my hair to see what it was, it wasn't just one piece of jelly, it was a whole wad of half-chewed cola bottles stuck together, all slimy and tangled in with my hair. And when I turned around to see who did it, right away I saw James Drolley looking right at me. He's kinda the leader of the idiots. But then, there were also quite a few of the other boys, also looking and laughing. So there's no way I could tell Miss Smith who it was.

Actually I'm not going to say anymore. I suppose it's just one of those things, but it did kind of mess up my morning.

* * *

When lunchtime finally comes I go straight up to the school library and I see Amber sitting by the computers. For some reason I suddenly feel really pleased to see her. I don't know why. But just as I'm about to go over to her I stop myself. She didn't text me this morning, and I'm only assuming she's here working on our case, but what if she isn't? What if she's actually just doing her school work, and she's not really serious about wanting to investigate Mrs. Jacobs case at all?

So I hesitate, not sure if I should go and speak to her after all. I almost turn around to leave, but then she looks up and spots me.

"Hey Billy! Over here."

Usually I wouldn't like it when people are loud in the library, but I don't mind now. So I go over to her, and sure enough it's not school work she's doing, but research into Mrs. Jacobs. This makes me very pleased.

"What are you grinning at?" Amber asks.

"I'm not grinning."

"Yes you are."

I'm pretty sure I wasn't grinning, but just in case I was, I make sure I stop.

"Now what are you doing? Are you ill?"

"No! I'm..." I concentrate on settling my face into a serious look.

"That's better. Now sit down, we've got work to do. Lots of work." She pushes a chair out next to her, and I sit down.

"I've been searching for *Henry Jacobs..."*

I lean in and examine her screen.

"Trouble is, there's loads of people on Facebook with that name. So we're gonna have to scroll through them one by one until we..."

"That won't work."

"What? Why not?"

"I looked last night. There's seven thousand three hundred and forty seven people called Henry Jacobs. And probably more who can't use computers."

"How do you know that?"

"I found a website that tells you. You type a name in, and it counts how many Facebook profiles there are for that name. And loads of them will have their security set to private, so you won't be able to see them anyway."

"Shit." Amber says.

"*And* even if you could see them, it's hardly likely he's going to have set up a Facebook account in his old name, if he wanted to disappear."

Amber frowns. "Alright then. What do we do then?"

"You could add search terms to his name," I say.

"Like what?"

"Well, if you type in '*Henry Jacobs*' plus '*Lornea Island*' plus '*disappeared*' then it helps to narrow down the results."

Right away Amber starts to type into the computer.

"But there's no point doing that either," I tell her. She stops and sighs.

"Why not?"

"Well it's obvious isn't it?"

Amber hesitates. "Is it?"

"Yeah. It's because the internet wasn't invented then."

She frowns again, deeper this time.

"The internet wasn't invented until 1983. Well, actually some people say it didn't really exist until the 1990s when Tim Berners Lee invented the world wide web, but either way it's not going to have any information on someone who went missing in 1979."

"Alright, alright. I get the point." Amber looks despondent.

"So what do we do then?"

I reach into my bag and begin to pull out a folder.

"We might not be able to search for Henry Jacobs, but we can search for Barbara Jacobs." I open the folder and start to read.

"Barbara June Jacobs is the granddaughter of the Charles Bennett, who opened the first silver mine at Lornea Island's Northend in 1899. While the Northend mine closed with the 1950 disaster, Northend Mining Corporation is still a major player in international ore mining around the world, particularly in Africa. Barbara Jacobs sat on the Northend Mining Corporation board of directors until 2005 when she stepped down."

"How do you know all that?" Amber asks, and I hand her the paper I'm reading. On it there's a picture of Mrs. Jacobs, only quite a bit younger, and wearing a red ball gown.

"She was on something called the Lornea Island Council. When you click on her picture, this is what comes up."

Amber spends a long time reading all the pages I've printed out. In front of her there's a packet of sandwiches. And just looking at them makes me feel quite hungry, because I didn't have time to make any lunch this morning. And also, because between Tucker and Steven, we don't have much food left in the house.

"Can I have a sandwich?" I ask."

"Huh?" Amber looks up. "Yeah sure. They're not very nice though. Tuna mayo, but the tuna was old. All I could find in the cupboard."

She goes back to her reading. And because I've already read it all, I take a sandwich and start to eat it.

"OK. So we know she's *old Lornea Island,* and she likes going to charity events. So she's rich, but we knew that already. What we don't know is anything about her husband, let alone how he went missing. Or even *if* he did. So how do we find him?"

Amber's right about the tuna. It's a bit nasty. I decide to wrap up what's left and give it to Steven later. Amber looks up.

"I did have one idea." I kind of say, with my mouth still half full of mashed up fish.

"What?"

I can't help but smile a little bit, because this is a really good idea.

"You know how I said the internet was only invented in 1983, except for people who don't regard it as the real internet until Tim Berners Lee...

"Yeah."

"Well. You also know about *The Island Times*, the biggest newspaper on Lornea Island? How you can search through old editions of the paper on the internet?"

"Yeah," Amber says, and already she's pulling up the website. I smile some more.

"Then you also know it only goes back to 2000, because they didn't do the internet before then?"

Amber stops. "Oh. *Yeah I knew that too.*" Even though I know she didn't. Not really.

"Well they still *made* the newspaper, back then. Still wrote it I mean."

"So?"

"So, you can still search it. It's just not on the internet. You have to go to the actual newspaper office and do searches there. They have a special room for it. On a microfiche machine. It says so on their website.

Amber stares at me for a moment, looking thoughtful.

"Show me." She says.

I lean across to use the keyboard, still talking while I type the address and the page loads.

"It's just like in those movies." I go on, because I'm not sure if she really understands properly.

"What movies?"

"You know the kind of movies. Where they're searching for something in files somewhere. And it always takes them forever, but then, right at the end they find it. Here you go."

Amber reads on the website about the *Island Times* reading room. And then suddenly she just gets up, brushing all her papers together.

"Come on."

"Where are we going?"

"To the newspaper office. I've got mom's car."

I'm a bit surprised by this, since we only get an hour for lunch, and we've already had fifteen minutes. We won't be able to get there and back in time.

"What about class?" I say.

"What about class?"

"Well, we might miss it..."

"So? This is way more important."

I totally don't know what to say to that, but Amber's already gone.

FIFTEEN

I STUFF my folder back in my bag. Amber hasn't put away the books she's used, so I quickly dump them onto the trolley that Mrs. Lopez uses to put the returned books back to where they go on the shelves, because you're not supposed to just leave them on the computer tables like Amber did.

Then I start to run, I can see Amber at the bottom of the stairs, and it doesn't look like she's going to wait for me at all. I just about catch her up in the lobby, and I'm about to say something when she stops.

"Wait here, I need to pee," she says, and then she disappears into the girls' bathroom. I'm starting to think that Amber is quite an annoying person.

But then something amazing happens. I start to look around the lobby – it's one of those spaces that you don't really look at much, even though you go through it every day. There's a long reception desk, empty, because the receptionists have a little room they work from. Then there's a few plants to trick parents and visitors into thinking Newlea High School is a much nicer place than it really is. And up on the wall there's all this wood paneling, with all the names of important people in the school over the years. Like an honors board. And for some reason I start to read down the names on the honors board. I'm not really paying attention, I'm just passing the time, when suddenly I notice something.

But before I can do anything about it, I'm interrupted by a voice right behind me.

"Hey Wheatley!"

I recognize the voice at once. It's James Drolley, the idiot from my class earlier. When I turn around he's with all the other boys who ruined Geography earlier.

"Hanging out by the girl's bathroom Wheatley? Why don't you just go in there?"

Drolley's friends all start laughing, as if what he said was actually a joke.

Though it isn't really. I don't reply. I get a bad feeling that they're not just going to walk by. It's lunchtime after all, they've got plenty of time.

And sure enough I'm right. They all stop and gather round me in a circle. Then James steps really close to me.

"Why'd ya get in the way?" Drolley asks. He pushes me in the chest. He's one of the smallest boys in the class, not much bigger than I am. I think it bothers him a bit.

"In the way of what?" I ask.

"In class you *fucktard!* I was aiming for Smith. Until you got in the way." He shoves me again, harder this time. The others laugh again.

"Go on James," one of his friends says. "Hit him." The boy's name is Paul. I used to be sort of friends with Paul, but then he got in with James Drolley and his gang instead.

There's no point answering any of them, so I turn away from Drolley, and look back at the wooden honors board again, not quite believing what I saw before. But then I get pushed really hard from behind, and I nearly fall over.

"*Don't fucking ignore me Wheatley.*" Drolley says. I only just manage to stay on my feet, and somehow my bag comes off my shoulder. Then suddenly Drolley is holding it. I realize it hurts where he pulled it from me.

"Hey," I say. I sense I need to concentrate now or things are going to turn bad.

"Give it back."

"Why?" James challenges. "You gonna make me?" He shakes my bag.

"You got any food for me Wheatley? I'm kinda hungry."

"No," I say. "I haven't got anything."

Drolley stares at me for a second. "Let's check shall we? Make sure you're telling the truth." Then he unzips my bag and looks inside. As he does so I remember the tuna mayo sandwich I wrapped up for Steven.

"Well lookie here..." Drolley pulls it out and opens the packet. "Mmmm. Tuna sandwich. My favorite. So you *were* lying Wheatley. You little fucking *shit.* You think you can lie to me?" He throws the sandwich to one of his friends, but with the packet open the two bits of bread separate and it all falls to the floor where Paul stamps on it.

"Awww fuck." Drolley says. "I can't eat that now Wheatley. You got any more?" He looks again in the bag, pulling out my books and folders to check if anything else is there. Then he pulls out the folder I made last night. I get a sudden, sinking feeling in my stomach.

"Hey, what's the fuck is this?"

On the front of the folder that Drolley is holding is a the logo Amber drew for the detective agency, only I've colored it in, and made it better. Arranged around the drawing are words, in a circle around the image of the magnifying glass. Drolley turns his head as he tries to read them.

"Newlea Island... Detective Agency?" His face lights up in delight, because – even though he's stupid – he knows when he's hit upon something he can use.

"Is that you Wheatley? Are you the *Newlea Island fucking Detective Agency*?" He opens it, letting some pages waft to the floor, and starts reading out my notes. I sense this is about to get really out of control when there's a sudden scream from across the lobby.

"*Fucking leave him alone you fucking gobshite faggots.*"

Before I know what's happening, Amber is amongst us, like some kind of wild cat. She shoves James in the chest so hard that he falls over on his butt. Then, before he can get up she makes like she's going to kick him with her massive boots. He scuttles away, looking a bit like a beetle, so in the end she doesn't actually kick him. Instead she turns to his friends. There's a sudden, stunned silence, but then the boys re-group, because it's still five against two, even though Amber is older than them.

"The fuck has this got to do with you, *Goth*?" Paul asks, but he kind of mutters it, and he's a long way back from her. Except she then turns on him.

"Fuck you! You motherfucking dumbass dipshit," she steps towards him, and he almost stumbles, he backs away so quick.

"You want me to rip your tiny dick off and stuff it up your ass?"

I take advantage of the sudden silence to gather together my notes and slip them back in the folder. When I look again Drolley is back on his feet. He's trying to make himself look brave.

"Are you part of it too, *Goth*?" Drolley says, now he's surrounded again by his friends. "Billy Wheatley's fucking detective *club*?"

"I said fuck off maggot-dick." Then Amber actually spits at him, but because Drolley is hiding behind his friends, it lands on Paul's bag. It looks for a second like he might have to react to that, but then she lunges forward like she really wants to kill them all, and they scatter out of her way. Then the others realize they can turn on Paul and laugh at him, now he's got Amber's spit on his bag. That way they can still be bullying, and pretend to themselves that they're not scared of Amber. Paul looks pretty miserable about it, but at least they're leaving now. As they do Drolley shouts over his shoulder.

"See you in class Wheatley. You can't always have a *vampire* to protect you."

There's an awkward silence as Amber and me watch them disappear, jostling each other and laughing loudly, as if there were never worried.

"I hate assholes like that," Amber tells me. "Really fucking hate them."

I wonder for a moment about explaining my idea for BullyTracker but decide it's not a good time.

"Come on. Let's get out of here," Amber goes on.

"Hang on," I put my hand on her arm to stop her, and she turns in surprise. But then I point to the honors board I noticed before.

"What?"

Newlea High School is really old. I didn't tell you that, but it is. It's been here for maybe a hundred years, or maybe longer. So the list of important people in the school goes way back too. And the honors board lists them all out, in gold letters. And one of those names, the gold glowing where a shaft of sunlight hits it from the skylight, is the name we've been looking for.

"Look at the honors board."

"*What?* Why?"

"Look at the list of school principals."

Amber frowns at me again, but I see her eyes begin to scan the list. And then she gets to 1972-1979, where the principal is listed as "Henry Arthur Jacobs."

"*Shit*," Amber says. "He was the school principal?"

SIXTEEN

It's not far into town but it's quite scary because of how bad Amber is at driving in traffic. She nearly kills three people, then a dog, then parks half on and half off the sidewalk. I don't know if I feel more worried about being out of school at lunchtime, or dying in a car wreck.

The *Island Times'* office is one of the big stone buildings in the centre of Newlea. I've never been in it, but I've seen it loads of times. It has that look of somewhere that used to be really important, but isn't anymore. It does still have a revolving door though, which is quite fun to walk through.

Inside we find two ladies behind a long reception desk. There are copies of this week's edition of the paper laid out all neatly, and an old man is giving some listing for the second hand section. I don't know why, you can just do it online.

"We want to search old editions of the paper," Amber says, when one of the receptionists turns to us.

"It says on your website you can do it here. You've some kind of reading room?"

"Sure." She studies us for a moment, quite suspicious. "School project is it?"

"Not exactly." Amber replies, with a smile. The woman doesn't smile back.

"Only if it's for commercial purposes I have to charge you."

"Oh. It's definitely a school project then," Amber says, and I feel her foot pressing into my leg.

I don't say anything. Honestly, sometimes I wonder if Amber thinks I'm stupid.

The woman comes out from behind her desk and leads us to a door in the corner of the room, it leads to a very small room where there's just a computer terminal and a couple of chairs.

"Where's the microfiche machine?" I ask.

"All the records have been digitized. We wouldn't be able to trust the original records with children." She wiggles the mouse to bring the computer to life.

"You put your search terms in there." She points at the screen. "You sure this is for a school project?"

"No it definitely is," Amber replies, and after a moment the woman leaves us to it. I'm still a bit disappointed we don't actually get to use the microfiche machine, but Amber sits right down and begins typing. She puts in the words:

Henry Jacobs

After a few moments the computer loads up results and we scan them. There's lots of mentions of 'Henry', and quite a few of 'Jacobs', but none mentioning them together. So I tell her to put them together properly, like this:

Henry + Jacobs

This cuts down the results to just three articles.

The first, from February 1979 has the headline:

Roadworks causing pupils to miss up to an hour's education a week, head teacher says.

We click to see the story, but it's not like a normal website. It takes us to an actual copy of the newspaper, laid out just like it was in 1979. There's only one mention of Henry Jacobs, and it takes a while to find it. When we do it says this:

School Principal Henry Jacobs warned that school buses are not able to get pupils to school due to the upgrading work on the main Silverlea to Newlea link.

We scan read the whole thing, but it doesn't seem very relevant.

"Go back," Amber says. "What's the next one?"

I click back and try the next link.

State-of-the-art building project to bring world-class gymnasium to Newlea High School.

This time the article is a bit more interesting.

Building work has commenced on a new project to construct a world-class gymnasium at Newlea High School. Henry Jacobs, School Principal, commented that students would now be able to play a range of sports in the new indoor facility.

There's a picture too, only instead of being a photograph, it's an artists' impression of all these children in a gym, dressed in old fashioned gym shorts. It's interesting because it's not just *a* gym. It's *our* gym. It's the *actual gym* we have to use at school.

"World-class facilities? Fucking hell, he was hopeful wasn't he?" Amber says. "Go back. Go to the next one."

I do what she says, and click the final link.

New Principal starts at Newlea High School

Dated February 1980, the article only briefly mentions Henry Jacobs, where it says this:

Mrs. Clarke steps into the vacancy left when Henry Jacobs quit his position of Principal in Christmas last year.

I get an excited feeling as I read on, expecting it to say what happened to him, but it doesn't. It just says how the new principal wants to move the school forward and prepare the students for the world, and things like that.

"Is that it?" Amber asks. "Isn't there anything more?"

We search for a while longer, trying different keywords. But nothing comes up. It's a bit disappointing after such a promising start. After another half-hour of searching we give up.

"I can't believe there's nothing more. How can someone disappear – how can the *school principal* disappear – and there's no mention of it in the newspaper?"

"I don't know," I say. "But at least it matches what Mrs. Jacobs said. How her husband went missing in Christmas 1979. At least we know she remembered that part right."

"Yeah, I suppose so," Amber replies, but she's clearly not satisfied. I've been getting worried about something else though.

"Hey, do you think we should maybe get back? We're going to get in trouble otherwise, for skipping class."

If Amber hears me she doesn't answer.

"It's just I already had to see Principal Sharpe once this month already...." I don't actually mean to say this, since Amber obviously already knows, but it just slips out. But it's OK because Amber just ignores me anyway.

"What do we know?" She says instead. She grabs her notebook and turns to a fresh page. "What do we actually *know* about what happened?"

I don't answer her, but again she ignores me. She answers her own question.

"We know Mrs. Jacobs says he went missing in 1979. At Christmas time. She said they were putting up the decorations, when he just walked out and never came back."

Amber writes on her pad *Christmas 1979* and then circles it. "And we know from the school honors board that Henry was school principal from 1973 to 1979. And from the *Island Times* that a new school principal started in 1980." She looks to me, as if it's my turn to add to the list of facts.

"And we know Mrs. Jacobs is crazy. So he might not have gone missing at all. He might have just... left."

Amber gives me a warning glance.

"Then why does she think he went missing? She wouldn't have hired us if there was no mystery."

I don't have an answer to this, so I think about it instead. I suppose it must count as some sort of evidence. At least a little bit.

"Well, maybe, but we don't know anything else."

"Actually we do," Amber says, and slowly she starts to smile.

"We do what?"

"We do know something else."

I frown and try to work out what she means. I don't much like the look of satisfaction on her face.

"Come on Billy. We've searched the newspaper right? For anything about him disappearing? And we've not found anything?"

"Yeah."

"So what does that mean?"

I really want to work it out, before she tells me, and I think I nearly do, but just not quite in time.

"It tells us that whatever happened wasn't a big thing. If he was – I don't know – murdered by a serial killer, or died in a big car wreck, it would have been all over the paper and we'd have found it. So because it *wasn't* there, we know that when he disappeared, it wasn't a big thing. It wasn't *news*."

I open my mouth to object to this, but I can't. It's quite clever actually.

SEVENTEEN

It's the middle of afternoon classes when we get back to school. I kind of expect to get into trouble walking into the lobby, but all the receptionists are back in their little room and they don't come out. It's strange though, standing in the empty lobby and looking up at the honors board. I stare at Henry Jacobs' name up there, picked out in gold letters. For a moment it's like I'm in the school, all those years ago. Someone who stood right here must know what happened to him, why he left...

"Hey Billy," Amber interrupts my thoughts. "Don't just stand there? Someone'll see you."

"Oh sorry,"

"When you get to class say you had a doctor's appointment. Say it's for something personal. That way they can't ask you about it."

I nod, and Amber leaves, to whatever class she has, and I go to Math. I decide to tell Mr. Duncan I had a dentist's appointment, and I'm all ready to pretend I've got toothache, but he doesn't really care, he just tells me to sit down. After that it's PD. And after that I get on the bus home. But all the time I'm thinking about how we can find out more about Henry Jacobs. I start to get some ideas too. But then, when I get home, everything changes.

It feels like an ambush. As I walk in the kitchen Dad and Tucker are there waiting for me.

"Billy," Dad begins. "Can you take a seat? We need to have chat."

From the sound of his voice I think I'm in trouble. For a second I wonder if he's found out about me skipping class, but how? Did Mr Duncan know I was lying about the dentist after all? And then I think that maybe it's *Tucker* who's in trouble. Maybe Dad's figured out about him lying about his name. Or not having a phone.

But then from the way Tucker's smiling at me, sipping on a beer, it can't be that either.

"Come on Billy, take a seat."

I still haven't taken my backpack off, but I do so now, and slip behind the kitchen table. Dad sits down opposite me. He smiles at me, but it's not a real smile. It's fake.

"What it is?" I ask.

Dad's smile falls away. "I need to tell you something. Some news. Some good news."

"What?" I ask again.

Dad looks away, and rubs a hand over the stubble on his face, so I know it's not really good news after all.

"What news?"

"You know I said Tucker would be staying here a few days?" He begins.

"Yes. That was last Thursday, so he's supposed to go two days ago..."

"Sure." Dad holds up a hand to cut me off. "Sure, I know. The point is he still needs..." Dad stops and rubs his chin again. When he continues he's changed the subject.

"Look, I got a call from Frank earlier. You know Frank, down at the harbor?"

I wait. I guess I must frown too, since Dad explains.

"You know Frank? The skipper of *Ocean Harvest*?"

For a second I don't know what he's on about, but then I remember. *Ocean Harvest* is one of the fishing boats. The big ones. I don't *really know* Frank though. It's just one time he did let me on board one time to do a species count of the fish in the hold.

"A space has come up. For a job."

I blink.

"It's just a try out, but it's good money. Real good money. If we get a good catch, it'd be enough to start saving. Putting something away, for... well for whatever."

Both him and Tucker are staring at me really intently now. I slide my eyes from one to the other.

"But *Ocean Harvest* is an offshore boat?"

"She goes out a bit further." Dad nods. "Sure she does. But that's where the money is. It's a modern boat Billy. It's totally safe. It just means I'll be away a bit longer." Dad lets his voice fade away. So I have to work out what he means.

"How long?"

Dad makes a face, like this is an awkward bit.

"Frank reckons it's a day and a half to get out to the fishing grounds. Then the same back. So it depends on the catch. Could be four nights. A week tops."

"A *week*? So who's going to look after me?"

Straight away I'm pissed at myself for saying this. I don't *need* anyone to look after me. Most of the time it's me looking after Dad. But a week is a long time.

And then I turn to Tucker. Or Peter. Or whatever his real name is. I see he's looking right back at me. Watching my reaction.

"It's what I was saying about Tucker," Dad goes on, but I hardly hear him. "How he needs a place to crash. Just for a little bit longer."

"But you said he was only going to be here a few days," I interrupt. "He should have gone home three days ago..."

"*Billy.* It's a good solution. He can keep an eye on you while he gets himself set up. I can show Frank he can rely on me. It's the opportunity we've been waiting for."

"Set up?"

"Sure. Tuck's gonna give it a go here on Lornea. Look for work."

"*Look for work*?" I can feel my voice go high again. It feels like it's betraying me.

"Come on Billy, I know this is a surprise. But you know I've been trying to get a place on a boat? We've talked about it."

"Yeah, but not on one of the big boats. You talked about the inshore ones."

"There's no fish inshore no more Billy. You know that."

I don't reply. I suddenly realize I'm breathing super hard.

"Come on Billy, we *need* this. I've gotta have some real money coming in. We got bills to pay. And if I can save a bit we can..." Dad doesn't finish his sentence. But I sense what he was going to say. It's to do with my idea for buying *Blue Lady,* and running whale watching trips for tourists.

I try to think fast. Maybe it *is* a good idea. But then I think about Tucker again. Or Peter. About how I'm going to be left alone with him, when I don't even know which is his real name. How can Dad think that's OK? I *have* to say something.

But I don't.

"When are you going?" I ask instead.

And this time Dad doesn't answer at once. He takes a deep breath and puffs it out. Like this bit's going to be difficult.

"We're leaving on the next high tide."

At once my eyes flick to the window. Because I'm sitting down at the table, I can't see the beach, but I don't even need to. I always know what the tide is doing.

"The *next* high? Tonight's high?" My voice has risen again.

"I know it's short notice Bill. One of the other crew phoned in sick. That's why Frank rang me. That's why I wanted to have this talk now. As soon as you got back from school. I wanted to speak to you before I go."

I calculate in my head. Next high tide is in two hours. It's a half hour drive to Holport, where *Ocean Harvest* comes in. He'll have to go in an hour and a half.

"I gotta help load up too." Dad goes on, like he's reading my mind. "I gotta leave now."

"*Now?*"

Why does my voice keep going so high?

I look out the window again. I can see the sky as it hangs over the sea. The light is fading now, and it highlights the clouds building into towering thunderheads. Mottled grey, studded with showers of rain. I think of Dad heading out there. Hundreds of miles out there.

"There's a storm coming." I say. I don't know why I say it, because it's not really true. It's just a bit of rain. At least, it is here. I don't actually know what it'll be like miles out to sea.

"She's a new boat Billy. She's safe. And... efficient. You get a place on *Ocean Harvest*, it's a safe income."

Suddenly Tucker joins in the conversation. So far he hasn't spoken a word, just stood there, drinking his beer.

"We'll be alright Billy," his voice sounds weird. Creepy. "We'll get to know each other." He grins at me, and I notice his incisors are really long. Yellow, but brown at the gums where he doesn't clean them properly. He takes a swig of his beer. I can feel tears forming behind my eyes, and I don't want Tucker to see them. I really don't want that. I turn back to Dad.

"I'm gonna go to my room. I've got homework."

Dad strokes his chin again a couple of times, then he just nods.

"OK."

I wasn't expecting that. I thought he'd stop me, but now he isn't I don't have a choice. I pick up my bag and go to the stairs. As I climb up I'm still hoping Dad's going to call me back. But he doesn't. So in the end I go into my room and I have to deal with Steven hopping all over me and pecking at my face. And then I haven't even taken his fish from downstairs, and I can't really go and get it right now.

So I wait. I'm still pretty sure Dad will come and see me before he leaves. So I listen out for the squeak of the floorboards in the stairs, the sound that tells me Dad's coming up. And I decide that when he does, I'm just going to tell him. I'm going to tell him about how Tucker isn't really called Tucker at all, and how he lied to me about not having a cell phone, when he does have one really. And when I think about that, I remember how I stuck that hair across my door, and how it wasn't there when I came back, which proves that he's been searching in my room.

And I know that when I tell Dad all this, he'll realize he can't leave me alone with Tucker. He'll sort it out. He'll work out who he really is, and he'll make sure he's not in our house anymore. I know he's been trying to get a place on a boat for a long time. I know he needs the money. But he'll realize he can't do it this way.

But instead of the squeak of the stairs, I hear another noise – the bang of the front door. So I creep to my window, and I peek out of it, since it might just be Tucker outside, and I don't want him to see me.

But it's not Tucker. It's Dad. He's throwing his kit bag into the back of the truck, and then climbing behind the wheel. And then Tucker gets in the other side, laughing as he does so. And then there's the noise of the engine firing up. I think I see Dad glancing up at my window as he begins turning around, but I pull back out of sight. And when I next look they're driving off down the lane.

EIGHTEEN

It's the next morning now. I feel a little better about things. Well, as better as it's possible to feel, given the circumstances.

I ended up staying up really late last night. Working. First of all I downloaded a new app to my computer. It's called *VesselTrack,* and you can use it to show where all the ships are in the world, in real time. So I've set it up to show me exactly where Dad is. At the moment this is where he is:

lat: 42.25495 lon: -68.13995

He's heading 077 degrees, and they're going at ten knots. That means they're about sixty miles away and still heading out. The weather isn't too rough though. The wind is force four and forecast to drop. That's hardly anything. It's worse than that here.

So I decided the more urgent problem is me being left alone in the house with Tucker. Or whatever his real name is.

I think about this first. I try to use logic to work it out, starting from what I definitely know. For example. I know that Dad thinks his name is Tucker. But I also know he has identification in his wallet where he's called Peter Smith. He can't be called both names, so one must be fake. You might think that the official identification - his driver's license - is the most likely to be the real one, but you're forgetting something. You see, Dad *grew up with him,* back in Crab Creek. So if Dad thinks he's called Tucker that must be true. Which means *Peter Smith* must be either a new name, or an alias.

I make a list of why people might use an alias. This is what I write:

Because he's a spy.
Because he an undercover policeman.
Because he's in the witness protection scheme.

Then I use google and find some more possibilities. I add the following:

Because he's an author and it's a pen name.
Because he's a celebrity and wants to travel incognito.
Because he's a criminal and wants to hide his identity.

Then I cross out the ideas that are impossible, or really unlikely. And the only one left is the last one. So Tucker is a criminal who wants to hide his identity.

Next I have a really good look around my room, to see if anything was missing from when he broke in. I don't think anything is. I do get the feeling that a few things were out of place – my desk drawers not quite closed as I'd left them, that sort of thing, but to be honest, it could have been Steven. But then, I have a good idea. I start to think about *why* Tucker might have tried to break into my room in the first place. The obvious answer is that he was looking for things to steal, because I already know he's a criminal. But since he's currently living in our lounge, it doesn't exactly make sense to steal things from my room, and just take them downstairs. So maybe he wasn't looking to steal something, but doing something else? But if that's the case, then what?

And then I work it out. Do you remember how he asked me, the morning after he got here, if he could use my computer? And then he said he wanted it to access the internet, because he didn't have a phone? But then I discovered he was lying about not having a phone. He *did* have one, only he was hiding it. I didn't understand why anyone would do that at the time. But I think I do now. It's all to do with how cell phones work.

I saw a documentary on it. And it's quite technical but this is the basic point: Cell phones connect to base stations by sending radio waves back-and-forth. Whenever your cell phone is switched on, it's constantly sending out messages, called handshakes, to the nearest base station, kind of like it's saying 'Hi, I'm over here'. It does this so the telephone company knows where to send all the calls and actual messages you get. Otherwise they'd have to send *every* call and *every* message to *every* base station, just in case all their customers happened to be standing next to it. And that would be crazy, because all the base stations would fill up, and they'd probably explode. But what this means is, when you have your cell phone switched on, your telephone company knows where you are. *And so do the police*. The police have access to the same system, and they use it to track down where criminals are. They do it all the time. And the thing is, it's not even a big secret – the criminals know about too. Probably because they saw the same documentary that I did.

The reason why this is important is this. When criminals are on the run from the police they have to leave their phones switched off. They can't even use the internet on them, because just having the phone on means it'll send a handshake message to the nearest base station, saying 'here I am!'

That's why Tucker/Peter lied about not having a phone – because he couldn't switch it on to use it. It also explains why he wanted to get into my room. He must have needed to use the internet again. So he broke into my room to try to find my computer. Luckily I had it with me at the time.

And then – because I find with me, good ideas often come in threes or fours – I have another good idea. I realize that, if Tucker doesn't want to turn his phone on because the police are using it to look for him, then there's a really easy way to get rid of him. All I need to do is find his phone and switch it on. It'll send a handshake to the nearest base station, and the police will see that and know exactly where he is. They'll come and arrest him. And because he won't even know about it, he won't be expecting them. And best of all, no one will ever know it was me.

I can't do it right now though. There's two reasons for that. First of all I don't want to get Dad into trouble. I'm not sure if it's illegal or not, but I don't expect they'll be very impressed he's gone off for a week and left me with a violent criminal. But there's another reason too – I don't know where Tucker's phone is. I haven't seen it since that time I searched his jeans. So I'll have to watch him carefully to see if I can get any clues where he might be hiding it.

And then I get *another* idea. Even better than just turning Tucker's phone on.

I wasn't sure at first if it would work, so I had to do some checking on the internet, and it was already nearly midnight by then. I know it was, because that's when I heard Dad's truck come back, and I looked out of the window to see Tucker getting out. He must have gone to a bar after dropping Dad off. I watched him with the light off, to see if he was drunk. But it was hard to tell.

Then I went back to work. I found some software that had a trial period, so it wasn't going to cost me any money. Then I took everything that was really important off my computer, just in case. I have it all backed up anyway. Then I did some testing, and checked it all worked. And then, at about two in the morning, I finally went to bed.

So when I go to school today I'm not taking my laptop. I'm going to 'accidentally' forget it. I'm going to leave it right here on the kitchen table, switched on, with the password disabled. Like I *meant* to put it in my bag, but forgot it at the last minute.

But I'm not really forgetting it.

It's a trap.

NINETEEN

It's really hard to concentrate at school because of wondering whether Tucker/Peter has fallen for it or not. The first lesson seems to take forever, and then in morning break I have a little bit of bother with James Drolley and his little gang. But then Mr. Stewart comes along. He's one of the gym teachers, and they always act like they're perfect students around him because they love gym, so they leave me alone.

At lunchtime I go and see if Amber is in the library. But she isn't there. I look out the window to see if her mom's car is in the parking lot, but that's not there either. Although that doesn't mean anything, because some days Amber isn't allowed to use it.

And then we have history class all afternoon, and we finish up with a test. At least that's quite fun.

Eventually the bell rings for the end of the day, and I get on the bus. And then just like normal I have to wait while everyone else gets dropped off, since my stop is the very last one on the route.

But finally the bus gets to the Littlelea stop, and the doors wheeze open. I get off and hurry down the little lane to our house. But then, when I see Dad's truck, and see how Tucker's parked it differently to how Dad does, suddenly I start to feel less excited and more – well, nervous I suppose. After all, Dad's hundreds of miles out to sea and I'm alone with a dangerous, violent criminal. And the thing is, last night when I was setting up my trap, I assumed he was just a *normal* criminal. But what if that's wrong? What if he's actually a computer-expert criminal? You know, the type in those movies who can disable alarms and open safes electronically. He doesn't look like one, I know, but then maybe that's a kind of disguise.

And then I remember the photograph in his wallet – where it showed his real name was Peter Smith. He actually *did look* like a computer expert in that photo. If

Tucker/Peter is a computer-expert criminal, then he's going to know I tried to trap him.

I start to feel short of breath. What if he's in there now, knowing I know who he really is? Knowing I know the police are looking for him? I think of those muscles he has all over him. I'm getting quite strong, but I'm nowhere near as strong as that.

But then I tell myself to be rational. He's not a computer expert, he can't be. People with muscles like that are never computer experts, even if they are in disguise. If Tucker/Peter is a criminal, and I remind myself that I don't know this for 100% yet, then he's the type who's good at fighting and violence. Or even the type who's not very good at anything much, given the police are looking for him.

So, even though there's no way I can know for sure, I decide it's unlikely that Tucker will have realized the computer is a trap. So I take a deep breath, and I unlock the front door.

* * *

Tucker is in the kitchen. I didn't expect that. He's standing next to the stove stirring something in a big saucepan. He turns around to look at me, his face impassive. I can't tell anything from it.

My computer is still on the kitchen table, but it's not where I left it. It's been moved to the end. The space where it was has been laid for dinner.

"Finally," Tucker says. "I was going to eat without you." He ladles up a spoonful of something red and lets it slop back down. If he's angry at me trying to trap him, he's hiding it well.

"I hope you like spicy shit." He flashes a smile, but it's only a half smile, just a flash of those yellow incisors and he goes back to looking – I dunno, it's a funny look. I don't know what it means.

I still haven't moved from the front door.

"Come on Billy. Take a goddamn pew. I wanna eat."

I don't move, except to look at my computer again. The lid is shut – I left it open, to look as inviting as possible, with the screen unlocked and the power plugged in, so that it would sit there, tempting him to use it.

"Tell me something. You have a good day at school? You giving the teachers shit? Talk to me."

I glance up at him, and notice how he was following my gaze. I'm not 100% sure, but I think he looks guilty for a moment.

"Come on kid. Sit down."

I don't have a choice, so I do what he says. Then I watch him as he goes to the refrigerator.

"You wanna beer? I won't tell your old man."

"I don't like beer."

Tucker shrugs and takes one for himself. Then he kicks the refrigerator door shut, grabs two plates and serves up two enormous portions of rice and the stuff he was stirring. It turns out to be beans with tomatoes. He sets one down in front of me, and then sits down opposite me. I wonder if he's going to try and make small talk, but instead he just starts eating, shoveling the food in fast. I try a little bit of the sauce, and though it's really spicy, it is actually quite nice. So I start to eat properly. Though what I really want to do is get my computer upstairs and see if my trap's worked.

"You hear anything from your old man?" Tucker asks after a few minutes. I look up and see he's finished already.

"No."

"You know whereabouts he is?"

This question could be a kind of test. I left the *VesselTrack* app on my laptop. Is this his way of letting me know he's seen it?

"No. Not really." I go back to my food. It's actually very nice. You wouldn't think someone like Tucker could cook so well.

"He told me where he was going. It sounds a long way, but it ain't really. And the weather's good. Better out there than here." I don't answer him. But I glance up at his face, and he gives me another half smile. I look back down again.

"You like sports?" He says suddenly.

"Pardon?"

"Sports. Football? Basketball? I dunno, *badminton*? You like it?"

"Oh. No. Not much."

Tucker chuckles.

"You're not such big talker are you Billy?" Tucker says, and again I don't say anything.

"Like your Dad I guess. He was always the strong silent type. Maybe that's what your mom saw in him. She came from a family of big talkers. Real flash bunch. You're lucky you take after him, you ask me."

I move another forkful of the food up to my mouth, but this time I don't taste it. I've never met anyone, other than Dad, who actually *knew* my mom. In a way I'd like to find out more about her. But this is hardly the time to ask.

Then there's a beep from my phone. It's the noise it makes when a message comes in. I slip it out and look at the screen, and straight away I see it's from Amber. Obviously I can't read it at the table with Tucker looking on.

"This is important," I say to Tucker, making sure he can't see the screen. "I need to..."

"Sure," he says. He inclines his head, like he's telling me it's OK to leave.

"It's just something from..." I stop quickly, annoyed at myself. I don't need to tell Tucker who it is, but now I've started I have to finish the sentence.

"From school," I say. It sounds a bit lame.

"No bother. You go. I'll clean up here." He leans back in his chair and beats his chest with his fists, like he's a gorilla or something. Quickly I take another couple of mouthfuls, and then put the fork down. I stuff my phone back into my pocket and pick up my computer. I'm about to head upstairs when I remember my manners.

"Thanks," I say. "For the food."

"Anytime kid. I told your old man I'd look after you didn't I?"

* * *

As soon as I get into my room I open my laptop. It doesn't ask for a password, but I type one in anyway. It's a secret password. It stops the software I installed last night from working. Then I get to work, opening the programs and scanning down the results.

Right away I can tell that I've got some results. My computer was used while I was at school. My trap worked.

TWENTY

THINGS CHANGE PRETTY FAST after that.

I put two different types of software onto my laptop. The first was something called *SpyCatch*. What it does is secretly record everything that happens to your computer. Every time someone uses the keyboard, it turns on the webcam and starts recording. Only there's nothing to tell the person using it that the webcam is on. It does it secretly. It doesn't even turn on the little red light. If you're using the computer, you'd never know that you're being recorded the whole time.

That's what I look at first. I open *Spycatch*, and it has a list of the videos it's made during the day, along with the time it made them. The first is at 08:47. I have to catch the school bus at 08:30. That means Tucker must have got up and used my laptop less than fifteen minutes after I went to school.

I *knew* it.

I click the file, and wait while the video player loads. Then there's a sudden image of Tucker, leaning in close to the computer. Actually seeing him there takes my breath away too. He *really did steal* my computer. And if I'm right about that, then maybe I'm right about everything else as well. I suddenly feel exposed, with him downstairs, and no lock on my bedroom door. So before I hit play I get up and drag my wooden chest in front of the door of my bedroom, just so there no chance that he can surprise me by walking into my room, and see what I'm doing. Then I plug in some headphones, so he can't hear me either, and I sit back down to watch.

Tucker doesn't have a top on, I can see his tattoos and his muscles. He's sitting down at the breakfast table, frowning at something just below the screen. It takes me a while to figure out that he's frowning at the keyboard. He must be trying to type, only he has to look at the keys when he does so. This makes me a lot more confident that whatever type of criminal he is, it's not the computer expert type.

I don't know what he's typing from looking at *SpyCatch*, but I've got that covered for later. Now I just keep watching, and for a long while he stares back at me through the screen. I can see his eyes moving left to right, so I guess he's reading something. I can see his lips move too.

Then suddenly he gets up. It's hard to tell, but he looks angry when he does it. Something about the way he pushes himself back from the table. Then he's out of the frame for a long time, and I'm about to fast forward the file when he comes back. He sits again, but he keeps shaking his head. Then there's this really long section of the recording where he's got his head in his hands. And then he's rubbing his face all over, covering his eyes. When I next see them, there's a moment when it looks like he's actually crying.

But then things go crazy. He starts swearing. I can hear it so loud I panic, but then I remember it's only in the headphones. I won't say the word, but he uses it over and over and over. It's the one beginning with F. He shouts it really loud.

And then there's a couple of minutes where he leaves the chair again. And then when he's back I see right away he's holding his cell phone. I snap to attention.

He's calmed down now. He just sits there, staring at the phone – not like he's using it, more like he's thinking about using it, because I can see it's still switched off. Every now and then his thumb hovers over the button, like he wants to turn it on, but something's stopping him.

Bang!

Then there's a moment that makes me literally jump. Real suddenly he slams the phone down against the edge of the table. It must have made the laptop jump too, because the image suddenly changes, like the screen got knocked and the angle of the camera changed. Now it shows the door of the kitchen, and I can't see Tucker. But then I can. Because the next thing I see is Tucker walking through the door, outside.

I'm baffled by this. He's still got no top on, just a pair of jeans, so he can't be going out for the day. I'm about to fast forward again, but then he comes back in. The next thing is the laptop is suddenly slammed shut, and the recording ends.

I rewind a bit and watch it again. This time I try to focus on whether he's carrying anything as he walks out of the kitchen. It's hard to tell for sure, but it looks as though he has something black in his hand – the cell phone. And it's definitely clear when he comes back that he's not holding it – I get a clear view of his hands as he walks up to the laptop to close it.

So then I minimize SpyCatch and think. For years now I've had a weather station mounted outside my bedroom window. It also has a camera that pointed down at the beach, and everything was linked to the internet so that people could actually find out the weather and actually see the surfing conditions on Silverlea beach, before they drove down from Newlea. But it wasn't a very good camera, it only took one picture every hour, and then some water got into the lens after a storm, so that the image was all misty. So about a year ago I bought a better camera on eBay, one that records actual video. You're supposed to be able to log in from anywhere in the world and see the view from outside my bedroom window, in real time, and high definition. The problem is, the camera was second hand, and

I couldn't find any instructions for how to set it up, so I never managed to get it to connect to the internet. I did set it up though, the camera had the same bracket as the previous one, so it's outside, actually recording right now.

So I go onto my other computer and I log in, then I rewind the recording all the way to 08:47 yesterday, and I'm a little bit surprised to see there's an image there. Nothing happens for a while, it's just the normal view of the clifftop, Dad's truck, and the beach below. But then, at 08:56:12 Tucker suddenly emerges into the frame. He's quite small, since the camera is zoomed out, but it's obviously him. He goes out to the front, by the cliff edge. He stands there for a second or two, and then he pulls his shoulder back, and throws something far out over the edge of the cliff.

You can't see what he throws from the image – it's too small. But I already know what it is from the laptop footage inside.

TWENTY-ONE

THE SECOND PIECE of software I installed is called *Keylogger Free*. It's something that logs your keystrokes – that's everything you type into the keyboard – and again it does it secretly so that whoever is typing doesn't know that they're being recorded. If you don't know about key loggers then you definitely should. They're used all the time by computer hackers and cyber criminals. They use them to get people's passwords or bank card numbers. There's a good chance your computer might have one on it right now. You should definitely check. People think that anti-virus software only protects them from viruses, but they also work against key loggers. That's one of the reasons it took me so long time to get everything set up the other night. I had to work out how to stop my own anti-virus system popping up. You do have a good anti-virus don't you? You really should.

Anyway, I look through the results now. It gives me another list of files, and I can click into the box titled 'keystrokes' and I can see exactly what Tucker has typed.

At 08:47 twelve seconds Tucker typed this:

Hounds Beach Classics Jewelry Store secrity guard

Then he deleted the word *'secrity'* and changed it to *'security'*.

Then he didn't type anything for a long time. I guess this was when he was reading. When he next typed it was this:

"Adam Smith security guard Classics Jewelry"

Keylogger doesn't have any pictures or anything, and I can't see where he typed it – in what program I mean. I would be able to if I had the full *Keylogger* software, but this is only the free trial version, and some of the features are restricted. But it's pretty obvious that he was searching online. So I copy what he typed and then go to Google and paste it.

I hit search. There's over 3 million search results. For a moment I think I'm going to have the same problem as before, not knowing which page to load. But then I notice something, right there on the first page of the search results, a few of the links are in a different color. You know the color that internet links change to when you've already looked at them? So it turns out I can see exactly which links Tucker clicked. The first one he looked at is from the *Western Enquirer* newspaper. I've never heard of it, but when I click it this is what it says:

Security Guard Killed in Armed Raid

A father of two died tonight after being shot three times during an armed raid on a Hounds Beach jewelry store. The raid took place on Tuesday morning, at Classics Jewelers, a family owned store which has been trading over 50 years. It's believed a masked man holding a pistol entered the store and demanded items from the display cabinets. It's believed Adam Smith, who was employed as the store's security guard, then challenged the raider, who opened fire. Mr. Smith was shot three times, dying later in hospital. The store has issued a statement confirming it was attacked this morning, and that it will be closed until further notice. It also offers its condolences to Mr. Smith and his family, and states that everyone involved is praying for him.

I stop reading. I check the date. The robbery happened two weeks ago. I think for a minute, then I read the whole thing again.

It all fits. It's pretty clear.

I do another google search, this time for *Hounds Beach*. I've never heard of it, but it turns out to be a little town about thirty miles up the coast from Crab Creek. That's the town where Dad comes from. And where Tucker comes from too. Where he was living until two weeks ago, when he turned up here.

I go back to Tucker's search, and read the rest of the links – they're all newspapers or news sites, and the only thing he reads on them are articles about that robbery.

I think about calling the police. I could add my bed to the barricade of the door, so that there's no way Tucker can get in before they arrive. But then I realize I can't call them. Because of Dad. The police will want to know how come he's away, and how come he left me alone in the house with a murderer. So instead I make sure I've got all the evidence saved and backed up, and I think about what to do next. Pretty quickly I get an idea.

TWENTY-TWO

OBVIOUSLY I SPEND the rest of the evening in my room, it's not safe to go downstairs with Tucker.

Slowly it dawns on me that I'm going to need proper evidence. I can prove that Tucker read a newspaper article about a robbery, but that doesn't prove he was the robber. And even my video of him throwing his phone off the cliff doesn't *prove* anything. It's not illegal to throw away a cell phone. Except for littering.

But if I could find his phone. Then I'd have evidence. Real evidence.

The cliff here at Littlelea is 60 meters high, but it's only the bottom part that's completely vertical. At the top, you can climb down a little way and there's lots of little ledges where bits of grass grow and birds nest. You shouldn't though, because it gets steeper and steeper, and if you slip there's nothing to stop you falling all the way down to the beach. Sometimes it happens to sheep. You never see them fall, but I find them on the beach, dead with all their bones broken.

I watch the video of Tucker throwing his phone, and I try to work out exactly where it might have landed. You'd think he'd have a good throw, but he doesn't stand right by the edge, presumably because he's worried about falling over. And he throws it at an angle, maybe to get it more out to sea. So after he releases it there's a moment when he leans forward – as if he's waiting for the splash – but it doesn't come.

Then I notice it's two in the morning, and I decide I had better go to bed.

* * *

In the morning, I have a really good idea.

I go downstairs like any normal morning. Tucker is still asleep in the lounge, and it feels weird to know he's a murderer and I'm alone in the house with him.

But I try not to think about it. I have breakfast, I feed Steven and then I make it look as if I'm going to catch the school bus, just like a normal morning. But instead of putting Steven back in my room, I take his box outside. Tucker is awake by now, so I shout to him that I'm going to school, but instead of going down the lane to get the bus, I grab Steven and carry him in the opposite direction, along the coast path to the beach. When I'm well out of sight from the house, I open the box and lift him out.

Steven is quite tame now, so there's no danger of him flying off and not coming back. In fact I'm more worried that when he does have to fly away he won't want too. Right now he just stands in front of me, stretching his wings and waiting for me to throw pieces of fish up in the air for him to catch. But I don't do that.

Instead I pull my cell phone out of my pocket, and show it to Steven. I let him have a good look, tipping his brown head onto one side, and inspecting it with one eye. He pecks at it gently.

"*That's it Steven,*" I tell him.

Then, when he starts to lose interest, I pick up the phone, and I pretend to throw it. And then quickly I hide the phone behind my back, so that Steven doesn't know where it is. He looks a bit confused for a second, but then he goes back to staring at me and squawking a little bit.

"*Find it!*" I say. But Steven ignores me. So I try again. Getting him interested in the phone, and then pretending to throw it along the cliff. This time Steven just holds his head on one side and watches me, like he thinks I've gone mad.

I try again, this time smearing a little of fish paste onto the back of my phone. We keep some for when Dad isn't able to get fresh fish from the harbor. This makes Steven a lot more interested. At first he pecks at the phone enthusiastically, and then he looks affronted at me when I throw it away.

It lands a couple of meters away, on a tuft of grass. Steven continues looking at me for a moment, then walks over to the phone and starts pecking it again, scraping little beak-fulls of paste every time.

"*Bring it here, come on Steven. Bring it back.*" I pull out a small fish from the Tupperware box in my bag, and hold it out to Steven. At once he flies back to me to take it, but I shake my head.

"*Uh huh. Bring the phone.*" Steven tries to prize his beak into my closed fist, but I don't let him, and instead I go to the phone and point at it.

"*First the phone. Then the fish.*"

I don't know if you've ever trained a herring gull, but you do need a lot of patience. It takes me an hour of this before he does what I want, picking up the phone in his beak and flying it back to me. I give him loads of praise, and he hops up and down squawking, and flapping a fish up and down in his beak before tipping his head back and swallowing it. And maybe an hour after that, I've got him reliably flying after my phone when I toss it away, then bringing it back, and dropping it, before I feed him a fish.

So then I move onto the next part of my plan. I pick up my phone, and this time I *pretend* to throw it. But I don't really. I just pretend that it's gone in the direction that I saw Tucker throw his phone on the video. And this time I hide my phone properly, slipping it into my jacket pocket and zipping it closed.

"Come on Steven! Find it. *Find it!*" I call, and I shoo him away up into the air. For a few moments he just beats at the air around my head, but I keep waving him away with my arms. Eventually he gets the idea and takes off properly, but he just starts to glide back and forth above me, riding the air currents rising up the cliff face. Again I wave towards where Tucker's phone must be, out on the steeper part of the cliff. But Steven won't go there. He just circles above me, and then after a while he lands and watches me.

After another hour I give up. Apart from anything else, I've run out of fish. So I walk back up the cliff path. I slow near the top, but as soon as I can see the house I can see that Dad's truck's gone. That's good, because it means Tucker must have gone out somewhere. So that means I'm able to go to the top of the cliff, at the spot where Tucker threw his phone from, and get a better sense of where it might have landed.

I stand there for a while. I consider throwing my phone down, trying to recreate Tucker's throw, this time with Steven watching? But I've kind of lost faith in Steven a bit, so I don't do that.

Instead I go to the storage shed we have in the yard, and I dig around until I find some rope. There's a length I salvaged a few years ago, after some fishing tackle got washed up on the rocks at the other side of the headland. It took ages, but I managed to recover about forty meters of it, only I haven't known what to do with it since, so it just sat in the shed. Now I tie one end carefully around our gatepost, giving it a good tug to make sure it's solid. Then I put knots in the rest of the rope so it's easier to climb. Then I toss the open end down the cliff so that it disappears out of sight. And then, with Steven still watching me, I begin to climb down towards where Tucker must have thrown the phone.

I get about five meters down when I wish I had some sort of harness. It's not the effort of holding my weight, it's because my hands start to get sweaty from nerves, and I realize that, if they slip on the rope, there would be nothing to stop me falling, and I'd end up like one of those sheep. But I force myself to go on, because I've started now.

Slowly I lower myself down, stepping on the ledges in the cliff face, or just leaning back against the earth. A few times I dislodge loose bits of mud and stones, and they tumble away below me, some getting caught on other ledges and some disappearing over the edge. It makes my hands feel even more sweaty.

There's a big ledge about five meters below me, and I aim to get there, thinking it might be where the phone ended up. I pay out more and more rope, telling myself to keep gripping it, because my hands are getting more slippery all the time. Eventually I get there, and I can relax a little. I look around at my feet, searching for the black plastic of a phone, embedded somewhere in the grass, but I can't see it. Eventually I know I'll have to go lower.

But as I do, stepping off the ledge, I realize I've been stupid. Looking above me I can't see anything except the cliff, so I can't keep check on the house and when

Tucker is coming back. It's a horrible thought. He could be there already, at the top of the cliff looking at this rope stretching out from the gatepost and leading out over the cliff edge. If he is, he's gonna know right away that it's me, because no one else ever comes to this part of the cliff, not since the footpath was closed. And he's gonna know exactly what I'm doing too, because obviously he knows he threw his phone down, and he knows it got stuck in the cliff, so he'll work out I'm looking for it.

And if he works that out, he'll know I know he's a criminal. And worst of all, I'm giving a really easy way to stop me. All he has to do is cut the rope.

I try to convince myself this is crazy – if he cuts the rope I'll fall and I'll die. And surely he wouldn't actually murder me? But the more I think about it, the more worrying the answer is. He was prepared to murder a security guard to get away when he robbed the jeweler's, so what's the difference between that and murdering me? And my death wouldn't even look like murder. People would think I was counting nest sites or something like that, and just slipped.

I get this sudden strong urge that all I want to do is pull myself back up the cliff face *right away*, and get away from the drop that's hanging beneath me. My hands sweat more, and the feel the rope slippery under my fingers. I try to calm myself, and move a few steps up, to a another mini ledge where I can take some of the weight off my hands. I try to slow my breathing. I look down at my feet, I scan the ledge, hoping against hope that maybe I'll find the phone here, so I can get off the cliff face. But there's nothing there but the scrappy rock-nests of terns and a few tufts of grass. I don't really care. I just want to get out of here.

Then I feel the rope move, like someone has grabbed it higher up.

TWENTY-THREE

RIGHT AWAY I start to panic. I can feel the vibrations from the serrated blade Tucker's using to saw through the rope. The ledge I'm standing on isn't wide enough for me to cling on to without the rope, and I flail around a bit pulling myself back up to the wider one, just above my head. But as I do so, I see what the real problem is. It's Steven, he's flown down to see what I'm doing and he's actually landed on the rope. The vibrations are him moving his wings up and down to keep his balance. I freeze, and feel it for a while. Steven settles, and pecks at the rope a couple of times. I feel how it makes the rope move. It's not Tucker at the top, the movement on the rope is just Steven.

I flick the rope, to dislodge him, and when he's flying around me again, skimming along the cliff face in the air, I feel the rope very carefully, just to be sure. It's not moving any more.

"Stupid bird," I call out. "If you want to be helpful, why don't you go and check Dad's truck's not there?" But he just peeps at me, and glides past my head with his wings outstretched.

But after my scare I start to gain a bit more confidence. Now I'm near the bottom of the rope I work out that I can wrap it around my body, and it works as a kind of harness. As long as I don't let go, it takes my weight quite well. I discover I can even traverse to the left and right, moving in little arcs, and covering more of the cliff face as I do it. And doing that I lower myself right to the limit of the rope, right before where the cliff goes fully vertical. And that's when I see it. On the final ledge before the cliff drops away to the rocks below I can see a Samsung Galaxy S9. It's the right way up, with the screen totally shattered.

I go to lower myself the last few steps to pick it up, but I can't quite get there. I've run out of rope. I try unwinding it from my body, but even holding the very end of the rope, I can't reach the phone. I'd have to let go completely, and if I did that there would be nothing to prevent me tumbling the rest of the way down. The tide is in below me, but I wouldn't hit the water, I'd fall straight onto rocks.

I look down now, seeing the jagged fringe of granite, like teeth, and then the blue of the calm ocean. I swallow.

I wonder if I can hold on with just one hand, and reach below me to pick up the phone. I don't want to, my hands are sweaty again now, but I force myself to do it. I bend down and slide my other hand along the cliff face, feeling my way down the rock and earth. But it's no good. I'm still too high.

I try to reach with my foot instead, and this time I get within a couple of meters of the phone, but no closer. I'm beginning to feel super frustrated when Steven suddenly comes in to land on the same ledge as the phone. I guess he got bored flying around watching me.

Effortlessly he steps over to Tucker's phone. He pecks at the screen a couple of times, and then looks at me. I hold my breath, hardly able to watch.

"*Come on Stevie. Get it boy.*"

He pecks at it again. With his beak he carefully lifts it up, and turns it over. As he does so he pushes it almost to the edge.

"*Careful boy. Just pick it up.*"

But then he seems to lose interest. Instead he lifts up one of his legs, pulls it into the softer feathers around his belly, and closes one eye.

"*Steven!*" I shout at him, and he wakes again. And then I pretend I've got fish on me. I pat the pocket of my jacket. Steven looks interested.

"Come on boy, get the phone."

All that training definitely taught him to do something, but he's not sure what it is I want him to do. I wish I could speak better Herring Gull. I pat my pocket again. I point at the phone, and eventually he moves back to it, and paws at it with one claw.

"*Grab it!*"

Then Steven finally does what I've asked. He gently grips the phone in his beak, it nearly slides out at first, but he gets it balanced, then tips his head back. Then he stretches out his wings, and before I can stop him, he takes off, right out away from the cliff edge.

He gets about five meters before it slips out from his beak and tumbles down. Steven arcs down after it at once, trying to snatch it out of the air, but he just ends up clattering into it. The phone spins further out from the cliff face and moments later splashes into the sea. For a second I hope Steven might dive in after it. Or it might float, but neither of those things happens. Instead there's nothing left except the mirror calm surface of the water, interrupted only by a small, growing ring of ripples where the phone disappeared.

TWENTY-FOUR

I CLIMB BACK up the rope to find Steven waiting for me at the top. I feel like shouting at him, but there's no point. And at least there's still no sign of Tucker. I pull up all the rope and put it back in my shed. And I find my goggles.

Then I climb all the way down the old cliff path to the sea. The tide's high, but it's a totally calm day. I clamber out on the rocks along the edge of the cliff base until I'm right below where I was just climbing. Then I strip off my clothes, and I slip into the sea.

I used to be really scared of the water. I could swim – Dad made sure of that – but I didn't much like it. I wouldn't go into any water except the swimming pool, and only then because there were lifeguards and I could touch the bottom the whole time. And it all got made worse when Dad was trying to teach me to surf, and I got confused, and thought he was actually trying to murder me. I had these therapy sessions after that, and they told me it was all linked to what happened when I was a baby, when my mom tried to drown me. I don't think the therapist helped much, but even so, I like the water now – swimming and diving. You can't really be a marine biologist and *not* like the water. It's kind of where it all happens.

I swim out now, with my goggles in my hair. I try to put myself right at the spot where the phone hit the water. It's hard to be exact, even though I took bearings, and even though I know the rocks really well. When I get to where I think the phone will be I put the goggles down over my eyes and duck my head under the water.

I'm lucky it's such a clear day. When there's a swell it churns up the sand and you can't see more than a few meters under the water, but now it's been flat for a couple of days, and the visibility is good. I can see all the way to the bottom, four or five meters down. The rocks and the sand are bathed in greeny blue sunlight. I take a deep breath and kick down for the bottom.

A couple of bass watch me as I descend. I reach out and grab hold of a rock. I didn't use to like touching things underwater, I felt like they were going to grab me and hold me down, but now I'm OK about it. Even long strands of seaweed that look like they're going to wrap around your feet, I know it's just plants. Underwater plants.

I hold onto the rock now. I look around. The water is cold down here, different to how it feels at the surface, where it's warmed by the sun. I feel my hair caught in the water as I look from side to side. I spot something on the sea floor, on a patch of sand. I swim over to it, but I run out of air, and I have to surface again before I can get to it.

My lungs hurt when I get to the top, and I have to float for a little while, getting my breath back before I'm ready to dive again. But then I take another big breath, and I push my head back under the water. I pull myself down with strong strokes. I have to hold my nose half way down and blow out hard, to equalize the pressure in my ears.

But this time I make it all the way to the bottom, and there in front of me is Tucker's Samsung Galaxy S9 phone. I grip it in my hands, making sure I'm not going to drop it like Steven did. And then I kick off from the bottom and leave a stream of bubbles flowing out of my nose as I coast back to the surface.

* * *

I swim back to the rocks, and clamber slowly out. I dry myself with a towel. I'm kinda frustrated with how much effort that took, but at the same time I'm quite pleased with my day's work. Then I carry the phone back to my bedroom.

The glass back and screen are totally shattered, and there's a couple of scuffs in the aluminum part too. I don't even bother trying to turn it on. There's no way it's going to work. Instead I pull open the drawer and rummage around until I find a paper clip. Then I press in the button to release the SIM card tray, and it pops out right away. And then I give a really broad smile.

Do you remember I told you I saw a documentary on cell phones? It talked about how most US cell phones don't use SIM cards because they use the CDMA network. That means all the data gets stored on the phone itself. So if the phone gets broken – like, for example, smashed against a table and thrown down a cliff into the sea – then all the data on the phone would be lost. But some phones, notably T-Mobile and AT&T use a different cell network called GSM. GSM phones store all the information on a little electronic chip that you slot into the phone called a SIM card. And on these phones it doesn't matter how damaged the phone gets, because all the information is on the SIM.

Tucker's phone is T-Mobile. And the SIM is still there.

TWENTY-FIVE

"BILLY! Where the hell have you been?"

I'm just stepping off the bus, outside school and I can't actually *get* off because Amber is standing there at the stop, yelling at me. There's something different about her too. I takes me a moment to work out what. Then I see it. Her hair isn't blue anymore. It's a kind of rich, dark red. I quite like it actually.

"I've been calling, messaging. Trying to get you on Skype. You wouldn't answer anything." She stares at me. I open my mouth to reply but don't know what to say. Eventually she moves enough so that I can climb down off the bus.

"Where were you yesterday?" she follows me now. "You weren't at school."

I didn't tell you, but I had to switch my cell phone off yesterday, when I was trying to train Steven, because Amber kept messaging me and making the phone beep. It was putting Steven off. I try to walk past her, but she falls into step beside me.

"Did you even get my messages?"

I try to keep looking dead ahead, but there's no way to escape her.

"I've been busy..."

"*Busy?* Doing what? How can you be *busy*?" Suddenly she stops, and when I don't do the same she grabs my shoulder so I have to.

"Hey, you didn't get another case did you? One you're not telling me about?"

"What do you mean?"

"From the agency. You didn't take my email off the website? You didn't get someone else to give you a case?"

"No." I screw up my eyes. It's actually quite a good idea, to remove her email. Just in case another email does come in. I thought about taking the whole site down, but Amber would see that and she'd go mental about it.

"Course not."

Amber stares at me suspiciously for a few moments. "You better not. We're partners, you know that?"

I kind of half-nod my head.

"I have to go to class."

"Fuck class, we have to go to work."

It's really hard to get used to the language Amber uses.

"I can't... I can't *not go* to class."

"Yes you can. What class is it?"

"Geography. With Mr. Parker."

"Mr. Parker's a fucking moron. You can skip it. Come on."

And so, without me really meaning to, I find myself turning around and following Amber in the complete opposite direction to the school. There's quite a few other students still arriving, and I feel like they all must be staring at me. But no one says anything, and soon we're around the corner and out of sight.

"Where are we going?"

"Smithsons."

I wait for her to explain further, but she doesn't.

"What's Smithsons?"

"I told you. I messaged you." Amber replies, and then she doesn't say anymore, she just walks really fast so that I can't keep up with her.

"Well can you remind me?" I ask, when I've caught up.

"You did read them didn't you?"

"Of course."

"Well then."

She's still walking really fast.

"Could you maybe remind me? Just a little bit."

Amber stops, but just for a second. Then she sighs.

"You're unbelievable Wheatley. Smithsons is the auto garage at the end of Main Street. It's been there for years." Amber turns to start walking again. But I stop her.

"So why are we going there?" I wonder if maybe she's crashed her mom's car. I wouldn't be surprised.

"We're going to speak to Gerry Smithson."

"OK. Why?"

"I thought you said you read my messages?"

"I maybe missed one. Or two. I've had some... Issues."

This causes Amber to stop for a second time.

"What does that mean?" She cocks her head to one side. It kind of reminds me of Steven, when he thinks I might be holding a fish behind my back.

"Nothing."

She keeps looking at me.

"Do you want me to read them now?" I ask this just to stop her looking at me like that.

"Fuck it. Read 'em later. For now just listen." Then she starts walking again, just as fast as before.

I have to half run to keep up with her.

"I figured something. If Henry Jacobs was the headmaster of Newlea High School back in 1979, then there must be plenty of people who were *in* the school at the time. Students I mean. And they might remember him, and what happened to him."

I think about this for a moment. It makes sense.

"So I worked it out, we need people who were aged between 13 and 17, forty years ago. So that would make them 53 to 57 today. And then I searched on Facebook for people who've put down their school as Newlea High School, and with a date of birth between 1963 and 1967." She looks at me and waits, like she knows I'm going to check the math. I quickly work it out, then I nod.

"Only, you can't *actually* do that, as you probably know – since Facebook doesn't show you people's ages." She gives me a smug grin.

"But even so, you can get a pretty good idea from how old people look. So then I started messaging everyone I could find who looked the right age and attended Newlea High School. I asked them if they remembered their school principal Henry Jacobs, or knew anyone who did. And Gerry Smithson, from the garage on Main Street, got back to me and said he remembered him. So that's why we're going to see him. OK?"

I do my best to process all this.

"OK."

"Good."

The garage isn't far, so even though I've got a bunch of other questions to ask Amber, I don't get the chance to ask them.

Smithson's garage is just off the road, behind a set of bright blue gates. There's a double-width opening to the workshop itself, through bright blue doors, where a couple of cars are lifted up in the air. There's music playing from a radio somewhere, and a man in greasy blue overalls is leaning into the engine bay of a battered looking sedan. Since this is Amber's idea, I let her take the lead.

"Are you Gerry Smithson?" She asks.

"Yeah." He's got his hands deep in the engine, but somehow also a roll up between his lips. "What you want?"

"I'm Amber. I sent you the Facebook message."

Mr. Smithson narrows his eyes. He looks confused.

"The detective?"

"That's right."

His frown deepens.

"You look older. On the computer."

Amber smiles at this, but the man doesn't. "Thanks," she says.

Mr. Smithson doesn't move. I'm not sure he meant it as a compliment.

"You said you remembered Henry Jacobs, from when you were at school? You said you wouldn't mind meeting? To speak about it."

Still Mr. Smithson hasn't moved, his hands are still in the engine.

"What the hell is this? Some kind of kid's project?"

Amber glances at me, then swings her bag off her shoulder. She roots around for a moment and then pulls out a small rectangular card. She glances at me again, and then holds it up so that Mr. Smithson can see. I have to lean forward to see what's on it.

"Not at all. As I said, we work for the Lornea Island Detective Agency. We're investigating the disappearance of one Henry Jacobs in 1979. You said you might be able to help."

It's a proper business card, and she's put the logo from the website in the middle. Below that is her name. It says:

Amber Atherton
Senior Investigator

Gerry Smithson looks from the card to Amber and then back again. Then he looks at me as well and I can tell how confused he is. I'm quite confused as well, but I try to keep it off my face.

"You said you remember Henry Jacobs?" Amber goes on. "He would have been the principal of Newlea High School from 1973 to 1979. You said you were a student there at the time?"

Finally Mr. Smithson takes his hands out of the engine and walks away to a bench. It's littered with oily tools and bits of car engines. He picks up a rag and wipes his hand. Then he turns back to Amber.

"Yeah I remember him."

Amber bites her lip and tries not to look excited.

"Could you tell us what happened to him?" She asks. But Mr. Smithson just frowns for a bit, then shrugs.

"Far as I know, nothing happened to him."

"But he stopped being the principal? A woman took over instead. She was called Mrs. Clarke?"

Still Mr. Smithson wipes his hands. Finally he shrugs again. "If you say so. I don't remember her. It was a long time ago." He stops, and I think that's all he has to say, but then he continues. "But I do remember Jacobs." He doesn't go on, doesn't explain the look he gives us.

"What do you remember about him? Was there something... memorable?" Amber asks.

I still haven't said a single word since we got here, and maybe Mr. Smithson wonders about this now, since he looks at me again. He's still holding Amber's card and he studies it again.

"So are you two like..." He hesitates, sounding really unsure now. "Look what's this about? This kid is way too young to work for any detective agency."

Without hesitation Amber replies. "Do you remember the case of Olivia Curran, the tourist girl who was murdered two years ago?"

He looks at Amber, confused. "Yeah, I remember."

"My colleague here may look immature, he I can assure you he was absolutely instrumental in solving that case." Amber pauses and looks to me, like maybe I should say something. But I don't know what to say, so I just nod in what I hope is a meaningful way.

"And since then he has solved many crimes. He is a most able investigator."

I look very serious and do some more nodding.

Now Mr. Smithson looks like he thinks he doesn't know if Amber is being serious or pranking him. But in the end he settles on the former, or maybe he just decides he wants to get rid of us as quickly as possible.

"How old would the guy be now?"

"Who?"

"Jacobs."

Amber takes an age to work it out, so I tell him.

"Seventy two."

At first I'm not sure if Mr. Smithson hears me, because he doesn't reply at once. And when he does it's to Amber again.

"And is he... Look is this..." He drops his voice, I suppose trying to make it so that only Amber hears him.

"Is he still *doing it*? At that age? Is that why the kid's here?"

Me and Amber look at each other.

"What do you mean? Doing what?" Amber says at last.

Mr. Smithson stares at us.

"Nothing." He turns away.

"Mr. Smithson, whatever it is you're trying to tell us, we need to know." Amber sounds really anxious now, like she's dying to hear him say something. But Mr. Smithson just looks from one of us to the other. I have to admit, I don't really know what's going on.

Finally Mr. Smithson speaks again.

"You swear you're nothing to do with the police? I don't want no trouble with this."

"No." Amber shakes her head firmly. "Absolutely not. You can tell us anything in the strictest confidence. We'll just use it for deep background." She gives him another smile, but it doesn't seem to settle him much.

"Look I ain't sure I wanna say this. It was a long time ago..."

"*What* was a long time ago Mr. Smithson?" Amber's eyes have gone really wide, her whole face pleading with him.

"Tell us Mr. Smithson. Please. What you have to say could be incredibly important."

He looks around again. Like he's hoping there's some way he can get away from this girl who's staring at him with her big doleful eyes, but she's leaning in close, hanging on every word.

"It didn't happen to me, right? Nothing happened to me. I just knew about it. *Everyone* knew about it."

"Knew about what?" Amber asks. "What did everyone know about?"

He puffs out his cheeks, than shakes his head.

"Jesus. I can't believe I'm saying this. It was forty years ago. What you want to go digging all this up for?" He takes a deep breath, but Amber is relentless.

"Please Mr. Smithson. It's important. We're working for someone connected to Henry Jacobs. They're desperate to discover what happened to him. Telling us is the right thing to do. Whatever you're still feeling, it'll help."

He laughs at this, but it comes out more of a cough.

"I don't need no *help*. I ain't even thought about school in forty years. And I sure don't see why I should be bringing it up now. Specially not to a pair who look like they should still be in school themselves..." He glances over at me as he says this. I get the sense he's not going to say anything now.

Mr. Smithson looks away and exhales slowly. But then he seems to come to a decision.

"Alright. But you didn't hear any of this from me, OK?"

"Absolutely. Of course." She makes a zipping sign across her lips, and he watches her, blank faced.

"Whatever." He starts to walk back to the car he was fixing when we came in.

"When I was in high school, Principal Jacobs had a reputation. That's what I remember. People said he liked his students a bit too much. The boys."

"What do you mean?" I'm really surprised to hear that it's me who's asked this question. And I think Mr. Smithson is too because he looks up at me for a moment. Then he continues.

"You say you're detectives. They used to call him 'Handsy Henry'. You fucking figure it out."

TWENTY-SIX

"WOW I WASN'T EXPECTING *THAT!*" Amber says as soon as we're far enough from the garage so that Mr. Smithson can't hear us.

"You know what he means don't you? By liking boys. It means he *messed around* with them. Interfered with them. Fucking hell! This is *massive*."

I don't answer.

"It means he was a pedophile Billy. This changes everything."

Still I don't reply.

"So what do we do now? Do we go back to Mrs. Jacobs and tell her? That her husband was a kiddie-fiddler? Do you reckon she'll still pay us?" She's walking fast again, and we're half way back to school already.

"I mean we've still got the check right? The 5000 dollars? We can still cash that?"

I don't reply.

"Billy? What do you think?"

Reluctantly I answer her.

"I think we have to be careful."

She spins to look at me. "What do you mean by that." But I hesitate. I don't know how to say this.

"We don't *know* he was a pedophile. We only know Mr. Smithson *heard* that he was. It's not the same thing."

"Course we do. Why would Smithson say so otherwise?"

I screw up my face, trying to make sense of this. I can't work out why I'm feeling anxious about this. Then I remember.

"I made a mistake. Once before." I begin.

Amber waits, her face screwed up into a deep frown.

"When I started investigating that murdered girl, there was this guy that used to hang around in Silverlea. He had a limp, and people thought he was a pedophile. And I just assumed he was too. And I thought that meant he was the murderer too. But it turned out he wasn't. And he wasn't even a pedophile. People just thought he was because of how he looked. So we have to be careful. That's all."

Amber doesn't reply to this, but I can see her thinking it over.

"OK." She nods, and we start walking again, in silence this time.

"Did you like the card?" Amber says after a while.

I shrug.

"I got them printed on the internet. I thought they might help convince people we're serious."

"It's alright." I can feel my face is still tight where I'm scowling.

"It was a good idea wasn't it?"

I shrug again.

"Did you like the design? Did you think it was alright?"

Honestly, I don't know why she doesn't just drop it.

Suddenly Amber stops dead on the sidewalk, and I take a couple of steps further on before I realize she's not beside me anymore. I turn around to see her rooting around in her bag. Then she pulls out a small box.

"Here you go." She hands it to me, and hesitantly I take it. I pull off the lid, and inside is another stack of business cards. But this time they have a different name on the front.

William Wheatley
Private Investigator

I look up at her. "William?"

"I thought it sounded more serious than Billy."

Amber grins at me, and I realize from my face I'm smiling too.

"You really think I'd forget you?"

I feel quite happy for a few moments, just looking at it. You couldn't tell, that it's not real I mean, because Amber is really good at design.

"They cost $35 dollars. We'll have to take it out of what Mrs. Jacobs pays us. When we've found out what happened to Henry. Which we will."

We set off again, and soon we're at the school gate. The only way back in is through the reception hall. Amber sticks her head round the gate to have a look, then pulls back.

"*Shit.* The receptionists are there. We'll have to wait till they go back to their office."

I feel a stab of anxiety, but Amber just leans back on the wall, waiting. She looks totally relaxed.

"Have you ever been caught? Doing this?" I ask after a while.

"Doing what?"

"Skipping class?"

"Not so much these days." She shrugs. I get a strange sense, that maybe she wants me to ask more. But I don't ask.

"Say," Amber says a few moments later. "If Henry *was* messing with kids, isn't that a pretty strong motive for someone to do away with him?" She looks at me and tips her head onto one side.

"I suppose."

"Like an angry parent who discovered what he was up to? Don't you think they might lose control? When they found he was abusing their kid? Maybe *they* killed him?" The light in Amber's eyes is dancing as she says this, and I can tell she half believes it already. I take a deep breath, and try to keep my thoughts clearer.

"Maybe."

I guess that doesn't sound enthusiastic enough for her.

"Come on Billy, you have to admit it's pretty likely?"

"I suppose it's possible," I accept. "But even so. There were hundreds of pupils in the school, and it was forty years ago. I don't see how we can know which ones he was abusing, and who might have found out about it."

Amber looks away, considering. "I suppose we could go to the police," she muses, and right away I start thinking about that too, since I've been considering it to solve my Tucker problem. But that's kinda complicated too, what with Dad still away on the boat...

"But what would we tell them?" Amber goes on. "We don't even know *for sure* that he disappeared. We need more evidence. Something concrete."

Then Amber suddenly reaches over and picks up my hand. I don't have any idea what she's doing, but then she turns my wrist over, and reads the time on my watch. It's weird to be touched like that. I don't like it, but then also, as soon as she lets my wrist go, I wish she was still holding it.

"Come on. It's break time. Let's risk it. Message me if you figure out what to do next."

Without another word she pushes herself off the wall, and strides confidently through the gate. I don't feel anything like so confident, but I follow her anyway.

We get about halfway through the lobby, almost joining the flow of students streaming past towards their next class. But at that moment there's a call from inside the receptionist's office.

"Miss Atherton?"

Amber freezes, but her voice is calm and clear. Unbothered. "Yes?"

One of the receptionists comes out, and I get the sense she's actually been hiding in there, where she knew she couldn't be seen.

"Principal Sharpe has been looking for you. You're to go to her office straight away."

"What for?" Amber doesn't sound so confident now, and the receptionist ignores the question. Instead she turns to me.

"And it's Billy Wheatley isn't it? The Principal would like to speak with you as well."

I glance at Amber, as if I'm somehow expecting she has some secret trick to get us out of this. But of course there isn't anything.

"Well go on then. Now please. She's waiting in her office."

TWENTY-SEVEN

"*Sit* down both of you!" Principal Sharpe says when we get in her office. We didn't have to wait outside this time, we got sent straight in.

She waits until Amber and I have taken a seat each in front of her desk, and then she sits as well, in the much bigger chair on her side. She looks calm, sort of. But when she puts her hands together, resting on the desk, I can see they're shaking.

"Miss Atherton. I came to look for you this morning. In your history class earlier, but you weren't there. Quite ironic, in the circumstances wouldn't you say?

I look up, not getting the reference. The receptionist wouldn't tell us why Principal Sharpe wanted to speak to us. I assumed it was for skipping class, but I can't see how that would be ironic.

Amber doesn't reply, she just studies the floor, and Principal Sharpe stares at her for a really long time. Then she slides her eyes over to me.

"And Billy. It seems you had something more important to attend to than your Geography class this morning, would you care to explain what that was?" She waits, and I try to think of something to say, but I can't tell her what we've been doing, so I don't say anything.

Principal Sharpe sighs. "I thought not."

She stares at us both for a few more seconds, then opens one of her drawers, and pulls out a sheet of paper.

"I was contacted last night by a concerned friend. Someone who thought there was something I should be aware of. Billy, this is beginning to get a little repetitive don't you think?

I try to work out what she means. This can't be about *BullyTracker*. She saw me take it down, and I haven't done anything on it since.

"I really didn't know what to think when I saw it. I can honestly say that. In all my time in teaching, I've never had a situation like this one." She glances at the window, and when she looks back she's smiling.

"So well done – for that at least."

I guess, like me, Amber has decided we're not supposed to say anything. It seems Principal Sharpe is just really into rhetorical questions.

"Miss Atherton, I understand you've been sending messages to former pupils of this school on social media sites, posing as some kind of investigator, and asking for information on former principals. Specifically Henry Jacobs? Is that correct?"

Amber looks up sharply mid way through the question. And when Principal Sharpe finishes, Amber hesitates for a while, but then shrugs and nods. Principal Sharpe waits to see if Amber is going to say any more, then when she doesn't she pours herself some water from a jug on her desk.

"I was forwarded one of these messages this morning. Would you like me to read it out to you?"

Amber shrugs again.

"Would you like me to read it to you?"

It turns out that question wasn't rhetorical after all.

"Not really." Amber says.

In response Principal Sharpe picks up the paper and begins to read.

"I'm a private detective and I'm looking for Henry Jacobs who was principal of Newlea High School who disappeared – *there's two 'p's in disappeared by the way* – in 1979. It says on your Facebook profile you went to Newlea High School then, so I thought you might remember him. If so please contact, blah blah." Principal Sharpe drops the paper on her desk.

"Blah."

There's silence for a moment.

"A private detective? I know many 10th graders take on part time jobs," she gives a cold smile. "I encourage it. But I've never heard of any working as private detectives before."

Principal Sharpe waits in silence, until finally Amber starts to say something, but I don't hear what it is, because she cuts her off immediately.

"And then I wondered, what *possible* interest could you have in a man who was the principal of this school *forty years ago*. So would you care to enlighten me?" She sits back in her chair and waits.

Amber's more cautious this time, but finally she replies.

"I don't mean this the wrong way, Principal Sharpe, but we can't talk about it."

"You can't talk about it?"

"No. Because we have a client and..."

There's a bang as Principal Sharpe slams her palm down on her desk. It makes Amber stop. It makes me nearly jump out of my chair.

"You have a *client*," Principal Sharpe repeats. "And who, pray, might that be?"

"We can't say that either."

"Of course not. Of course not. Because that would be a breach of confidentiality wouldn't it?" She leans forward again.

"Well perhaps I could ask you this – did your *client* contact you about this matter? Or did you approach her?" Principal Sharpe watches us carefully.

"She did." Amber answers in the end. "She wanted to find out what happened to him. She's been wondering all these years, and now she's getting old..." Amber stops and she stares open mouthed for a moment.

"How did you know it was a she?" she asks.

"How indeed? I have to say you're not particularly impressing me as a detective Miss Atherton. Neither of you." She looks to me for a second.

"Tell me, when were you planning on interviewing *me* about this matter?"

Amber looks up. "You? Why?"

Principal Sharpe's eyebrows go even higher. "Well I thought I would have been an obvious place to start. As the current principal of the school." She pauses, then goes on.

"And of course, given that Henry Jacobs was my father."

TWENTY-EIGHT

It's as if all the air in the room is suddenly sucked out, and replaced by new air that's colder, like it's from a freezer.

"Father?" Amber says after a long while. "What do you mean?"

"Well, it shouldn't be that difficult to understand, not for a *detective*. Your 'client' as you call her, is my mother, who I should point out is a very frail and confused old woman. So I was extremely concerned when I spoke to her last night, and discovered she is under the impression she had contracted a *professional agency* to locate my father."

Amber turns to me. Her eyes are as round as dollar coins. Then she turns back.

"Father? Henry Jacobs was your *father*?"

"I know, it's amazing. Even school principals have parents. I know this must come as a huge shock to you."

Amber turns to me again, her mouth hanging open. Then she turns back to Principal Sharpe.

"Well... Well what happened to him?" Amber asks. "Do *you* know?"

"*Of course I know.*"

Suddenly Principal Sharpe gets up from behind the desk and goes to a side table at the edge of the room. On it there's a tray with more glasses.

"Would you like a drink?" she asks us both, but doesn't wait for a reply. Instead she comes back, standing over us now, and pours us both a glass of water. While she's distracted doing so, Amber mouths to me:

She's Henry Jacob's fucking daughter!

Which obviously, I've already realized.

Then Principal Sharpe is talking again. "In normal circumstances I would say this is absolutely none of your business. But since my mother appears to have played her part in creating this *situation,* I feel bound to give you enough information to settle your curiosity. But after that this matter shall be closed, and it shall go no further than this room. Do we have that clear?

Neither me nor Amber really say anything to this, so Principal Sharpe says it again.

"Do I have your agreement on that?"

I quickly nod, and then look at Amber to see if she does the same, but if she did I missed it.

Principal Sharpe takes a deep breath. "Good." She sits down again behind the desk.

"My mother is seventy five years old, and unfortunately she's suffering from a rare form of dementia. Her memory is the most obvious symptom, but it also affects her personality. She can shift from one version of herself to another. I don't know if you noticed?"

I nod again. Principal Sharpe looks annoyed at the interruption. But then she smiles at me.

"People with her condition tend to lose their older, or more traumatic, memories first. And it's not uncommon that they become quite distressed and put time and effort into trying to recover those memories. They feel there's a significant gap, that needs to be filled." She laughs suddenly. "The irony is, there's often another part of their personality that still recalls those memories. So at times she knows what happened. At other times she doesn't. But the two parts of her no longer join up."

Amber and I wait in silence.

"My mother has always lived a very active life, she's certainly not one to sit around being distressed. And it seems that, when part of her lost her memory of what happened to my father that same part concluded it was a big mystery. And so she looked for help solving it. And then somehow got mixed up with the two of you, pretending to be detectives..."

She look levelly at me. I don't know what she's thinking.

"So what did happen to him?" Amber asks.

She glances at her, she seems annoyed.

"Nothing."

"Well where is he then?"

"There is no mystery, Miss Atherton. I'm very sorry to disappoint you."

"But... We found out he was principal here until 1979, then he disappeared and no one knows what happened to him." Amber pauses, maybe she realized that might not be quite right. "At least, we couldn't find anything about what happened to him. There was nothing in the *Island Times* about him."

A slight frown creases Principal Sharpe's face.

"Why would there be anything in the *Island Times*?"

"I don't know... We just thought... Well if something did happen it would be news."

The frown deepens.

"So what *did* happen to him?" Amber says in the end.

"I told you. Nothing happened. At least nothing dramatic. He and my mother separated, and he moved off the island."

For a moment it feels like Principal Sharpe is going to say more, but she doesn't. There's a few moments of silence before Amber speaks again.

"But... Mr. Jacobs, she said he disappeared. That he went out one night and never came back."

"No. That's not how it happened." Principal Sharpe drums her fingers on the desk. "Perhaps that's the dementia..." She stops and watches us. A few moments later she goes on.

"There's an element of truth in it. Perhaps that's why..." But then she stops again and sighs.

"My father did walk out. And it was at Christmas. It could have been 1979, I'm not sure without working it out." She takes a deep breath. "I can't believe I am explaining my childhood to two of my *students*." She takes a sip of her water.

"I was nine years old, and yes, for a few weeks we didn't know where he was. But it wasn't the first time he'd gone away like that. My mother thought he'd come back, like he always did, but this time he didn't. Then we got a postcard. From Hawaii. My father explained how he had met someone else, and moved in with her on the island of Maui. He continued to send letters, and birthdays cards for a few years. But then they dried up. It was very hard on my mother. It was very hard on all of us. But there's no mystery. And there never was."

There's silence for a while. Then Amber speaks.

"Palm trees," she says.

"I beg your pardon?"

"Mrs. Jaco... Your mother said she remembered something about palm trees. How they were important."

"Hmmm. Perhaps. They may well have featured on the postcards."

I zone out for a while. I'm getting this really weird feeling watching Principal Sharpe. All the time I've known her she's been this scary authority figure, but now it's as if I can see beyond this. That she wasn't always that way. Once she was just a kid, and bad things happened to her. But Amber doesn't seem to be thinking the same.

"Do you know if he's still there now?" She asks.

It takes Principal Sharpe a long time to answer.

"Excuse me?"

"Your dad. Is he still there now? In Hawaii?"

"I don't know. His communications dried up a few years after he left. And to be honest with you, after the way he treated us, I wasn't minded to care much either way."

There's a long silence while she takes another sip of water, and I see how much her hands are shaking. As she sets the glass down it spills and a drop falls on the paper she read from earlier. The surface tension holds it up like a translucent blob before finally it collapses, being absorbed and sucked into the paper.

I can't take my eyes of it.

TWENTY-NINE

We each have to go to class after that, but we arrange to meet up at lunch in the school canteen. There's nowhere to sit though, not where we can talk in private. That is until Amber asks a couple of first graders to move.

"Well? What do you make of all that?" she asks, when they've skulked away saying how they're going to tell a teacher. I think for a moment how to answer.

"She's actually alright isn't she? Principal Sharpe. Underneath all that..." I reach for the right word. "Fierceness."

"Yeah but," Amber interrupts. "Do you actually *believe* her?"

"Believe her?"

"Yeah. Cos I'm not sure I do." Amber takes a bite of her hot dog and ketchup squirts onto her plate.

"Why not?"

She chews for a minute, fast, because she wants to keep talking. "Because of what the guy in the garage told us." She takes another bite.

I think back to what the mechanic said. About how Henry Jacobs had a reputation for liking the boys.

"What's that got to do with it?"

"Like I said before. It's a motive. It's a reason why someone might want to kill him."

"But we know now that no one *did* kill him. He didn't disappear, he just left the island."

"That might be what Sharpe told us. But it doesn't make it true. What if he was actually murdered because of what he was doing to the students, and then whoever did it, sent a letter to Mrs. Jacobs, pretending it was from him and saying how he'd met someone else?" Amber opens her mouth wide and pushes all the rest of the hot dog in. Then she keeps talking, even though her mouth is totally full.

"Or, what if *she* did it? Mrs. Jacobs I mean. We already knew she's mental, and now Sharpe's confirmed it. But what if she's *really* mental. What if she actually murdered him, and then pretended to her daughter that he'd gone with the other woman? Isn't that possible?"

I think about this for a second. I'm not even sure that it is.

"Well? Isn't it?"

"I suppose it *might* be. But isn't it more likely he went off to live on Maui, like she said?"

Amber looks annoyed and turns away. Feeling a bit awkward, I take a bite of my own hotdog. I chew it carefully and swallow it down. Then I open my mouth.

"I saw a documentary on Maui..."

"*He didn't go to fucking Maui!*"

"What?" I almost choke on my mouthful.

"He didn't go to Maui. I can't believe you're being so dumb about this. He was a pedophile who *disappeared*. Doesn't that strike you as a hell of a coincidence?"

"But he send postcards. And birthday cards."

"It's easy to fake a birthday card Billy," Amber says, like she's some kind of expert in it.

"Is it?" I ask. "Wouldn't it be really hard? Wouldn't you need to go to actually Maui to post it, to get the right postmark…"

"*Oh come on Billy*! What the fuck's wrong with you?" Amber interrupts again. "Aren't you supposed to be the expert in all this? Didn't your dad lie to you about your mom for years? Didn't he tell you she was dead, when all the time she was locked up in some mental institution? I don't get how that can happen to you, and you can't accept this could have happened to Sharpe?"

I don't say anything to this. In fact I freeze a little bit, my hot dog quivering over my plate. Amber looks at me for a while then sighs.

"I'm sorry, I didn't mean to say it like that. It must be hard to have that much shit in your family history." She offers me a smile. "But don't you see? If it can happen to you, why can't it happen to someone else too?"

I still don't reply. But she's got it wrong. I don't mind her talking about everything that happened in the past. The problem is, there's so much going on *now*, with Dad hundreds of miles out in the ocean, and me living with a murderer. Maybe she's right, and I've just been too distracted to see this case for what it really is.

"Do you really not believe Principal Sharpe?"

She watches me for a long time before answering.

"I don't know what to believe. But I think we should keep on investigating. It's possible that Henry Jacobs never left the island. Or at least, never left the island alive."

I puff out my cheeks. Leaving Principal Sharpe's office I really thought this stuff with Mrs. Jacobs was over. That I could just concentrate on sorting out the

Tucker issue. And then everything else that I have to do. Suddenly everything feels overwhelming.

Then I can't stop myself. I reach into my pocket and I bring out the SIM card I found in Tucker's phone yesterday. It feels like weeks ago.

"What's that?" Amber asks.

"It's a SIM card."

"I can see that. What are you doing with it?"

Then I tell her. I just blurt it all out. I explain how this old friend of dad's turned up at our house a couple of weeks ago, completely unexpected, and how he won't leave. And how I suspected he was a criminal, so I tricked him into using my computer when I was at school and recorded how he'd murdered the security guard in the jewelry store he was robbing. And then how Dad's gone out on the *Ocean Harvest*, and left me alone with him. And then how he smashed his phone up and threw it down the cliff, and then how I found it. And when I'm finished, and the remains of my hotdog are left on the plate completely forgotten, and Amber's mouth is open in amazement. Then she laughs.

"Fucking hell Billy. There was me thinking you were useless at this detective stuff, when all the time you've got that going on at the same time. No wonder you've been distracted."

This cheers me up quite a lot.

"So what are you going to do?"

So I tell her about how the police will be monitoring his phone, so if I put his card into *my* phone it'll look like his phone is switched on. And then the police will see that he's here, on Lornea Island. And then they'll come and arrest him.

"Fucking hell," Amber says again. Then she thinks a bit.

"Well go on then," she says. "Put it in."

Her eyes are shining bright with excitement.

"I can't *here*."

She frowns. "Why not?"

"Because then the police will come *here*. I've got to do it at home, later on. So the police know that's where he is."

"So when you gonna do it?"

"Tonight I guess. I'll swap it over when I get home. Put Tucker's SIM in my phone. It doesn't matter what phone you use, as long as it's unlocked, it'll send out the same signal to the base station."

"OK." Amber looks thoughtful. Then she speaks again.

"I've got an idea," Amber's eyes shine brighter still. "I've got Mom's car today. Why don't I give you a lift home? Then I can help you do it. And I'll get to meet a proper murderer..."

THIRTY

HOOOOOOoooooNK. The white panel van goes shooting past the windscreen, the driver leaning on the horn, alarm on his face at the way Amber has veered into his lane.

"Asshole," Amber says, giving him the finger.

The good thing about going home with Amber is that I don't have to sit on the school bus and drop off half the school before I get home. The bad thing is I figure I've about a fifty-fifty chance of making it alive

"You have to be careful with the turn off the Silverlea road to Littlelea," I say, trying not to sound as nervous as I feel. "It's a left, and Dad always says..."

"I can drive you know." Amber shoots me a look.

Actually it's not just Amber's driving that's making me unsettled. Obviously I'm nervous about the whole plan to alert the police to where Tucker is. But there's more to it than that. The thing is, I've never actually had anyone from school come to my house. Not ever. It's not that I'm ashamed of where I live. It's just... Well, I'm a bit worried there's some things she might think are a bit odd. That's all.

I feel tense for the rest of the journey, and make a vague plan to try to keep her out of my room at least. And somehow we do make it alive. She stops behind Dad's truck. I notice again the way Tucker's parked it wrong, he doesn't turn it around, ready to go the way that Dad does.

"Jesus Billy, you live on the edge of the fucking cliff!" Amber is already out of the car and standing looking out over the beach below "It's amazing. You can see for miles!"

I don't really answer her. "He's here." I say instead. "Dad's letting him borrow his truck, so he must be in."

Amber spins around, and seems to notice the truck for the first time. Then she takes in the house and the yard.

"What's that?" she asks.

I frown, not sure what she means, then I follow where she's pointing. "Oh. It's the jaw bone of a sperm whale. It's not really..."

"Where the hell did you get that?"

"On the beach, but it's not relevant. We need to go inside."

Amber eyes linger on the bone for a moment, but then she spins around.

"Right." Then she looks at me and gives a grin. Her eyes are sparkling with excitement. Honestly, I don't know why she's so excited to meet a murderer.

We go inside, Tucker's not in the kitchen, but I can see the TV's on in the next room.

"That you *Billy boy*?" Tucker calls from the lounge. Me and Amber look at each other.

"Yeah," I call back, but not too loud.

"I made veggie lasagna. Figured you boys been eating too much red..." He appears in the kitchen. Straight away he notices Amber.

"...Meat. *Hi there*."

His eyes take her in. They don't focus on her hair, which by the way, is dark green now. Instead they run up and down her body.

"Say Billy, you didn't say you were bringing a *friend*."

I don't like the way Amber is looking at him either, like he's a white tiger in a zoo. Dangerous and rare, but beautiful.

"So? Aren't you going to introduce us?" Tucker's grin widens.

While I'm thinking what to say, Amber steps forward.

"I'm Amber. I'm a friend of Billy." She pushes a strand of hair out of her face and tucks it behind her ear. Her eyes are sparkling bright.

"Tucker."

"Billy's told me about you."

"Has he?" Tucker's eyebrows go up. "Nothing bad I hope?"

Amber half shrugs, but smiles to show she's kidding. Then the two of them just watch each other, like I'm not even here.

"Amber needed some help with her homework," I say, just to break the weird silence. "So we're going to go upstairs..." I know I said I didn't want her in my room. But when a plan goes wrong, you have to change it.

"Sure." Tucker glances at me, but then turns back. "Say Amber. You'll stay for dinner right? I made plenty." Tucker laughs. "You wouldn't think it, looking at the kid, but he eats like a goddamn horse."

"No, she's got to..." I start to say, but Amber talks over me quickly.

"That would be great. I love veggie lasagna."

"*Alright then.* Girl after my own heart." He smiles. He looks a bit like a tiger now. Or a cat, purring about something.

"I'll set up another place at the table. Give you a shout when it's ready."

They watch each other some more.

"Come on Amber," I say. Then when she doesn't move, I grab her sleeve and pull her towards the stairs, so hard she nearly stumbles.

We walk upstairs, and I sense how Amber is checking out everything in our house. She sticks her head into the bathroom, and then into Dad's room. I pause before I finally let her into mine.

"You might be a bit surprised," I say, "looking in here..."

"Why? What's in there? Is it like a museum filled with dinosaur bones? Or have you got a massive porn collection? That wouldn't surprise me Billy. Nothing about you would surprise..."

She doesn't finish what she's saying because at that moment Steven wakes up. There's a loud mewing sound, and then a big *thump* on the door.

"No. It's not that."

I open the door, and all at once I'm set upon by an overjoyed juvenile herring gull, flapping his wings and trying to rub his neck against mine. I catch him and smooth his feathers down to calm him, and tell him I'll get some food in a minute. Eventually I get him sitting on my forearm, mewing noisily. Then I look up at Amber. Her mouth is open, staring at Steven.

"You've got... A *seagull* as a pet?"

“He’s not a seagull. And he's not a pet. You're not allowed to keep wild birds as pets. I'm just looking after him until he’s ready to be released."

Amber looks around the room. I see her take in my collection of dried starfish, my fish posters, and then settle on Steven's nest, it sits in a plastic dog bed, his name written in black marker pen on the top.

"*Steven*?" She says. "Is that its name?"

"His name. Yeah."

"Why?" Amber asks.

"It was my Dad's idea. There's some actor called Steven Seagal and he thought it was funny."

Amber looks at me, screwing up her nose. "Jeez. Parents are so fucking lame sometimes."

At least we can agree on that.

"Does he bite? Can I pet him?"

"He won't if you're gentle."

I hold Steven out to her, and Amber gingerly puts her hands around him and lifts him up.

"He's heavy. *Hello Steven*!" She says to him. “I love his eyes! Big brown eyes. You're a handsome boy aren't you?"

Suddenly I feel a bit weird. I can't really explain it. It's like – It's not jealousy, or anything like that. It’s just, the way she’s going all soft over Steven. I kind of wish she was saying that to me. I shake the thought away, it's ridiculous. I sit down at my desk.

"What were you doing? Downstairs? Didn't I tell you he's a murderer? He's *dangerous*, and you want to have dinner with him?"

"Yeah but you didn't tell me he was hot."

I feel that strange thought again. Steven picks up on it, and shuffles awkwardly.

"Hey, it's alright baby," Amber soothes him.

I look away, then turn to my stereo. I switch it on, then I turn it up loud even though the song is some rapper or another. Amber looks up, questioningly.

"I never had you down as a hip hop fan."

"I'm not. I just don't want Tucker to hear what we're talking about."

"Oh. OK. Well anyway, *you're* having dinner with him."

"Yeah but I *have* to."

"Well?" She shrugs. "And anyway, what kind of a murderer makes veggie lasagna?" She asks the question in her cutesy voice, but more to Steven than to me.

"Hey little birdy man? Not a very scary murderer that's what…" So I have to talk to her quite sharply to get her attention back.

"Amber. It is possible for someone to be a murderer and also a good cook. The two attributes are not mutually exclusive."

Amber ignores me, stroking Steven's plumage. But then she very carefully she puts him down so that he stands on the carpet watching her and offering up one of his feet like I taught him.

Amber plays with him for a while, taking his foot and shaking it like she's saying hello.

"So anyway, *Sherlock*," She says at last. "What's gonna happen now with your SIM card?"

THIRTY-ONE

I REACH into my pocket and pull it out, folded into a square of paper so I don't lose it. I put it on the desk and look at it for a moment.

Amber watches me. Anticipation etched into her face. Her eyes shining with the thrill of it.

I reach into my other pocket and pull out my phone. I check it for messages, then when there aren't any, I press the button to power it down. While I'm waiting for that I open my drawer and root around for a bit until I find an electrical screwdriver. As soon as the phone screen has gone black I carefully prize the back of my phone, then slide my SIM card out of the slot. I replace it with Tucker's, then fit the phone's back case into place again.

"Is that it? That's all you have to do?"

"It's because he's on T-Mobile," I start to explain, even though I told her all this at school. "All the phone's data gets stored on the card, so the network will think it's his phone."

"OK, OK. How long do you reckon the police will take to start tracking it?"

I hesitate, because I don't actually know this.

"They might have some sort of alert set up, so that they know the moment it gets switched on." I consider this for a second. "Or they might not. I'm not sure."

I still have the phone in my hand, but I don't turn it on. I'm not sure why I don't.

"Seems a shame in a way. He's quite a cool guy. And, you know, he's pretty buff." Amber gives me a look to tell me she's joking. Or at least I think she's joking.

"Well go on then. Aren't you gonna turn it on?"

I swallow carefully. And then I press the button to power on the phone.

Nothing happens at first. The phone loads, and it's weird because it still *looks* like my phone. The photo it shows is my usual one, a dead oarfish I found on the beach the other day, but when I go to contacts, all my numbers aren't there, and instead there's lots of names I don't recognize. Amber is leaning in close to me, so that she can see the screen too. I can smell her too, and feel her hair brushing soft against my face. I hold the phone a bit further away, so she doesn't need to lean so close.

"Check the messages," Amber says, moving closer again.

"OK."

This time I don't lean away.

But when I check what she says, they're all my messages. A couple from Dad, and then lots from Amber herself.

"How come..." Amber begins, but I know what she's going to say.

"It's because the messages get stored on the phone once they've been delivered." I tell her. "They wait on the network until they get delivered, but then they just stay on the phone. Otherwise the telephone base stations would fill up. They might even explode."

"Oh." She sounds confused by this, but then she brightens. "How about the photos?"

I shake my head at once. I'm not actually sure of the answer, but I'm definitely not showing Amber my photos.

"So what do we do then? Just wait?" She sits back on my bed and crosses her legs.

It's funny really. I've never had anyone else in this room. Obviously Dad has been in here, and I suppose Tucker has too, but not when I wanted him too. And maybe when the police searched the house, when they were looking for Dad, they must have been in there. But other than that, there's never been anyone else in my room. And now there's *a girl*. A girl who's sixteen years old. I don't know why, but that thought keeps coming into my head. I risk a glance at Amber, I don't know why it feels like a risk suddenly. She's leaning over my bedside table, poking at my starfishes.

"Urgh," she says, and screws up her nose. I'd never noticed before, but there's something really interesting about the shape of her nose. I can't stop staring at it.

Then suddenly she moves away from me and goes to the window. It's a relief, at least, I think it is.

"I wish I had a view like this," she says. "You can see all the way to the end of the beach." She pushes the drapes out of the way so she can see better.

She half turns to me, still facing the window, but twisting her head and neck towards me. It means her chest is side on to me, and I can't help but notice how her blouse is pulled taut over her boobs. I hadn't really noticed that she really had boobs before, I mean I had, but I hadn't thought about them. I don't know why I'm thinking about them now.

I try to stop thinking about them.

"Did they?" She says.

"Did they what?"

"Did they close off the caves? Because of what happened to you?"

"Oh." I shrug. "I don't know."

She gives me a funny look, a kind of half smile, and again I notice how it makes her face look interesting. Kind of *pretty*.

"Billy? Are you alright? You look *weird* again."

"No, I'm not… I'm fine."

I turn away at once, but I notice I can still see her in the reflection of my computer screen. She turns away from the window, a bounce in her step. Her boobs bounce too. I wish I could stop looking.

"Well come on then."

"Come on where?"

"Downstairs. Lasagna will be ready. Bring the phone."

THIRTY-TWO

DINNER IS REALLY ODD. Tucker has set three places, and put glasses and a jug of water on the table. Then he offers us beer again, and Amber says yes, and gives me this innocent look as he gets it for her from the refrigerator. When we're both sitting down he pulls out a big tray of lasagna from the oven, and I have to admit it looks really good, all the cheese on the top is bubbling and crispy from the heat. He sets it in the middle of the table and then serves some to Amber first, then me, and then to himself.

It *is* really good. It's probably the best vegetable lasagna I've ever had, and that's a bit annoying, because it's one of the things I cook sometimes too.

"Mmmmm, this is, like, this is just amazing! Mr..." Amber says when she's tried it, not saying his second name even though she knows what it is, because I told her.

"It's just Tucker." He says. "The secret is you gotta pre-bake the eggplant. Get it good and tender."

"It's delicious. I wish my step dad could cook like this."

Tucker's eyes flick onto Amber.

"Step dad?"

"Yeah, my real dad died."

I remember Amber mentioned this once before. I don't know why she's bringing it up again.

"I'm sorry," Tucker says. Then he goes on.

"What happened?"

Amber doesn't answer right away. She actually sounds a bit strange when she does answer.

"Pancreatic cancer. Four years ago. Then my mom remarried, and they've had a new baby, so they don't have much time for me."

"Shit," Tucker says. Then he thinks for a little while.

"Cancer's a fucking bitch."

This time Amber doesn't reply, but after a moment she nods.

I don't say anything all this time. I'm thinking that we can maybe eat and then go outside. I could tell Tucker we need to fly Steven, or that we have to finish the work we were doing, but then Amber opens her mouth again.

"So you're like... You're like Billy's *uncle* or something?" She looks up into his face, her eyes round. She even flutters her eyelids a little bid.

"Kinda. Billy's dad and me were buddies growing up." He hesitates a moment. "You know anything about what happened to Billy?"

"Yeah, he's told me." Amber says, like she wants him to go on. But he doesn't.

"Well then you know it ain't so easy to talk about." Tucker sucks air through his teeth, like he wishes he could say more. Then he gives her a smile. There's a silence for a moment.

"What about you? You're not in his classes or nothing? You look a lot older..."

Amber seems delighted by this. "No I just... I decided to help him out, a few weeks back, with this project."

"Uh huh?"

"Yeah, we're working on it together." She turns to me. "Aren't we Billy?"

I wonder what she expects me to say to this, it's probably not a great idea to explain to a murderer on the run that we're actually private detectives. But in the end I'm saved from saying anything when there's a loud beeping sound from my pocket. It's a message coming into my phone. Only it isn't *my* phone anymore. Both Amber and Tucker look at me, expectantly, but I guess for different reasons.

I decide I'm best off pretending I haven't heard anything. "Yeah, it's for biology," I say, a bit too loudly, and then to cover that I quickly make something up.

"We're doing a count of grey seals out by the headland. Their numbers keep falling so we're gonna monitor them." I actually did do this, so I can talk for ages on it if I need to.

Tucker finishes chewing a mouthful of food. "Uh huh." He says when he's finished.

"Yeah. There's about a hundred at the moment. Or fifty breeding pairs," I go on. And that's true as well. "They have their pups later in the year, in October usually, so maybe the numbers will go back up again. I hope so because they're a sign of the overall health of the oceans."

Tucker nods seriously, then his face brightens. "Say. I saw a whale earlier today. Out in the bay."

"Really?" This is actually quite interesting. "Do you know what type?"

"I dunno, it was a way out. I just saw the spout and maybe half its tail."

"Fluke."

"What?"

"If you saw only half its tail, then that's a fluke," I explain.

"What you saying?" Tucker sounds a little bit angry, like I'm accusing him of something, so I have to explain again.

"Whale's tails are made up of two halves. Each is called a fluke." People are always getting that wrong.

"Oh," Tucker says. And then my phone with his SIM card beeps again. And as soon as it finishes it beeps again. So I guess two more messages have come in. Putting the new SIM in must have reset the phone to its standard message settings, because the notification message is super loud.

"You're popular tonight ain't you Billy?" Tucker says.

I don't reply, it's just occurred to me that maybe Tucker's SIM card holds the notification that Tucker has chosen for his messages. If so he might recognize the noise my phone keeps making.

Before I finish that thought another message comes in.

There's another silence.

"You sure you don't want to look at that? Could be your old man," Tucker says. So obviously then I *do* have to look. I slide my eyes over to Amber, hoping she can think of some excuse, but she's just smiling at me brightly.

So I have to pull the phone out of my pocket, and really carefully using my other hand to shield the screen so there's no way Tucker can see it, I glance at it. You don't get to see the whole messages, but it tells me four messages received, all of them from the same person. And what I can see of them, they're pretty weird.

"It's not Dad, I say, and slip the phone back, and as I do so it beeps again.

I eat the rest of my food as quickly as I can, but I can't go upstairs until Amber stops talking. She's on about her dad again with Tucker, and they keep talking right up till all the plates are washed and dried.

THIRTY-THREE

What the hell happened? Where are you?

THAT'S THE FIRST MESSAGE. It comes from a guy called *Vinny*. It was sent a week ago. It doesn't look like Tucker answered it.

We need to talk. Call me.

That's the second message. Sent a day later. Then the next one says

I ain't mad. I just need to know where you are.

Then there's a whole load more, all saying the same sort of thing. I show them to Amber, who's super excited.

"Who's *Vinny*?"

"I don't know."

"Why did all the messages come in now?"

"I told you. They get stored on the network until they can get delivered.

"That's so awesome. Do you think the police will have tracked the phone by now?"

"I don't know."

"What are you going to do now?"

"I don't know."

We wait for a few moments, and then Amber gets up and goes to the window, like she's expecting the police might turn up at any second, but of course they don't.

"Is there any way you can tell if the police have tracked the phone yet?"

I think for a moment.

"No."

"So is there anything you can do, now, to alert them?"

Again I shake my head. "I don't think so."

"Do you even still want to?" Amber asks then. "I mean. Are you sure he's definitely a murderer? He seems a really cool guy."

I look at her, a bit annoyed by this.

"Do you want to read the articles about the man he killed?" This shuts her up a bit and she comes back to the bed and sits down. Then she looks at her watch.

"I probably have to get back soon."

I don't reply to this. I'm still a bit annoyed.

"Why don't you phone him? He could probably tell you."

"Phone who?"

"This Vinny guy. He seems to want to contact Tucker pretty bad. Hey -" she hesitates, and turns around to face me. "Maybe he actually *is* the police. Or his probation officer or something. That would make sense, from how the messages sound."

I read them again, trying to see what she means. I'm not convinced.

"*I'll* call him, if you like,"

This is such a stupid idea I don't even consider it. But I do think of something else.

"We could *text* him back. Ask him what he wants? Maybe he'd tell us something more that way?"

Amber bites her lip, thinking this over.

"Go on then," she says.

"What do we say?"

It takes a bit of discussion, but in the end we settle on writing this:

What do you want?

I know that looks simple, but it's actually deceptively clever. It doesn't reveal anything about who we are, but it forces Vinny, whoever he is, to tell us something about what he wants. And just in case Vinny *is* Tucker's probation officer, which still seems unlikely, it will also alert him to noticing that his phone is back on, so that the police can track where he is.

I explain all this to Amber while she fiddles with the phone, but as I do so I begin to wonder if it's such a good idea after all. We actually don't know *anything* about who this Vinny guy is, or what he wants, and we're kind of messing in Tucker's business, and maybe we shouldn't do that. I'm wondering how to say all this to Amber interrupts me.

"Done. Message sent."

"What?"

She throws the phone down on the bed and shrugs.

"It's done."

So that's kind of that.

Then Amber stares at the phone, like she's waiting for something to happen right away, which obviously it isn't. I turn away and open my laptop, which I took upstairs with me this time. I turn it on, and type the password again, to stop it recording, then pull up the list of keywords Tucker has used.

"What you doing now?" Amber asks, leaning in close again.

I start to explain how it all works, how I downloaded *SpyCatch* and *Keylogger Free*, but I can sense Amber losing interest. "So it's just like spying on someone's internet search history?"

I hesitate. "Not exactly no..."

"I do that with my step dad all the time. He's so bad at deleting his search history. He gambles on this poker site. And sometimes he browses porn sites, he really likes Asian girls. So I've no idea why he's with my mom."

I don't know what to say to this, so I show Amber the newspaper pages on the robbery at the jewelry store in Hounds Beach.

"Shit," she says when she's finished reading them. "That *is* pretty bad."

I feel a bit better at this. Downstairs she was acting like he was Bruce Willis in *Die Hard*.

"Has he looked at anything else since then?"

"Hmmm?"

"Has he used your computer since then? Have you recorded him looking at anything else?"

"Oh." It's quite hard to answer this. I've used my laptop myself since installing the spyware, as well as leaving it out as a trap for Tucker, so his pages are mixed up with mine. Even so, I go to the list and we both lean in to look. I sort the results by time of day, selecting only the times when I was at school.

That narrows it down to about fifteen results on the screen. Fifteen separate webpages that Tucker's visited. But even then there's a problem. Most of them are impossible to read. You can see there's something there, but the program has blurred the words so you can't actually read them.

"Why can't you see what it says?" Amber asks.

"It's because I only installed the free trial version of the software. They only work for a few days then you have to pay."

"And you can't click them either? To see where they go?"

"Only the ones you can read."

Amber goes quiet for a moment, looking at the list more carefully. She puts her hand onto the track pad, and places the mouse pointer on the first legible name on the list. It expands to show the whole web address. Then she moves down, and goes to the second legible name, and then the third.

"Billy, these are all jewelry stores..."

"Are they?" I say. And then she clicks the link she's resting on.

The internet window opens and slowly a page loads. A video starts playing, showing a happy couple spinning around on Silverlea beach, and then a close up of their hands, with rings on the fingers. It's a store called Carter's.

"That's the jewelry store in Newlea. At the end on Main Street."

Amber frowns. She clicks back, and checks the next website on the list. Straight away I can see it's another jewelry store, also on the island. Then she clicks the third legible search on the list, and a third jewelry store website opens.

"Why is he looking at other jewelry stores?"

"Dad said," I begin, thinking back. "Before he went out on the boat, he said that Tucker was looking to give it a go here on Lornea Island."

Amber turns to look at me, her brow deeply furrowed.

"Like get a job?"

"That's what he said but..."

"... Maybe what he meant was, actually *do* a job. Like another robbery."

THIRTY-FOUR

THERE'S silence for a long while, then Amber stands up.

"I dunno. Maybe he's just looking for a necklace?"

"Look at him. Why would he want a necklace? And Dad told me he was *looking for work* here. This *is* his work."

Still she looks doubtful, but after a while she laughs.

"What's funny?" I ask, confused.

"You are. Everyone at school thinks you're this weird, nerdy geek, but then you've got the most full-on fucked-up home life that no one knows about. It's hilarious!"

Strangely enough, I don't laugh at that.

"You really think he's planning to rob a jewelry store here?" She asks a few moments later.

I shrug. "I'm not thinking anything. I'm just looking at the evidence. We know he robbed a jeweler's in that Hounds Beach place. And now he's looking at all the jeweler's stores on the island?"

"Maybe he's..." But her voice faces away. In the end she just stares at me.

"Fucking hell Billy. This is so fucked up."

* * *

Amber has to go home soon after that, so we don't get a chance to talk about what to do next. But she promises she's going to help me, with whatever it is. Like if we need to get more evidence that Tucker is planning to rob jewelry stores. Or if we just need to tell the police what we already know. Whatever we decide, she's going to help.

And then she goes downstairs. I watch for her out of the window. She takes a while, and I hear her laughing downstairs for a bit. But then she appears outside, gets into her car and drives away. Then I make sure the desk is securely in front of my bedroom door and go to bed.

I guess I must be getting a bit more used to living with a criminal, or maybe I'm just exhausted. But either way I get to sleep quite easily, and the next morning I wake up and I'm in quite a good mood. Maybe it's because I get woken up naturally for a change, instead of by the alarm on my phone, which obviously doesn't work because it doesn't have my SIM in it.

So I turn on my radio. It's tuned to Lornea Island 104FM. It's a music station, and I used to listen to it all the time when I was younger, but recently I've forgotten about it, until last night, when I needed it to make sure Tucker couldn't overhear what we were saying. But actually it's nice to listen to music, and some people say it's good for your brain too, it's something about helping the neurons to connect to each other. I don't think the evidence is clear, but it does feel nice sometimes.

After a while I get up and have a look at *VesselTrack*, and then my mood gets even better, because I see that Dad's boat is heading back from the fishing grounds. I work out he'll be back sometime tonight, which is earlier than he said. That's double good news because the boats only ever come back early if they're totally full of fish, so he'll have earned a lot.

Then I start to very quickly do my homework, because I've been so busy with all the Tucker stuff, and the Mrs. Jacobs stuff, that I haven't had a chance to do it, and there's two pieces I have to hand in this morning. So I'm doing all that when suddenly my phone rings.

I know what you're thinking, but I guess I'm still half-thinking about Dad, because I just assume it must be him on the phone, that maybe he's come back into range now he's getting closer to land. So without realizing what I'm doing, I answer my phone.

"Hi Dad!"

"Who's that?" The voice is all wrong. Right away I realize what I've done.

I lower the phone to look at the screen. The caller ID says 'Vinny'.

"I said who's that?" The voice says again. He sounds gruff, a bit angry.

"No one." I reply, desperately trying to work out what to do.

"Well it's definitely someone. And it's someone with Tucker's phone." The man goes on. "You know where he is?"

I don't answer, but I can't help thinking the answer. That's he's downstairs on the sofa, asleep. Then I have another thought. He might not actually be downstairs by now. I've been doing homework for a while now, and sometimes Tucker does get up early, and he's in the habit now of just coming upstairs and using the shower without being asked. And if he does that he'll hear me speaking on the phone, and wonder who I'm speaking to. So just in case I twist the volume knob to make the radio louder.

"Well? You know where he is?" The man on the phone repeats.

"No," I lie. "He's not here."

The man – I suppose I should call him Vinny, since I know that's his name - doesn't reply, and I wonder if I could just hang up. But I spend too long thinking about it and miss my chance.

"So where's 'here'?"

"Erm. I don't know."

For a stupid moment I wonder if Vinny might actually be Tucker's probation officer, like Amber thought last night, but I know he isn't. He doesn't sound anything like a probation officer would sound.

"How'd you get hold of Tucker's phone son?"

But then I'm not quite so sure. Suddenly he sounds a bit more friendly. So what if he *is* a probation officer. Or a policeman. How would you actually tell?

"Listen kid. I only want to speak to him. He don't have nothing to worry about, not from me."

I swallow at this because the way he says it, it kind of makes me think the exact opposite.

"Where are you kid? You don't sound like you're from round here. You got an accent. Tell me where Tucker is..."

Still I don't hang up, and I begin to understand why. I start to feel a bit braver. I work out that, whoever he is, there's no way he can tell where I am, just from a phone call. That's why he keeps asking me. Because he *needs* me to tell him. So I'm safe, as long as I watch what I say. And that means I'm able to start asking *him* questions. It might help when I speak to the police.

"Who are you? And why are you looking for Tucker?"

There's a long pause, and at the end of it Vinny laughs.

"Who am *I*? You got a nerve kid. And who says I'm looking for Tucker? I'm just looking *out for* him, you know what I'm saying?"

I don't answer.

"Tell me where you are you kid? Where's that accent from?"

I don't reply. I know what he's trying to do.

"Is that East Coast?"

Again I stay silent. I'm not going to be tricked into revealing anything.

"Tucker's a friend of yours is he?"

"*No.* He just knows my Dad, that's all." Straight away I realize I shouldn't have said that. I know it from the way he replies, sharp and fast.

"And who's your dad?"

I try not to answer, but Vinny just waits for me to speak, and it's weird how hard it is not to tell him, with the question just hanging there. And I can feel myself about to reply, even though I don't want to, when he speaks again.

"Who's your dad kid? What's his name?"

And somehow that makes it easier to not answer him. I shouldn't have let slip about Dad, but it's not enough for Vinny to know where we are, and now I'm not going to make a second mistake.

"Where's that accent son? You don't sound like you're from around here..." His voice has changed now. He doesn't sound mean, more like someone offering candy to a kid.

I decide the best thing to do it hang up, to be on the safe side. But then something really bad happens. Something really super unlucky. Just before I press the button to end the call, the song on the radio ends, and the DJ starts calling something out. And right away I know what he's gonna say, because I've heard it before, when I used to listen to *Lornea Island 104* a lot. There's this really old movie, you might have seen it. It's about the war in Vietnam, and a DJ in the army played by the an old actor called Robin Williams has this catchphrase. I reckon the *Lornea Island 104* DJ must have watched the movie a lot because he's always doing it too.

"Goooooooood Moooooorning..." I panic. I should just kill the call, but instead I dive across the room to switch the radio off. But I don't get there in time. "... Lorneeeeeee Isssssland!"

The room is suddenly silent. The phone has fallen to the floor, and I stoop down to pick it up, praying that it broke or stopped the call when it fell. But then I realise Vinny is saying something.

"What was that kid? What's goin' on..."

I don't wait long enough to hear it all. I fumble with the buttons until the phone's screen goes blank.

I stare at the phone for a few moments, and then the screen lights up, and the caller ID shows he's rung back. Hurriedly, and fumbling even more now, because my hands are really shaking, I manage to slide the back off and rip out the battery. Then I pull out the SIM card out too, and throw it away, it cuts through the air, like when you throw a playing card, but then it hits the wall, then drops down to the floor like a dead insect.

THIRTY-FIVE

AMBER CORNERS me as I get off the school bus, and asks if Vinny replied to the text, That's good, because it means I don't have to lie to her. I tell her that he hasn't sent any texts, and she looks disappointed, but then she starts talking about something else.

"I had an idea," she tells me. "About Mrs. Jacobs."

I have to get to class, so it's not really the time to talk.

"You remember how Sharpe told us about Henry Jacobs running off with another woman? But we know he was more interested in little boys."

"So?"

"So I figured that kinda proves how he didn't go off with a woman. You see what I mean?"

I try to follow her logic, but it isn't actual logic. As in anything actually logical.

"Why not?"

"Because he liked *boys*. So he wouldn't go off with a woman would he? Think about it..."

"Maybe he liked boys *and* women."

She gives me a look.

"That's how it works Billy," Amber says, then she drops into step with me, so we're both walking together down the corridor.

"What are you interested in?"

"What?"

"Girls? Boys? What do you like?"

Straight away I feel my face begins to heat up.

"What do you mean?"

"What I said. Handsy Henry liked little boys. So he's not going to like women as well. What are you into? Are there any girls you like?"

I don't look at her. I make a real point of it.

"No."

"Why not? Are you into boys?"

"*No!*"

"It's alright. I don't mind either way."

"I'm not..."

"Look my point is, people usually like one or the other. Except for bisexuals I suppose. And people that like to stick it into sheep. Maybe they like goats just as much, I don't know."

I open my mouth to reply, but she's off on one now.

"*Henry Jacobs.* If he was into boys, then I reckon it *proves* he didn't run off with another woman. Or if it doesn't prove it, then it pretty nearly does. Because he didn't *like* women! Not in a sexual way."

I don't know what to say. I think I just want this conversation to end. And then it does, but not quite how I wanted it to.

"Anyway." Amber says. "I gotta get to class. I had this great idea what we should do with Mrs. Jacobs. I'll tell you at lunch." And then she disappears.

* * *

I've had a bit of bullying to deal with recently. Ever since what happened in the reception hall, when Amber attacked James Drolley. It's not been anything too serious. But that kind of changes, in mid-morning break, when I'm going from one class to the next. Most of the classrooms in our school are in the main block, but there's also an annex, where the science labs are. To get there you have to go down this long corridor. And I'm walking down there when I hear someone calling my name. I turn around and see Drolley and a couple of others. Right away I know it's going to be bad. You can always tell.

"Wheatley. Where d'ya think you're going?"

I think about making a run for the classroom. But it's still break time. The teacher won't be there yet so I'll be trapped, and they'll be wound up from chasing me. So I wait for them, hoping to get it over with. Drolley's gang stop a few steps away, but Drolley himself doesn't stop. He keeps walking till he's almost on top of me, and then without slowing down or hesitating he punches me in the stomach. He punches me really hard.

It hurts twice as much because I wasn't expecting it. I double up. I'm still on my feet but it's knocked all the breath out of me and I can't get any new air in. I start to panic, trying to draw a breath, but it's like my lungs have broken.

"No vampire protector today Wheatley?" Drolley asks, then there's a fresh wave of pain as he hits me again. Then a third time. This time I don't stay on my feet, though I don't know how I go down. I just find myself on the floor, gritty against my cheek.

"Fucking little freak." I hear him mutter above me. And then there's a blow on my back, I think where's he's kicking me. I curl up into a ball, the kicks don't hurt as much as the punches, and now, finally, I'm getting some air in again.

It's bad, but at least it's quick, because then they're gone, laughing as they carry on down the corridor, and into the classroom. And slowly the pain recedes, and eventually I can get enough air in. I push against the wall of the corridor with my feet, and after a while I get to a sitting position. Quite a few of the other kids from my class have come by now, but none of them have done anything. They can't really, because Drolley will only pick on them if they do, so they just step by, like they're pretending they didn't see. And I know I have to get up too, before the teacher comes to take the class, because he'd ask what I'm doing here on the floor. And then if I told him what happened, Drolley would know I sneaked on him, and then he'd just do it again.

I'm sort of on my feet by the time Mr. Edwards comes by. He just gives me a strange look.

"Everything OK Wheatley?"

I still can't speak, so I nod, and he pulls a face. I've never got on with Mr. Edwards.

"Well don't hang around here looking *odd*. Get into class." And he waits so that I have to walk in front of him into the classroom. Normally I get in early, so I can get a desk at the front, but because I'm late there's none left, and I have to take one right at the back, right next to where Drolley is sitting, smirking at me.

So that's not very nice.

* * *

"You what?" I ask Amber, at lunchtime.

"It *has* to be her. It all fits."

I stare at Amber in amazement. "You actually think Mrs. Jacobs killed Henry Jacobs?"

"I'm sure of it."

"Why?"

"She found out he was a pedophile. She didn't like it. So *boom*." She mimes the action of a handgun against the side of my head.

"But what about the letters? The birthday cards Principal Sharpe received from her dad, who was living with another woman in Maui?"

"Faked."

I'm still staring at her.

"But why would she hire *us*? To find him, if *she* killed him."

"I know, it's crazy right? But what if she forgot? What if her mental state, whatever it's called, made her forget, but she really wants to know?"

"Her senile dementia?"

"Yep, that's the thing."

I realize I'm shaking my head.

"Look Billy, I'm only saying it's a possibility. This is how you investigate things. You make a hypothesis, then you test it."

"So how are you gonna test it?"

"We, partner, are going to go back to see her, and we're going to tell her we know the truth – that she killed him. And if that *is* true, it'll make her remember. She won't be able to hide it. And we'll record what she says, so we have the evidence."

"But..." There's so many reasons why this is crazy that I don't know where to start. "Principal Sharpe told us we're not allowed to speak to her again."

"She also lied about Henry Jacobs moving to Maui. You really gonna listen to her?"

"We don't know she lied, and she's the school princip..."

"Cos I'm not. Can't you see? She was covering for her mom. That's the reason she doesn't want us speaking to her. Because she knows what really happened to Henry Jacobs. She doesn't want us finding out."

"Or she just doesn't want her mother getting disturbed because she's got – what did you call it?"

Amber shakes her head to dismiss this at once, but then she stops.

"Actually it's a pretty big problem for her isn't it? Here's her mom with this dark secret, who's now going mental, and she could spill it out to anyone."

I open my mouth to protest again, how Principal Sharpe has letters from her dad which prove her mom didn't kill him, but I can tell I'm not going to get anywhere. Amber has convinced herself. So I try a different issue.

"How are you going to do it? We don't have any secret recording equipment."

And then Amber leans down to her bag, with a broad grin.

"Oh yes we do." She pulls out a tangle of black cables. "I borrowed this from the music department. All we have to do is tape this under your clothes and plug it into a phone. She's never going to search us is she?"

As she speaks I can't help but picture a miniature, secret microphone, like the type you see in spy movies. But the microphone she pulls out isn't one of those. It's like of those ones you clip onto a shirt, that the newsreaders wear. I guess you could call it discreet maybe, but it's definitely not secret.

"Why me? Why do I have to wear it?"

"Because I'm gonna be the one asking all the questions, so she'll be looking at me more, and she might see it."

"I don't know." I say, after considering all this.

"What do you mean you don't know? What is there to know?"

"I don't know if we should. I mean, after what Principal Sharpe said. What if Mrs. Jacobs tells her that we tried to speak to her again?"

"She can't stop us speaking to her. She's our client. Besides, you saw what a lonely old lady she is. She'll be pleased to see us. And, if we're wrong, it'll give us the chance to report back what we found out. We can tell her we discovered her husband moved away to Maui. If it is true, we should tell her that at least."

I think about this for a while. I guess it makes sense when she puts it like that.

"I can't go tonight." I tell her. "Dad's back and I want to see him.

"OK." For the first time Amber looks reasonable. "Are you gonna tell him about Tucker? About how he's casing out jewelry shops?"

I nod. I don't know *how* I'm going to tell him. But I know I do have to.

* * *

But then when I get home and look on *VesselTrack*, Dad's boat is still quite a long way out from the island, and I realize I misjudged how slowly it goes. I discover you can measure the actual distance on the screen, and since I know the boat's speed, I do my calculations properly this time, and I work out that *Ocean Harvest* will dock at about 10 tonight. I guess he'll have to help unload too, so probably won't get back here till midnight. I won't be able to tell him about Tucker then, so it will have to be in the morning, before I go to school. Then Dad can throw him out and I don't have to be part of it.

At least Tucker isn't here this evening. There's still half of the vegetable lasagna in the refrigerator, and he's left a note on the table saying he had to go out, and I should eat it.

So I catch up a bit more on my homework and tidy the house a bit, for Dad. It's not going to be easy to tell him about Tucker. Dad'll ask how I know about him, and he'll think I've been snooping, which he hates. I've just got to hope he'll understand it was the right thing to do, because of what I ended up finding out. But you never know with Dad.

I'm still thinking about this when, just before I go to bed, I break into Dad's emails. I actually do this from time to time, not because I'm being nosy, or snooping or anything, but just to keep an eye on things. A lot of the bills for the house come in by email, and I need to know if Dad's on top of them. So I scan his inbox a bit absently, and I'm about to click away when I see something that stops me dead. It's an email from Tucker, sitting in Dad's inbox. It's already been opened, I guess Dad in range of the shore now and he's seen it on his phone. So I click the message to see what it says. and after a moment it opens.

It's really short, just an email link and four words:

How about this one?

Confused, I click the link, and then my screen fills with a familiar looking website. It's the one with the couple spinning around on the beach, showing off the diamonds on their fingers. Carter's Jewelry. Tucker's sent it to Dad. Which means...

Which means I don't need to tell Dad that Tucker is looking for a jewelry store to hold up.

Because Dad already knows.

THIRTY-SIX

My dad isn't a bad person, I just want to take a moment to say that. It's just he's had a really tough life. When he was growing up his mom and dad had no money at all. So Dad couldn't afford to go to college, or even finish high school because he had to get a job or they wouldn't have been able to eat. Then he must have thought his life was going to get better when he met my mom, because she came from a family that had loads of money, and lived in this big house. But then my Mom went mad and murdered my sister, and tried to kill me, and her family blamed it all on Dad, so he had no choice but to run away here with me, in secret. So it didn’t really.

And if that wasn't bad enough, then Dad got involved in all the stuff that happened here. But that was just bad luck. He started dating this girl who seemed really nice on the outside, but turned out to be a murderer, and then Dad got blamed for the girl *she* killed. And even now, half the town doesn't really believe he was completely innocent even though she’s in prison for it. So if he's involved in Tucker's idea to rob a jewelry store then it's only because he's desperate. He just wants to earn enough money so we can both live here and have folk leave us in peace.

Even so I can't get to sleep for worrying. I keep trying to work out what to actually *do*. There's no point me telling Dad about Tucker, because obviously Dad already knows.

And I can't go to the police now either. Because if they came to arrest Tucker, they'll also look into his emails, and they'll work out that Dad is part of the plan too.

I can't even tell *Amber* about it, because... Well, because Amber's basically insane.

And I know that things like this always seem worse in the night, and not so bad in the morning. But even so I can't stop myself crying. Just a little bit. And once I start crying, pretty soon my pillow is all wet, because I'm crying quite a lot.

But after that I do feel a bit better. And just in time, because then I hear the noise of an engine outside, and I peek out the window, and I see Dad and Tucker getting out of Dad's truck. And I see how they're laughing and joking with each other, and Dad looks really happy. And I don't know what to feel about that. I'm pleased to see Dad again, and I want him to be happy. But I'm terrified about what he's going to do.

Quickly I wipe my eyes and get back into bed. I pretend to be reading a book, so that when Dad comes in, to tell me he's back and he's safe, he can't tell that I've been crying. I hear them both, still laughing downstairs, for quite a long time, but eventually I hear the squeak of footsteps on the stairs. I wipe my face again, and get ready for Dad to come in.

But then he doesn't. I hear the sounds of him in the bathroom. And then his bedroom door opening, and then shutting again. And then nothing. So I'm left there, holding the book I'm not really reading.

So eventually I just put it down, and try and go to sleep.

THIRTY-SEVEN

I'M a bit vacant in school the next morning, so when Amber catches up with me and tells me we're sneaking off for the afternoon to see Mrs. Jacobs, I don't even try to argue with her. It's easy to leave. There's a teacher by the gate, but she's only checking students who are walking in, and we're in Amber's mom's car, driving out.

Once we're out of Newlea she stops and tells me to take off my shirt. Again I do what she says without arguing. She's got some of that silver sticky tape that sticks to anything, and she pulls off long strips of it, and uses it to tape the microphone leads around my body and to my back. We put the actual microphone just below the neckline at the front of my t-shirt. When I put it all back on I can't move because the tape pulls and rips at my skin.

"Has that Vinny guy replied yet?" Amber asks as she's pressing the tape back down on my chest. "To the message we sent?"

I sense my body tensing up, and force it to relax. I'd forgotten about that.

"No."

"How about your Dad? Did he get back last night? Have you told him about Tucker planning to hit the jewelry store?"

"No."

"*Relax will you?* You'll put the tape off."

"I am relaxed. Just stop picking on me."

Amber doesn't mention it again.

I know why, it's because *she's* distracted. She's super excited about what we're doing. I've figured out how to tell with Amber. It's in the way her eyes go really shiny. She totally believes that Mrs. Jacobs murdered Mr. Jacobs, instead of him just going away like Principal Sharpe told us. And she really seems to believe she's going to persuade Mrs. Jacobs to confess to it. It's ridiculous. But then so is Amber half the time. But I suppose she *is* right about telling Mrs. Jacobs what we've learnt. Probably Mrs. Jacobs is too mad to understand, but just maybe she won't be, and maybe it'll even help her. And if that's the case then maybe we could hold onto the $5000 check. I still haven't quite decided what we should do about that.

We pull up outside Mrs. Jacobs' house and Amber fusses about with my wires again before we get out of the car. Until I knock her hand away, because Mrs. Jacobs will have heard us arrive, and might be looking out of the window.

"*Alright.* Easy Billy," Amber says. Then she presses record on her iPhone, and slips it into my pocket. And then she gives me an excited look, then we get out of the car and walk to the front door.

Amber rings the bell and we wait for a while, but nothing happens. I start to feel a bit relieved, because I don't really want to do this, now that I'm here. I think it's stupid, and I think we could get into a lot of trouble.

"Come on. Let's go back to school." I say. "She's not in. Even if she was, she wouldn't tell us anything."

Amber presses the doorbell again. And then she uses her fist to bang on the door.

"Shit," she murmurs.

"Come on," I say again. "Let's get back before we're missed..." But then the door suddenly opens. Just a crack, only as far as the security chain allows it. There's a rustling sound from inside, and we can see a strip of Mrs. Jacob's face. Just wide enough to see her eyes looking back, milky and a bit scared.

"Mrs. Jacobs? It's Amber. From the detective agency. We said we'd come to meet you?"

The eyes blink slowly. They look confused.

"Detective agency?" I didn't remember from before how old she sounds.

"The one you hired, Mrs. Jacobs." Amber is speaking really loudly now, and the poor old lady winces away from the sound, like it hurts her ears.

"To find out what happened to your husband."

The eyes come back again, blinking. Even though I can't see much I feel sorry for her, and I hope she won't let us in, because I'm worried about what Amber wants to do to her.

"To Henry, Mrs. Jacobs. Remember? Your husband Henry? He disappeared that Christmas. You asked us to find out what happened to him."

Then Mrs. Jacob's eyes rotate in their sockets as they inspect first Amber and then me. I feel awkward standing so close, it's like I can feel the wires of the microphone standing out through the thin fabric of my shirt.

"My husband?"

"That's right Mrs. Jacobs. We've got some news." Amber bites her lip hopefully. "Can we come in please?"

Suddenly the door shuts, and I feel slightly hopeful for a second that maybe she won't let us in. But of course she's just taking the security chain off. It rattles for ages, like she's struggling with it, and then the door slowly opens again, but all the way this time.

I'd forgotten how stooped over she is. And how crazy. She's only wearing one blouse today, but it's two buttons out of alignment. It makes her look lopsided. Amber slides a quick look at me.

"Thanks you Mrs. Jacobs. We appreciate it."

Mrs. Jacobs does a sort of smile, and then she stands back from the door. Amber walks in, and then I don't have any choice but to follow her in.

I remember the big hallway, the oil paintings. It all seems darker this time. Then I get a weird thought. I can suddenly imagine Principal Sharpe running around here as a nine year old who just lost her dad. But she's not like a real nine year old, she's like a miniature Principal Sharpe, just scaled down to be the same size as a child.

Then Mrs. Jacobs shuts the front door, making it even darker. She puts the security chain back on. It takes her ages again, and while she does it Amber and I just stand there waiting. But eventually she gets it, and that's a relief in itself. I wonder if she's going to take us somewhere crazy to talk this time, like into her bathroom. But again she leads us out into the garden, just like before.

"Could I get you a drink? Some coffee perhaps? Or some iced tea?" Mrs. Jacobs asks, and we both say no straight away, but she doesn't seem to hear.

"I'm sure I've got a soda somewhere. I won't be a moment." She waves her hand, and Amber and me are left there for a moment, looking around her garden again.

"What are you going to tell her?" I ask. The truth is I've been a bit distracted all day, with all the Tucker and Dad stuff, and I haven't really thought through what we're doing here.

"I told you," Amber say. "We're gonna tell her what we've found out and get her to confess ."

"But what about..." I don't finish what I'm saying because then Mrs. Jacobs returns with two cans of 7 UP on a tray. She sets it down and makes a big thing about giving us both coasters.

"I know what you young people are like with spillages," she says and winks at me.

I pick up my 7 UP and notice the tab is already open. I sniff it, a bit suspicious. But it seems alright, I get a nose full of fizz, so I take a sip.

"Now dear," Mrs. Jacobs says to Amber. "You said you found out something about Henry?"

I'm glad she asks Amber, because I don't have a plan for what we're supposed to say. I don't see how we can say how Principal Sharpe – her own daughter – told us about Mr. Jacobs running off with another woman. Nor how she – Mrs. Jacobs – must have *known* this, only now she's forgotten because she's gone mad. How's that going to make her feel? As it happens, I don't think Amber knows what to say either, because she starts off by explaining how we discovered Henry was the

Principal of Newlea High School when he went missing, and how we searched the newspaper archives for information about it. And all the time Mrs. Jacobs sits there with a whole series of looks on her face, from confused, to nodding, to angry.

"But I know all this!" She says, when Amber finally stops. Then she looks at me.

And that makes Amber look at me too. So I have to say something.

"We spoke to your daughter. Or rather, she spoke to us. She's our school Principal."

There's a moment when Mrs. Jacobs smiles, I suppose at the mention of her daughter, but then she looks totally baffled.

"*Your* school principal?"

"We go to Newlea High School. You know she's the principal there now?"

"Well yes. Of course. But..." she lifts a frail hand and points at me. "You're a student at Wendy's school?"

"We both are."

There's a moment of silence, then I try to smile. Amber isn't looking very happy. But what am I supposed to say?

"She told us..."

"But you're *detectives*. She told me you were detectives." Mrs. Jacobs spins in her chair and stares at Amber again, but she's more confused than angry.

"We *are* detectives. We're just students as well."

There's an odd moment when I don't know how Mrs. Jacobs is going to take it, but then she laughs.

"My my. Good heavens. I did think you were rather young." Mrs. Jacobs pauses, her face screws up again, like something's just occurred to her.

"But Wendy doesn't know what happened to Henry."

I'm not sure what she means by that, so I decide to correct her.

"Actually Mrs. Jacobs, that's what we need to..." But I don't get to finish my sentence because there's a sudden change in Mrs. Jacobs. She suddenly sits up straighter in her chair, appears less frail. And her voice hardens. It's like what happened the first time we were here.

"She doesn't know anything that girl. Never bloody did!"

It's like someone has magically just made Mrs. Jacobs vanish, and replaced her with someone else. Everything about her is different. Even the dullness has gone from her eyes.

"What did she tell you?" Mrs. Jacobs demands. "What did that *stupid girl* say?"

I look at Amber, trying to get her to take over again, but her eyes are wide and she just nods, urging me on. And I can feel Mrs. Jacobs eyes too. Piercing and sharp. Suddenly *mean*. I go on, as carefully as I can.

"She said your husband left the island with another lady. That he started a new life with her. In Hawaii. He wrote letters. To Principal Sharpe. That's how she knows."

Mrs. Jacobs eyes flare with something, surprise, perhaps. But she doesn't speak.

"I'm really sorry," I start to say, but then she interrupts me.

"*The goddamn hell he did!*" She suddenly explodes. "There's no way that man was ever going to leave *me*. I made damn sure of that."

There's a long silence. All I can hear is the birds tweeting, and the rolling of the surf at the bottom of the rock cliffs.

"Could you say that again Mrs. Jacobs." I hear Amber asking, but it's from a long way away.

"Say what again?" She snaps.

"What you just said. About how you made sure he wouldn't leave you? What did you mean by that?"

There's another shift in Mrs. Jacobs, and for a moment I think the sweet old lady is back. Or maybe I just hope that's what happens, because this version is scary. But I'm wrong. She's someone else again. Less angry, but more lucid.

"Henry was never going to *leave me.* I made him respectable. My family had all the money. Oh no..." her hand comes up again, even that looks somehow less frail than it did before.

"No. I killed him." She sits back and smiles, her lips drawing back to show her old, stained teeth and blood-red gums.

Amber's staring at me now, and there's all sorts in the look on her face. Like she's telling me how she told me so, and that I'd better be recording this.

"You... You did what?" She asks.

Mrs. Jacobs turns on Amber, and gives her a pitying look. It's like she doesn't have time for Amber's stupidity.

"*I killed him dear.* I warned him I would. If he kept on with that dirty fiddling he did. I told him what would happen. But he wouldn't listen. So I killed him."

She turns to me, and smiles again. I think I can feel my mouth hanging open.

"He'd have liked you, Mr. Billy. I tell you that. You'd have been one of his *special ones,* if you'd been around back then. Oh no. I couldn't let him carry on like that. We'd have been ruined when it came out. And it would have come out. Sooner or later."

"So what happened?" Amber asks. Her voice still sounds distant.

"I just told you! He promised me it wouldn't happen again. But I knew it would. I could *tell.* And sure enough, there he was, coming home from school again. *Working late!* I knew exactly what *that* meant. So I went to confront him, at the school. I got there just in time to see a boy leaving, his clothing messed around. So I went inside. I surprised him."

She looks each of us in the eye, and there's a strange expression on her face. Pride. Arrogance.

"Did you shoot him?" Amber asks, breathless.

"Of course not. Where would I get a gun from?" She rolls her eyes and turns to me.

"I pretended there was nothing wrong. I was just passing. I asked him to show me the building works – the new gymnasium, some of the money was coming from my family. And he agreed, mainly because he was feeling guilty about what he'd been doing. And then, when his back was turned, I hit him over the head with a brick. He went down like a sack of potatoes."

"It was easy. I rolled his body in the bottom of the hole and covered it with rubble. The next day they poured the concrete."

Mrs. Jacobs turns and smiles at me.

"And that was the end of Henry."

THIRTY-EIGHT

"Tell me you got that? Tell me you didn't sit on the phone and stop it recording? Tell me that didn't happen."

We're back in Amber's car, driving back towards school. I don't really know how to describe the atmosphere. We're just… stunned. After Mrs. Jacobs told us about how she killed her husband she went right back to being the sweet scared old lady she'd been before. With the same confused, milky look in her eyes. And when Amber asked her for more details she didn't seem to know who Mr. Jacobs was, let alone what happened to him. I'm not even sure she knew who we were.

I fiddle with the phone, making sure I don't do anything stupid like delete the file. And then I hit play. It's a bit hard to hear with the engine, but you can hear us alright, the two of us getting out of the car and going to the doorstep.

"Come on, let's go back to school," I hear my voice from earlier saying. "She's not going to tell us anything."

I guess Amber can't hear properly, because she turns abruptly into a parking area, off the road, skidding to a halt on the gravel.

"Turn it up," she says.

I do what she says. And then I adjust the slider at the bottom of the screen to fast forward to the part where Mrs. Jacobs confesses.

I killed him. I'd warned him I would. If he kept on with that dirty fiddling *he did.*

"Wow." Amber says. "Just fucking *wow*."

I don't answer. I just stare out the windshield. The parking area is one of those with a view out over the water. In the distance the mainland is a grey shadow on the horizon. Some way out a container ship is passing by, its massive hull streaked red with rust. Closer still there's a company of gannets feeding in the cold currents, that swirl round the southern tip of Lornea Island, folding up their long thin wings and diving into the water like arrows. I see them, I see it all but I hardly register any of it.

"We have to go to the police." Amber says. I don't answer.

"We *have to*. We know a crime's been committed. A *murder*. We can't not go to the police."

Still I don't say anything. I'm thinking.

"And to think, she put his body under *the fucking gym*! It'll still be there today. I was only in there yesterday for P Ed. That's sick. That's disgusting."

I'm watching the gannets now. They're kind of hypnotic. When they hit the water they can swim down as much as twenty meters. It's like they can fly under that water. I'd quite like to raise a gannet chick one day, but they don't nest on the island, they have these big stacks of rock out to sea where they form massive colonies...

"*Billy!*"

My head snaps around to look at her.

"We have to go to the police."

I open my mouth to reply to her. But I don't say anything. The thing is, I can't get out of my head what happened the last time I went to the police. When Olivia Curran went missing, and I thought that maybe this guy in Silverlea might have kidnapped and murdered her. I actually got a photo of what I thought was him dragging her body out of his house, rolled up in a carpet. Only it wasn't her at all. He was just renovating his house. It was just a carpet.

Without speaking I press play on the phone again. Mrs. Jacobs' voice rings out again. Just from the tone you can tell it's her nasty version.

I killed him. I put his body in the bottom of the hole and covered it with rubble. The next day they poured the concrete...

There's a laugh. I didn't notice it at the time, but it's there on the recording, clear as anything. Only it's more of a cackle than a laugh. Like Mrs. Jacobs is actually a witch.

"Billy? We *have* to go to the police."

I nod. "Yeah. I know."

THIRTY-NINE

ONCE WE'VE MADE the decision, we have to work out how. I mean, you can't just walk into Newlea Police Station and say you've got evidence of a murder. Can you?

Well actually it turns out you can. Or at least, neither of us can think of a better idea. So that's what we do. Instead of going back to school, Amber drives us straight to the police station, the same one where I was interviewed a couple of years ago.

It's weird being back. It doesn't feel like two years since I was last here, and I wonder if I'm going to recognize anyone. But the officer on the front desk isn't familiar.

"Help you?" He narrows his eyes like he doesn't like kids. I'd forgotten how the police are like that.

"We need to speak to a detective," I say, trying to sound firmer than I feel. "We have evidence about a murder."

The cop looks like he's trying to show this happens all the time, but I see his eyebrows going up in surprise.

"What evidence?"

In response I hold up Amber's phone and press play. Mrs. Jacobs' voice rings out inside the quiet of the police station. I stop the recording just after her cackling laugh.

"Who is that?" the officer asks, but I shake my head.

"We need to speak to a detective," I say again.

The officer stares at us for a long time before he does anything. He's obviously pissed, but we need someone more senior.

"I'll find someone you can speak to."

"Thank you."

. . .

Ten minutes later the same officer leads us to an interview room. He tells us to sit down and says someone will be with us shortly. It's even more weird being back in here – it's the same actual room I was in last time. It's still got the old fashioned tape-recorders they had before, the ones that actually use tapes. I point them out to Amber, but she frowns at me, like she's not interested.

"They're *analogue*!" I tell her.

She keeps frowning, and then she mutters, more to herself than me.

"This is so fucked up."

Then the door bursts open, and a man comes striding in. He's about to shut the door behind him, when he stops, noticing me. He holds his head still for a few moments.

"*Wheatley!* I knew I remembered that name." Then he closes the door, but he does so slowly, like he's taking the time to remember everything that happened before. I realize I know him too. He was one of the policemen I didn't really get on with when I was here before. Although there were quite a lot I didn't get on with. He sits down opposite us. Before he speaks again he looks carefully at Amber, but then he comes back to me.

"*Billy Wheatley*."

I don't reply. I don't remember his name. After a while he must realize this.

"I'm Lieutenant James Langley. We met before." He turns to Amber. "And you are?"

While she tells him her name I remember a bit more about him. He was the one who was in charge of the investigation to find the missing girl, but he wasn't very good. He got really angry just because I was trying to help.

"Frank tells me you've got something I should hear." He doesn't start the recorder on the desk, so it doesn't seem like he's got any better at being a detective. I think about pointing this out, but in the end I don't. Instead I re-play the audio of Mrs. Jacobs confessing.

Lieutenant Langley listens in silence with a stern look on his face. When it's finished he scratches at his ear.

"This some sort of joke?"

"*No*." I'm a bit confused by this. Why would I do this as a joke?

Langley thinks for a moment more.

"So who is that?"

"It's someone called Barbara Jacobs," Amber says. She sounds quite nervous. I'd forgotten she hasn't been to a police station before.

"And who's she talking about?"

"Her husband. Henry Jacobs. He was the principal of Newlea High School until 1979. That's when she killed him."

Amber falls silent, and Langley looks at both of us for a while, one after the other.

"1979, you say? That's..."

"Forty years ago," I have to interrupt. I can see him counting in his head.

"Right." He nods, then turns back to Amber.

"How'd you get the recording?"

Amber hesitates before answering. "We've been... We've sort of been investigating what happened to him."

Langley doesn't move.

"Why?"

"Because... We sort of thought... well..." Amber obviously doesn't know what to say, so I interrupt again.

"We started a detective agency," I say. I might as well just tell him. He's going to find out sooner or later.

"Then she hired us. She wanted to find out what happened to her husband before she died, because she's really old. Only it turned out that *she* killed him, and she's forgotten, because she's got dementia."

I feel Langley's eyes resting on my face, like he's sucking in all this information. Processing it piece by piece.

"*Who* did you say started a detective agency?"

I point to myself and Amber. "We did."

Lieutenant Langley's face change now. It stiffens, like he's trying not to show what he's thinking, but he's definitely thinking really hard.

"*You* started a detective agency?"

"That's right."

"You? Billy Wheatley? Started a detective agency?"

"Yes. And then Amber joined in too."

There's a pause.

"Why?"

"I think because she was bored. There's not much happening on Lornea Island and her mom is more interested..."

"No. Why did *you* start a detective agency?"

"Oh," I pause. "Well I didn't really mean to. I was just practicing making a website but then..." I fade out. He doesn't need to know *everything*.

But now Langley looks perplexed. He starts blinking lots. Then shakes his head just a little bit.

"And this lady... This Barbara Jacobs. She actually *hired* you? As a *detective*?"

I glance at Amber, I told her before we got here how we'd end up answering the same questions over and over.

"Yeah."

"Why? What did she want?"

"She wanted us to find her husband."

"The one she admitted to killing?"

I try to explain it again. "She forgot why her husband disappeared, because she's got dementia problems, so she hired us to find out. But then we found out... And, well." I point to the phone on the tabletop.

"And then how did you..." He stops. "*How* did you get this recording?"

"We worked out that she must have killed him, and then decided to get her to confess."

"I worked it out," Amber interrupts.

"Yeah, Amber worked it out." I admit, because that's only fair.

Lieutenant Langley sits silently for a moment, tapping the table with his knuckles. He doesn't look at us. Finally he gets up.

"Wait here."

He gets as far as the door, then turns around and comes back. He snatches the phone from the table.

"You mind?"

Both me and Amber shake our heads.

"I'll be right back."

As soon as he's gone I feel a bit anxious. He's just taken the evidence without giving us any sort of receipt. I think Amber knows this too, so we sit in silence, not even looking at each other.

We end up waiting for ages. Lieutenant Langley comes back several times to ask us new questions, or the same questions again. Sometimes he's on his own, and sometimes he's with other people. At one point the Chief of Police looks in. I met him when I got my medal, so I give a little wave to say hello, but he doesn't wave back, or even say anything, he just stares at us then walks out again.

Then they tell us they need to get our parents here, because they have to do formal interviews. I knew this part was coming, and I wasn't looking forward to it, but it can't be helped. At least Dad is back from the boat, so he's not going to get into trouble for leaving me on my own. And I start to wonder if him having to come to the police station again will remind him how the robbery he's plotting with Tucker is a bad idea. It actually might, and that would be an unexpected bonus.

Amber's step-dad gets here first. I haven't actually met him before. He's wearing a suit and he's really polite to the officers, but he looks super mad with Amber, like she's a pain anyway but this is something else. She has to go with him anyway, and the detective who waits with me explains how they want to interview us separately. They want to check if our stories match up, but I'm not worried because we're telling the truth.

Then Dad comes in. I haven't seen him for over a week. He hasn't shaved on the boat, so he's grown half a beard. It scratches at my face as he hugs me. He looks more worried than mad. He whispers to ask me what I've got mixed up in, but I don't get the chance to answer him, because right away Lieutenant Langley and another detective come in and sit down and begin the formal interview.

FORTY

I HAVE to go over everything I've already told them, all over again. And then when we're finished they want to go back and talk about specific parts of it in more detail, like what I thought the guy at the garage had meant when he told us Henry messed around with kids. It's really tiring, and they keep stopping and pausing the tape, then going outside and we're left there waiting for ages before they start again.

Dad keeps asking when we can go home, but they've always got one more question, until it's really late, and I'm so tired I can't keep my eyes open. Then Dad insists, and in the end they agree, but they say we have to come back first thing tomorrow. Then we get driven home in a police car. I go right to bed, since there's a weird atmosphere at home, with Dad and Tucker and everything. But we have to come straight back to the police station the next morning, and it just carries on like the day before. I sort of zone out of it all after a while, until, about lunchtime, when I get really hungry. Really hungry. I didn't eat last night, and I only grabbed some toast for breakfast. Then finally I say it to one of the detectives. I don't mean to, it just comes out.

"Can I have something to eat?"

It stops them in their tracks. Then one of the detectives, who's kind of looking after us, slaps the table.

"Sure. You like burgers?"

"Yeah."

"Alright then." Then he gets up and leaves.

That was about an hour ago. We've been left alone since then, just me and Dad, and we're not really talking. He's asked me a few questions about the detective agency, and I can tell he's annoyed about it, but he won't tell me off here. He can't.

Then, finally, the door opens and the detective comes back holding a Wendy's take-away bag. It smells amazing. Normally I'm actually not that fond of Wendy's. But right now I'd eat anything.

But then, before I can eat anything, Lieutenant Langley walks back in. He's about the only policeman we haven't seen this morning. In one hand he's holding a plastic folder full of papers. He says something quietly to the other detective, then takes the Wendy's bag from him, and closes the door behind him, so it's just him, Dad and me in the room. He sits down, and pushes the burgers to one side. Then he opens his plastic wallet and pulls out the papers.

"Billy, we need to have a little chat." Lieutenant Langley says.

It's so hard not to stare at the burgers, but I drag my eyes away and look at him.

"I've just got back from speaking to Barbara Jacobs." He looks me right in the eyes, his face not giving anything away. I glance at the burgers, hoping he'll get the idea. But he doesn't.

"She denies killing her husband. She told us he went missing in 1979 and she has no knowledge of what happened to him after that."

Again I look at the burgers. I can talk and eat pretty well. I wonder about saying that to Lieutenant Langley.

"Well that doesn't mean anything," I hear Dad replying. "Not when she's already confessed on the tape Billy made?"

"That recording was made without her knowledge or consent. We can't use it."

"But you're not just gonna drop it?" Dad says. "You heard what she said..."

"I didn't say we're gonna drop it. We're searching records to see if there's any evidence of Henry Jacobs after 1979. On Maui or anywhere else."

"And is there?"

I know I should be following all this more closely, but it's really hard because I'm so hungry. Suddenly my stomach gives a really loud grumble and Lieutenant Langley stops what he's saying and stares at me. Finally he understands, and pulls the burgers back in front of him. He peeks in the bag.

"You hungry Billy?" He says, and I kind of hold my breath. My stomach rumbles again.

He slides the bag across to me. At once I dive in, and pull out a bacon double cheeseburger. It tastes every bit as good as I'd been imagining.

I don't hear much for a few minutes. I'm too busy eating, but when I finish, I realize that Dad and Lieutenant Langley have been talking for a long time, and they're just finishing up.

"So what happens now?" Dad says.

"You take young Billy home is what happens now. And you make damn sure he keeps his nose out of this."

FORTY-ONE

THE REST of the day is a bit like when you get better from having a fever. You're kind of dizzy, and you're not sure what's real and what isn't. I get the sense Dad's not sure how to react either. He feels like he ought to be mad at me, but he doesn't know why, or even if that's the right response at all. After all, it's not exactly a normal situation.

He keeps trying to have a chat with me, but it never really goes anywhere. He keeps shaking his head and asking if I’m alright, but then he doesn’t know what to say next. In a way he takes it so well I actually consider telling him I know all about Tucker and what they're planning to do. But that would be a bit much, on top of everything else that's happening. So I keep quiet.

I spend the rest of the day moving Steven. It's actually something I should have done a long time ago, since he's easily ready. I put him outside, in a kind of pen that Dad built. He covered it in chicken wire, so that Steven wouldn't be able to fly off, but I take that bit off, because I actually want Steven to fly away if he wants to. But of course he doesn't. When I go back inside he just comes and sits on my windowsill, I pull the drapes shut so he can't see me. But I know he's still there.

And then I realize I'm actually really tired. Like exhausted. So I go to bed early, and for once I don't go on my computer at all. I just get into my bed and go to sleep.

I'm woken the next day by my phone ringing (I put my own SIM card back in it a long time ago), and I see it's Amber.

"You'll never guess what?" She says, when I answer it.

"What?" I reply. I'm still feeling really sleepy.

"The police have gone into the school. They're gonna dig up the gym."

FORTY-TWO

THEY DON'T CLOSE the school, they just shut off the gym hall. They don't even cancel gym classes, they just get moved out into the school field. In fact, it's almost like there's nothing going on at first – there's just a few police cars parked outside the gym hall, and an officer in uniform standing by the door to make sure no one tries to go in. But then the noise starts.

Deep, rumbling hammering noises, that you can hear from all over the school.

I don't tell anyone about what I know, I just listen to the noises, and rumors that have already started. Some people are saying how it might be Principal Sharpe the police are looking for buried there, which is bonkers when you think about it, but it tells you something about the intellect of some of the students at Newlea High School. Others are talking about how there might be bodies of students there, hundreds of them, murdered by teachers over the years. Like I said, a lot of the pupils here aren't that bright.

Even the teachers are gossiping about it, though they pretend they're not. They say how they just want us to get on with our work as normal, but when a television van turns up with a big satellite dish on the top, and the whole of my science class goes and watches at the window, Mr. Matthews doesn't do anything to stop us until he's had a good look too. So then we get to see this woman in a red dress with her microphone talking to a camera guy, in front of all the police cars. And then someone manages to get her interview streaming live to their phone and we all end up gathering around that, trying to listen.

"...The Lornea Island Police Department refuse to state at this point why they are interested in the gymnasium of Newlea High School, saying only they are acting on 'credible information'..."

Then Mr. Matthews does make us all go back to work. But it's impossible to focus, even on science class, with the noise of the concrete breakers. And the rumors keep flying.

I watch the full interview with the presenter in the red dress, later on at home with Dad and Tucker. But there's no actual news as such. Only that the police are looking for something, but they haven't found it yet. It's the same the next day, and the day after that. And then it's Saturday, so I don't go to school, although I keep an eye on the news websites to see what's happening. And then on Sunday night I'm upstairs and Dad calls me down to see something on the TV with him. I almost don't bother, but he says it's important. So I do go down. And this time there is actual news, as in something new.

But it isn't what I expect.

FORTY-THREE

ON THE TV Lieutenant Langley is sitting at a table with the chief of police on one side, and a woman I don't know on the other. There's a load of microphones in front of him on the table.

"What's this?" I ask Dad.

"Local news," he says. "Just came on."

"As you all know," Langley's voice comes through the speakers in a drone. "Over the last few days we've been conducting a detailed search of the foundations of the school gymnasium of Newlea High School. This was in response to credible information regarding the possibility of uncovering evidence related to a possible homicide." Langley pauses, and for a moment he looks at the wrong camera, then he seems to realize it.

"However, that search has not uncovered anything suspicious, and we no longer consider this site to be of interest in this investigation."

Then he starts to make an appeal for information from the public, but I don't really listen to that part.

"What does all that mean?" I ask, when the TV moves on to something else. Dad turns the sound down.

"Does it mean they couldn't find him?"

"No," Dad replies. "It means he wasn't there to find."

* * *

I spend the rest of the day trying to make sense of it. It's possible the police didn't look properly. Or that Mrs. Jacobs was lying to us. Or maybe that she got confused, and she never actually killed Mr. Jacobs at all. But I can't work out which. Then the police want to see me again, which is quite good, because at least they'll explain what's going on.

The patrolman at the front desk leads Dad and me out of the reception area straight away. I expect him to take us to the interview rooms like normal, but instead he goes upstairs where there's a big room full of desks. We follow the patrolman to a little cubicle at the end.

"Lieutenant Langley will be along any moment," the patrolman says. And then he leaves us.

Lieutenant Langley's desk is just like any normal desk, like the ones the secretaries have at school. There's a few neat piles of papers on one side, a coffee mug and a photo frame with its back facing us. I can't quite see it so I lean forward to get a better look.

"Sit still Billy. Don't touch."

"I didn't... I wasn't gonna..."

I don't go on. Dad seems angrier about the whole business today. It's like he was giving me the benefit of the doubt when he thought I might have actually solved a murder. Like he didn't have much choice about that. But now the police are saying there wasn't a body, he's not so sure about it all. I guess I'll have to find that out later though, since right now Lieutenant Langley strides in, wearing the same brown suit he always wears, with his detective badge on his belt. He closes the door on his glass cubicle and nods to Dad.

"Get you a coffee?"

"Sure."

There's a cabinet by the wall with a coffee percolator half full. Langley pours out two cups and puts one in front of Dad. I don't get anything.

"You've seen the news?"

I look at Dad, and he's nodding back.

"We didn't find nothing." Langley shakes his head.

"We pulled up the entire floor. Right down to the bare earth." He glances at me. "Guess you're not gonna have gym classes for a little while..."

"I don't mind that," I interrupt, and he frowns at me, like I wasn't supposed the say anything. Then he sits down behind the desk.

"Listen kid. The reason I've brought you in. We've been here before, and we're not gonna be here again."

He looks at me really seriously, but I don't know what he means.

"This website you made. This *detective agency*..." He stops and sighs. "You realize you need a license to operate as a private investigator on Lornea Island? Plus you have to be eighteen years of age. You could be looking at a fine of ten thousand dollars. We could lay charges for fraud. If Barbara Jacobs wanted, she could file a civil suit."

I'm not entirely sure what all this means, but it makes me feel nervous. I don't dare look at Dad, but he's the next to speak.

"Does she?"

Langley hesitates. "Not yet she don't."

"And what about you? You said you could lay charges...?"

Langley doesn't answer at once.

"We're not gonna do that either. But we are gonna have this little chat. To make sure we don't find ourselves in this situation again. And I mean ever." He turns to me.

"OK Billy? This ends here. No more inserting yourself into other people's business. No more *detective agencies*. No more... Period."

I open my mouth to speak, but think better of it.

"Cos if this happens again, we're not gonna be having a chat. We're gonna be throwing the book at you."

Still I don't reply.

"You got that?"

I nod.

"I need to hear it Billy."

"Yeah. I got it."

"Good." Lieutenant Langley takes a glug of his coffee.

"So what happens now with Mrs. Jacobs?"

"*Billy!*" Langley sets his coffee cup down. "Did you not understand what just happened?"

"Yeah, I did, I just want to know what's going to happen to Mrs. Jacobs..."

"No you don't. That's not your business. Listen to me, and listen good. The Lornea Island Police Department thank you for bringing this matter to their attention. And we ask you to step away. And if I hear you *don't* do that, I'm gonna personally see to it we file every damn charge we can."

There's a silence, but Dad breaks it this time.

"He understands, don't you Billy?"

Eventually I nod.

"Sure. I get it."

After that, Dad takes me to school. I think he's just dropping me off and I unclip my seatbelt on the road outside, but he keeps going, right into the parking lot.

"What's going on?" I ask. "Where are you going?"

"In to see your Principal." Dad says, swinging into a space too fast.

"Why?" I ask, but all he does is yank on the parking brake hard.

"Why do you want to see Principal Sharpe?" I ask again.

"What makes you think I want to see her?"

And so, for the third time in a month, I find myself summonsed to Principal Sharpe's office. But this time, I'm there alongside Dad.

FORTY-FOUR

SHE'S SUPER MAD. I see it right away. She has to struggle to be polite to Dad, because she's not allowed to shout at the parents in the same way she does to us kids. But she still talks to him in her real tight lipped way that makes it obvious she hates his guts.

"Do you know what this is?" She holds up a folder of documents.

The veins on one side of her neck are sticking out and throbbing.

"Mr. Wheatley?"

It's weird having Dad here. When we came in I thought maybe he would demand answers to what really happened to Mr. Jacobs, but it just feels like he's getting told off too.

"This is the school's insurance policy. I've spent the morning reading it. As well as case law on Section 12 of the 1983 Civil Rights Lawsuits. Do you know why?"

Dad looks at her, and for a moment it seems like he's gonna fight, but then he sighs. "No."

"Well would you like to know?"

Dad kind of waves a hand, like he knows she's going to tell him anyway.

"I've been reading this because the police, over the last week – and thanks to your son's harassment of my mother – have utterly destroyed the school gymnasium. At an estimated cost of..." She stops, and searches for a paper on her desk.

"Over *three hundred thousand* dollars. And apparently neither the police department nor the school's buildings insurance will pay for it. Which means it will need to come out of the school budget. Meaning every single student in this school will have their education suffer as a result."

She drops the folder on the desk.

"Well?"

Dad just shakes his head.

"*Well Mr. Wheatley?"*

"Well what?"

"Well, don't you have anything to say?"

It seems like he doesn't at first. I figure he doesn't want to get in a fight with my school principal. But then he replies, his voice calm and almost casual.

"Cops say they had a warrant. Which means they must've had some reason. So the way I see it, that's hardly Billy's fault."

"Oh yes. Mr. Wheatley. I forgot you're an expert on legal matters. With your background."

She glares at him, but he stares right back.

"What happened to me has nothing to do with this."

"No? You don't think so? Because I wonder if it's part of the problem. It's hardly a stable home life you're giving your son is it? Were you aware Billy was operating an illegal so-called detective agency?"

Dad's eyes flick over to me, then back to Principal Sharpe.

"No."

"I understand from Lieutenant Langley it's an offence to do so without a license. But he won't be pressing charges. For reasons I am unable to fathom, and do not agree with."

There's silence for a long while.

"I've also taken advice on what would be appropriate in respect of Billy continuing to attend this school. As I'm sure you can appreciate, in any normal circumstances what Billy has done is far beyond the threshold needed to expel him from the school. Well beyond."

This makes me glance up. I didn't think you could get expelled if you were a good student like me.

"And I sincerely doubt, if that were to happen, that any other school on this island would take him on."

She glares at me now, like she actually hates me, and I start to feel quite worried. I don't much like Newlea High School, but I do need to get good grades. Otherwise I won't be able to go on and study to be a scientist. And I'll end up like Dad, in dead end jobs. And if I can't even go to school on the island then I don't know what we'll do. We'll have to leave.

"However." And suddenly she looks really disappointed. "I have been persuaded by the state board of education that it might appear inappropriate for me to take any decisions in this case personally, given the involvement of my family." She stares at me.

"I argued strongly against this position as well. But the agreement we came to is this. In this instance the board will take no action. However, if Billy continues his invasion into my, or my mother's privacy, then I shall expel him, immediately, without any further warnings and all the negative repercussions that would bring. Is that clear?"

I look at Dad, to see if he's going to argue against this, but he's looking down at the floor. Then I feel Principal Sharpe's eyes boring into me, and I look up again. She smiles.

"Billy. I want you to listen very carefully."

I don't reply.

"I *clearly* asked you to leave my mother alone. I explained about the illness she is suffering from. Yet you ignored me. In doing so you have caused an untold amount of damage to this school, both financially and in terms of its reputation. Furthermore you have caused a lot of anxiety and stress to an elderly woman who has done nothing wrong.

"Billy, if you step out of line again. If you even think about stepping out of line, I will expel you with great pleasure. And if you go *anywhere near* my mother again you will be pursued in the courts for compensation for the damage you have caused. Is that understood?"

After a little while I nod.

But after that she lets us go. No detention, no nothing. It's weird. I get sent to classes, like nothing has happened. And then the afternoon is just like a normal Wednesday afternoon. Except gym class is held outside on the school field, not in the hall.

FORTY-FIVE

It's over a week now since all that happened, though it seems longer. Dad told me again how we had to have a *proper talk*, and how we had to make changes so that nothing like this ever happened again, but then he went out with Tucker, and didn't come back till late. And when they did come back I could tell they were drunk. Then a few days later Dad told me he had another trip on *Ocean Harvest* lined up. And how important it was he went, because he made such good money the last time. And when I asked him who was gonna look after me, he told me Tucker would still be here, and this time he'd make sure he kept a better eye on me. I felt like pointing out how we wouldn't need the money quite so much if he wasn't here, eating all our food, and living rent free. But I couldn't say that. So I just had to bite my tongue.

I haven't seen that much of Amber. She got grounded by her mom, and Principal Sharpe put her in detentions every lunchtime. And she has to register for every class, to make sure she doesn't skip anymore. It's kind of annoying, because I really wanted to see her to work out what really happened to Mr. Jacobs, if he's not buried under the school gym after all.

But then I decided maybe it was for the best. Maybe I should put all this behind me, and just forget it ever happened.

But then something *else* happens. Something pretty bad.

FORTY-SIX

It happens when I'm doing my homework. Only it's quite boring homework, so I decide to take a break to have a look through Dad's emails.

You'd think, when someone goes off on a fishing boat, they wouldn't be able to do emails, but actually it's the best way to keep in communication. There's loads of time when they're fishing that they're not actually doing anything, just waiting while the boat goes from one place to another, or when the nets are in the water. And even though cell phones don't normally work that far out to sea, they have this special network where they can bounce an internet signal from one boat to another, up to sixty miles out. But it's a bit like the internet in the old days, you can't stream stuff, but websites and emails work OK.

Anyway, the point is this: Dad uses his email a lot when he's out on the boats. I send him messages all the time, reminding him to take photographs and video if he sees any whales, and to note down his coordinates when he sees them.

So, when I look in his inbox, there at the top are the messages from me – some of them not even opened yet. And then there's the usual junk mail. And I'm almost about to close the page when a new email drops – like it's just been sent. It comes from Tucker.

I stare at it in surprise. Tucker is downstairs, right now. Watching baseball. He called up a while back to see if I wanted to join him. And obviously I just ignored him.

The subject of the email is this:

Fucking Whatsapp keeps cutting out...

Then right beneath that I can see the first few words he's written, even without opening it:

Agreed. Let's go for it...

So now I've got a problem. Obviously I'm curious to know what they've agreed, but to find out I need to click on the actual message. But if I do, the message status will change from *unread* to *read.* And if Dad happens to be looking at his email *right now,* it'll tell him someone else is looking at his emails. Normally that's not a huge problem, as I can change the emails back to *unread* once I've looked at them. But I can't do that if Dad's looking at his messages at this exact moment.

So I wait thirty seconds, to see if Dad opens the email. But nothing happens. That means he's either sailed out of range, or he's not looking at his phone. Maybe they had to haul the nets in or something. So I make a decision, I click on the message. I'll quickly read it, then change it back to unread, and Dad'll never know. But right then, like it sometimes does, our internet decides now is a good time to slow right down. The screen goes blank, and then a box opens on the screen, but without any text in it. It's almost thirty seconds later before the page finally loads, which makes me kinda anxious. When it does so, this is what the message says.

Agreed. Let's go for it day you get back. First thing, before it gets to fucking busy. It'll be way easier than hitting a bank and cash is cash. Don't stress it. We'll be sweet.

Then there's a link, and like before, it's to Carter's Jewelry in Newlea.

I read it twice, to make sure I get it alright. And then hurriedly I close the message and right click to restore it so that it looks unopened. My hand fumbles a bit because I'm nervous, and then the internet times out, making the screen go white, and a message appears in the middle saying:

Aw snap! Something went wrong when displaying that webpage

So then I have to reboot the router, which takes about four minutes, and all the while I'm thinking, I don't know if I managed to set the message to *unread* before it crashed. If I didn't, and Dad logs back on now, he'll see that someone else has already read it. He'll know someone's spying on him.

So when the internet finally comes back, I quickly log back into Dad's Gmail. And I'm right. The message is still there, still marked as read. I'm about it change its status to unread when I notice something else. Now there's a little arrow symbol next to the email. That means that something *else* has changed. Someone's *replied* to the message. That means Dad's seen it and he's replied to Tucker. And I can see the reply too, all I have to do it go to Dad's 'sent items box. And when I do that, this is what Dad's said:

I can't believe I'm saying this. But yeah. Let's do it.

FORTY-SEVEN

Let's do it? Let's do what?

Way easier than hitting a bank? What does he mean by that?

I follow the link again, and there again is the webpage from the jeweler's. This time I don't watch the video of the couple on the beach, but click around the site. Eventually I find a photograph of the front of the store, with its velvet trays of rings and jewelry displayed in the front window. I've never really noticed it before – I'm not really interested in jewelry – but now I see that it's quite a small place, and it's pretty impossible *not* to understand what Tucker means. He's talking about security. Carter's doesn't have all the security of a bank. It doesn't have those metal screens that drop down. It won't have a panic button. It's just a little family business. And that's why Tucker has chosen it. For a robbery.

Let's do it.

And Dad's going help him rob it. My first thought is why? Dad's making OK money at last, aboard *Ocean Harvest*, so why does he need to rob a jewelry store? But as soon as I ask the question, I know the answer. The place on *Ocean Harvest* is only temporary, until the regular crew guy gets better. As soon as that happens Dad'll be back scrubbing out the fish house. And I know how much he hates that.

Even so, you can't just start robbing places. Dad wouldn't even be thinking about it, if Tucker hadn't turned up. He'd just get another job, even thought it's difficult. And I'd help too. I'd get a part time job. Or I'd give up school and get a job. A proper one this time, not chasing around pretending to be a detective. Because look how that turned out.

• • •

And look what happened the last time Tucker did a robbery? That guy in the Hounds Beach place got shot and killed. What if the same thing happens here? Half the town already thinks Dad's a criminal. Oh god…

I click back to Tucker's message and read it again. This time I notice *when* they're going to do it. The day after tomorrow, when Dad gets back. I've got two days to work out how to stop him

I suppose I could tell the police. I spend a long time thinking that over. But I can just imagine what Lieutenant Langley would say if I tell them I think my Dad's going to do an armed robbery. He won't listen, and even if he did, it would just mean Dad gets arrested. How does that help?

I think about just telling the police about Tucker? They never did come to arrest him when I activated his SIM card. Maybe I didn't do it long enough? But I don't want to do it again in case that guy – Vinny – rings back.

In the end I phone Amber. She answers right away, and I just blurt everything out. Everything I've found out about Tucker and Dad, and everything I've just said here. When I finish she's quiet for a long time. When she speaks this is all she says.

"Shit Billy."

So I know she can't think of an answer either.

* * *

When I try to sleep it doesn't happen. So I get up. I track Dad's boat with *VesselTrack*, in the hope that maybe they'll run into bad weather and have to go around it, and then they won't get back in time to hit the jeweler's on the day Tucker wants. But that won't even help, because all they'd do is put it back a day. It's not like the jewelry store is going anywhere. And anyway, there isn't any bad weather, and it looks like Dad will get back right on time.

And then, sitting at my keyboard. I realize something I should have seen a long time ago. I think for a second, then I work so fast my fingers can't hit the keys quick enough.

FORTY-EIGHT

SOMETIMES I WONDER if I should actually be a lawyer when I grow up. I reckon I'd be good at it. Or maybe a newspaper reporter. If there still are newspapers when I'm older. Or anything at all. Maybe if we all get flooded by global climate change there won't be any world to be anything in. Maybe that would for the best.

I didn't go to school yesterday. What I was doing was much more important. At one point I heard the phone ringing downstairs, which must have been the school office wondering where I was, but I didn't answer it. And Tucker was out, probably casing out the jewelry store. Well. He can case it out all he likes. Because his plan isn't going to happen. He isn't going to rob anywhere, and neither is Dad.

When I finished working I printed everything out and organized it into three folders. Or maybe dossiers is the right word. I'm never quite sure what a dossier is, but it does sound a very nice word. So that's what I'm gonna call them. Dossiers. And in each dossier I made sure everything was in the right place, and all the images were properly labeled and everything. It took me ages, and that's why I couldn't go to school. I had to have it finished by this evening.

* * *

At seven o'clock Tucker shouts up the stairs to tell me Dad's called, and he's gonna go pick him up from the dock. It's about half an hour, there and back. I use the time to go over everything, but before I know it I hear the roar of the truck's engine in the lane. I'm nervous now. I could easily say I'm tired, or I have to work, and Dad wouldn't think that was odd. He wouldn't even mind, because he probably wants to go through all his plans with Tucker. But I can't do that that. If I just pretend this isn't happening then Dad's gonna rob the jewelry store. And everything we've built here will be ruined.

So I pick up the dossiers, and I walk downstairs.

FORTY-NINE

"Hey Billy," Dad flashes me a smile as he comes in. He looks tired, I wasn't expecting that.

"You keeping out of trouble?" He gives a little laugh, to show that's a rhetorical question. Or a sort of joke because of everything that happened with the school gym. He dumps his kit bag in the corner of the room. Tucker follows him in, doesn't say anything to me, but goes straight to the fridge and grabs two beers with one hand. He opens them both and hands one to Dad. The remains of our dinner are on the table.

"We left you some," Tucker says. "Not much though, your boy eats a goddamn ton."

I don't answer. It's not my fault if I'm going through a growth spurt.

Dad doesn't reply to any of it though, just helps himself to what's left from the pot in the middle of the table and starts eating.

I've got the dossiers in my arms, folded across my chest. "Did you catch much?" I ask, still standing by the door.

"So so." Dad replies as he swallows a mouthful. "Tough trip though. I'm gonna down this and hit the sack."

He wants to be fresh tomorrow. I have to do this now, or it's not going to happen. I start to hold out the dossier in front of me, then my nerve goes and I pull it back to my chest.

"We should have a little chat before you do," Tucker says to Dad, from where he's leaning against the counter top. "Just go over a few things before tomorrow."

I can't help but feel indignant at how openly he's talking about it.

"What's happening tomorrow?" I keep an eye on Dad as I ask, and sure enough he shoots an irritated glance over at Tucker, like he's a bit pissed at him for bringing it up. It gives me a burst of confidence. But maybe not quite enough, since I find myself still hugging the dossier against my chest.

"Nothing. Nothing important," Dad says, and keeps eating.

I'm still hanging back in the doorway, like I'm expecting to go back upstairs any second. And it's so tempting to do so. To not go through with this. But then if I don't, then Dad is going to do an actual robbery tomorrow, and there's no going back from that. He'll always be a real criminal after that. I have to stop him.

"Dad," I begin.

"Yeah?"

And then I step forward and drop the dossier on the table.

"Dad. I know what you and Tucker are planning to do tomorrow. And I'm not gonna let you do it."

There's a roaring empty silence. Like standing by a waterfall. I can sense how their attention has focused right onto me. Dad's just frozen, his fork loaded with food and half way up to his mouth.

"What's that Bill?" Dad says, his voice is calm, except for a slight waver he can't control.

"I said I know what you're planning to do. At the jewelry store."

Dad lowers the fork back down to the plate. His forehead is knotted in confusion.

"How'd you know?"

"Because I've been spying on you. And on Tucker. So I know he's a criminal. I know he uses a fake name, and that he's on the run from the police. And I know he murdered a security guard in a place called Hounds Beach..." As I say this part Tucker spits out the beer he's drinking, so that it goes all over the floor, and some of it over Dad. But I don't stop. I can't, not now I've started.

"And I know how you're planning to rob Carter's jewelry story in Newlea tomorrow. And I was going to go to the police, but I didn't think they'd listen to me, so I thought the best thing to do was tell you how I know about it and beg you not to do it..."

There's that silence again. But deeper and longer this time. Dad angles round to look at Tucker, like he can't believe I said all this. But then he wheels back to me.

"The *hell are* you talking about, Bill?"

He glowers at me, and then sends a desperate glance across at Tucker. And I can't believe it, because I see he's going to deny it. Only I can believe it, because I knew he would. It's why I had to make my dossiers. So I hand one to Tucker, then give the other to Dad, and then open my copy.

"OK. Page one. When Tucker first arrived he lied about not having a cell phone, and when I checked I discovered he had identity documents in the name of *Peter Smith.* That's the name he goes under now – but he can't use it with you, because you know his real name from when you were kids. So he's not using it now. Page two. Tucker had to keep his phone switched off, because the police were tracking it, so he was breaking into my room to use the internet on my computer. So I installed software that made it record video of whoever used it." I put a full page image of Tucker sitting at my laptop in the dossier. I deliberately chose a not-very-flattering one either, he was picking his nose at the time.

"Page three. These are the websites Tucker was looking at. They're all about a robbery of a jewelry store in Hounds Beach. Why would he so interested in this robbery, if he wasn't involved?" And what I've put on page three are all the articles from the newspapers about what happened to the security guard. The first ones about how he was shot, and then how he'd died later in hospital.

"Page four is..."

"Whoa Billy! What *the fuck* is this? What the fuck are you doing?" Dad interrupts me, and he has to do it really loud because I can't really hear anything too well. I'm kind of getting a bit emotional.

"Page four is..." I try to go on but it's hard to see because there's tears in my eyes.

"Billy stop!"

"...Is another still from the camera on my computer. This one shows Tucker on the *old* phone he pretended not to have. And then you can see on the next page how he smashes it up. And then there's the messages that he got on the phone, which I found when I recovered the SIM card..."

"*Billy that's enough.*"

"...They show... They show this guy called Vinny who's *desperate* to know where Tucker is. And I wondered if he might be Tucker's probation officer or something, only he said wasn't a probation officer when I spoke to him, he sounded more like a gangster or something so..."

"Billy!"

"Then the last page, that's all the messages that Tucker's been sending *you*. About the jewelry store in Newlea, and how you're going to rob it..."

I feel the dossier smashed out of my hands, and the blow knocks me back against the wall.

"Dad, don't do it. *Please don't do it*. If you do it you're gonna get caught, and this time they're gonna be right. All the people who say you're a murderer and a criminal. And they're going to send you to jail.

"And I don't want them to send you to jail."

FIFTY

"Billy you got this wrong. You got this all wrong."

I've stopped crying. At least, mostly I have. I can still feel how wet my face is. And I can feel the edge of the door hard at my back. Dad was right in front of me, but now he's backed off. His face is white, even with the tan he's got from being outside all week. It's like that's just dropped away.

"You've – I don't know how the fuck you've... But you've got this all wrong."

The way he says it, I want to believe him. Dad slowly flicks through his copy of my dossier. It's like he doesn't know where to start, but eventually he goes right to the end.

"This thing tomorrow. It's not a... It's not a *robbery*. I don't know where you... I don't know why you'd even *think* that?"

"Way easier than hitting a bank." I know Tucker's email by heart, so I recite it back to him. "And then you reply. *'Let's do this'*."

"That's... *Jesus* Billy. The fuck are you like? That's..."

He turns away and runs a hand through his hair.

"That's... Look I was gonna tell you. But not until we'd got it in the bag. Because it's such a goddamn long shot on this fucking island where no one gives you a fucking chance."

He breathes hard for a moment. Then turns back to me.

"We aren't gonna *rob it*. We're gonna try and raise a deposit. For a loan."

I try to make sense of this, but it's hard. "A loan?"

"Yeah. Tucker's been digging around, trying to find someone – anyone – who'd be willing to take some second hand jewelry as security for a loan. It ain't easy to do. When you got no track record, when you're guys like us…"

I screw up my face in confusion. "Why do you need a loan?"

Dad hesitates, then gives a deep sigh.

"For a boat Billy. We're gonna go in together and buy out the *Ocean Harvest*."

My head is spinning with all this. Is Dad making this up? Just on the spot, to hide what he's really doing? But if so, how come he's thought of it so quick? Dad's not the most imaginative guy you'd ever meet.

"You want to buy *Ocean Harvest*?"

"Yeah. I didn't want to tell you until I was sure we could raise the cash. But Tucker and me, when we were kids, we always dreamed that one day we'd run a boat together. If you have two skippers you can alternate, make sure the boat's always out working. It makes good business sense."

I stare at Dad, I still don't know whether to believe him.

"Billy, I know you don't like it when I'm away, so I thought it would help if Tucker was able to keep an eye on you, when I'm at sea. He won't always be living here. He'll get his own place, soon as we get the boat running and get some money coming in. But he'll be able to look in from time to time. Make sure you're OK."

Still I stare. I realize my mouth's open, but I don't feel able to shut it.

"Come on Bill… You wouldn't believe it, but I got the idea from you. You were going on about that other boat, the *Blue Lady*? That's never gonna happen. I don't have no accounts that a bank can analyze and decide if I'm a good investment. But this Carter's place. They're not so concerned about that. If you can put up something. And I've got a bit saved – and Tucker's got this jewelry - well, they make allowances. You know? They'll charge a bit more in interest. But we reckon we can earn that back. If we get a good run." He puts his hand through his hair again.

"I can't believe you thought I'd... thought I'd try and *rob* somewhere."

I'm silent for a few moments, and Dad is too. You can actually hear the clock ticking on the wall.

"But what about Tucker?" I protest suddenly. "Everything I found out about him. The fake name? The robbery in Hounds Beach? That was real. The security guard *died*."

"That's..." Dad begins, but then he stops. He turns to Tucker, who hasn't made a sound since spitting out his beer. "Tucker? What *is* that about?"

Tucker doesn't reply, but his eyes are running from side to side. Like he's trying to see a way out of here.

"Tuck? Tell Billy what that's all about. How you had nothing to do with – whatever that is."

Still he doesn't reply, and after a few moments Dad turns right around so he's facing him.

Still Tucker doesn't reply. And then Dad shakes his head.

"Aw shit." Dad says.

"Tucker. What the *fuck* have you done?"

FIFTY-ONE

"I DIDN'T SHOOT THE GUY." Tucker says.

"Aw shit!" Dad drops his head into his hands.

"I didn't. You don't know me well enough I wouldn't shoot anyone?"

"But you were there?"

Tucker is still for a long while, before finally he nods.

"Yeah. I was there."

Dad groans again. He screws up his eyes and presses them with his thumbs.

"Go on," he says finally.

For a while Tucker doesn't, but then he begins speaking in a voice stripped of expression.

"I was working out at Granville, in the steel plant. And that was going alright. But then they made a bunch of us redundant. And one of the guys, who I worked with, he kept going on at me that he had this job we could do, real simple." He stops for a second. "You remember Vincent? Vincent McDonald."

Dad stares. "Tell me you're fucking kidding?"

"I didn't want to do it. Not after I went inside, there was no way I wanted to go back. But Vinny was real insistent. Persuasive. And I had nothing else. I had bills to pay. A guy's gotta live."

"Inside?" Dad pulls him up. "You went to jail?"

"It was nothing. Just a couple of months."

"Why? What the hell d'ya do?"

Tucker hesitates. "I held up a liquor store. Or tried to. Look I needed the money."

"You fucking idiot! Oh man…"

They're both silent for a few seconds.

"Why didn't you tell me?" Dad asks in the end.

Then suddenly Tucker gets real mad. "Tell you? Fucking tell you? How the *fuck* am I gonna tell you? When you've disappeared into thin air like a fucking ghost?"

Dad opens his mouth. Closes it again.

"You know I had to do that. I had to protect my family... What was left of my family."

"And I wasn't family? *Fuck you man...*"

For a long moment they both just stare at each other, both of them breathing hard.

"You left me man. I drove you across the country and *you fucking left me.* And what's worse? You left me because you didn't fucking trust me."

Tucker's breathing now like he's just finished a running race. "So maybe that's why I didn't keep you up to date on everything that happened in my *fucked-up* life."

He turns away. Dad stares at the back of his head, and after a while he speaks. But now he's calmed down. He sounds defeated.

"So what's it about? This business in Hounds beach? What happened."

Tucker turns back. He rubs a hand on his face.

"I told you. I had bills to pay. And Vinny, he made out how he'd found this security guard in a little family jeweler's store out there. Came across him by accident but then began watching him. You see, security guards have to take breaks. They eat sandwiches. They have to go to the bathroom. But what they're supposed to do is vary when they do it. You know, one day go at ten, then next day at twelve, the next day don't go at all. Never get into a pattern. But this guard was lazy. He loved his routine. He *always* took a fifteen minute break at ten thirty. Like clockwork. I went and watched, just to check for myself. And it was just like Vinny said. Ten thirty, he was out the door, leaving this old dear behind the counter, all alone."

Dad's face is expressionless.

"All we had to do was go in there, wave a gun about, and we could walk out with enough gold that we wouldn't have to worry about finding work for a while."

Tucker falls quiet, and Dad gets up. He paces to the sink and runs himself a glass of water. He holds it in the air but doesn't drink any.

"Gold? Am I right in thinking that this gold is what we're gonna put up as security on our loan tomorrow?"

Tucker doesn't answer at first. Then he nods.

Dad takes a sip of the water.

"So when you told me it was left you by your aunt. That was just a crock of shit?"

It's only a tiny movement of his head, but Tucker nods again. Dad rolls his jaw around, like someone's punched it. Then he goes on.

"So what went wrong? In the store?"

Tucker rubs his face with his tattooed hand.

"This guy, Vinny. He's… well, you know what he's like. I thought he'd changed. I thought he was OK. But it turns out he ain't changed at all."

He stops. He can't even look at Dad now.

"Look, we talked it through beforehand. I told him I wasn't interested unless he specifically promised there'd be no violence. I didn't even want to go with guns, but he said we needed to have them, just for show." His tone changes. "Then, once we got in there, he..."

"He what Tucker? What exactly did he do?"

Slowly Tucker shakes his head.

"Everything was going just fine. We got to the store, and just like we planned. There's just the old lady there. The security guy is already away on his break. So we've got fifteen minutes – plenty of time. We get to it. We get the old girl away from the counter, so she can't go pressing any panic buttons. Vinny covers her with the gun. I fill the bags. It's good stuff – gold chains, rings, watches – you've seen it. We work fast, and it's going great. We're gonna be in and out in five minutes. But then the guard just walks right back in. I think he must be fucking short-sighted or something because he just walks right in, on top of us, ten minutes before he's supposed to be there. And he's fucking whistling, like it's the best day of his life... I dunno. Maybe he got served in the sandwich shop easier than normal. I don't know what the hell happened."

"And then what?" Dad asks.

Tucker gives a haunted laugh. "It's such a fucking shame, you know? Even when that guard turned up, you could tell he didn't want no trouble. He wasn't the hero type. He put his hands up the moment he finally saw what was going on. But Vinny freaked out anyway. He started talking how he was gonna execute him. I thought he was bluffing, I was telling him we had to get out of there. And then Vinny shot him. Like it was a game. Like it was nothing."

There's silence for a few moments, and I wonder who's going to speak next. In the end it's Dad.

"Then what?"

"I panicked. I ran. I went outside and jumped in the car. I swear to God I thought Vinny was there with me. But then I saw he was still inside the goddamn building. Still waving his fucking gun about like he's in a movie. So I just drove. I just got the fuck out of there. It was only later I realized I was still holding the fucking bag I'd been filling.

"And then I came here."

FIFTY-TWO

"WHAT A MESS." Dad says what seems an age later. "What a fucking mess."

He flicks through my dossier, on the kitchen table. He comes to the bit about Tucker's fake name. All my research into possible Peter Smiths.

"So how about this? How come you got a false ID?"

Tucker sighs before he answers.

"I don't."

Dad starts to hold up the dossier, but Tucker goes on.

"I don't. It ain't a false ID, I swear it."

"Well you wanna explain why Billy says you do?"

Tucker takes an age to answer.

"I don't have it anymore. I tossed it away. In a trash can in town."

"OK. You tossed it away, but how come you had it in the first place?"

Tucker sighs again and looks down at his feet. Then he lifts he head and looks straight at Dad.

"I stole it. After the robbery. I had nothing on me. No ID, no cash. Just a bag of gold fucking chains that I didn't know what to do with. And I couldn't go home. I didn't know who might be waiting for me there, Vinny or the cops. So I just took a long walk. Tried to figure everything out. That's when I decided to come here. To look you up. But I couldn't get here with no cash. Then I came across this restaurant, this little sidewalk café with tables outside and this asshole sitting there. He's real loud, on his cell phone shouting about some deal. I guess I realized he looked a little like me, even at the time." Tucker gives a rueful smile.

"Anyway, he's sitting there, drinking his frappucchino bullshit, and he's so fucking distracted with his conversation he doesn't notice he's got his wallet just sitting there on the table. I just slid it off and kept walking." Tucker stops.

“Look, I ain’t proud of it. I ain’t proud of any of it. But I had no choice. You understand that? Don’t you?” Dad doesn’t reply, so Tucker goes on.

“There was a few hundred bucks in it. Enough to get me here. And there was a driver’s license. Look I’m not saying we were separated at birth, nothing like that. But it was enough that I could pass for him if I had too. So I kept it. I thought it might be useful. But then I changed my mind, after you let me stay here. So I tossed it in the trash, like I said.”

Still Dad doesn’t say anything, but he looks at me, and down at the dossiers, the three of them, spread across the kitchen table and the countertop. I don’t know what he’s thinking, but I can’t get over how I’ve got it wrong. Everything in them is wrong. Again. Then Tucker goes on.

"You know we can still do it," he says quietly.

"Still do what?"

"We can still go ahead. Buy the boat. Start afresh. They're never gonna come looking all the way out here."

"That's what I thought," Dad replies, not looking at him. "When I came." There's a silence for a while.

"And it worked didn't it?" Tucker says. "They never did find you out here. Not until all the shit happened with that missing girl. And that was just..." He shrugs. "Bad luck?"

Dad doesn't answer. I don't know what he's thinking.

"Who's not?" he says in the end. I see the flicker of confusion in Tucker’s eyes.

"Who's not what?"

"Who's not going to come looking?"

Tucker doesn't seem to want to answer this, but Dad’s staring at him, so he has no choice.

"The cops. They ain't looking for me. It'll be Vinny they're interested in."

I think back to when I put Tucker’s SIM card into my phone. To ry and alert them to where he was hiding. Then Tucker goes on.

"There ain't no one who knows I'm here. And the jewelry's clean. I been researching it, there's nothing that can be traced. I don't see why we can't just go on like we planned. Turn it into cash and put it down on a boat. Like we *always* planned. Like none of this ever happened."

Dad's silent for a while, but in the end he turns to me. "We had this dream," he says. "When we were kids. Tucker and me, we used to sit for hours talking about it. Neither of us had any money. So we used to bait up the crab pots for the fishermen. We'd sit there, slicing up fish heads or smashing up mussel shells, and we'd talk about how one day this is what we'd do for our own boat. We'd catch crab and we'd surf and we wouldn't have to worry about nothing." A smile breaks out on his face.

“I guess I got caught up in that, these last few weeks. I thought here was a chance. My old buddy turns up unexpected, and like a miracle, he's got this jewelry. Some kind of inheritance. I didn't ask the details, because of this even bigger miracle. He wants to buy the boat with it. With me. I thought this is how it was always meant to be. A second chance." Dad shakes his head slowly.

"But there ain't no such thing as second chances." He looks at Tucker.

"Are there Tuck?"

Tucker sounds anxious when he replies. "I told you. We don't have to change anything. We can still go ahead..."

"No we can't. We never could."

"What do you mean?"

"The jewelry. I never really believed you, when you told me it came from some aunt I'd never even heard of before. I just didn't *care.* I thought if I don't know the truth, then it don't even matter where it really came from. But that's not right. It does matter."

"Why? The store's insured. Probably. So no one loses out. And we're going to *build* something with it. We're gonna invest it..."

"Because it's against the law. And because someone got killed when you stole it."

There's another long silence, then Tucker tries again.

"They ain't gonna come, the cops ain't gonna come all the way out here. They're looking for Vinny. And he don't know where I am, thank fuck..."

Suddenly Dad picks up one of the dossiers from the table. He flicks through it for a moment then turns to me.

"Billy, did you say you spoke to this Vinny guy?"

I feel both of them looking at me.

"You did. You said you wondered if he might be Tucker's *probation officer*, but he sounded more like a gangster. What did you mean by that?"

I have to tell them.

"When Tucker threw his phone off the cliff, I climbed down and rescued it. I wanted to know what he was hiding. And then I took the SIM card out, and I put it in my phone." I glance up, wondering if I need to explain how phones work, but it doesn't look like I do.

"And then when all these text messages from Vinny came in, we replied to them." I stop. I didn't mean to say 'we'.

But Dad doesn't seem to notice.

"Go on," he says.

"And I thought he'd maybe just text back, and explain who he was, and why Tucker was hiding from him. But instead he phoned."

"And you answered the call?" Dad asks.

I hesitate. I don't want to explain about how I was thinking it was actually Dad ringing, and how that made me happy because he hadn't rung me the whole time he'd been out on the boat. In the end I nod.

"What did he say?"

I take a deep breath before I answer. "He seemed... He seemed to be trying to find out where Tucker was."

There's a moment of silence after I say this. Tucker gets up. He walks to the window and glances out. It's dark outside, I don't know what he's looking for.

"I didn't tell him," I go on quickly, but I can't not think about what happened with the radio. "But there was…" I stop, swallow.

"What?" Dad says at once. "What happened?"

I have to go on. I have to tell them, so I explain how I wasn't sure if I got to the radio in time, before the presenter said 'Good Morning Lornea Island' in that funny way.

"Oh fucking Jesus," Tucker says, looking out again.

"When was this?" Dad asks.

"About a week ago. Before the thing with the school."

Dad looks at Tucker. He's running his hands through his hair, one after the other.

"Who is this Vinny?" I ask, since neither of them are speaking.

They look at each other. Finally Dad turns to me.

"He's an old acquaintance. We knew him in high school. Never had much to do with him mind, even then it was obvious he was a goddamn psychopath."

He glares at Tucker, who won't meet his eye.

"Who were you running away from? You came right the way out here. Were you running from the cops or from Vinny?

"I dunno, I wasn't necessarily running..."

"Bullshit. You come all the way out here to start a new life. You throw your phone off the cliff. Who were you most scared of? The cops or Vinny?"

"I don't see it matters. Vinny ain't gonna come looking all the way out here anymore than the cops are."

"Then why is he pumping Billy for information on your whereabouts?"

Tucker doesn't have an answer to this.

"Man you *drove away from a robbery without him*. You left him there. You don't think that makes you someone he's gonna want to get even with?"

Tucker gives a half shrug then a little shake of his head.

"But there ain't no way. I mean, even if he heard the name of the island, there's still no way he's ever gonna find me here. No one on the mainland ever even heard of Lornea Island, least not until that girl..."

"Not until that girl went missing, and the whole goddamn country heard about how they were blaming it on me. Think about it. He knows you and me were friends. He knows I disappeared to hide on Lornea Island? How long until he puts it together? Huh? Even Vincent McDonald's gonna work that one out."

There's a long silence.

"Oh fuck." Tucker says at last.

FIFTY-THREE

A FEW MOMENTS later Dad roots around in the kitchen cupboard and pulls out a flashlight. He checks the batteries work, then turns to Tucker.

"Stay here with Billy." Dad says, and moves towards the door.

But Tucker blocks him. "Stop," he says. "Don't."

Dad looks surprised. "What are you doing? I'm gonna go check the yard."

"With that?" Tucker nods towards the light. Then he sighs.

"If Vinny's come all the way out here to find me, you better believe he's gonna come with more than a goddamn flashlight."

Dad doesn't move.

"Don't you have a gun?" Tucker asks, and eventually Dad shakes his head.

"After I got shot I decided I didn't much like them." He hesitates a second, then looks directly at Tucker.

"You did an armed robbery. Where's the gun from that?"

But Tucker shakes his head, "I got rid of it. Tossed it in a river."

There's a silence.

"You could make a gun," I say, without really thinking if that's a good idea.

Dad turns on me at once.

"*What?*"

"If you had a 3D printer you could make one. I saw a TV program about it. You can download the plans from the internet."

Dad doesn't reply, but Tucker looks interested.

"You got a 3D printer?"

I shake my head.

"No. I wanted one but they're too expensive."

Tucker stares at me for a while, before looking away.

Dad flicks the flashlight on. "I'm gonna take a look outside. Make sure there's nothing out of place. Then we'll figure out what the hell to do next." This time Tucker doesn't stop him.

"Stay here with Billy."

I don't move, but watch the light from the flashlight flicking around outside. Neither me nor Tucker speak at all. I don't know about him, but I'm tensed up, half expecting to hear the bang from a gun. A few minutes later, Dad comes back inside.

"Well?" Tucker says, as Dad locks the front door.

"Nothing," Dad replies. "There's no one there. But we gotta make a plan. We gotta work out what to do."

We go into the lounge, because we don't have blinds for the kitchen window, and I think we all feel a bit nervous with the light on inside and just this black window open onto the night. I've hardly been in the lounge for ages, not now it's become Tucker's room.

"How about the police? Any way you can tell them where he is?" Dad asks.

Tucker's a long time in answering, but eventually he does.

"I don't *know* where he is."

Then Dad doesn't answer for a long while either.

"And how about you? You reckon maybe you should..."

"What?" Tucker says, when Dad doesn't finish his sentence.

Dad sighs. "I don't know. Maybe, go speak to them? Put your side of things. If you weren't involved in this guy getting killed... Maybe you're better off getting ahead of it?"

Then there's a really long pause while Tucker looks around the room. He drums his fingers on the coffee table, then finally scratches at the stubble on his chin.

"I dunno man. I think maybe it's too late for that. I already got a record. And what they gonna do to you? They're gonna want to know where I've been this last month. You really reckon they're not gonna pick you up for harboring a fugitive?"

"So what then?"

Tucker pauses again. "There ain't much choice is there?" He says in the end. "I just gotta leave. I gotta get outta here." His voice nearly breaks as he says it, and I'm shocked, because he looks like such a tough guy, and now suddenly he's nearly choking up.

He squeezes his palm against his eyes, as if trying to force them to stop making any tears, and when he pulls his hands down I wonder if I'm wrong, because there's no water there.

"It wasn't just your dream you know?" He looks at Dad. "The boat. I dreamed about that boat. All the time after you left me. That dream kept me going." His face is tense from where he's trying to stop himself crying.

"But I guess you're right. The idea that guys like us could ever get a break. It just ain't gonna happen."

Dad looks awkward for a moment. But when he speaks he's calm.

"Tomorrow," Dad says. "I'll take you to Goldhaven. You can get a ferry off the island. Find somewhere out of the way and set yourself up... It ain't easy but," he looks around the lounge. "Hell I managed it. It must be possible."

Dad turns to me. "You better get some sleep."

I look at him. "What about Vinny?"

"Tuck and me will take turns staying awake. Chances are he ain't within a thousand miles of here."

I'm not so sure about this, but I am exhausted. But I do feel pretty bad now. I turn to Tucker.

"I'm really sorry," I say. "For messing everything up."

Tucker's face stiffens for a moment, but then it softens into a sad, bitter smile.

"You didn't do nothing wrong kid. I brought this on myself."

"But I told Vinny where you were."

"He would have worked it out." Tucker shakes his head. "Everyone back home knows about your Dad and me. If I disappear, eventually he would have worked it out. It ain't your fault."

FIFTY-FOUR

THE NEXT MORNING I wake up in my bed, and for about half a minute I don't remember anything of what happened last night. Then I jump up and look out the window. I don't know what I'm expecting to see, maybe this Vinny character hiding behind Dad's truck. But everything looks normal. Right down to Steven waiting on my windowsill and flapping up and down when he sees me.

I go downstairs, and find Dad and Tucker already up and in the kitchen, or maybe they never went to sleep. Tucker is making breakfast, spreading peanut butter onto brown toast and throwing it on a plate.

"Here you go kid," he says, sliding the plate in front of me.

"Did anything happen?" I ask. "Did Vinny come?"

Tucker shakes his head. "No. And he ain't gonna come neither. Not when he knows I'm not here. You don't have to worry about that. You shouldn't have to worry neither."

"So what's going to happen?" I persist.

Dad looks exhausted, but he tries to smile. "You're gonna go to school, just like normal."

"And then what?"

"And then there's a ferry tonight that Tucker's gonna be on. So when you get home everything is gonna go back to normal. Just like it was before." He tries to smile again, but it doesn't come out very well. I know why. Everything before was pretty awful.

"But one thing," Dad continues, "You gotta stay in school today. I don't want you going off anywhere on your own, OK?"

I turn to Tucker. I suppose the truth is I've got quite used to having him around.

"Hey don't worry kid. I'm a big boy. I'll look after myself."

"Will we ever see you again?" I ask. "Dad?"

Dad doesn't answer, but after a few moments Tucker does. "You're a pretty good detective Billy. I reckon you'll always be able to find me."

And after that I have to go to school.

* * *

It's super weird being in school. I mean, it's super weird being in school anyway, just with everything that happened with Mrs. Jacobs and Principal Sharpe and the gym, without wondering what Dad and Tucker are doing. But at the same time, it's kind of nice to know that I don't have to worry about Dad trying to rob the jewelry store. I have to lie to my class teacher about why I wasn't in the last two days, but Dad thought of that and gave me a note, saying I was ill. Luckily you only need a doctor's note if it's more than three days.

"Pssst," I need you.

Amber grabs my arms as she speaks, and she pulls me behind the bank of lockers in the main corridor.

"What?"

"Where have you been? I've been looking for you? You haven't been in school for ages."

Oh that. I think.

"And you never answer your phone."

"Sorry. I've been a bit busy."

"Doing what?"

It's lunchtime, so I lead her to the library and when we find a quiet corner I explain everything that's happened.

"*Fuuuccckkk*!" She says, several times, as I tell her. And her eyes go wide and sparkle like they always do when she gets excited.

"So he's on the ferry tonight?"

"Uh huh."

"That means I won't get to see him again," Amber says, and the sparkle dulls a little.

"And they weren't going to rob the jewelry store anyway? They just wanted a loan?"

I don't answer.

"I never really thought they were going to rob it," she says. "He's a nice guy."

In a funny way I think I feel the same way. I mean, he looks scary, and obviously he's an armed robber and not far off from being a murderer, but at the same time, once you get to know him, he's OK. And I think he was quite good for Dad. In a way. I mean sure, Dad should have realized the jewelry was stolen, but at least he made a plan with it. At least he had some ambition. Now what's going to happen? He's just going to go back to scrubbing out the fish warehouse.

I'm so caught up thinking about all this, that it takes me ages to realize that there's something else Amber is worked up about.

"Will you please listen?" She says.

"What?"

"We need to talk about the Mrs. Jacobs case."

I half-hear what she says, but it's really hard. Partly because that all seems a long time ago, and not very important anyway, not compared to Dad. But also, we can't do anything more about it, we'll be expelled. I tell this to Amber now, but she just waves it away like it's nothing. So I tell her again.

"Billy!" Amber waves me away. She's getting frustrated. "Sharpe's only saying that because she's scared. Because we're close to the truth."

I stare at her, like she's gone mad. Then I realize she's right. We have to finish this.

"So what then?" I ask.

Then the twinkle comes right back into Amber's eyes.

"I remembered something. We made a mistake."

FIFTY-FIVE

"Right back at the beginning," Amber asks. "When we first met with Mrs. Jacobs, do you remember what she said?"

It's a stupid question really, she said lots of things.

"Can you be a bit more specific?"

"She was talking about her husband disappearing. Come on."

I try to remember. "She said it was at Christmas time." I try.

"And..?"

"And... He just walked out? But we know now that he went to live in Hawaii."

"Bullshit. If that was the truth, then why were the police so keen to dig up the gym? Don't you think they would have checked whether Mr. Jacobs was alive and well before making all that mess?"

I've never thought about it in those terms. "Did they say that to you? The police?"

"No. They didn't tell me anything, but it's obvious isn't it? You must have worked that out."

I don't say anything. I'm trying to think if there's a problem with Amber's logic, and if not, why I hadn't thought of it. I'm usually quite good at working things out.

"So what are you saying?"

"I'm saying there can't be any record of Henry Jacobs having ever lived in Maui, at least nothing the police could find. Otherwise they wouldn't have trashed the gym. Which means Principal Sharpe must have been lying."

Again I struggle to find the flaw in her argument, but the more I think about it, the more I see it's quite good logic.

"So what else?" Amber asks.

"What else what?"

"What else did Mrs. Jacobs say?"

I try harder to remember, but it's no good. "I don't know. It's too long ago."

And then Amber pulls out her notebook.

"Then allow me to remind you," she says, opening the book and leafing through the pages. "Here it is." She holds out the notebook for me to see. I can't read half of it because her handwriting is so bad, but I can make out these words:

Before Xmas children excited disappears

"So?" I ask.

"Look again. Don't you see?"

I know how much Amber is loving this, but I don't know what she's showing me. I shrug.

"*Children,*" she says excitedly. "*Plural.* Principal Sharpe had a brother or sister."

I think about this for a moment. I think I already knew that.

"So?" I ask again.

"So! So there's another witness we can speak to. Someone who isn't mad like Mrs. Jacobs or lying like Principal Sharpe."

I wait for Amber to go on, but there doesn't seem to be anything else. I can't help but feel disappointed.

"Is that it?" I ask in the end.

"What do you mean *is that it*?"

"I mean don't you have any more? Like where they are now, this brother or sister?" I don't bother to ask whether they're likely to want to speak to us. Although the answer to that is pretty obvious. But surprisingly, Amber doesn't sound annoyed, she sounds hopeful.

"I've been looking," Amber says, pointing to the computer, but I can't find anything. I lean in to see the screen more clearly. She's got multiple search pages open with terms like *Wendy Sharpe Lornea Island sister,* but none of the results seem to help.

"The problem is, I reckon, we don't know the name to actually search for." Amber goes on, but I stop listening, and read through the search results. One of them, about half way down the list, is for a genealogy website. It sparks something in my mind.

"I was thinking, maybe we could just *ask* Sharpe," Amber continues, and I tune back into her. "But I don't suppose she'll tell us. Not if she's been lying about everything so far."

I sit back. Trying to catch the idea that's forming. Or maybe the half-idea.

"So I know you're quite good at this sort of thing, and I wondered if you had any ideas for how to find them?"

I pull the keyboard towards me and start typing.

"What are you doing?" Amber asks, but I'm too busy to answer.

* * *

Do you remember I told you, my name isn't really Billy Wheatley? Or at least, it wasn't when I was born. My Dad changed it when he took me away after my mom tried to drown me. But since we were technically on the run, he didn't change it properly, not legally. But then, a few months after all that got sorted out, we had to make it legal. And the way we did it, we had to spend ages and ages at the records office, here in Newlea, trying to get all the paperwork sorted. And Dad doesn't really have that much patience for that sort of thing, so once we'd started, I ended up doing a lot of it. Or helping anyway. To be honest, the lady at the records office, Mrs. Richards, did a lot of it. I got to know her quite well.

* * *

"There'll be a birth certificate." I say, as I'm typing.

"You what?"

"If Mr. and Mrs. Jacobs had children on the island, there must be birth certificates for them. They'll be in the records office."

Amber's leans in close enough that I can smell her skin. "See, I knew you were good at this stuff Billy."

I glance across to see her mouth curving up in a warm smile. The light is beginning to dance in her eyes. "I didn't even know there was such a place."

"It's at the town hall. On the first floor, it's right at the back."

Amber grins a goofy smile at me.

"And you can access it from here? You can search it?"

I'm on the website now, Amber leans in, she sounds anxious.

"For some stuff… I'm just checking now." I sit back. "No. You have to go there in person."

"Oh shit. Well can we? Will they let us in?"

I think back to how Mrs. Richards would bake trays of brownies especially for when we had appointments. She'd put one on a plate for me, and then insist I took the rest home in a Tupperware. They were *really* nice brownies.

"I think we'll be just fine."

I start putting my things in my bag, thinking we're going to leave straight away, but then there's a problem. Nothing major, just a hiccup.

"We'll have to go after class," Amber says.

"Why not now?"

"I can't. Sharpe's got all my classes registering if I turn up or not. You know she's looking for any excuse to kick me out of school."

"But the records office closes at four."

We're both silent for a moment.

Amber turns back to the computer, frustrated. "Well how about tomorrow?"

"It always closes at four. It's ten to four, Monday to Friday."

Amber looks irritated. She clicks her jaw.

"Then you'll have to go. You can sneak out now before afternoon classes start."

I don't like this idea, but I don't immediately know why not.

"I'm not meant to miss class either," I remind her.

"Yeah but they're not recording your attendance," Amber says. "So you won't get caught."

I hesitate. If I do get caught, there's a good chance that Principal Sharpe will expel me. But more than that, Dad told me I had to stay in school. I haven't told Amber about Vinny. I didn't want to admit the part where I answered his phone call. And I can't really tell her now.

Amber turns to me and asks in a really pleading voice.

"Come on Billy," She says. "Just go and find out. We've got to know. This could be the key that explains everything."

I tell myself not to worry about things that aren't gonna happen. And I nod my head.

FIFTY-SIX

WE GO DOWN to the main entrance hall together and walk casually through, checking to see if the receptionists are behind their desk or not. Annoyingly they are. So we have to wait in the corridor the other side of the lobby.

"I'll tell you when it's clear," Amber says, then she ducks back into the hall and pretends to read something on the school notice board. I wait, wishing I'd managed to say no to this. I'm going to be finished if I get caught. But then there's a low whistle, and I don't have a choice, so I take a deep breath and step out of the corridor. The entrance hall is unmanned, the receptionists back in their room.

I keep walking, expecting any moment to hear them call out my name. I feel their eyes on my back as I pull open the door and step outside. And then even more so as I walk across the parking lot and out towards the gate. But I don't hear anything, just my footsteps. And then I'm past the gate and out of sight. I breathe a sigh of relief. Then I break into a jog. I want to get this over with as quickly as possible.

* * *

"Well well. If it isn't young Billy Wheatley!"

That's Mrs. Richards. I was a bit worried, as I was walking here, I thought that maybe she might have retired, or died. I didn't think she'd get another job, because apparently she's worked here forever. And I knew she wouldn't forget me.

"Hi Mrs. Richards," I say. "How are you?"

"Oh I mustn't complain Billy. I mustn't complain." she replies. "How are the 'projects?'"

"Good," I say. "How's Arthur?" That's her cat. I used to tell her about my experiments, and she'd tell me about Arthur, like it was sort of the same thing.

"Oh he's just swell," she smiles at the thought. "Naughty as ever. Like someone else I know." She looks expectantly. "Now what brings you here? I thought we had everything settled?"

Then suddenly I'm not sure what to say next. When I spoke to her before I was always getting *my* records. I'm not 100% sure I can get other people's in the same way.

"I'm doing another project now actually," I begin.

"Oh yes?" She smiles, and I think really fast.

"It's like a genealogy thing? For school. We've got to make a family tree of someone important, and..." I hesitate, but just a little. "I decided to do one on the school principal."

"OK." There's a waver in her voice, like no one's ever asked her this before, but it doesn't last long. I suppose, in fairness, I've done odder things.

"So I thought you might be able to help."

"Well..." She makes a big thing about sitting back in her chair. "I can show you anything that's part of the public record. That's the whole point of them!" Mrs. Richards says, and she sounds happy again. "What would you like to know?"

So I ask if she can find Mr. and Mrs. Jacobs, and whether they had any other children, and in no time at all we're both behind her desk, poring over document after document, all about the family.

"OK, so *Henry Arthur Jacobs* and *Barbara June Bennett* were married in 1970, right here in St Richard's Church in Newlea. Then four years later, 1974, we have a birth. A girl named *Wendy Amanda Jacobs*..."

"That's Principal Sharpe," I say out. Mrs. Richards nods, she's getting into this too. "Yes, she becomes Wendy *Sharpe* later on, through marriage." She goes back to the earlier records. "But this is what you wanted to know. Two years after Wendy is born there's another birth. March twelfth 1976, a little boy this time, one *Eric Henry Jacobs*."

I feel a wave of satisfaction and excitement. Amber was right. *Principal Sharpe has a brother, a secret brother*. It's exactly the information I need. And unlike Principal Sharpe he won't have changed his name by getting married, so we should be able to Google him. That's if I can't find out where he is right here.

"Can you tell me if he still lives here on Lornea Island?" I ask.

Mrs. Richards doesn't look at me, she's still scanning the screen. "Maybe, there might be something more recent... Here we go..."

"What is it?"

"There's a linked record for the boy. Eric. Let me just check..."

I wait. Then Mrs. Richards says:

"Oh!"

"What?"

"It's a... It's a death certificate. Dated eighth August 1992."

"Her brother died?"

"I'm afraid so. When he was just..." We can both see her screen, but she's quicker than me in reading the right bit of the records. "Sixteen years old. Oh how sad."

"Does it say how he died?"

"Well there is a cause of death but..." She stops, she looks suddenly worried. "This is a school project you say?"

"That's right." I try and stretch to see around her and onto her screen, but she seems to sense that maybe she shouldn't be doing this now. She leans forward to make it harder for me to see.

"And Wendy Sharpe is the Principal at your school?" Mrs. Richards asks.

"Erm. Yeah," I say.

"Didn't I see something about your school on the news? Weren't there rumors about... With the police digging up the gym? Say, this isn't anything to do with that, is it?"

"No." I reply, still trying to see round her. "Does it say how he died?" I ask again. I'm dying to ask if he was murdered but that might make her more suspicious.

"And shouldn't you actually *be* in school? Shouldn't you have class now?"

"I told you, this is a school project. So I can do it in school time."

But I can tell she doesn't believe me.

"Billy," she says after a moment. "It's lovely to see you here, but I think I should check with your school principal before I give you any more information. Given its personal nature."

"No that's alright." I say as brightly as I can. "There's no need. And anyway, I've got everything I need now."

I smile, because it's true. I've just read on her screen. Eric Henry Jacobs died by drowning.

* * *

On my way back to school I'm super excited. What Amber worked out was useful, but now it's really interesting. Not only did Principal Sharpe have a brother, but he died in mysterious circumstances. Obviously that's bad in the sense it means we won't be able to talk to him, but it's good because there's bound to be plenty on the internet about it. It happened in 1992, and the internet was invented by then, and sixteen year olds drowning is always news. So I need to hurry get back to school right away and get onto the computer.

But then I realize I'm being stupid. I don't have to wait until I get back to school. I've got my phone in my pocket and I can Google from there. So I pull out my phone and start to type in my new information as I'm walking.

I type in "*Eric Henry Jacobs*" and "*drowned 1992*" into Google. There isn't as much as I expected, but right away I see there are some results. The top hit is an article from the *Lornea Island Times*, from the really old version of their website. Walking slowly, with my phone in front of me, I read the first line.

The search for *missing teenager Eric Jacobs was called off today after police revealed he had been...*

But I don't get any further than that, because right then everything goes totally crazy.

FIFTY-SEVEN

I DON'T EXACTLY SEE it happen, because my eyes are on the screen of my phone, but I'm aware of it. A white car mounting the pavement in front of me. It happens so fast I don't even get time to pull my head up before the driver's door is open and a man jumps out. He's much too close to me. I'm about to shout out when he grabs me. He spins me around, and then his other hand is around my neck, cutting off my air so I can't even breathe.

"Come with me," he growls. "We're going for a ride."

I feel a sharp pain below my ribs. It hurts so much I think he might have stabbed me, and I can't help but cry out, but the moment I do his hand covers my mouth. Then something slams into my head. I'm dazed and scared and it's kind of hard to make sense of it, but I see enough to work out it's a gun.

"In the car."

The gun goes back into my ribs, pressing hard and really hurting. I don't even know if I do what he says, or if he just pushes me into the car. I do realize my phone slips from my hand and falls to the sidewalk. I don't pick it up. I don't have time. Then I'm in the car. Behind the wheel.

"Slide across." The man says. For a few seconds I don't even know what he means, but then he raises up the gun so that it's pointing into my face. I can see the hole in the barrel. I can sense the bullet inside being fired and flying out towards me. There's no room to get out of the way, no time to move even if there was.

"Slide across. Now."

I scramble to do what he says. Then he gets in too, pulling the door closed. The motor's still running, and before the door is even shut we're moving. He pulls away from the curb and seconds later we're past the school entrance, heading out of town.

There's a time when we're just driving, a million thoughts running through my head. I think about escaping, just pushing open the passenger door and rolling out, but we're moving fast already. Too fast. I glance across at the man. Right away he looks back at me.

I turn away at once, but try to process what I saw. I'm not good at judging adults ages, but he's kind of Dad's age. He's got short dark hair and stubble, and he's wearing jeans, the gun resting on his leg, still pointed at me. I feel a fresh flush of terror. I've had a gun pointed at me once before, but this is scarier. It feels like we only have to go over a pothole and he'll fire it, even just by accident. I sneak another look. He looks right back again. He's watchful.

"This is a rental. Don't do anything stupid and make me mess it up."

I blink, then I notice the sticker on the windshield. Island Rental Cars. It's the company we used to recommend to tourists.

"Who are you?"

"Shut up." The man says. He keeps driving. Fast, but not crazy fast, and I work out he doesn't want to draw attention to us. We're still going through Newlea, but soon we'll be out of town.

"What do you want."

"I want you to keep quiet so I don't have to shoot you." He resettles his gun in his lap. I wish he would stop pointing that gun at me. Over and over I imagine how it must feel as the bullet enters your body. I can't help it. And then the last moments of your life, in agony, as you actually physically die. It actually hurts just to think about it.

I try to distract myself by keeping track of where we're going. I don't know if it'll help, but I don' t know what else to do. We're past the limits of Newlea now, and there's just a couple of buildings left before the road cuts through the empty part in the middle of Lornea. The gas station whizzes past, and then we're into the forest. There's a couple of bends up ahead and then there's the long straight section that leads all the way down towards Silverlea. But instead of building up speed, the man slows as we get into the trees, and then when we get to a track on the left he pulls into it, and we bump thirty meters off the road, so we're hidden in the woods.

Then he stops the car, kills the motor and turns to me.

"Get out."

I'm too scared to do what he says, so he repeats it. Louder this time.

"Get out. And don't do anything stupid."

This time I claw at the door handle, and I'm surprised when it opens first time. I'd thought it would be locked.

When I'm out of the car he makes me walk further into the woods. It's mostly pine trees here, and they grow pretty thick, so there isn't much light. I stumble a couple of times, and both times I feel the gun pointing into my back to prod me forward. Both times really hard. It's like he wants to hurt me.

"That'll do." He says at last. "Turn around."

I do what he says, and see he's standing a few meters away now, the gun held casually at his waist. I frown in confusion. I don't know why we're here. Surely he doesn't just want to kill me?

"Who are you?" I ask again.

He doesn't answer. Just watches me.

"What do you want? Why have you brought me here?" Maybe he doesn't just want to kill me? I decided I have to get him talking.

"Are you Vinny?" I ask. "You are aren't you? I knew you were coming. You worked out who I was when you heard the radio."

The man finally breaks out into a grin at this. "*Good Mooooooorning Looooornea Issssland!* Yeah. I'm Vinny. That was real nice of you to tell me where to come." He's got really white teeth, like a Hollywood actor.

"But how did you find *me*?" I ask, a few moments later when he goes back to just watching me. It doesn't matter, I don't care. I just need to keep him talking.

It takes him a while, but he does.

"Tucker and your old man were close growing up. And I heard on the news he'd come out here, when he was mixed up in that missing girl case a couple years back. So when I heard Tucker's phone had made it to Lornea Island too, it didn't take much to work out he'd run to his old buddy. So then I flew out here and start asking around. See if I can find anyone who knows where *Sam Wheatley* is living. I met this nice lady in the grocery store. Said she had a kid in the local school that knows Sam Wheatley's kid. Described what you look like. So I've been watching the school. Today you sneaked out for the afternoon. *Lucky me*."

His voice fades out, but the grin stays on his face.

"So what do you want?"

Vinny doesn't answer. He puts his head onto one side again, and now he lifts up the gun, turns it sideways, and points it at me. Then he screws up his face, like he's not happy with something, and turns the gun so it's on the other side.

"I said what do you want?"

"And I heard you boy." He changes his position again, this time passing the gun to his other hand. He holds it out with his arm straight.

"We're here, in this nice little clearing in the woods, so that you can fully understand the gravity of the situation you're in. Afore we proceed any further. You do don't you? Understand the gravity?"

I don't answer. The way he's talking is freaking me out.

"I mean you could run. You could try and get away from me. Like your buddy Tucker did, but I don't fancy your chances because I will shoot you down."

He smiles at me again, showing his teeth. "You wanna try it? You wanna run?" He lowers the gun, like he's giving me a chance. I stare at him, I move my foot, not even getting ready to run away, but maybe thinking about it. But suddenly his arm locks straight, and before I can even think there's a flash from the barrel of the gun. At the exact same time I feel something cutting the air past my cheek, and then there's a massive explosion that bounces through the pine trees.

I put my hand up to the back of my head, not even sure if I'll feel a hole where

I've been shot, but when I pull it away there's only wood slivers. The bullet hit a tree just behind me. It can't have been more than a couple inches from my head.

"But I'm willing to bet I'm a good enough shot to stop you." Vinny goes on, with a little chuckle. He's relaxed his arm again, letting the now smoking gun aim at the forest floor.

"So let's not have any misunderstandings about this, shall we? Because I have other ways to get what I want. If you decide to not cooperate."

I'm too shocked and scared to speak, but slowly I realize he's actually waiting on an answer, so I try to nod, but my neck is so tensed up I can't really do it. If I had thought about trying to run, there's no way I can now. The fear is so thick I can't hardly breathe.

"Good. So now you're going to tell me where your friend Tucker is, and then we're going to pay him a little visit. And then if everything goes according to plan – and only if – then maybe I won't have to shoot you. How's that plan sound to you?"

Again he waits, and again I manage to force my rigid neck into something like a nod. I try to actually answer him too, but it comes out as just a noise.

"Good." I see the teeth again. They're like the teeth a movie star has, but for some reason they make him even more terrifying.

"So get talking." Again he straightens his arm, and the pistol is aimed right at my face. His arm is super steady, it's like it's mounted on a vice.

"One...Two..."

He doesn't wait. He doesn't give me any time, and I still can't get any words out.

"Three."

FIFTY-EIGHT

"HE'S AT HOME." I blurt the words out.

I don't even have time to think about lying or tricking him. I'm too scared. I don't even get to think if what I've just said is *true*. Dad and Tucker might have left for the ferry already.

"Where's home?"

"Littlelea." There's a flash of irritation on Vinny's face at this, and I take something from it. I don't know what exactly.

"Where or what is *Littlelea*?" He asks.

"It's where we live. It's in the south of the island. Overlooking Silverlea Beach. You just follow the road we were on before to get there."

"How nice." The white smile comes back now. "And is Mr. Nolan expecting any company, do you know?" As he speaks he waggles the gun to tell me to start moving back toward the car. When I do so he falls into step behind me, the muzzle pressing into my back. I struggle to think what to say. What's best to say. What's even the truth.

"I don't think so." I manage in the end.

"Well let's hope not. For your sake."

We walk until we're back at the car. Vinny unlocks it with the remote.

"Get in," Vinny says, pulling open the passenger door, so I do so. There's a moment as he walks around the back of the car when I realize he doesn't have the gun trained on me. I could do something, I could escape even, but I can still hear the sound of that gunshot, still feel the bullet whipping past my ear. So I don't. Then suddenly he's in the driver's seat again and he has the gun pointed at me, resting on his thigh.

"So let's go to Littlelea," Vinny smiles.

We rejoin the main road, and I desperately try to think. I wish I had my phone, maybe I could tap out a message, but it fell to the road when Vinny grabbed me. Maybe someone will find it? Maybe they'll work out I was taken? But even if they did, they wouldn't know who took me, nor where he's taking me.

Maybe Amber will work out I've taken longer in the records office than I should? Maybe she'll work out what's happened? But that's no good either. I glance at the clock on the dashboard of the car, she'll still be in class. And there's no way she could work out where I am anyway. Not in time to do anything.

"So how'd you get hold of Tucker's phone?" Vinny asks suddenly and I'm jerked back to the present.

"I found it," I hear my voice answering. I stop myself from explaining about how he threw it down the cliff.

"He had it switched off and hidden but I found it. I wanted to find out why he was here."

"Oh yeah?" Vinny smiles. "Well lucky old me once again. It seems I owe you big time." He falls silent for a few moments before going on.

"And did you? Find out why he was here?"

I hesitate. I'm aware that he's getting information from me, when I meant it to be the other way around. But there's no way not to answer him.

"I know about the robbery."

Vinny turns sharply towards me and studies me for a long while.

"And you know what he did?"

I want to say I know what *he* did, what Vinny did, in shooting the security guard, but I'm too scared to say that.

"I know he drove off and left you there." I say in the end.

"Yes he did." Vinny says, and then he's silent, and the silence unnerves me so I keep talking.

"But he didn't mean to. He panicked. After you..."

Vinny looks at me and arches one eyebrow.

"That what he told you?" He says.

I don't answer, instead I just nod.

"Didn't look to me much like he panicked. Looked more like he decided to leave me there to get picked up by the cops." He grins again. "But what he don't know is, I've got a good set of lungs on me. I had to run my way out of there, but I made it." Then Vinny's voice turns dark.

"What else'd Tucker say he did?"

I think for a moment, not understanding. But then I work it out.

"He took the jewelry. That you stole from the store in Hounds Beach."

"Yes he did that too." Vinny turns to me. "And now I'm going to get it back."

Right now we get to the turn off for Littlelea. I think that maybe I could just ignore it and we'll drive right past. But then we'll end up in Silverlea so that's no good. And anyway the turn off is clearly marked with a sign.

"Littlelea," he reads. "Should I be taking this turn?"

I nod.

I have a sudden idea. I don't know if it's a good idea, I don't have time to even think about it. The words come out of my mouth before I get the chance.

"I know where the jewelry is." I say.

For a second I think that maybe Vinny didn't hear, and I'm actually relieved because, obviously I don't know where the jewelry is, nor how it would even help much if I did. But then he turns to me, his eyebrow arched again.

"How's that then?"

And now he's said that I have to go through with it.

"He hid it. I saw him hide it. In the rocks, down by the beach where we live. When he first got here. That's why I was suspicious of him. That's why I took his phone."

Vinny seems to think about this for a long time, so I keep going. I'm still not sure exactly where this is going, but I'm committed now.

"I can take you to it. Tucker will never tell you where it is. If you kill him, you'll never find it. But you can have it, you can have it now." I point in front of us, at the road that leads down to the Littlelea end of Silverlea beach. It's at the foot of the cliff where our house is. There's nothing there but a dirt parking lot and the beach.

"I can make Tucker talk easy enough."

"Yeah but you don't need to. I can take you to the jewelry now. It's gold, I've seen it." Obviously I haven't, but I remember Tucker saying what it was. The mention of gold seems to work.

"He hid it?"

"Yeah. I guess he didn't think it was safe to keep it in the house."

We're almost at the turning now, and I think that Vinny is going to drive right by. Suddenly I'm desperate for him not too. It's not much of a plan that I've got, but it's better than nothing, and right now, nothing is the alternative. But it seems he senses it's a trap. We're level with the turning, and then we drive right by, his head cocked over, looking at me. But then he slows down.

"You better not be messing with me Billy. Like I said, I can find Tucker with or without you. I don't need you alive."

He stops the car, and then very calmly he slips it into reverse and backs up till he's level with the turn again. Then he looks at me again, a questioning look. I just nod. Then he turns the steering wheel and we set off again, rolling down towards the parking lot at Littlelea beach.

I try to think through what I'm doing. It wasn't a whole *plan* exactly, to bring him here. It was just a sense of something, I'm not sure what. Then I kind of work it out. It was when he didn't know where Littlelea was. He doesn't *know* the island. He doesn't *know* the beach. And I do. I know it better than anyone. So if I can get him onto the beach, then maybe I can lose him there. If I can get him into the rocks. I know every boulder, every crack of our cliffs. Quickly I decide where I'll pretend Tucker hid the jewelry, and then work out the quickest way from there up the cliff. If I'm lucky I'll be able to catch Dad and Tucker before they leave for the ferry. We can all get away. And work out what to do after that.

"Seems quite a public place to hide a bag of gold chains." Vinny says. He's stopped the car just before the entrance to the parking lot. It's empty, but there's space for maybe forty cars when it gets busy mid-summer. He taps his fingers on the steering wheel.

"Not really." I reply. "Hardly anyone ever comes here." I can feel my body filling up with adrenalin, getting ready for when I run. I'm desperate for him to let me out.

"Just park at the front. We have to walk to get there."

I feel him staring at me for a long time, suspicious as hell, but then we roll forward again and he parks where I said. Then he's first to get out. He looks around, scanning the little river that runs by the parking lot. At the steep cliff behind it. It's easy to cross the river since it breaks up into multiple streams when it hits the beach, each one studded with rocks. That's where we'll cross, I decide.

I get out the car too. Trying to make myself sound confident.

"It's this way. Down by the beach."

I sense he's more cautious here than he was in the car or the woods. He moves close behind me, and I feel the gun press into my back again. But he's doing it differently now, like he's trying to hide it, in case we see anyone. But that's unlikely this late in the season.

"So where we headed?"

I point about a third of the way down the beach, where hundreds of rocks of all sizes lay piled about and half-buried in the low-tide sand. I know every last one of them.

"Over there," I say, and keep walking. Vinny doesn't reply.

I lead him across the river, jumping across from one flat stone to another. Sometimes when tourists do come here they dam the river, or storm waves move the rocks, so that it's hard to cross, but I always come and put them back afterwards. I hear Vinny behind me swear, and turn to see him put a foot into the water. It gives me a jolt of confidence. He doesn't know the beach. I can lose him here.

Once over the river there's just a short stretch of sand before we get to the base of the cliff. You can't see my house from here, it stands too far back from the cliff top, but it's just above us now. I make a silent prayer that Dad hasn't left already.

"Kid are you messing with me?" Vinny asks. "'Coz if you're messing…"

"No, I'm not, I promise. It's just up ahead. He had to hide it above the high-tide line," I interrupt him. I turn a little so that I'm heading back up the beach, towards the area where short grasses partly cover the rocks. The sea never gets in here, but you still get cliff falls, so there's lots of boulders scattered around. I aim for the middle of them and prepare myself to run.

But now that I'm here, my idea doesn't seem so clever after all. I assumed that Vinny would just be following behind me, but actually he's actually holding me, with one hand on my shoulder, and the gun still pressed into the small of my back. I thought that when I got here I'd be able to run, and do it quickly enough so that I could shelter behind a rock before he could shoot me. Now I realize that's impossible. I try to shake him loose, just a little bit, making out I need his weight off me to help me balance, but he just grips me tighter.

We reach the rock I was aiming for. We start to walk behind it. My plan was to run from here, but there's no chance.

"So?" Vinny says when I stop. "Where is it?" I can tell from his tone he's almost at the point of flat-out not believing me, so I look around, desperate for anything that's going to help. I see stones on the floor, maybe I could pick one up and hit him with it? But he's twice the size of me, with a gun pressed into my kidneys. It's not going to work.

Then I see something – a piece of dried seaweed. It's not a lot, but it gives me a half-plan.

Casually I turn the piece of seaweed over with my foot. "I got it wrong," I tell him. "It's not this rock, it's that one." I point a little further down the beach, this time towards one of the bigger and most distinctive rocks structures on the beach, a sheer-faced slab that connects the cliff to the sand at forty five degrees, like a tennis court that's been tipped on its side. I hold my breath, praying he won't see what I'm thinking. "I'm sorry."

He doesn't react at first, but then I feel myself spun around, and he jabs the gun into my face.

"Last chance Billy boy," his teeth flash white in the sunshine, but it's a grimace now rather than a smile. "Or you're gonna be fish food."

We walk on, with Vinny gripping me even tighter than before, so there's no way to escape. I realize now he saw this coming. But this time I lead him more purposefully. The rocks we're headed to was one of my favorites, growing up. I used to have a rope tied to the top, so I could climb up, pretending to be a famous rock climber. Only it was difficult in some parts because you get so much seaweed growing on the rock. Actually you get different types of seaweed as you go higher, because the tide covers the lower part for longer. Some of the seaweeds are easy to see, but others are translucent, so you can't see them. But they're just as slippery.

We get to the base of the rock now where it disappears under the sand. At the top, where it connects into the cliff, there's a shelf of grass. It's actually not that bad a place to hide jewelry. I can sense Vinny's interest in it.

"It's up there." I say, pointing at the ledge. For a second he releases me, and I wonder if this is my moment, but I'm not quick enough, and the gun is pressed into my stomach.

"You have to climb up," I continue.

"Well OK then." Vinny says.

So I turn and put one foot carefully on the bottom of the rock slope.

"It's slippery," I tell him. "Be careful." But I don't tell him how to climb it.

The lower part of the slope is covered with bladderwrack. The best technique here is to find the limpets. They grip onto the rock like little pyramids, and you can use them as footholds and handholds. My feet find a couple now, almost automatically, and I scale the first bit easily. I turn to see Vinny is coming up behind me, but he's struggling trying to hold the gun and see what he's doing. I move a bit faster, accelerating higher and away from him. The limpets don't reach higher up and the bladderwrack gives way to the translucent seaweed. Its real name is Ulva something or other, but I used to call it *Witches Paper seaweed* because it's white when it's dry and nearly invisible when it gets wet. You can only really climb the dry bits, and I'm lucky because there's just enough patches of white left for me to climb to the top.

The other thing I used to do, when I was a kid, is slide down on the Witches Paper. You need a bit of rock that doesn't have barnacles or limpets, because otherwise you can really hurt yourself, so I never did it right here. But that isn't going to stop me now. I look back down the way I've just climbed. I'm ten meters up from the sand now, and nearly at the ledge where I'm pretending the jewelry is hidden. But I can't let us reach it, because if we do it'll be obvious I've been lying and there's nowhere else to go. So I take a deep breath. Vinny is about five meters below me, just getting to the top of the bladderwrack part of the slope, and he seems to be concentrating more on the climb than he does on me. If I'm going to do it, it has to be now.

With a scream that I don't intend I suddenly launch myself back down the slippery translucent seaweed and right towards Vinny. He looks up, and I see him raise his arm, not to shoot, but just to protect himself as I come sliding down towards him, but he doesn't have time. I hit him with my feet and then we're both falling and sliding the remaining way down the slope. I feel sharp pains as I'm dragged over patches of barnacles and the limpets. And seconds later we're tangled back together on the beach.

Vinny starts to shout something but I don't wait to listen. I'm already on my feet and running.

FIFTY-NINE

WHEN I HAD this plan I envisioned myself running so fast it would feel like flying, but now it's happening it's more like running in slow motion. I can't make my arms and legs move properly, and I feel this paralyzing terror that I'm going to be cut down by a bullet any moment. But it doesn't come, and when I turn a corner I get some relief. There's solid rock between me and Vinny, with his gun.

I *feel* the protection it gives me, cutting off the murderous bullets. I keep running, my legs pounding over the sand, and I speed up now. My feet start dancing over the rocks as I come to them. I've clambered these rocks so many times I know every angle, every solid step and every rock to avoid walking on because it moves or because it's coated in slippery weed. My leg hurts, and I glimpse red – blood – from where I must have caught it on something sliding down the rock face. But I don't care. I don't feel any pain.

I keep moving, my feet a blur, towards the cliff path. It's been closed for years because the steps cut into the rock have collapsed in places, but I've always used it. It's *my* path. It comes out at the top right by our house. The bottom of the path is fifty meters away. I'm going to get there.

But to my amazement, and horror, I'm not leaving Vinny behind like I thought I could. He's fast, *really* fast. At first I hear him shouting, but then he goes silent and I just catch the occasional hit of feet on sand or the splash as he jumps through the rockpools. Twice I glance behind me and I'm shocked at how close he is. I see the look of hard concentration on his face. I turn back, and try to run faster still, nearly at the base of the cliff path now. And for a moment there's near silence, just the sounds of the two of us panting and running through the rocky shore.

When I get to the path I can hear he's closer. Just a few meters behind me now.

I realize he could stop at any moment and line up a shot, and I think the only reason he doesn't is because he knows he's going to catch me. Up ahead the path cuts up the cliff in a series of stepped zigzags, and there's no shelter at all, not until higher up where brambles offer some protection. I flash past the sign saying *Danger, path closed.* I wonder for a second if that might slow him down, but I know it won't.

When I hit the slope I slow, you can't help it when you start going uphill, and Vinny closes still further until we're both climbing, him only an arms' length below me. He's so fast, it's moments before he's going to catch me. But in my haste to climb I'm loosening stones and small rocks and sending them cascading down the cliff behind me. And now Vinny has to deal with those as well as scrambling up the uneven steps. I do my best to loosen more as I go up, and for a few seconds the gap between us even widens a little. But then I hear Vinny let out a roar of rage. Then he must accelerate again because I sense him, getting closer and closer behind me. I'm not even a third of the way up the cliff before I feel his hand catching on my leg. I try to shake it off, but it tightens around me, pulling me to the ground. Gripping me hard.

I roll onto my back, and dig my hands into the dirt trying to stay where I am, and then I arch my foot to release it, and for a second he's left holding my shoe, and he slips a meter down the slope with it. Then he growls again, and he tosses the shoe. I see it bounce down the slope below him.

Then I see Vinny start moving up towards me again, but this time I'm ready for him. I push my palms into the earth to anchor myself, and tense my legs. As Vinny reaches me I kick out, hitting his face with my one remaining shoe. I see his chin jerk to the side as I connect, and he yells out in rage. I try to do it again, but miss this time, so instead I kick at his hand with my foot, while I scrape earth into my hands. He slips back and I crawl backwards up the cliff a few more yards. For a moment we both stop.

"You fucking little shit," he snarls, feeling his jaw. “You're dead.” And then he awkwardly pulls the gun up in front of him. There's no hesitation, but his face changes as he goes to pull the trigger, but as he does I scream and fling the handful of grit and stones from the path towards his eyes.

I don't wait. I hear him scream, and as I'm turning I see the dirt spraying into his face. But then I turn and again, upwards towards the top of the cliff, my house, and to where I'm praying my Dad hasn't left yet.

SIXTY

THIS TIME I open out a lead. When I scramble over the top of the path, onto the cliff top, I can't even see him behind me. I feel my leg hurting, and now my shoulder too, but the adrenalin is strong enough that they're hardly slowing me. Below me, not far below, I hear him coming again.

I only have one shoe on now, and my sock slips on the grass, giving me a lopsided limp. I'm exhausted. I want to stop to get some air, but I daren't. I stumble along the cliff top towards the house, and there, I see Dad's truck is still parked in the driveway. They haven't left yet. I feel a massive rush of relief. I try to shout out but I have no breath.

And then I see the front door of the house open and Dad step out. He's carrying Tucker's bag, and he swings it into the back of his truck. Then he turns back to the house.

"Dad!" I try to call out, but I'm so short of breath, no sound comes out. He doesn't hear me. It's like a bad dream. I start to feel the space behind me, where I know Vinny will appear at any moment. I have to cross open ground before I get to the house, there's no shelter to protect me from bullets.

But then something makes him turn – maybe the movement of me waving my arms – and he sees me. His face is confused. He waits a few beats, as I close the gap towards him, desperately waving my arms at him.

"Billy? What the hell are you doing here?" He steps forward, to get to me, moving himself out into the open.

"He's here. Vinny's here. He's got a gun!" I try to say, but the words don't come out loud. I so out of breath.

"I'm just taking Tucker to the ferry," Dad says, moving forward still further, half-smiling in confusing. "Why aren't you in school..?"

I wave my arms again, trying to make his step back. Finally he notices that something's wrong. "Hey? What happened to your leg? You're bleeding..."

I reach him now and just crash into him, pushing him back so at least we're behind the truck. Vinny must have got to the top of the cliff by now. I can feel him lining up a shot. But Dad resists me. I try to speak again, desperately sucking in air so I can form the words.

"We've got..." I pant. "Move... We've got to..."

"The hell are you saying?" Dad cuts in, starting to sound alarmed now. I still can't get more than two words out I'm so short of breath.

"The hell is it now?"

But before I can try again to explain there's another gunshot. I feel a huge flare of panic, and for a second I'm sure it hits me, square in my back, but then I realize it hasn't, it's just the way I've tensed up, in a spasm of panic.

I see snatches of Dad, trying to make sense of what's happening. I see his face, the emotions flowing across his features. Surprise, shock, fear. I hear more shots. Two. Three. I can't even tell how many. As I watch I can almost see the back of Dad's head explode and blood bursting out, I expect it to happen so much. I'm so freaked, it takes me time to see that this doesn't happen. I realize I'm screaming, and the only thing that stops me is a boot, a few moments later, struck hard into my ribs.

SIXTY-ONE

"Shut the *fuck* up."

I'm still so short of breath, it doesn't take much for me to do what he says.

"Get on your knees, hands behind your head."

It's Vinny, speaking through great panting lunges of breath. It takes me a second to see it's not me he's talking to now, it's Dad. I turn to look, still not sure if he's been shot or not, but I can't see any blood. Our eyes meet. I try to make him see I'm sorry. That I tried to tell him what was happening.

"Get on your *fucking* knees and put your hands behind your head." Vinny snarls a second time. He's got his gun held in both hands, pointed right at Dad. His eyes slide to me though now, like he's covering both of us. Slowly Dad does what he says, dropping one leg and then the other until he's kneeling in the dirt of our drive. I feel certain that as soon as he does, Vinny is going to shoot him. Execute him. It's like when he led me to the forest.

"No!" I call out, putting my hand on Dad to try to stop him.

"You too, you little shit." Vinny turns to me, aiming the gun at me now. It's amazing the power of it. It makes me freeze, imagining again the death it can deliver, with just a twitch of his fingers.

"*Kneel.*" Vinny says. I'm shaking, but I do what he tells me. Then Vinny steps carefully around. I see him glancing around, at the house, at the surrounding land, but there's no one around. Our closest neighbors are half a mile away.

"Well well. If it isn't Jamie fucking Stone. So this is where a rat like you goes to hide," Vinny says. He gives a nasty smile.

"Vinny," Dad replies. "Let the boy go. Whatever this is about, he's got nothing to do with it."

"Shut up," Vinny snarls. And Dad takes a breath of air, like he's going to say something else, but then does what he's told. Vinny looks around again.

"Where the fuck is he?"

Dad takes a second to answer this, and then when he does, his voice sounds weird. Cautious. Tense.

"Who?"

And then, so quick I don't really see it happening, Vinny has an elbow wrapped around my neck, and the barrel of the gun pressed against my temple.

"Where the fuck is your buddy Tucker?" Vinny spits out the question this time, I can feel flecks of saliva hitting my face.

I see Dad tense, on the verge of jumping forward, but stopping himself when he sees there's no chance.

"Tucker Nolan? I haven't seen him in years."

"Oh yeah? Well how come your boy already told me he's been living here. Two fucking rats. Now where the fuck is he?"

Dad's quiet for a second.

"OK, he was here. He got off the island this morning. There's a boat in an hour. If you go now you can get after him..."

"*Bullshit.* The truth or I blow the kid's brains out."

I screw my eyes closed, wondering whether I'll hear the bang, or my brain will explode before the sound hits it. It's weird how that's what you think about at times like this.

"OK," Dad's calm, trying to reassure Vinny. "He's in the house. He went to the bathroom."

I feel the hold around my neck loosen, and open my eyes. But I'm just in time to see Vinny's arm extend, and then he brings the gun crashing down onto the front of Dad's head. It's so quick, there's nothing he can do about it, no time to move out of the way. There's a sickening crack of metal hitting bone, and Dad slumps backward. Then, because of the way he's kneeling, so he can't actually fall backwards, instead he rocks, and then falls to the side. I don't know if he's unconscious or dead. I guess I must scream out again, because the next thing I know Vinny is shouting at me to shut up too.

"Unless you want the same?" He snarls, and lifts the gun to threaten me.

I'm quiet again. I look at Dad. He's lying on his side across the driveway. He's not moving, I can't see if he's breathing, but there's blood seeping out of a wound on his forehead. I turn to look at Vinny again, my eyes wide in terror.

But Vinny doesn't seem interested. He stabs the gun into the small of my back again, and forces me to move, half dragging me so that Dad's truck now stands between us and the front of the house.

"I know you're in there Tucker," Vinny calls out loudly. He's almost ignoring me now, but he keeps the gun pressed hard against me, and he's strong. He's unbelievably strong, his forearm wrapped around my neck, restricting the air I can get in. I think for a second that maybe I could drop my head down and bite his arm, but my chin is in the way, stopping me from moving. And then he changes his grip, tighter again, so that it's impossible.

"Tucker you *motherfucker*. Get your sorry ass out here."

Then we both wait, watching the front door. It doesn't move. I don't even know if I want it to. I just suddenly know I was wrong to lead Vinny here. I thought it would save me, but it hasn't helped. Not at all.

"Tucker... Don't make me come in after you," Vinny shouts now. Then suddenly he takes the gun from my neck and aims it at the house. He fires off three shots, shattering the kitchen window and then the windows of the lounge. The noise of it rises up and booms around the clifftop. Then when the echoes die out, nothing's changed.

"Tucker. Get out here now or the kid dies." Vinny shouts into the silence.

Nothing moves in the house. Dad's still lying still. I begin to wonder if maybe Tucker has escaped out the back. It's what I'd do. At least. I think it is.

"You know I'll do it Tuck. I'm gonna count to three."

I feel my eyes start to flick about, desperate for a way out of this. But he's gripping me tight. The gun is pressed against my temple again. Vinny forces me to my feet, so we're visible from the house. If anyone's there to see.

"One."

What if he's not there? What if he's gone? I don't want to die. Not like this.

"Two," he calls out. Then he speaks to me.

"Say goodbye boy."

He takes a deep breath. I struggle, but he tenses and stops me, it doesn't seem to take any effort.

"Three."

SIXTY-TWO

My eyes close. I don't expect to ever open them again. But when I do, I'm not dead. Instead I see my house. The front door is open, and Tucker's standing there. He's got his hands raised, and at once, Vinny aims the gun at him.

"You armed?" Vinny shouts.

"No." Tucker replies.

"Bullshit. Lift up your shirt."

But the second Tucker begins to move his hands, Vinny shouts again.

"*Slow down.* Do it *slowly.*"

Then, moving his hands very deliberately, Tucker does what he's told, unbuttoning, and then pulling open up his shirt until we can see his tattoo.

"Take it off. Drop it on the ground."

Tucker slips the shirt from his shoulders and lets it fall.

"Now turn around. Do it slowly."

So he does, turning a complete circle until he's back facing forwards. There's no gun, or any weapon on his torso.

"Now drop your pants."

"What?"

"Drop your fucking pants."

I see a dark look pass over Tucker, but he begins to unbuckle his belt, and then pushes his jeans down his legs. They get down to his knees so he's just standing in his underpants.

"All the way off. Shoes too. Do it slowly."

Tucker is slow to respond. But I guess he had no choice, because then he reaches down and pulls off one shoe and then the other. As he does so he slowly pulls out a kitchen knife out that he must have put into his sock. He holds it up, handle first, so that Vinny can see it.

"Toss it away." With his eyes Vinny indicates the direction he wants Tucker to throw it, away into the yard.

I watch as the knife traces a little arc and lands in the grass. I wonder if there's any way I can get to it, but Vinny is still holding me, and even if he wasn't, I don't know what I'd do with a knife. I try to imagine using it, but I can't.

"Keep going," Vinny says. His attention hasn't moved from Tucker. And as I turn back, Tucker is continuing to undress, until he's standing there just in his underpants.

"This ain't got nothing to do with the kid," Tucker begins. He sounds strangely calm, like this isn't that different from a normal conversation. "Nor Jamie neither."

"You made it to do with them. By hiding out here."

Tucker doesn't reply. He looks like he's about to, but then doesn't have the words.

"You knew I'd come for you. That's why you ran. You choose to hide here."

I stare at Tucker as Vinny says this, and for a second he looks back at me. But he turns back. I see him shake his head, very slightly.

"I didn't run. Least. I didn't mean to run. We were finished in there. It was going just like we planned it. It ain't my fault you decided to shoot the guy."

"He would have come after us. I was just doing the job properly. *Like we fucking planned.*"

Even from here I can see Tucker's nostrils flare in frustration. He doesn't have an answer again.

"Whatever dude. I don't think we're ever gonna agree on that one."

"Step forward." Vinny says, and Tucker hesitates.

"I said step forward." Vinny repeats.

"If it's the stash you've come for, it's in the truck. You can take it."

"Oh I will," Vinny says. "But you know I didn't come all the way out here just for a few gold chains. I can get that anywhere I want. There's a principle here. You don't split like that. Because there's consequences…"

I feel Vinny tighten the grip around my neck even more. He still has the gun pointed at Tucker. His arm outstretched now. I see in Tucker's face how the sight of the gun is affecting him. He can't even move his eyeballs. I guess it's because he knows this guy. He knows exactly what he's capable off.

"Now kneel." Vinny says. The atmosphere has changed. It's like we all know there's no more talking to be done. Tucker takes a long time to do anything, I can see him looking at his options. If he kneels down, Vinny is going to shoot him. But if he doesn't Vinny is going to shoot him. I suddenly realize I'm going to have to watch. I'm going to have to see Tucker's head burst open and his brains spray out. And then what's going to happen to me?

But then I suddenly notice another pair of eyes watching what's going on. Uncertain eyes. Nervous, almost reptilian eyes. I blink, not sure if I can trust what I'm seeing. But I can. I try to make contact with the eyes. I try to send a message. But the eyes are only watching.

"Kneel motherfucker," Vinny shouts out now. "And maybe I leave the kid alive."

I sense Tucker's turning to me, but I'm not looking at him now. I'm totally fixated on the other pair of eyes. The eyes belonging to a juvenile herring gull, sitting on the top of the house watching the whole scene unfold. A herring gull that doesn't like it when he sees me being threatened. I stare at Steven, desperate for him to understand. In front of me Tucker slowly kneels in the dirt. Vinny grips my neck tighter still and drags me forward, so that the tip of the gun is just a few yards from Tucker's head, bowed down, like he can't face looking at it.

"Mmmmmmmm," I suddenly say, as loud as I dare. "Hmmmmmmm-mmmmmmm."

Vinny shakes me. "Shut the fuck up kid."

But I don't.

"Hmmmmmmmmmmm. Mmmmnnnggg." I'm louder this time, and I see the reaction it has in Steven. His head stills, and I see him lean forward where he's perched, like he's contemplating taking off. Considering if I'm in trouble. But he doesn't do it. He still just sits there. I know I have to make Vinny hurt me. It's the only way to make Steven move.

So I moan again, and I push against Vinny, knocking his aim off Tucker for a second. It's not long enough for Tucker to react, but it annoys Vinny. He has no idea what's going on. He responds by shaking me, harder.

"Fucking keep it down kid. Unless you want me to shoot you first?"

"Mmmmhhhhhmmmggghhh" I shout it this time, and I struggle even more, and this time Vinny loses it. The side of the gun makes contact with my head, but it's more of a push than a blow since there's no backswing. Even so I see Steven's reaction to it. He steps forward from the ridge of the roof, his wings opening as he does so.

I don't hesitate. I know exactly what's coming, and I try with all my might to shake myself free from Vinny's grip. For a second it's easy for him to keep me overpowered, and I realize he's had enough. He's turning the gun now, to shoot me first, to rid himself of this pest. But right at that moment a flashing brown-grey-white creature smashes into him. He doesn't have time to even let out a cry before he's hit by five pounds of bird, slashing with his beak and the three claws on the end of each of his webbed feet.

Then everything happens so quick it's hard to make out. I feel I'm free, and I roll back. For a moment I see Steven all over Vinny's face, as he's lying on his back on the ground. And then Tucker is in there too. And I see a horrible moment when Steven's wing is caught at a horrible angle, and Vinny rolls on top of him, crushing him beneath his bodyweight. But when he's clear of the bird, his face slashed and bleeding.

But by then Tucker is standing over him with the gun.

SIXTY-THREE

It's just a few seconds, but everything has changed. I blink at the new reality in front of me. Tucker is holding the gun with both hands, and I can see them shaking. Steven is squawking and calling loudly, and he's dragging one wing behind him over towards his old pen.

I rush over to Dad. For a second I don't want to touch him, I don't know why, it's like I'm scared I'll find his skin cold. But that's stupid, even if he was dead, he wouldn't have had time to cool down. Then I don't have to think about that anymore because I see his chest is moving. I can hear the breaths, he's rasping as he sucks air in and out. There's a gash on his head, but it's like he's sleeping.

"He OK?" Tucker shouts to me.

I look up. He's keeping Vinny sat on the ground, the gun trained at his head. Vinny's bleeding from a gash to his cheek.

"I think so."

"Get him on his side." Tucker shouts again, but I already know. I've been to lots of talks at the Silverlea Surf Lifesaving Club about how to help people who've nearly drowned. I know all about the recovery position, and I roll Dad into it. It's harder doing it with a real person than it is with the plastic dummies we practice with.

When I can't do anymore I run back to Steven. He's sitting still now, one wing folded, the other laid out on the ground. It's clearly broken, and he's obviously in pain, but animals often make a lot less fuss than humans. I let him nudge my hand and talk to him in a quiet soothing voice. I tell him I'll fix it, that he'll fly again.

"Is that your seagull Billy?" Vinny calls out to me, still watched by Tucker. "Your trained seagull?" He laughs, like he can't believe the question he's just asked, or what's just happened. I don't answer him.

"Cos that is fucking weird," he goes on. "To be training fucking seagulls."

I still don't answer him, but I look over this time.

"At your age you should be going out getting laid. Not training fucking seagulls."

There's something about Vinny's voice that still scares me. A confidence. I look at Tucker, just as he resettles the gun in his hands that are trembling visibly now. I realize this is isn't quite over. I feel myself wishing Tucker would just shoot him. Just in the legs or something. Not because I want Vinny to die, it's just I'm still scared of him. Still terrified. It's like I can see what's going to happen. I don't know how, but somehow he's going to get the gun back. Vinny is the only one of us who's still calm. Composed.

"You got any more animals I should know about?" Vinny goes on. It's like he's enjoying himself. "A... I dunno, a ninja fucking rabbit?" He laughs at the idea, and I see him beginning to pull his legs underneath him, like he's preparing to get up.

"Don't move." Tucker says, but his voice wavers. He doesn't sound in control.

"Oh I'm just getting comfortable. I ain't gonna cause no trouble." Vinny slows his movement but he doesn't stop. He's testing Tucker, and since Tucker doesn't stop him, he fails the test.

Shoot him, I want to call out, but I don't. I begin to understand Tucker's problem. Now he has the gun, he's got a problem. If he shoots Vinny, he's shooting an unarmed man. There's consequences for that. Consequences that last forever. I can see the doubt in Tucker's face. I can see it in his arms, they're shaking now. I begin to think that, even if he did pull the trigger, he might actually miss.

Vinny stops moving now. He's moved his attention from me and Steven onto Tucker. He has all his attention on Tucker. I can see he's looking for an opportunity, and I'm terrified he's going to get it.

He glances sideways, at where the knife Tucker had lays discarded in the grass. Tucker doesn't seem to even register this.

"So," Vinny seems to have come to a decision. He's got a plan. "You've got my gun. But are you gonna use it? Because the way I see it. Those are your only options."

Tucker doesn't answer him. He just holds the gun on Vinny, like he's waiting for something. I don't know what.

"And it seems to me, the longer we sit here, the less chance you've got of using it. You know what I mean?"

Still Tucker doesn't answer. He just waits, not saying anything.

"Oh we can sit here as long as you like. Nice view and all. But sooner or later you're gonna have to make a decision." Vinny smiles again, he's getting more confident with every passing moment. He starts to move his legs again.

"Uh huh," Tucker says at once, and this time Vinny stops. But only for a second.

"You ain't gonna shoot me are you? You ain't got it in you."

"And you can't call the cops, because how would you explain all this? The bag of gold in your truck. So you gotta make a decision Tucker. Shoot me. Or don't shoot me. And if you don't, I'm just gonna get up and walk out of here."

"Stay on the fucking ground."

But this time Tucker looks away. In the distance there's a new sound. I can't place it at first.

"I already made a decision." Tucker says. And Vinny looks confused. He's heard the sound too, and at the same moment we both work out what it is. The sound of a car, maybe more than one car.

"I was gonna catch the boat today," Tucker says. "Keep running, but when you turned up just now, I changed my mind."

And then two marked police cars appear from round the bend and skid to a halt. Two police officers leap out of the first car, sheltering behind the open doors, their guns drawn and trained on Tucker. They shout out, screaming at Tucker to drop his weapon.

He looks at Vinny, and gives a bitter laugh, then lets the gun swing down and fall to the ground.

"You thought I couldn't call the cops. Well you got that wrong. Cos I already called them."

SIXTY-FOUR

THE POLICE RUN FORWARD, shouting, and before I know what's happened Vinny is leaning over the hood of Dad's truck with handcuffs on his wrists. Then they shove Tucker next to him. He keeps his eyes on Vinny all the time, and I can see him smiling. Vinny isn't smiling though, he looks super mad, like he'd have preferred it if Tucker had shot him after all.

Then they take them away, towards the cars. As they push Tucker into one he calls out to me.

"Tell 'em everything you know Billy. Tell 'em the truth."

Another police officer is crouched down by Dad, talking on his radio. I want to go over there, but I'm still sitting with Steven, stroking his feathers keeping him calm. Some time later a woman police officer comes over and starts asking me questions about what happened, and whether I'm alright, and why I'm sitting holding a seagull. There's an ambulance here by then too. The medics wheel a trolley over to where Dad's lying, and before too long they take him away. I want to go with him, and the police officer says she'll take me in her car to the hospital, but then she doesn't want me to take Steven. In the end she agrees that we can take him, but only as far as the vets in Newlea. I know the Newlea vets quite well, so that's OK. I know they'll look after him.

Then by the time we get to the hospital Dad's awake and they let me see him. But that's a bit worrying, because he's really groggy, like he's super tired, or drunk, but the doctors say that's normal and I don't need to worry. They've done scans and they don't think there's any serious damage, he just got hit really hard and knocked out.

Then I have to give an interview, right there in the hospital, in someone's office, and talking into a video camera. I have to explain everything that happened to me, right from the moment Vinny grabbed me from the side of the road, until the police came and arrested him. It's hard at first, because they interrupt me every now and then to ask questions about how I know Vinny, and how I knew he was looking for jewelry, and I have to remember what Tucker said, about being honest. I don't really know if it's the right thing to do or not, but once I start I don't really have any choice.

Then, because it's late by then and I can't go home, I get taken to a hotel with a lady called Gill. She's from the Child Protection Services. I already know quite a lot about them. She gets us rooms next to each other, with a connecting door, and she starts to explain how she's going to sleep right there and how I don't have to worry, but I just want her to go away so I can order dinner from the room service and eat it on the bed watching TV.

The next day Gill takes me back to hospital, and Dad's a lot better, he's sitting up and eating. They don't let him go home yet though, because they still want to observe him in case he gets concussion. So I spend a really long day just hanging around the hospital with Gill, answering the same questions over and over and over.

Finally Dad gets discharged and Gill lets me go home with him. We take a taxi but we don't talk much on the drive. I don't think either of us want to say anything that the driver will overhear.

It's strange getting home. Dad has to put boards up to cover the broken windows in the house. And while he does that I look at his truck. It has actual bullet holes in the sides. Some of them go all the way through one side and come out the other.

I wonder if Dad will want to talk, but instead he cooks us some food, and when we're finished eating he washes the dishes and tells me I should go to bed and get some rest. So I do, and I must be pretty tired, because it doesn't take me any time at all to get to sleep.

SIXTY-FIVE

When I wake the next morning Dad's already up and he's set the table for breakfast. It's only cereal and toast, and a carton of long life orange juice from the back of the cupboard, but he's still put a knife and a spoon and bowls and plates on the table. The thing is, it suddenly seems weird that there's just two places. After Tucker being here for such a long time.

"Morning Billy," Dad says. He sounds choked up too. I wonder if it's for the same reason.

They haven't told me anything about what's happening to Tucker. I kept asking – Gill, and the police officers – I asked whether he'll go to prison and if so, for how long. But they either didn't know, or they wouldn't tell me. But I know he will. You could tell from their faces, if nothing else.

And that makes me feel really guilty, because it's all my fault, when you think about it. If I hadn't interfered with Tucker's phone then Vinny would never have found out he was here on Lornea Island. Then Vinny wouldn't have come looking for him and then Tucker would never have had to give himself up to the police. Actually it's worse than that. If it wasn't for my interfering, Dad and Tucker would have got their loan by now and they'd be buying the *Ocean Harvest* already. They'd be setting up together in business just like they always wanted to ever since they were kids. Sort of like I wanted Dad to do, right at the start of all this.

I want to say something about all this, but it's all so big. I don't know where to begin.

"Morning," I say, in the end. And I sit down. For a moment I don't do anything, and then I pour myself a bowl of Cheerios, feeling uncomfortable because Dad's watching me. Then he gets up and makes a pot of coffee. I can hear him, pouring the water and getting a cup. Finally I can't take it anymore.

"I'm really sorry," I say, putting the spoon down. "I'm sorry I messed everything..."

"Stop," Dad interrupts me, his voice firm.

"You don't have a single thing to be sorry about." He takes the seat opposite me. He's holding his mug of coffee, squeezing it tightly with both hands, but even so I can see his hands are shaking.

"I'm the one who needs to apologize."

I don't really understand.

"But if I hadn't used Tucker's phone, then Vinny wouldn't have known he was here."

Dad takes a deep breath in.

"And you'd have got your loan. You'd be buying *Ocean Harvest*."

But Dad shakes his head now.

"You know, spending two days in a hospital bed gives you a little time to think." Dad begins, and I realize I need to stay quiet. I need to let him speak.

"I've let you down. A lot." He pauses, like he's choosing his words carefully. "Tucker's a good guy, at heart. But when someone like him turns up, unannounced, with a bag full of pearl necklaces and gold chains, saying how he wants to use it to make a new start... You've gotta wonder. You've gotta ask, where does that come from? And I didn't ask. I didn't ask because I didn't want to know the answer.

"But you did. You asked Billy. You asked me, and I wouldn't tell you, so you found out for yourself. Just like you always do."

He stops talking, but for a long time he keeps looking at me. I start to feel a bit self conscious. I didn't even know there *was* any gold.

"But I still messed everything up. Tucker's still going to go to prison because of the way I did it."

It takes a few moments, but in the end Dad nods.

"Yeah. And that's what should happen too. *He* made the decision to rob that jeweler's store. No one told him too. And with a guy like Vinny too. I hope he's not there too long, but he needs to spend a little time reflecting on that."

There's a silence for a moment. It's funny, Dad's laid out this breakfast but neither of us are eating any of it.

"And what was his alternative? Being on the run? That's no life."

I think for a few moments, until something strikes me. "But you went on the run," I say. "How come that was right then, but isn't now?" I think it's the first time I've ever actually asked Dad about this, what happened with mom and everything when I was a baby. He watches me, his eyes level.

"That was different. We went on the run because we didn't do it. Tucker would have been on the run because he did."

I consider this for a few moments. I suppose I see the logic of it.

"Eat up. I'll run you to school. But we gotta go somewhere on the way." I look up, surprised.

"Where?"

"Eat up. You'll see."

* * *

I get my bag and climb into the truck. You can see all the way through the bullet hole in my door, and there's a dent in Dad's door on the other side, so that bullet must be stuck inside the driver's door. I might try and get it out later.

"Where are we going?" I ask again, but Dad won't answer.

So I have to try to guess. We take the road towards Newlea, but then, instead of going all the way to school, we turn off towards the Holport where Dad works. It's also the road to where Mrs. Jacobs lives, so I start to feel a bit nervous. But when we get to the junction Dad takes the road that winds down towards the port itself. I look across at him, confused, but he keeps his eyes forward and doesn't say a word.

We stop on the hard, parking up above the basin where all the boats are moored up. I want to ask again why we're here, but there's a man waiting for us. A young guy in a suit. He's holding a plastic folder, closed, so I can't see what's in it. He shakes Dad's hand, and then he looks at me, and hesitates for a second until I put my hand out too. Then he leads us down onto the pontoon, and I start to get an idea where we might be headed.

But I still don't really understand it.

SIXTY-SIX

"I GOT TO THINKING," Dad says suddenly. He doesn't seem to care that the other guy can hear him. "If I can buy one boat with Tucker and get into fishing, then maybe your plan wasn't so crazy after all."

Up ahead of us the *Blue Lady* sits tied up, just like the last time I saw her.

"She's thirty nine feet long," the man starts to read from his clipboard. "Inboard diesel engine. She's not the fastest but she'll cruise at twenty knots. And with excellent MPG as well. Feel free to step aboard folks."

The guy holds out his hand to help Dad onto the boat, I guess he sees Dad's limp, but Dad ignores him and steps across on his own. Then he reaches out an arm for me to come over too.

"Come on Billy. You can show me around."

I don't know what to think, so I just listen as the salesman reels off all the specifications for *Blue Lady*, but I'm really impatient for him to open the door. I've seen the pictures on the inside so many times, but I've never actually *been* inside. I've never quite worked out how it all fits together.

"So you looking for personal use or..?" The salesman says, as he pulls out a set of keys. They're on a piece of string with a paper tag attached, the name of the boat written on it. "Or you looking to set up some fishing charter business?"

"Neither," Dad says, looking at me. "I was thinking about maybe running some whale watching trips. You know, run some tourists out there?"

"I gotcha," the salesman says. I think he's going to say that's a crazy idea but he doesn't. "My sister just got back from vacation in Florida. She went on one of those boats they have down there. She can't stop going on about it."

Just then another boat motors past and a small wave rocks the *Blue Lady* in her berth. I feel her, moving from side to side under my feet and I hardly listen to Dad or the sales guy any more.

"Are you serious?" I ask Dad, as the salesman unlocks the cabin door. "What about the money?"

"I definitely ain't promising anything, we gotta do a lot of work on that business plan of yours, and I still gotta speak with the bank. But I didn't think it could hurt to take a proper look." He hesitates and looks around.

"And she's a nice boat."

Dad climbs the ladder to the flying bridge, and the sales guy follows him up. So I go into the saloon on my own. It's light inside, since she has big windows. There's the little navigation area like I saw before, and then steps leading down into the cabin proper. I descend carefully, letting my fingers brush against the varnished woodwork. Up above I can hear Dad and the sales guy talking, but I can't hear what they say. I don't even want to though. Right away I'm lost in my own world. I'm down here while we're out at sea. I'm explaining to a group of tourists, super excited, about how we might see humpback whales, or minke, or fin whales, or sperm whales or even blue whales, or even maybe orca. I've only seen orca one time, from the top of the cliff. But that's only because I've never had a boat before. I've never had a way to get out to where they like to be, off the continental shelf.

It's warm down here, and there's a smell. It's a bit musty I suppose, but it's probably only because no one's had the *Blue Lady* open for a while. I hear a sudden sound below me, and I'm confused for a second, but then I realize it must be Dad and the sales guy turning on the engine to check it runs. There's a faint smell of diesel too, but overall I like it. It's nice. I sit down on the bed, right at the front of the boat, and I imagine what it must be like to sleep here, while the engine powers the boat along, cutting through the water, miles away from the land.

SIXTY-SEVEN

"What happened this time Billy?"

That's Amber. I'm back at school now, and she's just grabbed me in the corridor. She doesn't seem to be in a very good mood.

"You go out to find out whether Principal Sharpe's had a brother or sister, then I don't hear for you for *three whole days?*"

"I got kidnapped," I say, quietly, because I don't want the whole school to know.

"Yeah right. By aliens I bet."

"No, it was Vinny, Tucker's friend."

She stares at me, her head tipped right over on one side.

"You got *what?*"

She says that really loudly, and she's blocking the whole corridor now, her hands on her hips.

"Come with me," I say, walking towards the canteen.

"Why?"

"Because it's a long story, that's why."

I lead her to a table where no one can overhear, and I explain everything that happened. From when I was taken, on the way back from the records office, right up to when the police came and arrested Vinny and Tucker. Amber listens, only interrupting a few times where there are parts she doesn't understand. I don't know what I'm expecting when I'm finished, but it's not the reaction I get.

"I don't believe it," she says.

"You don't believe me?"

"Oh no, I believe it alright. I just don't believe how all the exciting stuff happens to you, *again*."

I can see she's joking, at least a bit, but it still annoys me. I guess I'm tired of the way Amber always thinks it's just a game.

"It wasn't *fun* Amber. I got kidnapped. I got shot at, I nearly got killed. I thought I was going to die."

"Yeah you said. Several times."

She turns away from me, her arms crossed over her chest.

"So what did you find out anyway?"

I don't follow this.

"What do you mean?"

"Did you even find anything out? In this records office of yours."

"Oh that. It isn't *my* records office."

"Oh, *whatever* Billy. I only asked if you found anything there?"

I feel my forehead start to wrinkle like it does when I get a bit annoyed.

"Yes," I say. "I found out that Principal Sharpe had a younger brother. He was born three years after she was, and his name was Eric."

From the look on her face, I'd say Amber would have preferred it if I'd not found anything out.

"And I suppose you've already talked with him have you?"

I look at Amber, feeling my forehead scrunch up even more. "Haven't you been listening? I was kidnapped, driven around at gunpoint and then stuck in hospital telling everything to the police over and over again. When exactly would I have had time to do any work on the case?"

"Oh here we go again."

I look away in frustration. I'm really not sure what her problem is.

"And anyway," I tell her. "I can't because he's dead."

"He's *what*?"

"He's dead. Principal Sharpe's brother drowned."

"*Drowned*? Fucking hell Billy. I cannot believe you didn't tell me this!"

I sigh, really loudly. "Amber I got kidnap..."

"How did he drown?"

I stare at her. "Give me your phone." I say in the end. She looks at me, openly suspicious.

"Why?"

"Because I need to search the internet, and I lost my phone when I was kidnapped at gunpoint." I reach across and grab her phone from the table in front of her. And then I open up her web browser, peer down at the little screen, and retype the google search I made for Eric Jacobs. It doesn't take long before I pull up the article I found, moments before I was taken by Vinny.

"Here you go." I angle the phone so we can both read it. "We can find out together."

The search for missing teenager Eric Jacobs was called off today after police revealed he had been suffering from depression in the days before his disappearance. It's believed Eric swam out into Lornea Sound in the early hours of last Tuesday morning near to his family home and leaving a pile of clothes on the rocks. It's now understood that Eric spoke to his family repeatedly in the days and weeks before, and seemed very low. Speaking on behalf of Lornea Island Police Department, Lieutenant Dale Collins said: "The Coastguard and volunteers have worked day and night in this case, but with the fierce currents off the southern tip of the island, it's now highly unlikely that Eric's body will be recovered. Our thoughts are with the family at this difficult time.

Amber looks at me once we've both finished reading. She's still pouting. "So what does that mean?"

I scroll down the screen a bit. "Look. It gives a number to ring if you're in need of help. For the Samaritans."

"So he killed himself?" Amber shakes her head. "Well that's a fat lot of use."

I don't reply, in fact I hardly hear her. I'm thinking instead about Eric. He would have been about my age. Thinking about it, he would probably have gone to this school too. He would have sat right here in this same cafeteria. He would have seen the same things I see, and yet, he chose to kill himself. He decided he preferred to swim out into the cold waters of Lornea Sound and let himself sink into the deep. That's terrifying.

"I wonder why he did it?" I start to say, but then I'm interrupted by Amber talking again.

"Or maybe he didn't? Maybe he was murdered too? Think about it... If he found out what happened to his dad, then maybe the old lady bumped him off too? To keep him quiet. I bet Principal Sharpe knows about it too, that's why she never told us she had a brother...."

"*Oh shut up Amber. Why don't you just shut up?*"

I don't mean to shout at her like that. I've just had enough.

"What? What's *wrong* with you?"

"Nothing's wrong with me, what's wrong with *you?* She didn't hide the fact she had a brother, we just never asked. And her brother's dead. He *killed himself*. You just don't know what it's like!"

"What what's like?"

"When bad things happen to your family. You just don't get it!"

Amber shoots me a funny look, but it's gone in a flash, then her face hardens again.

"Unless he didn't. Unless he was killed, because he was going to reveal what really happened to his dad."

"Just stop it! I told you, this isn't a game. It's people's lives. It's Principal Sharpe's *life*. We should never have gotten involved. It's not our business."

Amber stares at me. I shove her phone back across the table to her. Then I grab my bag.

"This whole thing, we got it wrong. We got it all wrong. It was never a big mystery, it was a tragedy. All along."

Amber's face is white with rage now, her eyes dark and sunken under her brows. I glower at her, wanting to keep fighting. But then I'm too angry. I stand up and stalk. I feel her eyes on me as I go.

I'm so wound up, I just walk at random round the school, which I never do normally, because there's lots of places I can't go. Or shouldn't go. Like the part of the school grounds at the back of the science block, where the basketball courts are. I don't like basketball, or any sport really, but that's not why I normally avoid it here. It's because this is where James Drolley and his friends usually hang around at lunchtime. And they do it because none of the teachers like coming back here, so they can do whatever they want. But I'm so annoyed with Amber's reaction to what happened to poor Eric Jacobs that I'm not thinking straight. And that continues when Drolley spots me.

"Hello Wheatley!" I actually nearly bump into him before I realize who it is. "You come for your daily dead arm have you?" He's got into this habit of punching me in the arm every day. He seems to think it's a kind of game we're playing, almost like we both enjoy it. I sort of told you about it.

"Which one do you want to do? Left or right?" He grins at me, and I can smell he hasn't cleaned his teeth in days.

Normally I'd talk to him, but I don't think I can today. I try to push past, but he steps in my way, blocking me.

"Where'd ya think you're going *Wheatley*? I ain't seen you all week. I must owe you three days worth of punches. Maybe four." He begins to roll his sleeves, and his friends abandon their game and gather closer to watch what's going to happen.

But today I'm just not in the mood.

"Let's do both arms shall we Wheatley?" Drolley grins again, and he lines up a punch. He's kinda got me trained so I don't even move, just to get it over and done with.

But then I don't know what happens. It's definitely something that's never happened to me before. I feel my hand tighten into a fist, and I pull it back behind me. Then, while Drolley is still grinning like an idiot, I spin myself around, and throw my arm forward with all my might. Dad tried to teach me once, how to throw a punch, and I kinda remember now, how you're not supposed to aim at the target, but through it. Behind it. That's what I do now. Then there's a massive, sudden pain in my knuckles as they smash into Drolley's face and keep going. And then I hear this shouting, and it's me. Yelling at Drolley, even though he's not standing there any more, he's sprawled on his back on the ground.

"Why don't you just stop it? Why don't you just *get lost*? I'm so fed up with you. You're just an *idiot*. Wasting everyone's time. People who are trying to be sensible. Trying to work in class or do useful things. Why don't you just...?"

I stop. I'm about to swear at him, and I don't want to, because that would be wrong. And I'm shocked by the scene around me. I'm panting like I've been running hard, and Drolley is still on the floor. His nose is split and gushing blood over his mouth and chin.

"Oh shit," someone says. I don't know who. "Wheatley's broken his nose."

"I didn't want to hit him," I say to his friends, they're all staring at me now, their mouths hanging open. "I don't want to hit anybody. I've just had enough of violence. I just want him to leave me alone."

And then I pick up my bag and walk on.

SIXTY-EIGHT

As soon as afternoon classes begin I know what's going to happen. First of all everyone's staring at me, and then a girl who's never even spoken to me before comes up and asks if it's true that I punched out James Drolley. I don't know what to say, so I explain that I didn't really mean to, it just happened. But instead of having a go at me, like I expect her to, because James Drolley is a much more popular kid than I am, she doesn't.

"I'm so glad someone's finally done that," she says instead.

I stare at her in amazement.

"He's such a jerk. Him and his stupid friends. They're always picking on me. No one ever does anything about it."

And then more people come up and tell me the same thing. Even Paul, who *is* one of his stupid friends, whispers to me that he's glad it happened. It's weird.

But from the moment Mr. Matthews, the teacher, comes in, I know I'm not going to get away with it.

"Billy Wheatley? Mr. Evans would like a word with you. Right away please."

Mr. Evans is the Deputy Principal. If I'm being sent there, it must mean Principal Sharpe isn't in today. That's something I suppose, but even so I feel my face flush hot with the injustice of it all.

* * *

"I assume you're familiar with the school policy on fighting?" Mr. Evans says, when I'm standing in front of his desk. And actually I'm not, since I've never had to consider it before.

"I suppose you're probably not allowed to do it?"

"No you are not. This school does not tolerate violence. Not in *any* circumstances." Mr. Evans replies. Then he fixes me with a stare and holds it until I have to look down at my feet. Then he waits what feels like a full half-hour before going on.

"However, I understand from several of Mr. Drolley's associates that he himself threw the first punch, and that you were merely responding to provocation. Is that correct Billy?"

I look up again, confused.

"No, he didn't…" But I don't get any further because Mr. Evans interrupts me.

"*I said,* Billy, that my understanding is that Mr. Drolley initiated the violence, and that you were simply defending yourself. And if that's the case it would certainly influence how I view your role in the matter. Now can you confirm, that is indeed what happened?"

I squint at him, really confused now. I'm pretty sure Drolley didn't actually hit me this time at all.

"If you say so."

"Good. Violence is never the answer Billy. Never." He keeps his eyes on me. "Not even when it seems that maybe it is the answer. It isn't. Are we on the same page?"

I don't know how to answer this. I don't know what page we're on at all.

"So if you have any more trouble with Mr. Drolley, you come directly to me. Rather than taking matters into your own hands. Is that understood?"

If I'm honest it isn't, but I nod anyway.

"Good," Mr. Evans says again. "Excellent. Now I have lots to do this afternoon, so I suggest you go back to class and we make sure this is the end of the matter. OK?"

And that's the end of it.

SIXTY-NINE

THERE'S some good news when I get home. Someone's posted my phone back to me. It had my name and address on a sticker on the back, so I was hoping this might happen, but I still think that's quite lucky because a lot of people would have kept it.

Then I sit down with Dad, he wants to go through the spreadsheet I made, about the whale watching business. So we check through every figure I used, like for how many people we could fit onto the boat, and how much we could charge them, and how much we'd need to spend on fuel. He makes me change loads of the figures, and then redo all the calculations, and with every little change the business ends up costing a little bit more to run, or making a little bit less money. So at the end it's all a bit depressing. Dad tries to stay positive, but I can see he's worried about it.

Then I go upstairs, and I can't stop myself thinking about my fight with Amber. I don't really argue with people, but with Amber it's hard not to. I decide her problem is she thinks everything's about *her*. That's why she's always dyeing her hair new colors - to make people look at her. She's desperate for attention. And she's not even a good detective. She jumps to conclusions too quickly. Like seeing conspiracies where there aren't any. And she just thinks everything is a game, for her entertainment.

But it's not a game. Not to Mrs. Jacobs. Not to Principal Sharpe, and it definitely wasn't a game to Eric Jacobs.

I think back to when this all began. I knew then we shouldn't have got involved. I knew we could never have actually found out what happened. We were never real detectives, and the only reason Mrs. Jacobs hired us was because she was too crazy to notice we were just kids. But even so we should have known we were messing around with *real* people, with real feelings, and real lives.

I think about how we told the police about Mrs. Jacobs 'confession'. I think I feel the most guilty about that. It wasn't ever a real confession. It was just a mad old lady getting confused because her memory was going. I feel my chest heat up with shame.

Then I remember the check.

The five thousand dollars from Mrs. Jacobs. I took it, but told myself I'd only pay it in if we actually found out what happened to Mr. Jacobs. I guess we never will now. I rummage around in my desk drawer until I find it. I look at the spidery handwriting. Five thousand dollars written out in black ink. I should tear it up. I'm about to do it too, when something stops me. It's the thought that she's got loads of money.

I'm not thinking of cashing it. Honestly it's the opposite of that. I'm thinking how she's got so much money, she probably hasn't realized that we *didn't* cash it in the first place. There'll be so many thousands in her bank account, she won't notice five thousand either way. Which means she'll think we've ripped her off. She'll think we tricked her into telling the police she killed her husband, and stole a load of her money.

I can just imagine how that would make me feel. If I was a little old lady I mean, and my husband had run away and my son had killed himself. I'd definitely feel even worse about all that if I also thought I'd been conned by some private investigators who were just kids.

So I know what I have to do. I slip the check into an envelope and put it into the pocket of my shorts.

So I'm all ready for tomorrow.

SEVENTY

I'M ON MY BIKE, cycling down to the southern tip of Lornea Island. There is a bus, but it doesn't go all the way to Mrs. Jacobs' house. It's quite remote where she lives. It's actually further than I realized though. And the hills are bigger too. But I'm nearly there now.

Last night my plan was to actually speak to Mrs. Jacobs. To apologize for everything we did - recording her without her knowing about it, and then getting the police involved and everything. But now I'm not going to do that. I'm just going to slip the check through her letter box and cycle home. She'll understand - well she won't understand, because she's mad - but what I'm saying is it won't make any difference if I speak to her or not.

It's a nice sunny day when I'm cycling, but then just as I arrive a cloud slides over the sun and makes it feels colder. It makes the house look spooky too. I didn't really see it when I came before, but it actually looks like one of those houses in horror movies, a bit run-down. Mrs. Jacobs has all the drapes across the windows, so that anyone could be in there, looking out, and I wouldn't see them. Thinking about that, I don't even know if *she's* home. I try to think back to whether there was ever a car here when I came before. I can't think though, and that makes me realize again that I was never actually very good at being a detective, since I'm not very observant. I get off my bike and I lean it against a tree. I feel quite uncomfortable now, with Mrs. Jacobs' big house towering over me.

I try to walk up to the front door confidently, listening to the crunch of stones under my feet. Then I can't find the letterbox, and I wonder if maybe she has one of those box ones at the edge of her property, that I didn't notice. But then I see it, a slim, cast iron slit right at the bottom of the door. I pull the envelope out of my pocket. I wish I'd written a note now, to explain why I'm returning the check. But she'll work it out. Or maybe she won't, but I'll know I've done the right thing.

I bend down and try to push the envelope through the letter box, but it's flimsy, so I have to use my fingers to push the metal plate back, and feed the paper through. And I'm just doing that when I suddenly feel my fingers gripped by the metal, tight against my knuckles.

I leap back in shock, but my hand is trapped. Then I realize what's actually happening. It's just the door opening. She must have heard me. Or maybe she *was* standing by one of the windows, watching.

I get my hand out now, and get back to my feet. And I see Mrs. Jacobs peering out at me from behind the front door.

"Mr. Billy?" She says. "What on earth are you doing here?"

SEVENTY-ONE

SHE BLINKS at me from the darkness inside the hallway. There's a trickle of blood from where the letterbox scraped at my finger.

"Mr. Billy?"

I want to just hand her the envelope and climb on my bike and cycle out of here. But I know if I do, she'll feel hurt again.

"I came to... erm..." I hold out the envelope.

"Oh – your hand! It's bleeding."

"It's nothing, it's just a scratch, from when..."

"Oh that wasn't me? When I opened the door? I am *so sorry* Mr. Billy. Let me fetch you a band-aid."

"It's alright..."

"Nonsense," she opens the door wide, and before I do much about it, I'm ushered inside. "Come through to the garden and I'll see what I can find."

So I swallow, and do what she says.

Her patio looks just like the first time I came here, with Amber, full of enthusiasm for investigating her mystery. Only this time I notice how she has a view of the water. Lornea Sound, the stretch of the coast where her son swam out to drown himself.

"Here you go dear," Mrs. Jacobs comes out holding a tray. On it there's a zip-up first aid kit, bright red with a white cross on it, and a pitcher of iced tea with two glasses. She sets it down, then sits and opens the first aid kit, finally pulling out a single band-aid. Then she takes a long while to get the band-aid from the little sleeve they come in, with her long wrinkly fingers shaking as she works. The cut on my finger isn't bad, I've already sucked off the blood and there's no more coming out. But even so, I take the band-aid when she finally holds it out to me, and wrap it around. She looks happy about it.

"So," she says, sitting down opposite me. "Mr. Billy, what brings you all the way out here?"

I think before I answer. About the check, which I've put back in my pocket now, about all the trouble I caused her by going to the police. About how she must look out every single day and see the swirling waters of Lornea Sound.

"I wanted to say I'm sorry," I tell her. I watch her for a second but then I can't. I lower my eyes.

"Sorry? What on earth for?" Mrs. Jacobs replies.

"For everything really. You see," I hesitate. I don't know if it's even worth me explaining, but so far today she hasn't done anything obviously crazy, so maybe she's having a good day. "We were never proper detectives. Amber and me," I tell her. "We thought we might be, but actually the world is a lot more complicated than we understood. We're just kids really."

Mrs. Jacobs responds by reaching forward and pouring out two glasses of iced tea. I watch to see if she's going to pour it all over the floor like last time, but she ends up with both glasses exactly three quarters full.

"You're rather clever kids," she says.

I don't know how to respond to this, so I sort of half-smile at her and take a drink. It's nice after all the cycling I've done, and the sun's come back out. I drink a bit more.

"And I think you've proven to be rather a good detective Mr. Billy." She says.

Again I've got no idea what she means by this, so I try to go on with what I came here to say.

"I wanted to say sorry about the police."

That makes her pause, just for a second, as she's lifting her glass to her cracked, thin lips, I see the withered definition in the muscles of her arm. It must be weird to be old, and have your body decaying all around you. And your mind.

"I rather brought that upon myself. I do sometimes get carried away, stuck out here all on my own, I get muddled." She takes a tiny sip then puts the glass down. There are coasters on the table and I notice how she puts it precisely in the middle of the one in front of her. I straighten my glass too, so that it's not overhanging the coaster she put for me.

"The doctors tell me I have *dementia*." She screws up her face at the word. "It's such a bore – I do hope they'll have found a cure before you get to my age. It makes me forget things. When I first called you I had quite forgotten what happened to Henry. I had myself in a right pickle about it."

She stops, so I ask her. "But you remember now?"

"Oh yes."

I want to ask her if he went to Maui, but I don't know if it's the right thing to do, to remind someone that their husband ran away.

"I remember where I buried him now."

* * *

I know you won't believe me, but at that exact moment another cloud goes over the sun, a really big, thick one this time, and everything really does go dark this time. Or maybe it's just feels like it because, sitting out here with Mrs Jacobs and no one else for miles around, is a little bit scary.

"Pardon?"

"I remember now where I buried him."

I swallow carefully. "Where?" I ask, because what else *can* I ask?

But then she starts talking about something completely different, so I wonder for a moment if I imagined what she said.

"You know, when Wendy and Eric were little they used to love it out here. They would play all summer long. Water fights, they used to love water fights. Do you enjoy water fights Mr. Billy?"

I open my mouth then close it again. Eventually I shrug.

"Not much."

"Eric loved it like nothing else. He would get himself soaked. And Wendy was very much a serious child, but that was one thing that made her loosen up." She's lost for a moment, absorbed by her own memories. I try to remind myself that, whatever she says, it's just the madness speaking. She doesn't *really* remember where she buried him, because she didn't bury him. They're just words.

"That's why I told you Henry was under the school gym. Because that's what I always told Wendy, when she was little. I thought it would be strange for her, the idea of playing out here otherwise."

Mrs. Jacobs looks around the garden, and then she smiles.

I know they're just words, but I can't help myself try to work out what they mean.

"Why would that be strange?"

Mrs. Jacobs waits until she sees my eyes fix onto hers, and then she glances down to the ground. It looks very deliberate.

"Oh come now Mr. Billy," She slides her eyes down a second time, and this time I follow them, and then notice the ground beneath my feet for the first time. It's made up of large stone slabs, each a half-meter square, their tops bleached by the sun.

"It would have been strange, don't you think? To grow up playing out here, knowing your father was hidden right beneath your feet?"

I don't believe her. Or maybe I don't want to believe her. "He's in Maui. Or he went to Maui, that's what Principal Sharpe told us."

"Because that's what we told everybody who asked. Not that many people *dared* to ask. You didn't in those days. It was more a hint here, a nudge there, to all the gossips on the island. Just enough that everyone knew *where* he'd gone, but no one felt able to talk about it." She laughs suddenly. "Do you know I even travelled to Maui? I posted back birthday cards, so they'd have the correct post mark, in case the police ever became suspicious. But they never did. Not until you got involved of course."

I don't reply.

"You don't believe me? Or, you're not sure what to believe any more?" She looks sad now. "You came here to apologize to me Mr. Billy, but it's me who should be apologizing. For everything *I've* done."

"Look at me Mr. Billy, tell me what you see?"

I do what she says, the first part at least. I see a frail old woman, with flesh that droops from the bones on her arms. The skin flakey and cracked.

"Tell me!"

I jump, shocked by how fierce she sounds. "An old lady?"

She smiles at this, then slumps back a little in her chair.

"An old lady who has lied her whole adult life. Do you know what that's like? A life of deception? I've plotted and schemed and connived and covered up, always believing myself and my children on the brink of a terrible peril if the truth were ever to come out. But do you know what's worse than being found out?" She looks away suddenly, and I see water forming in her eyes. When she looks back she's smiling through tears.

"*Not* being found out. Left to fade away, alone, and realizing that no one ever really cared. Mr. Billy, I *murdered* my husband and I hid his body and I made it my life's work to get away with it. Until I found out, I never *wanted* to get away with it. Not forever."

There's no way I can't not believe her now. I don't know what's happening to her, but it's not madness. Not craziness. She's telling me the truth now, I'm sure of it. I just don't have a clue what to do about it.

Mrs. Jacobs begins tapping her foot now, like she's getting impatient. "There's a shovel. In the shed over there," she points. "Would you be a darling and go fetch it?"

I don't move.

"Why?"

"Because I've put you in a pickle. You know where Henry is, but you can't tell anyone, not after going to the police once with your story of him being under the school gymnasium. No one will ever believe you without proof. "

I don't answer, I just listen.

"I'm sure you have one of those cell phones on you? They're all young people seem to look at these days. With a camera?"

I nod.

"Well then. A strong young man like you can easily prize up these slabs, and then you can get your proof. I don't suppose there'll be much left other than bones by now. But you can take a photograph. And then you won't have to worry about not being believed."

Still I don't move, but she just stares at me with a weird, horrible smile on her face. And even though I don't want to, I find myself slowly climbing to my feet.

SEVENTY-TWO

THE TOOL SHED is cool and dark. Neatly organized. It smells of cut grass from a big petrol mower that takes up most of the space. I find the shovel easily enough, leaning up inside the door. I pick it up, feeling its weight. I walk back with it, and I wait for more instructions.

"You might need to lift up a few slabs Mr. Billy," Mrs. Jacobs says. She's put the tray with the drinks on the lawn, and she's dragged the table over to one side. "I think you should start with this one."

I don't though. Not for a long time. I just stand there, with the shovel in front of me, wondering how I got into this, and how I can get out of it. I want to throw the shovel down, run back through the house and get as far away from here as I can. I could too. I don't suppose Mrs. Jacobs could do much to stop me. But if I did that, I still wouldn't know for sure. And even after everything I've been through, I do want to know the truth.

"If you put the edge between the slabs here, you should be able to lever them up." She comes towards me. I can see how frail she is. It kind of gives me the confidence to do what she says. I step forward and scrape away at the dirt that's built up between the paving slabs.

"That's it Mr. Billy. That's it."

I put my foot on the top of the shovel and force it down between the slabs. I lean back on the handle, pushing my weight into leveraging up the first slab. It resists, but only for a moment, then it breaks free, cracking the mud all around it. I get a glimpse of yellow sand underneath before the weight of it pulls the slab back down. I think I expect to see something horrific there, but it's just sand.

"You'll need to get your hands underneath it dear. Then you can drag it onto the grass." There's enthusiasm in her voice. A weird enthusiasm.

I lift the slab again, and this time I put my foot on the handle of the shovel, keeping the blade under the concrete so that I can get my fingers under each side. It's heavy, but not too heavy. I manoeuvre it away to the side and drop it onto the lawn. Then I look back. Now there's a glaring square hole in the patio. Squashed flat sand. Cut into it are channels dug out by ants, they look like a river seen from space.

"You'll need to lift a few more, and then dig down. Just a little." Mrs. Jacobs says.

With the first one gone it's easier, and the square of yellow sand quickly doubles then quadruples in size. I have to concentrate so hard on moving the slabs I can almost trick myself into not knowing why I'm doing it. But when I have six slabs moved she tells me to stop. I remember then.

"Now dig the sand out. Carefully mind."

I grab the shovel again, and gently scrape at the sand, cutting through the ant runs. I make myself think about them, instead of what I'm actually looking for. They're old runs, fortunately, I'm not disturbing an actual live nest…

"Come on Mr. Billy, put your back into it. He's further down than that."

Her words bring me back. I stop for a moment, but then I try to empty my head completely, and I crunch the shovel properly into the sand. I balance a load on the shovel, then lift it out. I start a pile on the patio. It's years since I made a sandcastle, but that's what I think of now. Summer days with Dad, when I was little.

Quickly the sand builds up. A couple of times I unearth a stone, and get a jolt of panic that it's something else. I can hardly look at the hole I'm digging. I'm expecting to see a ghastly death mask of Henry Jacobs, with flesh still falling from his face, and I wish now I hadn't started this. But it's hard to stop. Then my shovel hits something hard.

She claps her hands together and leans right over me.

"I think you've found him. Scrape the sand off Mr. Billy. Careful now."

I do what she says, revealing something buried in the hole.

The color is the off-white that bones turn when they're old. I know it well enough from identifying animal skulls I've found in the past. And from the shape I can tell this is a skull too. The back of it, although I've never seen a human skull before. Very carefully I insert the shovel to one side, and gently extract more sand so that more of the bone is revealed. I do this a couple of times more, until it's quite clear what I'm looking at – the rounded back of a skull, and part of a jaw bone. Then I stop and look at Mrs. Jacobs.

She's standing by the hole, watching what I'm doing, and she's got her hands clasped against her chest. And she's crying again.

"Oh Henry," she says, then she gives me a goofy look.

Then I put down the shovel and pull out my phone to take a photograph. I'm a bit worried when I do this, that she might try to stop me, but she doesn't even seem to notice. I pull the phone from my backpack, I frame a photo so that it's clear what it is, and I press the shutter. Then I take another shot, this time pulling back to get the hole and Mrs. Jacobs' house in the background – so the police know exactly where the body is buried. Then, since Mrs. Jacobs is still ignoring me, I attach the photo to a text message for Amber. I quickly type out the words.

You were right. Sorry.

"I'm going to go now Mrs. Jacobs." Again I'm half-expecting her to try something to stop me. But I guess she knows I'd be stronger and faster than her. So she just gives me a smile.

"Not yet dear," she says.

I don't know what she means by this.

"Why not?"

"She'll be here any second."

"Who will?"

And then a voice calls out from inside the house. The last person I was expecting to see.

"*Mother?!*"

SEVENTY-THREE

PRINCIPAL SHARPE MOVES QUICKLY, like a spider when a fly lands in its web. She puts herself between where I'm standing and the door. I look around, there's no other obvious way out.

"Wendy, how nice of you to arrive so promptly," Mrs. Jacobs says. Then she turns to me.

"Wendy installed a panic button. She said I had to use it if you or that girl ever came to harass me again. That was the word she used: 'harass'. I did tell her you've only been perfectly polite, every time we've spoken. But I did press it Mr. Billy, all the same. I pressed it when you first arrived." She tilts her head onto one side, and goes back to gazing into the hole.

Principal Sharpe takes in the scene. She's holding a purse, and she suddenly starts rifling through it, and I don't know what she's going to pull out, but then I'm shocked, and I guess maybe a bit weary to see it's a gun. It's only a small one, much smaller than the one that Vinny had, but it's still a gun. In my school principal's hands. She points it at Mrs. Jacobs for a second, but then she points it at me. I see the barrel wobble with how her hands are shaking,

"What's going on? What on earth is going on?"

"I wanted to introduce young Billy here to your father," Mrs. Jacobs says. She seems to be standing more upright now. Principal Sharpe puts her free hand over her mouth. Then she leans forward, looking into the hole I've dug.

"Oh Christ," she says. "Mother. What have you done?"

"I did tell you Wendy," Mrs. Jacobs says. She sounds totally calm. "That Henry was here. After they dug up the gym I told you. Don't you remember?"

Principal Sharpe doesn't answer, she just takes in big gulps off air, like she's struggling to breathe.

"And now I've decided to do the right thing."

"The right thing? This isn't the right thing." Principal Sharpe turns on her and snaps. "You stupid woman. *You stupid, crazy, deranged old woman.* The right thing was keeping your mouth shut."

Her eyes are crazy, swiveling this way and that.

"You're so *selfish*. You think you can excuse your part in this, so *you* get to disappear with a clear conscience. But you don't think about others, you never did!"

The gun isn't pointing at me anymore. Principal Sharpe is waving it all over the place, and her attention is on Mrs. Jacobs. I look behind her, at the door. If I can slip behind her I can run. Maybe I can lose her somewhere in the house.

"Have you considered it might be *you* I'm thinking about?" Mrs. Jacobs voice rises up now, like she's not calm anymore. "You think you can keep this hidden your whole life. But believe me, you don't *want* to keep it hidden."

"Oh right? You know what I want do you? You know best? I'll tell you what I wanted, I wanted you to stay on the fucking medication and not embark upon this absurd..."

"*Language*!" The tone of Mrs. Jacobs voice makes Principal Sharpe stop at once. It makes me freeze too, just as I'm about to sneak past Principal Sharpe's back.

"I did not bring you up to have cussing in my house."

"Mr. Billy," Mrs. Jacobs turns towards me. It makes Sharpe notice me as well, and she snatches her arm across so the gun is pointing at me again.

"We should really explain all this, since you've found yourself witness to an awkward family argument."

Principal Sharpe actually looks at me now, I mean actually looks at me. I think she realizes she's pointing a weapon at one of her students. That's not normal for school principals. It's hard to get back from that. There's a moment when she seems to acknowledge it with a twist of her lips. Then Mrs. Jacobs goes on speaking.

"Wendy here was just a girl when it happened. She was unlucky enough to interrupt Henry doing what he did with her brother. I don't have to tell you what that was, do I Billy? I don't like to speak about things like that."

I don't reply. I don't take my eyes off Principal Sharpe.

"I knew of course. About Henry and his *tastes*. I knew it was happening with some of the children at the school, but he always promised me it would stop, or that they liked it. Or that he'd be discreet – or whatever he thought I needed to hear. And times *were* different then. People didn't make such a fuss as they do these days."

"Mother!" Principal Sharpe's voice is a warning to Mrs. Jacobs to stop, but the old woman carries on.

"I confronted him about it, and... Well, you can see for yourself what happened." She gestures towards the hole in the patio, where the skull of Mr. Jacobs is still partially uncovered.

"Eric was too young to know what had happened. I told him that Henry had gone away, just the same as I told everyone else. But that was never going to work with Wendy. So I made it our secret. I said her father had been so naughty, I'd had to put him under the school gym, and no one could *ever* know. And you might think a little girl wouldn't be able to keep such a secret, but Wendy did. She sucked it inside herself. She absorbed it. That secret *became* her. She even decided to become a teacher, so as to take a job at Henry's old school, and make sure the gym was never dug up. It was a little late, by then, to tell her that he was never there in the first place."

Principal Sharpe glares at Mrs. Jacobs at that, and the hurt is visible in her eyes.

"And that might have been the end of it," Mrs Jacobs continues. "But then Eric started asking questions. Awkward questions."

"Be quiet mother!" Principal Sharpe warns again. But again it has no effect.

"He wanted to know where Henry was in Maui. Why he'd stopped writing birthday cards – Oh I couldn't keep disappearing to Hawaii. I should have had him move somewhere more convenient." She smiles.

"It became an obsession with poor Eric. This wondering about his father. And he sensed there was something - something between Wendy and myself, that we weren't telling him. I don't know, perhaps a part of him remembered what happened when he was little?"

"Mother, I'm warning you. I will use this thing." Principal Sharpe stops pointing the gun on me now and aims it at Mrs. Jacobs.

But the old woman either doesn't see or doesn't care. "Of course by then, Wendy was a young woman. She'd grown up with our secret, and the belief it had to be kept whatever the cost." She stops for a moment, looking sad.

"I argued to bring Eric into the secret. That he would keep quiet about it once he knew the truth, but only when he knew the truth. Wendy argued something different. Didn't you dear?"

I watch Principal Sharpe, her long, narrow chest heaving in and out.

"Eric was weak. He wouldn't have kept quiet. He couldn't have."

"You don't know that dear. You wouldn't give him the chance."

The two of them stare at each other. And then I notice something. In the darkness of Mrs. Jacobs's lounge there's a movement. A subtle, careful movement. I glance at Sharpe and Jacob's eyes, but they haven't seen it. They're too busy glaring at each other. So I look back, and try and make it out. And now I see it properly, and my breath catches in my throat. It's a figure, somehow familiar. A person, moving, with their back to the wall, sliding slowly and cautiously towards the door. And then the figure reaches the door. The light catches on purple hair.

It's Amber.

She stops. Her eyes meet mine and she raises a finger to her lips. I have to work hard not to stare. I look around her, hoping to see other figures, the police maybe, but there's no one. She's alone. Amber flicks her eyes to Principal Sharpe and back, warning me not to give her away.

"We agreed that Wendy should be the one to explain it to him," Mrs Jacobs continues, oblivious to what I've just seen. "So she took him for a walk, just at the bottom of the garden here, along the clifftop. Perhaps you'd like to explain what you did next, dear? What you did to your little brother?"

Principal Sharpe doesn't say anything. And after a few moments, Mrs. Jacobs continues.

"I don't know why she's gone coy about it. She was cool as a cucumber afterwards. Ever so matter of fact." She smiles tightly at me. "We have a boathouse, just around the corner, so we were able to tow his body out into the sound and weigh it down. And then pretend it was all a great tragedy, that poor Eric had been unhappy for some time, though that part was true enough…"

"He was like Dad," Principal Sharpe says suddenly. "Eric would have turned out like Dad."

"And you turned out rather like me." Mrs. Jacobs cuts her off.

I look from one of them to the other. They're not looking at me, so I glance again at Amber, to see what she's doing. I see now she's holding the poker from a fire set in one hand. I suppose she's planning to use it to smash the gun from Principal Sharpe's hand. I nod, trying to give her the message that I understand.

"What are you doing?" At once I snatch my eyes back to Principal Sharpe. She must have been watching me after all. She turns around, and Amber's there, in full sight. She's not close enough to swing the poker. Amber freezes, caught.

"Drop it!" Principal Sharpe says. "Drop it on the ground."

For a second Amber doesn't, and I feel my breath thicken. I know what Amber's thinking, about rushing forward, to try and take on Sharpe, and I'm desperate for her not too, because I know what guns can do. She'll get one step and then she'll die, right in front of me.

"Drop it!"

Amber does what she says. There's a clang as the metal poker falls to the ground.

"Get over there with the boy."

All of Principal Sharpe's attention is on Amber now. And I realize that maybe *I* could do something. But what? If I try to rush her, then she'll shoot Amber, or swing the gun and shoot me. And there's no weapons I can get. Nothing near to where I'm standing. And then the moment is gone, and Amber is next to me, her hands raised in the air. I hear her breathing, short and fearful.

"You will not win, either of you. I told you to stay away from my family and you ignored me but *you will not win*. You might think it'll be hard to explain your disappearance, but we'll find a way, won't we mother? That's what we do in this family."

She turns to Mrs. Jacobs now, and I realize that we've all taken our eyes off the old woman. Because now everything's changed. At some point Mrs. Jacobs must have picked up the shovel, and readied herself to swing it like an axe. Because at that moment that's exactly what she does.

It flashes in the light, as it cuts through the air.

SEVENTY-FOUR

THE BLADE of the shovel is turned sideways, so that it knifes through the air. It lands with a thud in the back of Principal Sharpe's head. Her snarl slackens and then droops away, and then something white passes behind her eyes. Then her knees buckle, and she flops to the ground. Through her hair a black-red line fills up and leaks blood onto the floor. It puddles out around her.

I think Amber screams, or it might be me. I'm not sure. But the next thing I know is Mrs. Jacobs has reached down for the the gun. She feels the weight of it, like she's selecting vegetables at the supermarket.

"Well that was easier than I thought," Mrs. Jacobs says. Her voice is calm, almost happy. "I'm sorry you had to see that, but I'm afraid Wendy's had it coming for a very long time." She steps forward and, slowly, she bends down to feel for a pulse at Principal Sharpe's neck.

"Where did you come from?" I ask Amber.

"I was following Sharpe," she says. "I was doing a stake-out outside her house. She drove here so fast I could hardly keep up with her. Then I saw your message."

"Did you call the police?"

Amber hesitates, but then she shakes her head. I screw my eyes shut.

The next moment there's an explosion of noise. My eyes open just in time to see Principal Sharpe's body jerk on the floor, and then the gun jump in Mrs. Jacobs hands. The noise of the shot bounces back off the house. Then she turns to us.

"Just making sure," she says.

The tip of the gun is still spewing smoke, like water flowing from a pipe, only rising instead of falling. I stare at it, transfixed. Then she points it at us, somewhere in the middle of where we're both standing, and I wonder which one of us she'll shoot first. And which one I want her to shoot first. It's weird how you think about things like that. How that matters. But then, awkwardly, she lets the barrel fall down and turns the gun handle first towards us.

"Well?" She says a second later. "Which one of you is going to take it?" She steps forward, holding out the gun in front of her.

"I've called the police," Amber stammers.

"I should hope so. This is definitely a police matter." Mrs. Jacobs smiles. Then she makes a decision. She hands the gun to Amber and then she steps back and looks at the body of her daughter, and at the hole where her husband lays buried.

"Would anyone like some more iced tea while we wait?"

Amber calls the police while she fetches it.

EPILOGUE (1)

We played Scrabble while we waited for the police. I was winning too, and I had a really good word lined up when they finally got there with all their guns and the shouting and everything. So I never got to put it down.

I found out later on that they never stopped investigating Mrs. Jacobs. Even after they dug up the gym and didn't find anything, they still believed she'd killed him because there were no records of him in Maui or anywhere else. They probably would have gotten around to arresting her even if she hadn't murdered Principal Sharpe. But that certainly sped things up.

It's amazing how quickly things move on in schools though. Everyone was really excited for a few days, but even just a week after it all happened, most people were more interested with who was going out with who, and where the next party is going to happen.

But by then I'd already moved on anyway. I was back looking at the whale watching business with Dad. And soon we got past the stage of just planning it, and went to the next stage. Dad rang all the banks on the island, and finally one of them agreed to discuss a loan. They want to actually do a meeting though, so we can lay out exactly what we need the money for, and how we're going to pay it back. I wanted to come along to show them, only Dad said it would be better if he went to the meeting without me, on account of me being just a kid and it looking a bit strange if I went through all the figures. So that's why I'm waiting outside the bank now. In Dad's pick up, with the bullet holes still in the sides. And hopefully when he comes out we'll be all set. It's pretty exciting.

* * *

"So? How did it go?" I can tell right away that Dad's trying to prank me, because he looked really unhappy walking out the bank, with his shoulders slumped down, and his new suit looking all uncomfortable.

"They didn't go for it." He gets in beside me.

"Don't wind me up. They must have." I can't stop smiling

"No Billy, they really didn't."

I can tell from his eyes. He's really not joking after all. "But, we can pay it back, it says so on the spreadsheet!"

Dad closes the truck door, then just sits there, not moving. Eventually he speaks.

"They're not prepared to lend the amount we asked for. They will give us less, but it's not enough. It doesn't buy us the boat." He stares out through the windshield, then he turns to look at me.

"I'm sorry kid…"

"But why?"

"Because we're… Because we're not their kind of people. I did tell you Billy. I got no financial history. No influential backers. No contacts. I did warn you this might happen." He puts his hands on the wheel, grips it hard.

"Well how much are we short?"

"Enough. Enough that it ain't gonna happen." Still he doesn't start the engine.

"But what if we spend less on the marketing? All that insurance stuff you added, maybe we don't need that? Maybe we can…"

"They liked the idea." Dad cuts me off. "Generally, they liked it. They said the business plan was solid. Well thought-out. But they don't make the decisions any more. They just go with what the computer says. And with my credit history. There's a limit. And it just ain't high enough." He turns to look at me.

"Look, we can try again, in a year or two, when I've put some cash away."

"But what about the *Blue Lady*? Someone else'll buy her. We won't be able to do it in a year."

Dad shakes his head. "I'm sorry kid, I really am."

"I can get it. I can get five thousand dollars."

"Billy, where the hell are you gonna get…"

"Is it enough? Is five thousand enough?"

Dad hesitates. In the end he shrugs. "If you really could, it would make a start."

Then he fires the engine. And without another word he drives me back to school.

* * *

I don't go to my lesson though. I've got much more important things to do. I go straight up to the library, and get on the nearest computer. But then I don't know what to search for. It's not exactly a common problem, is it? Trying to work out who Mrs. Jacobs' five thousand dollar check actually belongs to. I mean, first of all, she's just committed first degree murder in front of two witnesses, and admitted to another murder, so I don't know if the police will seize all her money. And then even if that doesn't happen, we were never quite a legal detective agency when she gave it to us in the first place - we never had a license to operate. And then even if that doesn't matter, then half of the money is Amber's. It's super-complicated. But in a funny old way, I'm quite good at super-complicated things.

EPILOGUE (2)

Amber comes round early. She's really excited about everything, and she's picked up Steven from the vets for me, because she's got a car and I haven't. His wing is healed, and the vet didn't charge anything, which was really nice of them, because vets are really expensive.

"They said they don't want to see or hear from you ever again."

"You're joking aren't you?"

"No. They said you cost them a fortune, you never leave them alone, and your bird is the messiest, most vicious animal they've ever worked on. I think they meant it."

I hardly listen, I'm too busy feeding sprats to Steven. His soft brown eyes are almost totally yellow now. He does look quite frightening these days.

"I'm just making sandwiches, do you want to finish off for me?"

"Where's your Dad?"

"He's finalizing things at the bank. He's going to meet us there."

"Well let's go then."

* * *

Amber parks on the edge of the harbor, midway across two spaces, and only moves the car when I point this out to her. Then she takes the cool box from the trunk, and I take Steven, and we walk over to the gate that leads out onto the pontoon. I see the security guard hurrying over, and I know what he's going to say, but he doesn't get a chance because Amber asks if he wouldn't mind holding the gate so she can get the cool box through. Then he just watches us walk down the pontoon like he doesn't know what to say. And even if he had tried something, the next thing is Dad turns up.

It wasn't that hard in the end. I found this website which was all about what happens to prisoner's money when they go to jail. Apparently it's only in some financial crimes like fraud where the police can seize your assets. So even though Mrs. Jacobs did murder Henry Jacobs, because the money they had came from her family, it's still her money. It was a bit more difficult to unravel the problem of the detective agency not being exactly legal. It meant that the terms and conditions we had on the website weren't 100% legal either, which in the end was handy, because there were still a couple of mistakes that we hadn't noticed, and I had to contact Mrs. Jacobs, in a prison on the mainland where she's on remand, to get her to say whether we had to give the money back, but then she said...

"So where's this boat I've invested all my money in?" Amber interrupts me, as we walk down the pontoon.

Mrs. Jacobs insisted that we'd done exactly what she'd paid us for, and that the five thousand was only ever an upfront payment. So she wrote a second check and insisted that Amber should have it. And then Amber said...

"Wow - that's beautiful. Didn't I tell you an island detective agency needs to have a boat as well as a car?"

Well, it turned out 5000 dollars wasn't quite enough for the bank after all, we needed almost double that. But you can probably figure out what Amber said.

* * *

It's a really lovely day for it. There's not much wind, and it's really bright sunshine. And Amber and me carry the cool box into the galley area, and we put all the food and drink into the fridge, which Dad gets himself used to the controls. Then, when we're ready, he starts the engine, and tells Amber and me how to untie the ropes. It's pretty fun, clambering on the deck and on the pontoon, following Dad's orders, and feeling how the boat dips under our weight as we clamber around. And smelling the tang of diesel in the air and feeling how the boat is humming, like it's just as excited as I am.

"Cast off bow line," Dad shouts to me, and I let go of one end of the rope. I pull it, so that it runs through the ring on the pontoon, and the front of the boat is untied then. Dad shouts to Amber at the stern, and she does the same, and then I get a tingle inside me as the engine note deepens, and there's a rush of bubbles coming out behind us, and then we start moving. I kind of miss the first bit because Dad gets me to bring all the fenders in and stow them away, in case it gets wavy out to sea, but I kind of see the rock breakwater pass by as Dad steers us out of the harbor and out into the actual sea.

"Billy, go and grab a beer from the fridge will you?"

I do what Dad says. Down below she's really stable. And there's this comforting throbbing sound from the motor, but you can still hear the sound of water splashing down the sides of the boat. And you can see it too, strikingly blue through the porthole windows. I take a beer and a couple of cans of soda from the fridge, then I take it back outside. I climb the ladder, to where Dad is sitting steering, with Amber beside him. I open the drinks and pass them around. Then Dad takes a sip.

"So Billy," he says to me, as we clear the last bit of the breakwater. "Where do we find these whales of yours?"

The End

THE APPEARANCE OF MYSTERY

BOOK THREE

ONE

The rain bullets down, blown near horizontal by the wind, and pushed with such force that it rattles off the deck like ball bearings. The man stands, hunched over in foul-weather gear, his feet forming a triangle against the inner edges of the cockpit. The yacht's self-steering equipment is struggling with the waves, some as big as houses, which are now rolling under the boat from astern.

Once again he fights to reset the steering gear. He lashes the wheel in place, then struggles forward and nearly falls down the companionway steps as the boat lurches sideways into a huge chasm between two waves. Inside the cabin is chaos. Water sloshes knee-deep across the floor, taking with it tins of food, cushions, the tattered remains of the foresail that was ripped earlier. The hull creaks eerily, noises he's never heard it make before. He jams himself down in front of the chart table and stabs on the chart-plotter. It's time to call up the latest forecast run. He can't help but feel his life now hangs upon what it tells him. The boat can't take much more of this. Neither can he. Slowly, sucking its data down from distant satellites, the data loads.

He blinks.

It's bad. Worse than bad, it's like a bad joke. It's worse than anything he's ever *seen*, let alone anything he's ever sailed through. His head goes light. For a moment everything around him – the crazy slewing of every surface, the raging noise of the wind, the rush of water sluicing all around him – is gone. Faded out, while he sees nothing but the forecast screen. *It can't be real*. But it is.

Twenty hours previously he made the decision to change course. The depression forming ahead didn't look dangerous, but it promised an uncomfortable ride. So he diverted south to give it a wide berth. It was a cautious decision that would add days to his voyage, but he was in no rush. And sailing alone, he had no one to answer to but himself. But since then, every new forecast seemed almost designed to mock his caution. First the depression deepened, then it too ducked south, chasing him faster than he could sail. Then it became a storm, then it deepened further, so that some gusts were raging at hurricane strength. He changed course again to escape from its predicted path, and now, finally, it should have been leaving him behind. But the new forecast reveals he's been sailing into a trap.

The storm's forward progress has slowed. So that he's still near to the center, where the winds are at their strongest. Worse, the storm has deepened again. The small Atlantic depression he planned to avoid is now a category four hurricane, and it stretches for hundreds of miles in every direction around him, with no chance of escape.

He sits still now – as still as it's possible to be when wedged on a boat lurching and skewing to crazy angles. There's a sudden whine from the pump as it struggles against its impossible load. The man takes in the chaos around him, and his eyes slide to the radio. But he looks away. He suddenly notices his own face reflected back at him on the inside of the window. The man looking back gives a strange smile. A gambler's smile. He makes one last calculation, then he rolls the dice.

He picks up the radio microphone and presses the button to transmit.

"Pan-pan, pan-pan, pan-pan. All stations." His voice doesn't sound right. It's still like a dream. But he goes on. "This is sailing yacht *Falco*. Yacht *Falco*. That's *Foxtrot, Alpha, Lima, Charlie, Oscar*. Position 32.37732 degrees latitude, -66.455457 longitude." He repeats the position reading twice, then pauses before continuing. Trying to calm himself down. "There's some, err, heavy weather out here. And I'm taking in water faster than I can pump it out."

He stops and listens for a moment, but the radio is silent. He repeats the message, sounding surer now. He waits. Repeats it a third time.

"All stations, all stations. This is a Pan Pan. Sailing yacht *Falco*..." *Jesus, is there even anyone out there?*

He stops. Forces himself to swallow down the sense of anxiety rising up from his gut. He listens again, but the radio is silent.

Again the man inspects his reflection. Why the hell is no one answering? Has he done something wrong? Forgotten something crucial? He goes to press the button to transmit again, but this time he's beaten to it.

"Yacht *Falco*, this is US Coastguard in Miami." The voice is calm. Confident. The sound of someone speaking from where it's safe and dry.

"We have your location as 32.37732 lat, - 66.455457 long. Can you give us some more details of your situation, over?"

The man feels a rush of relief. It's happening. He's doing it.

"Yeah. I'm taking in water faster than the pump will push it out. My steering gear is really struggling. There's waves hitting at all angles, and the forecast..." He stops, not wanting or able to express in words the growing horror of his situation.

"Understood *Falco*." The Coastguard operator doesn't need reminding about the forecast. "How many of you on board please? And are there any injuries?"

"Just me. I'm not hurt."

There's a pause.

"OK. I have you listed as a thirty-two-foot cabin-cruiser? That right? White hull, blue deck-house, *over*?"

"Yeah, that's me."

"And are you the owner of the vessel? Luis Fernandez?"

"Yeah."

"OK Luis. You've issued a *Pan Pan*, meaning you want to alert us you may need emergency assistance, but you don't require it at this point. Is that correct?"

The man hesitates before he presses the button. Is it correct? Should he tell them he's sinking now? His mind conjures up an image of a rescue helicopter, a flash of light and color in the black sky ahead. How long would it take a helicopter to get all the way out here? Might they even not send one at all in this weather?

What would that mean for his plan?

"I don't think so. But the waves out here… They're fucking crazy, I've never seen anything like it. They're coming from everywhere, sometimes they come together and double up. And if I get one of them over me I don't…" He nearly breaks up. "I don't think she's gonna come up through it."

"OK Luis," there's compassion now in the coastguard's voice. "That's understood. I have your position on screen now. I can see you're in some heavy weather. Can you tell me what emergency equipment you have on board in the event you have to abandon ship?"

The words abandon ship stun him into silence for a second. The sudden thought of being out there, in that boiling ocean.

"I think I got a life raft."

"OK. Can you ensure it's ready to operate if needed? Can you do that now for me. Soon as we're done?"

"Sure. I'll try."

"OK Luis. That's good." There's a pause, then: "OK Luis. I'm gonna keep monitoring this channel. Please keep us informed if the situation changes, and every half-hour even if it doesn't, *over*."

No reply.

"Yacht *Falco*. *Falco*. Are you receiving? Please keep us informed. Are you receiving?"

"Yeah. I heard you. Will do."

"Thank you. And good luck. US Coast Guard out."

The man listens as the channel goes quiet. Slowly he replaces the transmitter. Then he drops his head onto his left shoulder, stretching out the muscles in his neck. He holds it for a moment, then does the same on the other side. With the decision made, he feels better. He listens to the wind for a moment, then abruptly joins in with its whistling.

* * *

In his office overlooking the ocean, Lieutenant Oliver Hart sets a repeating countdown timer on his watch for thirty minutes. It's hard to operate the buttons, since his hands are trembling from the call he just took. He can hear the storm battering the outside of the building, and that's just here, nearly five hundred miles from the center of the first major hurricane of the season.

"Jesus fucking Christ," he mutters, as he picks up the phone.

"Hey Gail, you're not gonna like this, but I might have a shout for you. There's a cabin cruiser, out there in the middle of all this. Christ alone knows what he's doing out there."

On the other end of the line, a woman turns to her computer screen.

"Oh heck," she says, when the location pings up. "Oh my lord."

"Yeah." Hart takes a breath. "Just putting you guys on alert right now, but I got a bad feeling about this one. Guy sounded pretty scared."

"Sure Ollie. Thanks."

Hart puts down the phone and calls over his superior, Commander Sarah Withers. He's numbly glad it'll be her decision to send the chopper out if the Pan Pan is upgraded to a Mayday. Or when it's upgraded. Experience tells him it will be. Together they run the forecast simulations in the sector. They both note the yacht's position is right out on the limit of the range of the Sikorsky MH-60T *Jayhawk* helicopters stationed nearby.

"Jesus fucking Christ," Hart mutters again, as the images loop around. Commander Withers doesn't approve of the language, but she doesn't disagree either.

The watch on Hart's wrist suddenly bleats an electronic beeping. Half an hour has gone by.

"I asked him to call in every half-hour." Hart explains, and they both turn to look at the silent radio. For the next four minutes it stays obstinately silent.

"Call him," Withers orders, when five minutes have passed. Hart begins to transmit.

"Yacht *Falco*, Yacht *Falco*, come in please."

Without even knowing she's doing it, Commander Withers takes a lock of hair and twists it tight around her finger. She listens as Hart calls out again and again. But each time, there's no answering call. She thinks about the two pilots on call today for the *Jayhawk*. Both men are known to her personally. Both have young families. Yet there's no way they would refuse to take off, no way they would refuse a mission. It's a matter of pride. The control room has a window overlooking the beach. She turns to it now, seeing rain lashing down the pane. The ocean is a churning mass of dark blues, streaked with white. Ugly dumping waves break far further out than normal. She can overrule them. The final call on whether to launch is hers.

"There's no response ma'am." Hart's voice breaks into her thoughts.

"Keep trying," she orders.

He does so. But his words are met by silence. It's like there's nothing out there. Nothing left alive anyway.

After trying another twenty times Hart's watch beeps again. An hour has passed since the first Pan Pan. Hart looks up.

"Still no response ma'am? We have his last position…" The unspoken implication hangs loud in the control room. If the yacht has gone down, the man's only chance is if the chopper can get to him. And fast.

Commander Withers doesn't respond. For a few moments she doesn't even breathe, resentful for Hart's role in this. He's here simply to relay the order. Her order. Her responsibility. She thinks again about the men who will lift off into the sky in this madness. And without taking her eyes off the blackness of the sky outside, she gives a single nod of her head.

"We launch."

TWO

The ocean is like a liquid mirror. Not quite still, but nearly. The surface of the water with that thick almost gooey viscosity it gets when there's not a breath of wind. It's actually been stormy recently, so I've had to wait for a day like this, when I can get this far around the coast.

The water reflects the high cliffs above me, but it's also translucent, so you can see how the cliffs don't stop where they meet the sea, but keep plunging down. It's almost like I'm floating, twenty feet up in the air, above a forest of seaweed waving like trees in the underwater currents. The only thing breaking the calm are the dips from my paddle, which fan out behind me like watery footprints. That and the line of my wake, pointing around the headland showing how far I've come.

There's no one else in sight. There wouldn't be. A few years ago this part of the island was made into a marine nature reserve, so the fishermen aren't allowed to come here. You sometimes get people walking the cliff path, but it's a long way, and most of the time the path is too far from the edge to look down at the water. So I'm all alone, but I like it that way.

It's taken me an hour of hard paddling to get here, even in my new canoe, a sixteen-foot sea kayak that was abandoned in the boat yard. Well, sort of abandoned. You have to pay to store boats there, and the guy that owned it stopped paying, so Ben – he owns the boatyard – he said I could have it if I took it away. And there's an alley behind the fish warehouse that no one ever uses. So I spoke to the manager there and he didn't mind. So I cleaned it up and fitted it with some extra gear, like a compass and a solar panel to run a GPS – which I can take off so they can't get stolen – and then some storage tanks for samples. And I built a kind of rack to store it in the alley. And now I use it all the time as a base to run experiments from.

I won't be using the sample tanks today though. If I'm right about what I thought I saw, the last time I came here, then I don't want to capture it. I don't want to disturb it at all. It's way too important for that.

I already programmed my GPS to take me back to the exact spot where I saw it last time. Or where I *think* I saw it. But actually I don't really need the GPS, since I know where I'm going. It's a spot I've explored quite well, on account of the underwater caves. There's caves all around Lornea Island, and these aren't particularly special ones, so not many people even know about them. But they're quite cool because the entrance is underwater most of the time. Anyway, that's how I know where I'm going.

I hug the base of the cliff, not letting myself drift too far out. It means that even if there is anyone on the coastal path they won't see me, so it's like I'm invisible. But it also means I can't see my destination, because of the little rock headlands that cut off the view. So when I round the last one I get a bit of a shock. I'm not alone after all. There's a boat here. A small yacht. Anchored, with its sails down. I'm so surprised I stop paddling. And I almost think about turning around. But then I think. Sometimes people *do* come in here. It's such a beautiful place, and just because I like to think it's my personal area, doesn't mean it actually *is*. They're probably just having lunch and then they'll go. I just hope they haven't dropped their anchor on anything valuable.

I paddle past the yacht, not going too close, and then a few moments later I pass the opening of the cave itself, though only the very top of it is visible above the water. Then I angle back in towards my ledge.

A dozen paddle strokes later and the nose of the kayak crunches up against the wedge of rock where I always pull it out. I found this ledge a while back, and it's really handy. As long as you're here on a falling tide, it's quite safe to leave the kayak here. It's not very big, and it's quite hard to get out of the boat, but I'm well practiced now, and I step confidently out onto the black, slippery rock, my bare toes fighting to grip. Then I loop the kayak's painter around an outcrop of rock and tie it tight. That way it can't slide off and drift away, leaving me stranded here. That wouldn't be fun.

After that I sit down, my feet dangling in the cool water, and eat my sandwiches. Above me the cliffs bend and curve, and they're quite smooth, so it's like I'm sat at the bottom and inside an enormous spoon. But under the water it's a different story. The lower half of the cliffs are made from lots of different sorts of rock, and the weaker parts have eroded away over millions of years. That's what made the caves. But because the sea levels have risen, you can't see them unless you get into the water. Then you can actually swim into the cliff, and resurface. In some places it's like you're actually inside the earth.

I think about this while I set up my camera. How this place has been here, hardly changed for millions of years. And how it'll be just the same in another million years. Long after we're all gone. When all that's left of humanity is billions of crazy fossils. Maybe some other species will discover it all, and make up theories about the age of the humans, only they won't call us that, because they'll have some other name. I think about it while I load the camera into the waterproof case. It's that kind of place. It makes you think these sorts of thoughts. But then I stop thinking and concentrate. Because I don't have that long before the tide comes in. And I've got work to do.

I'm already in my wetsuit, and I guess what I'm really feeling is nervous. Not just about whether I might actually find what I'm hoping to find. But also nervous because the scale of this location does make it an intimidating place to dive. But then I take a few deep breaths to calm down. I spit in my mask and rinse it out. I pull my flippers onto my feet and then fit the mask and snorkel. Then I'm ready. I slide carefully into the water.

It's always the same sensation when you first go in. The chill of the water presses around you, and a few leaks trickle in through the suit. And even though what you can see suddenly expands to include this incredible underwater world, it also contracts because the mask cuts out your peripheral vision. I have to fight at first, to keep my breathing slow and calm. But when I do, I swim away from the ledge. It's like flying out from a mountain top. The rocky bottom drops away. Below me there are giant boulders, some as big as houses. Some reach almost to the surface, so I could easily swim down and touch them, but in other places the floor is way down beneath me, far out of reach.

A trio of large sea bass glide past, barely bothering to change their course to avoid me. Once they grow to this size there's nothing around here that eats them, and they're safe from being fished too, though I don't know if they've worked that out. But I ignore them too. I'm studying the rocks, trying to find the exact spot I was at last time. It was pretty close to the entrance to the cave – where the water shallows and there's more patches of sand. I just need to find the right one. Then I see the boulder I've been looking out for, with one side much redder than the other, and I know I've found it. I surface and take a breath, trying to take a bearing above the water too, from the cliff face.

Then I put my face back into the water and let my eyes adjust to the lower light levels. I dive down and hold on to an outcrop of rock. I study the sand. I'm looking for an irregularity that shows something is burrowed into the sand. Something that shouldn't be here, not this far north. The brown striped octopus, or *Octopus Burryi*, is quite common in the Caribbean and even as far up as the coast of Florida, but no one has ever seen one this far north. Not ever. So *if* I'm right, then this will be quite a moment for Lornea Island.

Although they're called brown striped octopuses, most of them are actually more speckled colored, at least most of the time, like the sandy bottoms they like to live in. But then they can change color too, so they can be hard to identify. I saw this one – or I thought I saw it – the last time I was here. The trouble is I was just leaving at the time. The tide had turned, and I had to get back to the kayak – and then I haven't been able to come back to check, because – like I said – it's been so stormy lately. But I made a really careful note of where it was, and I could see it was in a burrow, which means it *should* still be here.

The big problem is, I might have been mistaken. It could be that I just saw an *Octopus Vulgaris,* in fact it's quite likely given how no one has ever seen a *Burryi* this far north. Which is another reason I'm quite anxious at the moment.

That doesn't mean they're vulgar by the way, *Octopus Vulgaris,* it's just their Latin name. Really it just means they're common. If it was a common octopus, then I've wasted my whole day. But I've seen a lot of *Octopus Vulgaris* and I'm pretty confident I know the difference.

As I wait, my eyes adjust to make more sense of the grainy surface of the sand. Octopuses need oxygen, so they breathe water, just like a fish does. Only instead of slits covering their gills, they expel the water through a squishy tube that sticks out alongside their legs. But it means that even when they're hiding in the sand, keeping still, you can still see the tube if you look carefully, blowing water as they breathe out. And I see it now. It's the size of a dollar coin, and once I've spotted that, I can see the outline of the rest of the octopus around it. I'm already holding my breath, but I feel like I should do it more somehow. I get my camera ready up in front of me and fin slowly toward it.

As I'm overhead I see its eye. Octopuses are pretty smart, and this one knows I'm here. It's probably working out whether it should try to stay hidden, or escape. They like patches of sand near rocks, partly because they eat crabs and things in the rocks, but also because they can escape there easily too. Give them a crevice and you can't ever get them out, or even see them if they go really deep. So I gently pull the camera into position and fire off a couple of shots, because this encounter could be over very quickly. I gently reposition myself to get photographs from every angle, while it's still, and I swim down a few times to get closer-up images too. Then, when I've got all the pictures I can of the octopus hidden in the sand, I swim down and pick up a couple of good-sized rocks. And – I know you shouldn't really do this – I carefully drop the first of the rocks over the octopus, so that it lands with a gentle thud next to where it's hiding. It tries to pretend it didn't happen at first, so then I drop the second stone, watching it sway down through the water. And this one lands too close, because – in a sandy flash – the octopus is suddenly up and out of the burrow, its tentacles trailing behind it. I fire off lots of shots, and I'm super excited because *anyone* can see this isn't an *Octopus Vulgaris.* The eyes are the wrong size and they're slightly too low. And the webbing where the arms meet the body is much deeper. It's definitely an *Octopus Burryi.*

Then something even more wonderful happens. I expect it to disappear in the rocks, but instead it slows and then stops, still out on the sand. I guess it knows it can escape if it needs too, but it doesn't want to use up too much energy, or give up its territory if it doesn't have to. So I let myself drift very slowly closer again, taking photos the whole time. The best ones will be if I can get really close.

The octopus stands up on the tips of four of its tentacles, then slides them down into the sand, while the other four finger the rocks behind it. Then it blows the sand up, so that little clouds color the water. The colors of its body flutter and flicker to match the background, and gradually it sinks into the sand. And then it stops. Watching me, watching it.

I guess the time goes fast after that, because before I know it my camera tells me I've run out of space on the memory card. And then I check my watch, and a whole hour has passed. Which means I have to go or the tide will get too high for my ledge.

I don't want to go though, so I allow myself another five minutes, just watching the octopus, without taking any photographs. And then – and to be honest I'm feeling a bit cold now – I turn to swim back to the kayak. It's not too far, just the other side of the entrance to the cave really. And I'm not really thinking about anything as I swim, apart from what I'm going to do with the photographs, and who I'm going to send them to. And whether anyone will even believe that I took them right here, on Lornea Island. And that's when I get a shock.

Up ahead of me is another diver. It's a man, with a face mask and snorkel, and he's holding a massive spear gun out in front of him. He hasn't seen me, and I freeze at once. The good mood I'm in from seeing the octopus is instantly gone. And after a second I realize it's replaced by anger. I already told you how this section of the coastline has been designated as a marine reserve. That means you're not allowed to fish here. At all, and that definitely includes spear fishing. There's plenty of other places you can go if you want to do that, although I don't really approve of it. I mean, it's not exactly a nice thing to do to an animal is it? To shoot it. And the guns they use, powered by thick elastic bands, are incredibly powerful. When they shoot a fish the spear just punches straight through, like a dart bursting through a stretched-out piece of paper.

This guy looks like an amateur too. When you're spear fishing you're supposed to carry a buoy, so people can see you easily. But this guy doesn't have one. At least his catch-bag is empty, which means he hasn't killed anything yet.

I think what to do. The easiest thing to do would be to go back to the kayak, take the name of the yacht and then report the owner for illegal spear fishing in a nature reserve. But if I do that the chances are nothing will happen. I could take a photograph as proof – but I used up all the space on my card, and I don't want to delete any photos of the octopus. And even so, the guy's got a face mask on, so you wouldn't be able to see who it is, or prove his identity. And even if he did get fined, that's hardly going to stop him shooting some animals *right now*. Then I have a horrible thought. What if he comes across the *Octopus Burryi*? Some people actually eat octopus, even though that's hard to believe, and the one I've been watching was a good size. But if this guy shoots this one, the only *Octopus Burryi* ever seen this far north. Well that would be a disaster. I have to do something. And now.

I decide to confront him. I just have to be careful that I don't startle him. If I do he might accidentally fire the spear gun. And since it would go through me just as easily as a fish, I'll make sure I come up behind him so I can't get hit. So that's what I do. I fin fast to catch him, and swim up right behind him, kind of expecting him to notice me and turn around. But then I get really close, so I can just reach out and touch his shoulder. So that's what I do. Then he goes nuts.

All I mean to do is get his attention, and then point at the surface to tell him I need to speak with him. Instead he totally freaks out. He spins around like I've tried to attack him, and he flails out with his arms and legs. Something hits my mask so that it floods with water. So then I have to surface, and a second later he does too.

"Whoa. *What the fuck?*" The man says. He's got an accent, I notice at once, he's not from the island. Plus he's panting like he's been running or something. "You scared the fucking shit out of me!"

"There's no fishing here. It's a marine protected reserve."

The man pulls the mask from his head, and pants some more. He's got a ring of red around his eyes from wearing the mask. He must have been here quite a while.

"You're not allowed to spearfish here." I tell him again. He's younger than I thought. Early twenties maybe, not much older than I am.

"It's a marine…"

"Yeah, yeah. I heard you the first time." He interrupts me. "And anyway I wasn't fucking spear…" He doesn't finish the sentence.

"Yes you were. I saw you." Then I notice he isn't holding the gun anymore. I refit my mask and put my face into the water, looking for it. But it's not there. He must have dropped it.

"You had a spear gun. I saw it."

"Yeah well I don't now, do I?" Suddenly he starts grinning.

"I saw it. I saw what you were doing."

"Is that all you're worried about? Illegal fishing? *Fuck* man."

"It's nothing to laugh about. There's a $500 fine. If you don't leave right now I'm going to report you to the National Oceanic and Atmospheric Administration. *And* your boat's anchored. You're not allowed to anchor here either."

The man stares at me. He's got very clear dark eyes. His face breaks out into a smile again. A kind of sneering smile.

"OK kiddo. You got me. I thought this'd be a good place to bag a bass or two. But you rumbled me. I'll get outta here right now. OK?" He starts to swim away from me, backwards, towards the anchored yacht.

"What about your spear gun?" I ask. "You can't just leave it here. It's littering." We both refit our masks then and look down into the water. We're over a deep gully here, and the gun is only just visible, much further down than I can swim. The man lifts his head out of the water again.

"You can have it." He grins again, like he really doesn't care about losing it. "I'll buy another one." He laughs again. That's what really annoys me about the fine against fishing here. It should be much higher, because people like him, who are rich enough to have nice yachts, it's just not enough to deter them.

"Sorry buddy." He swims away, and I keep an eye on him as he gets to the yacht, and I return to the kayak. Once I get there I pull out my binoculars and watch him as he pulls up the anchor and motors away. I take a note of the name of the yacht.

It's called the *Mystery*.

THREE

The motor burbles as the boat pushes through the calm water. A slight swell – almost imperceptible here, but enough to push waves into the beaches along the island's east coast – ghosts underneath them. It causes the *Blue Lady* to roll gently as it cuts along, but it's not enough to upset the group of tourists sitting along the bench seat and looking hopefully around them.

"Are we *really* going to see dolphins?"

The voice belongs to a small child. A boy. Blond hair cut in a bowl style, and dressed in red pants and expensive Nike sneakers. Around his neck a pair of binoculars hang, looking absurdly over-sized.

"I'm sure we are," his mother replies. "You just need to be patient." At that moment a young woman steps past, the same young woman who checked their tickets as they climbed aboard, with a faded crew t-shirt and the name of the boat emblazoned on it.

"Excuse me Miss," the mother asks. "What are the chances of us actually seeing something? It's just we've been out here over an hour and…" she looks apologetic. "I know you said it's late in the season, but Charlie was so hoping to see dolphins. He just loves them…" She tails off, then looks around, like maybe they're actually surrounded by them and she just didn't notice.

The young woman breaks her stride and looks down. She takes in the hopeful look on the small boy's face. She crouches down.

"Hey Charlie. My name's Amber. How are you doing?"

Finding the young woman at the same level as him, the boy relaxes a little. "I'm OK."

"Just OK?" Amber's face takes on an indignant expression. "Why? What's up?"

The boy bites his lip, unsure whether this is one of those times when he's supposed not to tell the truth, or hide it.

"I just really really want to see some dolphins."

"You really *really* want? Wow that's a lot of wanting!"

"It's his birthday," the mom explains. Amber glances up at her and gives a reassuring smile. Then turns back to Charlie.

"So how old are you?"

"I'm five. But later on today I'll be six. Because I was born in the evening."

"Wow! That's awesome, I've got a kid sister just that age."

"It's his birthday treat." The mom cuts in again. "He didn't want a party or anything. He just wanted to see dolphins. I mean whales too of course. But mostly dolphins."

Amber takes a deep breath. "Well," she says, rocking back on her heels. She thinks for a moment, then points at the bridge, where a man in his forties is casually holding the wheel. He's suntanned and looks relaxed and capable.

"You see that man driving? That man is the skipper of this boat. He's called Sam Wheatley, and he just happens to be the best skipper on the whole of Lornea Island. Not just the best whale-watching boat skipper. The best skipper of any boat. And not just the best on Lornea Island either. Probably the best in the whole country. Or even the whole world. So if there are any dolphins around, and I mean any at all, he can catch up with them." Amber smiles again, and this time the boy smiles with her.

"And that's not all. Take a look in the cabin there." She points, and the boy's eyes follow her arm to see a teenage boy sitting at a chart table in the boat's cabin. In front of him are an array of technical looking screens, plus a laptop computer.

"*That,*" says Amber. "That is none other than Billy Wheatley. He's Sam's son, and *he* is only the best whale and dolphin *finder* in the whole wide world. So I promise. If there's *anything* around you're going to get to see it. OK."

Charlie's head nods up and down. His eyes wide.

"OK." Amber stands up and turns back to the mom.

"We would normally have seen something by now, but we are right at the end of the season."

The mom smiles, to show she understands, and appreciates the effort.

"OK then." Amber smiles and it looks as though she's about to leave, but she doesn't. She crouches down again.

"Hey Charlie, would you like a soda?"

"Sure! Mom, is that OK?" He looks anxiously up at his mother, who smiles at once, and nods her head.

"Pepsi?"

"Yes please."

Amber moves to the center of the boat where a chest is anchored down. She heaves open the lid, and from the bed of ice she picks out the soda, then takes it back to Charlie.

"So why do you like dolphins so much Charlie?"

"They're really smart! And I like the way they jump out of the water and do tricks..."

"I don't think they'll be doing any tricks Charlie," his mom says. "Even if you are lucky enough to spot some."

"I don't mind that," Charlie replies at once. "I just really want to see one. Do you really think we will?" Charlie's eyes shine up into Amber's, totally trusting that whatever she says next will be the absolute truth.

"Well…" Amber begins. "We did see some yesterday. And the day before, they came right up close to the boat. So I reckon there's a good chance. Whales too, a humpback mom and her little baby."

"A baby whale?" Charlie's eyes go round as coins, like up to now he hadn't thought such a thing could exist. "For real?"

"Course for real." Amber smiles, and the only thing that betrays a hint of anxiety is the way she glances at the flat water around them, before continuing.

"One thing I *definitely* promise you, if there's anything cool around, Billy is gonna find it. There's just no one better." Amber smiles again and stands up. To the mom she continues. "If he wants to come inside and see how the sonar works, you just give me a holler OK?" She pats the mother on the arm and moves away.

FOUR

THE DOOR to the cabin opens and then shuts again. I don't look up.

"Dolphins please," Amber says, her voice bright and cheery. "And if you could rustle up a humpback that'd be cool."

I ignore her and continue what I'm doing, which is reading an article on my laptop. It's in the scientific journal *Marine Biology Association of the United States,* and to be honest it's quite heavy going.

"Little kid, whose birthday it is. I also told him about the humpbacks yesterday, but it's dolphins he really wants."

"Uh huh." I keep reading as she talks. Then I suddenly stop.

"Humpbacks?"

"Yeah, you know the mother and the calf?"

Now I finally turn to look at her. I can't help myself frowning deeply.

"What? You don't remember? Jesus it's like you've left already. Like your brain's checked out and gone down under. You remember, the mother and calf?"

I continue to frown, and maybe I shake my head a little bit too.

"Oh *come on* Billy, don't be weird. They came right up to the boat?"

Now I know what she's on about. "Right up to the boat? They weren't humpbacks. They were *sperm* whales."

Now Amber frowns. Just for a second. "Oh. Yeah. That's what I meant."

"Sperm whales and humpbacks are *completely* different..."

"Yeah I know…"

"Humpback whales are in the *Balaenopteridae* family, part of the suborder Mysticetes. That means they have baleen in their mouths, instead of teeth. Whereas Sperm whales are of the *Physeteridae* family, suborder Odontocetes, which means…"

"Which means toothed whales, I know. I know. Humpbacks eat shrimp. Sperm whales eat fish – or cephalopods – which is squid in actual *English*. I know already. I just got them confused for a second."

I watch her for a moment.

"Krill."

"Huh?"

"Humpbacks. They mostly eat krill, not shrimp."

"Same difference."

"No it's not…"

"I'm kidding Billy. I'm pulling your leg. Lighten up."

I don't reply. I don't know why but I'm in a bit of a funny mood today. So I persevere.

"How could you get a humpback and a sperm whale confused?"

"Because I'm not an *asshole* like you. Will you please stop reading that and find me some dolphins? I've got a kid out there who's six years old today, and who really wants to see some." She goes to close my laptop, but I move it out of the way just in time.

"What are you looking at anyway? You should be out there enjoying this. It's the last trip we're ever going to do on *Blue Lady* 1. And you made this business such a success." She glances at the screen. The title of the article is *Molecular identity of the non-indigenous Cassiopea sp. from Palermo Harbour.* She reads it out loud, pronouncing it all wrong.

"What are they? Casio-whatevers?"

"They're jellyfish," I explain. "An invasive species that probably came into the Mediterranean through the Red Sea Canal…"

"Well that sounds riveting, but it's not exactly relevant to finding something exciting *right now.*" Amber sighs. "Honestly Billy, while you're getting excited in Latin in here, I'm out there chatting to *actual human people* who have paid you to see some whales. So would it kill you to find me some. Please?"

Reluctantly I close the screen on the laptop. Then I stare at her. I still can't believe she hasn't noticed them.

"What is it?" Amber asks, sensing something at last.

I try to keep a straight face, but in the end I can't, and I end up smirking.

"*What*?" Amber punches me on the shoulder, but not too hard.

"OK, OK," I laugh at her. "There's a small pod of spinner dolphins about a mile off. Bearing ninety degrees. I already told Dad."

"Where?" She jumps in front of the screens, then races to look out the window. Already a few of the guests outside are training their binoculars and shouting.

Then I shrug. "Course I could be wrong. They might be humpbacks. The way they're leaping out the water like that. And spinning around. Or maybe they're krill..."

"*Oh fuck off* Wheatley." Amber goes to hit me around the head this time, and I manage to duck out the way, only then I don't see her other hand, and she gets me and messes up my hair.

"So you gonna come out and look? Or stick with your nerdy jellyfish?"

I give her a look. "Amber, they're only *spinner* dolphins."

She stares at me for a moment, then she bursts out laughing. "What are you like, Billy Wheatley?" Then she picks up her megaphone and steps back outside.

FIVE

THE *BLUE LADY* tracks the dolphins, but they seem to be in a hurry to get somewhere, and the motor doesn't have the power to get them close enough for viewing without the binoculars. Then the animals stop, and change direction, so that their path takes them directly towards the boat. The excitement on board rapidly rises as the animals come much closer, leaping and spinning as they do so. But then, as if obeying a call only they can hear, they suddenly dive and disappear. Sam circles the boat, while the tourists wait with cameras poised. But after twenty minutes with the ocean's surface unbroken, it's clear they've slipped away.

And gradually the excitement ebbs away too, replaced by the beginnings of frustration for those hoping to get value for money out of their tickets. But for Sam and Amber it's simply a clear reminder – if one were needed – of why they made the decision to retire the *Blue Lady* at the end of the season, in favor of a faster, larger and better equipped vessel next year. Even so, they're both a little tense, as if both feel a strong desire for the old girl to go out on a high.

After some discussion with Billy, Sam steers the boat further out to sea into deeper water. It may be late in the season, but there are still whales about. They just need to know where to look, and be lucky. After another half hour of steaming as fast as the old motor can take them, Amber picks up the megaphone again.

"So. We've come out a long way now," Amber's amplified voice carries over the whole boat. "To where Billy tells me is the very best chance to have a whale encounter today." Amber does her best to keep her voice optimistic, but everyone can hear the 'but' that's coming.

"And here on the *Blue Lady* we do have an excellent record of viewing whales…" Her voice tails off. And then it comes.

"But these are wild animals and we can't *guarantee* sightings."

"My sister went on a trip from New York," a woman pipes up. "She said she saw whales before they'd even got out the harbor..."

Amber looks around at the sea around them. It's a little too long to be a casual glance, and the ocean remains stubbornly flat, empty.

"What we might be able to do…" she says after a while, still into the loud-speaker but turning now so she can watch Billy, who's still sitting inside the cabin. "Is get Billy to come out here and answer some questions."

The door is partly open, so there's no way Billy can't hear her. But he pretends not to.

"He's actually," Amber gives a smile, settled now on how to entertain the group. "He's off on a very exciting adventure next week. Isn't that right Billy?" She directs the megaphone at the open door, just in case he hadn't been listening. And when Billy continues to ignore the noise, Amber simply carries on talking. "He's been head-hunted. Sort of." Everyone can hear how Amber is enjoying herself now. They give her their full attention.

"Can we have a little show of hands? Who here has seen that show on ABC, *Shark Bites*?"

A few hands go up, one guy shouts back. "Yeah I seen it." Then a couple more hands rise up. Amber turns to answer the man.

"Well… *That* dude, the shark guy, *Steve Rose*. You know how he's actually a serious scientist, as well as a TV celebrity? Well he *heard about* our Billy here, and his incredible ability to find whales. And he's invited him along on a two-month research tour off the coast of Australia." Amber pauses to let that sink in, before she goes on.

"They're going looking for *great white sharks*."

An audible murmur goes up from the boat's seating areas.

"You wanna come out here and talk about that Billy? I'm sure the guys here would love to hear all about it?"

It seems that Amber's won, since, a second later Billy pushes up from his seat. He steps outside, but then he seems surprised to see Amber smiling and holding out the megaphone to him. Instead he moves to the rail, staring at the calm water on the port side of the boat. When he looks up, a few moments later, he sees the eyes of all thirty guests on him.

"I said, Billy," Amber goes on. "That you're off to *Australia*. To chase great whites. You wanna say anything about that?" She holds out the loudspeaker again, but he doesn't take it.

"Erm. I just…" He glances at the water again, frowning. "We're not really chasing… It's more of a survey… A population study…" He stops. He looks at the water again.

"Actually I think there might be some whales now. They might actually breach."

As he speaks the boat's motors slow. From the wheel Sam Wheatley calls out.

"Whereabouts Billy?"

"Just over..." Billy sweeps an arm over the ocean to their left, but it's a vague gesture.

"Somewhere..." At once everyone is looking where Billy is indicating. Suddenly expectant. But there's nothing to see. Behind them the land is just a gray smudge, low over the horizon. Around them the water is blue-black and oily smooth. It's empty.

"I don't see anything," someone shouts, a long moment later.

"It might have just been a shadow on the echo sounder. Or a shoal of fish." Billy replies, but he doesn't look confident. And after another thirty seconds of increasingly awkward silence, the ocean remains undisturbed. Billy shoots a glance towards the cabin and his laptop. Like he'd like to get back there, but now he's not sure how. All the boat's forward motion has now ceased. They're floating still on a near motionless ocean.

"So how do you find them? These whales?" A woman asks. "*When* you find them I mean?"

At once Amber sticks the megaphone in front of Billy, for a third time, and this time Billy reluctantly takes it from her. He turns it on, and speaks in an unenthusiastically- amplified voice.

"Well we have the fish finder, and the sonar, and you sort of recognize the patterns. But sometimes it's not whales it's just something else because the resolution isn't very high. Though you can get better sonar but they kind of have to be designed into the bottom of the boat."

"But you do see them? On most days right? That's what it says on your leaflet."

"Yeah," Billy replies, but again he sounds unconvinced. "It's just it's kinda late in the season now." His voice dies away and there's silence.

The guests fidget, and look around at the empty ocean. Then the woman from earlier calls out again.

"This whale watching trip my sister went on. She said they offered a guarantee. If they didn't see no whales they got a refund on their ticket price."

But if Billy even hears her, he doesn't reply. Instead he hands the loudspeaker back to Amber, then goes back to the rail of the boat and stares at the water again.

"Well, are you just gonna ignore her? What about this guarantee?" A man asks, probably the woman's husband, and his voice verging on mad. He's about to go on when Billy holds up a hand.

"Ooooh." Billy says.

A second later a few bubbles burst on the surface, less than ten feet from the side of the boat. It's enough to draw a few people's attention to that spot of water. And then, suddenly many hundreds of bubbles arrive, fizzing and boiling in a trio of circles. And then, almost in slow motion, the water stretches upwards and then splits apart as the black-and-white flecked bow of an enormous whale launches up and out of the sea. It climbs, higher than the top of the boat, like a missile emerging from the deep. Then it sweeps forward, hanging in the air for a heavy second before crashing back down, landing heavily and sending a curtain of green water showering over the boat.

There's screams all around. Yells of excitement and actual fear. A few of the quicker-witted watchers snap pictures, but most are too shocked.

"Maybe over there," Billy says, moments later and he points a little further away from the boat. This time everyone's ready as, exactly where he says, a second whale explodes upwards. It too hangs for a split second, then ten tons of whale land back into the ocean with another almighty splash.

"I *thought* they were humpbacks," Billy says, but by now no one's listening to him.

SIX

Flying is incredible. I always knew it would be, but to actually get to do it is amazing. I'm kinda pleased too, that it's my first time on a plane, and I've gone all the way to Australia. I mean, that's nearly half way around the globe. I even had to choose which way around I went. I decided on going west, not because it meant I got to fly over the whole country first, with a stop in Los Angeles, but because then we carried on across the entire Pacific ocean. I wanted to get a sense of just how big it was. Though as it turned out, you couldn't really see much, just lots and lots of blue. Anyway, we've just landed, so now I'm *in* Australia. I'm just waiting for my luggage. Then there'll be someone to pick me up and take me to the research boat. At least I really hope there is. Because if not I don't know what I'm going to do.

I end up waiting ages by the conveyor belt, quite a long time before any suitcases come out, and then even longer when, one by one, they bump onto the belt. And I get a bit worried, because at first I can recognize lots of people who were on my flight who are standing waiting with me, but more and more of them find their bags and load them onto trolleys and disappear, until finally it's just me left, and my backpack still hasn't come. It's just the three same cases going round and round, and there's no one left to take them.

So I don't know what to do then, but then I see a girl with dreadlocks and a backpack that looks a bit like mine, although it's smaller, and I guess I must look at her funny, because she tells me that backpacks come out on a special conveyor at the end of the baggage hall. When I ask her why she tells me it's something to do with the straps, and then she gets a bit angry because I explain how I tied all the straps down extra carefully and she tells me it's not her problem and walks off. So then I ignore her and go to where she tells me, and then I'm super relieved because my backpack *is* there, just abandoned lying against a wall, and none of the straps have come undone where I tied them. Honestly it doesn't seem like a very good system to me. I don't know what I'd have done if I got all the way here and found all my stuff had been left behind. I was a bit worried too, that it might have got damaged by the baggage handlers, because you hear bad things about baggage handlers, and I do have some quite fragile equipment inside. But actually it looks fine. I heave it over, and check the other side. It's just a bit dirty, but actually I quite like that because it makes it less obvious that it's new, so people won't know I've not done much traveling before.

Then I remember about the people waiting for me on the other side, and how I've been so long that maybe they'll think I didn't come after all. So I struggle into the straps and hoist the backpack on my back. I do have Australian banknotes, for the trolleys, but I decide not to use one, because it *is* a backpack, and the girl with dreadlocks wasn't using a trolley and she looked like she knew what she was doing. So I take a deep breath, and I walk as best as I can through the customs area. I totally expect to be stopped and searched, and probably arrested, because stuff like that *always* happens to me, but there's not even any customs officers there, so I just walk straight through. Then I have to go through some swing doors, and suddenly it's all mayhem. There's a big crowd of people all staring at me, like they think I might be the relatives they're waiting for. And I can't help but know they're all *Australians*. You can sort of tell. They all look a bit more tanned than normal people, and some of them are wearing flip flops – although quite a few people on Lornea Island do that in the summer too. I feel everyone looking at me, which I don't like, but I take a deep breath. I tell myself this is what growing up feels like. You can't have big adventures if you just stay home. Then I step forward, ignoring all the eyes watching me, and start to read the name signs people are holding up. There's quite a few, and I look for the one with my name on it. But soon I've read them all, and there isn't one. So I don't know what to do after that.

I walk up and down past the crowd – they're behind a barrier, except every now and then excited kids duck underneath because their relatives have just arrived and they run up to them and start talking in funny accents. But my backpack is actually pretty heavy, so it makes my shoulders ache. Even so I start to feel myself floating off the ground, like all this is some sort of dream, or maybe the beginnings of a nightmare.

Then I see a woman hurrying into the entrance of the terminal building, and looking around her, like she's late. I think I'd notice her anyway, because of how she's quite young and how pretty she is, but obviously I recognize her, though it's weird to see her in real life. She's dressed in a very relaxed way – in shorts made from jeans, with the material cut off really high up on her legs, which are very long and tanned. Then I'm doubly surprised when she notices me, but instead of continuing to scan the crowd, she breaks into a wide smile. That doesn't happen very much with me and women, especially not very pretty ones, so I'm a bit taken aback. Then she comes towards me, and even more odd – or not odd really, but it feels like it, she mouths my name at me, with a questioning look on her face. I feel myself nodding and walk towards her too, and we meet where there's a bit of a space in the crowd.

"Billy right?" The woman says. She's got a funny Australian accent too. Her blonde hair is tied in a loose pony tail, with strands of it falling out over her eyes. Up close she's *really* pretty.

"That's right."

"I'm Rosie. I'm so sorry I'm late, the bloody plane wouldn't start."

I don't say anything. I ought to – Rosie is the lady I've been emailing about the trip – but she's also the woman I've seen on TV so much, and it's kinda hard to make sense of both of those facts. Up close she smells like fresh flowers.

"You alright? Long flight huh?" She smiles again. Her lips open and her teeth are white and regular, except there's a little gap between the front two. I manage to nod in reply.

"Shall I grab a trolley for that bag? It looks like it's squashing you."

I shake my head and mumble something about being fine.

"OK. We might need a bigger boat though." She smiles again, to show how she's joking. Her cheeks go all round when she does it, and then there's little dimples too. She's actually *beautiful*, like a model, or even not like a model, at least not the ones in magazines, since you hardly ever see them smiling, like they're worried they're going to break their faces or something. Rosie seems quite happy to smile.

"You sure you're OK?"

Hurriedly I nod again, so I don't look odd.

"Yes."

"Alright then. Well let's get outta here."

She leads the way towards the exit. At first I fall into step behind her, and I can't help but watch the way her shorts lift up on the backs of her thighs, not so high that you can see her actual behind, but high enough to show the muscles in her legs. But then she turns to check I'm following her and I look away quickly. And then we walk outside, and I'm hit by a wave of heat. It's like a physical wall or something. We get hot summers in Lornea Island, but it's never like this.

She stops and turns to me.

"Hot huh?" She does that smile again. I force myself to try and smile back, even though my face feels all stiff.

"Come on. The van's got air con." She touches my shoulder and I feel a jolt go through me, like her fingers are electric. "It's just over there." She smiles again, but wonky this time, and it's even more pretty. Then she sets off again, and I follow, really trying to make myself relax. I know we've got a long car journey to where the ship is moored, so at least I'll have time to get to know her a bit before meeting everyone else. That's all I need, a bit of time.

"We had a change of plan by the way," Rosie says from in front of me. "I managed to grab a flight down with a mate of Steve's. So we don't have to do the drive."

Before I can even make sense of this she goes on.

"So we can all fly up together."

I feel myself tense up again.

"All?"

"Yeah. The other students are waiting in the van."

I feel myself tense up again. I'm not the only one on this trip. I'd kinda forgotten that.

"Don't worry Billy." Rosie tells me. "They seem really fun. It's gonna be a good trip."

Then we arrive at a minibus, and I see there's already three people inside, not including the driver. They all look about my age – well actually a little bit older – but I can't really see, because the windows are tinted. Then Rosie lifts the back of the minibus, and we try to stuff my backpack in, and I get a better look at them. But then it's a bit embarrassing because there isn't enough room, so we have to force it in the sliding door instead. The boy who's in there makes a big thing about pulling it in with both hands, and joking about how it takes up three seats all on its own. But actually there's plenty of room, because it's a minibus. Then I climb in and sit down too, next to the boy because it's the only seat I can get to, and Rosie slides the door shut behind me.

The boy holds out his hand. But instead of trying to shake mine, he tries to fist bump me, only it goes wrong because I was too slow working out what he was doing. Then he does something else, which I've seen rappers do on TV, and that doesn't work either. But he doesn't seem to care.

"I'm Jason," he tells me. His voice is loud and I can tell at once he's one of those super confident people. Then he introduces the others and tells me what colleges they're studying at, not letting them speak. I forget what he says, but luckily when I turn around to shake their hands they tell me their names again. On the seat behind me is a girl called Debbie. She has dark brown hair, and she looks quite round. I think she is studying at the University of Miami. And then on the back seat is another girl called Kerry. She's actually pretty too, I notice. Or at least you might think she was, if you hadn't just met Rosie to compare her with. She's studying at Stony Brook. Or it might have been the University of California. One of them is from there. I can't help but notice their bags – they all have backpacks too, but they're all quite a lot smaller than mine.

"So where you studying Billy?" Jason asks me suddenly.

"Erm," I say. And then I feel everyone go quiet, waiting for me to answer. "I'm actually just in high school at the moment."

There's another moment of silence, before Rosie interrupts from where she's just climbed in to the front of the minibus.

"Billy is the youngest ever graduate student we've taken on a trip." She says it in a kind way. "So you'd better all look after him." And that really helps break the ice a bit.

Then everyone starts talking about the subjects they're studying, and the teachers they know. I don't say much, even though I recognize some of the names. I suppose I feel a bit intimidated.

Then the driver starts the motor and drives us out of the airport. And I guess since we're all from America, and haven't been to Australia before, we all go a bit quiet and look out of the windows. It's funny how different the same things can look. I mean, we have freeways at home, just like the one we're on now, but it looks totally different. The road signs look different, and most of the plants and trees that we drive past look crazy different.

It's even more weird when we turn off the freeway and drive down a normal road. At one point we come to an open area, and there's a half dozen *actual* kangaroos. They're just standing in the open, grazing I suppose. Not fenced in or anything like that. We're all quite excited by that, so Rosie tells the driver to pull over so we can watch for a while. But not for long because she says that Steve's mate who's flying us doesn't want to wait too long.

So then we carry on, and eventually we come to an airfield. It's much smaller than the airport we landed at. And we're allowed to drive right into it, and even right up to one of the planes that's parked there. And it's not a big plane, it's tiny, and it's got propellers, one on each side, so it must be quite old too. Then we get out of the minibus and a man in a beige shirt that's hanging open so that we can see his chest, helps us to load our bags into the hold of the plane, just like it was a bus. He swears when he gets to mine. Then we all climb on board and we can just sit wherever we want. The plane is so small I can touch both sides of the cabin at once.

Then I realize the man in the beige shirt is actually the pilot, since he climbs on too, and sits down in the pilot's seat. I find myself hoping he'll do his shirt up, I don't know why, it just feels like he ought to, before he starts flying us. But he doesn't. He starts talking on the radio to the control tower, saying we're all ready to go, and asking for permission to take off. And I can hear the reply, and it's not a proper reply, they start joking about something, I think it's about a sports game or something that must be happening. Then before I really get a chance to prepare myself for my third ever take-off, and my first in a propeller plane, the motors go ridiculously loud, and we start bumping really fast to the end of the runway.

When we get there, I hope we're going to stop, just for a moment so I can collect myself before we take off, but we don't. The motors go even louder, and suddenly we're going straight down the runway. I can see it out of the front window, and when I look out of the side we're going so fast that the green and red of the plants and earth around us start to blur, and to be honest I start to panic a bit. But then we lift off and start going up. But this time it's not smooth and steady like it was in the Boeing 777 and the Dreamliner before that. This time we're going up much steeper. And from the cockpit the man in the beige shirt lets out a whoop, like he's really enjoying himself.

It's like going up a set of stairs. I feel my head go light, like I'm going to pass out, and I panic that the pilot will too. But then we level off, so abruptly I find myself staring at the pilot for signs of whether he looks relaxed or not. We're high up, but nowhere near as high as in a proper plane, more like as high as a hill. It makes me wonder if something really has gone wrong. But then the pilot turns around.

"We're just gonna buzz up the coast for an hour," he tells us. He has to shout over the noise, but he sounds calm enough. Maybe even too calm. Then he goes on.

"We saw a couple of hammerheads on the way down here. I'm gonna see if I can find 'em again for you." Then he turns back to his controls. And then I see Rosie unstrap herself and pull out a camera with a large zoom lens. Then she really carefully makes her way up to the front and sits in the second pilot seat. It's weird. I was so focused on being scared by the take off I'd forgotten about Rosie. But now I'm thinking about her again.

"This is so cool, isn't it?" I'm surprised when the girl in the seat next to me starts talking. She's the one who was sitting on her own on the back seat of the minibus so I didn't get to shake hands with her earlier. But she's holding out her hand now, pale and slim.

"We never met properly. I'm Debbie."

"Hi Debbie." I say. "I'm Billy."

"I know. So you're still in high school?"

"Yeah."

"Rosie was telling us about you. She said you're amazing. You're already doing loads of experiments and stuff?"

"Really? Well I have done some. I wrote a paper on the feeding habits of *Semicassis Granulata,* but I haven't had it published yet. I think I probably need to do a bit more…"

"Semi what?"

I'm surprised by the interruption. "*Semicassis Granulata.* You know, the sea snail? Some people call them scotch bonnet snails but I think it's better to use the Latin names because people sometimes use that name with completely different species of snail. Don't you think?"

"Yeah, I guess…"

"Well anyway, I established how they exclusively feed on *Fucus Serratus,* which no one knew before. At least I don't think they did." I glance at the girl, suddenly wondering if this is really basic to her. But she screws up her face.

"Fuscus..?"

"*Fucus Serratus*. You know? Toothed wrack?"

Her face still looks blank.

"It's a type of seaweed."

I think for a second. Maybe it doesn't grow where she lives. I don't think they have it in the Pacific at all.

"Did you say you were studying at the University of California?"

She brightens at this. "No. I'm from Boston. But I'm studying down in Florida. At the University of Miami. Marine Science." Suddenly she laughs. "Except I'm not studying that much. Not when I heard how *Steve Rose* was offering a month-long research trip. I totally stopped doing any actual work and spent all my time writing the best application I could. I couldn't believe it when I got picked."

I consider this for a few moments.

"My science teacher applied for me," I tell her. "He said it was one way to get rid of me for a month. I think he was joking though."

Debbie waits a moment, then laughs, like she can't quite work out if *I'm* joking. Then she keeps talking.

"I bet you're like me. I bet you've watched every one of Steve's programs. They're just so amazing. I can't believe we're gonna actually meet him."

I go quiet at this. Because she's right about that. I can't really believe I'm going to meet Steve Rose either. *Dr* Steve Rose. Though obviously the Dr is because he's a PhD, not just an ordinary doctor. He's kind of been a hero of mine for quite a long time. Since I started watching *Shark Bites.* That's his TV program. It has one or two series each year, where he does real actual experiments on board the *Shark Hunter*, and films them so ordinary people can see what actual scientists actually do.

"Yeah." I reply.

Suddenly the note of the motor changes and we roll violently onto our side. I grab the side of the seat in alarm, and looking forward all I can see is the turquoise blue of the ocean, coming straight towards us. I think I'm about to scream out in terror, but then I hear the pilot's voice again.

"There you go," He sounds totally calm. "Couple of mature hammerheads. Just like I promised."

He pulls out of the dive, only a few hundred feet above the surface of the water. I can't even spot them at first, even though I see Rosie clicking away with her camera. But then I see them, a pair of silhouettes of the sharks, swimming slowly near the surface below us, their tails flicking left and right in a lazy pattern.

We circle around them for a few minutes, banked right over. And the others are all really excited, but I'm quite pleased when we leave them behind and carry on, because it means the little airplane levels out, which feels a lot safer.

A few moments later I'm still trying to calm myself from all the drama of the plane diving down to see the sharks.

"Have you ever seen *Charlie and the Chocolate Factory*?"

I turn back to Debbie. "Huh?"

"You know. Willy Wonka. That film where the kids get to go round the chocolate factory. That's what this is like. Like we've all won a golden ticket."

She's not pretty, but she does have a nice smile.

SEVEN

THE AIRFIELD where we land is right next to the water. It's the kind of blue you never get on Lornea Island. The kind of blue you see on travel shows and magazine articles. An impossible turquoise so deep it glows. I can't stop staring at it, thinking how beautiful it looks, even though I'm fairly sure we're about to crash into it. I suppose it might even be a nice way to go. It's only at the last possible moment that the tarmac comes into view underneath us, and we bounce down onto it. Then we get out, in this tiny place with just a shed for the actual airport, and we pile into Rosie's really smart 4x4 and she drives us to the dock where *The Shark Hunter* is tied up. I actually noticed it from the plane, you couldn't miss it.

It is weird though, seeing it for real. It's much bigger than the *Blue Lady*, more like a small ship than a boat. The bow and sides are really high, so it has an actual walkway to get on board. And there's a row of neat portholes running down the side, and then at the back there's a platform that's lower to the water. That's where Steve does a lot of the experiments. There's also a steel shark cage lashed there, and a yellow crane for lifting it in and out the water, and next to that a smart gray inflatable boat with a seventy horsepower motor. I know how the ship is packed with loads of other scientific equipment too because I've seen it on *Shark Bites*. I can't believe it's going to be my home for the next month.

I keep looking, expecting to actually see Steve Rose as well, but then Rosie tells us he's ashore doing some last minute jobs. So we have to help get the ship ready to leave. There's a whole pile of supplies on the dock, and we have to carry them all into the galley. And when we're done with that Rosie takes us to see where we're going to sleep. I have to share a cabin with Jason, which I'm a bit surprised about since it didn't occur to me I might have to share. There's an upstairs and a downstairs bunk, and there's a funny moment when he asks which one I want. I say the bottom one, thinking that he'll want it too, but he says he wanted the top one anyway. I guess he isn't thinking about what happens if the sea is rough, but that's OK, because I'd rather he falls out than I do. So I don't mention this, but quickly unpack my clothes. There's nowhere big enough to put my backpack, so I have to leave it on the bunk. Then we get called to the saloon. I hope we're gonna eat, because I'm hungry by now, but actually it's that Steve's come back.

I see him as soon as I walk into the saloon. He's deep in conversation with another man in a black t-shirt. In a way he's smaller than he looks on TV, even though he's also normal sized, and quite big. I don't know if that makes sense. It's just a bit weird seeing him actually standing there. I don't know who the second man is, but he seems to be good friends with Steve, from the way they're laughing together. I get ready to introduce myself, and the others do too, but for a while it's like Steve hasn't noticed us. Or perhaps he thinks it would be rude to stop talking with the man in the black t-shirt. Then Rosie comes in, and Steve notices her right away.

"Babe! You're back. How'd the pickup go?" He comes over to Rosie and puts his arms around her. I'm pretty surprised by that. Then even more surprised when he slides his hands down her back. His hands come to a rest on her bare skin, where her top doesn't quite meet her jeans.

"No problems." She pushes away from him. "You want me to introduce you to everyone?"

"Mmmmm. Sure." He tries to hold onto her, but she wriggles away. "No wait. Let's catch it. Dan, you wanna get set up? We'll do it as a *walk up*. Make it authentic." I guess the man in the black t-shirt is called Dan, since he nods his head and gets to work opening a black plastic case on the floor of the saloon. He pulls out a big TV camera and starts fiddling with it, while Steve turns back to Rosie.

"I missed you babe." It's like he hasn't noticed us students at all.

"I was only gone a day," Rosie rolls her eyes at him. I find myself hoping she's going to push him away again, but instead she leans in and I'm really quite shocked to see that she kisses him. On the lips and everything.

"I missed you too honey." She says when they finish. And it's like she's joking. Or partly joking at least.

I'm still wondering about that when Dan, the man with the black t-shirt, seems to be ready.

"OK guys," he says to us. "I'm gonna need you to climb off the boat, walk down the dock, turn around, line up all together and then walk toward me in a nice straight line, you reckon you can do that?"

I'm not sure what he means, and I guess I'm not the only one, since none of us move.

"Anytime around now would be good." He laughs at this, even though we don't. And then he beckons us to follow him. So we all walk out of the saloon, right past Steve, who doesn't even look at us, and onto the deck of the ship. Then we walk down the gangway, onto the dock and walk away from the boat.

"That'll do," he shouts from behind us. "Now turn around and line up."

We do what he says. And see him leaning into the camera.

"Tallest two in the middle."

We rearrange ourselves. Then wait for what happens next. He's got the camera on his shoulder now, and he's looking into the eyepiece.

"You couldn't manage a smile could you? Come on girls. This is gonna be your TV debut."

I look across at Debbie, in time to see her fix a smile in place. She looks a bit nervous too.

"OK, now walk towards me, keep in line."

We do what he says, and it feels really awkward knowing that he's filming every step. It's almost like I can't walk properly, but it helps to have the others beside me, and to be concentrating on walking in a line. I don't know what's going to happen when we get to the boat, I'm expecting Dan to shout 'cut' or something, but instead, just as we arrive level with the stern of *Shark Hunter*, Steve jumps down from the deck, not using the gangplank, and opens his arms out wide.

"Guys! So nice of you all to join us!"

And suddenly he's amongst us, shaking hands with me and Jason and hugging the girls. And then he gives us hugs too, as Dan comes in closer with the camera.

And then, a few moments later, Dan does shout 'cut'.

"OK mate," Dan says to Steve. "Let's just do it one more time with the *Hunter* in the background."

So then we have to line up again, just like before, but this time we've got Dan and the camera behind us, filming as we're walking towards the ship. And again, just as we draw level with the stern, Steve leaps down and greets us in exactly the same way. *Exactly* the same.

Then we all go back onboard, and I'm not sure if we've really met Steve at all properly yet. I definitely didn't get to say what I wanted to say, which was to thank him for the opportunity. But I don't get long to think about this, because straight away Steve wants us to get going. So he goes up to the bridge, and starts shouting instructions, and then Rosie and Dan show us how to release the mooring ropes, and coil them up properly, and drop them into the lockers out the way. And as we're doing it I notice that Dan's filming this as well. Twenty minutes later both he and Steve seem happy, and the land is sliding away behind in our wake as we steam out to sea. It's late too, the sun is dipping down over what's left of the land. I'm not sure what to do next, but then we all get called into the saloon again.

I'm still hungry, but now I see Rosie has laid the big table for dinner. There's eight places. The four of us students, and then Dan the cameraman, and also Bob, who's the captain of *Shark Hunter*. I've seen him on the TV show. He always seems really grumpy, and he's always worried about the dangerous things that Steve wants to do for his experiments. Then there's places for Rosie and for Steve too. That's all of us on board.

Rosie tells us to sit, so we all do, and then Steve comes in, carrying a crate of beers, that he throws down on the table. He rips open the plastic and throws one to each of us in turn. I don't really want one, since I don't drink very much, but I don't get a chance to say so, and then since I don't know what else to do with it I open it anyway.

"Now are we ever gonna bloody eat?" he calls out. And then Rosie tells him to shut up, but in a playful way, and then she asks Kerry to help her serve up. And then we've all got big plates of sausage risotto in front of us.

Steve does most of the talking while we're eating.

"Sorry about before," he says. "We have to do our little bit of stage management here on the *Hunter*. It's a pain in the ass, but it's all in a good cause. And you will get used to it. After a while you won't even notice Dan. He'll just blend into the background. Won't you mate?"

Dan doesn't reply but holds his beer up in a toast. It's a kind of mocking thank you.

Then Steve starts talking with Jason and Kerry, who are sitting either side of him. He asks them to tell him about themselves and why they wanted to come on the trip, and the rest of us end up listening. And while I think it's going to be awkward, it isn't actually. Unlike before, when he was being filmed, he's actually listening to what they're saying and then he asks sensible questions afterwards. And he's careful to talk to all of us, and when it gets to my turn he tells me I'm the youngest ever crew member of the *Shark Hunter,* but that he specifically wanted me on board because he'd heard of my ability to find whales off Lornea Island. And I get the sense that the other students are quite impressed that I have my own boat and whale watching business. Even if I am still in high school.

And the dinner is nice too. I'm not at all surprised that Rosie is a good cook.

After we've eaten, Steve divides us up into two watches. We have to work six hours on, six hours off, twice a day. When we're on watch we're completely responsible for the safety of the ship and we have to do exactly what our watch leader tells us. When we're off watch we can do whatever we want, as long as we don't fall off the bloody ship – or that's how Steve put it. He suggests that we sleep, because he says how hard he's going to work us. I get put in a watch with Debbie, and I'm a bit disappointed that Captain Bob is our watch leader, because Rosie is the leader of the other watch, with Kerry and Jason. Steve says that he and Dan will kind of float between both watches.

After that Steve says it's time for dessert, and Rosie brings out some chocolate pudding.

"And I hope you can all cook," Steve says, before we can get started. "Because we all take turns with making the meals, and doing the washing up. And all the other chores too. That's how we work aboard this ship. Like a big family."

The chocolate pudding is really delicious.

We're on the first watch, and Captain Bob explains all the things we have to do while the ship is under way. It's funny, he has such a grumpy reputation on TV, but in actual fact he's not grumpy at all. He's just a bit quieter than Steve, but actually he's really nice. In fact he's really interested in hearing about everything that me and Dad have done with *Blue Lady*, and how he's now helping on the build of

Blue Lady II. And Debbie is nice too, even if she doesn't know much about seaweed.

The place we're going to is called Wellington Island. You've probably heard of it, since it's pretty famous. It's a fur seal colony about two hundred and fifty miles off the coast of Victoria, and it's so well known because every year when the fur seals have their pups, you get lots and lots of sharks, of all different species, coming to prey on them. Steve says it's the largest concentration of sharks on the whole planet. And that's why we're here. We're going to carry out a population survey of the different species of shark to see how many there are, and their ages. Steve has been doing this exact same survey for nearly a decade now, and that means he's gathering really important data on whether shark numbers are increasing or decreasing, so we know if the populations are stable or not. It's also why he needs us students. Our job is to watch out over the water, all the time, to spot the sharks. And then when we see them, to make sure we're accurately recording what size and species we spot. That's why I've been spending so much time watching shark videos on YouTube, so I can tell the difference between a mako and a porbeagle and a bull shark and a tiger shark, just from their dorsal fins. Obviously we don't just have to tell the difference from the surface. We're also going to use aerial and underwater drones. And obviously Steve does a lot of work from in the water, either with the shark cage or without it.

At the same time, Steve is going to record a whole new series of *Shark Bites*, his TV series. So he'll have lots of other experiments for us to do, which will help to show the viewers how real scientists do real science, aboard a proper research ship. Obviously this part isn't quite as important as the actual data gathering role that we're doing. But it will be quite interesting to see how TV works as well. And to actually be on TV of course.

The voyage lasts nearly a whole day, or four watches. I had hoped we'd do some experiments as we went, but in the end we mostly sat around playing cards, and doing what Dan calls 'pieces to camera'. They're basically just little interviews, where we sit at the bow of the ship and he asks us questions and films the answers. I only had to do one, but Debbie and Kerry did two each, and Steve did loads of them, so we didn't see too much of him. I expect he's getting the TV work out of the way before we arrive and he's too busy with the science.

Rosie comes up with the idea of a competition to see who can spot the island first, and our watch wins, although we could actually work that out from the chart plotter, which shows our position and how we're getting closer to the island, and even our estimated arrival time. Anyway it's Debbie who spots it first, which still feels exciting. From a distance there isn't much to it, and even as we draw closer, I'm not sure I'd really call it an island now we're here. It's more like a large flat area of rocks that only rises a few meters above the water. It's uninhabited, by humans at least, and there are no trees or bushes. Not really any plants even, it's pretty much just rocks and seals.

As Bob steers us in close we can get our first proper look. There are seals *everywhere*. Every flat surface is covered in them, the adults brown and fat and basking in the sun, while the pups are a much fluffier gray white color. And the water around the island, where a light swell is rolling onto the rocks, is packed too, with seal heads coming up for air or diving down, or just resting there. The noise is amazing, it sounds a bit like a sports stadium full of people, but where everyone is screaming and squabbling with each other. The smell is worse. A mixture of fish, rotting in the hot sun. And seal poop.

"You get used to it," Steve tells us, about the smell. "I promise in a few days you won't even notice it."

We all look dubious about this, but even Rosie says it's true, and I'd trust her.

"At least they look cute," Kerry says. She points at a pair of pups, who are standing up on their tails and flippers, watching us glide by. "Can we go up to them? On the island itself?"

Steve shakes his head. "Uh huh. We can't land. It's protected. Plus it's generally too dangerous to get on and off with the waves. And if you get too close to a pup, the parents will generally try to kill you." His eyebrows flick up as he says this, and Kerry looks disappointed.

"How many seals are there here?" I ask, as we slide by a little rocky outcrop. We're in the calm water now, in the lee of the island.

"We reckon there's a hundred thousand breeding pairs," Steve says. "Give or take."

"Though we're getting closer to an exact figure," Steve goes on, as we all stand watching the amazing scene. "One of our first jobs will be to carry out an aerial survey. We'll get the drone up, fly over the island, then we'll use artificial intelligence to count them. Anyone want to volunteer for that one?"

I feel a burst of excitement. I do an annual seal survey of the colony on Lornea Island. We have about two hundred breeding pairs of grey seals. I've tracked the population for six years now, and it's increasing a little bit every year. I'm about to tell all this to Steve, when Jason pushes in front of me.

"I'll do it. I'm great at drone flying."

"Alright then." Steve gives him a smile I've seen a few times already. He's impressed by Jason. "We'll get you on that soon as we're anchored up."

Then suddenly a light gust of breeze plays over the deck, and with it a change to the smell, it's sweeter, stickier, but still pretty horrible. Steve's nostrils twitch as he tastes it.

"You smell that?" He says, and we all do.

"That's the smell of death. That's why we're here."

I don't know what he means by that, and he doesn't go on, because by then Bob wants hands to help him with dropping the anchor in the right place. He doesn't need us though, just Steve and Rosie, poring over the screens to make sure they're in the same place as previous years. Eventually there's an almighty rattling as the anchor is released, and then a few moments later, silence – for the first time in twenty four hours, as the motor is stopped. Then a few moments later, Steve calls us all to the stern platform of the ship for a briefing.

He points over to the island.

"You see the neck of this little channel here? Where the water meets the rocks, but where it's not so steep? That's the only place where the seals can get in and out of the water. We call it *death alley*. If they want to feed their pups, they've got to eat, and that means passing through this channel. And as the pups learn to swim, that's their only route too. Now the sharks know that, and the seals know that they know. So this is where it *all* happens. That means we stay here, twenty four hours a day, every day, for the next three weeks. We're witnessing and documenting what we see. And I promise you, it's gonna be quite a show."

He stares at the water for a while, as if there's already something happening, but actually there isn't. It really doesn't look that much now. It's a calm area of water, shaped in a vee and which cuts into the island. At the point of the vee the rocks are lower, but along the sides the rocks are steeper like the rest of the island. We're anchored mid way across the mouth of the vee.

"You're gonna see nature at its rawest and at its meanest. You're going to see some daring escapes. And you're gonna see brutal deaths too, because we've got some big bastards swimming around here and they are *hungry*. But we're not here to be sentimental. We're here to get an accurate count. I cannot stress how important that is. The validity of our data depends upon accurate observations. We need accurate species identification. You see a shark – and you'll see plenty – I need to know what species it is, I need to know if it's alone or in a group, and I need to know how old it is." He stops.

"Anyone. How do we tell how old a shark is?"

Kerry's first to answer, which annoys me, since I know too.

"Length. We have to estimate the length."

"That's right. Now apart from swimming up to it and holding out a tape measure, who can tell me how we go about estimating the length of a large, dangerous shark?"

All the hands go up now, because he's talking about Chumley. Steve grins. Everyone knows about Chumley. We've all been wondering where it was hiding.

"That's right. Our old friend Chumley. Our life-size cardboard cut-out of a white shark. Only he's not made of cardboard because he'd go a bit soggy in the water if he was. No, he's made out of finest marine grade hardwood. Chumley goes in the water, anchored front and rear in front of a camera buoy, and then we'll be able to use the measurements marked onto him to get an idea of the size of the sharks as they swim past. It might sound a little rough and ready. But it does the job."

Then Dan interrupts him.

"And it looks good on TV."

Everyone laughs at this.

"We're also going to have underwater and aerial drones, and we'll get you all involved in those. But the core task. The main reason you're here, is to scan the water, keep a close eye on the sonar, spot those sharks early so we can get the monitoring equipment in the right spot."

We all know this. It's all we've been talking about, since we got on board, and now it's actually happening, it's really exciting.

"Any questions?"

There's a pause. I think we're all just itching to get started.

"None. Good. In that case I'm gonna take a swim before we get down to it. Anyone want to join me?"

And with that Steve pulls off his t-shirt. I think he's joking, and I think everyone else does too. Except Dan maybe, who's already got his camera up and pointed at Steve. And the next thing, Steve raises his arms above his head, and then he does this real elegant swan dive right into the water.

He's a bit crazy is Steve.

EIGHT

We all watch the water where he dived, which is just a mass of bubbles, and I can't be the only one that's worried we're going to see a flush of red appear in the water, as he's eaten by a shark. But actually nothing happens. The bubbles slow and then stop completely, and Steve doesn't even surface. We all glance at each other, getting more and more concerned but not knowing what to do. But at the same time I sense Dan's camera pointed at us now.

Jason and Kerry are nearest to where he jumped, and they peer over the side of the ship. I see Jason fiddling with his t-shirt, like he's thinking about pulling it off, to dive in too, and try to save Steve I suppose, but he's not sure and to be honest I don't blame him.

Eventually he does rip it off, and Kerry takes her t-shirt off too, but they look down into the water for any clue for where they should jump to find him. Someone – I don't know who – asks whether he might have hit his head on the bottom. But then suddenly there's a roar of laughter from the other side of the ship, and when I turn I see Steve there, treading water and laughing.

"Come on you pussies. You're not afraid of a few fish are you?" Then he climbs out the water, and shakes himself on the deck. He picks up a towel and rubs his head.

"OK kids. How about we put the cage in? You can take a swim in there? Get used to the water gradually?"

So then we prepare the shark cage. First we unstrap it, from where it's been secured for the voyage, and then we hook it to the top of the crane, and finally we winch it out over the water, then down. It's about the size of an elevator, and it's got floats at the top, so that it hangs suspended just under the surface. There's a hatch at the top, where you climb in and out. Soon we have it hanging down off the back of the boat, bumping up gently against the stern on fenders. Then Steve tells us to get in there. So I have to go and find my swimming shorts.

By the time I'm back Jason is already in there, and Debbie joins him. I watch as she climbs over the bars on the top of the cage, dressed only in a red swimsuit, and then lowers herself into the water through the hatch. She screams out at the temperature, even though it's not cold here. Not compared to Lornea Island at least.

Then Rosie comes out. She's wearing a yellow bikini with red flowers on it. I've not seen her in a bikini before, and even though I'm trying not to look, I can't help but see she has a prominent curved scar across her tummy. It's about the size and shape of a football. And it's pretty obvious what must have caused it.

"Eyes off my woman Billy," Steve says suddenly.

I jerk my head around, panicked that I've been caught staring at Rosie.

"I wasn't…" I begin, but I see that Steve is smiling really broadly, so he must still be kidding me around.

"She gets a bit self conscious about it," he goes on. "But she must feel relaxed with you lot. Sometimes she won't strip off the whole trip."

I frown. I don't understand, and she gives him a sweet smile.

"It's hot," she says. They stare at each other. I can see it means something but I can't tell what.

"Well come on then," Steve says in the end. "Are you gonna tell 'em the story or shall I?"

Rosie's hand goes to the scar, and her fingers follow its raised lip, but she doesn't speak.

"It's a love bite," Steve says. "From a striped tiger. That's how we met, I was working nearby and ended up interviewing her to get details of the shark. She was so bowled over by my considerate and caring approach she moved in with me."

Rosie rolls her eyes.

"What happened?" Kerry asks. "With the actual shark I mean?"

Slowly Rosie pulls her hand away. She starts tying up her hair.

"I was just swimming. Off the beach in Aswell Bay. I wasn't even that far out, and I was heading back to the shore, when I saw this flash of silver or blue, and the next thing it was like I was punched in the stomach. It didn't really hurt, I actually thought it was my friends playing a joke on me, but when I put my hands down I saw they were covered in blood."

She finishes tying her hair and shrugs. "I managed to get out onto the beach, and then I passed out. And when I came to Steve was there. He hasn't left me alone since."

I watch – a bit more carefully this time – as Rosie steps out onto the cage after Debbie. She seems to know where to put her feet better, and she lowers herself into the water with no sound. And then it's my turn. But before I climb off the boat, Steve calls out, and when I turn to look he throws me a diving mask. I only just catch it, which is lucky because it's a good quality one, with real glass. Steve tosses masks to the people in the cage as well, and I fit mine in place. Then I climb over the railings of the ship, and lower myself carefully down onto the roof of the cage. It feels weird, a little bit exposed, as though a shark might jump out of the water and snatch me before I can get inside the bars where it's safe. Then I get to the hatch, where the others are swimming, and jostling around.

"Come on Billy, it's lovely and warm," Rosie says to me. Her hair is slicked back over her forehead, and she's putting her mask on. I sit down on the edge of the hatch and let my feet swing back and forth in the water. Then I take a deep breath and plunge in.

At first I can't help feeling a bit panicky. It's not the sharks so much as the sensation of being surrounded by bars on all sides. Underwater they look magnified, and inside the cage there's a tangle of limbs and the bodies of the other swimmers, so that it feels like being caught in a net. So I fight my way back to the surface and take a breath. From here you can see the side of the ship, and it kind of reminds you how we're in the ocean now, and in an ocean known to be full of very dangerous sharks. Again I have to fight back the panic. But after a few moments I realize we're quite safe inside the cage, and I dive down to look underwater.

You can hold onto the bars, which makes it easy, and I do so, looking through them and out into the blue water. Looking horizontally it's beautiful. Shafts of light are glittering through the water, as the sun's rays are refracted and penetrate the surface. Down below though the blue quickly turns darker, and right below us it's almost black. But as my eyes adjust I can see the bottom is actually in sight, maybe thirty or thirty five meters down. A bed of rocks, long snaking seaweeds waving up at me. I look around, there's loads of shadows, but I can't see anything that's definitely a shark.

When I come back to the surface I see I've missed something. Steve is pulling on diving flippers. At first I assume he's joking again, but then I notice Dan is setting up to film him.

"Anything about?" He asks. And it's Rosie who answers.

"Nothing I can see. But please be careful."

With that Steve looks to Dan, who gives a thumbs up signal. And then Steve fixes his mask in place. He stares at the water below him for a long while, then rolls forward. He hits the water with his hands protecting his face.

Then he surfaces, and swims closer to the cage. We're all still inside it, and Steve's outside, and I can tell I'm not the only one looking past him, and kind of expecting to see a fin arcing through the surface of the water. It feels weird, knowing *I'm* safe, but that I might see him get eaten. And then Steve slips down under the water and out of sight, and I almost panic, because it looks like he's been sucked under, a bit like a fish sometimes just gently pulls on some bait and eats it without making much fuss. But then I remember I can look underwater myself, so I refit my mask, and I sink down.

I've got this real irrational fear that I'm going to see him being torn apart by a pack of sharks – but of course I don't. But what I do see is pretty crazy anyway.

He's swimming underneath the ship, checking out the propeller and the rudder. And then he pivots in his own length and he starts swimming straight down.

He's not wearing any kind of scuba gear, just his mask and his over-sized flippers. But he doesn't seem to need air. It's like he can breathe underwater. I have to pull my head up to breathe, several times, while he's underwater, just to keep watching him. And I'm quite good at holding my breath these days. One time I lose him, but then I see he's right the way down at the bottom now. He looks in a few of the darker places, and I can see now that they're caves under the water. A couple of times we see a white flash as he looks up at us, and the light catches his face.

In the end I have to take three breaths before he starts to come back toward the surface, flexing his flippers really casually, as though he's in no hurry. Then when he surfaces he's just very quiet for a few breaths.

"Anything?" Dan asks, after a while.

Steve shakes his head. "Couple of seals. Didn't see anything toothier." Steve replies. "Looks pretty though. Gimme the water housing and I'll get some shots looking up."

So then he goes down again, this time with a video camera locked into a waterproof housing, I get out of the cage and dry myself off.

"Don't try that at home." Rosie interrupts me.

"Sorry?"

"Free-diving in shark infested waters. Steve's a national champion. He won the Aussie free diving championships two years running." She wraps a towel around herself so that her scar is covered.

"And he's a crazy lunatic very probably with a death wish."

She smiles at me, to say how she's joking.

NINE

I GET to help tow Chumley out into position, using the inflatable boat. We anchor it at the mouth of death alley, a couple of meters under the surface of the water at high tide. Then we set up the camera buoy about ten meters in front. It has a solar panel that transmits video footage of the cut-out shark back to the boat. The idea is that when real live sharks swim in front of or behind Chumley, we can measure them against the scale that's marked on it. I've always been quite dubious about how accurate it is, but Steve tells us they've tried lots of different systems, and this is the best anyone's come up with. It's even become the standard, with other scientists copying the technique.

It's quite scary being out there in an inflatable boat though. It has double thickness rubber, but Steve says it still wouldn't survive a proper attack by a big shark. Just as we finished I asked Steve why he didn't have a stronger boat, but he laughed and said it didn't matter because no small boat would survive a proper attack by a big shark. And right after that Dan said we had to go and pretend to anchor Chumley all over again, because he wanted to film it from the air this time.

Back on the ship we stay in our watches and begin monitoring. I spot a few fins, mostly of bull sharks and a couple of makos, and there's a couple of moments of excitement when sharks swim past Chumley, and we get to measure them off. But none of them seem to be eating anything. So even though we start off being super alert to every tiny splash in the water, after a couple of watches where nothing happens we all get a bit bored.

"They're biding their time," Steve explains it to me, a couple of days later. I'm sitting on the observation deck with the rest of my watch and he's kind of sneaked up on us. He seems to do that all the time, just appear out of nowhere. We've not seen too much of him actually, since he's been busy with some TV stuff, and the seal survey.

"The seal pups are still being nursed, fed milk by their mothers, so they don't need to get into the water yet." Steve picks up my binoculars and puts them to his eyes. He looks around for a few moments then drops them again. "The adult seals are cautious, good swimmers, they're hard to catch. So it's not worth the sharks using up energy. But soon the pups will have to go into the water. To learn to swim and to fish. That's when it all kicks off.

No one answers him. And he doesn't really need to say it, because we all know. It's what we're all waiting to see. But I think we're all kind of dreading it too. Hoping it won't happen this year.

"What are you most hoping to see?" Steve turns to me, but then he puts the binoculars back up to his eyes. And I'm not quite sure what he means.

"I think I'm most interested in how the science is actually done," I say. "Seeing it firsthand I mean."

"Uh huh?" He sounds a bit bored by my answer. "I meant what species are you looking forward to seeing? What *excites* you?" He goes on scanning the calm water of death alley.

"Oh," I say. And for a moment I can't think of an answer, so Debbie gets in before me.

"I want to see a great white."

Steve doesn't drop the binoculars, but seems to tighten his grip on them.

"Yeah," he says after a few seconds. "Me too."

Suddenly he starts speaking again. "You know the mechanical shark they built for *Jaws*? The movie? You know they could hardly use it because it broke down so much. They had to come up with all these creative ways to suggest there was this monster shark without actually showing it. And by not actually showing it the movie ended up much more suspenseful than it would otherwise have been?"

No one answers this, but he doesn't seem to mind.

"Turned it from being just another piece of Hollywood trash into a worldwide phenomenon. And it's never been the same since. Nowadays, the whole goddamn world knows what a white shark is. And half the world is terrified to go into the water, case they get eaten by one." He's still scanning the water as he talks.

"You know how many people each year get killed by sharks? All sharks I mean. As opposed to, say, *cows*?"

No one knows which of us he's speaking to, but Debbie answers. "It's about ten isn't it?"

He clicks his tongue in irritation. "Not quite. The average is six. Yet *twenty two* people are killed by cows. Not counting the millions who die from heart disease from all those Big Macs." Then he drops the glasses and smiles, a bit ironically. "And how many sharks do you think are killed by humans?"

I answer this one. "It's about thirty two million."

Steve looks right at me.

"Yeah. It is. Or about that." he says. "Some estimates run even higher. Killed for their fins, for sport, or just caught as by-catch in nets. Either way, we're many orders of magnitude more dangerous to them, than they are to us."

He stops talking and scans the ocean with the binoculars again.

"Everyone loves to hate the great white…" He drops the glasses again.

We're all silent for a while.

"You know what's really ironic though?" He goes on. "Even considering how famous white sharks are, we still know shit all about them. Relatively speaking. Even us scientists. Take this place for example. I've been coming here every year for a decade, and it's always the same. We see the odd bull shark, the odd mako, but no white sharks. Not a sniff. Not until the pups go in the water. But the very moment they do – like to the *hour* – the whites are here. It's like they can tell *exactly* when to turn up. I don't know how they do it. But they do. Every year."

He turns back to Debbie.

"So you'll see your white shark. And when you do…" He hands the binoculars back. "It's gonna be quite a show."

And with that he wanders away.

TEN

For the next two days I work six hours on, six hours off. I record everything that happens in the log book. I spot our first blue shark, and even get to measure it using Chumley. But apart from that not much happens. I end up helping Jason with the seal survey, and I help Rosie make dinner when it's her turn, because she's supposed to do it with Steve but he's too busy. That's because he's always tinkering with the shark cage, or some of the other equipment, or filming pieces to camera with Dan. When we're off watch we play a lot of cards.

"Rock, paper, scissors to see who makes the coffee."

That's Steve again. It's about ten o'clock in the morning, on our fourth day at the island. It's my watch and so far it's been a quiet morning.

"Come on. Everyone. We'll have two rounds, and then a final. Whoever wins makes the coffee."

Steve likes this, doing sudden games. I think it's to keep us interested, because otherwise all this waiting around would be boring. My first round is with Kerry, and I win that, so then I have to play Rosie in the final. I'm a bit distracted by her warm eyes on me while I decide whether to go with scissors or paper. I make a late decision to use scissors, and it means I win again. Or lose, depending on how you look at it.

"Yee ha! We have a winner!" Steve shouts. "Congratulations Billy, you get to make six cups of coffee!" So then I have to go inside and busy myself with the coffee machine. I don't mind. I wouldn't have minded if he'd just told me to make it. The truth is, even though there isn't much happening, I'm feeling really happy just to be here. I can't really say it, not to Jason or Kerry at least, because they're doing their best to pretend this is all something really normal to them, but I've never done anything like this and it's awesome. Everyone is really nice, and smart, so that I feel I'm learning, all the time, wherever I am on the ship and whoever I'm talking to. It's like the total opposite of school. I hope this is what college is like, but I kinda doubt it. I think this is just something special.

When I come out again, they're still playing silly games. I-Spy this time. But a kind of silly, ironic version. I hand out the coffee and do my routine scan of Chumley, and around the ship with the binoculars. I check the clipboard to see if anything has been added to the sightings since I went in.

"I spy…" Rosie begins, "with my little eye, something beginning with 'S'."

"Is it *ship*?" Kerry asks.

"Nope."

"Sea?"

"No."

"Seal?"

"*No*," Rosie replies, but from the way she starts giggling, we all know that it was really.

"Is it Billy's scissors?" Kerry starts laughing now. "Billy's invisible…"

"*Shark*."

There's something immediately different about Steve's voice. He's not playing nor joking, and we all turn to where he's pointing. About fifty yards from the boat there's a slight disturbance in the water. I didn't really have enough time to see it, but I can tell it's where a dorsal fin has just disappeared.

"Did you see what it was?" Someone asks. I don't catch who, I'm too busy getting the binoculars trained on it.

"Uh huh. Just saw the fin go under." Steve replies. He looks at the island. Reaches for his binoculars. "Well, well, well."

"What?" That's Rosie talking. She's looking where Steve is pointing. At the island now. It's a bit hard to see because the sun is in my eyes.

"There. Just at the edge of the water. It's one of the pups, it's going in."

"I got it," she says. I squint, and she moves closer to me. So I can look down the length of her arm.

"*There.*"

Then I see what she's looking at. The seal pups have been rapidly losing their gray-white fur, and instead taking on the blubbery appearance of the adults, but they're still much smaller. I see a couple more flop into the water now. They make more splash than the adults.

"*Shark!*" This time it's Captain Bob. He's standing on the flying bridge, which is the highest part of the ship.

In an instant Steve is up there with him. The whole atmosphere is totally different now.

"Where?"

"Off our port side. A hundred feet out. Coming straight towards us."

Rosie and I go to the other side of the ship. I can see something but it's hard to tell what. It looks like someone is pulling a piece of lead pipe through the water. You can see a little bit of white foam where it breaks the surface. Then it sinks down, and we can't see it again. Steve freezes.

"What was it? Did anyone see?" Someone asks. It takes me a while to realize it's Kerry. She's asking because it's their watch, and she's supposed to note down sightings as they happen. That way nothing gets missed. But no one replies to her.

"Did anyone see? Shall I put it down as another unknown?"

"No," Steve says. Put it down as *Carcharodon carcharias*."

At once I feel the hairs on the back of my neck stand up. Rosie freezes too, when she hears the name, and when no one else reacts, our eyes lock together.

"What's that?" Kerry asks.

"*Carcharodon carcharias*." Steve says again. "The most famous fish in the sea." He smiles at me.

"I don't know what that is." Kerry complains. I see Jason frowning too. So I have to tell them.

"It's the Latin name. *Carcharodon carcharias*. It means *Crooked-Tooth Shark*.

"Yeah but what is it?" Kerry asks, frustrated now. So I tell her."

"It's a Great White."

Then the fin comes up again, at a slight angle this time, so we can all see exactly what it is.

"Dan? You filming this?"

"Yes boss."

"Good." Then Steve calls out. "Let's get the drone up, shall we?"

Moments later we're all gathered around the screen while Steve flies the drone low over the silhouette of a large shark, lazily working its tail back and forth. We can see so much more from the air. It cruises by our stern twenty feet away, and even without the drone we can see the shadow of it under the water.

The shark doesn't notice us, nor the drone at all. Or if it does, it doesn't care. It's just cruising towards the vee of death alley. It doesn't seem to be in a hurry.

"Right on time. Just like every year." Steve says. He hands the controller to Jason.

"Keep on it Jason. There's some seals in the water just ahead. See if you can zoom out and get them in the shot too." Jason does what he says, so then we see the shark on the screen, and a little way in front of it, a single adult fur seal swimming back to the island. The shark seems to notice it, and speeds up just a touch. I realize we're all holding our breaths.

"Poor thing doesn't have any idea it's there." Rosie murmurs, but I don't think anyone but me hears her.

The seal swims quite close to the shark, but then it casually banks right, and it moves out of shot. The shark cruises on, again it doesn't look like it cares. But it does seem to be going somewhere. It's moving casually to where the baby seals are, at the head of death alley.

"Oh god," Rosie goes on. "I really do hate this bit."

"Pan the camera up a bit." Steve directs. He's got one eye on what Jason is doing, and another on the scene, and he keeps taking sightings with the binoculars too. He sounds totally calm and focused.

Jason pans up with the camera again, so now we can see three baby seals following each other in a circle. They're playing, a bit like puppies do, chasing each other around and around. They're actually really cute, the seal pups, even now they've lost their baby fur, they still have oversized flippers and really big eyes, and they move in a kind of ungainly way.

"Come on. Get out of the water. Just get out," Kerry says.

Then the first of the pups darts into shallow water and the rest follow, and for a few moments it looks like they're going to be safe, because surely the shark won't be able to follow them. But then it changes direction, and jets out away from the rocks directly towards the shark. The others follow, and suddenly all three are in the frame with the shark again. They turn, and begin playing their game of tag again. We all hold our breath.

Then one of the pups breaks off. I guess it's coming to the surface to breathe. The shark moves its head, just a tiny bit. But then, in a horrible instant, everything happens at once. The seal goes to dive again, but as it does the shark suddenly massively accelerates. The first we see of it is the great tail surging from side to side, and then in a split second it's closed the distance to the seal pup. And it's just *gone*. The greeny-blue of the water in the frame begins to fill with a cloud of red. Then beyond the blood we see the head of the seal caught on one side of the shark's mouth, and its tail emerging from the other side. Then the shark shakes its head, and then there's just a piece of the seal's tail left. Then the shark angles away. Jason keeps the drone camera pointing at the red water, and the very back of the tail sinks down out of view.

There's silence on the boat. Apart from Steve, who whistles.

"OK gang. Make a note of the time and location. I got a look as it came past the stern of the boat. We're ten foot wide and there was a good foot hanging out either side. So that makes it a twelve foot white shark. And I don't think it's going to be the last. Things are going to get busy from now on."

And they do. From that moment on we see an average of one attack per hour. Weirdly they seem to follow our mealtimes, with most happening in the morning and the evening, and then a smaller peak at lunchtime. The white sharks do most of the killing, and the other species come in to scavenge on the bits of seal left over. We're kept really busy recording all the attacks and trying to work out which species it is, and where we can, which individual sharks are attacking. I start to realize the real benefit of Chumley. We have the drone, and also a remote controlled underwater vehicle, but the first has a very limited battery time, and the second is very slow. So it's hard to get them in position in time. But most of the sharks have to swim past Chumley to get into or out of Death Alley, so it gives us two definite chances to confirm the species and check their size. Steve's right, it's a really good system.

But even while we're busy, I can't help but feel a bit confused about what Steve's doing. He's even busier now that the sharks are attacking, but most of the time he isn't helping us with the survey, or doing any science really. Instead he's doing even more of the TV stuff. I kind of got the impression earlier that he had to get the filming out of the way before everything kicked off. But now that it has, I don't really understand why he's still doing it.

This afternoon for example, he had Dan film him going down in the shark cage. There weren't any sharks nearby, they were too busy eating seals, and when I asked Dan about it he told me not to worry because he was going to edit in some footage he'd taken earlier from one of the camera buoys. To make it look more real. That wasn't my point at all. And when I tried to explain, and ask what was the scientific purpose of it he said he didn't have time to go over it.

I asked Rosie about it, and she told me I shouldn't worry, but that if I want she'll get Steve to sit down with me and explain how it all works. But I tell her not to, because he's obviously busy, and I don't want to look naive. We agree that the important thing is I concentrate on doing the jobs I've been given to do. So that's what I do.

I already told you about the clipboards. We keep them on the observation deck, tied on with lanyards and loaded with special waterproof paper and a wax pencil on a piece of string. We use these to record sightings and attacks as we see them happen, with as much detail as we can, so that we don't miss anything when it gets busy. And then, when we have quieter moments, it's my job to compile all the data into Steve's laptop. He has an Excel spreadsheet, where he's recorded the raw data like this for all the sharks they've seen over the last ten years. I'm only updating this year, but I've discovered you can look back at the earlier years. And it's very tempting to compare the data.

The only problem is, you can't compare it very easily. It's the way Steve has laid out his spreadsheet. He's put each year in a separate sheet, so you can't easily see them side by side. But it wouldn't be too much work to put all the years into one sheet and use pivot tables, and then you'd be able to analyze the data easily. You could see how many of each shark was seen each year, and in more detail too – for example you could look at how many male blue sharks were over three meters long. Or how many females had a successful attack at dusk. I think this would be really useful, so I decide to ask Steve if he minds me changing the sheet. I'll tell him how I can save his version first, just in case something goes wrong – even though it won't. But whenever I try to talk to him he's busy doing something with Dan. So in the end I decide to use my initiative and take that as a yes.

And that's when I start to see something odd in the numbers.

ELEVEN

The sharks don't attack at night, except when there's a very clear moon. Steve thinks it's because they simply can't see the seals. So it's dark when I knock on the door of Steve's cabin.

"Yeah," he calls out.

I hesitate, because I'm not 100% sure of what I have to tell him. So he calls out again.

"What is it?" He shouts out now.

I open the door, to see him sitting at his desk typing into his computer. It's the only light on in his cabin, and it's casting a glow onto his face. He glances up, sees it's me, then looks back at the keyboard.

"Billy. What can I do you for?" He starts typing again. Using just two fingers.

"Erm…" I begin. "I think I've noticed something odd. A problem maybe."

"Uh huh?" he's still typing. "Are we sinking?"

"No. At least… no. It's…"

"Run out of beer?"

"No."

"We're on fire?"

"No…"

"Good. So it's nothing super urgent?" He hits a couple more keys, then looks up. "Huh?" He peers over the top of his work glasses. "It's just I'm kinda busy here."

"Oh." I say. I wonder if maybe I shouldn't be wasting his time.

"You know, actually doing *proper scientific work.* For once." He smiles suddenly. And I guess I must look confused, because then he goes on.

"Rosie mentioned how you had some questions. About how it all works."

"How what works?"

"How *it* works. The whole thing. This whole deal." He sweeps his arm around the cabin, but I still don't understand.

"Look you wanna come in? I need a break anyway. I'm trying to get this paper finished. It's looking at how reef sharks adapt their attack habits as they grow older. They're like Spielberg's velociraptors. They *learn*…"

I don't understand what he's talking about, and I guess that shows on my face too.

"Jurassic Park? The movie? Tell me you've seen that one?"

"I think my dad's watched it."

"Jesus you kids make me feel old. Well never mind. Get your butt in here. We need to talk."

So I walk into his cabin, and then there's nowhere obvious to sit, except on his bed. And I feel a bit uncomfortable sitting there, because I know that Rosie sleeps in here too.

"You wanna beer?"

I shake my head, but he goes to the little fridge anyway, and gets one for himself.

"So. Billy. Young idealistic Billy. The lovely Rosie tells me you have concerns about whether I'm devoting too little time to pure scientific research, because I'm always playing around making cheap trash TV?" He bursts open the beer and takes a swig.

"Well…" I begin. "No…"

"Because I was too. When I first got into this game." He stops, and looks at me for a long time, so I don't remember what I was going to say. It doesn't matter, since I don't get the chance.

"You sent me a paper. Or your high school science teacher did, on your behalf. On the feeding habits of *Semicassis Granulata,* the scotch bonnet snail. How it feeds exclusively on just one type of seaweed. I read it. I don't think it's quite ready for publication, but it's got promise. And the thing that excited me most, was how no one before had even found a *Granulata* in the Atlantic. They're Pacific snails. At least I thought they were, until you came along, and showed me otherwise. But the problem is…" He stops and rolls his shoulders around, like he's stiff from being hunched up in front of his computer screen too long.

"The problem is nobody gives a damn. About snails I mean. Or seaweed. Or anemones. Or about just about anything that lives in the sea. Unless that is, it eats *us,* or at a pinch, if we eat *it*. The consequence of this is we know almost nothing about ninety-nine percent of what lives in the oceans. And even then, the one percent we do know about… Like our old friend *Carcharodon carcharias,* we don't know much more about them."

He takes another swig of beer.

"And you know why?

I think about this quickly, so I can answer before he tells me.

"Because they're hard to study?"

He glances up. Surprised, then shakes his head. "No. No they're not *that* hard to study Billy. Not with all the technology we have at our disposal. The problem is they're *expensive* to study. No one wants to pay for it. So we have to do what everyone has to do if they want a career in this game. We make a pact. A little deal with the devil."

He stares at me again, and I feel a bit uncomfortable with his wide blue eyes staring into mine.

"This entire trip is funded by our income from six episodes of a television program. Me, you, none of us would be here without it. The science is just an add on. Sure for guys like you – and for me I might add – it's anything but. But it simply wouldn't happen if it wasn't for the TV cash. So if we don't treat the TV side of things seriously, the science disappears.

I try to consider what he's saying. I get it, but it's hard.

"What about universities?" I ask, but he kind of ignores me.

"You know there is nothing inherently special about the shark Billy, but it does capture the public attention in a way that very few other creatures do. And it's my job to use that. Our job. To harness that interest, and to use it to drive forward the sum of knowledge of all the other species that would otherwise be ignored." He takes another big swig from his beer can.

"And that is why, during the daytime, I'm a ridiculous caricature of a scientist, jumping in and out of that ludicrous shark cage and hamming up the danger in order to drive our ratings. And it's also why, at night I stay up till the small hours doing my real work. Do you understand Billy?"

I don't answer at first, because I don't want to sound rude.

"Yeah, I kind of understood that already." I say in the end. "But it isn't why I came to see you."

Steve looks confused by this. He doesn't move for a long while.

"Oh." He says in the end. Then he takes a deep breath. "OK Billy. So why *did* you come to see me?"

Then I take a deep breath too, because what I have to say is really hard.

"Well, this is going to sound a bit odd. But I've noticed a problem in your data."

He frowns.

"What problem Billy?"

"Well it's a bit weird really…"

"Go on." He kind of makes himself smile, even though he maybe doesn't want to. "I like weird."

"OK. It's just I noticed how all your sharks got bigger by ten percent four years ago."

"What?"

"Well actually it's 9.8% but that's just an average obviously, and I rounded it up…"

"What did you say?"

I pull out the print out I made earlier. The boat has one computer terminal with a printer attached, and Captain Bob let me use it.

"Here. I thought there must be a problem with the formulas in the Excel sheet, but I went through the whole spreadsheet checking them, and they all seem OK, so I can't work out *where* the error is coming from..."

"There is no error Billy."

"...Because it doesn't make sense that you'd get this *uniform growth* in all the sharks. It just wouldn't make..."

"There is no error Billy," Steve cuts in, his voice suddenly hard. I stop talking.

"Of course it makes sense," he says. "You're not thinking."

I look at him now, I mean really look at him. His whole demeanour has changed. It's suddenly like he's earnest and *serious*. It's almost like he's talking to me as if I were a *scientist* too. It makes me feel nervous, but in a good way. But it doesn't help me think of anything sensible to reply.

"Think about it. Were you the same size two years ago as you are today? Or were you maybe a bit smaller?"

I frown. I don't understand what he's getting at.

"I'm not *much* bigger."

"But a bit bigger, yeah?"

I shrug. "Yeah." I don't see how this is relevant.

"They're *growing* Billy. That's why they're bigger."

I stare at him, like he's joking, because it's obviously not *that*. "They can't be. I mean, obviously some are, but not the *entire population of sharks*. The younger ones sure, but adults will already be full size. Adult size."

"Billy, sharks don't have an adult size. I thought you'd know that."

"Well..." Suddenly I can't believe I've been so stupid. "Don't they?"

"No. They don't. Come on Billy, this is basic stuff. Sharks – like most fish – they don't stop growing. The older they are, the bigger they get, allowing for differences in diet and sex. It's the whole reason we can use their size to age them so accurately." He seems to relax now, and he rasps his hand across the stubble on his chin. Meanwhile I feel my face begin to burn hot.

"Well yeah, I mean I know they'll still grow a bit every year, but they still do *most* of their growing when they're..."

"No 'buts' Billy." Steve cuts me off. "That's just the way it is."

I try to assimilate what he's saying into how I understood the problem. It kind of makes sense, but somehow it doesn't quite fit.

"But if it's just that *all* the sharks are growing, why would we only see it in the data four years ago? Wouldn't we see it every year?"

Steve shrugs again. But then he sighs. "OK, that does sound a little odd, when you put it like that. But you also have to remember we're only getting a *very small* sample size here. It's quite possible that the sharks we happened to see before that year were smaller, and the ones we happened to see afterward were larger. Wouldn't that explain it?"

I frown again, trying to keep up. "Well I guess… I guess we could run a statistical analysis to see if…"

"There's not enough data for that!" Steve takes the print-out from me suddenly, and studies it for a moment, all the time still rasping his chin.

"Look I tell you what, I reckon this could just be my clunky old database. Sometimes you get a little gremlin in the data. And I'm pretty sure I remember that *was* a good year for shark growth. But let me have a look at it? I'll figure out what's going on here." He doesn't give the paper back, instead he puts it down on top of his own papers, by the side of his laptop. Then he smiles at me.

"And while we're here chatting, how about we give you a turn flying the drone tomorrow? I've noticed how Jason's kinda taken over. I'm sure you'd like a bit of drone flying huh?"

I think about this. It's true, Jason has been hogging the drone, even though I'm a good drone pilot too. But I don't really mind, I have a drone at home anyway.

"Or if you prefer," Steve says suddenly. "That offer of a swim still stands." He grins. "I'm not kidding either. I'll take you out for a dive, any time you like. I promise you, getting in the water with those creatures, unprotected. It's like nothing else. And it's safe enough, while they're concentrating on the seal pups." He raises his eyebrows, actually waiting for an answer.

"Erm. I'll think about it," I say.

"Do that. But don't think too long." He points at me, and then he turns his hand over like he's squeezing something. "Sometimes you've gotta stop thinking and just grab life by the balls." He grins again. "You know what I mean?"

I nod.

"OK. Well I better get back to this paper. The science isn't gonna do itself." He waits until I take the hint and get up to leave.

And – still not really understanding what just happened – that's what I do, closing his cabin door behind me.

TWELVE

It's late by then, but I don't feel like sleeping, so I take a walk around the ship's deck. I can't go far, since it's not that big, but it's a nice starry night, and much cooler than in the day. I end up doing two laps before I have an idea of what I need to do. Even though it feels kind of crazy.

After that I go and check the store room. I figure I might as well get what I need when most of the crew are asleep. The store room isn't really a room, more a kind of large closet, but it still has almost everything you could need for measuring and weighing and experimenting, plus a good set of tools for fixing things that go wrong. But even after a long search I can't find what I'm looking for, which is kind of odd.

So then I go and ask Captain Bob, who's still up in the bridge, and he tells me there's a box of odds and ends under the companionway steps, and I'll probably find one in there. So I go and pull that out and search through it. And it's full of bits of old radios, and slightly rusty tools, and a compass that's had paint spilled on it, so you can't read the bearing very easily. But I still can't find what I'm looking for. So eventually I head back to my bunk, and go to sleep. I figure I'll work it out in the morning.

And when I wake up, I have an idea.

"Debbie," I ask, when we're both quite slow finishing breakfast. There's just the two of us there. "How tall are you?"

"What?"

"It's just obviously I couldn't help notice you were quite short, so I thought you might know your height. You know, *accurately*."

"*What?* What the hell is that to you?"

"Oh I don't mean it in a rude way. I mean I'm really short too, but I don't know how short, or at least, not *exactly,* because I keep growing. So I wondered if you did. Know, I mean?"

Debbie stares at me in a way that's not very polite, frankly.

"Do you know?" I try again.

"Yes!"

"Well, would you mind telling me?"

She gets up from the saloon table and picks up her breakfast things to take them back into the galley. I think she's not going to reply at all.

"You'll have to tell me why."

"Oh. OK, sure." I get my own bowl and follow her to the sink. "Well it's a bit weird," I say. "But I need to check something with a tape measure, only I can't find one anywhere on the whole boat. Don't you think that's odd?"

Debbie screws her face up, confused. "Why would that be odd?"

"I don't know. Just, we've got pretty much every piece of equipment you could imagine on board. And yet we don't have a tape measure. I thought it was odd."

"Well. Maybe there was one, and it fell overboard."

"Yeah," I say. "Maybe."

She turns away.

"So… Do you know?"

"Yes. Of course I know. But you haven't told me what you want to measure yet."

So then I tell her. About the data, and how all the sharks got ten percent bigger four years ago. Well nine point eight percent bigger.

"So I just want to make a tape measure so I can double check that there isn't a mistake with Chumley. Like the measurements we're reading from him aren't wrong."

Debbie stares at me now, like I've grown a jellyfish on my face.

"How could it be wrong?"

"It probably isn't. But it's the only answer I can think of. And I need a tape measure to check it. And I don't have one."

Debbie turns to go.

"So do you know? How tall you are?"

She stops. "I'm five foot. OK?"

"Five foot exactly?"

"Yes."

"Like properly exactly? I mean could you tell me in centimeters?"

"No! I don't know. I've never had to be a *tape measure* before." With that she stalks off. Which isn't much good to me.

I ask Jason too, because he's quite tall, and maybe he might know, but he just says he's about six foot one. But then I have a better idea anyway. We're not really allowed to access the internet on board, because our connection is by a satellite phone, and it's really expensive, but I look anyway, to see if I can just print off a measuring stick. Only I find you can't, or at least not easily, because the size you see an image that's on a computer screen depends upon lots of factors, like the size of your monitor, so it's not accurate enough.

But then I stop being a complete idiot and realize I can use the monitor itself. I type the brand and the model name into google along with the word 'dimensions' and it tells me exactly how wide and high it is. Both the actual screen, and the screen and the frame around it. So now I have four reliable measurements. I mark those off on a piece of paper, and then I fold it in half at each point, so that I get eight measurements, and from that I make a scale. Then I grab some thin white rope from the storeroom, and I mark that off with measurements all the way up to twenty meters. My very own tape measure.

Next I go to speak with Rosie.

"You want to do what?" She says.

"I want to take the RIB and check the measurements on Chumley."

"Why?"

"I just think we should check it."

"Why?"

I shrug. I don't tell Rosie about the problem in the data, and I don't think I ought to yet. I should let Steve see if he can figure it out first. I mean, it could be really embarrassing for him if it turns out that some of the data he's published is inaccurate. Besides, it's more likely that I'm wrong anyway.

"And how are you going to do it?"

"Well if we just take the boat over to the buoy, and pull it up, I can quickly measure it, and then we'll get it back in position and..."

"Aren't you busy enough? Haven't we given you enough to do?" Rosie breaks into a smile now. She means it to be incredulous I know, and it's not her fault it makes her look so pretty, but it still distracts me.

"Yeah I just... I like to be thorough."

She laughs, and I think she's going to say no. But then she shrugs.

"OK. Well I don't think anyone's using the boat right now. So if it'll make you happy."

So then I go off and get us life jackets, and roll up my rope tape measure ready to use, while Rosie connects the hoist for the rigid inflatable boat or RIB. It's stored on the back of the ship, so there's no chance of the sharks mouthing it to find out what it is, and puncturing it. But it makes it a bit of a hassle to launch.

But when I come back there's a problem. It's Steve – and Dan obviously – it turns out they need to use the boat after all to get over to the island. Steve wants to do some filming close up to the seal colony. Normally Steve would tell us this at breakfast, while he explains the plan for the day, but apparently he didn't this time. It's obviously annoying because it means Rosie and I can't use the boat now after all, and I think Steve senses my disappointment since he comes over to talk with me about it.

"Hey Billy, how's it going?" He looks a bit tired, and it occurs to me that maybe he was up late going over the data, trying to find the error. But he doesn't say anything about it.

"Did Jason get you set up on the drone yet?"

I shake my head.

"Well maybe I'll have a word."

I'm about to tell him that I don't mind, that I've flown my own drone a lot, when he goes on.

"Say, you've got your buoyancy aid on, why don't you come along?"

I'm a bit surprised by this. Since there isn't room for us in the boat when Steve and Dan are filming.

"We're gonna take a little walk through the colony, see what we can see."

"Through the colony? Actually on the island? I thought you said we weren't allowed…"

"We're not allowed. I never said we didn't though. Come along. And I'll grab Jason now to hand over the drone. Bring it along, it's always good to get some extra footage."

I can't help but feel a bit excited."Really?"

"Sure. It'll be fun."

So then I get in the inflatable boat after all, but not to do what I wanted to do.

THIRTEEN

ROSIE DRIVES THE RIB, while Dan films her closing on the island, and Steve tells me what he's doing.

"We want to grab some shots of the pups close up," he shouts, over the roar of the motor. "While a few still have their baby coats on. It's too dangerous to go when they're all young, since fur seals are so bloody territorial, but now the numbers have thinned out we should be OK. You need to keep your eyes open though, when we're in the colony. You got that?"

I nod. "What do you want me to film?"

"What's that?"

I ask again, shouting this time so he can hear me.

"Oh right, with the drone. Whatever really. Dan'll grab most of what we need, but any aerial footage you can get will work too. Just keep the drone up high, so you're not getting Dan in the shot."

I think about this. I reason that I'll need to keep it flying quite low, and pointing away.

"OK, we're coming into the landing area now." Steve's voice cuts into my thoughts. "Get ready to jump, and don't fall in."

Rosie uses the motor to hold the front of the boat close to the rocks. There's hardly any swell in the neck of Death Alley, but even so the water is sucking and frothing as it rises and falls around the rocks, and it's not easy to step out. Steve goes first, and he's able to wedge his big boots into a couple of cracks in the rock and hold out his hand for me to follow, the drone case on my shoulder. Then Dan follows him, and Rosie backs the boat back out into the water.

"Take the RIB back to the Hunter," Steve shouts to her. "We're gonna be quite a while."

Then we walk a few steps inland. It's so cool. I've been monitoring the seal colony on Lornea Island for years, but they're only common grey seals, and I've never actually gone into the colony, I've always watched through binoculars. Now I'm actually walking through one of the biggest colonies of fur seals, in the whole world. And now there's hundreds and *hundreds* of seals, all around me. The noise is incredible. And the smell is back – Steve was right, we got so used to it from the ship that we didn't notice, but now we're up close it's stronger than ever, a little bit of drying seaweed, but mostly fish guts and seal poop. The rocks are mostly flat, but we have to pick our steps carefully, avoiding walking in front of any of the adults. The seals turn around to watch us as we step past. They don't look totally happy that we're here, but they're kinda lazy too, so while they're bending around to keep their eyes on us as we pass, they're not doing anything more than that.

When we reach one of the higher parts of the rock we stop, and Steve talks with Dan. He tells him to get set up with the tripod, and then he beckons me over to where a seal pup is lying on its own, and watching us. It's probably four weeks old, one of the later ones to be born, and it's still covered in a gray fluffy fur, so that it looks more like a cuddly toy than an actual wild animal.

"Beautiful aren't they?" Steve grins at me. Very carefully he reaches out a hand and, keeping his eyes fixed onto the huge, soft eyes of the seal, he lets it sniff at his fingers.

"Alright buddy. We're not here to hurt you." Steve's voice is soft and soothing. "We're just gonna use you for a few moments. Tell your story." The seal heaves itself forward a little bit, to move away, so Steve pulls his hand back.

Quietly he stands up and turns to Dan. "OK. Let's do it."

Then he squats down again, and Dan drops to one knee to get the camera at the same level.

"Rolling," he says.

"We're here in the largest fur-seal colony in the world…" he begins, in his TV whisper. I sort of tune out and concentrate on getting the drone out of its case, as quietly as I can. I'm a bit worried about the noise when I fire it up, but I'm quite a long way away from Steve now, and he's using the microphone anyway, what with all the noise of the seals around us. So then I take off, and fly low above the colony, using the screen in the controller to see where I am.

"And now we've come across this little fella," I hear Steve continue. "At four weeks old he's already graduated from his mother's milk to fish and squid. Hence why he's all alone here, waiting for his mother to come back and feed him. In itself that isn't unusual, but what he doesn't know, is that when she went into the water earlier today, she had an encounter with one of the many prowling great whites in these waters." Steve twists to face the camera.

"This little pup's mother isn't coming back, which means he faces a slow death by starvation." He stares seriously into the lens.

"OK, got that," Dan calls out, after a few long seconds. Then Steve gets up at once and stretches his legs.

"OK. Get a close up of its eyes will you? Make it look tragic. Then we'll go again." He turns to me.

"So Billy, obviously we don't know if the mother is coming back or not, but we'll cut this in with footage of an adult being attacked in the water. Make it look like that's this pup's mother. So that we're telling a story that's not *literally* true, but that speaks a truth about the lives these animals live."

I nod. I wasn't really paying attention, it's a different drone to the one I'm used to and it takes a lot of concentration to fly so that I don't get into Dan's shot. And the images on the little screen of the controller are amazing, especially the way I can go anywhere I like. But I start to notice that there's not just seals and seal pups and seaweed and rocks on the island, there's a surprising amount of trash too. Plastic and fishing buoys.

Steve crouches down again.

"But as bleak as things look right now for this pup, it's not quite all over yet. Because we've witnessed an incredible behavior among these animals that makes them seem almost human." He stands up and walks a few paces away from the seal, to where another adult is lying. "Once the neighboring parents realize it's been left alone, there's a good chance they might actually adopt him as if he were their own pup."

Steve turns to the camera, still crouched right down by the seals. "At first glance it seems to make no evolutionary sense – why risk your life looking after the genetic offspring of other individuals? But when you consider the wider picture, things come into a different focus. If there's a real possibility of being eaten alive, every time you go out for lunch, it starts to make sense to have a back-up plan for your kids. So you look after your neighbor's pup if the worst happens to them, and hopefully they'll do the same for you..."

"Hey look at that!" I interrupt him. I don't mean to, but there's something I've seen on the screen.

"Billy! What the fuck?" Steve stands up. "What is it?"

I'm closer to Dan, so I turn the controller to show him the screen. The drone's still in the air, hovering over another part of the colony.

"There. That seal's stuck." It's hard to point because both my hands are busy flying the drone, so I fly lower. I descend right over the large male seal, its tail and side flipper completely tangled in the fishing net.

"Shit, is it dead?" Steve asks. But then the seal looks up at the drone, like it's annoyed by the buzzing presence.

"OK. Not dead, but definitely fucked."

"Should we release it?" I ask, and we both look over at where the drone is actually flying. It's probably a half mile away from us, right on the other side of the island. Steve shakes his head.

"Too far away, we can't get there. Too dangerous to cross the whole colony. Even if we could, it's definitely too dangerous to approach an adult male."

I don't reply. But I guess I must have that look on my face.

"It won't be able to swim with that net round it," I say in the end. I pull the drone back, so we can see how it's caught from another angle. "You could probably just cut that line there, and the rest would fall off."

There's silence for a minute. Then Steve swears loudly. "Shit Billy. Alright. All-fucking-right. Dan, you fancy taking a walk?"

Dan's already joined us, but he shakes his head. "Can't get the main camera all that way across these rocks. Besides, don't you want to wait until this one's mom comes back? Finish the adoption narrative?"

Steve looks at the pup he was filming, and the neighbor which has moved away from the noisy humans. He clicks his tongue in irritation.

"You got the handheld camera?"

"In the bag."

Steve nods. Then he makes a decision. "OK. Dan you stay here and get some footage of the pup. Billy, land the drone and grab the hand held cam. We'll *try* and get over there, but I'm not promising. I can't take any risks with you."

So that's what we do. I bring the drone back and land it and pack it away, while Dan gets the handheld camera ready. It's just like a little handy cam, but apparently it's a very expensive one, and Dan makes a big point about how I have to have the carry strap around my neck at all times, in case I drop it. And even then he doesn't look happy. Then me and Steve set off. Without the drone up it's actually very hard to see exactly where to go, and we can't just walk in a straight line, because of the rocks and all the seals lying in the way.

"Stay close Billy," Steve says, when I drop behind a bit. It's amazing as you walk between the seals just how different they are. From a distance they all look black, but closer up there's all sorts of different patterns and colors. It's like when you see a crowd from a long way away, all the people look kind of the same, but if you walk through them you realize they're all individuals. All different.

"Jesus will you keep up? I'm gonna have to tie a rope to you." Steve hisses at me. So I have to catch him up again.

It takes us about twenty minutes to get across the island, and then another ten to find the seal with the fishing net wrapped around it. But then we do, hidden in a little dip. The net of the rope has cut into its skin, so that it's weeping blood. And it seems angry about it. It's making a horrible bellowing sound, and lurching around, every time we try to get close to it. Steve shakes his head.

"This don't look good," he mutters, and I don't think he's talking to me. I start filming anyway, not sure what else to do, but Steve doesn't even seem to notice. He keeps walking around the seal, looking at it from all angles but never getting close. In the end he stops and pulls the diving knife he carries around his leg from the holster. Then he seems to remember I'm here.

"Stay back Billy," he says. He doesn't have his TV voice on now.

He starts whistling tunelessly as he edges towards the back of the seal. The fishing net – blue nylon rope – is bunched up in a big ball on the rocks, and there's only a couple of lines from it that are wrapped around the seal, but they're wrapped around pretty tight.

"Poor bastard must have dragged the whole lot out the water." Steve moves so that he's by the net, and he takes hold of the line to the seal. Gently he lifts it up. At once the animal goes into a huge convulsion, its massive body trying to writhe, but it's constricted from doing so. It lumps back down. If either of us get trapped underneath it would be like being hit by a truck.

"Easy boy, easy." Now we're up close it's clear this is one of the bigger seals we've seen. Easily two meters long and probably 600 pounds. 250 kilos. As Steve edges closer it occurs to me it could easily knock him out, and then I wouldn't know what I'd do. I bite my lip but keep pointing the camera.

Steve moves closer, keeping a close eye on the animal's tail flukes, which are the most likely part to hit him. Then he slides the blade of his knife up the rope, until he's almost touching the animal's side. Then, watching its eyes, he slides the blade under one part of the rope, where it's wrapped around the skin. Then he turns it outward, against the rope, and gently begins cutting. It's lucky the knife is so sharp, and the tough rope just melts from the blade. But there's lots more places where the seal is caught, and some where the rope is deeply embedded into the skin.

A couple of times the seal lurches, still trying to get away, even though Steve is trying to release it. But Steve's able to see it preparing to move by leaning its weight forward, and each time he steps back, and waits for it to subside. And slowly he's able to strip off the main part of the net, until only one section remains, where it's cut into the skin. But he cuts it so he has a free end, and then he nods to me.

"Move back a bit. I'm gonna rip it out."

I don't answer, but I just nod.

And then before I'm really ready, Steve pulls the rope. Instantly the animal convulses with pain, and lets out a roar, and then it pulsates forwards as it turns on Steve, but he's faster. He scrambles away until he's close to me. Then finally the seal quietens down, perhaps understanding that it's free at last. It twists its head and licks at the wound like a dog. Steve scrambles closer to me, then crouches down again. He's breathless as he speaks, and at first I don't realize what he's doing. But luckily I work it out quick enough.

"Even right the way out here, we can't escape from the issue of plastic debris in the waters. This alpha male would have paid the price with its life, had it not been for one of our student helpers, young Billy Wheatley, who spotted it with the drone. It was a long way away and I didn't think we stood any chance of saving it, but he insisted, and as a result..." He beckons to me, and after a moment I realize he means to take the camera. I let him and he turns it around, so now the lens is pointing to me.

"It's got a fighting chance to see another day. Thank you Billy." He keeps filming me a bit longer, then cuts the recording with his thumb.

"Good job Billy. Now let's get the hell out of here."

It's getting dark by the time we get back to the Shark Hunter, so there's no point me asking again to go and measure Chumley, and because it's been a pretty full on and amazing day, I'm relieved to get back to my bunk.

But the next morning it all goes off.

FOURTEEN

It begins as I'm having breakfast. There's a shout from Debbie on the observation deck, because it's her job to check all the equipment, and when she gets to check the feed from the video buoys she notices the problem.

"What's happened to Chumley?" She calls out.

And then, because it's Rosie's watch, she goes over to the screen to see what the issue is, and then I look as well.

The screen's working, and obviously the camera suspended under the camera buoy is working too, because we can see the water. And that looks like it always does in the morning, with the shafts of sunlight shooting through it. But there's no big wooden shark.

"Where the hell is Chumley?" Rosie asks.

We look out to where it should be moored, tethered at the front and the back between two orange buoys. We see at once that they're still in place, and they don't look like they've moved, like the anchors on them have dragged or anything like that. So then we decide to go over in the RIB and see what's happened. And that's actually easier than it would normally be, because Steve decided not to lift the RIB back onto the back of the ship last night when we got back from the island, because it was too late. So then Rosie drives the RIB over there and Debbie and me pull the first of the orange buoys on board the RIB to see what's happened. It's quite heavy, which means the anchor is still in place, but as we get the rope on board we see that the point where Chumley used to be tethered, he isn't. Instead the loose end of the rope is frayed and hanging loose in the current.

"It must have been bitten through," Rosie says, as she sees it.

"By what?" I ask.

No one answers that.

"But where's Chumley?" Debbie asks.

"It must be tied to the other buoy." Rosie replies. So then we throw the first orange buoy back in the water, and motor over to the second. But when we pull that up we see exactly the same problem. The rope which should be tethered to the front of Chumley is loose, its end twisting in the current.

"It looks cut," I say, the moment we get it on the RIB. I grab it and inspect it. You can see the marks of a serrated edge.

"Bloody hell," Rosie says when she sees too. "To take both ends out – that's almost deliberate. They must have taken against him."

"Who? What?" I ask. I don't know what she means.

"I can see how one side of the tether might have been taken out. That could have been an accident, one of the sharks mouthing a little to see what it was, but both sides. It must have been a deliberate attack."

"Well where is it now?" I grab a scuba mask from the locker under Rosie's seat, press it to my face and use it to peer down into the water. Through the blue clear water I can see the rocks, twenty meters down. The rope of the buoy arcs down to the concrete filled tire of its anchor. I pull my head back out the water, my hair wet now and plastered over my forehead. "I can't see it down there."

"It's got neutral buoyancy, so if it broke free it would have drifted away," Rosie replies. She looks around. "It could be anywhere."

There's a silence on the little boat, then she slaps the inflated tube with her palm.

"*Fuck it!* That's a really big loss. That means we've lost the consistency of having the same measuring system this year." I'm surprised by how mad she suddenly is. I've never seen Rosie angry before this.

We leave the orange buoys in place, but we un-clip the tether lines from the anchor lines, so that we can have a better look at the damaged ends back on the *Hunter*. Half an hour later we're all gathered around them, on the saloon table, and drinking coffee. We've also got Rosie's laptop open and replaying the feed from the camera buoy from last night. Of course it's dark, but we want to see if there's anything we can see, like the flash of a white shark's belly, from when it happened. We watch the whole night on 16X speed, but you can't see anything, the screen is just black the whole time. Until the morning, and then as the water lightens you can see how Chumley is just gone.

"It looks cut to me," I say, looking again at the end of the line. The rope is quite thick, like the stuff that climbers use, and the edges have funny marks on it. Steve inspects it too.

"Wait here," he says a moment later. Then when he comes back he's carrying the jaw from the shark he keeps in his cabin.

"You can identify a shark by its teeth. A mako has long pointed teeth, for catching prey at speed. A nurse shark has rounded teeth for crushing shellfish. But a white shark, like this guy here, see how the teeth are triangular and heavily serrated?" We lean in to see what he's showing us.

"These are teeth designed to saw through meat and bones. To tear away mouthfuls of flesh." He puts the rope inside the mouth and pushes the jaw together so that it clamps down. "And you've got to remember there would be thousands of pounds of pressure." He pushes down harder, and at the same time tugs on the end of the rope, so that it comes away. It kind of looks like the jaw has cut through the rope, even though it hasn't.

"I think from the marks on the rope we can identify this as the work of a white shark." Steve says. And then everyone starts asking him if he's ever heard of this sort of thing happening before – because for all the reputation of Great Whites as attacking humans and boats and things, us scientists know it's not usually true. They much prefer seals. And Steve goes on about how it's possible that one of the white sharks here saw Chumley as a threat, or just got pissed off with seeing it. And how next year they'll need to tether it with steel wire instead of rope. And how they probably were just lucky that this didn't happen before.

And I can't help but notice how well he's taking the loss.

FIFTEEN

I SPEND the morning with the binoculars. I'm supposed to be looking out for sharks, for the population survey, and I am doing it, but at the same time I'm also searching for Chumley. It's occurred to me that it might have washed up in one of the gullies or inlets that make up the rocky shore of the island. But after I've scanned the whole coastline – or at least the part that's visible from the ship – I can't see anything. So then, when I get my half hour for lunch, I go back to the saloon.

Since you don't have to work the entire time you're on the boat, and since we don't have easy access to the internet, Captain Bob has a little library. It's not really a library, it's just a wooden chest with paperback novels and copies of marine biology journals, and a few old magazines like *Surfer* and *National Geographic*. And there's one article I'm looking for in particular. It's one written by Steve a couple of years ago, and it's about here – about Wellington Island and the fur seal colony and how he does this population survey each year of the sharks. I know about it because everyone was looking at it earlier in the voyage, but actually I first saw it two years ago because I subscribe to *National Geographic*. Back then I thought it was super cool. And certainly I never realized how significant it might be.

It doesn't take me long to find, and when I get it I study the pictures. The one I'm looking for shows Steve, with his top off, fixing the tether lines to Chumley on the deck of *Shark Hunter*. You can see Rosie at the other end, and she looks really pretty in a bikini top and white shorts. I remember noticing that when I first saw this article, though back then I never imagined I might get to meet her one day. Anyway, that's not what I'm looking at now. I examine the photo again. They're both standing on the observation deck of the ship, and Chumley is leaning up against the railings. I think for a moment, then pick up my measuring rope from my bunk, and take it, and the magazine, outside. I prop up the magazine sort of where I think the photograph must have been taken from. Then I go and lay my measuring rope in a straight line where Chumley is in the photograph. Then I go back to the magazine, and I check again, and I have to make some adjustments, but in the end I get the measuring rope on the actual ship, exactly where Chumley's measuring marks are on the photograph of the ship. I check to see if they match up.

It's not perfectly exact you understand. I can't tell to the centimeter that it's off. Which is kind of how much I was expecting it to be. But it is off. By nearly half a meter. Ten meters on Chumley is marked off at nine and a half meters on my rope. You can tell because the upright posts that make up the railings are installed at half meter intervals. I check it again, making sure I haven't accidentally run my rope past another of the railing posts. But there doesn't seem to be any doubt. The measurements on Chumley are wrong.

"What are you doing?" Rosie's voice interrupts me. I close the magazine in a hurry and kick my measuring rope out of place. Then I turn to look at her. Her forehead is a little bit wrinkled where she's screwing up her face, and she's still in a bit of a bad mood, like everyone is, because we all know the data we're going to collect this year isn't going to be that good. She doesn't look suspicious at all though. Just curious about what I'm doing. I'm so tempted to tell her, but I know it's Steve I need to speak to, not Rosie.

"Nothing," I say.

Of course he's filming all afternoon with Dan, out in the RIB and then in his shark cage, and over dinner they're busy editing and going over what they've shot, so it's late by the time I knock on his door. Even so, I get the feeling he's been expecting me.

"Billy," he smiles this time and doesn't make any sarcastic comments. "Come in. Sit down."

I do what he says, sitting on the bed again. He shuts the lid on his laptop, then steps out from behind his desk. He pulls the chair out from under the desk and spins it around with one hand, so it has its back towards me. Then he sits on it, backwards, like he's trying to be cool.

"So what can I do for you?"

"It's about Chumley." I say. And then I wait. He waits too, but has to break the silence eventually.

"What about Chumley?"

I pause again, just to make the point.

"He's not as long as you said he was."

Then there's a really long pause before Steve speaks again, and he tries out a weird mix of expressions on his face.

"What makes you say that?" He says in the end.

Then I just hand him the copy of *National Geographic*, folded from where I've been holding it, open on the page with his article. He unfolds it and looks at it for a while, then looks back up at me.

"I measured it. I couldn't find a tape measure so I had to make a measuring rope, and then Chumley went missing, so I couldn't measure the actual Chumley, but in this photograph you can see how long it is against the railings of the ship, so I could put my rope against the railings and work it out. And... and the scale's wrong."

Steve goes back to studying the photograph. Then he tosses the magazine onto the bed beside me, and looks to one side. After a while he turns to look at me again. But neither of us speak. Not for a long time, I just feel his big brown eyes gaze into me. And I just stare back.

Eventually he sighs.

"You ever see *Killer Shark* on NBX?" He says suddenly.

The question surprises me. "That other TV shark show?"

"One of them Billy. One of them."

I don't reply because I want to work out why he's asking this.

"Well? You ever see it?"

In the end I shrug. "Sometimes."

"You like it?"

I shrug again. "Not much. It's a bit..." I can't think of the word.

"Hyperbolic? Overblown?" Steve suggests. "Shite?"

"It's just it... Well they're not actual scientists are they? It's just... sort of an entertainment show."

Steve nods. "Yeah. Russell Owens, the guy that hosts it, he's a total fucking asshole. I met him about seven years ago. We were both holed up in some harbor in a storm. The Caribbean I think. We had a few beers together, we got talking. He seemed real interested in what we did, and I thought we were just chatting. But then a few months later I heard how he'd refitted his boat – daddy's money of course – and talked his way onto the network. Then he started grabbing a big chunk of our ratings."

I frown again. I don't get why this is relevant.

"He took *my* formula, combining the thrill you get from interacting with sharks with real front-line research into how they live..." He locks his jaw for a moment. "And he never bothered with the second part. He just makes out sharks are deadly killers out to get anyone who goes in the water. And that's that." Steve pauses a moment, and shakes his head.

"And the network chiefs, they... here's the thing Billy. They don't really give a shit. That's the hard cold truth of it. There's only one thing they're interested in, and that's *ratings*. A couple of years after Russell came along they wanted to cancel my show. And it was only when I convinced them..."

He looks aside again. Like he wants a way out of telling me this. But he knows there isn't one.

"Which of these sounds more dangerous Billy? A ten meter great white – or a nine meter great white?"

"Well it sort of depends whether they're in a cruising mode or an attack mode…"

"Yeah, OK." He holds up a hand. "You might know that, but what's a regular viewer gonna think?"

I don't answer. I don't really know.

"Bigger is *badder* Billy. The bigger the shark, the bigger the mouth. The bigger the mouth the bigger the *teeth*. It's a no brainer."

"What's a no brainer?"

"The TV guys were gonna replace my show with Russell's. So I went to meet with them. I gave them the full bullshit about how it was important to educate people about sharks and other marine life – because we all have to live on this planet – but I wasn't getting anywhere. You could see it in their eyes. Until I said one thing." He holds up one finger.

"What one thing?"

"I didn't even mean to say it. It just slipped out. I told 'em that with our scientific background we were better placed to track down and film the larger specimens. And they just *jumped* on it."

"What do you mean?"

"They thought I meant *Jaws*. They thought I was telling them I was gonna find the actual Jaws, from the movie. You know, thirty five feet long, made of fiberglass a remote control mouth. That's what they really want. That's all they want. And somehow they got the idea that since we were rooted in science, we could get them the bigger sharks. More *dangerous* sharks. The sharks that people want to watch." He puffs out his cheeks, and then exhales slowly.

"But that's nonsense."

"Yeah it's nonsense. It's total fucking bullshit."

"So what did you do?"

"You know what I did. You just told me what I did. I started finding bigger sharks."

"But how?" I can feel my face is all screwed up from frowning.

It takes him a while to answer. "By then we were already using Chumley. We wanted to bring some kind of rigor to the job of estimating the sizes of sharks. And other people were already doing the same… with their own Chumleys." He tails off. "So I changed the scale."

"You changed the scale?"

Steve nods.

"You faked it?"

He hesitates, but then nods again."

"Oh my God," I say. "You did it four years ago?"

"Yeah."

"And that's why the sharks grew by ten percent that year?"

"Uh huh."

"Or nine point eight percent?"

"If you say so."

"So they didn't *really* grow by that much?"

"No Billy. They didn't."

I'm stunned. After a while I can feel my mouth hanging open, and I quickly close it. I mean I kind of knew this already, but to hear him admitting it is amazing. Shocking.

"But you've written articles. *Papers.* On the population sizes of white sharks. And other species. And it's all based on the data measured by Chumley. The data will be inaccurate."

"Only a little. Not enough to make a real difference."

"But it's still wrong!"

Steve rubs his face. I hear the bristles of his stubble rasp under his fingers.

"I meant to correct it. At first I mean. But then I realized I couldn't. I always had students like you helping to gather the data, and they might notice if the papers we published then used different data. So I had to keep it the way they recorded it. And it… worked!" He shrugs. "I gained a reputation for being able to track down the bigger sharks. I could take it to the TV guys, it *worked* Billy…"

"But."

"No. No buts. It *worked.* The TV guys – they all play fucking golf together – they loved it. I got bigger sharks, they got bragging rights. They put *Shark Bites* in the prime time slots, and we won the war of the ratings against Russell *Fucking* Owens."

I'm silent for a long while.

"But the data is wrong." I say in the end. But Steve snaps right back.

"And if I didn't do it, there wouldn't have been any data at all."

We both stare at each other for a moment, both breathing hard.

"But… I say again."

"No Billy. That's just the way this is."

I don't speak for a while. I'm trying to make sense of this.

"Welcome to the murky muddy world of how science really *fucking* works. I'm sorry it's such a…"

"Does Rosie know?" I interrupt him.

"Huh? *What?*"

"Does Rosie know what you're doing?"

"No. *God no.* No one knows. Rosie? Why the hell would she…" He shakes his head. "Look, *I* repainted Chumley. Alone. I figured if anyone did notice the scale was off, I could just say it was a mistake I'd made. But no one noticed. Least not until you came along."

I think about this. Somehow I'm pleased that Rosie doesn't know.

"And she's not gonna know either," Steve suddenly interrupts me. I look up.

"No one's gonna know."

"Did you cut Chumley loose?"

He looks away, rubbing his chin again.

"Yeah. Rosie told me you wanted to measure it. So I sneaked over last night. I towed it around the other side of the island. Anchored it up there."

I don't reply. I pick up the copy of *National Geographic*. I flick through the few pages of Steve's article.

"It's half a meter Billy. No harm no foul."

"It's not though is it?" I say. "Not if we're *aging* sharks from their length. It doesn't just mean they're a bit smaller than we think, it also means the population is *younger*, and that might have important consequences for the health of the population."

Steve raises his eyebrows at this, but he doesn't reply. Then suddenly he jumps up and walks to the back of his cabin. He opens a cabinet and pulls out a bottle of whisky, and two glasses. Without asking me he pours two drinks and hands one to me.

"I don't like whisky."

"Try it. One day you will."

I take a sniff, it nearly burns the inside of my nose out. I put the glass back down. Steve smiles.

"You know Billy, one lesson I've learned in life is this. There's always something good that comes out of a crisis." He pauses to take a sip of his own drink. "And you know what's good about this crisis?"

I frown up at him, but don't answer.

"You're what, seventeen years old?"

"Sixteen."

"Sixteen? Shit. I didn't know we took kids that age."

I hesitate. Then I tell him. "Actually I'm not sixteen for another month, I just put that I was on my application form, because you had to be sixteen to apply."

Steve considers this for a moment, then he raises his glass in a kind of toast. "Well there you go. Everyone's gotta bend a rule here and there." He shakes his head and seems to relax. "You know Billy, this is the start for you. The beginning. Of your whole *career,* and I can help. You know this… *celebrity* thing, it's bullshit, but it does mean I know folks. In every Marine Bio school in the country. In the whole world come to that. And it's a *very* cliquey world. So your little piece of detective work here has gained you a very powerful ally. It's gonna open a lot of doors." He raises his glass again. "Can we at least toast to that?"

I don't move. And after a few seconds Steve picks up my glass and holds it out for me.

"Come on Billy. This is a fourteen-year-old single malt. I had it shipped in from Scotland and it costs a fortune." He holds it closer, and eventually I take the glass from him. The liquid inside it is golden and so thick it clings to the sides of the glass. I sniff it, and a cough catches in my throat. Steve smiles. Then – I guess I'm curious now – I bring it to my lips and take a sip, and a dribble of fire fills my mouth.

"Atta boy! To your career Billy! To taking a few risks. To grabbing life by the goddamn *balls* and squeezing it tight."

He clinks his glass against mine, and takes a large sip from his glass. I put mine back to my mouth, and pour a proper sized sip in this time. I let it fill into my mouth, and then throw it back, feeling it burn down my throat.

I can still taste the whisky the next morning, when my alarm wakes me for my shift. I swing out of my bunk, making sure not to wake Jason, who has one leg draped over the edge of his bed and is snoring gently. Then I dress as quietly as I can, and slip out into the saloon. Debbie is on the same shift, and she pushes a cup of coffee towards me. Then she says something but I don't hear it, because I'm still thinking about last night.

"I said good morning," she says again.

"What? Oh yeah. Morning."

We don't say anything after that, but both sit and drink our coffee. Normally I'd have a bowl of cereal too, but I don't feel hungry this morning. So when we've finished our coffees we head out onto the observation deck to begin work. The sun hasn't risen yet, but there's already light in the sky. We start monitoring the sharks at sunrise, and go all the way through to sunset. It doesn't matter if we miss some that appear before sunrise, what's important is we follow the exact same methods as previous years, so that the data is comparable. That's why the loss of Chumley is such a blow.

"Shark," Debbie calls out. I look up from the screens and follow her outstretched hand. About twenty five meters away there's a disturbance in the water. It's hard to see anything about it from here, and it's not by any of the camera buoys. But we have the drone ready to fly so I grab the controller, and it buzzes up off the deck. I fly it over the disturbed area. This early in the day, the water's still a bit dark to see clearly, but there's something black floating in the water.

"What's that?" Debbie asks, and I bring the drone lower.

"It's the back half of a seal," she says. We've seen lots of them now, but they still make you feel a bit queasy.

"Go up again, see if we can see what did it." So then I fly a bit higher again, until we see the shadow of a shark turning slow circles around the half-seal. We're all experienced now in seeing what type of shark it is from the outline, and without even checking with me, Debbie writes it down as a male white shark.

"Look, it's still got the other half in its mouth." She notes down the time and nature of the attack on the clipboard, and I bring the drone back.

"Say Billy, did you ever find your tape measure?" She asks, as I plug the drone in to recharge. I shake my head.

"You wanted to check the measurements on Chumley didn't you? Guess there's no point now anyway, what with it getting lost and everything."

I think about this for a moment, it's just occurred to me how I could use the drone to try and find it. But... But what exactly would be the point? I know now that Steve put the wrong measurements on it. The question is what I should do about it.

"I don't get why we need it anyway," Debbie's voice interrupts me. "We should use the drone to measure them. Fly the drone at a known height over every shark that comes in there, and take a picture. We could work out the exact length of all the sharks super easy." She shrugs. I'm quiet for a bit, then I look up at her.

"That's actually a really good idea."

"I know it is. You're not the only smart one Billy."

"No, I mean it's a *really* good idea." I say.

She rolls her eyes. "I said I know. I'm actually gonna tell Steve about it, see what he thinks."

Something about this makes my face drop.

"What?" Debbie asks. "I thought you liked the idea?"

I try to make myself look positive again. "I do."

"Well? What is it then?"

I hesitate. I know I shouldn't say anything. But in the end I can't help myself.

"There's no point."

"What? Billy, are you alright? You're acting super weird this morning," Debbie says. "Even for you."

And then I don't say anything for a while, because I haven't decided if I should say anything to anyone or keep it quiet. And then I know what I'm going to do. I can't not.

"He'll just lie about it anyway."

"*What*? What does *that* mean."

And then I tell her. This early it's just the two of us on the observation deck, so I tell her everything. How I found the inconsistency in the data, and then how I wanted the tape measure as a mistake on Chumley was the only way I could think of to explain the problem. And then how Steve discovered what I was doing and made it look like Chumley was attacked, just to stop me measuring it.

"No way, I don't believe you." Debbie says when I'm finished. And for a while I wonder if it's better, even now, that she believes him and not me. But then I pull out my phone and open up my voice recorder app, and scroll through my recordings until I find the one I made last night, taping Steve as he admitted what he'd done.

"I wasn't sure if he'd admit it or not, so I taped him." I press play, and we both listen to the part where Steve admits to getting up in the middle of the night to hide Chumley. I stop it before he tries to bribe me.

Debbie's mouth is literally hanging open. Opening and closing like a fish just pulled from the water. "Oh my God. Jesus Billy! What the *actual fuck*?" Debbie says when I stop. "Oh my God!?"

I look at her, I don't say anything.

"What are you gonna do?"

I don't know the answer to this. It's all I've been thinking about since I worked out what's been happening.

"I mean like, if you tell anyone, it's gonna totally *waste* his career. But if you don't, it's like you've uncovered this massive scientific fraud. And you didn't do anything."

She actually smiles as she says this. And I know why. It's because she knows what a massive thing this is, and it's a kind of relief that this is my problem not hers.

"So what are you going to actually do?"

"I don't know."

I spend the whole day thinking about it. On the one hand it's not like he's a *murderer* or anything. On the other hand what he's doing is wrong, and it's totally against the ethos of scientific endeavor. I mean, look at it this way – what if all scientists behaved like Steve? I have this book that Dad gave me for Christmas one year. It's called *On the Shoulders of Giants*. It's all about how all the great scientific advances are built upon other work that other people have done. So that all scientists don't have to start right at the beginning with finding out the boiling point of water, or giving all the fish names. So if Steve's work is based on a lie – even if he thinks it's only a little one, then it still matters. Because we don't know what might be built upon his research. And his little lie will get amplified every time someone builds upon it. And it could bring everything tumbling down.

And it's not as if it's *that* little a lie anyway. Given how we only know the age of sharks from their size, his lie doesn't just affect the shark's size, it also affects the sharks' ages, and from that the whole health of the population. We – all the scientists working in this field – think that the average age of white sharks is actually older than it really is, all as a result of Steve's lying. I don't think I can just ignore that. Even if I wanted to. I don't think anyone could.

The truth is, there's never been any decision to make. All the thinking I've been doing, I realize, it's just because I don't like the conclusion. But there's no decision about what I ought to do, and therefore no decision about what I'm going to do. It's just it makes me sad.

Once I've made the decision I figure I just have to get it over with as quickly as possible. I wait until the day is over, and everyone's gone to their bunks, then I go into the work area and I download my audio clip onto the computer and I compress it down, so it doesn't take as much data to send. Then I write an explanation of what Steve's been doing, and add in the photographs I took of the railing of the ship, with a photo I took of the article in the National Geographic with Chumley. Then I attach two data files, the raw Excel sheet with all the recordings of the shark sizes over the last four years, and a second where I've calculated what the actual sizes should be, in case they want to correct their articles. Then I send it to the *Journal of Marine Biology*, which is where most of Steve's papers on shark population have been published. They're the experts in things like this. They'll know what the right thing to do is.

Then I do nothing. The next day it's like nothing happened at all. Steve doesn't say anything, but he's friendly and a bit more attentive than normal, even though he's still doing lots of filming. I work my shift, trying to avoid talking too much to Debbie, and then afterward I hang around on the observation deck, and then it's my turn to cook dinner. And then I go to bed early. But the day after that things go crazy.

SIXTEEN

I'M ALMOST FINISHED with my morning watch when Captain Bob comes to find me. His face is a weird kind of white color, even through his tan.

"Billy, you need to come with me," he says. "I don't know what you've done, but Steve is saying he wants to throw you overboard."

We'd had a busy morning – busier because we still don't have Chumley to help us estimate the sizes of the sharks – and I'd almost forgotten what had happened, so I feel my lips curl up in a bemused smile.

"I'm not kidding, and I don't think he is neither. He's raging mad. What'd you do?"

I don't get the chance to tell him, since then Steve comes around the corner.

"Where the fuck is that *fucking* kid?" He sees me as he speaks, and then lunges towards me. Bob is quick to move his body across mine.

"Whoa there Steve, think what you're doing."

"Let me at the little *fuck*."

I try to shrink back out of the way, but there's nowhere to go on the ship, and I'm not going to go in the water, we've just seen the biggest female white shark we've yet seen, and her hunt wasn't successful this time.

"*Steve!*" Bob says. "You need to calm down. What the hell is this all about?"

Steve doesn't reply. He just stands there, too close and with his chest heaving up and down. "Ask the fucking kid."

Then he turns and stalks away. He slams the door frame with his palm as he walks through it, and then he's gone.

So then everyone is looking at me, standing right at the back of *Shark Hunter,* with Bob still standing in front of me.

"What did you do Billy?" Rosie asks, her face white with shock. I feel myself thinking it's unfair the way she says it. As if she's blaming it on me. I look at the others, they all look totally confused, except Debbie. She looks scared.

"Steve was lying about the sizes of the sharks. Exaggerating how big they were." I say.

There's a silence. Then Rosie starts shaking her head.

"What?" Her forehead creases in a frown. "What are you talking about?"

I don't reply, and she goes on.

"How could he? When we were making the observations? And anyway *why* would he? What would be the point?"

"He says it was to make the TV series more exciting. People like bigger sharks."

Rosie starts to answer this, but then she stops. She screws up her face.

"But *how* could he? The observations, we made them."

So I explain. About how he changed the markings on Chumley. There's silence again when I've finished. Like everyone is stunned.

"So what did you *do*?" Rosie says after a while. So then I go on to explain how I sent an email to the editor of the *Journal of Marine Biology.* How it was the only responsible thing to do.

"Jesus Christ," Rosie says to that. "You've fucking ruined him."

After that Captain Bob takes over. He takes me to his cabin and he locks the door. He tells me how I have to keep out of Steve's way, and he'll try to calm him down. And then he's gone for a long time, but after a while I can hear shouting from somewhere else on the boat. Eventually Captain Bob comes back.

"We need to get you off the boat Billy," he says. "You're not in danger, Steve isn't going to throw you overboard anymore, but…" He hesitates just long enough to sigh, "he's refusing to let me take you back to the mainland. So I've put out a call on the radio to see if there's any other boats nearby that'll take you. And you're in luck, there's a Swedish couple on a yacht that's only a couple of hours away. They're on a passage to Port George, you can get a bus from there to Melbourne and the airport. You'll have to figure the rest out yourself."

"What about the study? I'm supposed to be here for three more weeks, doing the shark population survey?"

"I think we can safely say that's over. For you at least. I don't know if we're gonna stay to complete the work. I don't know anything right now, except I need you off my ship to avoid a murder."

"But…" I think about this. "Who's going to go with me?"

"No one's going to go with you."

"But…" I stop. Suddenly I've run out of questions.

"You better go and pack your stuff ready for when they get here. I just hope it's soon enough before Steve changes his mind again."

Captain Bob escorts me from his cabin to the front of the ship where my bunk is. On the way we pass Rosie in the corridor. Her eyes are red, like she's been crying. I open my mouth to speak to her, but I don't know what to say, and anyway she turns away, like she won't listen.

When we get to my bunk Bob turns, to leave me there alone.

"Aren't you going to wait with me?" I ask. "In case Steve tries to throw me overboard?"

He thinks about it for a moment.

"Just pack your stuff Billy."

So I do what he says. Shoving all my clothes into my backpack, and powering down my computer, which is charging on my bunk. When I look up I see Jason standing in the doorway.

"I guess you can have the bottom bunk now," I say to him. It's kind of a joke, but he doesn't laugh. Instead he shakes his head.

"Dick move, Billy." He says. "Fucking dick move."

SEVENTEEN

I WAIT BACK in Captain's Bob's cabin while he logs onto the internet and looks for a ticket back from Australia to the United States. I don't have any money, so I'm worried about how I'm going to buy it, but he says I shouldn't worry, and he'll sort it out. And when that's done he goes out, so I just sit there, watching out of his little window. After an hour I see the sail of a yacht on the horizon, and slowly it comes closer. Finally the sails come down, and I see a woman on the deck, staring over at us. Then Captain Bob comes back to the cabin, unlocks the door, and leads me out onto the deck.

I'm surprised because everyone's there. It's like I'm the entertainment. Even Steve, and I get the sense that everyone is kind of on his side, which seems pretty unfair, given how I didn't do anything wrong.

It's Steve himself who insists on driving the RIB to take me over to the Swedish yacht. I can see how Rosie and Captain Bob don't like the idea, but he waves them away. So a little bit nervously I step into the boat and Jason lowers my giant backpack behind me. Without a word Steve fires the motor and flicks the painter clear. He puts loads of power down, pushing a huge vee into the water and making the bow rear right up, so I have to hold on really tight. Then we plane super fast toward the yacht and he doesn't even look at me. It's far too noisy to talk. Then, just before we're going to smash into the side of the yacht he throws the throttle into reverse, so we stop in our own length. It's really reckless driving.

On the yacht there's a man and a woman, both in their sixties. You can see on their faces how curious they are, about what's going on, but they don't say anything, except how we should pass my bag up. I'm nervous as I stand in the RIB, to pass it up, because Steve could easily fire the motor again, and I'd lose my footing. But he doesn't. And then it's my turn to climb up after my bag. Still Steve hasn't said a word, and I look at him now, thinking he must want to say something, and this time he meets my eye. His jaw is set hard, and his eyes don't waver as he stares at me. But still he says nothing. I turn back to the yacht, and climb aboard. By the time I've finished shaking the hands of the Swedish man and his wife, Steve's spun the RIB around and is already speeding back to the *Shark Hunter*.

The Swedish couple are called Eric and Agnes and they're really nice, especially Agnes. She tells me how Eric used to work in insurance, and she was a teacher in a primary school in Gothenburg, but now they're retired and sailing around the world. I was a bit confused at first, since I thought Gothenburg wasn't a real place, but where Batman lived. But then we worked out it wasn't Gothenburg but Gotham City, and she thought that was really funny. Then she told me lots of stories about their trip, about how they were really worried about pirates in the Malacca straights, and how they nearly got shipwrecked in a storm off the coast of Kerala in India. Eventually she asked me about what happened to me on *Shark Hunter*, and I told her the whole story. Then she frowned a lot, and didn't say much for a while.

Eventually she asked if I was tired, and said I could lie down in the bunk in the forepeak. Because they don't have guests on the boat much they use that cabin for storage, but she makes me a bed in among the spare sails and supplies. Then, when I wake up, we're really close to land, and I help out on deck getting the fenders ready.

Agnes takes me in a taxi to the bus station, and she waits until the bus to Melbourne comes up. A local lady explains to us how I have to get a second bus to the airport, and it's pretty easy to just follow her instructions. Then at the airport I just have to go to the Qantas desk, and there's a ticket waiting for me. Actually it's two tickets, the first to Los Angeles, and then another one to Boston.

It takes thirty eight hours in total before I get back to Boston, and from there I have to get another bus down to the ferry terminal, and then wait another four hours before the boat leaves back to Lornea Island. And then I have to get another two buses on the island, the first to Newlea, the capital of Lornea Island, and that feels weird, because normally it feels like quite a big place, but after all the travel it suddenly feels really small. Then I catch the local bus that stops at the end of my road in Littlelea. Finally, almost three days since I waved goodbye to Agnes, I'm outside my front door, and fitting my key into the lock.

EIGHTEEN

It's really hard to stop myself calling out to Dad, even though I know he's not here. But I don't, and instead I just pause and listen. The whole house is cold and quiet. Dad knows what happened now. He actually offered to come back with me, but I told him not to, because it's important he stays to work on the new *Blue Lady II*. She's still on the mainland, in a boatyard there, and Dad's saving money by working on the fitting out himself. It's only a few weeks before he's back, and I told him I'd be OK, and I had lots of school work to catch up on anyway. But I don't do that straight away. Instead I dump my backpack in the kitchen and go upstairs for a bath. Until I remember that there's no hot water. There's no food in the refrigerator either, so I heat up some beans from the cupboard. Then I wait for an hour and have another go at a bath, but the water still isn't hot, so I only sit in it for a little while before I get cold and have to get out. Then I just give up and go to bed.

It's weird waking up the next morning. Obviously I know where I am, but it still feels wrong. Too quiet I suppose. And still. I guess I'm just disorientated after all the traveling, and before that being on the ship with lots of people everywhere and Jason sleeping in the bunk over my head. Here I might be at home, but I'm completely alone.

I don't get up for ages. There doesn't seem to be any point. I'm signed off school – Dad said I should phone them and explain what's happened, and see if they'll let me back early. But I don't do that. Instead I search the house for food again, and in the end I give up and catch the bus into Silverlea. There I go to the store and I buy as much food as I can get in my backpack. Then I bring it home and decide to watch TV, but I see that *Shark Bites* is on, just an old one on repeat. And then I can't *not* watch it, because I know all the people on it now, except it's a different group of students. I see how well Rosie gets on with them, and that makes me feel rotten. So I go back upstairs and run a bath again. And this time the water is actually *really* hot, because I forgot to turn the water heater off, which would make Dad mad if he was here. But he isn't, so I have a really full bath, and when I eventually get cold, I just let some of the water out the plug and turn the faucet on again to top it up. But then I end up all wrinkled. So I have to get out. And even though it's still early I go to bed and sleep again.

On the third day I decide to do something more useful than eating and sleeping and having baths. So I call Amber. I figure she'll want to know what happened, and she'll probably be quite pleased that I'm back, because I can help her with the job of sorting out the old *Blue Lady* and putting her up for sale. I dial her number.

"*Billy*!" It's nice to hear her voice. "How you doing? I mean..." She stops and changes to a really bad Australian accent. *"G'day mate. How's it hanging down under?"*

"I'm not there. I'm back."

"What? Oh." Amber switches back to her normal voice. "Why? What happened? You didn't do something terrible did you?"

"*No.* I didn't do anything. Well I didn't do anything terrible." So then I tell her what happened, and about what Steve was doing. And because it's Amber I give her the longer version, because I know she'll want to know everything. But then half way through my explanation she stops me and asks if I can hurry up a bit.

"Why?"

"Nothing, it's just you've caught me right in the middle of something."

"Oh." I say. "What?"

"Nothing. I'm just... I'm just with someone, that's all."

So then obviously I have to ask who.

"*Billy*!" Amber says.

"What? Who are you with?"

She doesn't answer that. "Look, I'll call you later," she says instead. Then she adds: "I'm sorry it didn't go well with the shark guy. I'll call you later." And with that she calls off. So then I don't know what to do. After a while I make myself a really large sandwich, and then I feel a bit sick so I have another bath.

I wait that evening for Amber to call, and even though I check my phone to make sure it's not stopped working, she doesn't call. I mess around on the internet for a bit, and then I go to bed.

The next morning when I wake up I'm determined to do something more useful, and I decide to ride my bike down to Holport where the *Blue Lady* is moored. I can make sure nothing's happened to her while I was away, and see if Amber's made any progress with cleaning her up for selling. So that's what I do.

It's nice to get out of the house, and it's nice to remember that Lornea Island is actually a really nice place, even if it's not as hot and the colors aren't as bright as Australia. Actually the colors here *are* pretty spectacular. We've got all the fall colors here with the leaves turning into thousands of different shades of orange in the trees. And when I ride down the hill into Holport it looks small and familiar and homey, because I've been here hundreds of times before. I punch in the combination at the gate on the pontoon, and then push my bike as I walk out, because the security guards don't like it if I cycle.

Blue Lady is in the last berth, right at the end of the pontoon, because that's the cheapest one you can get without having to get a mooring. When I get there she looks fine, pretty much exactly as when I last saw her, but I hoist my bike onto her little stern platform anyway and pull out my keys to open the cabin.

She feels small after spending so much time on *Shark Hunter*. And she smells a bit musty inside, but everything is in order, and Amber's done a good job tidying. I begin to feel a bit foolish for coming all the way out here for nothing. But then I notice something a bit strange – we've got a new neighbor. For ages the berth next to ours belonged to an old guy who kept his fishing boat there. But then he died from a stroke, and his family sold the boat, so there was a space next to us. But now there's a yacht parked there. I didn't register it as I wheeled my bike past – probably because I was checking how *Blue Lady* looked. But now I look at it, and I see it's a bit familiar. I have to think hard to work out why. But then I realize. Ages ago – when I was photographing the octopus – it was the boat that belonged to the guy who was spear fishing in the marine reserve. At least, I think it is. It certainly looks like it. Because I want to make sure, I walk out of the cabin for a better look.

And that's when I see that someone's actually living on board. You can always tell – boats that are empty have covers over everything, and they're all boarded up and dark. But this one has washing strung out on the guard rail, and a large red towel hung over the boom. And now I listen I can hear music too, coming from the yacht's cabin. I look at the name on the front, and sure enough the name painted there is *Mystery*. That looks a bit shabby too. Like the rest of the yacht. I frown. I feel quite bad about this. Like this is all I need.

I'm still feeling annoyed as I make myself a cup of coffee and turn on my laptop – not for any particular reason. I can get the internet on board *Blue Lady* because I tether my cell phone to my laptop. I couldn't do that in Australia, because we didn't have a cell phone signal out by Wellington Island, and even if there had been, it would have cost a fortune. But then I don't know what to look at online. So I shut it down again and drink my coffee. I did think I might end up sleeping on board *Blue Lady* tonight, because we have a little bedroom set up, and there's always some dried packet food in the galley. But I'm not sure I want to now, knowing that the other boat is right next door, with that man living on it. So that means I now have to cycle back quite soon before it gets dark. And it's mostly uphill on the way back. So even though I'm feeling a bit sorry for myself now because everything keeps going wrong, I still wash up my coffee cup, and make everything tidy, ready to leave. Then I hoist my bike back onto the pontoon and leave it there while I lock the cabin door. Then I climb off the *Blue Lady* and start to wheel my bike back up the pontoon. But then just as I'm passing the new yacht I get unlucky again. Because a man bursts suddenly out of the cabin.

He can't not see me, and I can't not see him. And that interrupts what he's doing, which seems to be laughing and being chased. And because I interrupt him doing that he looks a bit surprised and even a bit embarrassed. But only for a moment, before the person who was chasing him comes out of the cabin too. And then I'm the one who's surprised. Really surprised.

"Amber?" I say. And she stops laughing too.

NINETEEN

"BILLY! WHAT ARE *YOU* DOING HERE?" Amber stops. Her face, which was full of smiles as she climbed out of the yacht's cabin is suddenly white. It's like I'm her mom and I've caught her doing something bad.

"What do you mean? I told you I was back."

"Yeah but... You didn't say you were coming *here*."

"I wanted to check the boat." I think for a second. "What are *you* doing here?" That seems to me to be the more pertinent question. She looks suddenly embarrassed. And then the man answers before Amber anyway.

"You're Billy? *The* Billy?" His accent takes me right back to when I saw him before, spear fishing in the reserve, but this time he's not angry and his smile is different.

"You work with Amber? On the *Blue Lady*?" His whole face seems to smile with him, and I can see – even though it annoys me a bit – that he's very handsome. "Amber has told me everything about you." He glances across to her, and smiles again. I sense he's both comforting her and teasing her at the same time. "I mean *everything*. Amber never shuts up about you."

She pushes him now, from behind. "Shut up Carlos." But he just laughs. "I mean every *little* thing. The way he says it, it rhymes with beetle. He grins again, until she pushes him harder.

"Seriously. *Shut up*." Amber looks miserable, and she won't meet my eye. There's a moment of awkward silence, but then he seems to smile his way through it.

"No I really mean it. She told me how you have the boat together, and how you run a business. And how you find whales, even when no one else can find them. That's super cool man. Super cool."

He reaches over from the cockpit of the yacht to shake my hand. And he fixes me with his eyes until I do so. Dark eyes that seem to compel me to do what he wants. I move across and shake his hand.

"I'm Carlos," the man says. He rolls the 'r' in his name so that it burrs. *Carrrrrrrlos.*

I look again at Amber, but she's got her head hung down now.

"Say, we were just gonna have a beer." Carlos says. "Why don't you jump up and have one too? If you're not doing anything I mean..?"

I look at my bike. If I don't go soon it's going to get dark. And though I have lights the roads aren't safe for cycling after dark. "No, I have to..." I stop, as an idea hits me. "Say, Amber have you got your car here? Could I maybe get a lift? When you go home?" If I can get a lift I won't have to cycle up the hill. But Amber doesn't answer. She looks embarrassed instead.

"What?" I ask, since I don't understand the way they're looking at each other.

"Hey, nothing man," Carlos waves a hand to dismiss any problem. He turns to Amber. "We can run him home later on, can't we babe?"

Babe? – He says the word so casually I almost miss it. But obviously I don't, because no one has ever called Amber babe before, without her hitting them. I stare at him, and then at Amber. She pushes him on the shoulder again and looks like she wishes she was a hundred miles away. In the end she turns to look at me and rolls her eyes.

"What?"

I don't reply.

"Oh for fuck's sake. I'll run you back Billy. Just stop looking at me like that."

So then I don't have any other choice, even though I think I'd rather not have a beer. I put my bike back onto *Blue Lady* and when I've locked it safely I climb onto the yacht. I seem to spend half of my time on yachts these days. Both Amber and Carlos have already gone below, but I can hear them talking, and the yellow glow from the lights looks quite welcoming.

"Come on down Billy, it's cold out there." Carlos calls to me, his voice friendly now. I climb into the cockpit and look down into the cabin. It looks cozy down there, but it's a lot less tidy than Eric and Agnes' yacht that I sailed on in Australia. There's a funny smell too, though I'm not sure what.

"Come on, get down here," Carlos says again, clearing some space on one of the bench seats. So I climb down the ladder and sit down next to Carlos. Amber is half sitting, half-lying on the other side, and she sits up too.

"Have a beer," Carlos says. He reaches into a cupboard behind his seat and pulls out a bottle. It's funny, I never really drank beer before Australia, now I quite like the taste.

"So..." Carlos says. "Amber was telling me you were over in Oz, but had to come back?" He waits.

"Yeah," I say in the end. "I never really explained the whole story though."

"Something about the wrong size sharks?"

"Yeah."

Carlos raises his eyebrows, and stays quiet. And then I start to explain what happened. It's a bit weird, even though I've never met Carlos before – apart from when he was spear fishing – he seems a lot more interested than Amber does, and he asks really sensible questions, and he seems to know quite a lot about sharks too. I'm kind of surprised by that, given what happened when I first met him. And by mistake I sort of tell him that, which makes him confused.

"How do you mean?" he says, his accent suddenly stronger. "Have we met..?"

"Well not met exactly. But in the nature reserve..."

"Huh?" He leans forward, suddenly he seems quite agitated.

"You were spear fishing in the reserve. And I stopped you."

He frowns deeper, and then slowly it must dawn on him. "That was *you*? You were that kid!" He bursts out laughing. "Oh man! You were that kid!" And Amber doesn't know what he's talking about, so he explains it for her, even though she's being so weirdly sulky.

"I tried to do some fishing. When I first arrived. I didn't even know I was inside a nature reserve. Billy here put me right. He scared the shit out of me in the process though." He laughs again, as if this is the funniest thing ever, and both me and Amber look at him as if this is all getting a bit weird.

"So anyway," Carlos continues once he's calmed down. "You were telling me how this guy had the wrong measurements on the sharks, and you figured it out."

"Yeah," I continue my story, explaining about Chumley and how Steve needed bigger sharks for his ratings. Carlos listens intently, and it's obvious he's paying more attention than Amber did the other day, but then he suddenly hunches forward and leans over the table. From the mess everywhere he pulls out a metal box and pops off the lid.

"Go on," he says, since I hesitate a bit. Inside I see something strange. There's a packet of tobacco in there and rolling papers, plus a bag of some dried green plant.

"So how did you get off the ship? This *Shark Hunter*?"

"Err..." I try to keep talking, but now I'm watching him as he pulls out three papers, deftly licks one of them and joins it to the other two. I guess I must go quiet after that because he looks up again and smiles.

"Do you smoke, Billy?" he asks.

"Err..." I say again, and then Amber opens her mouth. It's the first thing I've heard her say. "Hey... Maybe you shouldn't..."

"It's alright," Carlos cuts her off with another grin, which he turns back onto me. "Billy doesn't mind, do you Bill?"

I don't get the opportunity to answer this, and I don't know what I'd say even if I did. Instead I watch his fingers as they work. I guess he's concentrating, because he doesn't seem to notice that we've all gone quiet. I don't think Amber likes the silence, because she's the next one to speak.

"Is your Dad back?"

I'm surprised by the question. I thought she already knew.

"No. He's still on the mainland. He's working on the new boat."

"When's he back?"

"Few weeks."

The silence comes back. Really I want to ask *her* questions, like what the hell she's doing on this boat, and why this guy called her babe and she didn't punch him in the face. And if she's just going to sit there while he takes *drugs*. The thing is, I can't. I can't ask her any of that.

Carlos pulls out the bag of marijuana – I know what it is – and he opens it. He pulls out a pinch of the dried plant and tears little pieces off, then he sprinkles them along the length of the papers he has laid out in front of him. I can smell it, it's really strong. I realize now, that's what I smelt when I first stepped into the cabin, I just didn't recognize it.

"You ever been to Europe Billy?" Carlos looks up suddenly and smiles at me. I have to look away from his hands really fast.

"No."

He goes back to his work, and then because I can't just leave a long silence I ask him:

"Is that where you're from?"

"Yeah." He leans back and picks up the joint with both hands, then he rolls it into a tube and licks the glued edge. He twists it, and moments later he's tapping a perfect little cylinder on the top of the table.

"Yeah, my dad comes from Genoa. It's a city in Italy, on the west coast. He has a factory there where they make metal things, you know – parts for motors. But my mother comes from Barcelona. So I am fifty percent Italian and fifty percent Spanish." He chuckles. "And maybe ten percent crazy no?" He looks up at Amber and smiles. So then I have to ask something else.

"What does she do?"

"What? Who?"

"Your mom?"

"Oh!" He looks pleased with the question. "She is an artist."

He glances at Amber again.

"Like Amber, only not so good."

I feel a bit awkward hearing that, since Amber isn't an artist. She is studying design, but it's hardly the same thing.

"Yes. It's true. She makes pottery and glassware, and also some paintings. She sells to the tourists that come every year. She has a little studio off Las Ramblas. It's very cool." Then he seems to have an idea. "Hey I can show you? If you like. If you come with me, next year?"

For a moment I think the offer is aimed at me, but then I see from how Carlos twists around in his seat and looks at Amber that he means her. He gives her a really broad smile now and I watch as her face changes from looking annoyed to biting the corner of her lower lip. It's a gesture I've seen lots before. She only does it when she likes the sound of something. But she doesn't reply.

"Do you know Las Ramblas Billy?"

I frown. Annoyed that I don't know what he's talking about.

"It's a street in Barcelona. A very famous street. You can see everything there. Arts, fabulous architecture. Entertainment, shopping. You'd love it."

"Oh," I say, dubious about this. I don't even *like* any of those things. But I don't answer. I'm more interested to know what he meant by if Amber comes with him next year.

"What are you…" I start. I'm trying to think of a polite way to ask what he's doing here, and when he's going to leave, but I'm distracted by him tearing a corner off a magazine cover and rolling it into a tiny tube, and then inserting it into one end of the joint. I didn't know they did that.

"What are you… like how did you get here?" I ask in the end. It's not quite what I meant to ask.

"I sailed here."

"What do you mean?"

He shrugs. "I sailed here."

"You *sailed* here?"

"That's it."

"What, like all the way here?"

"No Billy," Amber cuts in and I hear the sarcasm in her voice. "He sailed half-way here, and he's still out in the middle of the Atlantic."

I glower at her but Carlos seems to find this an awesome joke. But then he goes on like he hasn't heard her at all. "Yeah. I came out the trade route. Out of the Mediterranean and down to the Canary Islands. Then across with the north east trade winds." He looks up and smiles. I can't help but look around. It's quite a small boat to cross a whole actual ocean. And he's not very old either, I mean older than me but not by that much. As I look he balances the joint on his lower lip, so that it hangs down, and then picks up a closed Zippo lighter. He flicks his arm, faster than my eye can follow, and suddenly it's open and there's a flame standing upright, bright and steady. He puts it to the end of the joint and it crackles and glows orange and white. He snaps the lighter off.

"Did you come straight here?" I ask. I'm sort of mesmerized by the drugs, but I'm also interested now. I mean Lornea Island is very nice and everything, but it's a long way to come from *Europe*.

"No. I crossed to the Caribbean. Hung around there for a while. Then I've been working my way up north. I planned to cross back on the northern route before it got too late in the year, but the weather set in early. So now I'm kinda stuck here until the spring." He shrugs, and then takes a deep draw on the joint.

"Stuck here till the spring?" I repeat.

"Yeah. I have to wait until the weather gets better. Don't want to get caught in a hurricane."

His eyes go wide as he's saying this. Like a hurricane is some sort of bogeyman.

"So you're staying here until the spring? Aren't you going to go home, and wait there?"

Carlos laughs. Then waves an arm around the boat's cramped interior. "I am home. This is where I live, man."

I look around the boat again. This time I notice details. The rug he has on the floor, the line of jars – peanut butter, chocolate spread – in the galley. He's got a Samsung phone, just like mine.

"And what a place to get stuck huh?" His voice cuts across me. "*Lornea Island*. I swear I never even heard of it until I saw it on the chart."

The way he says it, it sounds like he doesn't like it very much.

"There is one good thing though, about getting stuck." He looks across to Amber and raises his eyebrows. She sees and rolls her eyes a bit. But though she's trying not to show it, I can tell she wants him to go on. "Because otherwise I wouldn't have met Amber here." He smiles again and then offers the joint across to me, holding the lit end upwards. I totally wasn't expecting that.

"Erm. I don't..." I say, or something like that.

"Go on."

"No I..." I sense that Carlos finds it funny how uncomfortable I suddenly am.

"You sure?" He's still leaning across the cabin holding the joint out to me. "It's really good stuff. I got it from this guy in a bar in town here. It's OK for a place like this."

"No thank you. I don't do... drugs." I say, in the end. I wince a bit at how it must sound. But I'm not gonna start taking drugs just so I don't sound uncool.

"Hey don't worry man." He pulls the joint back, takes another draw on it, and then exhales a big cloud of blue smoke. "Best way to be."

Then he surprises me again by holding out the joint to Amber. I mean it's not *that* big a surprise, or at least not that he offers it. The surprise is that she takes it. She actually hesitates for a few seconds, then gives a bit of a sigh and takes it from his fingers. I really have to bite my lip to stop myself calling out to her.

"It's alright Billy," she tells me in an irritated voice. "It's only a bit of dope."

I don't reply – I don't think I can. Instead I try not to watch, but I can't help seeing how she puts the joint in her mouth and sucks some in. Carefully, trying to look natural.

"So what did you think of Australia?" Carlos asks suddenly.

"Huh?"

"Down under. What did you think?"

I don't know what he means. I've just explained to him how everything went totally wrong.

"Apart from the shark thing I mean."

It's really hard to concentrate, since I'm still watching Amber handle the joint.

"What did you think of the people?"

"Sorry?"

"I'm thinking of sailing there. Next year. Just... keep going, after I cross back to Europe. Just keep going." He shrugs. "It's amazing, people think it's such a big deal to cross an ocean but it's not so hard..." He talks some more but I stop listening now. I can tell some people would think he's charming, but I think I've decided now. On balance there's just something about Carlos that I don't like. And now he's just annoying me.

"When did you say you were going home Amber?" I ask suddenly, and she jerks her head around to scowl at me, like I'm the one being rude.

"What?"

"You said you'd give me a lift. Once we'd had a beer. Well I've finished my beer, and it's probably best if you don't smoke too much drugs before you drive. So I'm asking if you're going home soon?"

I catch her, glancing at Carlos, and I see him smirk. I don't know exactly what it means, but he doesn't try to hide it, and I decide I don't really care what he thinks. He's the kind of guy who goes spear fishing in a marine reserve. And smokes drugs.

"I wasn't going…" Amber starts to say, but then she stops herself before I know what she meant to say. Then she takes a really deep breath, and she even smiles a little bit. "Fuck's sake, Billy," she says in a voice a little more like she normally sounds. "Come on, I'll give you a lift home."

She looks at Carlos again, shakes her head and passes him back the joint. For a moment I see something pass between them. And then she gets up.

TWENTY

IT TAKES ages to actually leave. First Carlos seems to think he's going to come with us, even though I don't want him to, and there's no point because then Amber would have to come back here and drop him off, before going home – and also because there's no room for him and my bike. And then it takes ages to get the seat down in Amber's car, which is only small, and fit my bike in, because we don't have the tool to take my wheels off. But finally we fit it in, and me and Amber get in the car.

"So," I ask as she starts the motor. "What are you playing at?" I try to keep the anger out of my voice.

"I'm giving you a lift home?" She replies, not looking over.

"I don't mean that. I mean hanging out with that… that…"

"With *Carlos*? Is that what you mean?" Now she looks.

"Yeah."

"What's wrong with him?"

The list is so long I don't know how to answer. I start with the obvious. "Smoking *drugs*?"

"Oh grow up Billy. It's just a bit of dope. I've been smoking it for years."

"*What*? When?"

"When you're not looking. I do have other friends you know."

I shake my head at this. For a start it's not actually true.

"You know, in my class. At college." Amber graduated last year so we're not together at Newlea High School any more.

"You smoke drugs at college?"

"Not *at* college Billy."

"Well where then? You can't do it at home. Your mom would kill you, especially with your sister…"

"Oh for God's sake Billy, does it matter?" This silences me. And we sit like that for a long while, pulling up the hill out of Holport. At least I don't have to cycle up it.

"Babe?" I say, when we've driven a few miles. "So is he like…" I don't want to say it. "Is he like your..?"

"I'm dating him Billy. If that's what you're asking"

Dating? Amber?

She carries on. Unusually for her she's going quite slowly. I wonder if it's because she's worried about being affected by the drugs.

"Where did you… How did you…?" I don't seem to be able to finish any of my questions. I could be affected too. I could definitely smell the smoke so some must have got inside me.

"When I was sorting out the *Blue Lady*. Carlos was in the berth next door. We got chatting."

"What about?"

"Just *chatting* Billy. The way people do. Some people."

I ignore this. "Does your mom know?"

"Course she does." Then she sighs at me. "It's cool Billy. Honestly. We're just… having a bit of fun."

I can't help wondering what exactly that means. I've already seen it involves drugs.

"Has she met him?"

"Who?"

"Your mom?"

"What? *No!* Jesus can you just drop it? We've only known each other a few weeks. We're not exactly at the meeting each other's parents stage."

"But he said he was going to show you his mom's studio? In Barcelona?"

"He was just… It's just a thing." She leaves that hanging for a while, but then explains. "He said when he sails back next year I should come with him. You know, for the adventure. I always wanted to see Europe."

I consider this for a while. "But what about your college course?"

"I don't know."

"How long will it take? How much would you miss?"

"I don't *know* Billy. It's just… talk at the moment. You know, we're feeling each other out."

The expression brings a horrible image to my mind and I turn to look at her. I know she sees it too and keeps her eyes on the road. "I didn't mean *that*."

There's a silence between us, and I watch the trees go past in the dark, out of the window.

"I am eighteen," she makes me look at her again. "It's not exactly unheard of for eighteen year olds to be dating."

"I know."

"And the only reason I *don't* date much is because the guys on Lornea Island are so fucking weird." She glances across at me, then snorts a little laugh. "And because I spend all my time with you."

I'm about to protest that she doesn't have to spend time with me, it's just that we both help Dad run the whale watching business, when she carries on.

"I thought you'd be happy for me."

"I am." I say. "Happy for you." Even though I can tell I'm not really.

"I can't exactly date you, can I!" Amber jokes. But neither of us laugh.

Finally, as we get to my house Amber asks me what I'm going to do. I think she means right now at first, but then I see she's talking about more generally.

"I suppose I'm going to call the school, tell them I'm back early," I say. "Go back to class."

"Yeah. You should," Amber says, and then we're both silent for a few seconds, before she pushes open the door.

We have to wrestle to free my bike. Then I don't ask her, but I kind of expect she's going to come in – I don't know why, it's just that she normally does. She knows the inside of our refrigerator better than I do, and she always finishes off the Diet Coke. But then she goes back to the driver's door.

"Aren't you gonna come in?" I say.

"What for?"

I don't know what to say to that, so I just shrug. "I suppose you have to get home?"

"Yeah," Amber says. And then she won't meet my eye. She kind of shuffles the keys in her hand.

"Yeah, something like that."

TWENTY-ONE

I HAVE a good think as I sit in the bath. After a while I start to wonder if I've been a bit harsh. After all, Amber is eighteen, and it's true that most of the guys on Lornea Island aren't exactly the sort of people she should date. And maybe I over-reacted about the drugs too. I mean, it's only marijuana, not heroin. Lots of guys at school smoke it, or they say they do – they're probably lying. But I'm sure I read how half the states in the country have legalized it now for medical use. I'm not sure what it's for, but Amber can be quite a stressed person, so maybe it could help with that.

In a way I change my mind about Carlos too. He says he didn't know you're not allowed to fish in the marine reserve, but it *was* only reclassified recently, and he wouldn't have got to hear about it over in Europe. And it's not as if there's signs up or anything. If he just sailed up there, he might have just thought it was a nice place to drop the anchor and do some fishing. There's something else too, it takes me a while to work out what, but in the end I realize I do know after all. I feel a bit guilty over how I told the Journal of Marine Biology about Steve. I know it was the right thing to do, but maybe I should have told him first. Maybe to warn him or something. I don't know.

In the end I make a decision. Actually two decisions. The first is, instead of phoning the school tomorrow like I said I was going to, and asking if I can come back early, I'm just going to go in, like normal. Now I think about it, I don't know why I didn't work this out before. I had to spend ages persuading them I could go off on the trip in the first place, because of all the school I'd be missing, so they're hardly going to complain now I'm coming back earlier than planned.

The second thing is that I'm going to apologize to Amber. It's not that I really *need* to, but she is my best friend, so I'm going to cut her a bit of slack.

After that I feel a bit better, and I practice holding my breath underwater for a while. I've been doing this for ages now. Dad got me into it, he used to do it for his surfing, sometimes when the waves are big he gets held under for a long time. I don't like surfing that much, but it's good practice for snorkelling and free diving. I can do over a minute easily now, and my best time is one minute fifty nine seconds.

Actually I think there's another reason I'm a little bit funny about Amber. It's definitely not true now, but a few years ago, when we first met, I used to have a bit of a crush on her. Not that much, but she can look quite pretty from some angles, when she's in a good mood, which isn't very often. We did this thing where we opened a detective agency together. We were really immature back then, her more than me obviously, because I'm very mature for my age. But I definitely don't now, have a crush I mean. I think of her more as a sister. And that's why I'm being a bit protective of her now. Or over-protective maybe. Whichever, I definitely think I should say sorry.

So then I get out of the bath and fix myself some dinner, and get an early night so I'm fresh for school the next day.

* * *

I catch the bus which gets me into Newlea at 08:33. Then I realize I've been a bit dumb, because even though school starts at 08:45, the first class that it's actually worth me going to isn't until 10.30. I'm not going to go back just to sit through registration. So instead I head over to Amber's house. It's only a few blocks away, and I know she doesn't start college until 11:30.

I feel a bit nervous as I walk up to Amber's front door. I'm not exactly the best at saying sorry. But even so I'm determined to do it. I glance at my watch: 08:45. I just hope she's up already. She's not exactly the earliest of risers.

I knock on the door anyway. Then it's Gracie who answers.

"Hi Billy," she says.

I like Gracie. She's Amber's baby sister, only she's not a baby anymore, she's six. But she's really funny. She comes out with us on the *Blue Lady* sometimes, and I'm teaching her about all the birds and the different types of whales.

"Why aren't you in Auster-rail-eria?" She demands, cocking her head on one side.

I try to give her a relaxed smile. "It's a bit of a long story. Is Amber up yet?"

"I don't know. I like stories. Can you tell me it?"

"Sure. Sometime, but not now. Because I really need to see Amber. Can you see if she's up yet?"

Gracie looks at me funny, then shrugs. "Not really."

I'm confused by this. It's not like Gracie to be awkward. "Why not?"

"Because she's not here."

"Not here? Where is she then?"

Gracie shrugs her shoulders. "Don't know. Maybe she's at college?" She adds a little hopefully, but that can't be right because Amber doesn't have any classes that start this early. There's no point telling this to Gracie though, because she can't tell the time yet.

"Have you had breakfast yet?" I ask instead.

"Yep."

"Did Amber go out before or after you had breakfast?"

Gracie tips her head on one side again, but doesn't answer.

"Before or after you had breakfast?" I say again, in case she didn't get it the first time, but then she giggles.

"I'm just trying to work out if…" But I don't get to finish what I'm saying because at that moment Amber's mom comes to the door, I guess to see who it is.

"Oh hi Billy, you're back are you?" For a second I think I'm going to have to go over the whole Australia thing again, but instead she just looks at me expectantly. So I ask her if Amber left for college already. But Mrs. Atherton frowns at that.

"No… Well I don't think so. But she stayed with a friend last night, so I don't know. A girl called Jane that she knows from her course."

"Jane?" I think. Amber didn't mention anything about a Jane yesterday, and I've never heard her talking about one before.

"That's right." Amber's mom gives me a breezy smile, kind of like she wants to get rid of me from her doorstep. I think some more. Amber did say she'd made some friends on her course. Even if it was in the context of them smoking drugs together.

"Erm, do you know where Jane lives?" I ask. "It's just I need to speak with Amber this morning. If I can."

Amber's mom lets out a long sigh, she does that a lot when she's talking to me. It's why I don't much like talking to her.

"I don't have the address. Why don't you phone her?"

"Yeah OK, I'll do that." I start to turn around, a bit disappointed, when Mrs. Atherton goes on.

" I know it's somewhere in Newlea though. She has been there a lot recently. She was studying there yesterday afternoon and it got late so she just stayed over," she gives me her *you-know-teenagers* look, which is a bit ironic because I'm a teenager too.

"Hey, there's no problem is there?" She says now. I guess she notices my face. And I decide I won't drop Amber in it. Obviously she hasn't told her mom about Carlos after all.

"No." I say. "There's no problem. It's nothing urgent." I turn to go, until Gracie distracts me.

"Bye Billy!" she says. So I turn around and wave.

"Bye Gracie. Have a nice day!"

And then I walk back down the drive and back towards the school.

TWENTY-TWO

I walk towards the school. I can feel my face tight, my brows knitted together. I guess I'm just angry that Amber lied to her mom, about being at this Jane person's house, if she even exists. And that she lied to me, about whether her mom knew about Carlos. I guess she figured that if I thought her mom knew about him – and didn't mind – then I'd be more likely to not mind either. Well if so, that plan's backfired.

I see the school up ahead of me. And something makes me slow down. I'm not in the mood for school now. I pause for a moment and think. I suppose it's *possible* that Amber dropped me off last night, and then went to this Jane person's house instead of going home. My hand finds my phone, automatically, inside my pocket. I could call her. Though I don't know exactly how I'm going to ask. It might look like I'm snooping. And I'm definitely not snooping. I'm just concerned with who she's hanging out with. I'm just looking out for her.

So I let go of my phone and think a bit more. There is another way I could find out where she stayed the night. If I'm quick.

I turn around and break into a jog. It's only a couple of blocks to the bus station, and there's buses to Holport that go every half an hour, which means there's one in five minutes. I'm out of breath when I get there, and it's just pulling out of the station so I have to run out in front of it and wave my arms. The driver gives me a mad look, but he pulls up and the door hisses open. I show him my pass and swing into the first empty seat, feeling my heart beat hard in my chest. It's about a half hour on the bus, but I don't really get the time to think whether this is a good idea or not, because it's going to be touch and go whether I get there before she leaves for college. If she's been there at all, that is.

The bus takes an age. I have to work really hard not to curse when people get on and take ages to pay. Why can't they just get a pass like I've got? Or at least have the right change ready. But finally we pull into Holport and I hammer the button to make the bus stop, then jump off as soon as the doors open. It's quicker for me to run down to the harbor rather than wait while the bus goes around the whole town. I race through the alley that leads to the fishing harbor, and then along the dockside until I get to the main marina where *Blue Lady* is moored. And looking out I see the mast from Carlos' boat *Mystery* alongside her. Then I stop. I have to put my hands on my knees to catch my breath. Then I check the time. If Amber *is* here, she could be leaving right about now to drive to college. I have to make sure she doesn't see me before I see her.

I scan all the normal spaces where she parks her car, and then I see it. She's got it parked right against the window of the chandler, which they hate, because it blocks people from seeing into their display window. I trot up behind it, and glance in the rear window. The seats are still down, from where I had my bike in there last night. Otherwise it just looks like Amber's car. I check the doors, and they're locked. Then, feeling a bit stupid, I go to the front and feel the hood. To see if it's hot, which would mean it's been used recently. The hood's cold. So much for *Jane*.

I look around. I feel a bit stupid and frustrated now. Like I don't know what to do next. I think I expected to see Amber getting into her car, ready to go off to college. And maybe I hoped she'd see me and realize she'd been busted, and maybe apologize for not telling me the truth. But all there is here is Amber's car. I look again out into the basin at where the *Mystery* is moored. I can't see much from here, since she's moored right at the end of the pontoon. But I could go out there. I could even pretend I was just checking something on *Blue Lady* – that would give me the perfect excuse, and then I could casually glance into the cabin windows of *Mystery* and see if Amber's there, and she'd know she's been busted. I pat my pockets again, feeling better just to have a plan, but then I realize something awkward. I don't have the keys to the boat. I was meant to be going to school today, not coming down here to Holport, so I left them at home. That means I can't pretend to be grabbing something from *Blue Lady,* because I won't be able to get in. But at the same time, I really want to check in the windows of *Mystery* now. To see if Amber's there, and what she's actually doing.

Which just leaves one thing. My kayak. I can paddle out to the *Mystery* on the other side of the pontoon – where they won't be able to see me – then paddle around the top and go right up alongside them. Then I can look right into the windows and see exactly what Amber is doing.

I run around to the alley where it's stored, and unstrap it, from where it's hung off the ground. I lower it down, right onto my trolley-wheels, and then pull it down to the launch ramp.

I don't take my shoes and socks off. The water inside the harbor is always flat, and I figured out a way to launch without even getting my feet wet. As the kayak slides out into the water, and floats off the wheels, I pull them out and collapse them, then stash them in the front of the boat. Then I pull it alongside the ramp and jump in, and then paddle quietly out. I have to duck under the walkway to the pontoon, and then paddle out past the sterns of the boats on the opposite side to where *Mystery* and *Blue Lady* are berthed.

When I get to the end of the pontoon I slow down. From here they *could* see me, if they were looking out for someone. So I stay real close to the tied-up boats to make use of the shelter they provide. I work my way towards *Blue Lady*. Once I'm in her shelter I speed up again, until I get to her bow. Here I stop and peer round. It's a bit difficult to peer round actually, because there's three feet of kayak that sticks out in front of where my eyes are. But I figure that, in the unlikely event they see anything, they'll think it's just any old kayak, they won't know it's me. And when I can see, the *Mystery* looks all tied up and empty. No one on deck.

Trying to keep my paddle splashes to a minimum I slip forward, out of the shelter of *Blue Lady* and across the gap between the two boats, until I'm under the overhanging bow of *Mystery*. I go straight around to the far side, away from where she's tied up against the floating dock. It's dangerous here. I make sure the hull of the kayak doesn't touch the side of the yacht, or worse, bash into it, because that would make a lot of noise inside the yacht. I can touch it with my hands though, just as long as I'm gentle. So I ship my paddle and pull myself carefully along the length of the yacht, towards the middle, where the windows are. Here I realize I've misjudged things a bit. I can't actually see into the window after all because I'm too low down in the kayak. The only thing I can do is stand up. And I don't know if you've ever stood up in a kayak, but they're not designed for it. They're stable enough when you're sitting down, but as soon as you move your weight high up, they become really unstable. It's OK, because I'm quite good at balancing, plus I've got the side of the yacht to hold onto. But I've got to be careful.

Very carefully I get to my feet, and pull myself level with the window. It's then I notice something weird. As I pull myself along the side of the yacht's cabin, the paint starts rubbing off in my hand. I feel a stab of concern that Carlos could accuse me of damaging it, even though it's his fault for not painting it properly. I try to ignore the little bit of blue where I've rubbed the white paint off and get to the window. Then there's a kind of drape, fixed inside with Velcro. It's half drawn, which is annoying, because I have to move even more, and I'm already a bit off-balance. And as I pull myself forward even more I hear a noise. I recognize it. And now I hear it I don't know why I didn't notice it before. I guess I was concentrating too much. But even so it makes me feel like a plug has been pulled underneath me, and all my emotions are draining out. And when I finally look into the window, I already know what I'm going to see.

It's still a shock though. The kind of shock where it takes me about five seconds for my eyes to make sense of what I'm actually seeing. It's all limbs, and movement. And Amber's hair – dyed black these days – splayed out on the floor behind her. Her mouth open, gasping. They're naked, having sex. Right there on the floor of the cabin. In a way it's lucky that Carlos is on top of her, because that means I don't get to see any of Ambers 'bits' – I'm not a pervert, I don't *want* to look. But it's such a shock I can't look away at once. It's like my eyes are drawn to it. To Carlos' butt – tanned just like the back of his legs, I guess he must have done naked sunbathing while he crossed the ocean – rising and falling. And the thought of what's actually happening. I'm just about to recover enough to pull my head away when Amber turns her head. I don't know if she's heard something, or noticed something, or if head moving is just a thing girls do when they're having sex, but either way, I can't let her see me. I just *can't*. I whip my head back, and then, forgetting I'm standing in my kayak, I go to step away too, and it's too much. Even for my good balance, and the fact that I'm holding onto the side of the yacht, because then I'm not holding onto the side of the yacht anymore.

As I fall, I feel the kayak's hard plastic shell thump into the yacht's hull. I feel the bump even through my falling feet.

And then I'm in the water. It closes over my head.

TWENTY-THREE

"WHAT ARE YOU DOING?" The large man asked, while trying to fit the seatbelt over his ample stomach. His companion, younger, fitter and dressed in a significantly shinier suit, continued what he was doing, which was leaning over the car's touch-screen and programming the GPS.

"I'm putting the address in."

"You don't know where Jimmy the Fish lives?"

"Sure I know where Jimmy the Fish lives. I just wanna get the traffic information."

The bigger man paused for a moment.

"It's just a couple blocks."

"Yeah... you say that..." The younger man's voice faded out as he continued to press at the touch screen.

"And?"

The younger man ignored him, concentrating on the screen.

"And what?" The big man pressed. "If it's just a couple of blocks..." Now his voice faded out too, but in his case it was out of frustration, sensing too late how he had fallen into a familiar trap.

The large man balled his hands into fists and forced himself to stay calm. His name was Tommy Battaglia, but many people knew him as Tommy *the Teeth*, at least behind his back. The reason for this was obvious every time he opened his mouth. As he passed through puberty he'd developed significantly more teeth than was normal. Had he gone to a dentist he might have learned the problem was relatively common – and the fix was too – but by then he was already living on his wits on the streets, stealing cars for the Old Man. There wasn't much time for dentists. Besides, the intimidating look the extra teeth gave him came in useful as he graduated to holding up goods trucks running protection rackets. Now, over three decades later, his mouth was just a mess of overcrowded, oversized and filthy teeth at awkward angles to each other. And his breath always stank.

"Jesus Tommy, will you chill?" The younger man said, well aware that Tommy had already dropped it, but still hoping to provoke a further reaction. The younger man was called Paulie, and there was nothing wrong with his teeth. Indeed on being told he had to work with Tommy he'd been to see his dentist for additional whitening treatment, so that his set of perfectly straight teeth shone white in what he proudly regarded as an above-averagely-attractive face.

"There could've been a crash," he went on. "Or they could be fixing the street. Or..." He ran out of possibilities and fell silent, annoyed that he couldn't think of anything further to irritate his companion. When he found out he was being sent to work with *Tommy the Teeth* he was angry. The move came in the reorganization that followed the Old Man's death. It was a surprise passing, at least some aspects of it. The death of someone who had been known as 'the Old Man' for as long as anyone could remember couldn't be considered surprising. But the manner of his passing – peacefully, in his own bed – was not how anyone would have guessed it would happen. Furthermore what came next was a series of shocks that had totally restricted the whole organization. Rather than power shifting down the family, the Old Man had given instructions that his replacement should be the son of his most faithful advisor, Angelo Costello. For Paulie this was a welcome surprise, and an opportunity. Paulie had been nothing to the Old Man, just another lowly foot soldier whose face he couldn't have picked out in a line up. But Angelo was Paulie's family. Technically they were only second cousins, but as kids they'd known each other. Sure, they'd lost touch since then, when Angelo was sent off to private schools and then onto whichever Ivy League college it was he went to. But they'd *played* together when they were just little kids. They were family.

So it was disappointing that, instead of getting the position of some authority Paulie felt he warranted, he'd been paired up with Tommy *the Teeth*. He took it out on him by taking every opportunity he could to piss him off.

"And if so," he went on now, suddenly remembering the basics of how the GPS worked, "the computer – which is fed data about traffic flows from all round the city – would take that information and direct us a quicker way. And *then* I wouldn't have to sit here staring at your ugly fucking face." He clicked the button marked 'go' and the screen changed to a map, showing their route in red ahead of them.

"There. That was painless wasn't it?" Paulie said.

"Just drive the fucking car," Tommy said. Then added under his sour breath. "Fucking jerk."

Paulie pressed the start button on the Toyota, whistling to himself. They'd argued over start buttons too. Tommy had whined about how every car had them these days. When Paulie had asked him what was so bad about push starts, Tommy had replied how they were harder to hot-wire. Paulie grinned to himself at the thought. It was true, push-button starts *were* harder to hot-wire – but then who the fuck cared about jacking cars these days? Tommy, in the twilight of his life, was harking back to his younger days. Back when he was the future. Well that was ancient fucking history now, Paulie thought, with a buzz of excitement. *He* was the future now.

"What's got you so fucking pissed anyways?" Paulie asked, tiring of his whistling before it had time to irritate Tommy.

"I ain't pissed."

"Yeah you are. You're like a bear that's been kicked in the balls."

Tommy turned, grinding his mismatched teeth.

"It's this fucking bitcoin *bullshit*," he said suddenly.

Paulie glanced across. He hadn't been expecting an answer.

"What about it?"

"What about it? I don't trust it."

Paulie hesitated while he negotiated a junction.

"OK." He shrugged. "Then sell it."

"I don't trust selling it. And it's a fucking hassle. Scrabbling around on my goddamn cellphone. I don't see why we can't just get paid in the old way." Tommy shook his head.

"What? Cash?" Paulie allowed himself a laugh. "You want an envelope stuffed full of hundred dollar bills at the end of every week?"

"It worked fine." Tommy growled with enough menace to remind Paulie there was a point beyond which it wasn't wise to push him.

"Maybe." Paulie drove on for a while, wondering whether they were there yet or not. He decided to keep going. "But it wasn't exactly conducive to modern life. When was the last time you took a vacation Tommy?"

Tommy looked across, his face dark.

"I don't do vacations."

"Yeah I know. But say you did. And say you wanted to buy a flight. How you gonna do that with your pile of cash?"

Tommy glowered. "Go to a travel agent."

Paulie shook his head. "They're *gone* Tommy. They don't exist. They all got changed into *vegan* coffee shops. Or maybe you didn't notice?"

Both men were silent for a moment.

"Airline desk then. At the airport," Tommy said.

"Oh yeah. *Very* convenient. So you go all the way down to the airport, at great fucking expense and inconvenience. And what do you find, huh? There's a long fucking line, or worse, the desk's closed?"

Tommy didn't answer. Instead he tried to adjust the seat, which got stuck.

"Why'd you drive this fucking Jap car?" he asked.

Paulie ignored him. "And if it is open, the ticket's five times the price. Oh yeah, and the moment you pay with cash you bet your life you've got an alarm ringing under the desk. Bend over big boy, you're gonna get a glove up your ass." He grinned, catching sight of himself in the rear view mirror and enjoying the sight. He ran a hand over his hair, shaved high up the sides and the top combed back and held in place with gel.

"At the very least," he said, forgetting for a moment whether he was still trying to wind Tommy up, or in a rare moment where he actually enjoyed talking to the guy. "You're gonna be drawing attention to yourself. You don't get none of that with bitcoin."

"Yeah. I get it. I just don't fucking trust it."

Paulie smiled. The truth was, *he'd* been surprised, and just as ready to join the general outrage when one of Angelo's first changes had been to make all payments within the organization via a crypto currency. He hadn't known what the fuck Bitcoin was. But since then its value had nearly doubled, effectively doubling his, and everyone's income. Suddenly the new boss had seemed like a fucking genius, and everyone was wishing the Old Man had brought it in, or died sooner so they could have got into Bitcoin when it was tripling its value every few months.

They were there. Paulie turned the car into a residential street, and drove along it, looking up through the windshield for the apartment where Jimmy the Fish lived. He stopped right outside, just as a young couple exited from the communal doorway. Paulie waited until they had walked past the car. He watched them until they were twenty yards away down the street and hadn't looked back.

"I'll look over it for you. If you want," he said suddenly. "Show you how it works." He wouldn't admit to himself why he was suddenly being nicer to the guy, but on some level he did know. Whether or not he liked spending time with Tommy – and the answer was he didn't – there were times when it felt good to have someone with his years of experience backing you up. You simply didn't get to his age in this life if you weren't careful. And lucky. He might look like the monster from a horror movie, and have bad breath to match. But he knew the business. He knew the fucking trade.

Tommy looked uncomfortable. He didn't say anything but suddenly he reached into his jacket and pulled out his gun, a 9mm Sig Sauer P938, that Paulie knew would have been meticulously sourced with all identifying features removed. Paulie didn't react at all. Instead he just watched as Tommy released the magazine, ensured it was full of rounds, all loaded correctly, then slid it back into position. Then he pulled back the slider, checked the chamber was clear and loaded a round ready to fire. Every movement was automatic, beautifully practiced.

"I mean it," Paulie went on. "I know we don't always… exactly see eye-to-eye. But there's a reason Angelo put us together. I can teach you shit like this and…" Paulie hesitated. He wasn't going to spell it out for the guy. "You know, you've been doing this a while. You pick stuff up." He shrugged. "That helps me too."

Tommy reached into his jacket again, and this time pulled out a silencer. He held it up and sighted down it, checking it was clear. Finally he grunted.

"Yeah sure."

Paulie nodded. "Obviously I'll take a commission. I ain't gonna do it for free."

* * *

The two men got out of the car and walked to the intercom. Paulie pressed the buzzer for Jimmy's apartment and waited.

Moments later an electronic voice responded, "Who is it?"

"It's me," Paulie replied. "Paulie. Let me in will you..."

He was met with a short silence.

"I wasn't expecting you…"

"Just buzz the fucking door Jimmy," Paulie slammed his finger back on the intercom, glanced at Tommy and shook his head, like he couldn't believe the way the fucker was reacting. A few seconds later the buzzer sounded, and Tommy, who already had his hand on the outer door, pushed it open. They went inside.

There was no elevator. Tommy glanced up the stairwell before they began climbing, listening for any sound that wasn't right. They moved quietly, their eyes darting this way and that, checking everything. They made their way along the passageway until they were standing outside Jimmy's apartment. Here Paulie tapped on the door with the back of his hand. Straight away it opened, and a skinny man, wearing just jeans and a vest looked out. He clocked Paulie, but then Tommy too, and his nose started twitching, like a rabbit sniffing a fox.

"We come in for a moment?"

"You didn't say you had Tommy with you." Jimmy sniffed.

"You didn't fucking ask."

Paulie grinned at his own response and went to push past the skinny man, but he stepped back from the door at that moment, so that Paulie almost stumbled into the room. Tommy stayed by the door, closing it behind him. The apartment opened right into the living room. The TV was on, the sofa drawn close-up to it, and looking worn out. The remains of a pizza sat in a cardboard take-out box on one arm, and around the floor, and the rest of the sparse furniture, were scattered beer cans and dirty plates. But the most striking feature of the room was the wall given over to a giant fish tank. It divided the room from the kitchen, and reached from the counter top all the way to the ceiling. And was filled with tens of thousands of tiny tropical fish, and aquatic plants, and beautiful features. Everything about it was lovingly maintained, the water sparkling clean.

Jimmy rubbed his face.

"You wanna sit down?"

Paulie took his gaze off the fish tank and eyed the sofa. "Not particularly." He turned to glance at his partner. "Tommy, you feeling tired at all? Wanna put your feet up?"

Tommy, who hadn't moved from the doorway now responded with the barest of movements of his head.

"No, we're good," Paulie interpreted.

"OK." Jimmy replied. He was struggling to lift his eyes from the floor. "Well what's the problem? I wasn't expecting no one to come. I still got plenty of product."

"Oh we know that."

"And I don't owe nothing. I'm up to date on payments. So I don't get what this is about."

"What you watching?" Paulie ignored him, instead turning to the TV. "Is that *Breaking Bad?*"

Jimmy didn't reply, until Paulie turned and asked him a second time.

"Yeah."

"Oh man, I love this show." Paulie looked back at the screen, genuinely animated now. "This is series three right? The one with the chicken shop guy? The guy who runs the whole fucking drugs scene in New Mexico. I just love that. The idea you can run a whole organization from a chicken shop." Paulie smiled, and turned back to Jimmy.

"I mean I worked in a chicken shop. KFC, just for a few months you understand. But it's a busy fucking job. You ain't got time to be shifting product on the side, believe me." He turned back to the screen, where two sinister looking men were having a meeting in the booth of a fast food restaurant.

"I told Tommy here he has to watch this, but he's more into wildlife shows. Ain't that right Tommy?"

Tommy didn't move at all, but Paulie goes on.

"Oh yeah, he loves something called *Blue Planet*. Guess maybe you'd like that too?" He gestured to the fish tank again, but Jimmy didn't answer, his eyes were full of a cautious fear.

"But the problem we both have, we don't have much *time* for TV, because we're always working." Paulie snapped back around until he was facing Jimmy directly. "Unlike you, or so it seems. You've got all the time in the world. Time to be watching *Breaking Bad* at…" he glanced at his watch, a heavy metal Rolex. "Three twenty on a Thursday afternoon." Paulie shook his head. "I ain't sure Angelo's gonna like that. He likes his guys to work hard, you know? He likes to get value."

"I was just… I have people coming around. Customers."

"Oh yeah." Paulie gave the appearance of suddenly understanding. "Oh I get it. This *is* work for you guys. Sitting around, watching Netflix. Every now and then the doorbell goes and you do a little deal. You *are* working. Yeah you're really putting the hours in. I'll be sure to report that back."

Jimmy pulled his face into a unconvincing smile of thanks, then it dropped away.

"In fact, now I come to mention it," Paulie went on, spying the TV remote and picking it up. "One of those *customers* who came around – keeping you so fucking busy – it turns out he wasn't no customer after all. Least, not in the normal sense of the word." Paulie seemed to have lost all interest in Jimmy directly. He paused the show, then clicked *back*, to check which episode was showing.

"Series three. Didn't I say?" He turned to glance at Tommy, who drew back his lips into a kind of crooked half-smile to acknowledge Paulie's accuracy.

"No," Paulie turned back to Jimmy again. "He was actually a guy doing a favor for Angelo. You ever hear of mystery shopping?"

"Huh?" Jimmy replied. For a moment he'd been distracted by the sight of Tommy's teeth up close. But now he was back, worried by what Paulie was saying.

"*Mystery* shopping. Say you own a chain of stores, and you wanna improve customer service. So you roll out all these rules saying how staff have to be respectful to their customers, and serve them inside thirty seconds, or whatever the hell you wanna do. But how do you make sure it's happening? How do you know your staff are doing what you tell them?"

"I dunno," Jimmy said after a while.

"*Mystery shopping.*" Paulie smiled, almost warmly. "You send someone in who *pretends* to be a customer. You get them to report on how they got treated. All the big stores do it. I guess Angelo learned about it when he was studying the MBA the Old Man sent him on. Anyway. That's what he's been doing. With you."

Jimmy did a good job of keeping his face from tightening up, but his eyes betrayed his fear. Paulie scrutinized it, enjoying the fear now on clear display. Then he carried breezily on.

"So this guy – or it might have been a girl – I don't even know myself. Maybe they bought from you all the time, or maybe it was just the once. Who the fuck knows?" He shrugged. "What's important is, they *did* buy from you. And they took their little baggie of coke right back to Angelo. And he had it *tested.*" Paulie stopped and stared at Jimmy. Jimmy swallowed.

"And do you know what?"

Jimmy breathed several shallow breaths before answering. "Look I can explai…"

"Turns out someone had cut the product."

The change in Paulie's tone seemed to lower the temperature in the room, and an ominous silence descended. Jimmy didn't answer. Instead he glanced over at the door, the only escape route in the room. But Tommy was still blocking it, and he was no longer smiling. His eyes were black and his heavy frame gave no chance for Jimmy to get by.

"See," Paulie continued. "Angelo provides the product to you at a very specific level of purity. He likes to do it that way because it gives his customers a product they know. A brand identity, if you like. You know how important brands are Jimmy?"

Jimmy didn't reply.

"They're *very* important. That's why Angelo's so fucking hot on them, because he's a real smart guy." For a second Paulie considered why, if Angelo was so smart, he didn't appreciate him – Paulie – more, but he shook his head to dispel the thought. Forced himself to concentrate.

"So when our mystery shopper turned up with product cut with *boric acid,* and..." He pretended to think for a while. "what was the other thing Tommy?"

"Powdered milk."

"Yeah, *powdered milk.*" He winced. "Well, it really upset Angelo because it damaged the brand. His brand. He took it personally."

Paulie sent a sideways glance in Tommy's direction, just for a split second, but in response, the big man reached into his jacket. He pulled out his gun, then reached in a second time and withdrew the silencer. He casually screwed the two together, then let his hands fall by his lap, the weapon hanging casually from his large hands.

Jimmy, who had watched the entire performance, turned back to Paulie. "It was just the one time. I swear it. I was short of the money I owed to Angelo and I needed to make it up. That's the only reason I did it."

Paulie put a finger to his lips, like he was a judge, hearing Jimmy's case.

"I swear to you. I swear it Paulie. It was just the one time. You know loads of guys cut it all the time, but I don't. I know Angelo don't like it. I swear I respect that."

"You respect that? You respect Angelo?"

"Yeah. Fuck yeah. I love the guy. I understand. I fucked up. It won't happen again. And I'll make it up. Whatever it takes. I swear to God I will. On my mother's life."

Paulie didn't answer, and for a few moments there was silence. Apart from a whining sound escaping from Jimmy's lips.

In the end Paulie shook his head. "You know Jimmy I believe you. It *was* just the one time, or our mystery shopper would have picked it up. And you've never been behind on the money. Which reflects well..." He sniffed.

"But you know how things are Jimmy. With the Old Man gone, and Angelo in charge, he has to make sure nobody thinks of the transition period as an *opportunity*. To take advantage. He has to build his reputation."

"Yeah but you can talk to him. Paulie. You've got his ear, he *listens* to you. And you *know* me, from the old days. It ain't *ever* gonna happen again, I swear to you..."

"Oh I know that," Paulie cut in, his voice suddenly quiet. "I know that for a fact."

Jimmy opened his mouth to protest further, but something stopped him.

"That's why we're here," Paulie went on. "Having this little chat. We're here to make sure nothing like this happens again. Ever."

Paulie turned to glance at Tommy, who now lifted the pistol so that it was pointed at Jimmy. His arm was steady, his eyes still dead.

"Paulie, *what the fuck*? Cutting ain't *nothing*. I'm a good earner. You *know* that! It don't make no fucking sense to *shoot me* for this."

Paulie stepped away from Jimmy before he replied. "Like I said Jimmy. We're not making the decisions. We're just here to pass on a message from Angelo."

With that Paulie took two steps back until Jimmy was left alone on the far side of the room. He turned his head to Tommy and his raised gun. He seemed transfixed by the sight of it, unable to move.

"Tommy? Don't do this. Everyone cut with the Old Man, you know that! It wasn't..."

He was silenced by two muffled clicks that came in quick succession. The gun bucked, even under Tommy's expert grip. But Jimmy never heard the shots. Not properly at least. Instead his shocked and terrified brain tunneled in on the fact that the bullets hadn't hit him, but had instead slammed into the thick clear glass of the huge fish tank behind him. He turned, in time to see a crazy network of cracks spreading out across the front until they reached the sides and corners. For a moment little else happened, inertia keeping the water in place, but then the wall bulged and finally the weakened glass gave way, collapsing outward.

Within a second thousands of gallons of water, shattered glass and tropical fish surged out in a huge wave. It was close enough to engulf Jimmy, knocking him to the ground and surging across the room's filthy carpet. Tommy was far enough away that he didn't have to move, but Paulie had to leap clear, laughing as he did so.

Then Tommy casually unscrewed the silencer and put the gun away, while on the floor around him, ten thousand tiny fish flapped and wriggled on the carpet. As Paulie turned away he stepped on a dozen of them.

"Oh," he said, looking down in distaste. "And you might want to think about getting another nickname."

TWENTY-FOUR

One week later the silver Toyota pulled up outside another apartment, this time the cheap brown-brick block where Tommy lived. Paulie leaned forwards and looked up through the windshield at the second floor, then he leaned on the horn for a long blast.

Inside Tommy went to the window of his bathroom. He was naked except for a towel wrapped around his waist. As he did so his phone, balanced on the windowsill rang out.

"Yeah?"

"Where the fuck are you? I told you Angelo wants to see us."

Tommy pulled back the blind in the bathroom and looked down, just as Paulie hit the horn again. This time the sound blared up from the street. A moment later it also sounded through the ear piece of the cell phone, routed half way across the country and bounced up and down into space.

"Alright, alright. I'm coming. What does he want?"

"How the fuck should I know? Just get a move on."

Two minutes later, Tommy came out of the door of the apartment building and crossed the street, tucking his shirt in as he walked. Paulie watched the way he lumbered and shuffled with obvious disgust.

"I got neighbors you know." Tommy said as he clambered into the car.

"Yeah. You got an appointment to see Angelo too. Which of those is more important?"

Tommy answered by pulling hard at his seatbelt, then swearing as the mechanism locked.

"Fucking Jap car," he said.

. . .

Paulie kept to the speed limit, and soon they pulled up outside a pair of iron gates that protected a large house that overlooked the water. The gates offered the only way past a ten foot high wall, and security cameras were mounted on each post, and at regular intervals along the length of the wall. The cameras on the posts looked like a pair of vultures. For a moment the two men waited as they swung to inspect them, their motors humming. Then the gates swung open. Paulie drove in, through a well-kept garden, and up towards a heavy stone house. He parked in a bay between a Cadillac and a Porsche. They both got out.

A thick-set man in a dark suit already had the front door open for them. He checked around the grounds, then lifted a hand-held radio to his mouth and spoke quietly into it. As Tommy and Paulie came up to the door the man nodded at them, and ushered them inside. They stepped into a wide hallway decorated in a traditional style. A blue-painted vase – it looked Chinese, or at least expensive – sat on a massive oak dresser that was stained near black. Inside the glass doors was a display of antique pistols.

"Hey Barney," Paulie said, unbuckling his own gun with no hesitation, "What's happening?" He put the gun on the table while the man took the weapon carefully, checking the chamber was empty, before slipping it into a drawer. Then he turned to Tommy.

A little reluctantly Tommy reached for his own gun. Giving up your weapon before going in to see the boss was a new rule of Angelo's. It still felt weird, disrespectful somehow, like it implied how you might be tempted to use it otherwise. In the Old Man's days you simply had respect. If there was any doubt that you might not have respect, well in that case you would never get this close before someone put a bullet in your head. As he had done a thousand times in recent months, the realization that times changed passed through his mind. He released his gun from the holster, pulled the slider back to show it wasn't loaded, and handed it handle-first to Barney. As he did so a look passed between the two older men, both were survivors from the old regime.

"I'll take care of it," Barney said quietly, and Tommy nodded.

"You know what this is about?" Paulie asked brightly, as Barney led them down a corridor, and up some stairs.

"Nope," Barney said without turning around. At the top of the stairs was a large landing, with some chairs arranged, not dissimilar to a doctor's waiting room. There was even a low table with magazines.

"Wait here. He won't be long." Barney turned away and walked back downstairs, leaving Tommy and Paulie alone. Paulie sat down, but Tommy went to the window and glanced outside at the harbor. Then he looked around the landing, taking in the differences that Angelo had made since the Old Man's death. Some of the paintings were missing, he saw. The Old Man had developed an interest in art in his later years. Classical stuff, always Italian painters, and probably not as valuable as it was intended to look. But even so, Tommy had appreciated them, especially the couple of times the Old Man had taken the time to explain them to him.

"The paintings are gone," Tommy said.

Paulie glanced up from a magazine called *Jet Ski Rider*. "What? Oh yeah." He shrugged. "Angelo probably sold 'em. Good thing too. It used to be so fucking dreary in here."

Tommy frowned, but didn't get the chance to say anything more, because at that moment a door opened and another man, dressed impeccably in a dark blue suit and silk waistcoat walked out. He looked at Tommy first, and there was something in his eyes, a silent respect, but it was Paulie he spoke to.

"Angelo's ready for you now. Please come through." The man's voice was very quiet and very calm. He didn't wait for an answer, but led the way into a huge office, half paneled with oak, and with one wall given over completely to books. The largest piece of furniture inside was an enormous desk, not dark like the rest of the room but painted matt white. A young man with blond hair sat behind it, frowning into an Apple laptop. An iPad sat beside it, balanced on a frame. He was dressed expensively but casually – a white cotton shirt with the sleeves rolled up showed off his tan. Tommy noticed he wore nothing on his feet.

Angelo glanced up as the three men walked in. He offered a brief smile but continued working, and only after a few moments more did he push the computer away and get up. He walked first to Paulie, and embraced him warmly. Then he nodded at Tommy, but didn't touch him.

"Sit, please. Take a seat," he said, indicating the chairs in front of the desk. Tommy and Paulie did so, while the man with the blue suit took his own seat too, over by the wall.

"Thanks for coming by. I appreciate it." Angelo spoke with a nasal tone that made him sound whiny, but his eyes were sharp and alert.

"No problem," Paulie answered. He considered adding a casual 'cuz' to the end, but his nerves failed him. He settled for a breezy reply instead. "What's up?"

Angelo didn't answer at once. He went back behind his desk and sat down. He leaned forward. Then sat back. He seemed about to speak, but then looked away. Everyone waited.

"I got a little job for you," Angelo said in the end.

"Sure." Paulie felt his chest inflate. This was the first time he'd actually been in to see Angelo since he took over. Mostly the orders flowed down through the ranks. So whatever this was, it sure wasn't 'a little job'. It was something bigger. It was an opportunity.

The room fell silent again. And for a moment they all watched Angelo as he stroked his chin.

"It's a little different. It's gonna take a bit of explaining."

"No problem." Paulie glowed inwardly.

Another silence filled the room.

"The Old Man, before he… passed. He was having a few issues. Down at the port." Angelo said at last. "I'm sure you know about it." He stopped for a moment, as if realizing that maybe this was something they wouldn't have known.

"Nothing serious," he went on. "Just the cost of bringing product in was creeping up. You know? Guys getting too greedy, you know what I mean."

"Sure," Paulie said enthusiastically. The truth was though, he had no idea. He'd always been way too low-level to be party to any information like this. The fact that he was hearing it now was giving him a huge sense of excitement.

"To tell you the truth, I wonder if it didn't contribute in some way to... you know..." Angelo didn't finish the sentence.

"To his heart attack?" Paulie finished it for him, and immediately wished he hadn't, as Angelo looked up sharply.

"Yeah." Angelo dropped his head again. Everyone did when the subject of the Old Man's passing was raised. It was an unspoken mark of respect, that Paulie dimly realized he'd just violated in some way. He cursed himself, told himself to be more careful.

"Anyway," Angelo went on. "After he died, I wanted to take a look at it. See if we could sort it out." As Angelo started talking again it looked like he didn't really care about respecting the Old Man. But why would he, all this was his now...

"So I asked Paulo, he handles things down with the Colombians, I asked him if there were any alternatives to our regular routes. You know we generally have it come in on containers?" Angelo said this casually, as if it was common knowledge, but Paulie felt a buzz of thrill again. He didn't know. He knew that high up in the organization this was what got discussed, but he'd never been present before when it was. He forced his face to stay neutral. He glanced at Tommy, and was disappointed to see he was almost looking bored.

"So we had another look at flying it in," Angelo was continuing. "I went down there, to meet with him. We looked at small aircraft, coming in to airfields. No customs to pay off. Or even dropping it from the air..." With his hand he mimed an aircraft flying over his desk, but then winced. "I didn't like it. You have to file and record flight plans. Planes are tracked. It's... messy." Angelo shook his head. "But then Paulo had this idea. We were sitting in this restaurant in Caracas. Overlooking the harbor, and we were watching these sailboats, and then Paulo turned to me and he says 'why can't we just sail it in?'" Angelo looked suddenly at Paulie.

Paulie didn't know what to say, so he decided to stay quiet. After a worrying silence, Angelo continued.

"So we looked into it. Now me, I don't much like sailboats." Angelo glanced out the window as he said this, where Paulie knew he had a large motor cruiser moored on a dock outside the house. He knew because he'd heard about the parties. Word was Angelo threw the most amazing parties, for his closest friends. They were little short of orgies, limitless amounts of coke and girls imported from Eastern Europe and South America.

"But Paulo, he knows a bit about them. He said how a load of retired folks travel around in them. How they go where the hell they like. Without having to tell no one *where* they were going. And how the whole customs thing is kind of voluntary – you come into a harbor, and if there is any customs guy, he don't know where the fuck you've come from. You tell them if you've come from the next town down the coast, or across the whole fucking sea." He paused again, as if reliving the original conversation.

"But we couldn't ask these guys. These old timers. I mean they're pretty unlikely smugglers," Angelo laughed suddenly. "And they're rich enough anyway. They don't need the money. So I left Paulo with a challenge. Find me someone who could do a test run. Just a token amount. See what the costs were. See how it works."

There was a soft electronic ping as an email hit Angelo's computer. His eyes moved to it without moving his head. He read the first few lines, then went back to his story.

"Then two weeks later Paulo calls me up, tells me he's found the perfect fucking guy. An Italian, he's sailed his boat all the way across from Europe, and now he's heading here, to the States, before going back home again. He's alone. And best of all, he's *totally* up for it. So we check him out. Paulo takes him out for dinner and while they're doing that we get on the boat, and sweep it. It's clean. *He's* clean. It all checks out. So we have to make a decision. I figure we give it a go, and we load him up. Ten keys." Angelo snorted loudly, like it was a reflex action to the mention of cocaine.

"Then I think, *fuck it*. Let's really do this. So we put a bit more on board. *Eighty keys*." He paused, to let the implications of such a large amount sink in. "We bury a tracker in there, make sure he sees it. Make sure he knows we're gonna be on top of him the whole fricking time. We agree how he's gonna come in this little harbor north of Florida. We're gonna move the product the rest of the way by truck."

Angelo smiled wistfully. "Eighty keys. If we can get that in without paying off the guys at the dock. That's..." He stopped suddenly, as if realizing revealing his profit margins was going too far. "That's a sweet fricking deal. That's what it is. So anyway. Paulo waves the guy off at the port, and the both of us watch this tracker as the guy sails north." With this Angelo turned the iPad around, and pulled up an app. It showed a map of Central America and the southern United States. Marked out on it, was a dotted line, showing the route taken.

"He goes up through the Caribbean. Shoots east of Cuba, and everything's looking good. But then he changes direction. On the computer. I'm like – what the fuck? And I call up Paulo. I ask him – what the fuck? And he tells me the guy's *phoned him* – from the sailboat – to say he's skirting round the back of some bad weather."

Those words are left hanging for a few seconds, as Angelo seems to become more present again. He looks at the two men in front of him, then chooses Paulie and lets his eyes rest there. "And look, you can toggle on the weather. On the map here." He does so now, spinning the iPad around so he can see it better himself. Suddenly the screen changes, to show the weather systems overlaying the route.

"And it's not bad fricking weather the asshole's sailed into. It's a goddamn hurricane."

There was another silence. Paulie wondered if he was expected to do or say something, maybe even give a snort of laughter at this unknown man's stupidity, but he knew nothing at all about boats, so wasn't sure if this was appropriate or not. In the end he settled for scratching awkwardly at his nose. It seemed to do the trick since Angelo continued.

"At first the guy ain't concerned. He reckons he can get around it, or below it. Or it'll somehow miss him – or whatever. But all the time I'm comparing where this little boat is and where the weather guys say this storm is. And I can see he's not gonna get around it. The whole fucking lot is gonna land on top of him. But what can we do? We can't get out there. We just have to wait. Then the guy phones again, says he's damaged the boat. The steering or some shit. So he has this idea he's gonna call the Coastguard to get some help. Obviously Paulo tells him *that* ain't happening. Not with eighty keys of finest Columbian on board. But when he does the guy panics, says he'll throw it over the side. So the whole thing's going to *fuck*." Angelo's voice hardens suddenly. "And I'm thinking, how we gonna get eighty keys out of the ocean? And clearly we ain't."

He was silent for a moment, thinking. Then Angelo shook his head again. "The next thing, there's *another* call from the guy. He tells Paulo he's gonna have to issue a mayday, the boat's fricking *sinking*. He's right in the middle of the hurricane and his boat's going under." Angelo held up both his hands in surrender. Then he sat back in his chair. "And that's the last we hear from him. We found out afterward he did issue a..." Angelo searched the air for the word. "Not a *mayday*, something else..." He turned to the man in the blue suit. "What'd they call it?"

"A Pan Pan," the man said.

"Yeah. Fucking Pan Pan. The Miami coast guard picked it up, and when they didn't hear anything else, they sent out a helicopter to look for him. But by the time it got there, the yacht was already sunk. Gone. About four hundred miles out."

The story seemed to be finished, and though Paulie was beyond thrilled that Angelo had shared it with him, he had no idea why he had. Even so, he had to say something.

"Fuck," he said.

"Nah," Angelo replied, unexpectedly. He waved the comment away with his hand. "It's only eighty keys. Not a big fucking deal. Just a shame because it would have been nice to bring that in..."

He paused again.

"But shit happens. Shit fricking happens."

There was another silence as they all considered the wisdom in this.

"But then I had a think about it," Angelo went on, leaning forward suddenly. "And I wondered something. Why would a guy, who's on a *sinking* sailboat – in a goddamn hurricane – why would that guy bother to make a call?"

"What?" Paulie frowned.

"Why would he call Paulo? I mean what does he think we're gonna do? He issues the *Pan Pan,* which is this call you make when you want to alert the helicopter, but you don't know for sure if you need it – you know, you wanna put them on standby. Then he calls *Paulo.* He tells *us* he's sinking. But he doesn't make the Mayday call. It's never registered. Doesn't that strike you as odd?"

Paulie considered. With zero experience in shipping in the product, and even less in sailing, he had no real idea, but at the same time he sensed how this meeting was some kind of test. If he could only think of the right thing to say.

"Guys like that. They know they've gotta show respect," he replied, giving it his best shot.

Angelo's brow furrowed just enough to make Paulie know he'd got it wrong. "I fricking wouldn't," he said dismissively. "What? I'm about to drown and I got time to make one call? I make the mayday call. Every fricking time."

There was another silence, and eventually Paulie shrugged. "Sure," he said, feeling an ache in his guts. He shifted awkwardly in his chair. "Yeah, me too."

There was another long silence, during which another email came in. Again Angelo glanced at it, gave it a few seconds of attention, then looked up again.

"And then I got a call." He smiled now, just a subtle twisting of his pale lips.

Paulie was totally lost now. He tried to keep the anxiety off his face.

"Just a call. From one of my guys – you don't know the guy." Angelo dismissed that idea out of hand. "My guy wanted to let me know about this funny story. How one of *his* guys got offered a half key of coke. By some guy. Some Italian guy, but *Italian* Italian, not Italian American, you know what I mean?" Angelo glanced at Paulie and raised his eyebrows. "The funny thing was, he didn't want enough for it. What do you make of that?"

Paulie began stroking his chin now. Finally he had a glimmer of where this might be going.

"Italian guy?"

"Yeah."

"The guy on your boat. The sailboat. He was Italian, right?"

"Yup."

"Italian Italian?"

"Uh huh."

Paulie thought some more.

"They ever find the wreckage?"

Angelo shook his head. "The Coastguard wrote it down as lost at sea. Sunk."

"They didn't dive down? Make sure?"

"Too deep. We looked at that, as a way of getting the fucking coke back. Too far out."

Paulie stroked his chin some more.

"So maybe… Maybe it didn't sink?"

"That's what I'm thinking."

"So then where is it?"

"Good fricking question." Angelo grinned now. "I asked my guy to find out about this Italian guy, but no-one knows jack about him. So they dig around a little and the only thing they hear, is some other guy reckons he's living on a boat somewhere."

"A boat?"

"Oh yeah. A *sailboat*."

"Where?"

"They don't know exactly. But…"

Paulie glanced at Tommy. An understanding forming at last for what the job was.

"You ever been to Lornea Island?" Angelo asked.

"I don't do vacations."

"Well you're about to have one." He spun the computer around to show them the screen. "It's a long shot. There's a dozen places the guy could be hiding, *if* he's on the island. Marinas. Little creeks. Shit like that. Or he could have left. Or more likely he could have never been there in the first place, because he's fish food. But I need someone I can trust to go and check it out." Angelo sat back in his swivel chair and looked at the two men in front of him.

"Danny here will give you some pictures of the boat, and the guy." At the mention of his name, the guy in the suit stood and walked silently over with an envelope. Paulie pulled out the photographs of a white sailboat with a blue painted cabin. Another of a smiling young man. He stared at the photograph with a hatred and an electric thrill, hope spreading throughout him like the blossoming of a flower. When he and Tommy had been ordered to visit Jimmy the Fish, he'd been disappointed the command had been to give him a warning, and not to put a bullet between his eyes like he dreamed of doing. Paulie yearned for the ultimate chance to prove his loyalty, and his competence. And here at last was his chance.

"And if we find him? What do you want done?" He frowned as a horrible thought crossed his mind. Every time he thought he understood what Angelo was saying, he got it wrong. Might the same have happened again. Might Angelo just want another warning delivered? "Not like Jimmy the Fish?" He said.

"No, not like Jimmy the fucking Fish." Angelo angered at once. "This asshole stole my coke. I want his balls cut off and his head in a fucking box." For the first time in the meeting, it was Tommy that Angelo looked at. Paulie followed his gaze, and saw how the big man was staring calmly back, completely unmoved by the order to take another man's life. He felt a surge of jealousy. Then Angelo spoke again.

"Oh. And even more than that. I want those eighty keys *back*."

TWENTY-FIVE

THE WATER'S cold but I don't even notice. I feel – as I'm falling through the air – how the side of my kayak crashes hard into the hull of the yacht, knocking it with a thump that must reverberate throughout the entire boat. And then I'm under the water, gulping down mouthfuls of stale marina seawater before I think to close my mouth. Normally it's peaceful when you go underwater, but now I'm panicking. I've got to get to the surface, get back in my kayak and get out of sight before they get out on deck to see what's happened. I flap my arms, but it's more like a bird learning to fly than swimming. Finally my head breaks clear, and when the water drains from my eyes I look around. The kayak is right next to me, but capsized.

Moving fast I place my hands on either side, near the front, so I can lever myself back on board without capsizing it again. At the same time I glance to the cockpit of the *Mystery*. They're not there yet. I think. They're *naked*. They'll have to get some clothes on before they come out. And maybe there's other things too. I'm not exactly sure if you can just stop having sex if you're interrupted in the middle. Like with dogs. Or when you go to the toilet. No, I know that's stupid. Or just wishful thinking, because I really, really, *really* don't want Amber to see it was me who was spying on her. I don't know how I'll ever explain this if she does.

I scream at my brain to calm down. Thank God I've practiced this. Sometimes I watch tourists who come and do kayaking on their vacations, and if they fall out they usually can't get back in at all, all because they don't know the technique. You have to pull yourself up and twist onto your butt all in one smooth movement. I do it now, and slither back into the kayak. When I'm in I grab the paddle and start going as *hard* as I can. Fortunately the front of the kayak is already pointing away from the pontoon, and since going straight is quicker than turning, I just keep going, straight across the open water towards the rock breakwater on the other side. It divides this part of the harbor from the channel back to the sea, but there's a second channel too, which leads to the commercial harbor. Then I realize if I get to the second channel I can hide there, behind the rocks, so I paddle harder on my left side to swerve over to the entrance. But there's about twenty feet of open water I have to cross before I get there. So I just paddle as fast as I can, panting like crazy and expecting to hear Amber yelling out my name at any second.

But then I'm out of sight, behind the tall barrier of rocks. I stop paddling, my chest heaving up and down. I didn't really plan where to escape to, but actually it's worked out well. As well as being hidden, they can't get to me here, nor can they get over here to see who I am, at least not without walking all the way around the marina basin.

I listen, in case I can hear them shouting, but there's nothing – no sound at all. And after ten minutes of just waiting there, I loop the kayak's painter around a pointed rock, so it can't drift away, then carefully climb out. Then I scramble up the breakwater, so I can peek through a gap at the top. I'm really careful, in case they're on deck watching out, but quickly I see they're not. The *Mystery* is there, just as it was before, but the deck is empty, and so is the pontoon. They must have… Well, I don't know what they must have done. I wonder for a second if maybe they didn't hear me after all, it's hard to believe, given how hard the kayak crashed into the hull of the yacht. But then they did look pretty absorbed in what they were doing.

Yuck.

I decide not to think about that. So I focus on my situation instead. Which isn't great. I'm soaking wet. It's late in the year and I don't have any spare clothes. And the only way I can get home is on the bus. Plus, now the adrenaline from nearly being chased has worn off a bit, meaning I'm already quite cold. On top of that, I can't just paddle back to the ramp I launched from, because to do that I'd have to go past the Mystery again, and they would only have to glance out the window and they'd see me. And when I think about *that* I realize something else too. If they do suspect it was me, Amber only has to check where I store my kayak to see if it's there or not. So on top of everything else, I have to return it as soon as possible.

I'm feeling glum as I pick my way back down the rocks and into the kayak. Then I paddle all the way up the channel until I get to the commercial harbor. It's where the fishermen unload their catch, and I'm wary here, because they get super mad when tourists come in here, getting in their way. But I'm lucky, there's no one here at the moment. There's another problem though – there's no slipway here to pull the kayak out. I paddle around a bit, wondering what to do, but then figure I might be able to just pull it up the wall, since the tide's quite high. So I stop by one of the iron ladders and loop the painter around my hand. Then I climb up and when I get to the top I try to heave the kayak after me. It's made of tough plastic, so it's strong enough, but it's pretty heavy and I can't do it. For a little while I get really annoyed – I'm getting really cold now and this is just frustrating. But then I tow the kayak, back down in the water, until it's under one of the mini cranes the fishermen use to lift out the boxes of fish. You're totally not allowed to use these, but like I said, there's no boats in right now, and I know how to use them. I lower the winch, then climb down another ladder, hook it on and climb back up. Then I fire up the crane and winch it up. Then, finally, I can tie the wheels back on, and get it back in the alley where I store it.

The whole time I'm working, I keep a pretty careful watch out for Amber and Carlos, but I don't see either of them. So I'm fairly sure she doesn't see me either. It's some consolation, as I squelch around to the bus stop in the town – the one that's well away from the harbor. I almost freeze to death waiting for the bus, and I'm worried the driver won't let me on, because I must look a bit crazy. But by then I'm only kind of damp rather than dripping wet, and the driver doesn't even ask. Then I sit right by the vent for the heater, and I think without that I'd probably get hypothermia and maybe die.

I have to change buses at Newlea, but there's a waiting room, and inside I find a big radiator, which I sit on. The Littlelea bus is cold though, and it's horrible when I have to get off, because it's a bit of a walk from the stop to my house and my clothes feel heavy and damp. But fortunately the house is warm, because I left the heating on full before I left. And as soon as I'm inside I run myself a bath.

* * *

I try to decide whether Amber saw me, and if so what to do about it. On the one hand, there's no way they wouldn't have heard when the kayak hit the yacht's hull, but they probably couldn't tell what it was. Not least because they were distracted. I definitely didn't see them run onto the deck, but I didn't notice the windows. They could easily have looked out when I was getting back into the kayak, or when I was paddling away with my back turned. But on the other hand I was pretty quick, so if they did see me, it would have been the back of my head they saw. In that case, they might not have recognized me. And if Amber *did* recognize me, then she'll know that *I saw her* too, and more importantly, saw what she was doing. And I don't think she'll want to bring that up in a hurry. So even though I don't exactly feel good about how today went, I decide the best thing to do is try to forget it. And if Amber ever mentions it, to pretend I don't have any idea what she's talking about.

I still feel a bit glum, though. I reach out of the bath and pull my cellphone out of my damp coat pocket. It's a Samsung Galaxy S7. It's supposed to be waterproof to 1.5 meters, or nearly five feet, but I've never actually tested it before, on account of how cell phones are so expensive and I didn't want to risk breaking it for no reason. But actually it looks just fine. That cheers me up a bit. And now that I've shown it does work underwater, I try it again, holding it under the bath water. It's actually really cool. You can see it perfectly even when it's totally underwater, actually better than normal, because the water magnifies it a bit. You can't use the touch screen though – but I read before in the instructions how that's normal, because of how the water breaks the electrical connection. Or something, I don't remember the details.

I play with it a while, then grab a towel and dry it again. And then I think for a while.

I think about Carlos. There's something about him I don't like. Something I don't trust. His story about sailing across the Atlantic, for example. I don't believe for a minute he did that. I'm sure he's lying.

I start with Google. Carlos never told me his surname, but I remember he told me his dad comes from a place called Genoa in Italy. I check where it is on the map, and then start googling combinations of words that might find him. I try 'Carlos, *Mystery*, Genoa' – but nothing comes up. Then I remember how he said his mom is an artist in Barcelona. So I add more words to do with that. But still nothing relevant comes up, which isn't completely unexpected, but is a bit odd all the same. So then I decide to focus on the boat. If you have a boat you have to register it, and the most likely places, if Carlos is telling the truth, is that it's registered either in Genoa or Barcelona. Then I have a bit of a problem, because everything I can find about registering boats in Italy is written in Italian, and everything about registering boats in Spain is written in Spanish. And I don't speak either Spanish or Italian. But with the help of Google Translate, I mostly figure it out. But again, I don't find anything.

Then I get out of the bath. You really need a proper computer to do actual research like this, and anyway, the hot water has run out again, and the bath is getting cold.

As I dry myself off I have another idea: Amber's Instagram page. Amber is *super* into Instagram. I don't know why I didn't think of it sooner, just about the first thing she does when she meets someone – anyone – is to follow them on Instagram, and then tag them in every single photo she uploads.

It takes me a while to log on to Instagram because I don't have an actual account – I don't do any social media, and I deleted all the fake accounts I set up before to let me follow other people. But when I'm in I scroll back through Amber's timeline, expecting to see hundreds of photos of him. But there's nothing there. There's no-one called Carlos mentioned anywhere. No one tagged. No photos of him. Nothing. Confused, I go to Amber's Facebook page and check there. I figure that maybe Europeans don't do Instagram? But I can't find him on Facebook either. Or at least, if he is there, Amber hasn't friended him. Which is crazy, because I already saw they were way more than friends.

I look back over the notes I've made. I realize I've found precisely nothing about who he is, or where his boat comes from, or anything at all. It's like he doesn't exist. Or maybe like he doesn't *want to* exist.

TWENTY-SIX

I GET UP EARLY the next day and empty my backpack, ready for the day ahead. Then I pack some food – there's not much left in the house but I find an apple and make a sandwich from two crusts and some cheese. I can always stop by the store to get something nicer. Then I go upstairs and I kneel down beside my bed. I reach underneath and pull out my spy box.

Inside there's a tangle of black cables, and several Tupperware boxes from when I was organized, for a while at least. I went through this phase, a couple of years ago, when I was a bit obsessed with James Bond-style gadgets. Not the killing types – just the spy ones. It's really amazing when you think about it, when they made the films originally, the inventions that Q gave to Bond were just made up – no one thought it was possible to actually build them. But now, you can just buy them, on the internet. And they're not even that expensive either. Although as I found out, if you do buy the cheap ones, you often find the instructions are in Chinese, or if not in Chinese, then written by someone who is Chinese and doesn't speak English very well.

I empty the box onto the bed. I bought most of this stuff just after Amber and I set up our detective agency. We had to shut it down, because we found out it's illegal for people under the age of eighteen to operate as private detectives on Lornea Island. I was fourteen at the time, and Amber was sixteen, so we weren't even close. Plus you need a license which we also didn't have. But for a little while we didn't know any of that. Even so, we did get an actual case, and we did actually solve it. Sort of. We spent most of the money we earned in buying the original *Blue Lady*, but Dad wouldn't let me spend all of it, so that's when I went a bit mad buying all the spy gear.

But then the problem was I had no one to spy on. The agency was shut down, and Amber figured out pretty early on to sweep her house for bugs. Then Dad told me if I didn't stop surveilling him he'd take all my electronic devices outside and smash them with a hammer, even my laptop. So after that they just ended up here in this box under my bed.

I pick through them now, thinking what might be useful. I pick out my cell phone charger, which actually *is* a cell phone charger, but also has a secret listening device in it, my tracker, and my endoscope, which is a long cable with a camera lens built into the end. Then I stand up, and right away I notice myself in the mirror. Without thinking I've just got dressed normally, so I sort that out. I throw on a baseball cap, and get changed into some clothes I don't normally wear. Finally downstairs, I grab one of Dad's heavy overcoats. It's too big for me, but it makes me look older.

Then I go out and catch the first bus to Newlea. Forty minutes later I'm standing on the harborside looking out over the boats in Holport marina.

* * *

The *Mystery* is exactly where I last saw her, the second-to-last boat at the end of the pontoon, with only the *Blue Lady* outside of her. There's no one about. Keeping as unobtrusive as I can, I unlock the gate to access the pontoon, then make my way down towards the end. There's nothing I can do to avoid walking past *Mystery*, and I'll just have to hope Carlos doesn't see me. Or Amber. If either of them do it's not a disaster, because today I have the keys, and I can just say I'm going to do some work on *Blue Lady*. And in a way I am. Even so, I try to make my footsteps as quiet as possible as I walk past the yacht, and I'm relieved when no one comes out from the cabin. I do see the hatch is open though, and I hear music playing from inside.

Normally I love jumping onto the *Blue Lady*, feeling the way she gives a little under my feet. But today I'm focused. Very quietly I open the door to the cabin, slip inside, then close it behind me. I don't want anyone to know I'm on here. Then I finally breathe properly for the first time in five minutes.

I slip out of my backpack and Dad's overcoat, and unpack my gear. The first thing I do is set up the endoscope. I only had to pay $49.99 for it, which is a bargain, but on the other hand it is just a camera lens fitted to a long wire, with a USB plug on the other end. I run the cable up to one of the port-side windows, that looks out onto the side where the *Mystery* is moored. I open the window just enough to poke the camera outside, and gently close the window again, so that the camera lens is held in position, looking out over the yacht. Then I go back and plug the other end into my laptop, and turn it on. I have to go back up and adjust it a bit, but in the end I'm happy. I've got a nice clear view of the whole of the yacht's cockpit. No one can go in or out without me seeing them, but there's absolutely no chance that anyone can see me watching *them*.

Feeling a bit better about life now, I brew up some coffee, and open my bag of donuts.

TWENTY-SEVEN

THE THING ABOUT STAKEOUTS – and you never see this in movies or whatever – is just how incredibly boring they are. You always get things set up, and then expect that something is going to happen. But it never works like that. It's a bit like fishing in that respect.

Anyway, twenty minutes later I've brewed and drunk my coffee, and eaten three donuts, and even though I've got one left I don't want to eat it because then I'll feel sick, or sicker than I feel already. And even though I've been watching the screen the whole time, absolutely nothing has happened. So I unplug the camera from the laptop and plug it back into my phone instead. I do this so I can still see the feed from the camera, just on a smaller screen, but I can connect the laptop to the internet.

I don't actually know *why* I do this, since there's nothing I need to do on the internet, but like I said, stakeouts are boring. Then I decide to google *Steve Rose.* I suppose I want to see if anything has happened about his scientific fraud. And fairly quickly I find it has. I watch a news report which says his TV series has been canceled by the network. The report doesn't say why, or anything about how he cheated when he reported the size of the sharks, it just says it's down to unexpected and unforeseen events. I check my email next, since I haven't heard from any of the guys in Australia. That's a bit odd, because we all agreed how we should stay in touch, after the cruise finished, but then I had to leave early, and I haven't heard anything from any of them. I check my inbox and my spam folders, but I can't find anything. I wonder for a while about emailing Debbie, to ask if she knows any more. But I decide against it.

Instead I eat my last donut.

Then I have to go to the toilet. Actually it's called the head. That's what toilets on boats are called. This is actually a bit of a problem. The head on the *Blue Lady* is a marine toilet that uses seawater to pump out whatever you put in the bowl. And for reasons I don't think I need to explain, you're not supposed to use it in a marina. Normally it's not a big issue, because there's a public washroom by the end of the pontoon, but I don't want to walk past the *Mystery* again if I don't have to. So I make an exception and use the head, and then pump very quietly so that no one will hear me from the pontoon. It's OK, because it pumps out on the starboard side of the boat, which is the side not facing the *Mystery*. When I get back I'm feeling much better. And when I check the screen of my phone, I see that something's happening.

I actually almost miss it, because the image is so small. But on the screen of my cell phone I see a little image of Carlos swinging a backpack over his shoulder, and stepping over the rail of the *Mystery*. On the little screen it looks so harmless I almost go to the window to check, but I force myself not to. At least not until he goes out of sight from the camera. To be sure I count to thirty and then I peek out the window. There's no one in sight. So I quietly walk outside and jump onto the pontoon, keeping my footsteps light so it doesn't rock too much under my weight. I jog toward the stern of the *Mystery* and peer around it. And sure enough I see Carlos' back disappearing up the ramp.

I look at the yacht now. The hatch is now closed, and I'm 99% sure that means Amber isn't on board. After all, her car wasn't here when I arrived, or at least it wasn't parked in any of the normal places. Plus she's got college. Though that didn't stop her the other day.

I wait until I see Carlos open the gate at the end of the pontoon and shut it behind him. Then, when I'm sure he's gone, I climb onto the *Mystery* and try the hatch. It's locked. That's good. It means Amber definitely isn't here. But it also makes it hard to get in. Hard, but not impossible. I jump off the yacht again and fetch my backpack. I open the front compartment this time, and I pull out my lock breaking kit. I told you I had a phase when I was obsessed with spy gear. Well I also bought a lock-picking kit. It was pretty good fun. It had see-through versions of all the common lock types, and the right tools and instructions for how you could open them. For weeks I was obsessed with it. It was a bit like when Dad bought me a Rubik's cube when I was small. I just played with it week after week until I'd memorized all the different ways to solve it. I could even do it blindfolded. Well, nearly blindfold. But picking a lock is a bit like solving the Rubix cube. You just identify what stage you're at, and then perform a sequence of moves to shift it to the next stage until it opens. The lock on Carlos' yacht is a common Yale lock, so there's only three stages to solve. I do it in less than three minutes.

I slide the hatch back a little way and look inside. Seeing where he lives makes me pause a bit. I realize I'm sort of crossing a line by going down there. So before I climb down, I get off the boat again and check along the pontoon, to make sure he's not coming back already. The pontoon's empty, but I'm still a bit anxious, since I don't know where he's gone, or how long he'll be away. For a while I consider setting up the endoscope again, so that it's pointing down the pontoon, and I'll see when he returns. But the cable isn't long enough. It's annoying actually, because I could have got a much longer one for another twenty dollars. But it's too late now. I decide I'll just have to be quick, and I'm wasting time worrying about it. I abandon the idea, and climb back onto the yacht.

This time I slide the hatch right back and step down into the warm interior. I cast my eyes around. The place is a bit of a mess. There's a cereal bowl on the saloon table, along with a sailing magazine folded back against the spine. He must have been reading it while he ate. I glance at the article, about cruising in the Caribbean, but it doesn't look relevant. Then there's clothes all over the benches. I notice the carpet on the floor. I can't help but think how I saw Amber lying on it yesterday, and I have to shake my head to clear the image. Then I see his computer on a shelf – an Apple Mac, and right away I pull it out and open up the lid.

I'm annoyed when it asks for a password. I've never owned an Apple computer but I know that if you don't actually know someone's password, there's not much you can do to break in. I try a couple of obvious things – like '*Mystery*' and 'Amber' but then I give up, because I don't want it to send Carlos a password reminder – he'd figure out pretty quickly what's going on. So then I shut the lid again, and look around for what I came here for.

Of all the spy products I bought, my favorite is my phone-charger-listening-device. It's a Samsung charger – or rather it *isn't* a Samsung charger, but it looks exactly like one. You can use it like a normal cell phone charger if you want to – it works just the same – but it also has a secret listening device built into it. I can dial into it and then listen to whatever the secret microphone on the charger picks up. Or, if I want, I can have it listen all the time, and then text me to say when it's picking something up. I think it's awesome. The only problem is, people have lots of different types of cell phone – Apple, and Samsung and Nokia and Motorola – and they all use different, branded chargers. So if you were a proper professional detective you'd need to have a whole range of different charger listening devices, because otherwise the person you were trying to spy on would see right away that someone had switched their charger for a different brand. And they might get suspicious.

However, I know that Carlos has a Samsung phone, just like mine. I noticed it the last time I was in here. The last time his phone was plugged in and charging on the little chart table, by the companionway steps. I look here now, and obviously the phone's not here – because he's taken it with him. But I don't care about that. I can't help smiling when I find the USB end of the cable, he has it taped down with a piece of gaffer tape. All I need to do is switch over his charger for mine, and I'll be able to hear every word he says when he's in the boat. I quickly follow the cable back to where it's plugged into the socket in the side of the yacht. And then I stop.

Where Carlos' real charger is plugged in doesn't look anything like my surveillance charger. I'm so annoyed with myself I hit the side of my head with my palm. Of course. Mine's made to look like a normal charger, but his is a *European* one. His has round pins, instead of the normal flat ones. The only way I can plug my charger into the boat is by using an adapter. And I don't have an adapter. Even if I did, it would look fairly suspicious. But the bigger issue is I don't have one.

I sit down on the bench. Defeated.

I think for a moment about slipping my tracker device into his jacket, or his shoes. But that's no good either. It's a non-starter. I do *have* a tracker device, but when I bought it I didn't understand how you need a monthly subscription to make them actually work. They're like cell-phones you see, they work on the same data networks. And I just used the three months free trial that came with it, but never signed up for the ongoing subscription. I suppose I could sign up again now, but I left the tracker at home on my bed. So that's out too.

I'm about to leave when I think I might as well check the drawers by the chart table, to see if there's anything interesting there. And it's lucky I do, because right away I find something.

TWENTY-EIGHT

It's the boat's registration papers. Or rather, it's *a* boat's registration papers, but it can't be this one. The papers are written in Italian, but I was looking at papers like this last night, checking to see where the *Mystery* was registered. And it is Genoa, after all. But the name of the boat isn't *Mystery*. It's *Falco*.

I stare at the papers, trying to remember what all the Italian words mean. It doesn't make any sense. The class and size of the yacht on the papers looks right for the *Mystery*. Then I notice something else. There's a little box where the description of the boat is given. This is what it says:

Scafo bianco con timoneria blu

Even with my little Italian lesson last night I wouldn't know what this means, but alongside it is a little diagram to help. It shows a side view of the yacht – and it's shown in two colors. The lower part of the hull is painted white, just as this boat is. But the upper part – the sides of the cabin – they're blue. Right away that makes me remember something. Just before I fell in, when I was coming alongside in my kayak, I noticed how the paint was loose on the side of the cabin, and underneath was another color. I wasn't paying much attention to paint back then, so I climb outside now. I quickly check around me, that there's still no sign of Carlos coming back, and then I walk around to the window that I looked through when I saw Amber and Carlos having sex. I crouch down and scratch at the paint. Most of the places it doesn't come loose, but there's a couple of areas where the new paint hasn't bonded properly, and underneath the white, the color is a light blue. Just like in the diagram. I rock back on my heels. This boat isn't the *Mystery*. Or rather it's *a* mystery, because until very recently it was called *Falco*.

* * *

I sit there for a while trying to make sense of it. I have some ideas but nothing that really makes sense. That's when I'm disturbed by a noise. It's the clang of metal, and it's familiar to me. Almost too familiar in fact – I'm so lost in my thoughts I almost ignore it, but then I realize it's the noise the gate makes at the top of the pontoon. It sticks a bit, so you have to give it a good old pull, and when it shuts it makes this metallic clang. So suddenly I know exactly what it means. It means Carlos is coming back.

I stand up at once, and I can see a tall figure walking briskly between some of the smaller boats. I see glimpses of dark hair. It's him, already half way down the pontoon.

I feel a surge of panic. I want to get off the boat as fast as possible, but stupidly I've left my bag down in the cabin. So I sprint back down there, cursing myself for being too casual. I chuck all my gear back into my bag. I accidentally miss with my charger, and it falls on the floor under the cooker. I have to kneel down to retrieve it, losing valuable seconds. The pontoon isn't very long, and he'll be here in seconds, so I can't do anything about putting everything back the way I found it, it's too late for that. I throw my bag on my shoulder, run back up the steps and jam the hatch back hard. I feel it catch behind me and – thank God – the lock re-engages.

Then I swing over the side of the yacht and onto the pontoon between his boat and mine. I land just as Carlos comes around the corner from the main length of the pontoon. He sees me at once, and stops.

"Billy?" His voice is not unfriendly, but it's suspicious, or at least pretty curious. "What are you doing here?"

Just as I'm about to reply with my excuse from earlier, that I'm here to work on the *Blue Lady*, I notice something awkward. It's hard not to. His yacht is now rocking from side to side. It's from where I just ran to the side and jumped off. I realize I need to explain it somehow, otherwise he's going to know I was on board.

"I'm just..." I think fast. "Say did you see that RIB go past?" I try to make my voice sound annoyed, then shake my head. "They were driving way too fast. The speed limit for the harbor is four knots. And that's in the main channel." I point out vaguely at the water behind me, hoping he'll blame the rocking on the wake of the boat I just invented.

But Carlos just steps closer, giving me a strange look now. He looks behind me, at the still water. "What RIB?"

I open my mouth to repeat the lie, but I don't say anything. I've just made a stupid mistake. If a RIB had gone past the wake would be obvious, and it would make all the boats rock, not just his. I close my mouth, and shrug instead. But then maybe he does believe me, because he suddenly breaks into a smile.

"Ah Billy... Billy.... You really do love your rules, don't you?" He swings his backpack off his shoulder, and I see it's full of groceries. He shakes his head again. "You working on your boat?"

I can't quite believe my luck. I nod my head. "Yeah just some… stuff I had to do."

Carlos nods, like I don't need to say any more. And I'm about to turn away and climb back aboard *Blue Lady*, when he goes on.

"Say Billy, you weren't here the other day were you?"

I freeze. "What?"

"Yesterday. Morning, about eleven. Someone knocked on the side of the boat." Carlos smiles as he asks me, smiling openly, and looking me right in the eye. I feel guilty panic rising inside me. I force my face into a confused look, like I decided last night, but I feel my face flush deeper.

"The wrong side of the boat." Carlos goes on.

"The… what?"

"Yeah. They were in a… canoe I think. Crashed right into the side. Then whoever it was fell into the water. Amber thought it might be you."

I blink at him.

"Me?"

"Yeah."

"Amber thought that?"

"Yeah."

"She was with you?"

"Guess so."

I swallow. "No, it wasn't me."

I try to meet his gaze, because that's what someone who wasn't guilty would do. But he won't stop staring at me. It feels like my face is melting under his stare.

"The water's kinda cold for swimming huh?"

I'm about to answer, but then I figure this might be a trick. So I consider before I do. "I wouldn't know. I haven't been in for ages."

This time I manage to keep eye contact.

"Oh no?" He says. He's not smiling as much now, and I feel I'm winning whatever battle we're having. But then, just the wrong moment – I feel I need to sneeze. I will the itching to go away, but it just gets stronger and stronger, and in the end I can't help myself. I turn away and sneeze right there in front of him, and then, as I'm wiping my nose afterward he snorts a kind of laugh.

"Nasty cold you've got there Billy," he says, and suddenly his voice sounds bored. He doesn't say anything else, but he vaults elegantly over the guardrail and onto the yacht. I hear him whistling as he unlocks the hatch. And I know – he knows.

* * *

OK, he knows. Or at least he *thinks* he knows. But he can't prove anything. That's what I tell myself, when I'm back inside again, and watching the yacht through the endoscope feed. And even if he could prove it – if they took a photo of me, or something, when I saw them having sex – it's not illegal to kayak in the marina.

It's not even illegal to look into people's windows. What *is* illegal is to change the name of your yacht.

Well, actually it's not. People change the names of their boats all the time, when they buy them usually, or if they just get bored of the old name. But they don't do it very often, since it's supposed to mean bad luck. But if you do change the name then you also have to change the registration documents. That's obvious.

And anyway, the *Mystery*, or *Falco*, or whatever I should call it now, isn't just a boat, not in the sense that most people who have boats. Carlos actually *lives* on it. So it's more like someone changing the name of their house. No, not the name, the *address*. It's like someone changing their identity. And why would anyone do *that*?

I ponder this for a while, but my head keeps replaying the encounter I just had with him, and each time I feel more and more embarrassed. He was so casual when he asked whether I'd been looking in the window yesterday, it's like he was playing with me. I realize now that he saw through my excuse about the RIB too. He knew I was on board his yacht. And he didn't even care. He thought it was funny.

And then it's like this feeling that's been bubbling away underneath breaks up to the surface, just for a moment. I've been an idiot about this. I'm *being* an idiot. I'm seeing a problem where there isn't one, not really. OK, so Carlos and Amber were smoking dope. It's not such a big deal. I *knew* she smoked dope before I met her anyway, she told me. We stopped talking about it, but that was just because of how I didn't approve. To be honest, I'm quite unusual in my class in *not* smoking drugs these days.

I go back to watching my laptop screen again. It's showing the feed from the endoscope again. And at that moment Carlos comes out up onto the deck. He steps onto the roof of the cabin and I watch him hanging some washing out. It's a couple of t-shirts and he tosses them over the boom, arranging them carefully so they don't crease. He has his head tipped over to one side, and it takes me a while to work out why, but then I see the reason. He has his phone jammed between his shoulder and his ear, and he's speaking into it while he works. And like normal he's laughing and smiling. Then he finishes the washing and goes back down below, transferring the phone to his hand now. I feel a burst of frustration – if only my phone charger listening device had worked I could have called it up now. I could find out who he was speaking to, and what he was saying. I'd *know* if it was suspicious.

Then I have a sudden idea – but I have to be quick if it's going to work. I snatch up my own phone and dial Amber's number. As it connects I realize I have no idea what to say if she picks up – but I don't have time to worry. Because – just as I expected – she doesn't pick up. Instead the call goes to her voicemail – the line's engaged. It's *Amber* that Carlos is talking to, I'm sure of it. I hang up, not leaving a message.

And then, finally, I properly wake up to what I'm doing. It's suddenly like I'm looking down on myself from above. And I don't like what I see. I should be at school, but I'm actually here *spying on my best friend.*

And not even for any reason. I thought I was going to find out something bad about Carlos, and that maybe Amber would decide to stop seeing him. But he hasn't really done anything wrong. OK, he anchored in the marine reserve – but if I'm going to be totally honest with you, even I've done that a few times, before I discovered the ledge for the kayak. Oh yeah, and he changed his boat name. So what? Maybe he changed it and he just hasn't had a chance to tell the Italian authorities. It's hardly a big deal.

And if Amber knew what I was doing, not just trying to watch her having sex – I shudder again at that thought – but also breaking into his boat, and planting electronic listening devices. She'd go crazy. She'd be so mad. I don't think she'd ever talk to me again.

And deep down I know there is a reason why I'm doing all this. I'm jealous. Of her getting on with her life, and being happy with Carlos, when I've gone and messed mine up by doing what I did in Australia.

So then I take a last look at the yacht on the screen of my laptop, then I unplug the endoscope lead from the laptop and loop the cable up. The screen goes black, then automatically closes. So the only thing showing is the article about Steve Rose, and how he lost the TV show. How *I* lost him his TV show. I feel sicker now than when I ate all the donuts. I feel miserable as I gather my stuff together and tidy up the boat. And then I climb off, and I go to catch the bus home.

TWENTY-NINE

Tommy and Paulie stood side-by-side looking out over the narrow strip of water. Where it met the land it was bordered by a wide strip of thick, gray, low tide mud. A rickety wooden jetty reached out a small way, the far end only just reaching the brown water that swirled around the seaweed-covered uprights. Somewhere around here was the open sea, but the open horizon was lost somewhere down the maze of marshy creeks that made up this section of the island's coast.

Behind them stood a different vehicle – this time a gray-brown, unmarked panel van. It was a couple of years old – neither new, nor old enough to stand out in any way – and was parked by the only building for miles around, a locked and apparently abandoned boat house.

"What'd you say this place was called?" Paulie asked.

Tommy consulted the map gripped at his side in one big hand.

"Bishop's Landing."

"Bishop's Landing." Paulie repeated, deadpan. "Well if he did land here, he didn't stay long before he fucked right off again."

Tommy's hand clenched into a fist around the edge of the map, but he said nothing. They were both getting grouchy. On the boat over Paulie had been full of enthusiasm. Clearly he regarded this as his big chance to impress the new boss. But that had slowly ebbed away as they'd followed dirt track after dirt track to the hundreds of possible places you could hide a yacht.

Tommy wasn't used to working with such ups and downs. He was the sort of guy that labored at a task for as long as it took to get it done. But then that way of thinking seemed kinda old fashioned these days. He turned, ready to walk back to the van to try the next creek down.

"You coming?"

"I dunno," Paulie said. *"Fuck this."*

Tommy's big face creased just enough to indicate he was losing patience. Unlike Paulie he no longer dreamed of achieving a position of real power in the organization – if he ever had. These days he had a different dream. Of a modest apartment, somewhere near a golf course, down in Florida. Far enough away that he wouldn't have to spend all of his days looking over his shoulder in case some kid came after him, looking for revenge, for what Tommy might have done to his father. But with the Old Man's death, and Angelo deciding he had to work with Paulie, any chance of retirement seemed a long way off. Maybe after this though. Maybe if they got a good result, recovered the coke…

"Fuck this," Paulie said again.

"Yeah you mentioned," Tommy snapped suddenly. Then he took a breath. Whatever success here meant, getting angry wasn't going to help it any time soon.

"Hey, maybe we should pack it in for the day?" He offered. "Find a motel? Grab a beer?" He didn't mention the hooker he was also thinking about, if he could find one.

"No." Suddenly there was a spark of enthusiasm in Paulie's face, which hadn't been there most of the afternoon. "No, I got an idea how we can speed this up." He turned to Tommy. "Tell me, what's the best place to hide a body?"

Tommy sighed as the beer and food slid from his mind. "Paulie, we've got to *find* the guy before we waste him…"

Paulie looked irritated.

"No, I don't mean… It's a metaphor."

"A what?"

"Come on, just humor me. What's the best place to hide a body?"

Tommy stared at him. After a while he shrugged. "A lake," he said at last.

"A *lake*? No…"

"Yeah a lake. I put more bodies in lakes than anywhere else…"

"What the fuck? What are you even talking about?"

"I'm telling you. You stick a guy in a lake, gym weights zip-tied round the thighs and shoulders, he ain't ever coming up again. Don't matter how much he puffs up."

Paulie considered this for a moment, torn between making his point and not looking like this was both news to him and unpleasantly morbid. "OK. Sure. Lakes are good. But that ain't what I mean. I'm talking about a *metaphor*. I ain't looking for the literal answer."

"A metaphor?" Tommy repeated again.

"Yeah. It's like… a saying."

"A saying?"

"Yeah."

"*What's the best place to hide a body*? That's a saying?"

"Yeah."

"Well it ain't one I've ever heard."

"Jesus fuck." Paulie looked around, as if searching for something to punch.

"How about we just get on with it?" Tommy lumbered away, shaking his head.

They walked back to the van and climbed in. Tommy into the passenger seat, Paulie behind the wheel. Then Tommy studied the map, looking to see which of the dozens of possible spots left to check was closest. After a while he glanced up, wondering why Paulie hadn't started the van yet.

"I mean it," Paulie said instead. "*Metaphorically* speaking, what's the best place to hide a body?"

Tommy studied his partner for a while, wishing he'd taken the chance to retire when the Old Man was alive. He'd have let him go, Tommy was almost sure of it.

"So you're saying you don't want an actual answer, you want to know what the answer would be *if* this was a popular saying?"

"Yeah."

"Which it ain't."

Paulie winced involuntarily.

"Yeah."

"In that case I don't know."

"Oh fuck's sake, I give up, alright? The answer is, the best place to hide a body is *in a graveyard*."

Tommy thought about this for a while. "Kinda public isn't it?"

Paulie screwed up his nose in irritation. "Yeah but..."

"And you gotta dig the grave and fill it in one hit, which could be two or three hours work depending on the ground conditions. And you get people turning up to graveyards at all hours. It's risky."

"Fuck's sake Tommy. It's a saying. It ain't real. The point is it's the last place anyone would think to look, and if they did, all they're gonna find is a load more bodies anyhow."

Tommy blew his cheeks full of air. He thought how easy it would be to carry out DNA tests on any remains, how there would be a hundred other bodies there, and how the cops would know exactly the date they went in the ground, making it easy to get a time of death by comparison. It seemed a fucking stupid place to him, saying or otherwise. But he let it go.

"If you say so. I don't necessarily agree."

Paulie exhaled slowly, counting in his head as he did so. "OK. I'm just saying we could be wasting our time driving down these shitty little dirt tracks checking out Parson's fucking creek..."

"Bishop's..."

"Whatever. We should be looking in the bigger places."

There was a pause while Tommy thought about this.

"Why?"

"Because of what I just said. If the best place to hide a body is where there's a load of other bodies, then it follows that the same goes for a yacht. The best place is to hide it with a load of other yachts. In a marina."

Tommy hesitated, but in the end he couldn't not say it. He hadn't spent three months getting wound up by Paulie without learning nothing about being a pain in the ass himself. "But the best place to hide a body is in a lake. Zip tied with gym weights…"

"Shut the fuck up Tommy. Or I'm gonna shoot you in the fucking head and zip tie you to gym weights."

Tommy shut up. But as he did so he was smiling inside.

"How many marinas are there on this fucking island?" Paulie went on. "Any marked on that map?"

Tommy looked down at the map. There were several, but they'd been checking the smaller, more tucked away places first. "Uh huh," he said.

"Well? Where are they?"

"There's two in Newlea. One in a place called Catterline. And then one in… Holport."

"OK then, let's go."

"Which one?"

"I don't know. Fucking pick one."

Tommy rolled his eyes, but stuck his finger down onto the map, then checked to see which of the towns his finger was closest to.

"Holport," he said.

"Well, let's go to fucking Holport." Paulie said, and fired the engine.

THIRTY

TWENTY FIVE MINUTES later the van cruised by the road which fronted the public harbor in Holport. A forest of masts bristled from the yacht basin, and Tommy gazed out at them, bored. Paulie swung the car into a bay facing the water.

"Now what?" Tommy asked.

"You see it?"

"See what?"

"The yacht. Do you see it?"

"I dunno. I see a lot of yachts. They all look kinda the same."

Paulie didn't answer. Instead he yanked on the parking brake and pushed open the door. Tommy waited a moment and watched where he went, down a ramp that led to the floating pontoon where the boats were moored. But he didn't get very far. A large steel gate barred his way. Tommy watched while Paulie shook it, gently at first but then harder. Then he started looking at whether it was possible to climb over, but it didn't look easy. When Paulie went back to shaking it ineffectively, Tommy sighed. He got out of the van and opened the sliding door. Inside were a number of canvas bags. He opened one and rummaged around.

Moments later he joined Paulie at the gate, carrying a large pair of bolt cutters. Wordlessly he fitted them to the lock.

"What you doing?" Paulie was incredulous.

"Opening the gate."

"*Fuck no.* You wanna just announce we're here on fucking Twitter?" Paulie roughly pushed him out of the way, and continued to stare through the mesh. There were a dozen or more yachts that could have been the one in the photograph, but they were too far away to see properly.

"Well how are we gonna take a look?" Tommy asked. The sooner they checked this marina, the sooner they could eat and finish this off tomorrow.

Paulie didn't reply.

"We get these boats checked," Tommy pushed. "Then we can get some dinner." He'd spotted a bar on the way into town, it looked like the sort of place with a chance of finding that hooker he'd thought of earlier.

"I got an idea."

"Yeah?"

"Yeah. Lose the bolt cutters."

Paulie waved away any further questions, and walked back up the ramp. After a while Tommy followed him, and shaking his head, he returned the cutters to the bag. When he looked up again, Paulie had crossed the street, and was outside the window of a yacht brokers.

"Wait here," Paulie said, when Tommy got there.

"Why?"

"Because I don't want to look like we're a pair of fags. That's why."

Paulie pushed his way inside.

Tommy felt his hands bunch up again, but he did what he was told. As he did so, he realized he usually did these days. They might have been put together as partners, but he was increasingly finding himself the junior partner. The reason for it was clear, and had fuck all to do with who had the most experience. The reason Paulie felt entitled to push him around was because he was Angelo's second cousin. And both of them knew it. Paulie had Angelo's ear.

He watched Paulie inside, unable to hear what was being said. A woman had risen from behind her desk to greet him, and now they were talking. Paulie was expressive, looking relaxed and flashing a smile. Now he touched her shoulder lightly. She was attractive too, Tommy noticed, better put together than any hooker he was likely to find.

The woman was slipping her coat on now. She picked a large bunch of keys from a hook on the wall and came to the door. Tommy turned away as the door opened, and the woman and Paulie stepped out.

"It's a lovely boat," the woman was saying. "How long have you been on the lookout?"

"Oh, you know," Paulie replied, with a leer in his voice. "I'm always on the lookout."

The woman threw her head back, showing an elegant neck. She gave a little laugh, flirting back. Tommy kicked at the wall, hating the both of them.

"Fucking Paulie," he muttered as he waited, before following them at a distance. The woman led Paulie back down to the ramp and stopped at the gate. Tommy watched as she casually unscrambled the combination lock, and led Paulie through and onto the pontoon. They stopped at the third boat along, which Tommy now noticed had a *For Sale* sign hanging from the back. When they got there she fiddled with her large bunch of keys, while Paulie slipped out his cell phone. Moments later Tommy's buzzed in his pocket. When he pulled it out there was a message with just four numbers on it.

"Fucking Paulie," Tommy said – out loud this time.

THIRTY-ONE

From inside the cabin of the *Mystery* came the rhythmic sound of carrots being chopped. Slowly, carefully, methodically. Carlos held the knife with an eccentric grip, his fingers curled over the sides of the blade leaving most of the handle exposed. He watched as he chopped, as if drawing some meditative power from severing each slice. And only when he was satisfied they were all a uniform size and shape did he place the knife down and tumble the carrot pieces into a pan. Then he washed and dried his hands, then stepped around into the saloon area and stood over the table.

Amber tried to ignore him, her eyes fixed on the screen of her laptop. A notebook was open beside it, her handwriting black and spidery. After a while though she had to glance up, and she saw Carlos watching her. She looked away at once, but not quick enough to miss the edges of his mouth turn up into a satisfied smile.

"What?" She tried to make her voice irritable.

"How do you mean?"

"Why are you watching me?"

"I'm wondering if you're really going to do that all evening."

"I told you," Amber replied. She kept her eyes on her work, though she'd lost the thread of what she was doing already. "I have to get this done."

"Yeah. You said."

Carlos didn't move. He didn't stop watching her either.

"And I can't exactly do it with you standing right there."

"Hey, I only have this small boat. Where would you have me stand instead?"

"You said you'd cook me dinner. Maybe you should do that?"

"Yeah." He shrugged.

"Well? Where is it?"

Carlos was silent for so long she had to glance up again. He wore the same thoughtful look he'd had while he was chopping the vegetables.

"I decided I wasn't hungry," he said, as he held her eyes on his. "Not that sort of hungry anyway."

The corners of his mouth curled up again. His teeth appeared, gleaming. Then his eyes dropped, taking in how her body was arranged on the bench seat. He took his time, then lifted his eyes back to her face.

"I gotta do this project, I'm already behind."

Carlos reached forward to stroke a strand of her hair behind her ear. He let his hand touch her face. "Do it later."

"Do *this* later."

"Let's do this now. *And* later."

"Carlos! You're insatiable."

"And you're irresistible."

Despite herself, Amber smiled. The top she was wearing was borrowed from her mom. Every time she wore it, Amber thought it was disgusting, the way it plunged at the neckline, putting her mother's boobs on display. She moved her position now, taking care to keep her chest in his view. Then she turned back to the screen. "Well you're the reason I'm behind with this project, so you're just going to have to suffer."

Carlos didn't reply. Instead he slowly began pressing the lid of the computer closed.

Amber caught his wrist and stopped him. But she didn't let it go. She uncurled her legs and let them drop to the floor, and used his weight to pull herself up. Then, facing him, she carefully placed his hand onto her breast. She watched his eyes as she did so, seeing the pupils dilate, the mouth break open. She felt his breath against her face. She let go his wrist to hold his face with both her hands, and angled his mouth down towards hers. She kissed him, feeling his hard body pressing against hers. Then, just as his other hand wrapped around her she twisted away. She had to take a moment to compose herself before she could speak.

"I really have to get this done. And I *am* hungry. So get cooking." She lifted her hand and shooed him back to the galley.

This time he gave up.

"OK. But afterwards I am going to make love to you." He pointed at her with one finger, as if this were a stern warning.

"We'll see how good dinner is."

"Oh it will be good." He banged a frying pan noisily onto the galley stove, playing at being angry. "It will be more than good." He turned on the gas and it ignited with a blue whoosh.

"And not just the food will be good."

Amber laughed, then turned back to her work. The feeling surging through her body was incredible. The anticipation for what was to come so powerful.

Somehow though, she felt calm too – relaxed – and she was able to absorb herself back in her work, while the little cabin filled with the sounds and smell of cooking.

"Why'd you have to do that now anyway?" His voice broke into what she was doing, and he slid into the seat next to her. Glancing up she saw a pot now bubbling on the stove. He frowned at the screen.

"I told you. My mom's going off the island for a couple of days. Some work thing, and I have to look after Gracie. So I need to get this done now, because I won't have time later."

Carlos turned away and pulled out a small plastic bag half-filled with a fine white powder. "So your Mom's away huh?" He formed the side of the bag into a funnel, and poured a small stream of the powder out onto the table top. "Meaning you have the house all to yourself?"

"To myself and my six-year-old sister." Amber's eyebrows rose meaningfully. "Who will totally drop me in it with Mom if I bring my *boyfriend* home."

Amber stopped. She hadn't meant to use that word, it had just come out. She glanced at him, suddenly anxious.

In return he gave her a smile she couldn't read, then reached for her college ID card, which was on the table. He used it to cut the pile of powder into four smaller piles, and began arranging them into neat lines. Amber watched him, her eyes hesitant.

"I'm actually supposed to be there tonight," she went on. She didn't mean to say it. The situation – watching him with the drugs maybe – it had suddenly made her nervous.

"Where?"

"Home. Mom wanted to talk through Gracie's routine. Like…" Suddenly she was on more comfortable ground. "Like I don't know how to look after my own sister? It's just because it's the first time Mom's gone away and Gracie is a bit special…" She stopped as he neatly rolled a bank note, and placed one end into his left nostril. He leaned forward over the first line and in a second it was gone. Then he switched to the other side and a second line disappeared. He sat back, opened his mouth, and a shudder went through his body. Amber saw those dark pupils dilate again, wider this time. He held the note out to her.

Amber hesitated. For a moment she imagined what her Mom would say if she knew what Amber was actually doing, instead of being told how to look after her sister. But at the same time she didn't need instructions. Since Mom had split up with Pete – the man whom Amber had never agreed to call her step dad – and gone back to work, Amber had played a big part in bringing up Gracie anyway. Sometimes she wondered if she ought to tell Mom what the girl liked to do. She smiled as she accepted the note. It felt delicate between her fingers. Like something precious.

She looked down at the two remaining lines. Of coke. *Cocaine*. Just saying the word made her head spin a little. She risked a glance at Carlos, who was sat back now against the seat, his eyes half-closed, his hands relaxed on the table and twitching just a little. Maybe she shouldn't do it? Maybe she should be keeping her head clear? But then cocaine didn't make you groggy the next day, not like dope did. And she'd looked after Gracie when she was high before. A few times. Moreover, *having sex* on cocaine was something else. It was incredible. Being with Carlos was strange – he was older, and so much more experienced, she felt almost like a child playing a role sometimes. But the coke stripped away all her self-consciousness. The social anxiety she hid so well – but certainly felt, the lack of confidence she disguised with attitude – it all just disappeared. The coke allowed her to feel like the experienced lover a man like Carlos would have as his *girlfriend*.

She placed the note in her nose and leaned down over the line.

There was an instant shift as the chemical hit her, like the cabin's interior rotated around her brain. She had to bite her lip not to call out. Then the colors popped around her, as if each exploded into a more vibrant version of itself, one after the other. Her hearing sharpened. The sounds of the cooking crackled and fizzed, like it hadn't been there before, but was now loud and vibrant. The smells seemed to fill every inch of her, she could pick out individual tastes, like they were laid out on a plate. When she looked up into Carlos' warm tanned face he glowed. He was impossibly handsome.

Amber reached down and pulled her mom's top over her head. She threw it on the seat opposite and leaned in to kiss him. "Come on," she said. "Let's fuck."

For a second he looked almost too comfortable where he was to oblige, but then she ran her hands over his body until she reached the hardening bulge in the front of his jeans. Then she left one hand there and wrapped the other around his head, pulling them together. They broke apart, a few moments later, only for him to smoothly move her work stuff to one side, and drop the table down to give them more room.

* * *

"Where are you getting it from?"

His eyes narrowed. "What?"

Amber blinked her eyes, suddenly aware she had asked the question out loud. She was naked now, lying under a blanket, Carlos on his back smoking a joint.

"You know. The… The coke. It's just, everyone I know says it's hard to get hold of. Here on the island."

He shrugged, relaxed again. "I met a guy in a bar."

She was quiet for a moment. But the truth was she had a load of questions. And she loved to talk after sex, it felt like an extension of the intimacy.

"But isn't it expensive? And dangerous – like you don't know what might be in it?"

"Don't worry about it."

He smiled easily, then rolled onto his side, facing her now. The joint crackled as he sucked on it, then handed it over. He began running his finger in a circle on her bare shoulder.

It was distracting, but she loved the effect her body had on him.

"I'm not *worried*. I'm just interested. I think you're interesting."

"I think you're 'interesting' too," he said, his eyes concentrating on the path his finger took. It followed the curve of her breastbone, and onto her throat.

She took a hit on the joint. Carlos had told her how the downer of the marijuana helped to balance the high of the cocaine. It made it easier the next day, when she stopped taking it. The hot smoke felt familiar, and she pulled it in deep. She closed her eyes and felt waves rolling up and down her body. She realized she ought to slow down, he rolled his joints stronger than she did.

"Well if you're worried about running out, don't be. I got a guaranteed supply."

Amber held it out for him to take again.

"I wasn't worried about that." She spoke easy at first, but then her voice tightened. *Was that what he thought? That she was just here for the drugs?* She shook the idea away, it was just the dope hitting. Sending strands of paranoia through her mind. She looked to his face, trying to read what he was thinking.

Carlos screwed up his face, like he didn't recall that he'd even said it. Then he shrugged his shoulders again and took the joint. He reached beyond her to tap the ash from the end into a saucer he used as an ashtray, then rolled over again onto his back.

"It *is* kind of expensive," he continued, his own voice easy and relaxed. "But I don't exactly have to pay for it."

Amber – still preoccupied with the flow of thoughts in her own mind – almost didn't register what he said. But then it cut through.

"Hmm? Why not?"

She glanced across, and saw him smile up at the roof of the cabin.

"When I said I got it from a guy in a bar. It wasn't an actual guy. In an actual bar."

Amber felt herself focusing now. "What do you mean?"

"OK at least, it wasn't a bar here. It was somewhere else."

Amber propped herself up, letting the blanket fall away, but unconcerned by that. "I don't understand."

"There's nothing *to* understand." Carlos seemed to have realized what he was saying too, and changed his mind about saying it. "Better you don't."

"What? But I want to." Suddenly the conversation was much more than just easy post-coital chat. She wanted to understand him. He was mysterious enough, turning up – literally – out of the blue, a European. She needed him to open up to her.

"Come on Carlos. Tell me."

Carlos contemplated for a while before replying. "You really want to know?" He turned to her, measuring, thinking. His eyes were dark, unfathomable.

"Yes. I do."

He hesitated. A long time. "OK," he said in the end. "I stole it."

"You stole it?"

"Yeah." He laughed carelessly. "I didn't exactly plan to. It kind of just happened."

Amber stared at him. "Who did you steal it from?"

"It's fine. They aren't ever gonna find out."

"How can you say that? Who did you steal it from?"

Carlos lifted a hand and pressed it against his temple. He looked like he wished he hadn't spoken.

"Look, I met some guys, they asked me to carry a couple of kilos from Venezuela to Florida. That's all. But on the way I got caught in a storm, and they think I sank. So that's it."

"That's it?"

"That's it."

Amber lay back down. She felt her body shaking. From what? Fear? Excitement?

"But is it safe? I mean, where is it?" Suddenly she looked around the cabin, as if she might have missed bales of cocaine amongst the general disorder.

"Not here. It's safe."

She opened her mouth to continue, but he reached forward and placed a finger on her lips.

"No more. There's nothing to worry about." Then he thought for a minute. "Actually there is one thing to worry about." He gave a careless laugh.

"What?"

"Your little friend Billy."

She frowned, "Billy?"

"Yeah. I caught him, climbing off the boat, the other day. The hatch was locked so he didn't get inside. But he was spying again. He might have an idea where it is."

Amber groaned. "Oh God. Billy." She remembered the mixture of feelings she'd felt on seeing him flailing about in the water. Laughter, but also horror at what he must have seen. Then she registered what he'd just said.

"Billy? How would *he* know where it was?"

"Oh nothing. Just the first time I met him…"

Carlos stopped speaking, and smiled instead.

"What?" Amber asked. "What is it?

But this time Carlos didn't answer.

"I'm hungry now," he said instead, jumping naked to his feet and leaving her with the blanket. He walked to the galley and stirred the pot. "For food this time." He began gathering plates from the rack on the wall and glanced back at Amber. She took the hint and got up too, though she used the distraction of his cooking to dress again before replacing the table and setting it so they could eat.

* * *

They ate in silence. Carlos seemed to enjoy it that way, and Amber forgot her concerns. No doubt she would consider what he had told her later on. But perhaps it was better this way. That there was no 'man in a bar'. Besides, she knew, from how the last few nights had gone, that Carlos wasn't yet done for the evening. She let her mind focus on that. She found it strangely exciting to listen to the sounds of the food being cut, and the careful way he moved it to his mouth. And the feel of his dark eyes on her as she ate from her own plate. When he was nearly finished he reached for a chunk of bread, and used it to mop up the sauce on his plate, but instead of eating that himself he leaned over and offered it to her, holding it close to her lips. When she parted them he placed it gently inside, and then pushed it in with his finger, his eyes never leaving her face. Still neither of them spoke. After that he took both plates and moved them into the sink, then he reached down and peeled her mother's top up and over her head for a second time.

THIRTY-TWO

"I REALLY DO HAVE TO GO," Amber said, nearly two hours later. She felt warm and comfortable, her buzz fading gradually with the help of another joint.

He watched her. "Why?"

"I told you. I have to be home tomorrow before Mom leaves. She's on the early ferry."

His eyes dropped. "Go from here."

She shook her head. "I was supposed to be there tonight, remember?" She smiled at him, trying to make it an indulgent reminder of what they had done instead.

"OK *go*." He pretended to sound put-out. Or perhaps he actually was a little. But then he softened. "You want me to take you?"

Amber's brow furrowed. "You don't have a car."

"I can take yours."

"Then how will you get back here?"

His eyes revealed him thinking about it, but then he rolled away, defeated. She took the moment to slip out from under the blanket and retrieve her underwear. But she heard him roll back again to watch her.

"Stop staring. Haven't you had enough?"

"No. I never have enough."

She leaned forward to pull her panties on, feeling awkward at how it must make her look. "Well that's all you're getting tonight." She found her bra, hanging from the corner of the chart table, and quickly strapped it on. Then she put on the rest of her clothes. It would be OK, she thought, if he offered to walk her up the pontoon to her car. But as she dressed he showed no signs of moving. On the other hand, she kind of understood why he might be tired. She grinned inside at the thought.

"You come here after school?"

"College."

"You come here after college?"

"No I have to look after Gracie. Remember?"

He stared stone-faced, like this was an incredible hardship. And she had to laugh.

"It's only three days. You'll cope."

"Maybe you'll have to send me some photographs of yourself. To keep me sane."

"Maybe I'll do that."

Suddenly Carlos pulled himself up and sat up against the seat. The blanket that had been covering him slipped down to show his stomach, toned and tanned. Amber found her eye pulled towards it. He reached above him and grabbed the bag of coke.

"Quick one?"

"I can't. I have to drive."

"Just a quick one."

"Carlos!"

He stopped, and put it back. "OK. I'll come with you. See you to your car." He stood now, naked again, but made no move to dress.

"You going to come like that?"

He shrugged. "Why not?"

She laughed again, and made a decision. "Don't worry. I parked just across the street. And it's only Holport."

"No really, I'll come." He looked for his jeans now, but casually, as if expecting her to deny him. And she waved him away.

"No. It's fine. I have to get going. I'll see you in a few days."

She placed her hands flat on his bare chest and breathed in deeply to taste the smell of him. She kissed him, long enough to feel him becoming aroused again, but not long enough to delay her departure.

"I had fun tonight," she said.

It was cold and quiet out on the pontoon. Her footsteps echoed on the boards and the wooden walkway sank a little as each footstep pushed it down into the dark water. The low level lighting of the pontoon reflected off the surface, giving it the look of black mercury. At the end she quickly unlocked the gate and swung it shut behind her, then crossed the street and went around the corner to where her car was parked. Then an uncomfortable thought hit her. Her little car – purchased with money left to her after her dad's death, and usually pretty reliable, had recently been having trouble starting. One time last week she'd even run the battery flat trying to get it going, and only been saved because she was at college, and half a dozen of her classmates had been there to give a push start. She'd meant to get it to the garage, but instead had rushed off to see Carlos. Now, suddenly, alone on the deserted dock, and with the time past midnight, she felt exposed.

She unlocked the car, and settled into the seat, then slipped the key home. She held her breath as she turned it, hearing the motor protest as it was suddenly commanded into life. Something spun loudly, under the hood, then whined, but the motor wouldn't fire. And then, just as she was about to stop and try a second time, it caught. She pumped the gas, feeling relief flood through her just as gas flooded through the motor, and then it was revving normally, the little motor sounding eager to go. She relaxed, puffed out her cheeks, and fitted her seatbelt. Sweet little car. She looked to the sky, silently thanking her father. There was no reason to look in her rear view mirror, and even if she had, the two men inside the dark-colored van were as good as invisible. Just watching her at this point.

Amber kept the revs high as she moved out of the space, and drove out of Holport. As she climbed the hill out of town, she wound down her window, letting the cold night air flow into the car. She hoped to weaken the effects of the drugs she had taken, but it hardly mattered. Mom would be asleep by now. She glanced down at her cell phone, which she'd kept on silent. Three missed calls from Mom. Could have been worse. Then she noticed the battery was low, so she fumbled the connection to the charger she kept plugged into the cigarette lighter. She'd need it tomorrow, for college.

A few seconds later she realized her mistake.

College. She had to hand in her project for college. She'd mostly finished it, but she had to use her college ID to hand it in.

"Shit." She spoke out loud. She fought to clear her thoughts. She'd definitely put the laptop and her notes in her bag, she could see the corner of her notebook poking from the top of the bag on the passenger seat. But not her ID card. It was on the side, where Carlos had been using it to chop up the lines of coke.

She considered if she could get it later. Surely they knew who she was? But then this wasn't school. The office where she had to hand in the project probably wouldn't know who she was, and if she didn't have the card it would mean the coursework was late. She'd get marked down. And her grades were bad enough anyway.

She clenched her fingers around the plastic of the wheel, then bunched her hand into a fist, and hit it. The impact felt weird, like it wasn't totally her own hand – the drugs were clearly still affecting her. Probably that was why she forgot.

But then what did it matter? It was late anyway. Another ten minutes wouldn't make any difference. And she would get to see Carlos again. She smiled again. There was a junction up ahead where a smaller road met this one. And with no one about this late, she slowed, and swung around in a u-turn. She almost felt relaxed now, wondering what he would be doing? Probably he would have gone to sleep. Well she'd wake him up.

• • •

She pulled into the same spot she had left only minutes before and hurried back around the corner. But before she crossed the street she stopped. Two men were leaning over the combination lock on the gate which led to the pontoon. One was large, one small, and they had a small flashlight. At once she slunk back into the shadow of the building behind her. There was no reason to feel fear exactly – there were many boats kept on the pontoon, and people could visit them at any time. But equally, there was no way she wanted them to see her. It was late. And they would probably be as startled by her sudden appearance as she was by theirs.

The gate swung open, and the two men stepped through. One was carrying a large bag. It comforted her further. They were just boat owners, probably getting ready for an early start. Maybe to catch the tide. That thought spurred her into action. Mom would definitely ask her what time she got home. And the later she did, the more of the moral-high-ground mom would claim. Amber stepped forward to get the card and get on her way.

Even so she opened and closed the gate quietly, using her palm to prevent the metal ringing out. She could still make out the silhouettes of the men half way down the pontoon. She watched, expecting them to disappear at any moment, as they climbed onto one of the boats. But they were still walking forwards. They must have one of the boats out near the end, where the *Mystery* and *Blue Lady* were kept. That was awkward, she hoped they would find their boat, and go inside their cabin before she had to walk past. But then they came to the last boat before *Mystery* and *Blue Lady* – the last boat which could possibly be theirs – and to her surprise they walked right past that too. Suddenly her irritation hardened into something else. Confusion. Then quickly to concern.

There was no reason for anyone to be visiting either the *Mystery* or the *Blue Lady* at this time of night. No reason at *any time* really. But in the middle of the night? Her concern grew, beginning to feel a lot like fear.

She ducked left, onto one of the smaller offshoots of the pontoon, so that she was hidden if either of the men looked behind them, and she watched from behind the steep bow of a fishing skiff. And she was glad she did, as one of the men turned now and studied the pontoon behind him. She froze. Then he flicked on the flashlight, and carefully probed the semi-darkness behind him.

What the hell? Amber thought, as she ducked her head back in. She suddenly thought to call Carlos, to warn him. Of what exactly she wasn't sure. But everything about the situation suddenly felt awfully wrong. But when she went to her pocket to get her cell it wasn't there. She'd plugged it into the charger in the car.

Shit.

When she dared to look up again, the two men *had* disappeared. She looked around, straining her eyes in the gloomy light. They couldn't have. Unless they'd jumped in the water… but then she realized. They must have climbed onto a boat. But the only two boats there were *Mystery* or *Blue Lady.*

Suddenly Amber realized she was shivering, and it wasn't the cold making it happen. But it wasn't only fear that overcame her, it was confusion too. A part of her mind, which screamed out the need to stay rational, told her to question whether what she had seen was actually real. Could it not be some sort of delayed hallucination, from the dope and the coke? And the story Carlos had told her, about where the coke came from? She forced herself back onto the main branch of the pontoon, and hurried forward. And now her own footsteps began to confuse her. They didn't sound or feel real either. Like when she'd hit the wheel in her car. Everything felt like she was playing some role in a movie, or stuck in a dream. It convinced her that whatever she'd thought she saw was a hallucination. A crazy dream.

As she reached the bow of the *Mystery* she was almost relaxed again. She would surprise Carlos. She would grab her ID card, and she'd get home. And maybe another time she'd tell him of how her mind had played tricks with her.

But then she heard them.

It was shouting, or not quite. But raised, angry voices. Thuds. All muted because they came from inside the cabin of *Mystery*. But *definitely* real. Then a voice. Loud, but measured. In control.

"You move I put a bullet through your fucking head."

Amber blinked in surprise, the words were so out of context. The sound was coming from inside the boat, and it wasn't her they were speaking to, but still she felt suddenly vulnerable, standing here on the pontoon. So she retreated until she was hiding behind the concrete upright that the floating part of the walkway was anchored to, against the rise and fall of the tide.

Back here it was harder to hear. There were only fragments of voices. She considered what to do. She thought again of her cellphone, all the way back in the car. Should she get it? Who would she call? What would she tell them? And had she really heard what she thought? She figured she had to go forward again. To find out what was actually going on, before she could decide what to do.

She stepped cautiously, keeping her tread as light as she could to not cause the pontoon to sway too much. This time she went past the bow of the *Mystery*, crouching low, and feeling her legs trembling, until she reached the mid-point of the yacht. There she ducked down, so that she was below the height of the cabin windows. There was nowhere to hide on the narrow strip of wooden boards, but she could hear again, the voices coming out through the open hatchway.

"Luis. You've been very careless."

Amber dared to lift her head a little. And through the narrow cabin window she got a snapshot of what was happening inside. The two men were standing opposite Carlos, who was seated, and dressed only in his jeans. He had his hands unnaturally placed on the table in front of him.

The two men were both dressed in suits. It looked odd, in the cabin of a boat, but somehow it looked threatening too, or perhaps that was just the way they were standing. Then Amber saw the smaller of the two men move, and suddenly she could see his hands too. In one he held up Carlos' bag of cocaine. Her heart beat faster in fear. Then she gasped when she saw his other hand. In it he held a long black gun. She'd watched enough movies to know it had a silencer fitted.

The man removed a glove, and then opened the bag. He touched the tip of one finger into the powder, pulling it out with a small amount stuck to the tip. He tasted it, and looked to Carlos.

"Oh dear Luis." He shook his head, as if pretending to be disappointed. Then he turned to the bigger man, which prompted Amber to do the same, and she saw he too had a silenced pistol.

"Luis, Luis..."

Along with her horror, Amber registered that the smaller man was repeating the name *to* Carlos, as if he had his name wrong. It confused her. Another thing that made no sense. She strained her ears, desperate to understand what she was watching.

"I do believe you had an arrangement to deliver something for our employer." Still it was the smaller man speaking. He had greasy hair, slicked back, and a black earring in each ear. Should she be remembering details like this? Or trying to forget them? Amber had no idea. It felt like her brain was thinking through treacle.

"I don't know what you're talking about." Carlos replied. Her fear was intensified by just how sullen he looked. How different to how he'd been all evening.

"Oh Luis. You maybe wanna take a moment. Consider if *fucking around* is something you wanna do here?"

Why do they keep calling him Luis? Amber fought to understand. *And why doesn't he correct them?* The two possible explanations collided in her mind. They knew him by a fake name. *She* knew him by a fake name.

Then the smaller man put his gun down and lifted the bag she had seen earlier onto the table. Now she saw it was more of a sports bag than the sailing bag she had imagined she saw. He unzipped it and pulled out a small white plastic tube. He opened that and drew out a plastic spatula. Then he dipped that into the bag of cocaine and pulled out a heaped spoonful. Carefully he dropped it into the tube and screwed the lid back on. He shook it gently. He seemed to be enjoying his work. Then he turned to Carlos and smiled.

"This little test here will confirm if this is our product or not. If it turns blue, we'll know you've been a naughty boy." He began whistling as he waited. Then he held up the vial. Amber saw that the liquid inside was now a soft blue color.

"Oh dear," Earrings said.

Then there was a buzz of movement inside the cabin. It happened almost too fast for Amber to follow, but she caught how Carlos suddenly lunged forward, towards the bigger man who still had his gun. He was quick, but the big man was quicker. He moved left, out of the way, and at the same time, delivered a blow to Carlos' head. It stopped him at once, and he dropped back down to where he'd been sitting, as if he was about to lose consciousness. Then the big man snarled. His teeth were crooked and discolored. The younger man, with the earrings, looked unconcerned – almost bored – during the whole moment.

"No need for that, Luis," Earrings said. "We just want to have a little talk."

A bubble of hope filled in Amber as he said this, she was desperate to believe it, but as Carlos looked up again, she saw there was blood running down the side of his head now. He dabbed at it, looking at his finger disbelievingly. She knew then there was nothing hopeful about what was happening in front of her.

"I gotta tell you Luis," Earrings picked up the bag again and shook it thoughtfully. "You can save yourself a whole lot of pain right now, just by telling us where you stashed the rest of this. You wanna do that? It here on the boat?" his eyebrows lifted hopefully. But Carlos didn't respond at all, save to lift his eyes and glance angrily at Earrings, and touch his head wound a second time.

"No? You know I'm kinda glad about that. Give us a chance to settle a little row we had earlier, don't it Tommy?" This time Earrings turned to look at the bigger guy, who looked madder than ever.

"You see. Tommy here – they call him Tommy *the Teeth* by the way, on account of the fucked up state of his mouth – you don't want him breathing on you, believe me." He sniffed. "Now Tommy here, he don't have no style. If it was up to him, he'd be breaking your fingers by now. One by one, until you tell him where you put it. And maybe that would work, and maybe it wouldn't. Maybe you'd tell us what we want to hear, but maybe you'd give us some bullshit story and then, when we cut your fucking head off, we wouldn't have no idea where you'd stashed it." He stopped talking and picked up the bag of coke again. He opened it and dipped his finger in a second time, but this time he pulled out a little mound of powder balanced on his fingernail. He held it to his nose and sucked it up. For a second he screwed his eyes shut. Then he went on.

"And I can't have that. I came here to recover what you stole, and that's exactly what I'm gonna do. So I told Tommy he wouldn't be breaking your fingers like normal. One by one, until you squeal like a fucking pig. We'd be doing this my way." Earrings looked at Carlos's hands, both still palm-down on the table in front of him.

"So maybe you wanna say a little thank you for that," he went on.

Carlos didn't reply, and after a second, Earrings repeated himself.

"I said maybe you wanna say a little thank you, that I'm not gonna be breaking your fingers." Amber felt herself holding her breath, and even willing Carlos to do what the man asked, there was such an air of menace to him. But still Carlos was silent and still. Then in a sudden blur of movement, Amber watched as Earrings lunged forward and swung the handle of the gun down hard on Carlos' fingers. He hit him again and again, until there was blood bursting from the hand, and Carlos had it clamped to his chest. There was noise now, the sound of Carlos screaming, and swearing in Italian. Through tears of shock Amber watched as the other man – Tommy – calmly picked up a magazine from the shelf, folded it twice and jammed it into Carlos' open mouth.

THIRTY-THREE

WITH A SUDDEN JOLT Amber realized she had to do something. If she didn't she was going to watch her boyfriend tortured and murdered, she was sure of that. She dropped back down to the deck to get space to think. What the hell should she do? The police. She could call them, she *had* to call them. But she had no phone. She wept for her decision to plug it into her car, before screaming at herself to think. She could run to get it. Better still, call the cops *from* her car, where she would be safe.

But something stopped her. And she knew what. Holport was too small to have a police station, the cops would have to come from Newlea. That was a half hour by car. And how long would they take just to get ready? Before they even set off? Lornea Island wasn't the sort of place where the cops sat around expecting this kind of situation. It might be forty minutes, an hour, before anyone got here. They were torturing him – actually torturing him – now. This wasn't going to last that long. And while she fought for answers she heard the nightmare unfolding further.

"*Motherfucker*," Earrings snarled, as if he were the one who had been injured. Carlos still had the hand clamped to his chest, his eyes screwed tightly shut. Even from where she stood, Amber could tell it was badly damaged.

"So like I said," Earrings went on suddenly, as if nothing had happened. "I told Tommy we were gonna do this in a more intelligent way." Then he turned away and began rummaging in the bag they'd brought. He pulled out a small black case. He placed it on the table, and undid a zip all the way around its edge, folding the lid back. The contents were too small for Amber to see clearly, but it looked like the kind of kit vets carried about with them.

"You see Tommy's way is OK. But science has come a long way since he started out in this business." Earrings smiled now. "Tell me Luis. You ever see a movie where they use a truth drug?"

He waited for Carlos to answer this, then when he didn't he busied himself by selecting a syringe from the case, and then a small glass bottle. Eventually Carlos did reply.

"Yeah." His voice sounded awful. There was blood smeared all over his chest, from his broken hand.

"Good. And let me guess. It probably showed a guy getting injected, and afterward just spilling his guts. Am I right?"

Carlos breathed hard before replying. "Something like that."

"I thought so." Earrings ignored him for a moment, rolling the bottle thoughtfully in his fingers. After a while he went on. "It don't work like that, not in real life. I mean, just imagine for a minute if it did – you wouldn't need courts, you wouldn't need lawyers. None of that. Just stick the needle in and out comes the truth." He chuckled now. "Maybe one day."

"But what most people don't know is how they're trying to do it like the movies. You know, the CIA, Secret Service, all that bullshit. They ain't ever gonna tell us exactly what they're up to, but I heard, from a guy who's brother was in the military — special forces — that," he stopped. "Well, it don't matter *how* I know. I just know." He pressed the needle of the syringe through the lid of the bottle, then inverted it and pulled back the plunger. The syringe filled with a clear liquid.

"This is *sodium thiopental*. What it does is slow down how your brain sends messages from one part to another. It's like thinking through glue. You see, you have to consider how a lie works. You have to make up a new reality. You invent it. A lot of different parts of the brain have to work together. And that takes effort. But you pump enough of this stuff in and you lose the power to keep lying." He held the needle upwards and squirted a jet upward, clearing the air.

"But I told you, they ain't got it quite like the movies yet. Not as simple." He frowned, and looked pained. "You see, it's kinda dangerous. The dosage is real important. You need a lot before it starts working, but if you give *too* much, then the guy's heart is just gonna stop. Just like that. Second thing is this. *It don't always work*. A guy like you, who's holding onto a really big lie? Well it's *possible* you could keep it inside, even when the drug is working. If that happens we're no better than with Tommy here breaking your fingers."

Carlos didn't respond, his gaze was still on his damaged hand.

"But what no one can do is lie about *everything*. The brain just doesn't work like that. That's the real beauty of this system. If we ask you questions that don't seem to relate to that secret you're holding onto, it simply won't occur to you to lie to us. Which means we just need to take a roundabout route and we'll find the truth." He turned to the other man.

"Are you gonna hold this fucker down or what?"

Amber looked at the man called Tommy in time to see a dark look run across his face, but he stepped forward and grabbed Carlos. He spun him around, as easily as if he'd been a child, and gripped him by the throat. Amber thought he was going to strangle him there and then, and she could see Carlos, gasping in pain. But while Tommy held him, Earrings moved forward and carefully pressed the syringe into his upper arm. He pushed down the plunger, then pulled the needle out again. When Amber saw it again, the barrel of the syringe was empty. Then Tommy released his grip and sat back down opposite.

"Now we wait," Earrings said.

Outside Amber gagged and she tasted sick in her mouth. She was breathing as hard as if she were the one being tortured. She thought again about the police, wishing she'd left earlier, and almost fantasizing they were already on their way, or here. A fleet of squad cars coming to the rescue. But she knew they weren't. And if she left now to call them, Carlos would die. Her boyfriend would be dead before they could arrive. They would arrive to find his body…

The sick came out. First a mouthful, and then everything she had. It spewed onto the pontoon, and over the side into the black water. She saw fish, attracted by the movement, or the smell. She recognized what she had eaten earlier, it made everything she was watching all the more unbelievable, yet real.

Finally she stopped heaving. She stared at the mess on the decking, and blinked in horror. She *had* to do something. She couldn't just hide here, watching a murder. But what? She looked around her, searching for ideas. There was a plastic bollard at the junction of the pontoon, giving out just the barest yellow light, sufficient so that users could see enough to not walk into the water. But it was fixed down, it couldn't help her. There was a hose, for boat owners to clean the salt off. But what could she do with a hose? The two men inside were armed with guns. Huge guns, with silencers attached. The thought of that impacted her for the first time. It registered that what she was witnessing was the work of actual professional killers. The thought made her almost moan out loud.

The flare gun. On the *Blue Lady* there was a flare gun. If she got that maybe she could… The rush of hope died almost as fast as it arrived. There were two of them. They had real guns. They were professional killers. She felt tears pressing out of her eyes at the sheer frustration of it. If she couldn't think of anything then Carlos was going to die. The man she loved was going to be killed in front of her eyes.

"OK Luis," she heard Earrings start up again. "You should be about cooked now. Let's say we ask you a few questions." Amber raised herself up on her knees, just high enough to see into the cabin.

"What's your name."

"Luis," Carlos breathed in reply. "Luis Fernandez."

"That's great Luis. That's real nice. Thank you for that. And do you know why we're here?"

Amber watched, as the man she had known as Carlos leaned back now, his head lolling around on his shoulders, like it was too much of an effort to hold up. "Yeah," he said in the end.

"OK, and you wanna tell me why?"

Another pause, then Carlos replied. "I was meant to deliver… A load of cocaine. But I didn't do it."

"And why didn't you do it?"

"I dunno. I decided not to. I decided to take it back home and sell it there. I didn't think anyone would ever find me."

"That's OK Luis. We understand. A stupid fucking decision, but we understand. But tell me, where is the product now? Where have you hidden it?"

For a while it seemed Carlos hadn't heard. Or that he had heard, but the pain in his arm was blocking out everything else. But in the end he lifted his head very slightly, his eyes barely open.

"Is it on the boat?"

"No," Carlos managed in the end.

"Where is it then?"

"I buried it," Carlos said. The effort it took to speak was clear.

"Oh?" Earrings said. He turned to Tommy and his eyebrows went up in surprise.

"Where'd you bury it?"

Carlos was having trouble breathing now, it took him a while to answer.

"In the woods."

"The woods? What woods?"

Carlos took a few breaths before he was able to continue. "No not the woods, by a stream."

Earrings frowned now. "What stream?"

"Or maybe…" Carlos panted again. "Maybe it wasn't a stream. More of a lake."

Earrings' frown deepened. "A lake?"

"More of a sea really. Yeah that's it," Carlos went on, warming to it now. "The sea of tranquility I think it's called. On the *fucking moon.*"

He sat back now, and stared at the mess of his hand.

"On the moon? You buried our product on the moon?"

"I might as well have, for all the chances of you *fuckers* finding it," Carlos continued, and he forced a grin before his face went slack.

But Earrings didn't look bothered. "On the moon huh? That's nice. That's a real nice hiding place. Ain't no one gonna find it there." He nodded to himself, before going on. "Say Luis, anyone else know you borrowed a little bit of coke? Huh? Or is it just you?" Earrings kept his voice casual.

Outside Amber immediately realized the danger in the question. And she stared at Carlos, willing him to see it too. But he just shrugged.

"No," Carlos shook his head, then stopped. "Yeah." He narrowed his eyes as if something had occurred to him but he wasn't sure what. "Amber. I told Amber."

The sound of her own name crashed into Amber's brain. She looked about again, she felt like she were tied to a train track, watching the locomotive charge toward her, unable to do anything to prevent what was coming.

"OK Luis," Earrings said again, keeping his voice pleasant. "Amber's that chick you were banging earlier?"

"Yeah."

"You mind if we talk about her for a while?"

Carlos didn't respond.

"She looks like a nice lay?"

Again he was silent.

"Nice, tight little ass on her anyway."

No response.

"Oh come on Luis. It must feel good, slipping one into an ass like that?"

Somehow Carlos managed another shrug.

"OK, good. You're a lucky boy. Now, does she got a surname?"

A look passed across Carlos' face, like he thought for a moment this might be something he shouldn't say, but then he forgot.

"Atherton."

"Amber Atherton. So maybe you got the coke hidden up at her place? That right?"

It took a while for Carlos to answer. It looked like a huge effort.

"I ain't telling."

"No?"

"No. No way."

"Where's she live, anyway? Just out of interest."

Amber prayed that he would refuse to tell them, but this time he hardly hesitated.

"It's in Newlea. I don't know the address."

There was a silence before Earrings continued the questioning.

"This her?"

Carlos looked confused, as something was thrust in front of his face. Amber saw what it was, her college ID card. "Hey," Carlos slurred. "Where'd you get that?"

"Why it has her address on it, right here! Thank you Luis. And you said she knows where the product is hidden? Is that right?"

"Must have left it here." Carlos was mumbling now, so that it was hard for Amber to hear him, but then he brightened, his voice clearer. "Yeah that's right. Must be right."

"OK Luis. That's great. Now, shall we ask a few more questions? Would you like that?"

Carlos was silent for a while. Then, with a big effort he lifted his head. He ignored Earrings, and stared at the bigger man.

"Hey Tommy!" he called. The big man narrowed his eyes, and tightened his grip on the gun. "You know something?" Carlos went on. Amber held her breath, unsure what was happening now.

"You're one dumb motherfucker!" Carlos broke into something of a grin, though it looked like the effort of it was nearly killing him. "You know that? Working for a fucking jerk like this?"

The atmosphere in the little cabin had changed, it was like the power had shifted, subtly but significantly. Amber watched in confusion.

"This guy's a fucking moron, so what does that make you, huh? A guy that takes orders from a fucking moron." Carlos laughed again. And he didn't stop talking.

"And I bet… I bet that's how you got those teeth, from blowing him off?"

"Is that it?" Carlos lifted his good hand and mimed the action of a blow job. "He gives you head, and you get so fuckin' excited, you knock your own teeth out?" He grinned now, manically.

And suddenly Amber knew what he was doing. He was *goading* them. He was doing everything he could to provoke them into killing him now. He knew there was no chance of getting out of this alive, and he just wanted it over with.

And finally it was enough to spur Amber into action.

THIRTY-FOUR

SHE STOOD and ran the few steps to the *Blue Lady* then leapt on board. There was a fire extinguisher mounted on the inside of the spray shield which protected the cockpit, and she ripped it off and swung it against the glass of the cabin door. It smashed at once, and she reached inside for the lock, grabbing her sleeve to protect her wrist against the glass still lodged in the window frame. From the inside she turned the lock and the door swung open.

She moved directly to the locker where the distress flares were kept. They were required by law to keep several types, and for obvious reasons they had to be accessible in the event of an emergency. Never for an emergency like this though. It took her precious seconds, but soon she found the type she was looking for – the rocket flares. She grabbed one, and ripped open the packet as she jumped back onto the pontoon.

She had no time to consider what she was doing, she simply acted. She ran the two steps across the walkway, and swung herself aboard the *Mystery*. She planted her feet on the two side benches of the cockpit, looking straight down the hatchway into the cabin. It took her a moment to make sense of the view that met her.

Carlos was still alive. But she was there just in time. The bigger man, the one called Tommy, had his gun, but the man with the earrings was now holding a huge knife, the kind explorers use to chop through jungle vines. They seemed to be arguing, horribly, about how they were going to kill him. Then Earrings grabbed Carlos and held his head back, exposing his neck for the knife.

"Let him go or I'll fucking fire this!" Amber yelled, holding out the plastic tube towards them.

All three of them looked, bewildered by the interruption. The big man was the quickest to move, he turned his gun towards her.

"Don't fucking move!" She yelled again, and it slowed the man's arm. The flare had a pull-cord, and she already had it stretched taut, so that just a tiny extra tug would detonate the flare. She had no idea what effect it would have in the cabin, and there was no time to think. No time to think anything. The big man continued to swing the weapon towards her, and she knew he would fire. A fraction of a second seemed to stretch out forever, but as the barrel of the weapon levelled on her she pulled the cord as hard as she could.

The result was instantaneous. It was as if her arm itself shot out fire. It ripped apart the air around her and a yellow-orange trail exploded downward into the yacht's cabin. It didn't explode. Instead it hit the door of the bow cabin, which was closed, but then bouncing first one way then another, moving too fast, and too bright, for her to follow its path, but with the effect of a pinball machine. For a second, maybe two it ricocheted inside the small cabin, fizzing with eruptions of fire and sparks with every surface it hit. And then it did explode. Suddenly the entire space was just a thick red glow, so bright Amber had to shield her eyes. Then she felt a wave of heat roll from the cabin, forcing her to drop away.

When she looked again, the cabin was still too bright to see into, and she blinked in horror at the thought she had killed them – all three of them. But then the flare, perhaps damaged by its fractured trajectory, started dimming, and eventually she saw recognizable shapes emerging from the red light. And then she saw movement. And then – with a bang – the brightness suddenly dimmed significantly. It took her several seconds to work out what had happened, but as her eyes adjusted further she saw the reason. The bigger man had kicked shut the door to the forward cabin. And the flare was now shut inside, still burning but its light hidden. Suddenly the cabin looked almost normal, apart from the smoke now pouring up the companionway steps, and the three men inside picking themselves up from the floor. Then the man with the earrings saw her. Their eyes locked together.

"Fucking crazy *bitch*!"

He was pushing himself up off the floor, and they both saw the gun at the same time, right next to his hand. He had dropped the knife by now, and grabbed for the weapon. Amber had taken just the one flare, and now had nothing to defend herself. As he turned the pistol onto her again, there was nothing else she could do but turn and run.

* * *

Amber jumped down to the pontoon, and nearly fell flat on her face. The narrow walkway that ran between the two boats was greasy and slippery from where she had emptied her stomach earlier. But some part of her brain remembered this just in time, and her arms went out to help her balance. She skidded a few feet, but somehow stayed on her feet and began running. But still, it felt like running through glue, every step took an age and with each one she expected to hear the muffled shots, to feel the bullets thudding through her exposed back.

She was nearly at the corner, where the narrow offshoot of the walkway met the main pontoon. But just as she reached it she felt something zipping through the air in front of her. Then she heard the noise, louder than she expected, but still clearly the muffled report of several shots being fired. She screamed and dropped to the decking. For a second she froze. Then something in her terror made her glance behind, as if she wanted to die facing her executioner. She saw the man preparing to leap down from the yacht. Once he was level with her on the pontoon he surely couldn't miss. She turned again, and forced her limbs to work, clambering away from him on her hands and knees but knowing it was hopeless.

Then another bang sounded behind her, and Amber froze again. But again she worked out she hadn't been hit, and when she looked back a second time she saw the man sprawled on his back on the walkway, where he had slipped in the sick. She didn't need a second invitation. She scrambled back to her feet, and fled down towards the land.

It only gave her a short head start, and seconds later Amber realized the other mistake she had made. *The gate.* She should have gone to unlock it before attacking them. Now it blocked her way, and he would catch her up as she tried to open it. Or at least, she would be an easy target, pinned against it like an animal in a trap. It was a fatal mistake, she moaned out loud at the realization.

There was nothing else she could do but keep running. She pushed her legs to run faster and faster, aware of how the muscles burned but the pain almost irrelevant. And she arrived at the gate sooner than she thought, slamming into it to slow down, and feeling the metal crack into her forehead. Her hands and fingers were shaking, almost more than she could control, as she tried to unscramble the combination lock. She was aware of herself screaming out in frustration. And she could hear him, the sound of footsteps running hard behind her as she lined up the numbers. *One. Two,* three numbers now… How would it feel when the bullet hit? Would she even feel anything? Her fingers wouldn't stop shaking again as she tried to set the fourth number. She spun the dial too far, and then had to turn round and go the other way. And all the time the footsteps were coming closer, his voice shouting now. Why wasn't he firing?

The lock opened and the latch on the gate released. She pushed through, just as she felt the man's weight arrive behind her. As she went through the gate she gripped its edge with both hands and turned and slammed it hard behind her. She felt the crunch as the metal caught on something rather than fitting into its frame, and when she looked she saw fingers were trapped between the gate and its frame. There was a scream of pain as the man tried to pull them out, but Amber put all her weight behind it now, shoving it shut. She willed the mechanism to catch, but the fingers were preventing it. She moved position, to try and increase her pressure, but he took advantage, pulling his hand out. The gate caught, shutting properly now, and she spun the combination on her side. For a second they stared at each other, close enough to touch, but with the steel of the gate between them. Then Amber turned again and fled once more, up the ramp and off the pontoon.

When she reached the land she didn't slow. She sprinted across the road and around the corner to where she had left the car. She slammed into the side, and began fumbling for her keys. But then she remembered something – her unreliable car. An image flashed through her mind, herself pinned in the driver's seat while the motor turned over, advertising where she was but leaving her powerless to escape, until he lined up his shot through the windshield.

Then she did hear a noise, the metallic ringing of the gate opening again and crashing back on its hinges. She turned again to the car, praying it would be OK, but as she tried to slip the key into the lock, her hands fumbled them, and they dropped to the street. She looked down to recover them, but it was dark. And she heard his footsteps again, ringing out as he climbed the ramp.

She left it, and ran again. This time with no idea where she was going. In seconds he would be around the corner and see her. And really there was nowhere to run. No one lived here, at night it was just empty warehouses and closed up shops. In a panic she ducked down behind the nearest car, but it would take him only moments to see her. He would hear her frantic panting. Then a section of the wall beside her registered in her mind. It wasn't just wall, there was a narrow alleyway cut into it. It led to a space behind a small boat storage yard, and wasn't used for anything. She only knew of it because it was where Billy kept his kayak. It was hidden enough that no one vandalized it there. With no time to decide, she went for it. She sprinted into the dark alley at full speed and didn't slow down. It was another mistake. First something caught at her feet – perhaps rope, perhaps something else, but whatever it was, it sent her flailing forwards in the darkness, traveling far too fast. Then a crashing blow hit her on the front of her head. Dimly she was aware of falling, and a sharp pain on her temple. But then instead of the pain increasing, the opposite happened. All the pain, and all her feelings lessened. They drifted away. Her range of vision shrank quickly down as the blackness around her was replaced by a different shade of black that only existed in her head. Her knees crumbled underneath her.

She welcomed it. And then she felt nothing.

THIRTY-FIVE

It was the cold that woke her. Creeping through the flesh of her side, deep into the bones. Her eyes opened. She didn't recognize what she saw. Her whole body hurt. Everything was cold, so cold. Her knees and hips felt stiff and her head – she went to move a hand to touch her forehead and it snagged against the rough brick of the wall that she lay against. Her eyes refocused and saw another wall just opposite, and above her a strange, green plastic roof, beyond that the sky a pale blue. The roof wasn't flat but curved and… Her brain unscrambled it to make out the hull of a kayak. Billy's kayak. Why…?

Some of it began to come back to her. She had been running, trying to escape from the man. The man with the earrings. Little black balls in each of his ears. But why…? Why had she been running? And then it all hit her, like the wake from a boat suddenly hitting a calm shore. Each one pushing a fresh flood of horror into her mind. She had left Carlos on the yacht, but then returned to collect her ID card, only to find two men torturing him. The man with earrings had been about to cut his throat. She had tried to stop them. She had fired the flare into the cabin, but… It hadn't worked. She must have escaped – she remembered running into the alley – but what about Carlos? Had they gone back to him. Was he… Was he *dead?*

Her breath caught in her throat. She felt the beginnings of a panic attack, and only just managed to get it under control. She told herself to breathe. She counted ten breaths, and only once she felt her heart rate dropping a little did she allow the question back in. Was Carlos alive or dead?

She had to find out. She struggled to her feet. She had to duck to keep out of the way of the kayak and she realized how she must have run square into it the night before. From the way her head throbbed she must have knocked herself out. She turned and looked at the small space where she had spent the night. The men must have looked for her, she reasoned, but she had been hidden. She hadn't planned it, but under the kayak jammed into the alleyway was the perfect hiding place. Yet at the same time, it was no wonder everything hurt, no wonder she felt colder than she had ever been in her life.

Then a fresh wave of fear struck. What if the men were still looking for her? What if they were still out there, with their guns ready. Perhaps even right by the entrance to the alley, if so they must have heard her already. But no – that made no sense. It must be hours later. It was dark when they chased her, not long after midnight she reckoned, though the thinking caused real pain in her temples. And now it was daylight. They wouldn't have searched for this long.

She felt for her cell phone, to check the time, only then remembering how she had left it charging in her car.

She stepped carefully to the entrance of the alley, still expecting to see the men at any moment. What she could see of the street looked normal. Even so she felt terrified as she peered cautiously around the corner. Nothing. The street looked as it always did. She could see her car, exactly where she had parked it, and a dozen yards further away, a man in blue overalls whistled as he swept the entrance to one of the small warehouses. She stared at him, longing to run over and tell him what had happened, plead for him to help her. But fear stopped her, and as she thought about it, she realized it was impossible. Her story, as she understood it, seemed too incredible. Too unbelievable. Instead she slipped out of the alley, and very cautiously made her way down the street and back over to the waterfront. She had no idea what she was expecting to see, only a deep sense of dread and certainty that somehow Carlos must be dead. She blinked back tears at the thought of that, the sheer impossibility that this had now happened.

Soon she reached the yacht basin. At first everything here looked normal too. But then looking out she saw out by the end of the pontoon, one of the yacht masts wasn't pointing straight upwards, instead it was raked at a 45 degree angle, and when she followed it to where it should meet the deck of the boat below, she saw that it was half hidden, and lying at a strange angle. The *Mystery* was still in its berth, but now it lay half-sunk. What was left of its structure above the water was blackened and twisted. Burned. Amber felt tears flowing freely down her face now. He was dead.

"You all right Miss?"

She swung her head round in alarm. A man was standing, staring at her, a small brown dog stood next to him holding an orange ball in its mouth.

"Oh." She wiped the tears away as best she could. "Yeah. Yeah I'm fine."

If anything the man looked disappointed with her answer. Like he was hoping for someone to gossip with.

"Come to see what happened?"

"Huh?"

"The yacht," the man said. "The one that sunk. I suppose you saw the flames last night? All very dramatic wasn't it? We don't often get excitement like that in Holport."

Amber stared at him, unable to reply, but shocked by the lightness of his tone.

Her lover had been murdered. By professional killers, and she had only just escaped with her life. And he thought it was just some local excitement. She barely heard how the man was still speaking.

"They reckon it was gas. With that kind of explosion."

"Explosion?" Amber forced herself to concentrate.

"Oh yeah. I heard it all the way from the top of the road. And then there were all sorts here. An ambulance, the fire service… All very dramatic."

She didn't want to but Amber forced herself. "The man… The man who was on the yacht, do you know what happened to him?"

"Well yeah. They think he left the gas on and didn't notice. There's always someone doing something stupid like that…"

"Yes but, did he…" Amber couldn't make herself form the word.

"I mean..." She looked around. There was no police cordon. No police cars even, if a man had been *murdered* here the night before, surely the police would be here in force? There would be something. She turned again to the old man, this time barely daring to hope.

"I mean, did he survive?"

The words caught in her throat, and the man looked at her differently.

"Oh I'm sorry Miss," the man said now. He studied her, and Amber felt how she must look. "You didn't … You're not *involved* in anyway?"

Everything about the situation screamed at her to be cautious. Whatever this was about, it involved drugs, professional killers.

"No… I was just... It's just so horrible." She forced herself to smile, and it seemed to work, since the man seemed content to return to his gossiping voice.

"The owner of the yacht you mean?" The man said. "They took him away in the ambulance. Seems he managed to drag himself out before the fire got too bad. They found him lying on the pontoon. He was in a pretty bad way though."

Amber blinked.

"Where is he? Now I mean?"

The man shrugged, looking confused again. "He'll be at the hospital. Had pretty nasty burns I heard…"

Amber stopped listening. She barely registered about burns, only that he was alive. Carlos was alive! She covered her face, squeezing her eyes tight shut and only then remembered the old man standing next to her, and how she must look. She tried to compose herself, but she realized her hair and clothes must be in a state, She looked at him now to see his curious expression as he watched what she was doing.

"You sure you're okay miss? Because if you know anything about this… I heard they found drugs on the boat as well."

"Drugs?" Amber dropped her hands.

"Yeah. There's a security firm looks after the marina. I spoke to the guard – I walk Elvis here every morning and night, so we know each other – and he said the guy from the yacht was a pothead. Been smoking weed out there ever since he turned up. The guard wasn't surprised this had happened. Not at all…" The old man shook his head, but he kept his eyes on Amber, clearly suspicious of her now. And this time the only urge Amber felt was the one to get away from him as quickly as possible.

She nodded her thanks, and walked back across the street, towards her car, feeling his eyes on her back the whole way. At the car she felt for her keys, then remembered how she'd dropped them the night before. She turned, and saw the man, still staring at her, and as she watched he slipped a cell phone from his pocket, but then she noticed a flash of silver from the ground by her feet. She crouched down, making a hasty attempt to look like she was tying a shoe lace, and gathered her keys gratefully into her hand. Then she stood, unlocked the door, and climbed inside.

She slipped the key into the ignition and said a silent prayer. Then she turned it. The motor turned over once, twice, three times and then the motor caught. She put her foot flat to the floor, revving it hard and sending a cloud of gray smoke from the tailpipe.

In the rear-view mirror she caught sight of the man, still staring at her but now with the phone at his ear. Then she slipped the car into drive, and pulled out of the space.

THIRTY-SIX

SHE DROVE towards the hospital in Newlea. But as she did so, her head filled with questions, and new fears. There would be police there at the hospital with him. They would want to know about the drugs. What should she tell them, to avoid getting Carlos into more trouble? What should she say to avoid incriminating herself? Worse, she was the one who had fired the flare that had put him in hospital – might the police be interested in that. Or should she just tell them everything, and hope they'd believe her? A worry surfaced in her mind. She didn't even know his name, not for sure anyway. Who should she ask for? Would they let her see him?

Then her thoughts were interrupted by the ringing of her cell phone, still plugged into the car charger.

"Oh shit."

For a second she left it, but then she grabbed the device and hit the button to accept the call.

"Mom?"

"Amber, where the hell are you? I've been calling you all morning. I have to get the morning ferry, I told you that and if you're not here, who the hell is going to look after Gracie…"

"*Mom!*" Amber tried to stop her, but it was no good.

"Don't you *Mom* me. I told you to be here last night so I can explain about Gracie's piano lessons, and you didn't come home *again*. So I texted you and said you better be here by seven at the latest and it's already 8:30 and where the hell are you?"

"Mom…" Amber's thoughts raced as she tried to compress everything that had happened into a reply to cut into her mom's anger.

"I meant to come back…"

"Where are you now?" Her mom snapped, ignoring her.

Amber looked about her. The truth was she had been driving with no awareness of the road around her. "I'm... I'm on the road into Newlea."

Her mom sighed. "Well that's something. Get a move on, and I can still catch my boat."

Then the call went dead.

Amber sat without moving for a long while, watching the tarmac flow towards her like a dream. She gripped the wheel hard, and opened the window wide, but still couldn't be sure whether she was dreaming everything or if it was real. As she came into Newlea she passed the hospital, turning her head to stare at the drab, squat building she had seen hundreds of times before but never really noticed. But rather than turning into the parking lot she kept going until, ten minutes later, she pulled up outside her house. She screwed her eyes tight shut again before pushing open the door and walking up the drive.

Her mom answered the door before she could get her key out.

"I'm so angry with you Amber."

"It's not my fault."

"Oh nothing is ever your *fault* is it Amber?" Her mom was as mad as Amber had ever seen her. She had her suitcase ready in the hallway, and she picked it up now, and carried it through the front door and out to the trunk of her car.

"I've written instructions for Gracie and left them in the kitchen. She has piano at five today, not six, and you need to be at the school by two thirty latest to pick up. Have you got that Amber?"

"Mom! I need to talk to you. Something's happened."

"Have you got that? Her piano lesson has been brought forward. Can you at least *acknowledge* me Amber? Is that too much to ask?"

"Mom, it's important."

Her mom paused, the suitcase resting on the lip of the car's trunk. "What is it?" She demanded.

Amber struggled to think how to tell her. How could she possibly put into words everything that had happened the night before?

"Well?"

Eventually she shook her head. Her mom sighed, and went back to wrestling the suitcase into the trunk.

"Was it really so much to ask? Three days? Without you making a drama of it?" With a grunt she got the case in, and slammed the trunk shut.

"It'll be just my luck if there is traffic and I'm late for the ferry." She shouted this back at the house, where Gracie was now standing in the doorway. "I'll see you in three days honey. You can call me anytime on my cell. And Amber will look after you, I promise." She smiled sweetly at the little girl, but the smile fell away when she turned back to Amber. "And you'd better. Unless you wanna be grounded for ever, 18 years old or not."

With that she stalked around to the driver's seat. Amber followed her, but before she could say anything more her mom had yanked the door shut.

Amber gave up and walked slowly back toward the house. She smiled at her sister, and put her arm around her. Together they watched their mom's car disappear down the street. Gracie waved at the disappearing vehicle.

"You should have been here earlier." Gracie told her, she didn't sound upset.

"Don't you start midget." Amber replied, but she rubbed her sister's shoulders affectionately and they went inside together.

"What happened to your head?" The little girl asked as they went into the kitchen. There was a mirror hanging by the entrance and Amber caught her reflection. Her hair was a mess, tangled and matted, and the skin on her forehead was split and bruised raw.

"I had an argument with a kayak."

"A kayak? Why did you have an argument with a kayak?"

"Because I like arguing with kayaks."

Gracie looked at her with a confused expression. "You know I don't have school today?"

"Yeah. I know that."

"Mom wrote it on the list, in case you forget."

"I didn't forget."

"She said I should do my math homework. That you'd help me. But I figured we should do something else, like ride our skateboards, and then maybe watch a movie with popcorn."

Amber smiled as much as she could. She touched a finger gently to the broken skin on her forehead. "I might pass on the skateboards, but I'll watch you while you ride yours."

"Okay," Gracie replied happily. "I'll go get it."

"Sure. But give me a moment. I'm just gonna take a shower."

THIRTY-SEVEN

THE MCDONALD'S, which they had picked up from the drive-through in Newlea, was partly a prop to justify their presence on the quiet suburban street, but more a much-needed breakfast after the night which had gone so fucked up. Paulie fed fries one by one into his mouth like a drip of starch and salt, as he stared blankly through the windshield of the panel van. Tommy took huge bites out of a Big Mac and chewed the meat contemplatively.

"I'm just saying it was a fuck up. That's all," Tommy said, sucking in another bite. "And if you'd done what I said, we would have been outta here by now. Instead of sat here, wondering what to do next."

A few more fries found their way up to Paulie before he replied. "Shut the fuck up," he said.

Tommy obeyed only because he was shoving the rest of the burger in. After a few moments he opened the bag and pulled out a second burger. He unwrapped it and lifted up the top half of the bun. He began picking off the limp pieces of lettuce.

"And what was that bullshit of cutting his goddamn head off?"

Paulie ignored him.

"I mean, you figure Angelo really wants his head? Like, literally? What you think he's gonna do with it? Mount it on the wall?" He shook his head. "Plus it's gonna start rotting the moment you cut it off. I heard the brain is the first part to decompose. You'd need to pack it in ice or something. Or it's gonna start to smell like..." He stopped, and put the top back on the burger.

"Didn't I tell you to shut up?"

Tommy shrugged and took a bite, chewing more slowly this time, and watching the street through the windshield. The front door opened in one of the houses opposite, and a man stepped out. He was dressed in a suit, and carrying a briefcase. He walked to a car and zapped it unlocked, then opened the rear door to put the case inside. Then he climbed into the driver's seat. The car backed off the driveway and pulled away.

"OK. You wanna remind me why we're sitting here? And not sorting this fucking mess out?"

"This is sorting it out," Paulie replied, then he added, "and it ain't a fucking mess."

Tommy stayed silent, which served to irritate Paulie further.

"And what would you recommend? With all your years of fucking experience?"

Tommy shrugged. "We go to the hospital and take him out. We might have to leave his head in place, but least we'll know he's dead."

"Oh yeah. That's a great idea Tommy. Real good. Except that hospitals are all covered with cameras these days. They'll have you matched up on facial recognition in no time."

Tommy pondered this. The rise of surveillance had done for some of his better friends, and it wasn't an area he understood these days. Plus, it hadn't escaped his attention which one of them Paulie had expected to go in there. He changed the subject.

"Anyway. It's not whacking Luis Fernandez I'm worried about. It's going back to Angelo without the product."

"We're not gonna go back without the product," Paulie sounded frustrated. "The girl knows where it is, remember? All we have to do is find her, and she'll tell us where it is."

Tommy didn't look fully convinced by this, but he let it go.

"Maybe," he said, then shook his head. "I still don't understand how she managed to get away."

"I told you, she broke my fucking fingers." Paulie grabbed a handful of fries and stuffed them into his mouth. His fingers looked fine to Tommy.

"And I don't see why she's gonna come back here. Seems to me this is the least likely place she's gonna wind up. She'll be at the hospital. Or the cops."

Paulie said nothing.

"I mean she must've got a good look at your face, when she was breaking your…"

"Shut the fuck up man."

Tommy gave up and arranged his jacket so that it acted as a cushion against the hard plastic and glass of the van's door. Just as he was arranging his large body as best he could, Paulie spoke again, but it sounded like he was trying to convince himself.

"She ain't gonna call the cops. Her boyfriend's smuggling eighty keys of cocaine. That's the last thing she's gonna do."

Tommy shrugged again, like it wasn't really his problem, and closed his eyes.

Two tedious, empty hours later Paulie nudged him awake.

"What?"

"Open your eyes you fucking imbecile. She's here."

Outside the little Mitsubishi that they had seen Amber driving the night before pulled into the driveway. Tommy pulled himself upright, but neither man made any move to get out. Instead they watched. Amber's car pulled up on the curb, and she got out. But before she could reach the house, the front door opened and an older woman – presumably her mom – stepped outside. She was clearly angry about something from the way she was yelling and waving her arms about.

"What the fuck?" Paulie said under his breath.

Then Amber and the older woman went back inside. But the door stayed open, and moments later the woman reappeared, this time struggling with a large suitcase. Then Amber re-emerged as well, and the two of them carried on their argument all the way to the trunk of another car, this time a BMW compact that sat on the driveway.

"What they arguing about?" Tommy asked, his voice still a little sleepy.

"How the fuck should I know?" Paulie snapped back. Then a small child appeared in the doorway.

"Who's the kid?" Tommy asked.

"Again. How the *fuck* should I know?" Paulie repeated himself. But already he was beginning to form an idea.

The argument continued, but clearly the older woman was in a hurry to leave. And moments later she drove off in the BMW, leaving Amber and the child together. She was a girl, maybe five or six years old. Then they walked back into the house and shut the door.

"Well well. What's going on there?" Paulie asked, his voice different now, suddenly interested again. Tommy stared at him, frowning. He had been interrupted mid dream.

"Wait here," Paulie said five minutes later, when nothing else had happened. He pushed open the door of the van.

"Where you going?" Tommy asked.

"Just do as you're told," Paulie shot back. He slammed the door shut.

Tommy did what he was told. It was what he did. That had always been his job. But he was getting more and more pissed at doing what he was told by a fucking idiot like Paulie. With a fingernail he cleaned some of the remains of his burgers from his teeth, but he didn't leave the comfort of the van's cab.

Outside Paulie crossed the road and stopped on the sidewalk. He looked both ways but the street was empty and quiet. It looked as if most of the occupants had already left for work, or for school, and the house in front of him – the address on the girl's ID card – had no more vehicles on the drive, only Amber's Mitsubishi parked outside. He walked up the driveway. Ignoring the front door for now, he cautiously approached the window of whatever room it was that overlooked the street. He moved to the side, stole a glance, then pulled back against the wall. He saw enough to know it was a sitting room. A second glance confirmed it was empty, so Paulie stepped closer, and this time he used both hands to shield his eyes as he peered inside. It looked ordinary. A sofa, and a couple of armchairs were angled around a TV, and a collection of toys were strewn out on the floor. Through the open doorway Paulie could see into what looked like the kitchen. The light was on, but he couldn't see anyone inside. He rolled back, so that his back was against the front wall again, and thought. He *had* to get the girl, *Amber Atherton,* to take them to the cocaine. Anything else was inconceivable. Last night *had* been a fuck up, and he couldn't afford another one.

"Can I help you?"

Paulie froze, then slowly he turned around. The front door was open now, and the little girl was on the step, staring at him. He didn't answer, he had no idea what to say.

"I asked if I can help you?" The girl repeated herself. She didn't look scared, just alert. Paulie's mind raced.

"Why are you looking into my window?"

"Oh I'm just…" He pushed himself away from the wall, and forced a smile. He had no idea how to finish the sentence so he didn't. "I dunno. Say – was that your mom I just saw leaving?"

"Yeah," the girl answered.

"Oh. How about your dad? Is he about?"

"He doesn't live here anymore."

Paulie's smile became a little more real.

"Oh," he said. "So your mom, where's she gone?"

"She's gone away. For *three days.*" The girl emphasized this, like it was a pretty big deal.

"Three days? Why's she done that then?"

"She had to. She didn't want to," the girl said, in a very matter-of-fact way. "It's for work."

"Oh right," Paulie thought for a moment. "So who's looking after you then?"

"My sister."

"Your sister? That's Amber right?"

The girl looked immediately suspicious. She tipped her head onto her shoulder. "How do you know that?"

Paulie considered. This was better than he could have possibly hoped for. "Oh she's a friend of mine," he said airily.

"*You're* Amber's friend?" The girl replied.

"Yeah." Paulie shrugged.

"You don't *look* like one of Amber's friends."

He laughed, beginning to enjoy himself. "Well how do Amber's friends look?"

"Better than you."

Paulie stopped laughing. He looked around the street again.

"What do you want anyway?"

"Excuse me?"

"Why are you looking in our living room window?"

Paulie ignored the question. "Where is Amber? Right now?"

"She's upstairs. In the shower."

Paulie glanced up, he realized the room above them was the bathroom. He could hear the water running.

"In the shower?"

"Yes! Like I just said."

Paulie studied the girl. From her face it was obvious she hadn't fully bought his nice-guy act. But then he didn't really give a shit about that. He allowed himself a few more seconds to consider, then made a decision. He pulled out his phone.

"Who are you calling?" The girl asked, but Paulie ignored her again. As soon as the call connected he began speaking. "Tommy, shift over and back the van up the drive. Do it right now."

"Who are you talking to?" The girl asked. "Why are you telling them that?"

"Don't ask why you…" Paulie bit his tongue into the phone. "Just… *do it.*"

Paulie slipped his phone back into his pocket, and turned back to the girl. He smiled again, trying not to make himself look creepy, which he knew he could do, from practicing in front of the mirror. Over the road, the van's motor started up. He glanced at the front door of the house, taking in which way it opened. Where he would need to stick his foot to block it.

"So what's your name then?" He asked the girl.

"*My name?* What's your name?"

"My name?" He thought. For some reason the name of his first pet came to mind, a mouse he'd been allowed to keep when he was about six. "Jason." He smiled again, thinking of the way it had scampered over his hands as a kid. "Come on. It's not going to hurt to tell me your name is it?"

The girl tipped her head over again. "No, I suppose not."

"That's right." Paulie glanced at the van. It was taking an age for Tommy to actually get moving. The guy was a fucking liability.

"OK then," he said. "So what is it?"

The girl noticed the van, moving now in front of the house, and slowing. She didn't seem to connect it to the strange man talking to her.

"It's Gracie."

"That's a lovely name," Paulie said absently. But his eyes were on the van now. It had stopped at an angle in the street. Then the reversing lights came on, and with a screech, it bumped up to the sidewalk and began backing fast onto the driveway. It stopped only a few feet away.

"What's he do…?" Gracie began, but she never got to finish her sentence, because suddenly Paulie was upon her. He threw one arm around her, picking her off the ground, and with the other he flung open the rear door on the van, then he pivoted and dumped her inside, his weight falling onto her, silencing any chance of a scream. Moments later Tommy was there.

"The fuck are you…"

"Shut up." Paulie cut him off and rolled off the girl. Now he had one hand clamped over her mouth.

"Get in here and tie her up. Make sure she doesn't make a fucking sound," Paulie commanded, then when Tommy hesitated he swore at him, until the big man was inside. He easily held the girl down with one giant arm, while with the other he searched for tape.

And when he was satisfied the situation was under control, Paulie climbed out, checked around the still-empty street, and stepped inside the house.

THIRTY-EIGHT

AMBER LET the warm water run down through her hair and eyes. At first it pooled pink at her feet, as it washed the dirt and blood from her hair, but soon it ran clear. She stood for a long time letting the warmth unlock the tension in shoulders and back. She didn't know what she was going to do, but whatever it was it would have to wait until her Mom came back and she could give Gracie back. She reached for the shampoo, and squeezed a generous handful.

Then there was a noise from downstairs.

Amber opened her eyes. She listened. But there was nothing else. It was just Gracie she decided. Slamming a cupboard door, or jumping off the table. She was that kind of kid. Amber listened for a second, but there was nothing – it was nothing – so she went back to letting the water run over her. And ten minutes later she turned off the flow and reached for a towel. She wrapped it around her and stepped out of the shower, then when she had dried herself she left the bathroom.

Right away she sensed something wasn't right. It was the quiet. Too quiet. Amber felt the hair on the back of her neck rise up. She called out downstairs, "Gracie!"

There was silence.

Amber tried again, louder this time. "*Gracie?*"

Again there was no reply.

Amber wrapped the towel tighter and looked down the stairs. The front door was open. Not wide-open, but just a little ajar.

"Gracie?" Amber called again, worried now. She stepped down the stairs, a slight sense of floating, unreality. She passed the entrance to the living room and looked inside. No Gracie. She wasn't in the kitchen either. And the house was silent. She went to the front door, feeling the slight flow of wind on her bare legs and feet. She gently pushed it wider open, then stepped onto the doorstep and looked around. Outside the street looked completely normal, but still there was no Gracie. Amber called out her name again, but quieter now, not wanting to draw too much attention while she stood there in a towel. Then she rushed back inside, up the stairs and threw some clothes on, and a minute later she was outside the house calling loudly, and checking every possible place the girl could be hiding. But she wasn't there.

Eventually Amber went back inside, reasoning that she hadn't properly checked the house – Gracie had any number of hidey-holes she liked to squirrel herself away in, dressed as a pirate or a princess, and lost in her own world of make believe... And that's when she saw the note. Scrawled on the back of a letter and pinned under a coffee cup on the kitchen work surface. Amber stared at it in disbelief, somehow realizing what it meant, even before her brain had deciphered the words:

You've got what we want. Now we have what you want. Let's make a swap.

Underneath there was a cell phone number.

Amber stared at the note in shock. They had her sister?

* * *

Her thoughts were a cocktail of confusion, hope and horror mixing what made sense with what she wanted to believe. It could be some sort of a joke. Her sister was always getting into some sort of scrape or another. So Gracie must have written the note to trick her. But of course that made no sense. It wasn't in Gracie's handwriting, hers was neater than that. It was something else then. Something separate to the crazy and bizarre turn her life had taken in the last twelve hours. But this thought only served to connect the total horror of what she had witnessed the two men doing to Carlos with *the fact they had her sister*. Her six-year-old sister.

Those men had her sister. Without thinking any further she dialled the number.

"Yeah?" It was a man's voice. Amber didn't recognize which of them it was, but then she didn't really give a fuck.

"Where's my sister? You mother*fucking* piece of shit..."

"Whoa there. Calm down lady."

"*Fuck you asshole*. Tell me where she is right now or I swear..."

"Bitch, you're gonna calm down or your sister's gonna get hurt. Which is it gonna be?"

Amber stopped talking. She could hear her own breath coming in short stabs. She wiped tears from her eyes.

"That's better, now how about we start again? You're Amber Atherton right?"

Still breathing hard, Amber confirmed it.

"It was you fired that flare into the boat last night? Damn near broke my fingers too, on that goddamn gate…"

"Fuck you. I should have fucking cut them off."

"Yeah well fuck you too. We don't have to make friends here lady. We just have to do a little business."

"Where is she? Where's Gracie?"

"All in good time. Here's how this is gonna work, it's real simple. We get the product back, you get the little girl back. How's that sound?"

Amber's mind went blank. "I don't know what you're talking about."

"I think you do. You've put plenty of it up your fucking nose."

There was a moment of silence, but inside Amber's mind it all came together. "I don't know where it is, so there's no point you holding onto Gracie…"

"Well we think you do."

What the fuck were they talking about?

"You think I do what?"

"We think you know where he hid it. No, we *know* you know…"

Amber felt like screaming in frustration. "What? How would I know?"

"He told you."

"No he fucking didn't."

"He told us he told you."

"*What*? This is insane. You're insane. Why would he say that, when he didn't? He told me he bought it from some guy in a bar."

There was a pause, and the voice – she realized it was the man she'd called Earrings now – he suddenly sounded considerably less sure of himself.

"Well you fucking better know. For the sake of your sister."

Amber caught sight of her reflection in the mirror again. Her cut forehead. This couldn't be real.

"Look this is madness. I've got nothing to do with this, and my sister has got even less. I swear to you I don't have any idea where he put it. Now please, I'm begging you, let her go."

But the man's voice was surer again now. "Don't feed me that crap. You know where it is. Or if you don't, you better fucking find it."

"But I…" Amber was interrupted this time.

"And don't even think about calling the fucking cops. If you do that we'll cut the girl up and mail her back to you in six different boxes. Then we'll hunt your mom down and kill her too."

"But…" Amber stopped talking as she realized the line was dead.

This was a dream. It had to be. There was no other possible explanation for how her life could explode into such utter chaos and horror in such a short time. But the girl in the reflection staring back at her was too real, her forehead still bleeding. It was no dream. Her next thought was to call the police. She almost didn't connect it with the final command of the man on the phone to not involve the cops. Instead she considered what she would tell them. About the drugs. About what she had seen the night before. About how they now had Gracie –

these two killers – and how the police *had* to act. But all she saw were the problems. It would take so long. She would have to tell her story to one person, and then another, higher up, before they even started searching. And that was *if* they believed her. And how would they find these men? What was to stop them doing what they'd threatened long before the police caught them?

The reality of what they said suddenly made Amber's stomach turn. At first she just felt ill, but then she realized, with blank disbelief, she was actually going to throw up again. She only just got to the sink in time before the little that was in her stomach came up with a thick stench of bile.

And once she'd started, she retched over and over, her body locked into a rhythm of convulsions that made her eyes and nose water and which she feared might never end. And when it did she stared miserably at the mess in the sink for a while. This wasn't real. This couldn't be. Amber almost forced herself to call out Gracie's name again, but the note was there staring up at her. Ugly writing. She saw the machete the man had carried, heard the popping of the guns they had fired at her.

Somehow she had to come to terms with the horror of all this. And the faster she did, the better the chance for her sister. Slowly, gradually, her brain began to turn to addressing the situation in a more practical way. *Had* Carlos told her where the coke was hidden? She forced herself to revisit the conversations they had had. Carlos had introduced the cocaine into their relationship casually, and with only a little bit at the beginning. They'd smoked a joint, and then he'd pulled out a little paper slip folded into four.

"You ever tried this?" He'd said, and he'd laughed when her eyes went round with surprise. That had been three weeks ago, and they'd only done it a handful of times since, until last week, when she'd turned up to find him with a larger bag of the powder, and much keener to snort more of it.

But all he'd ever said about *where* it came from was the lie he'd told about buying it from a guy in a bar in Holport. She only knew that was a lie yesterday, when he'd finally admitted that he had stolen it. And probably – it was obvious now – he'd told the lie to protect her. The thoughts came rushed and ill-formed, and refused to stay long enough for her to properly interrogate them. A cold panicky urgency took over. Horrible imaginings about where her sister was right now, and what they might be doing to her.

He hadn't told her where it was. She was sure of it. And surely she would remember something like that? Especially now. If he'd mentioned where he'd hidden a huge load of cocaine, she wouldn't have forgotten…

Suddenly she stopped dead. He hadn't told her where it was, she was right about that. But he had said something. Something about Billy. About how *he* might know where it was.

Amber blinked at her reflection in the mirror for a long moment. The battered girl blinked back at her. Then she grabbed her keys and ran out the front door.

THIRTY-NINE

"I DON'T UNDERSTAND," I say, but Amber just keeps on shouting and waving her arms about. She's still outside the front door, where moments before she began hammering like the world was ending. Her car is parked half in our hedge, the driver's door wide open.

"Slow down Amber, you need to slow down."

"I don't have time to fucking slow down. I need you to tell me where it is, where he put the cocaine."

"What are you talking about?"

"*Arrgh!*" She pushes past me into the kitchen, where she paces up and down.

"Billy, will you just listen to me, please?"

I stare at her, not sure if I've heard right. "Did you just say cocaine?"

"Yes." She pauses, for the first time since she got here, and I take the moment to pull out a chair and sit down. Then she tells me the story again, a little bit slower this time, but it still sounds absolutely crazy. Something about Mafia hitmen and shipments of cocaine, and then the craziest bit of all. About her sister, Gracie, being kidnapped.

"And then I remembered," Amber says as she finishes the story. "Carlos – or Luis, or whatever his name is – he told me how you knew where he had stashed the cocaine."

I stare at her, still not sure if this is some kind of weird joke, or more likely, a reaction to the drugs she's been smoking. Like a bad trip. It's kinda what I feared.

"Amber… " I try to keep my voice as neutral and un-threatening as possible, which I think you're supposed to do with people on drugs. "Is this all real, or just in your head?"

In response she lets out another loud scream. When she calms down enough to speak she pulls out a letter from the pocket of her jeans.

"For fuck's sake Billy. Look at this." Then she turns it over, and there's something written on the back. The handwriting is bad so I can hardly read it.

You've got what we want. Now we have what you want. Let's make a swap.

I read it out loud, then look up at her. I'm still confused.

"Who wrote this?"

"*They did*. The Mafia guys. The guys who tortured Carlos. Who chased me. The guys who've got Gracie. And who are actually going to kill her if we don't tell them where their fucking drugs are." Suddenly Amber bursts into tears, great big sobs that make her whole body heave up and down.

I pretend to read the note again, but actually I'm just trying to get some time to think. I study the handwriting first, to see if it might actually be Amber's. She has really distinctive writing, she wants to be an artist and she's really into graphic design. So if it *is* her, she's done it with her left hand.

"So?" Amber says, pulling herself together. "Do you know where it is?"

"Where what is?"

"The drugs. The cocaine. Carlos told me you know where it is. So do you?"

I consider, just for a half second, but already she has her fists clenched again and she's making a moaning noise.

"Why would I know?"

"Because you *have to* know," Amber says, her voice suddenly sounding even more desperate. "You have to know, or they're going to hurt Gracie. Or even worse..."

I'm baffled. Honestly I didn't think Amber was really talking to me at the moment, on account of how I didn't approve of her relationship with Carlos, but then she turns up here screaming all this crazy stuff at me. It's just hard to take.

"Would you like a cup of coffee?"

"No I wouldn't like a fucking cup of coffee. I'd like some help finding my sister."

We sit in silence for a few moments. When I think it's a good moment I try again.

"Amber, I did a little bit of reading about marijuana the other day, and how it can cause symptoms of paranoia. You see people think it's not that strong, but the strains they're growing now are very powerful. And they actually cause hallucinations, where things seem really real even though they're not..."

At this, Amber sits abruptly down at the table across from me. She leans forward and takes my hands in hers. They're ice cold.

"Billy," she pulls my hands towards her, and stares, her eyes clear and earnest. "Billy we've been through a lot haven't we? Together I mean?"

She waits, and in the end I nod, because there's not much else I can do while she's holding onto me like this.

"Good. And I swear to you, I promise. This isn't a hallucination. It's totally real, and I am *desperate* for your help."

Looking at her now I see there's a cut and a bruise on her forehead. I frown at it now.

"What happened there?"

She doesn't hesitate. "I told you. The kayak."

She doesn't take her eyes off me as she speaks, pleading with me. Her chest heaving up and down.

"Where you ran into it?" I check. "When they were chasing you?"

She nods. It looks nasty actually. It's certainly not part of a hallucination, unless I'm having one.

"What did you say happened to Carlos? While they were chasing you?"

"I don't know. The yacht caught fire. It sank. I spoke to a guy who says he got out. But I don't know. I don't even know if he's alive. I don't even know if that's his *name*."

She hesitates for a minute. Then, still staring right at me she goes on.

"Which means you were right by the way. About not trusting him."

Again I consider, this time for a little bit longer, while Amber continues to stare earnestly at me. I did always think there was something not quite right about Carlos.

"And you actually saw them? You saw the guns they had, and… this machete?"

"Yeah. I saw it. I saw it all."

I feel myself blinking quite a lot.

"Well you have to go to the police," I say in the end. I can't think of anything else *to* say.

But Amber lets out her frustrated scream once again and looks away.

"I *can't*. I told you. If I go to the police they're going to hurt Gracie. That's what they said…" It looks like she's going to continue, but instead fat tears appear again in each of her eyes. This time she wipes them away.

"But don't they always say that?" I ask. "Kidnappers? They always say not to go to the police, but actually it makes sense to ignore them and go anyway. And we have quite good contacts with the Lornea Island police force, I'm sure they'd listen to us, what with all the murderers we've caught already."

Amber gives an animal-sounding howl at the word murderer.

"I'm sorry," I say. "I'm sure they're not going to… do anything to hurt Gracie. Why would they? She doesn't know anything about this. She is only six years old."

"Because Billy, they think I know where their cocaine is. And they're professionals. Actual hitmen. They've probably killed dozens of times before."

"Then call the police," I say again. "That's why you have to call them. They're the experts. They'll know what to do."

Amber screams again, but this time, when she's finished, she pulls out her phone and slides it on. But then she stares at it, as if she's forgotten how it works.

"What do I call?" She asks.

"Nine one one."

She breathes heavily, staring at me. "You're right. The police will have people for this. They'll know what to do."

I get up, relieved to have my hands back, and that this madness is starting to come under control. I start making coffee. Even if Amber doesn't want any I need some. "Yeah. They'll know."

"Okay," she says as she takes a deep breath. "If you think it's the best thing to do, I'll call them. I just want Gracie back. I don't care what happens to me, or even to Carlos. I just want her back safe."

I listen to this as I pack the grounds into the machine.

"Sure. Did they have island accents?" I ask, a little offhandedly.

"What?"

"The mafia guys. Did they have island accents?"

"Why do you ask that?"

"I don't know. I was just wondering."

Amber thinks for a moment, her fingers poised to press the digits. "No. I don't think so, at least. They sounded from the mainland."

"Oh," I say.

"Why? What are you thinking?"

"I'm not thinking anything." I say, and I'm really not.

"Are you saying the island police won't be able to handle it?"

"No..."

"Well you're saying something. And you might be right. I mean they were totally fucking useless with the Principal Sharpe thing, back when we were running the detective agency."

"No, I really didn't mean that. I was just..."

"And if we do get the police involved, they'll never let them get their drugs back. They might hurt Gracie out of spite. They might kill her... Oh my God Billy."

"No, I wasn't saying that. I really wasn't." I look at her. "Call them. If this is real you have to call them."

Amber looks like she's barely heard me. But then she nods, and this time she dials. She keeps talking as she does so.

"You're right Billy. I'm glad I came here. I just want Gracie back as soon as possible. Unharmed. And I thought you really might know where the cocaine was being hidden, because Carlos said something about it. About the first time you met, and then I thought we could just give it to them in exchange for Gracie, and that might be the safest thing."

As Amber speaks I suddenly get the strangest feeling. It's like a really bad thought. Or really important. But I don't know what. I don't know what it is, just that there's something.

"911, what's your emergency?" I hear through the phone.

"Oh hi," Amber begins. She pauses, screwing her eyes tight shut.

"Hello ma'am please state which service you require..."

Amber opens her eyes, ready to speak, but then I suppose she sees my face. And I must look wrong, because then she doesn't speak after all, least, not into the phone.

"What is it?" She says instead, talking to me.

I don't reply. I try to figure out what it is I just thought of. But I can't get it.

"Billy? What is it? What are you thinking? Have you remembered something?" Amber says, as the voice on her phone repeats their call.

"Ma'am, are you OK? Which service do you require?"

I still don't really know what it is I'm thinking, but a shape has come into my mind. Or rather a series of shapes. Landscape. Or more accurately, a seascape. It's like my brain is playing me a video. The way water is cut in half by the sharp bow of my kayak, and the rhythmic splashes either side of paddle strokes.

"Billy? Talk to me. What have you remembered."

"Ma'am? Are you in danger? Are you unable to speak?"

"Billy…" Amber begins. But I hold up a finger to keep her quiet.

"*What?* Did he tell you? Did Carlos tell you where it is?"

I think some more. And now I know where this is going. It's like I'm retracing the trip I took out to the nature reserve, when I went to photograph the octopus. The *Octopus Burryi.* The time I first saw the *Mystery,* and the man who turned out to be Carlos – or Luis – spear fishing in the reserve. Only, because it's a nature reserve, there's loads more fish there than anywhere else on the island. And if Carlos really was an experienced spear fisherman, there's no way he would have been that far away from the yacht without any fish.

"I think I know where the dope might be," I say, my voice hushed.

"Ma'am…"

"I'm fine. Wrong number," Amber stabs her finger down to kill the call. "Where?"

I tell her. I explain about the time how I saw Carlos spear fishing. Only he had an empty bag, and how seeing me made him jump. Jump so much he actually dropped his spear. Like he'd been caught doing something he didn't want anyone to see.

Before I've even finished she jumps up to her feet. "Well where are they? These caves? Let's go. Let's get it." So then I have to explain because Amber hasn't been to the caves. Not many people have, on account of how they're actually very hard to get to, because you're not allowed to anchor nearby, and because that side of the island is very exposed to swells. Plus you need a spring low tide to actually access the caves, unless you've got proper diving equipment.

Then I stop and think because that might be relevant. And yes, it *was* calm the day I saw Carlos, because I wouldn't have gone otherwise, but it was definitely low tide too. It wasn't an issue for me, but I noticed how low it was when I pulled the kayak up on my ledge.

"But how would Carlos have known all that?" Amber says now. "How would he even know about the caves?"

I shrug. "They're marked on charts. But, I don't know…" Understanding why people hide drugs where they do is not really a specialty of mine. "Maybe he was desperate to find somewhere, and he just got lucky? He probably didn't want to come into the harbor with all the drugs on board."

She nods at this. "So when can we get it?"

I walk to the window and look out at the beach below. The swell isn't huge, but it's still way too big to get access to the caves. "The tides are good," I say. "We're on springs. But the waves are too big. We'd need to wait for the swell to drop."

"Well when will that happen?"

So then I pull up the lid of my laptop, and open up the site I use for the weather. There's an icon that switches the display from showing the weather for the next few days to showing the expected swell. It's actually more accurate than the weather forecast, since it's not really a forecast at all, it just shows what swell is actually already there, and which will just keep rolling until it hits the coastline.

"Hmmm." I say.

The site shows the east coast of the island, and the sea around it is colored in various different shades of yellow and red and even purple. When it does that, the waves here get huge. I wouldn't even think of going to the nature reserve unless the waves showed as green for a couple of days, just to be on the safe side.

"Oh shit," Amber says. I didn't notice her leaning over my shoulder. "Is that another storm?"

"Yeah," I say. "Looks like it."

She runs her hands over her hair.

"Well we don't have to get it *for* them," she says now. "We just need to tell them where it is."

I don't answer her. Instead I click to see the higher resolution models. Then I type in my password. You have to subscribe to the site to get the most detailed information, and even though I'm not a member, the surf lifesaving club is. And they let me use their password, as long as I log out once I've used it, otherwise they can't log in. And looking at it now, I see there is a narrow window of time when the wave height shows as green, or less than half a meter of swell. It's tonight, and it's only for a few hours, before the wind kicks in and the wave height builds. But it's there. Then I let my mind imagine being out there at night, with a storm coming in. It wouldn't be nice.

"I'm gonna phone them." Amber's words bring me back to the present. "I need to get Gracie."

FORTY

"AND DON'T EVEN THINK about calling the fucking cops," Paulie spat into the phone. "Or we'll cut the girl up and mail her back to you piece by piece." He quit the call, and when the connection was dead he slammed his hand on the dashboard.

"*Motherfucker!*" He shouted.

Tommy, driving the van a little too fast on the road out of Newlea, glanced across. He waited for Paulie to go on, but he didn't.

"Well? She say where it is?"

Paulie didn't reply.

"The coke? She tell you where it is?"

"Not yet."

"*Not yet*? The fuck's she waiting for?"

Paulie ignored him again, so Tommy asked him a second time, but Paulie snapped back.

"Will you shut the fuck up? I gotta think." He noticed their speed. "And slow down, we don't want to attract any attention."

Tommy did what he was told, easing off the gas a token amount. He glanced in the rear view mirror at the girl, her hands and legs bound with tape, half her face covered with the silver material. She was staring back at them, he could see her eyes.

"Sure. Because kidnapping a kid ain't gonna do that," he said in the end. Then when Paulie didn't react, he went on. "Attract attention I mean…"

"Fuck you Tommy. She's the broad's sister. With her we've got *leverage*."

Paulie went back to thinking.

"You call it leverage? I'd call it a big fucking problem."

"Yeah well what would you know about it?"

"What would I know? I been working with the old man since you were in short pants, you think I don't know how to..."

"And the old man's *dead*. In the fucking ground. And your new boss, who happens to be my cousin, put me in charge since he knows you ain't smart enough to take a shit unsupervised. So watch your fucking mouth."

Tommy considered correcting Paulie, that he was Angelo's *second* cousin. But he settled for saying it in his head. First *or* second, the asshole had a point.

Paulie checked the speed again. "So slow the fuck down, or I'll be telling Angelo you have a loyalty problem."

It looked like Tommy wasn't going to reply, but then he changed his mind. "Yeah. You're in charge alright. And you're doing a great job too. With your CIA bullshit interrogation methods. And now kidnapping a random little kid? It's a great fucking operation you're running here. First class."

"She ain't random."

"And you know what? I'm gonna be sure to report back all the details of the amazing job you're doing..."

"She *ain't* random," Paulie insisted. "The broad knows where the coke is, that dumb fuck told us so last night. And he did so precisely *because* of my methods. We tried your way, remember? Breaking his hands up. He told you to go look on the fucking moon. Let's tell that to Angelo shall we?"

Tommy had no answer to this, so Paulie went on, laughing now. "What you gonna do, go back to Angelo and suggest building a space rocket?" He mimed being weightless for a moment, floating in space, but he did it badly.

"What about the cops?" Tommy said in the end. "They're gonna be looking for this kid everywhere. Probably already are."

Paulie shook his head. "No. The bitch is dumb, but she won't go to the cops. Not if she wants the kid back in one piece. Besides, she's up to her neck in it."

Tommy glanced across. He didn't feel the same confidence.

"Even so, what we gonna do with..." He jerked his thumb towards the back of the van. "We can't leave her in the van. She's gonna need food. To go to the bathroom. She might bang on the sides, attract attention..."

Paulie interrupted at this.

"Well she might now, you dumb fucker. You've given her the idea."

"Jesus Paulie. I'm just *asking*. What's the plan? I assume you have got one?"

"Course I got one."

"Well? What is it?"

For a long time Paulie didn't answer. But just as Tommy opened his mouth to speak again, Paulie cut him off.

"We go somewhere quiet and wait till she calls us back. Tells us where the coke is."

"OK. And if she don't?"

"She will."

Tommy might have pursued his line of questioning further, but at that moment they drove past a junction where a police cruiser was waiting to join their road.

They both fell silent, trying not to look as they swept past. Then they both studied the mirrors, to see the cruiser pull out behind them, two uniformed officers visible.

"Watch your speed," Paulie said.

"I *am* watching my speed," Tommy replied. The police cruiser didn't have its blue lights on, and it hung back, not obviously watching, nor interested in them.

"OK *boss*," Tommy asked, "So where exactly does this plan of yours say we hole up and wait?"

Paulie kept his eyes on the cruiser for a long while. Then glanced at the dashboard to check their speed. Then he grabbed the map they'd been using earlier. Suddenly he smiled.

"I know just the fucking place."

FORTY-ONE

THE VAN BUMPED down the track, until eventually they arrived back at Bishop's Landing. Just as before it was totally empty, the only signs that anybody ever came here were the jetty reaching out into the creek – the tide higher this time – and the old wooden boathouse. Climbing out the van, Paulie crouched down to inspect the tire marks on the ground. The only ones he could see were theirs from the other day. He stood up, nodding with satisfaction, and pulled open the sliding door of the van. He ignored the frightened grunts and squeaks from the kid, and instead pulled a large crowbar from a canvas tool bag.

"Wait here. Watch that," he told Tommy, gesturing to Gracie with the crowbar. Then he stalked over to the boathouse.

The double doors were secured with a padlock. Paulie studied it for a moment, noting how it looked rusty all over. Then he inserted the end of the crowbar under the clasp, and leaned on it hard, until the screws began releasing their grip on the weather-softened wood. He felt Tommy watching him, critical of his technique, and he ended up frustrated that even with the clasp half off, he still couldn't wrangle the door open with his bad fingers. He nearly reached for his gun, but finally, and with a lot of grunting, the clasp was on the ground. He resisted the urge to give it a kick, thinking, rightly, that all he would do is add a couple of broken toes to his tally. He nudged it aside instead, then yanked open the door.

Inside was dark and musty. A small open fishing boat that had seen better days took up half of the room downstairs. Next to it, a tractor stood with its motor partly stripped down. Above them a small mezzanine floor was visible, reached by dusty wooden steps. Paulie climbed them carefully into a small workshop area. Everything looked old, and every surface was covered with cobwebs. He pulled a finger across the worktop, and inspected it in the half light. His fingertip came back black. Paulie smiled. He looked around again, then jogged lightly back down the steps and outside.

"No one's been here for years," Paulie said, as he got back to the van. "We'll stash her here and wait for the broad to tell us where the coke is."

Tommy looked around, trying to find fault with the location. But he stayed silent.

"Come on, give me a hand."

Together they carried the bound Gracie into the boathouse and up the stairs, where they lashed her to a beam with more carpet tape. Paulie began to feel very pleased with his morning's work. Until Tommy opened his mouth again.

"How do you know the broad is gonna phone?"

There was no time for an exasperated Paulie to reply, because at that very moment his cellphone rang.

* * *

With a grin, Paulie answered the call, then put it on speaker. At once Amber's voice rang out from the speaker.

"Is this the motherfucker who's got my sister?"

Paulie felt himself smiling, feeling very happy.

"Yeah, it is," he replied. "And is this the dumb broad who thinks she can just steal eighty keys of coke and get away with it?" He glanced at Tommy, his eyes dancing. Tommy stared blankly back.

A pause.

"Where is she?"

"Somewhere safe," Paulie turned back to the phone. "Where's our product?"

"Let me speak to her. I need to know she's OK."

Paulie looked at the girl, her mouth covered and her whole body wrapped with carpet tape, holding her against the post.

"She can't talk right now. She's kinda tied up." He chuckled out loud at the joke, glancing again at Tommy to see if he appreciated it too, but still his face was blank. Humorless fucker.

"I'm not saying anything until I speak to her," Amber said.

Suddenly Paulie's mood burst.

"Well then you clearly don't feel too strongly about seeing her again, because I'm making the rules here, and she's fucking tied up. Literally." He frowned. It was unbelievable he had to explain his joke to these idiots.

"Well you piece of shit," Amber spoke carefully, after a moment. "I don't know what eighty kilos of coke is worth but I bet it's millions. And I sure as hell ain't telling you where it is unless I speak to Gracie. So unless you want to be down several million dollars, you better untie her. *Asshole*."

There was a moment of silence, during which Paulie regretted putting the phone on speaker. He felt Tommy watching him, and he tried to consider. In the end he sighed.

"For fuck's sake. What the hell?" He indicated to Tommy to pull the tape from the girl's mouth. "No loss to me bitch," he spat at the phone, while Tommy unwrapped the tape. He noticed how he did it carefully, not just yanking it away. But then the kid did look in a pretty bad way. She had grime all over her face, with little lines running from her eyes where she'd been crying. And judging from the stench she'd already pissed herself. When the tape was released she said nothing. Stupid little chin quivering.

"Well?" Paulie said, a moment later. "Ain't you gonna say nothing?"

"Gracie?" Amber asked. Are you there? Are you OK?"

The little girl began crying again, but she managed to get out a single word. *Amber*.

"Oh my God. Don't worry," Amber said down the line. "We're gonna get you. I promise you…"

"Alright that's enough," Paulie cut in. "Tape her back up, and let's stop fucking around." He snatched up the phone and switched off the speaker.

"First of all, you better not have gone to the cops, because if you have, the girl dies. Do you understand that?"

There was a pause, then Amber's voice came through again.

"Yeah."

"Have you gone to the cops?"

Another pause. Then a strangled reply.

"No."

Paulie thought for a second. He wanted to ask how he could know she hadn't gone to the cops, but there was no way she could prove it. He tensed a little, as if sensing how this had slipped out of control. But he suppressed the thought. Then he realized the girl on the end of the line was crying. For some reason this settled him a bit.

"OK. So where is our product?"

"It's hidden."

"Hidden where."

"Where you won't ever find it."

"What?" Paulie sighed.

"I'm not telling you until I get my sister back."

"Well you ain't getting her back until you tell me."

"I'm still not telling you."

There was another pause. Paulie felt the tension returning. How the fuck was he supposed to break this stupid deadlock?

"Why not?" He asked in the end.

"Because if I just tell you, how do I know you'll give Gracie back?"

Paulie considered. He gave the best answer he could think of.

"You'll just have to trust me."

"*What?* Why would I trust you? You're a fucking *hitman*. You've *kidnapped* my sister!"

The beginnings of a smile crept onto Paulie's lips as he heard the word. He'd never thought of himself as a hitman exactly.

"And anyway, it's not that simple," Amber went on.

"It sounds pretty simple to me." Paulie said, meaning to ask again where the coke was so they could get on with this. But then a second thought broke in too. Wasn't this what police negotiators taught? To make things *complicated*? To slow things down, to give them time to track down the location of the perpetrators. He tensed. The thought crossed his mind to consult with Tommy. If only the guy wasn't such an asshole.

Then there was another pause, and this time Paulie heard a second voice in the background, barely audible.

Tell them they're gonna need a boat.

"You're going to need a boat." Amber repeated.

"Who the hell is that?" Paulie snapped back at once. "I just heard a voice. Have you called the fucking cops?"

"No!" Amber replied.

"You better fucking not… Your sister's as good as dead."

"No, please," Amber cut in. "I swear I haven't. It's… Oh fuck, Billy can you speak to them?"

"*What*?" Paulie asked, but he didn't get any further as there was the muffled sound of the phone being manhandled, then the second voice came on the phone more clearly.

"It's just it's a bit complicated," the new voice said. Unbelievably it sounded like another kid. A boy this time.

"Who the hell is this?" Paulie demanded. "What the fuck is going on?"

"I'm a friend of Amber's," the boy replied quickly. "And it's complicated because of where it is. The cocaine I mean. Or where we think it is. Where we think he must have hidden it."

"Where?"

"Well we can't say that. But even if we could it's very hard to actually get to."

"*What?* Why?"

"Well if there's eighty kilos, then it's going to be quite big, and obviously quite heavy – well eighty kilos – which is quite heavy unless it's packed into smaller parcels, which it usually is on the TV. But there'll still be a lot of them. And there's a lot of swell on the way, and wind, and that's going to make it very hard. You'll need quite a lot of time to get it out…"

"Get it out of where? The fuck are you talking about?"

Another pause. Paulie felt Tommy watching him. Even the fucking girl.

"I can't tell you where it is. I already said that."

"Why… *Fuck that*." Paulie frowned, and turned away so Tommy couldn't see his face. "How old are you anyway?"

There was another pause, then the boy's voice continued, sounding confused.

"I'm sixteen. Well nearly. But I don't see why that's relevant."

"Sixteen? What the…?"

The dumb bitch has gone to another kid for help... Paulie felt his stress levels rise. How in the world was everyone so fucking *dumb.* He told himself to calm down. This was nuts, but it was *good* nuts. There was no way the cops would put him on the line with a sixteen-year-old kid. Not in a million years. So all he had to do was figure out a way to make the exchange. But now the damn kid was talking again.

"So we're thinking, if we give you the instructions for how to get it, in exchange for Gracie, then you can get it when the weather is right…"

"Shut up," Paulie said. "Just shut the fuck up." The voice went quiet. Paulie tried to think. But the more he tried, the less he had any idea about what to do next. The more he felt Tommy's eyes on him. The more his fears about the police grew, listening in behind the voices on the phone.

There are no cops. It's just a couple of goddamn kids.

Stop messing around and get this done.

"This ain't happening on the phone," he said suddenly. "There's a restaurant, on the road out of the ferry port. It's got a big fuck-off anchor on the sign, you know it?"

A pause, then: "Do you mean *The Schooner*?"

"I don't know. Does it have a fuck-off great anchor on its sign?"

Another pause. "Yes."

"Then I mean *The Schooner*. We're gonna meet you there in *one hour*. Just the two of you. We see a single sign of the cops, the kid dies. You make sure you bring whatever you need to get this fucking coke back. If not, the kid dies. Is that fucking clear enough?"

There was another pause, a long one this time. Finally the kid broke it. "One hour is a bit tight from here. Could we make it ninety minutes?"

"*Fuck sake.*" Paulie looked at his watch. "Let's do 3pm. Does that work?"

"Erm." The line went quiet, and Paulie could hear them conferring. "OK," the boy said.

"Fucking wonderful." Paulie hung up, and turned back to Tommy, his chin jutting out in a challenge.

"What'd you say that for?" Tommy asked.

"Because it's all part of my fucking master plan. And I'm hungry. So let's just get the hell out of here."

FORTY-TWO

NEITHER OF US say much as we drive towards Goldhaven. We both know the restaurant they mean, it does well with tourists who come off the boat because it's kind of the first big place you come to, with parking and a big anchor on the sign that kind of tells you what they serve. In my bag I've got a map, and a chart, which shows the location of the caves, plus a print out of the weather that I just made, and a set of time tables. I don't know how I'm going to explain it all though, we haven't discussed a plan. Amber just wanted to get here as soon as possible. She's driving really carefully too, given how she hasn't actually stopped crying. I realize after a while that she's checking the mirrors all the time, not because she's driving carefully, she's seeing if anyone is following us.

As we pull into the parking lot I check too. There's a dozen or so cars here, a couple of trucks and small vans, but nothing that looks especially suspicious. At least, I don't really know what would look suspicious. Amber finds a space and stops the motor. She looks at me.

"You need to clean your face," I say. She nods at me, and pulls open the glove box. She finds some tissues, and then what I suppose is a make-up purse, and I go back to scanning the parking lot while she sorts herself out.

"OK," she says a moment later, even though she looks like she's going to burst into tears again. "Let's go."

It's a weird feeling crossing the parking lot. It's like we can really feel how we're being watched. But I've got no idea where we're being watched from. I've never been to *the Schooner* before, but it's obviously not the type of place where you get shown to a seat. So when we get inside we look around the restaurant, which is nearly empty, seeing where we ought to go. And when Amber shakes her head, that she doesn't recognize anyone, we go and sit down in a window booth so we can keep an eye outside. Then we wait. No one comes to the table to serve us. I've got the maps in my bag under my table, and I can feel my hands sweating, fiddling with the straps. Neither of us says anything.

Then the door chimes, and two guys walk in.

I know it's them from the way Amber stiffens. One of them is quite small, and kind of looks normal, in a sort of gangster way with a shiny blue suit on. But the other one is massive, a great big lumbering giant of a man, and when I look at his face I see his teeth are all messed up. It's obvious they see us right away, but they look around anyway, as if pretending they don't. And then I realize they're checking out the restaurant. The big, ugly guy goes over to the restroom, but it's not because he needs it, because he opens both doors, then comes right back out again, and shakes his head at the smaller guy. Then they both come over to where we're sitting. They don't ask or anything. They just sit down.

"Well ain't this nice?" The smaller one says. He's got a round black earring in each of his ears, and I remember now how Amber told me about this. How she never got this one's name, but called him Earrings. Neither me nor Amber reply.

"What's your name?" Earrings asks, looking me up and down.

"Billy."

"Nice to meet you Billy." He gives a kind of snort of laughter. "You really are sixteen."

I don't correct him.

He drums his fingers on the table top.

"Where's my sister?" Amber asks suddenly.

"Don't start with that already," Earrings replies. He drums his fingers a little more. Then he suddenly smiles. "Let's start afresh shall we?" With this he picks up the menu, pretends to study it, but I see his eyes flicking up and glancing at Amber and me. He looks kinda nervous.

"So how is this gonna work?" Amber tries instead, but he ignores her.

"Pancakes. That's what I'm gonna have." He raises a hand and clicks his fingers, grinning at me now. The waitress, who's ignored us so far, comes over. She's got a bored look on her face, like she really hates tourists, but this is the only job she can find. A lot of the restaurants on Lornea Island have staff like that.

"Yeah? What can I get you?"

Earrings orders the Schooner All Day Breakfast Special, which is a big pile of pancakes with blueberries and maple syrup. The other guy, the really scary looking one, asks for a burger. Then Earrings turns to us.

"How about you guys? You want anything?"

"I'm not hungry." Amber says. She looks like she wants to say something else, but can't since the waitress is still here.

"You sure? It's on me. My treat." Earrings looks at me. "You like pancakes?"

I've not actually eaten much today, on account of how I've kind of run out of food at home again.

"I'll have some fries," I say. "And a coffee. Actually and a burger too."

I feel Amber staring at me, then Earrings looks at her again.

"I told you, I ain't hungry."

The waitress gives us all a look, like we're the weirdest bunch of tourists she's seen all season, but she isn't going to worry about it. Instead she scribbles the order down and goes away. There's a moment of silence. Until Earrings launches into a speech.

"OK. I accept we none of us got off on the right foot. And that's kinda my fault. I accept that," he says.

"But none of this is difficult. You got what we want. We got what you want. It couldn't be more simpler. Amber – you mind if I call you that?"

He waits, until she gives a shrug. "OK. We don't wanna hurt your kid sister. There ain't nothing in it for us, going down that route. And as of right now she's fine. She's somewhere safe. And just as soon as we get our product back, you'll get her back. OK?"

I look to Amber to see if she's going to answer, and when she doesn't, I figure it's up to me.

"OK," I say.

"Now, let's just deal with the cops issue. Have you contacted them?"

"No."

"You sure about that?"

"Yeah."

"Good. Because if anything happens to us, then little Gracie ain't gonna be found. Not before she runs out of food, or water, or whatever else she needs."

"You piece of shit asshole motherfucker." Amber interjects.

"Jesus!" Earrings says. "I'm trying to be nice here."

I decide to keep things on track. "So how is this going to work?"

But he doesn't answer, because at that moment the waitress comes back with our drinks. We're all silent while she works out who ordered what, and she's a bit useless, but eventually we figure it out. Then she goes away, only he still doesn't reply, and I'm beginning to think he doesn't actually know how to do this. But then he surprises me.

"You said we needed a boat. I'm guessing he's hid it underwater somewhere?"

"Not really..." I say, before Amber's elbow jabs into my side and shuts me up.

"Or an island?"

Amber stares at me, and I don't say anything.

"OK – but we need a boat to recover it?"

I look to Amber – we already told them this. After a few moments she relents, and nods her head.

"Yeah," I say, turning back to Earrings. "But we've got one."

"Good. Thank you." I'm pretty sure he doesn't hear my last comment. He dumps sugar into his drink, and stirs it thoughtfully. Then he turns back to Amber.

"Amber. Honey. I can see you ain't so comfortable telling us exactly where it is while we've got your sister. I understand that. But you should understand how we're not going to release her until we have the product back in our possession. So the way I see it, that only leaves one option. We're gonna have to recover the product together. Then you get what you want, we get what we want. And we all go off into the sunset together. Only not together." He smiles sarcastically. "Anyone disagree with that?"

Amber doesn't answer, but I don't think it means she agrees exactly.

"You wanna maybe discuss for a minute?" He waves a hand at the two of us.

Amber looks at me now. But only for a second. She turns back to the man.

"OK."

"Good. *Great.*" Earrings looks kinda relieved.

"So. Either of you know anything about boat hire services?"

"I've got a boat," I say again.

"Not a fucking row-boat kid. I'm talking a proper boat. Like with a motor."

"It is a real boat," Amber interrupts. "It's a thirty-two foot fishing boat. The one next to the yacht you sank last night."

Earrings looks at the guy with the teeth, who looks blank. So then he shrugs.

"OK. So you've got a boat. Where do we need to take it?"

I glance at Amber. I've still got all the charts, the tide tables, and the weather readings in my bag. She gives the smallest of nods, and I'm about to pull them out.

But I don't get the chance, because as mad as all this is, right then things go *completely* nuts.

FORTY-THREE

"*Billy*!" A voice calls out from across the restaurant. "Billy! What a coincidence! Mate!"

Even though I know him so well, it's so out of context it takes me a few moments to register who the voice belongs to, and he's already walking quickly over to our table before I get it. It's Steve. Steve Rose. You know, from *Shark Bites*.

"Jesus, this is... this must be *meant to be* or something." He's grinning and shaking his head in disbelief. As soon as he reaches us he holds out his arms like he wants to hug me, but then pulls one back so it's just a handshake he expects. I don't really mean to hold out mine, but I do anyway. Then the next thing is he grips my hand so hard it pulls me out of the booth, and onto my feet, and then he won't let go, pumping my whole arm up and down.

"What an amazing coincidence. You know I just got off the ferry... and I was hungry because the food is..." He screws up his face. "Well I bet you've been on it often enough to know." He stops shaking my hand now, but doesn't let me go.

"Hey, Billy. What are we doing here? How about a hug huh?" And then without waiting for me to reply he wraps his arms around me and squeezes.

"Steve?" I manage to say when he lets me go, but he interrupts me at once.

"No. No, no. Let *me* speak Billy." Only then he doesn't say anything. He holds up a finger, and I can see in his eyes how he's working out what to say.

"Hey! Buddy!" Earrings says from behind me. Not in a nice way either. But Steve doesn't notice. He's ready to speak now.

"Billy... *Jeez!*" He stops, and gives a goofy grin. "Look I wanted a little time to work out exactly *how* to say this, and now you're here already, and I don't have it straight in my head, but..." I take a glance behind me, and see that both Earrings and the big guy are now looking totally freaked out. Then I see a flash of black metal, as Earrings pulls out a pistol from his jacket. I blink in disbelief as he holds it on the table, covered by the menu.

"Steve!" I interrupt him, as loud as I dare, because I really think Earrings is going to shoot him if I don't.

"Hey sorry, my manners, huh?!" Steve gives another grin. But then instead of leaving he turns to the others. He sees Amber then reaches out his hand again. She shakes it, but her mouth is hanging wide open while she does so.

"Hi. I'm Steve. Steve Rose. Nice to meet you."

There's a second, and then she doesn't answer, so I have to.

"Err, this is Amber?"

"*Amber!* Billy's told me all about *you*." He flashes a different smile at her, I remember it from the research trip - he used the same smile on the girls there too.

"Don't worry, it's all good." He winks at her now. Then he turns to the others, to the two kidnappers.

"How ya doing guys? You must be friends of Billy's? Any friends of Billy are friends of mine." He turns back to me. "I mean that Billy. I really mean that. I know I was kinda mad when you left, but I'm past that now. I swear to you."

He turns back to Earrings. "Sorry buddy. What'd you say your name was?"

Earrings has his mouth open pretty wide now too, and suddenly everyone is looking at him, waiting for an answer.

"Jaso… Justin." He says in the end. He doesn't accept Steve's hand, I guess because he's still holding the pistol, so Steve leans over and kind of hugs him, like this is the beginning of a beautiful friendship.

"I'm Steve. *Great* to meet you Justin. Really great." He nods, like he really means it, then turns to the big guy. The one who Amber told me was called Tommy. He's kinda squinting at Steve, like he recognizes him, but the person he thinks he is, doesn't make any sense. Which it doesn't.

"Hey big fella, I'm Steve. Steve Rose." He holds out his arm again, rock-solid muscles holding it still and firm.

The big man stares at it but can't ignore it. He lifts his own hand and shakes. There's a moment when the big man gives a weak half-smile, and I think Steve gets to see his teeth, but he pretends not to notice. Then there's a weird silence.

"*The* Steve Rose?" The big man says in the end.

Steve grins. He glances back at me, like the both of us were expecting this reaction.

"Uh huh…" He nods.

"The shark guy? From the TV show?"

"That's right buddy. Well, except I don't actually *have* the TV show at the moment, since it was canned, mostly on account of your friend Billy here." He turns back to me, and quickly holds up both his hands. "Though I'm totally not holding that against you Billy. What you did was right. I was the one who was out of order." He hesitates for a minute. "Actually that's kind of why I came." He stops now, screwing up his face like this is causing him pain.

Then he turns to the others again. "Look fellas, I don't want to interrupt your little…" he hesitates for a second. "What is this, a late lunch or an early supper?" He gives a little laugh. "Whatever it is, I do need to speak to Billy. I've come a long way to find him. Actually, all the way from Australia." He glances at the kidnappers again and smiles. The contrast between his Hollywood white teeth, and the big guy's oversized yellow ones is kinda horrible.

"Yeah, that's where we were filming, ain't that right Billy? But I didn't treat him so well, and things kinda blew up, so I had to come here to apologize. In person. You know what I mean?"

There's another stunned silence. Earrings – or possibly Jason – breaks it.

"What the fuck is this?" He says.

Steve raises his eyebrows, like he's doesn't think the profanity is really appropriate.

"Hey buddy, I'll just be a minute OK? No need for that kind of language." He tries to laugh the moment away, but he looks pained now. Justin/Earrings doesn't seem to care about his language.

"Who the fuck are you?" He asks now, loudly. "And what *the fuck* do you want?"

Steve doesn't answer. I think he finally understands that something isn't quite right here, but the moment doesn't last long.

"It's the shark guy," the bigger kidnapper says now. "From the TV. You know, he does diving with killer sharks? Don't even use the cage half the time. Guy's a legend."

Steve laughs again, and it's like he's happy to be back on familiar ground. "Hey, when you understand these creatures as well as I do," he says to the big guy now. "Well, you kinda know when you're putting yourself in a dangerous situation and when you're not."

"I don't give a fuck who it is," Earrings snaps back, trying to take over again. "I wanna know what the fuck he's doing here?"

"Hey, so not everyone's a fan," Steve says. He stays talking to the big man. "Listen buddy, you want an autograph or a selfie or anything you just say. Right after I speak with Billy here."

"He don't want a fucking selfie. And he don't give a rat's ass who you are. Just get the fuck outta here."

"Whoa," Steve says. He looks around us all, then finally settles his gaze on me. "Billy, is everything OK here?"

I swallow. Then I notice how Earrings is looking at me. Threatening. Like he's warning me how things are gonna get bad if I don't get rid of Steve right away.

"Yeah," I say cautiously. "Sure Steve. Everything's OK. We're just having lunch."

Earrings nods and turns to Steve. He's still got the gun hidden under the menu, I can see by the way the paper doesn't lie flat.

"It's all fine," I go on. "Maybe we could meet up later, and you can tell me what you want to say?"

Steve pauses, but then he nods his head. "Sure OK. I mean I've mostly said it already. It's just…" He winces. "It's just I had to come tell you how I was wrong. And you were right. About how the science mustn't be compromised. No matter what. And how it may feel I've lost everything right now, but I haven't. What you did was give me a gift. You've put me on the right path."

There's a weird silence again.

"OK." I say, in the end. And then I realize that Steve's about to go. And suddenly I don't want him to. I mean, I feel like I need to get him to see what's going on here. So he can call the police, or do something to help us.

"OK," I say again. I've got no idea how I'm going to tell him.

"OK," Steve repeats. "Well I've got your number – I didn't want to call you in advance, I thought you maybe wouldn't wanna speak to me… But maybe I'll call later. We can speak then?"

"OK."

"OK." Steve gives me a smile. Then he looks at the others. "Alright. Great to meet you…" He glances up at Earrings, and I can tell he's searching for the name he gave him. "Justin."

Earrings doesn't move, and Steve turns to the big man. He looks blankly, like he can't remember the guy's name, even though he never gave it in the first place. But now he gives a sort of half smile, like he's a bit star struck. He shows his crooked teeth again.

And suddenly I know what to do.

"*Carcharodon carcharias,*" I say.

"What?" Earrings says at once. I see the tendons in his arm tense, as he grips the pistol tighter. And Steve gives me a weird look. I glance over at the big guy and repeat what I said.

"*Carcharodon carcharias.*"

"What's that Billy…" Steve starts, his face scrunched up in a frown. I know he understands what I'm saying, but I need him to make the connection. I slide my eyes across to the bigger guy's mouth, full of its horrible crooked teeth.

"*Carcharodon carcharias.*"

Then I see Steve silently following my gaze, and moments later I know he's made the connection. It's the Latin name, for great white shark. *Crooked tooth.* Steve doesn't know what it means, but he knows we're in danger.

Then suddenly he smiles again. "*OK.* Well look, I'm real sorry to interrupt you guys..." He starts to back away, but he glances at me with a look that tells me he understands. I don't know what he's gonna do. I don't know what he *can* do. But at least someone out there knows something bad is going on.

Steve raises his hand, to wave goodbye. But then he doesn't get a chance.

"Don't you fucking move," Earrings snarls.

FORTY-FOUR

THE NEXT THING, Earrings jumps out of the booth. He moves incredibly quickly, and before I know what's happened I see he's got the gun pressed into Steve's stomach. He's shielding it from the rest of the restaurant with his own body, but I see him twist it, digging it in hard.

"I don't know what the fuck just happened there, but you better take a seat."

Steve is obviously shocked because he does nothing to resist, and Earrings is able to walk him back to the table and shove him down next to me. Then Earrings takes his seat opposite, using the menu again to cover the pistol. I see the big guy has also got a gun out now and he's doing the same.

"And whatever it was, you just joined our little party."

We all sit there in silence, while Earrings takes it in turns to point his gun at each of us, making sure we see it. Actually though, I think he's working out what to say next.

"OK. Here's what's gonna happen. You're gonna tell me *right now* where my product is, or this gets very messy, very fucking quickly. Are we clear?"

I glance at Steve. His eyes are wide and he's white-faced, blinking in amazement. Then I look at Amber. Her eyes are red and raw from all the crying she's been doing. She looks back at me, and after a few seconds she nods her head. So then I tell them.

"It's in a sea cave down the east coast of the island. At least, that's where we think it is."

"Where? *Specifically*?"

"It's hard to explain. You can only get there by sea. I can show you though. I brought a chart."

Earrings is cautious. "OK. Bring it out. Slowly."

I do what he says, moving really carefully in case he thinks I'm tricking him and going to bring out a weapon. I pull out the chart, unfold it, and point to the area of the national park where the caves are located.

"Just there."

Earrings looks at it, then turns the chart round for a better look.

"That a road? Why can't we drive there?"

"No, it's a footpath." Because it's a chart, there's not much detail about the land, so it's hard to see. "We could walk there, and I suppose you could get down the cliff with ropes, but even then, the entrance to the cave is underwater, so it's easier by boat."

"Why'd he put it here?" Earrings asks.

I don't know the answer to this, but I guess it's fairly obvious. "Because no one ever goes there?"

He thinks for a while."Are you fucking with me kid?"

"No."

Then he glances at Steve, then back at me. "How's he fit into this?"

"He doesn't. Not really."

"Then what the fuck is he doing here?"

I hesitate. "It's a bit of a long story…" I stop, expecting he won't want me to tell him, but he waggles the gun under the menu, so I figure he does.

"Well… We were doing a population study of sharks. Off the coast of Victoria. In Australia," I begin. He doesn't stop me, so I keep going. "Basically counting the number of individual animals from each species and estimating their size. Because if you know the size of a shark you can make an accurate estimate of its age, which are the two variables you need for a population study. Only then I discovered how he'd been overstating the size of the sharks we were counting. Not just on the trip I was on, but earlier trips, meaning the data was unreliable. And… well it was just really bad science…" I look at Steve, in case he wants to add anything.

"I came to apologize," he says. "I was unprofessional, and I behaved badly and I came to see Billy to apologi…" But Earring's cuts him off, speaking to me.

"Does any of this have anything to do with our current problem?"

"No," I say. "I don't think so."

Earrings stares at us both.

"Then spare me." He looks back at the chart. "My product. You reckon it's in a sea cave? How do we get there? How easy is it to get at?"

"That's the problem," I say. Actually I'm relieved to get back onto the point. "We need the right combination of low tide and calm weather. And although it's calm now, the forecast is for strong winds to come in from tonight, so if we don't go now, more or less now, we might not get another chance for a week. And even then it's going to be quite difficult, and we'll need diving equipment, because we can't actually go into the cave with the boat. We'll have to swim in and take it out that way."

He thinks. "Swim?"

"Yeah. The entrance to the cave is underwater, even at low water."

Earrings stares at me, like he still isn't sure whether to trust what I'm saying.

"Swim," he repeats, after a while. Then he looks at his friend. "You said this asshole was some TV shark expert?"

"Yeah," the bigger guy replies.

"Goes in the water without the cage. Free diving expert?"

"Yeah. I think so."

Then Earrings turns to Steve. He just waits.

"I'm the Australian Speed-Endurance Apnea National Champion." Steve shrugs. "Three years running."

"The fuck does that mean?"

Steve doesn't answer for a moment, but eventually he has no choice. "It's a distance event. Basically it's how far you can swim underwater, on one breath."

"Well? How far can you go?"

"Two hundred fifty meters."

Earrings shrugs. "How far's that?"

"It's five lengths of an Olympic swimming pool."

"Whoa. On one breath.?"

"Yeah."

Earrings weighs this up, impressed. Then he looks at me. "How big is the cave?"

"What?"

"The cave, how fucking big is it? How far do you have to swim underwater to get in it?"

"Oh, nowhere near that far. *I* can do it."

"Perfect. Looks like the two of you are going for a swim then. Let's fucking move."

FORTY-FIVE

Earrings makes us all stand up, keeping us covered with his pistol. There's an awkward moment when the waitress comes hurrying over, because she thinks we're walking out before our food has even arrived, but then Earrings pulls out a hundred dollar bill and throws it on the table. I think she's going to say something but instead she just gives him a look, like she hates mainlanders. Then she turns away to the kitchen to cancel our order. And we leave the restaurant.

They march us over to a gray panel van. The big guy opens the rear doors and we're forced inside. We're made to kneel, facing the front, with our hands behind our backs, and while we're like that something is wrapped round our wrists, it feels like a plastic zip tie, and they do it tight too, so that it cuts into my skin. Then they do our ankles too, so we're stuck, kneeling there on the cold floor.

"Roll over onto your butts," Earrings says. And when we do he inspects us.

"Cell phones," he says next. "Where are your cell phones? I know you've all got them. Hand them over."

Then we all look at him, since obviously we can't move at all. I think I kind of look down at my pocket though, and the next thing Earrings is patting my jeans, which feels weird, until he finds it, and then he puts his hand into my pocket.

"You'll get it back," he says, like he's irritated by the way I try to squirm away from him. He does the same to the others, then switches all the phones off. Then he slams the doors shut, and we're left there in silence.

But it's not for long, because then they both climb into the front, and turn round to look at us.

"So. Tell me more about this cave," Earrings says to me.

"What about my sister?" Amber replies, before I get a chance to do so. "You can't have this all your own way. If you don't tell us where she is, we're only going to lead you to the wrong place." She looks at me while she's speaking, a warning.

There's a pause, and Earrings tries ignoring her. "The boat's in Holport right? Next door to the other one, the one she blew up."

"I mean it." Amber says. "You can have your fucking cocaine. I swear it. But I want my sister back first."

I think he's going to ignore her again, or tell her to shut up, but there's something about her voice, she sounds serious.

"OK." Earrings lets out a long sigh. "A deal's a deal." He smiles now. "We'll pick her up on the way. She can come out on the boat with us. Does that satisfy you?"

Amber doesn't reply, but she nods, and I get the sense that just maybe things aren't as bad as I think, because maybe these people are reasonable.

"But if you don't get me back my product, I'm gonna make you watch as I drown her, right in front of your face." Earrings stares right at Amber. "You get me?"

Amber's face goes a little whiter, then she nods, and with that Earrings turns to the front and starts the motor.

The big man keeps his gun trained on us from the passenger seat as we set off, bumping our way out of the parking lot. I can keep track of where we are for the first ten minutes or so, just because we're on the main road south. But after that we take a turning and I lose track. Then we take another turning, onto what must be a dirt track, because the three of us are thrown about in the back.

We can't use our arms properly to protect ourselves, so we get banged around, and I start to worry that with the bumps the big man might accidentally pull the trigger on his pistol and shoot us. But there's nothing we can do except try to stay as wedged as possible until the van finally comes to a halt.

"Stay there," Earrings says. I think for a moment he's talking to us, but then I realize he means the big guy, who stays where he is, keeping the gun fixed on us still.

Then nothing happens for a few minutes, until the back door is suddenly thrown open, and there's Earrings again, but he's carrying something this time. It takes all of us a few seconds to work out it's Gracie – bound and gagged. Amber lets out a scream, and Gracie starts kicking on Earrings' shoulders.

"Move up," he orders, gripping her tighter. "And stop fucking wriggling."

We do our best to budge along, and he leans forward and puts Gracie down into the van. He doesn't do it gently.

"Asshole," Amber snaps, but she doesn't really even look at him, instead she shuffles herself over and manages to get Gracie up and sitting next to her, and then she's cooing over her sister, talking to her in a soft voice. Then the back doors of the van slam shut again, and I realize I didn't even get to see where we were.

"So. About this cave then?" Earrings asks again when he's back in the front. "Where do we go?"

I tell him, and answer all his other questions, about whether the boat is fueled and ready, and whether we have all the equipment we need on board. I explain how we keep spare wetsuits and snorkeling gear on board, for the tourists to use when the weather's warmer. Then he takes my bag, and makes me show him on the chart the exact location of the caves, and how to read the coordinates. And after he's studied everything, he steps out the van and makes a phone call that I can't hear. And then he climbs back in, and we're off again, back down the incredibly bumpy track.

When we're finally back on the main road again, the big guy finally turns back to the front. He glances back every few moments, but it looks like his neck hurts or something, twisting around all the time. And the noise in the van gets louder too, back here we can hear the tires on the road pretty loud, and Steve uses the distraction to turn to me and ask very quietly what's going on. I don't want to say anything at first, since I think it will attract the attention of the big man, and he'll watch us again, but he doesn't. So keeping my voice as low as possible I do my best to explain to Steve what this is all about, and where we're going. Right away Steve narrows in on the practicalities, like where we are going to anchor the boat, and how easy it will be to find the stuff in the cave. Obviously I don't know many of the answers to this, and I start to worry – what might happen if we get there and can't find the cocaine? Because, until this point, it hasn't even occurred to me that it might not even be there. Or that we might find it, but not be able to get it out. Or that it'll already be too rough to get in there. But Steve stays calm and almost sounds relaxed.

"It'll be a breeze," he says.

"But what if the weather gets bad, or swell comes in earlier than the forecast?"

"It won't. And even if it does, we got this. Piece of cake."

I don't really understand his optimism, but I do know he's done some pretty crazy things in his life. So maybe this is just quite tame by comparison. I hope so. Then he changes the subject, and starts talking about why he came to see me. He tells me how his whole life has fallen apart since I emailed the journal. First the editor contacted him to say they were going to retract all his papers. Then the TV network canceled his show, and then he was fired by the university where he does teaching. Basically his whole academic and scientific life is ruined as a result of what I did. I watch him as he explains it all.

"Only it wasn't what *you* did, Billy," he insists, quietly, but firmly. "The fault was mine. It was all mine." He's not laughing now, his face is grim. "It just started off as a little exaggeration which wasn't supposed to impact the data. And by the time it did, I didn't feel like I could stop it. I should have stopped though. A long time ago."

I don't know what to think about it really. I mean, I don't think I'd know what to think about it even in normal circumstances, but with everything else that's going on, it's just a bit much.

"But why did you come here?" I ask.

"I told you," he replies, and he grins now. "I had to tell you face-to-face. That you were right. Not just right, but brave. Incredible really. You stood up for the science, while all I cared about was my career. Whether I got another series of *Shark Bites*." I guess I must look confused because he shakes his head.

"What I'm trying to say is, this whole business has made me realize something. I thought everything was going good, but it wasn't. I was on the wrong path. The cheating path. That's not who I am. Not who I want to be anyway. So I had to do the right thing. And that began with coming here and apologizing to you. Mano-a-mano."

"Why didn't you just email me?" I ask. Steve doesn't answer that, so I don't push it. Instead he sits there, bound up next to me, and looking a bit sorry for himself. Still I don't know what to say.

"How's Rosie?" I ask in the end.

"Oh yeah, she's good. Real good," Steve replies, smiling again. Then, a moment later he adds. "Actually she's left me. But again, it's only what I deserve."

"Oh," I say.

It's not really possible to talk with Amber, she's got her whole attention on Gracie. Amber's somehow gotten her hands in front of her, and now she's got Gracie on her lap and she won't stop holding her. She's peeled off Gracie's gag too, with her teeth, and she just keeps talking to her in a very quiet voice. Gracie says she's thirsty, but when Amber asks Earrings for some water, he tells her no. Well that's not exactly what he says.

And then, just from the glimpses of the world outside that I can see from where I'm sitting on the floor, I realize we're coming down the hill into Holport. And soon Earrings is backing the van into a parking space, then he kills the motor. There's silence for a moment.

"OK boys and girls. You get the drill by now. We're gonna cut off those ties, then we're all gonna walk out to this boat nice and quiet. And if anyone tries anything then we're gonna start shooting. So let's remember to be good. Huh?"

FORTY-SIX

THEY GET OUT, and a few seconds later the back of the van opens. They've parked right next to the ramp that leads down to the pontoon, so it's not far to go. The big guy leans in, and uses a box cutter to free our hands. He does it carelessly, even though he could easily cut our wrists with it, and I get the sense he's done it before. I don't know if that makes me feel more or less anxious, but it's nice to have my hands and feet free again.

Then they make us all get out too, and they walk us down the ramp towards where the *Blue Lady* is moored. I risk a look around, hoping that someone will see us and think it's odd, the way we're walking, but it's late in the day already and there's no one about.

We get to the gate. I think maybe I can trick them by not saying the combination, but they don't even ask, and put it right in.

As we walk past the other boats, I check each one, in case anyone's aboard. I know most of the other owners, at least the ones who use their boats regularly, but I don't see anyone, and then I feel the muzzle of the gun in the small of my back again, and Earrings growls at me to speed up. Then I see the *Mystery*. She's still in her berth, only she's mostly underwater with just a bit of her cabin showing. As we get closer you can see the deck and the rest of her a couple of feet down.

"Keys," Earrings says. I don't realize he's talking to me, because I'm still looking at the sunken *Mystery*.

"Gimme the keys. Now." He digs the muzzle of the gun harder into my back, and I dig in my pockets and hand them over.

Earrings gives them to Tommy, who climbs onto *Blue Lady* and glances up and down the deck. I don't know what he's looking for, but after a few seconds he unlocks the cabin and disappears inside. A couple of minutes later he reappears and calls us aboard.

I always feel good when I step onto my boat. Even now, with a gun being pressed into my back. I feel at home suddenly, and a bit more confident. I ask right away if Gracie can drink something now.

Earrings looks annoyed at the question, and ignores me. Instead he tells Tommy to go and lock Gracie up somewhere. But then Amber won't let her go, and tells him there's no way she's leaving her again. So then Earrings tells him to lock them up together, and I see him taking them to the fore cabin downstairs. And I see as well that he sees a bottle of water and takes it with him. That just leaves me and Steve and Earrings. I look around the boat. I notice the broken window where Amber broke in to get the rocket flare.

"Come on. Get this fucking thing moving," Earrings says, irritated.

I brace myself, then try something that I thought about as we were coming down the hill.

"I have to radio the harbor masters office," I say. "We're not allowed to go to sea without letting them know."

"Sorry Billy," Earrings says. "But I don't think that's going to be possible." He steps into the cabin, and I see at once why not. The radio is fixed to the wall above the chart table, or it used to be. I see now that it's been smashed off, and it's only just hanging in place. I suppose Tommy must have broken it when he came on board first.

"Just get us out of here."

So we do. I start the motor, and a couple of minutes later Steve releases the mooring lines, while I climb up to the bridge. I slip the motor into reverse, and back the *Blue Lady* out of her berth, swinging her around, and taking care not to get too close to the sunken *Mystery*. Then when we're clear, I push the gear lever forwards, the prop bites, and a gentle trickle of bubbles pushes out our stern.

Tommy is back now. He's sitting in the saloon, and he doesn't stop watching us the whole time. Earrings is watching me too while I steer the boat. I keep the speed to six knots as we leave the harbor, so I don't draw any attention to ourselves, but still there's nobody about anyway. Nobody really uses their boats at this time of year. And even the fishing boats won't be going out with the bad weather forecast.

When we are out past the breakwater I push the throttle forward and take the *Blue Lady* up onto the plane. She's quite a heavy old boat, and doesn't do it easily. After a while I notice Earrings is gone, and when I look for him, I see him at the stern, making another phone call.

"How long till we get there?" He shouts up at me suddenly.

I look at the electronic chart display. At least Tommy didn't smash that.

"We're seven nautical miles away," I call back, over the noise of the motor. "We'll be there in about half an hour."

He repeats this into the phone, then calls up again.

"What's our coordinates? Now?"

I consider giving him a fake position. But I still think our best chance is to do what they say, so I read out the numbers and watch as he repeats them into his cell. When he's done that he hangs up. He climbs the ladder back up the bridge, and then he pats me on the back, with the side of the gun.

"OK. Good. This old tub go any faster?" He almost sounds like he's enjoying himself. I shake my head, but he ignores me, and pushes the throttle forward with the side of his gun. We surge forward a tiny bit faster to *Blue Lady*'s top speed. I never go this fast as we use a lot more fuel, but I'm not stupid enough to tell him though.

Earrings makes me keep *Blue Lady* at full tilt as we race around the coast. The sea is mostly flat, but there's a growing breeze, pressing dark gusts of wind onto the cliffs, and the further round we go, the more they're pushing a light chop onto the surface of the water. That, combined with the sun having already dropped below the island on our starboard side, gives an ominous feel to the trip, like it's not just darkness that's approaching, and a storm, but some malevolent force. Finally we get close to the cliffs where the sea caves are, and I'm pleased to be able to slow the boat down. I bank over into a turn so we roll back off the plane without our own wake catching up and flooding the cockpit. Earrings who was sitting examining his gun, looks up sharply.

"We here?" He asks. I nod.

He looks around. "Where's the cave?"

I point. There's just a tiny bit of the roof of the entrance visible. The water looks dark and uninviting.

"Good. You better get on it."

"We've got to anchor first," I tell him. "It's not like parking a car."

He says something else, but I ignore him. This is actually one of the most difficult parts. It's not just that you're not allowed to drop an anchor here, the bottom is so rocky that it would be easy to get it stuck. I motor slowly around, going as close to the cave entrance as I dare, and keeping a check on the depth gauge. All the while Earrings is moaning, but in the end Steve comes up to help me, and even tells him to be quiet.

Then Steve kind of takes over, checking the depth. I remember the sandy area where I watched the octopus. It all seems a very long time ago.

"There's a clear area," I tell him. "Somewhere around here. If you go forwards you should be able to see the sand beneath us."

So Steve goes forward, still covered by Tommy with his pistol, and through a combination of shouts and arm signals, we position the boat as close as we can to the mouth of the cave. Now we're nearer it's clearly visible above the water as a black arc. Then Steve releases the anchor and there's the familiar hammering of metal on metal as the chain slides out. I put the boat in reverse to help the anchor hold, and when everything seems okay I slip it into neutral. We're about thirty feet from the base of the cliff, which is now deep in shadow. And we seem to be holding. Earrings keeps asking what we're doing, but more quietly after Steve asks him if he wants to be on a shipwreck. When we're happy the anchor is secure, I kill the motor. Everything goes eerily quiet after that, especially with the whistle of the building wind, and the slapping of the choppy swell against the side.

We're way closer to the rocks than I'd ever be comfortable coming in any normal situation, and the anchor could still drag. But now my concern shifts to going into the water. The light has properly gone now, and the water looks black. I can't help but think about the big boulders down there, and what might be lurking amongst them. I know we don't have any really dangerous animals come here, but snorkeling at night somewhere so exposed is still scary. Earrings doesn't seem worried about this though. He almost seems to be enjoying it.

"Well?" He says. "Hadn't you better get in the water?"

So I take Steve to the locker where the wetsuits are kept and we each of us get kitted up in a suit and diving mask and snorkel. I manage to find a couple of waterproof flashlights too, with rechargeable batteries, and I'm relieved that Dad's always hot on keeping them topped up. The whole time we are watched over by Tommy and Earrings, who are impatient and keep telling us to hurry up. Finally we're ready though, and we go over to the stern, where the diving platform is just above the water level. The sea isn't smooth now at all, and the gusts are stronger now, and cold.

I'm about to lower myself into the water anyway, when Earrings takes hold of my shoulder.

"Hey kid. You're not planning anything stupid are you? Remember we've still got your friend Amber and her kid sister. If you do anything other than recover our product and bring it back to us, you're gonna get them shot. You understand that don't you?"

I look out at the black cliff face, with the ink black water slapping up against it.

"Sure. I get it."

"Good." He lets go of my shoulder. "Clever kid."

I look at him, and then slip down into the water.

FORTY-SEVEN

THE FIRST THING that hits me is the cold. I'm not in my proper wetsuit, just one we use for the tourists. They're fine for the summer, but not much good this late in the year. I expect a trickle of water down my back, but it's more like a flood. I suppose it's good in a way, since it clears my head. It makes me super aware of what we're trying to do.

The second thing I register is the light levels. I've done a lot of snorkeling, here and in other places. But I've only ever been in the daytime. Now the light is low even on the surface, and when I put my head down and look below me, I can hardly make out the bottom. The rocks and caves I'm floating over are filled with shadows. It seems deeper. It seems scarier too.

I click on my flashlight. It casts a yellow glow a few yards ahead of me, lighting up the water, and the particles suspended in it, but it doesn't penetrate. Then I see Steve's flipper slipping into the water beside me, and suddenly the whole of him crashes downwards, and then all I can see are a billion bubbles, blue, black or gold where they hit the light. I pull my head up, and wait until he surfaces. He spends a few moments adjusting his mask, then turns to me.

"OK Billy, lead the way," he says. He doesn't sound scared, more a kind of grim calm.

We swim on the surface, away from the boat. I try to talk at first. I want to ask him if he's got any ideas for what we should do, now we're able to talk without them listening, but it's too choppy, and I keep getting mouthfuls of water. So instead we just fall into line, me leading the way and Steve on my shoulder. It's comforting having him there, and I think he knows it. After a while I duck my head under the surface and use the snorkel, because I'm worried about swimming right onto the rocks where they get shallow, and Steve does the same, so I can look across and see him right there.

Suddenly I feel Steve's hand on my back. I stop, surface, and look up. We're close to the cliff face now. Thankfully the waves are still quite small – it's just chop really, not real swell, and it's slapping against the rocks, rather than crashing as real waves would do. Or will do in a few hours time. I point at the entrance to the cave. It's visible even in this light as a darker semi circle set into the bottom of the dark cliff face. It doesn't look like the sort of thing you'd want to swim into, but I know that just under the surface of the water is a large tunnel, several meters across. Most of the time the entire entrance is well under the water and you'd need proper diving gear to get through, but because it's coming up to low water, we'll be able to swim through.

"How long do we swim underwater for?" Steve asks. He has to shout over the noise of the waves hitting the cliff.

"It's not too long," I reply, reminding myself how I've done this a half-dozen times in the daylight and it's easy. The first time I was really worried, but it's not that far.

"It's only about ten foot."

"Okay," Steve calls back. "Piece of cake. You take the lead and I'll follow."

I take a couple of good deep breaths, then roll forwards into the water and swim towards the darkness. As I get up to the cliff face I dive down, seeing how the light illuminates the face of the cliff, and then how it disappears as I move inside the underwater tunnel. I force myself to stay calm, and kick with my legs, letting my flippers propel me forward. All I can see is the yellow puddle of light from the flashlight, and it's hard to know if I'm going too deep, or too shallow, and I'm going to crash into the tunnel's roof. Then suddenly the light changes, I see something reflecting from above me again, and I know I must be inside. I give a couple more kicks, then push up to the surface.

Right away everything has changed. The noise of the chop slapping against the cliff face has gone. Instead there's different sounds. The noise of water droplets falling from high above me, and ringing out as they hit the surface of the pool. I shine my light around. The ceiling is mostly low, but in a few places it stretches high above me. Where the walls meet the water mostly they just drop straight down, but in a few places around the cave there are ledges, some quite large, and at the back the water shallows and even forms a little beach of round pebbles. Then beneath me I see the yellow glow of Steve's flashlight, which gets brighter and brighter, until he surfaces beside me. He exhales calmly, and joins me shining his light around.

"Wow," he says. "This place is cool." His light has a second bank of LEDs that give out a wider source of light, and he switches to this now, so that the whole cave is dimly illuminated. I know how the walls here are actually amazing colors, from the mineral deposits from water running down the inside of the cliffs above us, but mostly now it looks different shades of black.

"So where do you think he'll have stashed it?" Steve asks.

I don't answer. Instead I push the beam of my flashlight around the ledges, hoping to see something that will tell me I haven't made a horrible mistake. But there's nothing. At least nothing obvious.

"Maybe it's over by the beach?" I give a couple of kicks, and send myself gliding smoothly through the calm stillness of the pool. Soon my hands feel the pebbles below me, and I pull myself forward and out of the water. Steve does the same, until we're both clear of the water.

There's only beach here because the tide is low right now. And even so it's pretty tiny, just a strip of stones that meets the cave's back wall, and where it does, the headroom dips right down so that you can't stand. It's about the only place I can think of where the drugs might be hidden, and I crawl towards it hopefully.

My flashlight works better here, picking out the detail in the rock, and I explore the many little folds and crevices, all the time expecting to see packages of drugs. It *has* to be here. But after ten minutes Steve and I have each explored the whole length and found nothing. So then we re-enter the water, and between us we search the whole perimeter of the cave, hauling ourselves out onto each of the ledges and checking wherever we can with our flashlights. All the time I call out to Steve to ask if he's found anything, and my voice echoes back at me. But every time he shouts back that there's nothing, and I can hear how his voice gets more and more grim.

After another twenty minutes, we meet back at the little beach.

"So..." Steve begins. "Are there any other chambers in here? Maybe somewhere else he could have stashed it?"

I shake my head, then remember how it's dark, and he won't see me. "I don't think so. At least, I've never heard of any," I say. I've got it wrong, there's nothing here. That means we've got to go back to the boat empty handed. I don't know how the two men are going to take it. But it's not going to be well.

I fall silent and try to think. Steve shines the flashlight around again.

"So, if it's not here..." he begins, and I can hear how he's trying to keep his voice positive, but it's beginning to sound anxious. "How far is it to swim outta here? Where's the nearest we can get out the water and call the cops?"

"We can't," I say. "Amber's on the boat. And Gracie."

Steve doesn't answer at first. "Look, maybe one of us swims for help. The other goes back, try to convince them to let us all go?"

"No. And it's miles anyway. It's cliffs all the way to Hunts Beach, and Holport to the north."

"How far?" Steve insists.

It's barely worth answering him, with the incoming weather it would be suicide.

"Ten miles?" I guess. "You saw how long it took to get here. That's basically the closest place to get out."

He doesn't answer, and I figure he's given up the idea. I'm sure he could swim that far in good weather, but at night, along the foot of a cliff with a storm pushing him against it? There's no way...

"I can do that," he says, his voice doesn't sound anywhere near as confident as before. "It'll take me a couple of hours, but I can do it. And come back with the police."

"But what do *I* do?" I hear how petulant I sound in my own echo. I don't mean to. It's just I'm not sure what he expects me to do. Steve falls silent again. And as he does so I get the glimmer of an idea. Then Steve goes on.

"You could tell them you're still searching. Make them believe it's gonna take two or three hours, and they just have to sit tight…"

"Underwater!" I interrupt him suddenly. "We haven't looked underwater."

"What?"

"He must have known – Carlos I mean – that people sometimes come into these caves, because they're marked on the charts. So he wouldn't have just left it on the beach or on the ledges. He'd have hidden it properly. So maybe he anchored it under the water."

Steve doesn't say anything at first. But then he refits his mask.

"You take the left side, I'll take the right."

So then we push back into the water, and this time do our best to search the bottom with our flashlights. Inside the cave it's not as deep as outside, and the bottom is more regular than the seafloor outside. And this time it doesn't take me long to find it.

The drugs are in small packages, each about the size of a loaf of bread, and held down by what looks like a piece of old fishing net. The corners and edges are weighed down by rocks. Steve must see it about the same time I do because he comes swimming over, and together we dive down. We both tug at the rocks, but he's able to stay down much longer, and I have to resurface to grab a breath. By the time I sink down again, Steve has shifted enough rocks so the corner of the netting is loose. He pulls out one of the parcels and points upwards with his flashlight sending me to the surface again.

This time we surface together, and Steve hands me the parcel. It's quite large, and surprisingly heavy. It's wrapped in a combination of clear plastic and parcel tape.

"This what you were looking for?" I can hear the grin in Steve's voice. "Go get the bag. I'll go and grab a few more."

It takes no time to fill the net bag that we brought, though it's obvious we can't get it all in.

"I can hold the flashlight in my mouth," I say, "Then I can take a package in each hand." But Steve shakes his head. "We'll have to do two runs anyway. And it could be hard to swim against the wind." He shines his light on the package, inspecting it. In the half light I see him shaking his head. "We might as well get this first batch back. They'll be wondering where we are."

So then we pull the neck of the bag tight and take a few deep breaths, ready to swim back through the entrance and into the open sea.

Straight away I'm struck by how the weather has worsened outside the shelter of the cave. The waves hitting against the side of the cliff are bigger now, perhaps two or three feet high and I can see the *Blue Lady* is not riding well on her anchor. She is lying stern towards us and the lights are on, making it obvious how much she's rolling around. It must be pretty uncomfortable to be sitting waiting.

Talking is impossible again, even swimming is hard, and I just follow Steve, aiming for the boat. I'm glad it's him towing the bag.

Then there's a new light. The big flashlight, the one we keep clipped to the wall above the chart table. It's shining from the stern of the boat, its light playing over the sea. I guess it must be Earrings looking for us, then I hear him shouting too, his voice almost lost to the strength of the wind. There's no point trying to shout back, we're better off just swimming, and Steve obviously thinks the same, because he stretches out ahead of me, even with the extra weight he's carrying. By the time I get to the ladder he's already on board, and then he reaches an arm down to help me. I climb up just in time to see Earrings, holding his pistol with two hands, and looking angry.

"Hey!" He shouts. "I asked you a question." Steve ignores him and keeps helping me on board, physically pulling me up the ladder until I'm kneeling on the deck. But then suddenly Earrings steps forward and whacks his gun across the side of Steve's head. It makes a noise like a loud crack.

"I asked what took you so long."

I don't think the blow was as hard as it sounded. The boat's moving so much, it took the power out of it. But even so Steve touches his fingers to the side of his head, like he's feeling for blood.

"That was just a warning," Earrings says, regaining his balance. "Now answer me, or you're gonna get something a lot worse."

"You wanna calm down a little?" Steve tells him. He goes back to the ladder and pulls the bag up from where he'd clipped it on. "It was well hidden. The kid did good to find it at all."

Earrings stares at Steve, like he still wants an answer to his question. But eventually the sight of the bag wins out. He kicks at it suspiciously, then bends down to shake it open. But it's tied shut, and he can't open it without lowering his gun.

"Open it," he tells Steve, who doesn't move.

"I said open it."

Slowly Steve does what he's told. He picks at the knots around the neck. It takes him a few moments.

"Where's Amber?" I ask, but no one answers me.

"Where's Amber and Gracie," I go on. "You've got your drugs…"

"Keep it shut kid," Earrings snaps, then turns back to Steve. "Is that it? Where's the rest?"

"Still inside."

"What? Why the fuck didn't you bring it all..?"

"We brought as much as we could. I told you to calm down. We're doing exactly what you asked, in very difficult circumstances."

This seems to silence Earrings for a moment. He picks up one of the packages, and inspects it one-handed. I glance at Steve. I can tell he's judging whether

Earrings is distracted enough for him to launch an attack at him. I'm terrified by the prospect, but at the same time I try to make myself ready to help if I can. But then the other man, Tommy, steps out of the shadows of the cabin.

"Hands where I can see them," he says. He's got his pistol trained on us as well.

Earrings glances up, and sees he can use both hands safely. He shoves the pistol into his waistband and inspects the package properly. I don't know what he's looking for, but he seems satisfied. At least for a moment. Then he shakes the other parcels free and kicks the empty bag towards Steve. Then he pulls out the gun again.

"Well? What the fuck are you waiting for? Go back and get the rest."

There's a moment of silence, and I look back at the water. I suddenly realize I'm tired. The last thing I want to do is go back in there. But I don't have any choice.

"Hold on," Steve says.

"What for?" Earrings replies.

"I want to know the plan," Steve says. "You've got what you wanted. I want to know how you're planning on letting us go."

"What the fuck are you talking about?" Earrings says.

"Exactly what I said. We've given you this," he points at the drugs. "I'm no expert but I know it's worth a ton of money. And all we want is for you to let us go. But how do we know we can trust you?"

I glance at Earrings face, and I see it's twisted into an angry sneer. "I don't care if you trust me or not. We've got the girl and the little kid locked up in the front. So you better do what the fuck you're told."

But Steve doesn't move. "Not until you tell me the plan. How are you gonna get out of here, and how are you gonna release us?"

There's a standoff that lasts a long time. I get the sense that me and the other guy, Tommy, are just waiting on the rocking and rolling deck to see what happens. I think for a second that Earrings is simply going to shoot Steve, and my next thought is super selfish – how I'd have to go into the cave on my own if he did that. But Earrings doesn't. I guess he figures he might not get the rest of the drugs that way.

"OK." He says in the end, "this is the *plan*." He shrugs like it's no big deal to tell us. "You get the rest of it, then we'll take you back to the marina." He stops and I sense he's making it up as he goes. "We'll lock you in the boat, that'll give us enough time to get away and out of town. After that you're on your own. That good enough for you?"

I look to Steve. I've got a host of questions, but Steve just stares at him a long time. In the end he nods his head.

"OK, now get back in that goddamn water and get me the rest of my packages."

Slowly Steve gets up. He ties the bag around his waist, then turns to me. "Billy, you ready?"

FORTY-EIGHT

I'M ALREADY COLD, but I know better than to say anything. Instead I nod, and try not to look at the water as I step carefully back to the ladder. I've still got my flippers on, so the easiest way is to jump back in. I don't want to, but there's no choice, and I step off, and plunge into blackness. Another bucket full of water flushes through my suit, and I come to the surface gasping for air, then fit my snorkel and mask.

Steve takes the lead this time, now he knows the way, and he makes me swim fast, which helps to warm me up. I try to talk to him as we go, but he shakes his head, and swims away, not even hesitating at the entrance to the cave, but ducking straight under the water. That makes it easier to get through the tunnel too, as all I have to do is follow the yellow glow in the water ahead of me.

Once we're back inside the cave, I expect him to stop and talk to me. He must have some kind of plan, at least, I hope he does. But straight away he dives down, and this time I watch from the surface, as he works underwater, moving the rocks and un-snagging the remaining packets of cocaine. It's amazing how long he can stay down. I thought Dad was good – he used to practice staying underwater to help with when he surfed big waves – but Steve is like a seal or something. He only needs the one breath before he's recovered it all, and then he ferries it to me on the surface, and I pack it into the bag. Five minutes later and we're done. But then, instead of heading back through the entrance and swimming back to the boat, he points at the little beach at the back of the cave, and swims that way instead. And there he pulls off his mask and snorkel.

"We need to do something," he says as I get there too.

"What?"

"I don't know. But something. Or this isn't going to end well."

"Why do you say that?" I ask, but I know the answer really, it's just I don't want to think about it.

"Did you hear him?" Steve asks.

Then I don't answer, and the next thing, he's shining the light right into my face. "Jesus! Billy! Are you OK? You're white." Suddenly he grabs me, and start rubbing up and down on my arms and chest, using friction to warm me a bit. I think he's going to stop, but he keeps going, for what must be four or five minutes, and actually I almost get hot.

"There," he says, he's out of breath now. "That better?"

I nod.

"Good. Now I need you to concentrate. Did you hear what he said, when I asked what the plan was?"

I nod again, though this time I remember how he can't see me. "To lock us in the boat while they escape."

"Yeah, but did you notice how he had to make it up on the spot? There was no plan. Or if there was, it wasn't that."

I'm feeling a little bit better now I'm warmed up. My head is starting to function again. "So what do you think they'll do? When they get the drugs back?"

Steve clicks his light to the lamp mode again, casting a dull yellow glow that illuminates the cave better. He shakes his head. "Billy, we've seen their faces. Not just a glimpse either. There's only one thing they were ever planning to do."

I don't need to ask what he means. I already know. It's obvious. But then I have to check, because all this feels impossible, sitting here in a cave with Steve, a bag packed full of cocaine at our feet.

"What?"

It takes him a while to answer. But then he doesn't hide it.

"They're going to murder us, Billy. If we give them this cocaine, they're going to take it, and they're going to shoot us. And if we don't go back, they're going to execute your friend and the little girl."

There's a moment of silence. I know he's right, but it's surreal to hear him say it out loud.

"So what do we do?" I ask, in the end.

"We need a plan."

I feel a faint flickering of hope. Not strong. "OK… What?"

He's a long time in answering, and the glimmer fades.

"Billy I'm sorry but I got nothing."

The hope is snuffed out completely. I feel the gloom around us pressing down.

"We've got to stay positive," Steve says. "There's more of us than them. They're outnumbered. That *has* to work in our favor. We have to find a way to make it work in our favor."

I try to do what he says, to be positive. But I can't help but want to protest. We might outnumber them technically, but Amber and Gracie are locked in the bow compartment. And Gracie is only six. And two grown men. Armed men. Then it's like he's been reading my mind.

"Your friend, Amber. Can we get a message to her? Is there a window in the bow compartment?"

I think, to answer him, but he's already moved on.

"Maybe we can tap out a message to her, through the hull? Would she know Morse code?"

"I don't think so," I say. "I do though."

His head jerks around to look at me.

"What? I'm a bit rusty, but I taught myself when I was a kid. I thought it might come in handy."

Suddenly he gives a snort of laughter. "Shit Billy, why doesn't that surprise me?"

I don't know what he's talking about. And I'm still wondering when he stops laughing. Again his voice is hard, bitter.

"If only we had a *weapon*." He starts hunting around him, looking for stones, but here it's just pebbles. "We can take rocks from the bottom. If I can get close enough, maybe I can knock the cocky one out with it. The fucker with the earrings."

He's talking to himself mostly, and it gives me the time to imagine how it might go. The bigger guy, Tommy, he watches all the time. He's always holding his gun, and he's got a kind of competence about him that terrifies me. If Steve tries to attack Earrings with a rock, even if he manages to get one blow on him, the other man will just shoot him.

I watch now. He's crawled down to the water's edge, where there's some larger rocks. He selects a couple now, feeling the weight, and then he puts them in the bag.

"Come on kid," he says.

I feel like asking if that's it? That's the plan. I thought we were going to come up with something for how to get us out of here. And now it just seems I'm going to get to watch Steve get shot and killed when he tries to beat two big guns with a rock.

"It won't work!" I say out loud, and Steve stops.

"It's dark, the boat is rocking. There might be an opportunity."

"But what if there isn't?"

"Listen Billy," finally his voice snaps, and he sounds angry. "If you've got a better idea I'd love to hear it."

I don't, so I stay silent.

"Come on. When we get there, you need to look for a chance to distract them. I don't know how, just anything. Wait until I've got the rock and I'm close enough to..."

Suddenly I remember.

"I've got it!" I cry.

He turns to stare at me.

"I know where there's a weapon!"

FORTY-NINE

"WHERE?" Steve asks. He doesn't move at all.

"When Carlos – or whatever his name is – when I saw him here it must have been after he hid the cocaine, because I didn't see it at all. All I saw was he was spear fishing, and this whole area is a nature reserve."

Steve stays silent.

"He hadn't shot anything by then, he probably wasn't even trying to, he just had the gun for protection, but I didn't know that, so I swam up to him, to tell him about the nature reserve, and how he wasn't allowed to fish here, and he was so surprised that he dropped the spear gun. It was in deep water and he didn't even try to get it. I know, because I waited so I could watch him actually leave. It's still there. I know where it is."

Suddenly I'm in such a hurry to leave I find myself tugging at Steve's shoulder. But still he hesitates.

"How do you know where it is?"

"I saw it below me. After he left. It fell into one of the holes, and I was annoyed because it was too deep for me to get, and I thought it was littering. But I know exactly where it is."

He hesitates again.

"One of the holes? How deep?"

I stop. The truth is I don't really know. I've just assumed that Steve will be able to get it, even in the dark, because he's a free diving champion. I hadn't thought that I'd have to go down there.

"Maybe fifteen feet?" I say. But really I'm already working it out. It's got to be more than that, because the tide is higher today. "Could be twenty."

There's a short pause before he answers. But he nods his head. "Twenty feet is OK." I don't tell him I didn't measure it, It could be more than that.

"Show me where it is."

So we take the bag, and once again we descend under the surface for the quick swim through the underwater passage that connects the cave to the sea, but this time, once we're outside we don't swim directly back to the boat, but instead I try to work out where Carlos dropped the gun. I know what I need to look for, in order to find it, but it's so dark beneath me that I can hardly see the seabed, let alone recognize the features. And it's so choppy and rough on the surface now that just swimming in the same place is difficult. I sense Steve alongside me – we're both careful to keep our lights shining down, so that no one on the boat can see what we're doing – but the light only helps illuminate the tops of the shallower sections of rock.

I stop, pull my head out of the water and think. The octopus was on a shallow piece of sand near to the cave's entrance. I'm able to locate that quite easily. Then I take myself back. The *Mystery* was anchored further out than *Blue Lady* is, and further to the north too. I try to make the same swim now, and all the time I'm pushing my head down into the water and straining to see as much as I can.

Eventually we're treading water over roughly where I think the gun must be. But it's hopeless. Even shining the flashlights down just reveals water, the light doesn't reach the bottom.

"It's somewhere around here. Down there somewhere." I say to Steve, but I shake my head as I speak. I don't even know if he's going to bother trying. It's obvious now that this is impossible. Yet he hands me the bag with the drugs in, and then he floats on his back for a minute or so, saying nothing. I don't know how he's even managing to do that, with the way the swell is buffeting us both around. And something makes me not interrupt him, just wait for what happens next. Then he rolls over and I see his eyes through the mask, fixed and staring. He gives me a thumbs up. And then he rolls forward, and disappears under the water.

Right away I use my snorkel and mask to watch him descend. He's got his flashlight on, and I see it sinking down. Slowly down, further and further. And I wonder if I really am in the right place, or if I've just sent him towards the empty bottom. Or worse, a section of the reef where it's way too deep for anyone to reach. Still the light is dropping away below me. Then finally I see how it lights up the rock around him, he must have got to the sea bed.

A wave overtops my snorkel, and I get a mouthful of salty water. I nearly panic, and come to the surface choking and coughing to clear my airways. Then I blow hard through the tube to empty it, and look down again. The light is moving now, slowly crabbing along the seafloor. It's hard to see but it looks like he's making his way along a crevice in the rock. That worries me. I don't think there were any crevices where the gun was dropped. It was more like a round hole in the reef. Then I worry about something else. I'm breathing normally, or as normally as I can through the snorkel in such choppy water. But Steve's just got one breath. I decide to hold my own breath, as a way of measuring how long he's been down there. So I push the snorkel from my mouth, and instead pinch my nose closed.

I keep watching as the light, far below me, crabs further to the right. Then it stops. I wait, still counting in my head. I get to twenty before I can feel the pinch on my chest, the need to get more air in. I try to ignore it, to will it away, but it just grows stronger and stronger. On forty I know I have to release my grip, and breathe again, but I also know what it means for Steve. He's been down there far longer than I've been holding my breath, and now the light isn't moving. I realize it hasn't moved for thirty seconds or more. I begin to panic at what that means. Maybe he's unconscious? Maybe he's already drowned.

I splutter and resurface, gasping at the air, but disgusted at myself that I couldn't even count to a minute. I fight to calm myself and look down again. But this time there's nothing. I don't mean there's no movement. I mean there's no light at all. I turn my own flashlight off, so it's not blinding me. But still I can't see anything. It's just an ocean of blackness.

The feeling in my stomach is sheer, cold terror. I look up and around me, but it's just empty sea. There's a rare break in the clouds, and the moon is visible, the sloppy swell breaking its reflection into shards of light on the water. A little way away the *Blue Lady* is still riding her anchor, her deck lights still rolling in lumpy arcs. Behind me the cliffs hang dark and threatening. But there's no sign of Steve, no head above the water. I look underwater again, unable to breathe myself now. But nothing has changed. It's still just darkness.

There's literally nothing I can do. Something must have happened down there. Free diving is dangerous, even in normal times, all sorts of things can go wrong, and I'm powerless to help. Even if I could get that deep I'm too late. Fear spasms through me. He's probably already dead. He's ahead of me. By what? Fifteen minutes?

What do I do now? Should I go back to the boat anyway? Give them their drugs, and let them shoot me? At least I might get to see Amber again. Or is it better to try and swim away. I'll drown before I reach anywhere, no question about that. Or should I try and go after Steve. Perhaps Steve found it, before he ran out of air. Perhaps I can swim down. I fight to take a breath, ready to duck forward and dive down. But even as I do, I know I'll never make it. I couldn't get the spear gun in daylight, in good weather, when I was calm, and when the tide was lower. It's impossible now.

Ooooffff.

Suddenly something punches me in the stomach. I get another mouthful of seawater, and then something surfaces right in my face, gasping for air, just like I am. For a second I don't realize what it is, then with an explosion of joy I see it's Steve. Neither of us can speak, but then I see the gleam of his teeth in the dull light, and then he holds up a long metal spear gun in his hand.

"I got lucky," he says, panting through the wind and the waves. "Flash light failed, but only after I saw the gun."

I don't answer. I feel sick, from thinking he was dead. "It's a good one too," he says, a minute later, after he's done breathing hard. "Christ alone knows how you found the spot where it was."

Dimly I appreciate the compliment. I must have put us right above it.

"Come on. They won't be expecting this," Steve says. And without stopping to tell me the plan he starts swimming again, back to the *Blue Lady*.

FIFTY

AGAIN WE'RE PICKED out from the rear platform of the boat by the spot light, but we get closer this time before they see us. I can't see which of them is operating it, but I'm worried they'll see the spear gun. It's quite big. Steve stopped on the swim to load it, pulling the thick elastic band back and clipping it onto the spear. It only has one shot, but the force is deadly. I've seen them go right through fish, even large ones, and I've watched videos online of people shooting other things, trees and TVs and they go through anything.

When we reach the ladder, Steve pushes me to go first, so I climb aboard, and see if there's anything I can do right away to distract them. Earrings is right there, clamoring for the bag with the drugs, while Tommy is hanging back, his feet spread wide to compensate for the roll of the boat. I feel how he watches me, the pistol loosely aimed in my direction. His attention focused completely on watching me.

"Where's the other one? The shark guy?" Earrings asks. I don't know the answer.

"He's right behind me. Or he was."

"And where's the coke? Where the fuck is my coke?"

Steve had the bag, so I don't know the answer to this either, but then his voice suddenly sounds out, from the water. "It's here."

For some reason he's appeared on the port side of the boat. Then he swims back to the ladder at the stern, and we all watch him climb up onto the platform, using both his hands. Then I see the bag is tied around his waist this time, and he slowly hauls it up behind him. But I can't see where he's got the spear gun. Has he dropped it? After all the effort it took to get it. But then he gives me a look, and I notice there's a thin line tied round his foot. With spear guns you have a line that connects the spear to the gun, else you'd lose the spear every time you fired it. It's this line he had round his ankle. He must have cut it with the propeller blade. The gun must be suspended in the water below him.

Earrings doesn't notice anything, least I don't think so. He's only interested in the drugs.

"Is that all there is?" He snaps when he gets the bag open again. Steve nods, gradually moving his foot. Once he gets into the cockpit he might be able to hide the gun behind one of the bench seats.

"It looks light."

"It's all there was," Steve replies. "You're welcome to go take a look yourself. But right now we're cold and the boy needs to get out of his suit and warm up."

Earrings glares at him, but then turns away and opens the bag further. I keep my eyes on Steve, and see how he's watching both of them. But Tommy is keeping his eyes fixed on Steve. Then Earrings kneels by the bag, pulling out the packages and tossing them inside the cabin where the first batch are piled up.

"How many's that?" he asks Tommy. I glance up, and see the flicker of irritation on the bigger man's face. He still doesn't take his eyes off Steve and me. But he counts the packages anyway. Using his feet.

"Fifteen."

Earrings seems happy with this, and Steve tries again.

"Come on buddy. We've done our part. Let the kid get dried off. He's freezing cold."

Earrings doesn't make any sign he hears. Instead he pulls out his cell phone and clicks the screen on. He stares at it for a moment, then clicks it off again. He looks disgusted.

"No fucking signal," he shouts, more at himself than anyone else.

"Come on man. This kid's gonna get hypothermia if he doesn't get warm now." I don't know what Steve's plan actually is, but I try to go along with it. I make myself start shivering, which isn't hard, because I really am cold. My teeth start to chatter. That makes Earrings look up.

"Like I give a fucking shit." Earrings replies. Then he turns away, and looks out towards the open sea for a moment. I don't know what he's looking at, but then he suddenly yells out.

"Over there!"

Suddenly I realize we're not alone. Because not far away I see the navigation lights of another boat. Not far away at all. I feel a rush of relief. Maybe Amber's somehow managed to get out, and used the radio – but no, didn't Tommy smash it up?

"At fucking last," Earrings says.

"What's going on?" Steve demands, but Earrings ignores him again. Then Tommy steps over to Earrings' side of the boat too, and for a moment all three of us are staring out into the darkness. The other boat has deck lights and the windows of the cabins are illuminated too. It looks like another private fishing boat, but newer and bigger than *Blue Lady*. My dad calls them gin palaces. It's coming close. Then I look back at Steve, just in time to see him swing the spear gun over the gunwale, and gently place it on the deck. Then he slides the loop of cord off his foot.

"Who's that?" He asks again, when he's done.

"None of your fucking business." Earrings replies.

"You said we were going back to the port. You'd leave us there."

"Yeah well I fucking lied didn't I?" Earrings turns again to watch the other boat. A spotlight plays on us, picking us out one by one. Then, when the boat is within hailing distance a voice calls out, across the water.

"Why aren't you answering the radio?"

Earrings looks at Tommy, annoyed, then he shouts back. "Tommy smashed it up."

Then there's laughs, rolling over the water. "Tell Tommy he's a fucking idiot."

I can make out figures on the other boat now. At least four men, and there's enough light to see that two of them are standing on the top of the cabin, holding on with one hand and with proper automatic assault rifles slung around their necks.

"Are they with you?" Steve persists.

"Course they're with us," Earrings snaps, then looks annoyed at himself for bothering. He shouts again.

"Tell Angelo we got fifteen packets back. He better be fucking grateful!"

There's a pause, while the other boat's motor roars as it struggles to hold position. Then the voice comes back.

"Tell him yourself! You think he'd let anyone else skipper his new boat?"

Suddenly Earrings seems incredibly happy. He almost seems to forget we're here. "Tommy, you hear that? Angelo's here himself. We're done here. We fucking done it."

Then the voice comes again. "Who's the civilians?"

Earrings stops smiling at once. He glances at Steve and me, then yells back. "No one. No one important."

There's a long pause, while the other boat's motor roars again. In the reflected light I can make out the name *Mea Culpa*, painted across the stern. I see the men scurrying across the deck. Then the voice rings out again.

"Then get rid of them. Angelo wants this sorted fast. Bad weather coming."

The light gets brighter as the other boat comes closer still, but they're pointing the other way from us.

"We'll turn around, come alongside." The voice says now, and the spotlight abruptly breaks away, like they want to give some privacy, and we're back to just the low-level deck lighting on the *Blue Lady*. We all heard what the man said, and we all know what it means. Earrings turns to Tommy.

"Well, you heard him. Get it done."

No one moves. No one speaks. Until Tommy does so. The longest sentence I've heard him speak.

"I thought we were gonna let them go," he says in the end.

Earrings turns to look at him. When he speaks, his voice is a snarl.

"Yeah well, we ain't."

"We made a deal."

"Angelo didn't. So stop fucking around. Shoot them."

There's another silence.

"What about the two in the cabin?" Tommy asks. "The girl, and the kid?"

"What about them? Shoot these two, then shoot them as well. It ain't fucking hard."

Earrings stares at Tommy, who's relaxing and tightening his grip on the gun.

"Yeah but the little girl… She's nothing to do with this."

"The fuck are you saying Tommy? You just got a *direct order* and you don't wanna do it?" Earrings stares at Tommy. They're both holding their guns, and I could almost believe they're more likely to shoot each other.

Then Earrings snaps. "You don't want to shoot a six year old kid? Fine. I'll fucking do it. But shoot these fuckers now while I get this sorted." Earrings bends down, and sets his gun on the deck so he can use both hands to move the drugs into one pile. He snorts angrily while he works. Terrified, I look up at Tommy. He's looking right back at me. He raises his gun.

"Shit," he says. "Sorry kid. I wish there was another way."

My mouth opens to speak. To tell him there is another way, that there must be. But no sound comes out. With his other hand Tommy pulls back the slider on the top of the gun, pulling a bullet into the chamber. He shakes his head slowly.

"Fenders!" I say, the word garbled in my mouth.

"What?" Tommy lowers the gun a fraction.

"You'll need fenders. If you're going to have that other boat come alongside. You'll need fenders, or we'll smash holes in each other. I know where they are."

I can hear my breathing, desperate, fast, in-and-out as I watch Tommy's reaction. The gun tips sideways as he gives a little half-shrug. "OK…" He turns to Earrings.

"Paulie," he says. "These guys, they're not soldiers. They're not involved. This isn't the way the Old Man did things."

But Earrings has finished what he was doing now. He picks up his gun again, and this time he holds it out. His arm straight, pointing directly at me. "Yeah, and how many times I gotta tell *you*, the Old Man's gone. New times. New rules."

Then there's a strange sound, or two strange sounds. The first is the release of pent up pressure on the elastic of the spear gun, the second is the sound of the metal harpoon piercing first the flesh of Earring's shoulder, then the wood of the wheelhouse structure behind him, pinning him in place. Then there's a clatter as the gun he was holding falls to the deck. The noise distracts Tommy, who turns to look, confused by what's just happened. It gives Steve the time to react. He dives at Tommy, tackling his legs and in a second they're both on the deck together, Steve's voice screaming out.

"Get the gun Billy!"

I'm a bit slower to react, and Earrings goes to pick up the gun before I can. But suddenly he can't move. He's stuck in place by the spear, and I'm able to crawl across near to him and pick up the gun. I hold it, shaking in my hands and aim it at him for a second, then I spin around and point it at the moving tangle of limbs and bodies that is Steve and Tommy. In the dim light it's impossible to make out who's who, or which of them is winning.

"Freeze!" I shout, as loud as I can. It works, and then Steve rolls away. I can't see where Tommy's gun has gone, but he's looking right at me. In a flash Steve is by my side. He carefully takes the gun from my hands, then holds it out towards Tommy.

"On your knees."

The big man doesn't respond.

"I'm telling you. Get down right now. Or I'll shoot your legs out from under you."

"You can't win this." Tommy replies. Still not doing what Steve says. "Don't you see they're armed on that boat? Fully automatic assault rifles. They'll cut you to pieces."

"Last chance motherfucker," Steve ignores him. "Get on your knees or I'll shoot your legs out."

This time Tommy does what he's told. I don't know if I just started hearing it, but now there's the sound of Earrings moaning. He's trying to move, but he can't.

"Now lie down. Hands behind you. Billy, come here."

Steve holds the gun pushed up against the back of Tommy's head, while he makes me tie his hands together. I'm pretty good at knots, but even so Steve checks it. Then he rolls Tommy over again, and I tie a second rope, securing him to the chest where we keep the drinks, so there's no chance he can move. It's all happened so quick, the other boat is still finishing its maneuver to turn around and come alongside. It's coming back now, the searchlight clicks back on, and wobbles around, trying to pick us out.

"Billy, get the motor started. We've got to get out of here," Steve shouts now. And when I hesitate he yells it again. "Now! I'll dump the anchor."

Then the searchlight rests upon us. And I feel the glare as it must pick out Earrings, still pinned to the side of the cabin, calling out now. I don't hesitate any more.

The motor on the *Blue Lady* fires first go, and straight away I see Steve has released the anchor. He doesn't bother trying to pull it in, it would take too long to get all the chain back on board. Instead he frees the end of the rope and casts it overboard.

"Go!" He shouts at me, and I don't hesitate. I ram the gear lever forward and the boat rears up as the power pushes the bow high. The *Blue Lady* is heavy though, and she takes a while to coax onto the plane. And in this weather I have to work hard to keep her straight through the chop and swell.

"Lights," Steve yells, "lose the lights." I do what he says, hitting the switch, then grab a look behind me, and see the search light flailing around, trying to locate us. I guess they maybe take a few moments to figure out what's happening, because they don't move at once. It gives us a head start – not much, maybe a hundred yards before I see the bow of their boat lift up too, white against the black of the cliffs. And then we're both flying along, charging out into the deeper water and the approaching storm.

"They're onto us!" Steve shouts into my ear from beside me. I stare at him. I don' t have anything to say. "Here, let me steer. Go release Amber."

I do what he says, dropping down the ladder from the bridge to the cockpit. I see how Tommy is being bounced around, tied to the floor, and then I see the other man, Earrings, and how he's still pinned to the side of the cabin, and how each time the boat lands from a wave he's screaming out in agony. But I don't have time for him, instead I make my way inside and up to the bow cabin, where Amber is screaming too. I work as fast as I can to unpick the knots that Tommy tied to keep the door closed, but it's hard with how much the boat is moving. We'd never normally go full tilt in swell like this, and I've never seen the inside of the boat crashing around this much. Finally the rope is out the way, and the door falls open.

"Billy! What's happening?" Amber looks desperate. She's still holding Gracie, trying to calm her down, but not really getting anywhere.

"We're getting away." I breathe. "We've escaped." There's a huge crash, as the boat lands in a trough between waves. We slow then accelerate again. It's horrible this far forward. "Sort of escaped. They're chasing us."

"Who is?" Amber asks, but already I'm heading back to help Steve.

When I get back out of the cabin I see the other boat has already halved the distance between us. Its search light keeps picking us out, and then losing us as both boats crash up and down. And then, every time the light is on us I hear the rat tat tat of their weapons, firing at us.

"Get down," Steve shouts, from up on the bridge. Too late I drop to the deck, pulling Amber and Gracie with me. But it doesn't matter as we must be impossible to hit in this water state.

"They're closing fast. Bigger boat. It rides the swell better," Steve yells down. "Hold on. I'm gonna try to out corner them."

Without any more warning he suddenly sends the boat into a hard turn to starboard. Their light loses us at once, and we stretch out our lead by a boat length or two. But it doesn't take much for them to pick up our wake, white against the dark water, and find us again. Steve tries again, but this time whoever is steering the *Mea Culpa* is quicker, and turns harder, cutting the distance again. Another rain of bullets flies across our stern.

"Shoot them!" Steve yells. "Shoot back." I don't know where the gun is, until I remember I left it on the floor by the bow cabin. I stagger back to get it, and then see Amber already has it. She's white faced in the doorway of the cabin, before I pull her to the floor. Then there's a series of loud cracks, and I realize we've been hit by a volley of bullets. They don't hit anything vital – at least I don't think they do – but it's impossible to know if they've hit us below the waterline.

She shrugs me off, and aims at the boat behind us. She's quite good with guns, but it's obviously hopeless. The men on the following boat are protected by its bow, high up out of the water, and by the fact that both boats are leaping and crashing through the seas. What's also obvious is there's no chance of us escaping. The other boat is faster and more maneuvrable, and we're hopelessly outgunned. Then Steve makes a shallow turn, and for a moment the side of the chasing boat is revealed. Amber aims again, and empties the rest of the magazine behind us. Obviously she does enough to worry them, and for a moment they turn away from the chase. But only enough to put them on a parallel path. It looks like they're going to come level and then rake us with fire. It means we're in a straight race. And the *Blue Lady* is being overhauled at a frightening rate.

"You got a life raft on this tub?" Steve shouts down.

"Yeah!" I scream back at him.

"Then go get it. Get ready to throw it over." He takes his hands off the wheel for second. At once the boat rears wildly, and he has to grab it again, hard.

"What do you mean, throw it over?"

"It's dark enough that we can get it in the water without them seeing, if we put it over the other side. Then jump in after it. They'll keep chasing the boat."

I try to make sense of this.

"Just do it Billy. Now!"

His words jerk me into action. We have two life rafts on board – we have to, because of the passengers we carry – they're stored in explosive canisters on each side of the boat. The idea is they're super easy to get ready, and they self-inflate when they hit the water. And we have to do drills with them, so we know exactly how to operate them, just in case an emergency happens. I clamber around the side deck now to reach the port side canister. The other boat is now creeping alongside us on our starboard side, so I'm hidden from view. I rip open the buckles, my fingers are shaking. Then Steve makes a sudden swerve to port, widening the gap between the two boats. The other one is slower to respond again, allowing us to pull ahead.

"Don't pull it yet. I'll tell you when," Steve yells. "Put a life jacket on the kid." He turns around and shouts to Amber. I don't hear what, but I see her go off to the stern locker and pull it open.

"What about you?" I shout up.

"Can't leave the wheel. She won't stay straight."

"So what are you gonna do?" But he doesn't hear me. I turn and look at the water flashing past beside me. Whenever we've practiced deploying the life rafts we've been stopped, in calm water. I don't even know if it will work properly at this speed.

I check the other boat. It's about a hundred yards away now and closing again. We're going along the lines of swell, so the boats are crashing up and down less. Their superior speed is working against them now.

Then I see what Amber is doing. She's holding a small green plastic gas container. We keep it there to run the little outboard for the inflatable tender. Only she's got the top off, and she's sloshing it around, over the cockpit, and then inside the cabin. The smell of gasoline is suddenly everywhere.

"What are you doing?" I scream, over the noise.

"Distraction." Steve yells.

"You're going to set the boat on fire?!"

"Not just this one Billy. Are you ready there?"

I glance again at the flashing water. I check I've got all the buckles free. I just have to pull the quick release handle, and the canister will roll overboard. In theory it will self-inflate.

"I asked if you're ready Billy?"

"Yeah."

"OK Amber. Light her up. I'll make a hard turn to port. Release the raft and jump all together."

There's no time to argue. I crouch over my task, my whole hands shaking with fear and adrenalin. Then I see an orange glow appear behind Steve. He waits a couple of seconds – long enough for the glow to brighten, and then he leans the *Blue Lady* into a hard port turn.

"Goooo!" Steve screams. And I don't hesitate. I yank my handle as hard as I can, and I watch as the final catch holding the canister in place tears away, and the whole barrel rolls over the side, splitting open as it does so.

"Go Billy. Jump now!" Steve yells. The other boat anticipated our turn, because they're closer than ever, and shooting at us again.

"What about you?" I call again, as behind me I see Amber and Gracie on the side of the boat. And then they're gone, into the water, and immediately lost in the darkness.

"Don't worry about me. Just jump." Steve screams back to me. Still I don't do it. The whole of the cockpit of the *Blue Lady* is now alight, smoke flooding out the cabin and flowing out behind us.

"Jump Billy."

I push myself up, and leap sideways off the boat.

FIFTY-ONE

I HIT THE WATER HARD. It's like being smashed by a wave, and then tumbled underwater. It's so dark I'm totally disorientated. I don't know where up is. And I didn't even think to take a breath. I don't so much panic as feel incredulous, am I just too far underwater? Is this how I'm going to drown? But then one of my hands breaks the surface, and a reflex kicks in – I struggle to get my head up. And at once it's quieter. Then I spin around, just in time to see an incredible sight.

The *Blue Lady* is a fireball. Already it's fifty feet away, and flame and smoke billowing out the back. I can still see Steve on the bridge, at the wheel, his body silhouetted against the flames. The other boat is still alongside, still both at full speed. But just as I look, the *Blue Lady* cuts hard to starboard, away from the chasing boat, like Steve's making one final desperate effort to escape. At once the driver on the second boat follows, like he's used to it now. But then Steve must throw the wheel as hard as he can around the other way, because just as the second boat begins turning, the *Blue Lady* suddenly cuts back and turns the other way. But now there's no room for her to do so. The two boats are going almost directly towards each other. A second later they collide, the *Blue Lady* riding right up and on top of the other boat. They both slow, and finally stop, and I see they're locked together. I can hear shouts, screaming. There's people jumping into the water. And then there's a massive explosion.

I have to shield my eyes, as the night sky is lit up. Bits of boat shoot up, high in the air, then fall like solid pieces of rain. Both boats are stopped now, dead in the water. And both are on fire. It's mesmerizing, almost beautiful. But horrible because I know Steve is on there somewhere. I get a mouthful of salty water, and I realize I'm screaming, shouting out his name. Not because he might hear me. Not because he might still even be alive. Because I know there's no chance. He was right in the middle of the two boats. And now there's nothing left. I fall silent. I know I'm crying, my tears mixing with the salt of the ocean. And I know there's nothing I can do. Then I remember Gracie and Amber. I turn around.

I can't see anything behind me, not even the land, let alone her and Amber swimming somewhere out in the dark. But then there's a flash of red in the darkness. The life-raft has a built-in light that operates automatically. I lose it for a second, then catch it again, rocking from side to side about a few hundred yards away. I don't know what else to do, so I begin to swim towards it.

My shoulder muscles are sore and stiff from my swimming earlier, and it takes me a long while. I try to keep my eyes open, watching for Amber or Gracie floating somewhere in the water around me, but it's pitch black now. The still burning boats are so bright they make it hard to stay focused on the beacon on the raft. But finally I get there, and I feel for the fabric ladders that hang underneath. And when I pull myself inside, I see Amber staring back at me, sitting on the bottom of the life raft, with little Gracie resting on her knees. She doesn't say anything. She just gives me a weak smile, and I know she's crying just like I am.

EPILOGUE

I'M STANDING on the edge of the cliff. It's the one outside my house, only it looks funny because there's fog rolling in off the sea and rising up all around me. I can feel the breeze it's riding on, cold and wet. It's pushing my hair back from my forehead. I don't know why, I hold out my arms. I can feel my jacket flapping where the wind catches it. I step forward. Close to the edge now, so as to really feel the wind. Then I take one more step, right out into the nothing ahead of me. And then I'm falling, my arms still stretched out beside me, my jacket flapping harder as I accelerate down.

But then something weird happens. Instead of just falling down, I start to fall outwards, away from the cliff face, and over the rocks and beach below. I don't flap my arms, I just hold them outstretched, and they work as wings, like I'm a bird, soaring on the air currents. Like my pet herring gull I used to have, Steven.

I get the hang of it. I dip one arm, and I turn that way, gaining speed. The sand and water race towards me as I swoop down to it. So I dip the other hand, and I'm level again, flying effortlessly above the Littlelea sands. I breathe. Pulling the fresh, cool, damp air deep inside me, and feeling its invigorating touch.

I breathe more. I rise up, high above the beach now. Above the dunes, higher than the cliffs even. I look down on our little house. My bike dumped in the drive, where I should have put it in the shed. Dad's truck forced to park at an awkward angle — no, still moving, like he's just arriving. But he shouldn't be here… I float in the air, hanging above the truck as the door opens and then Dad gets out, staring up at the sky, squinting against the sun. He's animated, calling my name up to me so that gently I float back down to earth, calling out his name, while he calls out mine. *Billy, Billy, Dad..!*

"Dad?" I open my eyes.

"Billy," my Dad actually replies. His face is lined with dirt, and his hair looks long and streaked with oil. He takes my hand. "Billy! Are you OK? Jesus you gave me a scare." He shouts, away from me. "Hey, he's awake! A little help here..." Then he turns back, squeezing my hand, and smiling.

"Where am I?" I ask, but I already know the answer. The white-painted walls and tubes running into my body give it away.

"You're in hospital." •

"In Newlea?"

"That's right."

"What happened?"

"That's what I've been wondering. What we've all been trying to piece together. You've been out of it for three days. You nearly died."

I stare at Dad in wonder. "What of?"

"Hypothermia. Amber said you lost consciousness in the life raft."

"Amber," I repeat. "Is she alright?"

"She's fine. Pretty cut up, but fine."

"Cut up? Why?" A thought hits me. "Is... Is Gracie... Did she not..."

"Don't stress, Gracie's more than fine. Thinks it was all a grand adventure. No, it's Amber's boyfriend who didn't make it. The guy that started all this mess." Dad takes a breath. "He passed away."

"Oh." I say.

"Yeah. He was pretty badly burned by all accounts, so maybe..." He doesn't finish, but I know he means it's maybe better that way. I don't know about that, so I don't reply.

"Listen, what the hell did you get up to anyway? I leave you counting sharks in Australia, I come back, you're chasing drug smugglers down the back of the island? The cops say they've made the biggest drugs bust here in ten years because of what you did."

It's too long a story to answer this, so I stay silent again.

"Not just the cocaine either, but you've given them the whole gang behind it. They fished most of them out the water. There's one guy — they found him tied to an ice-box — according to the cops, he's been telling them everything. Details on the whole lot of 'em. Enough to put them away for years."

I almost go to smile, but then how it happened. How Steve drove the *Blue Lady* into the other boat. How he must have burned to death too. And then I don't think I'll ever smile again.

But I have to ask. I need to know for sure. "Steve Rose," I blurt out. "Did he..." I begin. But I guess I must be weak still, since I can't finish the sentence.

"Did I what mate?" A voice cuts in. A voice I know.

"Steve?" I don't know if I'm still dreaming, but I can't be. I'm not flying.

"Hey Billy." He's got one of his arms wrapped in white bandages, but lifts it up and waggles the fingers in a greeting. There's more bandaging on his face and chest.

"What mate? You look like you seen a ghost!"

I don't reply. It kind of looks like I have."

"This is nothing. There was a good few seconds after the boats hit before the fire kicked off. Wetsuit got a bit melted but figured it would be OK for a little swim." He laughs. "What? You didn't think you'd get rid of me that easy, did you?"

* * *

A while later Amber comes in. She's quiet and withdrawn, but she leans over the bed and gives me a big hug. I can see she's been crying a lot. Then her mom arrives with Gracie, who's clearly loving all the attention. It looks like Amber and her mom need to put in a bit of work before they're going to trust each other again, but at the same time, I can see her mom is trying hard. I guess I'm going to have to help though too, making sure Amber's OK after everything that's happened. But I know she'll come through. She tough, is Amber.

Then they all leave, and two detectives come in. I don't know them, since they're from the mainland, but they set up a recorder and say they need to take a statement from me about everything that happened. It takes ages, because so much *has* happened, and they want to know every detail, and they've got a million questions about everything I tell them. At first I try to ask them questions too, but they won't tell me anything because it could influence what I say, apparently. But then I realize I don't care anyway, because they're just a bunch of criminals, and I'm not interested in criminals. So then I just lie here and do my best to remember it all, but I get more and more tired, and slowly the voices of the detectives just drift away until they go completely quiet. And then later on, I know I must have fallen asleep, because the detectives are gone, and everything's dark.

The next time I wake up it's daylight.

"How are you doing, Billy?" Dad asks me, when he sees I'm awake.

I smile back at him, just enjoying the quiet for a moment, the way the sunlight is hitting my bed covers.

"What time is it?" I ask after a while.

"I dunno. Morning, sometime. But don't worry about it. You just rest as long as you need."

"No it's not that. It's just I'm starving hungry."

Dad smiles at this. "OK. I'll go get you some breakfast."

But then I notice that Dad's not alone in the room. Steve's here too, and from the way they have their chairs arranged, they must have been talking. He gets up now, and ambles over, holding out a bag of grapes.

"Here. I keep getting given things. Trials of being a celebrity huh?" Then he glances at Dad. "Well, you know, a minor one."

I take the bag and try a couple of grapes. They're nice and sweet.

"I'll go get you some breakfast," Dad says again, but this time I stop him. There's something I feel bad about.

"Hey Dad, I'm sorry about all this. And about you having to stop working on *Blue Lady II*. Just because of me."

Dad shakes his head. "I didn't."

I'm confused by that. "Why not?"

Dad shrugs. "I didn't have to stop because she's finished. She's all fitted out. All ready." Then he glances at Steve, a little bit strangely. "Actually we've been… talking about that, Steve and I, about whether we could maybe do something. I don't know exactly what, but if you didn't want to just go back to running the whale watching trips. We could…" He stops.

"What?"

Dad shrugs again. "I dunno. I really don't know. But we were just… it's just an idea. Something to kick around over the next few weeks."

I want to ask more, but then Steve speaks again.

"Hey listen Sam, you stay here, I'll go grab some food for the both of you. You look like you haven't eaten in days too." He goes to the door and I think he's going to walk out, but then he stops again.

"Hey Sam, I didn't say this before but…"

Dad's quiet. He does look tired.

"I just wanted to say, that's one helluva kid you've got there." Then Steve then taps on the door twice before pulling it open and stepping through. When he's gone I look back at Dad, but he won't meet my eye, but then he does and I can see he's welling up with tears. He doesn't say anything but picks up my hand and gives it a squeeze.

And then I squeeze him back.

Made in the USA
Coppell, TX
22 September 2023